EPIC

AZTEC MYTHS & TALES

ANTHOLOGY OF CLASSIC TALES

Foreword by Anthony F. Aveni

FLAME TREE PUBLISHING

TALES

This is a FLAME TREE Book

Publisher & Creative Director: Nick Wells
Editorial Director: Catherine Taylor

Publisher's Note: Due to the historical nature of the classic text, we're aware that there may be some language used which has the potential to cause offence to the modern reader. However, wishing overall to preserve the integrity of the text, rather than imposing contemporary sensibilities, we have left it unaltered.

FLAME TREE PUBLISHING
6 Melbray Mews, Fulham,
London SW6 3NS, United Kingdom
www.flametreepublishing.com

First published 2023

25 27 26 24
3 5 7 9 10 8 6 4 2

ISBN: 978-1-80417-589-7
Special ISBN: 978-1-80417-341-1

The cover image is created by Flame Tree Studio based on artwork by Slava Gerj, Gabor Ruszkai and Doni Hariyanto. Internal images are courtesy Shutterstock.com and the following artists: Svetlana Parshakova, Zvereva Yana (page 12), Emre Tarimcioglu and Karlionau (story headers).

A copy of the CIP data for this book is available from the British Library.

Printed and bound in China

EPIC TALES

AZTEC MYTHS & TALES

ANTHOLOGY OF CLASSIC TALES

Foreword by Anthony F. Aveni

FLAME TREE PUBLISHING

Contents

Mayan Myths

Myths of the Incas & Peru

Myths of the Pueblo Indians

El Dorado

Foreword

MYTH IS A WORD that carries a dual meaning. For many of us, it's 'just a story' that usually deals with natural phenomena and supernatural beings. For others it's a false belief, delusional, 'all made up.' In the latter sense it becomes fake, a product of fanciful imagination in need of debunking by science and replaced by the 'real' truth. But those who tell stories like the indigenous oral tales from the two American continents that appear in this volume, relate events they experience to beliefs and practices in their daily lives that capture essential truths about human existence. However, they must be carefully read, because the written versions that appear here are the product of colonizers and they are prone to encapsulate a European world view.

Modern people tend to assume their human ancestors, who lacked the benefit of superior technology and accumulated wisdom, misread what they sensed in the world around them, so they populated it with needless spirits and based their child-like interpretations on false premises. The widely held Pan-American indigenous belief that all nature is endowed with life, that its properties are transferable to people, appears to have little value for us, even if such stories prove effective in guiding the everyday life of the storyteller.

Let me illustrate by referring to one of my favourite creation myths in this volume, the Mayan creation story from the *Popol Vuh*. The environment where the tale is told is the karst topography of the central Yucatan peninsula, a land riddled with huge caves and natural sinkholes, a fitting stage for the encounters of the Hero Twins sent by the gods of the Upper World to confront the Lords of the Underworld to determine who will control the world in between, where people will be created and destined to live following the anticipated first sunrise.

To get to the palace of the pestilence-bearing rulers below, the twins first must survive a dangerous route consisting of encounters with rivers of pus and blood and houses filled with bats. The confrontation of the forces of good and evil finally culminates when the Twins perform a sacrifice. One of them excises the heart of the other, then magically returns him to life. Enthralled with the possibility of coming back from the dead, the evil lords plead: "Do it to us!" The twins dutifully follow the request, tearing out the hearts of the evil ones, except they omit step two. So goes the defeat of the Lords and a world destined to be free of the pestilence they would otherwise have brought upon impending humanity.

The stories of the *Popol Vuh* extol the qualities of the hero. Unlike our archetypal Hercules and Odysseus, who exhibit courage and physical strength, their culture values cleverness and trickery, using one's wits to outsmart the foe. These qualities are shared by other Native American cultures, among them the North American Tlingit Raven and Navajo Coyote.

As an astronomer, I imagine the gifted Maya storyteller and avid young listeners circled about a campfire under a clear night sky spinning his yarn. As he tells of the twins' victory, he points overhead and narrates the creation event that follows, to the Maya constellation of the Hearth of Creation, where the first fire to warm the nascent earth was kindled. Contemporary Maya still connect the eastern star in the belt with the southernmost stars, Rigel and Saiph, in what we call Orion, that outline the hearth enveloping the smoke and fire at the centre, We recognize it as the Great Nebula in Orion, visible to the naked eye as a fuzzy patch in the middle of the stellar triangle. There is a wonderful surprise in the Maya story of the great cosmic fire of creation. Modern astronomy teaches us that the Orion Nebula is actually a vast cloud of dust and incandescent hydrogen gas, a ten thousand-degree fire where stars are being born, many of them surrounded by cosmic disks out of which future planets are likely to emerge. And so, tales imagined long ago and retold for generations yet hold meaning for us. There is truth in myth.

Anthony F. Aveni
Russell Colgate Distinguished University Professor of Astronomy, Anthropology and Native American Studies, Emeritus, Colgate University

Publisher's Note

AS THE TALES from Mesoamerican and ancient and indigenous North and South American mythology and folklore are principally derived from oral storytelling traditions along with a few surviving fragments of ancient manuscripts, their written representation has depended on the research, transcription and interpretation by those who first put them to paper or first translated them – and most of these were conquistadors, colonizers, Christian writers and well-meaning but often misguided European historians and archaeologists of the nineteenth century. The text and stories in this book derive from a mixture of these sources, and you can learn more about the sources and authors at the back of the book. This collection presents a selected cross-section of information about and stories from all over this wider region, with the aim of representing the breadth of ancient indigenous culture, civilization, religion and storytelling inherent to these peoples, for both enlightenment and entertainment, rather than for scholarly education. For the purposes of retaining the integrity of the source texts, most variances in spelling have been left unaltered, though punctuation has been rationalized and BC/AD now rendered as BCE/CE to reflect current practice.

EPIC

AZTEC MYTHS & TALES

ANTHOLOGY OF CLASSIC TALES

Foreword by Anthony F. Aveni

FLAME TREE PUBLISHING

TALES

Mesoamerican & Andean Civilizations

Introduction

MESOAMERICA and wider Central and northern South America encompass many countries, all of which possess their own rich tapestries of sacred narratives, thrilling stories, tall tales and fascinating mythologies, rooted in ancient civilizations.

Of those civilizations it is the Aztec and Mayan that are perhaps best known today, but explore further and the stories of other cultures, from the Muisca of Colombia and the Inca of Peru to even the Pueblo peoples of the Southwestern United States, are every bit as exciting. The region has long been a source of immense fascination for Western societies, from the Conquistadors of Spain and Portugal in the fifteenth and sixteenth centuries, to more modern explorers of the nineteenth and early twentieth centuries intent on uncovering the secrets of the region and its peoples. Writings of these latter-day adventurers and scholars form much of the pages that follow, giving insight to the cultures, beliefs and way of life of these incredible civilizations.

For example, Lewis Spence (1874–1955), the prolific folklorist and scholar, was one of few in the early twentieth century who accessibly presented the fascinating history and mythology of Mexico, Central America and Peru. So it is from his work that much of the deeper introductions to the culture, civilization, religion and mythology of these ancient nations is drawn. Another example of an author whose work we have presented is the bishop Diego de Landa (1524–79) – a very problematic character due to his anti-idolatrous destruction of Mayan manuscripts, and yet his documenting of Mayan culture has preserved invaluable information still worth reading. However, it must thus be remembered that these texts are thus of their time and filtered through Christian and colonial lenses and must be read with that in mind.

The First Civilizations, A Summary

THE FIRST HUMAN BEINGS had reached Mesoamerica by at least 15,000 years ago. Agriculture appeared by c. 5000 BC, and village life by 2000 BCE. Common traits throughout the region led anthropologists to propose the idea of Mesoamerica – a cultural area whose diverse societies shared maize-beans-squash agriculture, monumental architecture, organized religion and a 260-day ritual calendar.

The first civilization in Mesoamerica appeared around 1250 BCE on Mexico's tropical eastern coast. The Olmec (1250–200 BCE) created many cultural traits, which featured throughout Mesoamerican prehistory. These included the rubber-ball game, monumental architecture and sophisticated pottery and jadework decorated with images of gods and supernatural beings. The two main Olmec centres were San Lorenzo and La Venta, whose sites were adorned with giant monolithic stone heads and zoomorphic sculptures. Between 500 BCE and 700 CE, the Zapotecs of southern Mexico's Oaxaca Valley flourished in their hill-top city of Monte Albán. The city housed perhaps 25,000 inhabitants at its peak between 500 CE and 700 CE, with the elite building 20 pyramid-temples and a ballcourt around the great central plaza. In Zapotec religion, clouds represented transformed ancestors, and worship focused on Cociyo, god of lightning. As with other Mesoamerican gods, Cociyo was revered through ritual bloodletting and sacrifice carried out with obsidian lancets. Further north, in the Valley of Mexico, the great urban metropolis of Teotihuacán emerged around 100 CE and flourished until around 700 CE. Teotihuacán's great economic and ideological influence on Mesoamerica was due partly to its size and partly to its exploitation and trade in the dark volcanic glass obsidian, which was the 'steel' of prehistoric Mesoamerica. Covering *c.* 20 sq km (7 sq miles), and housing c. 200,000 people, the city of Teotihuacán was dominated by the Pyramid of the Sun, the Pyramid of the Moon, the ceremonial avenue known as the Street of the Dead and the great Palace of Quetzalcoatl, the 'Feathered Serpent.' Archaeological evidence indicates that Teotihuacán shared both trade links and cultural ties with the Zapotec city of Monte Albán.

The Classic Maya

The Classic Maya civilization (*c.* 250–850 CE) flourished in the tropical lowlands of modern Mexico, Guatemala, Belize and Honduras. The Maya were never a unified empire, but rather a series of autonomous city-states each ruled by a royal dynasty and a god-like king. They possessed Mesoamerica's most sophisticated glyphic writing system, a complex dual calendar and a vigesimal (base 20) counting system. The Maya built great ceremonial centres like Tikal and Palenque, whose astronomically aligned architecture was the backdrop for an elaborate ceremonial life, including ritual bloodletting and human sacrifice. Internal dissension, Teotihuacán's collapse and possibly climate change have all been suggested to explain the Maya collapse around 850 CE.

The Aztec

Following the demise of Mesoamerica's Classic cultures, a new militaristic era began. It was the warrior society of the Toltecs at their capital of Tula (950–1150 CE) that set the scene for the tumultuous post-Classic period. Most significant were the Aztecs (1325–1521), Mesoamerica's last imperial civilization. Aztec society was hierarchical, ruled by a divine emperor and nobility. Long-distance trade by the Pochteca merchants (often doubling as spies), conquest and tribute (everyday and luxury items) constituted the backbone of their economic success. Aztec religion was dominated by the tribal war god Huitzilopochtli, the rain/fertility god Tlaloc and the supreme deity Tezcatlipoca, the Lord of the Smoking Mirror. Human sacrifices to these and other deities were considered debt payments to the gods whose acts of self-sacrifice had brought the present world into being.

Tenochtitlán and the Great Temple

The Aztec built their capital of Tenochtitlán (modern Mexico City) on an island in Lake Texcoco in the Valley of Mexico. Like Venice, it was built on reclaimed land, criss-crossed by canals and connected to the shoreline by great causeways. At its peak, the city housed up to 200,000 people. In myth, the city was founded around 1350 when Aztec priests saw an eagle perched atop a great cactus – a sign given by Huitzilopochtli. The Aztec expressed their imperial destiny by building the 'Great Temple' in the heart of Tenochtitlán. Temples were considered godhouses or teocalli, and embodied the Aztecs' cosmic essence and identity. The Great Temple had two shrines on its summit, dedicated to Huitzilopochtli and Tlaloc (representing blood and water), and thus materialized cosmic myths relating to both deities.

Rebuilt and enlarged by successive emperors, the Great Temple was a symbolic recreation of the mythic mountain Coatepetl and the human sacrifices which took place there recapitulated the cosmic victory of Huitzilopochtli over his sister, the moon goddess Coyolxauhqui. The presence of the shrine and offerings of jade and seashells to Tlaloc suggests that the temple was also conceived as a great mountain symbolizing water and fertility.

Myths of Origin

Mesoamerican myths placed society at the centre of the universe, legitimizing the social order and sanctifying the will of divine rulers. Myths gave sacred meaning to ideas of birth, marriage, war, sacrifice and death, interpreting them as re-enactments of previous events in a universe governed by cyclical time.

In the highlands of Central Mexico, creation myths reflected a landscape where frost, drought, earthquakes and volcanoes threatened civilized life. The Aztecs believed that the universe was conceived in an elemental struggle between light and darkness, with cosmic principles being embodied in Ometeotl and Omecihuatl, the male and female lords of duality. Their four offspring, Xipe Totec, Huitzilopochtli, Quetzalcoatl and Tezcatlipoca were joined by Tlaloc, the rain god, and Chalchiuhtlicue, goddess of water, in a series of cosmic battles which saw successive worlds created and destroyed.

The Aztecs believed in five creations or 'Suns,' each identified by the cataclysm which engulfed it. The first creation (Four-Jaguar), presided over by Tezcatlipoca, was destroyed when Quetzalcoatl knocked Tezcatlipoca into the primordial waters and the earth was consumed by jaguars. The second creation (Four-Wind), was ruled by Quetzalcoatl, and ended when Tezcatlipoca cast Quetzalcoatl off his throne and destroyed the world with hurricanes. The third creation (Four-Rain), was governed by Tlaloc and destroyed by fiery rain sent by Quetzalcoatl. The fourth creation (Four-Water), belonged to Chalchiuhtlicue, and ended with a flood, its human inhabitants turned into fish. Tezcatlipoca and Quetzalcoatl then changed into two great trees, raising the sky above the earth. Quetzalcoatl created human flesh by mixing powdered bones with divine blood. The world remained buried in darkness, however, until the gods gathered at Teotihuacán to create the fifth, Aztec, world (Four-Movement). The deity Nanahuatzin hurled himself into the cosmic fire and was transformed into the rising sun, remaining motionless until his fellow gods sacrificed their blood to give him the energy for his daily journey across the heavens.

Popol Vuh, the Book of Maya Creation

In Mesoamerica's lowlands, Maya creation myths also embodied natural phenomena in epic tales of successive world eras. The *Popol Vuh*, the sacred 'book of counsel' of the Quiché (or 'Kiche') Maya of Guatemala, is a unique masterpiece of Mesoamerican literature, preserving ancient creation stories which tell how the creator-gods Gugumatz and Huracan shaped the earth, dividing mountains from water and separating sky from earth. Their first world creation failed when the jaguars, deer, birds and serpents they made were unable to speak or praise their makers. Their second attempt also proved unsuccessful when, made from mud, the beings dissolved in the primordial waters. With the help of sorcerers, Gugumatz and Huracan tried a third time, carving their creations from wood so as to speak and look like real people. When the manikins forgot their makers, the vengeful gods turned the world upside down, forcing pots and grinding stones to turn against the unworthy creations. The fourth and final creation saw the gods fashion human flesh from multicoloured maize brought by the fox, coyote, parrot and crow. They transformed the maize into the first four men able to honour their makers – the mythic founders of the four Quiché Maya lineages. Jealous that their creations were too perfect and might one day be rivals, Gugumatz and Huracan diluted the mens' uniqueness by clouding their vision and inventing women with whom they could procreate.

Aztec Origin Myths

One Aztec myth tells how the ancestors emerged from the sacred earth at Chicomoztoc, legendary mountain of 'the seven caves,' and place of cosmic genesis for many Mesoamerican peoples. An alternative legend relates that the Aztecs took their name from an island called Aztlan in northwest Mexico, and began an epic migration south-east to the Valley of Mexico, in the year '1 Flint' (1116 or 1168). During the journey, the Aztecs were guided by a speaking idol of their war god Huitzilopochtli, who prophesied future greatness for his people, conquering all others and receiving tribute of gold, emeralds, quetzal feathers and cacao (chocolate). The Aztecs continued their wanderings to Coatepetl ('serpent mountain'), where, in a form of mythical rebirth, the god Huitzilopochtli was magically conceived by Coatlicue, the Earth Mother, from a ball of precious feather down. The unborn god was forewarned of an attempt by his jealous sister, the moon goddess Coyolxauhqui, and her 400 star brothers, the Huitznahua, to kill his mother and himself and retain their cosmic supremacy. Forestalling the murder, Huitzilopochtli was born in adult form, springing from his mother's womb as an invincible warrior. With a flaming fire-serpent, Huitzilopochtli cut off his sister's head, mutilated her body and scattered his star brothers to every corner of the sky. According to legend, the Aztecs then continued their journey southwards into the valley of Mexico and founded the city of Tenochtitlán.

The Sacred Calendar

Mesoamerican civilizations devised a dual calendar system which fused real and mythic time in two intermeshing calendars. Like interlocking cog-wheels, the sacred and secular calendars created a unique date every day for a 52-year period (i.e. 18,980 days) – the so-called 'Calendar Round.' Each day had a patron deity which exerted influence over people and events.

The Mesoamerican calculation of time integrated observable phenomena in the real world, such as cycles of growth and decay, and the movements of celestial bodies, with ideas of cosmic fate and mythological events. Time itself was cyclical; every physical action possessed a supernatural aspect. Everyday events and their consequences could be explained, enhanced or sometimes avoided by a precise and seemingly endless series of calculations based on knowledge contained within the dual calendar system.

The Maya Calendar

Maya mythology gave emphasis to the ritual significance of gods, signs and numbers, which marked the passage of time. The Haab or solar calendar had 18 'months' each of 20 days, with five unlucky days called uayeb added on to make a total of 365 days. Running in parallel, and intercalated with the solar year, was the sacred calendar, or Tzolkin, made up of 260 days divided into 20 'weeks' of 13 days. The origins of the Tzolkin may be as an approximation of the nine-month human gestation period. Each 'week' had its own deity or deities and every day its own god or goddess. The association of each day with its supernatural patron signified a specific symbolic value: the day Kan meant 'maize' and 'abundance'; and Caban meant 'earth' or 'earthquake.' The last day of each solar month was designated the 'seating of' the next month, whose supernatural influence could already be felt. Thus, the 'seating of' the month Pop preceded One Pop, and instead of Twenty Pop came the 'seating of Uo,' the succeeding month.

The Aztec Calendar

The Aztecs possessed a similar but distinct calendrical system also composed of two intermeshing day-counts. The ritual calendar, or tonalpohualli, was a 260-day cycle composed of 20 'weeks' of 13 days (called trecenas), each with its own number and a glyphic name such as ocelotl (jaguar), cipactli (caiman) or tecpatl (flint). The cycle of 20 days rotates with 13 day numbers, giving a unique date to each of the 260 days in the calendar, such as One Acatl (One Reed) or Thirteen Ozomatli (Thirteen Monkey). This sacred day-count was recorded in the tonalamatl, books made from barkpaper, which served as ritual almanacs. Like modern astrological horoscopes, these were interpreted by professional diviners who foretold a person's fate according to the good or bad qualities associated with their date of birth. For example, Seven Rain was fortunate, but Two Rabbit was unlucky. If a birthdate was deemed inauspicious, it could be changed. The tonalpohualli was intercalated with the xiupohualli or solar year, which, like its Maya counterpart, was composed of 18 'months' of 20 days with the five unlucky days known as nemontemi. Each 'month,' known in Central Mexico by the Spanish term veintena, possessed its own festival, which was closely associated with the agricultural year. Each Aztec year was named after the 'year bearer,' one of the four possible day-name and number combinations of the tonalpohualli which occurred on the last day of the eighteenth month – and was either Rabbit, Reed, Flint or House.

Counting Time, Maya Numbers

The Maya developed the concept of zero, representing it as a shell. Their vigesimal (base 20) counting system increased from the bottom to the top in vertical columns, unlike our decimal (base 10) system, which progresses from right to left. From 1 to 19, they wrote numbers using a bar-and-dot system, in which the dot = 1 and the bar = 5. Using positional notation, the first position counted from zero to 19, the second position had units with a value of 20, the third had units worth 400, and so on. In this way, 1 kin = 1 day, 20 kins = 1 uinal, 18 uinals = 1 tun (360 days), 20 tuns = 1 katun (7,200 days) and 20 katuns = 1 baktun (144,000 days). This sophisticated system recorded calendrical, genealogical and mythological dates, sometimes encompassing millions of years. The Maya also invented a 'Long Count' of years whose mythical starting date was 3114 BCE. This allowed time to be calculated in a linear fashion in basic units of 360 days (tuns). Correlating this with our modern calendar allows us to calculate historical dates for named Maya rulers, such as Yax Pac, king of Copán, who died on 10 February in 822 CE.

Gods and the Spirit World

In Mesoamerica, gods and myths emerged from an Amerindian worldview, reflecting a natural philosophy where ideas concerning life and death were linked symbolically to the earth, sky and sea in a grand cosmic scheme. As civilization developed, ancient spirits became powerful deities, controlling every aspect of sacred and secular life.

In Mesoamerican worldview, the earth was sacred, the sea the 'mother of fertility' and the sky an untouchable realm of gods and spirits whose influence reached down to affect all earthly life. This was a universe ruled by cyclical time, where myth was a living reality and everyday life punctuated by ceremonies which recapitulated the legendary events of the past. In pre-Columbian times, and still today, the rhythms of nature and human life-cycles were united with social, economic and political life, and every part of the natural world was infused with spiritual force. The shimmer of lakes and rivers, the lustrous sheen of jade and pearls, the iridescence of bird feathers and the crimson glow of human blood, were manifestations of the fertilizing cosmic power that permeated all existence. Throughout Mesoamerica, gods were deifications of natural phenomena – sun, moon, rain and wind – and intimately associated with human concerns of birth, death, fertility and war.

The Nature of Gods

At the heart of the Mesoamerican life was the symbolic equation of blood-for-water. Humans offered their blood to the gods and the gods reciprocated by forestalling drought, frost and, crucially, by sending rain to the earth to fertilize the crops. The daily worship of ambivalent but all-powerful deities was essential to keep the world in motion and the universe in balance. Exemplifying the uneasy relationship between Mesoamerican peoples and their deities was the supreme Aztec deity Tezcatlipoca, Lord of the Smoking Mirror. He was patron of royalty and warriors, master of human fate and inventor of human sacrifice through which he could be revered. Capricious by nature, cruel and generous by turns, he watched the world through his magical obsidian mirror, seeing into the very thoughts of his subjects. The Aztecs regarded themselves as his slaves, and their emperor as a living manifestation of the god. Equally bloodthirsty was Huitzilopochtli (Hummingbird of the South), the Aztec war and sun god, often depicted carrying his serpent-shaped spear-thrower. His association with war and death is reflected in his name, as hummingbirds were the souls of fallen warriors who accompanied their patron's solar image as it journeyed across the sky. Where these two gods sanctified the shedding of human blood, other Aztec deities were concerned with water and fertility. Chief among these was Tlaloc, an ancient rain deity, worshipped throughout Mesoamerica under different names, such as Cociyo amongst the Zapotecs, and Chaak amongst the Maya. In Aztec belief, Tlaloc was associated with mountains where rain clouds gathered and mists lingered, and where young children were sacrificed to his cult – their tears an augury of the coming rains. So influential was Tlaloc that the lush and brilliantly coloured Aztec paradise or heaven was called Tlalocan. The god's consort was Chalchiuhtlicue (She of the Jade Skirt) who summoned hurricanes and was associated with the breaking waters which precede childbirth. Quetzalcoatl, Feathered Serpent, was also an ancient deity whose imagery is found in Olmec art and at Teotihuacán. During post-Classic times, the Maya knew Quetzalcoatl as Kukulkan (also Feathered Serpent), and the Aztec regarded him as a wind god, who announced the rains.

Blood for Rain at Acatlán

Today, in remote parts of Mesoamerica, echoes of ancient blood sacrifices can still be heard. In villages like Acatlán, Zitlala and Ostotempa in the Mexican state of Guerrero, young men don jaguar costumes and helmets to fight or dance in honour of the supernatural jaguar. These ceremonies occur in early May, when the soil is parched. Although now Christianized as festivals of Santa Cruz (Holy Cross), they may be a survival of the springtime Aztec ceremony of Toxcatl, which celebrated the god Tezcatlipoca and his jaguar alter-ego, the monstrous Tepeyollotl. Most such events see the jaguar-men dancing or whipping each other with ropes, or a single jaguar-man being chased by villagers. But in Acatlán, where the Aztec language of Nahuatl is still spoken, events are more violent. Before dawn the villagers make a pilgrimage to the nearby summit of Cerro Azul (Blue Mountain), clear a sacred arena, then decorate a stone altar with blood-red and orange flowers. At midday, with the sun at its zenith, groups of jaguar-men engage in violent fist fights during which blood is spilt and contestants knocked unconscious. The villagers explain that only by shedding young and potent blood for the jaguar deity can he be persuaded to release his own blood in the form of fertilizing rains.

The Civilization of Mexico

IMMEDIATELY PRIOR to the Europeans' discovery, there was in America a widely disseminated belief that at a relatively remote period, strangers from the east had visited American soil, eventually returning to their own abodes in the Land of Sunrise. Such, for example, was the Mexican legend of Quetzalcoatl, to which we shall revert later in its more essentially mythical connection. He landed with several companions at Vera Cruz, and speedily brought to bear the power of a civilizing agency upon native opinion. In the ancient Mexican *pinturas*, or paintings, he is represented as being habited in a long black gown, fringed with white crosses.

After sojourning with the Mexicans for a number of years, during which time he initiated them into the arts of life and civilization, he departed from their land on a magic raft, promising, however, to return. His second advent was anxiously looked for, and when Cortés and his companions arrived at Vera Cruz, the identical spot at which Quetzalcoatl was supposed to have set out on his homeward journey, the Mexicans fully believed him to be the returned hero. Of course Montezuma, their monarch, was not altogether taken by surprise at the coming of the white man, as he had been informed of the arrival of mysterious strangers in Yucatan and elsewhere in Central America; but in the eyes of the commonalty the Spanish leader was a 'hero-god' indeed.

A Peruvian Prophecy

The Mexicans were by no means singular in their presentiments. When Hernando de Soto, on landing in Peru, first met the Inca Huascar, the latter related an ancient prophecy which his father, Huaina Ccapac, had repeated on his death-bed, that in the reign of the thirteenth Inca white men of surpassing strength and valour would come from their father the Sun, and subject the Peruvians to their rule. "I command you," said the dying king, "to yield them homage and obedience, for they will be of a nature superior to ours."

But the most interesting of American legends connected with the discovery is that in which the prophecy of the Maya priest Chilan Balam is described. Father Lizana, a venerable Spanish author, records the prophecy, which he states was very well known throughout Yucatan, as does Villagutierre, who quotes it.

The Prophecy of Chilan Balam

Part of this strange prophecy runs as follows: "At the end of the thirteenth age, when Itza is at the height of its power, as also the city called Tancah, the signal of God will appear on the heights, and the Cross with which the world was enlightened will be manifested. There will be variance of men's will in future times, when this signal shall be brought.... Receive your barbarous bearded guests from the east, who bring the signal of God, who comes to us in mercy and pity. The time of our life is coming...."

It would seem from the perusal of this prophecy that a genuine substratum of native tradition has been over-laid and coloured by the influence of the early Spanish missionaries. The terms of the announcement are much too exact, and the language employed is obviously Scriptural. But the native books of Chilan Balam, whence the prophecy is taken, are much less explicit, and the genuineness of their character is evinced by the idiomatic use of the Maya tongue, which, in the form they present it in, could have been written by none save those who had habitually employed it from infancy. As regards the prophetic nature of these deliverances it is known that the Chilan, or priest, was wont to utter publicly at the end of certain prolonged periods a prophecy forecasting the character of the similar period to come, and there is reason to believe that some distant rumours of the coming of the white man had reached the ears of several of the seers.

These vague intimations that the seas separated them from a great continent, where dwelt beings like themselves, seem to have been common to white and red men alike. And who shall say by what strange magic of telepathy they were inspired in the minds of the daring explorers and the ascetic priests who gave expression to them in act and utterance? The discovery of America was much more than a mere scientific process, and romance rather than the cold speculations of mediaeval geography urged men to tempt the dim seas of the West in quest of golden islands seen in dreams.

The Type of Mexican Civilization

The first civilized American people with whom the discoverers came into contact were those of the Nahua or ancient Mexican race. We use the term 'civilized' advisedly, for although several authorities of standing have refused to regard the Mexicans as a people who had achieved such a state of culture as would entitle them to be classed among civilized communities, there is no doubt that they had advanced nearly as far as it was possible for them to proceed when their environment and the nature of the circumstances which handicapped them are taken into consideration. In architecture they had evolved a type of building, solid yet wonderfully graceful, which, if not so massive as the Egyptian and Assyrian, was yet more highly decorative. Their artistic outlook as expressed in their painting and pottery was more versatile and less conventional than that of the ancient people of the Orient, their social system was of a more advanced type, and a less rigorous attitude was evinced by the ruling caste toward the subject classes. Yet, on the other hand, the picture is darkened by the terrible if picturesque rites which attended their religious ceremonies, and the dread shadow of human sacrifice which eternally overhung their teeming populations. Nevertheless, the standard of morality was high, justice was even-handed, the forms of government were comparatively mild, and but for the fanaticism which demanded such troops of victims, we might justly compare the civilization of ancient Mexico with that of the peoples of old China or India, if the literary activity of the Oriental states be discounted.

The Mexican Race

The race which was responsible for this varied and highly coloured civilization was that known as the Nahua (Those who live by Rule), a title adopted by them to distinguish them from those tribes who still roamed in an unsettled condition over the contiguous plains of New Mexico and the more northerly tracts. This term was employed by them to designate the race as a whole, but it was composed of many diverse elements, the characteristics of which were rendered still more various by the adoption into one or other of the tribes which composed it of surrounding aboriginal peoples. Much controversy has raged round the question regarding the original home of the Nahua, but their migration legends consistently point to a northern origin; and when the close affinity between the art-forms and mythology of the present-day natives of British Columbia and those of the Nahua comes to be considered along with the very persistent legends of a prolonged pilgrimage from the North, where they dwelt in a place "by the water," the conclusion that the Nahua emanated from the region indicated is well-nigh irresistible.

In Nahua tradition the name of the locality whence the race commenced its wanderings is called Aztlan (The Place of Reeds), but this place-name is of little or no value as a guide to any given region, though probably every spot betwixt Behring Strait and Mexico has been identified with it by zealous antiquarians. Other names discovered in the migration legends are Tlapallan (The Country of Bright Colours) and Chicomoztoc (The Seven Caves), and these may perhaps be identified with New Mexico or Arizona.

Legends of Mexican Migration

All early writers on the history of Mexico agree that the Toltecs were the first of the several swarms of Nahua who streamed upon the Mexican plateau in ever-widening waves. Concerning the reality of this people so little is known that many authorities of standing have regarded them as wholly mythical, while others profess to see in them a veritable race, the founders of Mexican civilization. The author has already elaborated his theory of this difficult question elsewhere, but will briefly refer to it when he comes to deal with the subject of the Toltec civilization and the legends concerning it. For the present we must regard the Toltecs merely as a race alluded to in a migration myth as the first Nahua immigrants to the region of Mexico. Ixtlilxochitl, a native chronicler who flourished shortly after the Spanish conquest of Mexico, gives two separate accounts of the early Toltec migrations, the first of which goes back to the period of their arrival in the fabled land of Tlapallan, alluded to above. In this account Tlapallan is described as a region near the sea, which the Toltecs reached by voyaging southward, skirting the coasts of California. This account must be received with the greatest caution. But we know that the natives of British Columbia have been expert in the use of the canoe from an early period, and that the Mexican god Quetzalcoatl, who is probably originally derived from a common source with their deity Yetl, is represented as being skilled in the management of the craft. It is, therefore, not outside the bounds of possibility that the early swarms of Nahua immigrants made their way to Mexico by sea, but it is much more probable that their migrations took place by land, following the level country at the base of the Rocky Mountains.

The Toltec Upheaval

Like nearly all legendary immigrants, the Toltecs did not set out to colonize distant countries from any impulse of their own, but were the victims of internecine dissension in the homeland, and were expelled from the community to seek their fortunes elsewhere. Thus thrust forth, they set their faces southward, and reached Tlapallan in the year 1

Tecpatl (AD 387). Passing the country of Xalisco, they effected a landing at Huatulco, and journeyed down the coast until they reached Tochtepec, whence they pushed inland to Tollantzinco. To enable them to make this journey they required no less than 104 years. Ixtlilxochitl furnishes another account of the Toltec migration in his *Relaciones*, a work dealing with the early history of the Mexican races. In this he recounts how the chiefs of Tlapallan, who had revolted against the royal power, were banished from that region in AD 439. Lingering near their ancient territory for the space of eight years, they then journeyed to Tlapallantzinco, where they halted for three years before setting out on a prolonged pilgrimage, which occupied the tribe for over a century, and in the course of which it halted at no less than thirteen different resting-places, six of which can be traced to stations on the Pacific coast, and the remainder to localities in the north of Mexico.

Artificial Nature of the Migration Myths

It is plain from internal evidence that these two legends of the Toltec migrations present an artificial aspect. But if we cannot credit them in detail, that is not to say that they do not describe in part an actual pilgrimage. They are specimens of numerous migration myths which are related concerning the various branches of the Mexican races. Few features of interest are presented in them, and they are chiefly remarkable for wearisome repetition and divergence in essential details.

Myths of the Toltecs

But we enter a much more fascinating domain when we come to peruse the myths regarding the Toltec kingdom and civilization. These exhibit an almost Oriental exuberance of imagination and colouring, and forcibly remind the reader of the gorgeous architectural and scenic descriptions in the *Arabian Nights*. The principal sources of these legends are the histories of Zumarraga and Ixtlilxochitl. The latter is by no means a satisfactory authority, but he has succeeded in investing the traditions of his native land with no inconsiderable degree of charm (*see* pages 217–21). But it is time that we examined the claims put forward on behalf of Toltec civilization by the aid of more scientific methods.

Did the Toltecs Exist?

Some authorities have questioned the existence of the Toltecs, and have professed to see in them a race which had merely a mythical significance. They base this theory upon the circumstance that the duration of the reigns of the several Toltec monarchs is very frequently stated to have lasted for exactly fifty-two years, the duration of the great Mexican cycle of years which had been adopted so that the ritual calendar might coincide with the solar year. The circumstance is certainly suspicious, as is the fact that many of the names of the Toltec monarchs are also those of the principal Nahua deities, and this renders the whole dynastic list of very doubtful value. Dr Brinton recognized in the Toltecs those children of the sun who, like their brethren in Peruvian mythology, were sent from heaven to civilize the human race, and his theory is by no means weakened by the circumstance that Quetzalcoatl, a deity of solar significance, is alluded to in Nahua myth as King of the Toltecs. Recent considerations and discoveries, however, have virtually forced students of the subject to admit the existence of the Toltecs as a race. The author has dealt with the question at some length elsewhere, and is not of those who are free to admit the definite existence of the Toltecs from a historical point of view. The late Mr Payne of Oxford, an authority entitled to every respect, gave it as his opinion that "the accounts of Toltec history current at the conquest contain a nucleus of substantial truth," and he writes convincingly: "To doubt that there once existed in Tollan an advancement superior to that which prevailed among the Nahuatlaca generally at the conquest, and that its people spread their advancement throughout Anahuac, and into the districts eastward and southward, would be to reject a belief universally entertained, and confirmed rather than shaken by the efforts made in later times to construct for the Pueblo something in the nature of a history."

A Persistent Tradition

The theory of the present author concerning Toltec historical existence is rather more non-committal. He admits that a most persistent body of tradition as to their existence gained general credence among the Nahua, and that the date (1055) of their alleged dispersal admits of the approximate exactness and probability of this body of tradition at the time of the conquest. He also admits that the site of Tollan contains ruins which are undoubtedly of a date earlier than that of the architecture of the Nahua as known at the conquest, and that numerous evidences of an older civilization exist. He also believes that the early Nahua having within their racial recollection existed as savages, the time which elapsed between their barbarian condition and the more advanced state which they achieved was too brief to admit of evolution from savagery to culture. Hence they must have adopted an older civilization, especially as through the veneer of civilization possessed by them they exhibited every sign of gross barbarism.

A Nameless People

If this be true it would go to show that a people of comparatively high culture existed at a not very remote period on the Mexican tableland. But what their name was or their racial affinity the writer does not profess to know. Many modern American scholars of note have conferred upon them the name of 'Toltecs,' and speak freely of the 'Toltec period' and of 'Toltec art.' It may appear pedantic to refuse to recognize that the cultured people who dwelt in Mexico in pre-Nahua times were 'the Toltecs.' But in the face of the absence of genuine and authoritative native written records dealing with the question, the author finds himself compelled to remain unconvinced as to the exact designation of the mysterious older race which preceded the Nahua. There are not wanting authorities who appear to regard the pictorial chronicles of the Nahua as quite as worthy of credence as written records, but it must be clear that tradition or even history set down in pictorial form can never possess that degree of definiteness contained in a written account.

Toltec Art

As has been stated above, the Toltecs of tradition were chiefly remarkable for their intense love of art and their productions in its various branches. Ixtlilxochitl says that they worked in gold, silver, copper, tin, and lead, and as masons employed flint, porphyry, basalt, and obsidian. In the manufacture of jewellery and *objets d'art* they excelled, and the pottery of Cholula, of which specimens are frequently recovered, was of a high standard.

Other Aboriginal Peoples

Mexico contained other aboriginal races besides the Toltecs. Of these many and diverse peoples the most remarkable were the Otomi, who still occupy Guanajuato and Queretaro, and who, before the coming of the Nahua, probably spread over the entire valley of Mexico. In the south we find the Huasteca, a people speaking the same language as the Maya of Central America, and on the Mexican Gulf the Totonacs and Chontals. On the Pacific side of the country the Mixteca and Zapoteca were responsible for a flourishing civilization which exhibited many original characteristics, and which in some degree was a link between the cultures of Mexico and Central America. Traces of a still older population than any of these are still to be found in the more remote parts of Mexico, and the Mixe, Zaque, Kuicatec, and Popolcan are probably the remnants of prehistoric races of vast antiquity.

The Cliff-dwellers and a Connection to the Pueblo Indians

It is probable that a race known as 'the Cliff-dwellers,' occupying the plateau country of Arizona, New Mexico, Colorado, and Utah, and even extending in its ramifications to Mexico itself, was related ethnologically to the Nahua. The present-day Pueblo Indians dwelling to the north of Mexico most probably possess a leaven of Nahua blood. Ere the tribes who communicated this leaven to the whole had intermingled with others of various origin, it would appear that they occupied with others those tracts of country now inhabited by the Pueblo Indians, and in the natural recesses and shallow caverns found in the faces of the cliffs erected dwellings and fortifications, displaying an architectural ability of no mean order. These communities extended as far south as the Gila river, the most southern affluent of the Colorado, and the remains they have left there appear to be of a later date architecturally than those situated farther north. These were found in ruins by the first Spanish explorers, and it is thought that their builders were eventually driven back to rejoin their kindred in the north.

ZFarther to the south in the cañons of the Piedras Verdes river in Chihuahua, Mexico, are cliff-dwellings corresponding in many respects with those of the Pueblo region, and Dr Hrdlicka has examined others so far south as the State of Jalisco, in Central Mexico. These may be the ruins of dwellings erected either by the early Nahua or by some of the peoples relatively aboriginal to them, and may display the architectural features general among the Nahua prior to their adoption of other alien forms. Or else they may be the remains of dwellings similar to those of the Tarahumare, a still existing tribe of Mexico, who, according to Lumholtz, inhabit similar structures at the present day. It is clear from the architectural development of the cliff-dwellers that their civilization developed generally from south to north, that this race was cognate to the early Nahua, and that it later withdrew to the north, or became fused with the general body of the Nahua peoples. It must not be understood, however, that the race arrived in the Mexican plateau before the Nahua, and the ruins of Jalisco and other mid-Mexican districts may merely be the remains of comparatively modern cliff-dwellings, an adaptation by mid-Mexican communities of the 'Cliff-dweller' architecture, or a local development of it owing to the exigencies of early life in the district.

The Nahua Race

The Nahua peoples included all those tribes speaking the Nahuatlatolli (Nahua tongue), and occupied a sphere extending from the southern borders of New Mexico to the Isthmus of Tehuantepec on the south, or very much within the limits of the modern Republic of Mexico. But this people must not be regarded as one race of homogeneous origin. A very brief account of their racial affinities must be sufficient here. The Chichimecs were probably related to the Otomi, whom we have alluded to as among the first-comers to the Mexican valley. They were traditionally supposed to have entered it at a period subsequent to the Toltec occupation. Their chief towns were Tezcuco and Tenayucan, but they later allied themselves with the Nahua in a great confederacy, and adopted the Nahua language. There are circumstances which justify the assumption that on their entrance to the Mexican valley they consisted of a number of tribes loosely united, presenting in their general organization a close resemblance to some of the composite tribes of modern American Indians.

The Aculhuaque

Next to them in point of order of tribal arrival were the Aculhuaque, or Acolhuans. The name means 'tall' or 'strong' men, literally 'People of the Broad Shoulder,' or 'Pushers,' who made a way for themselves. Gomara states in his *Conquista de Mexico* that they arrived in the valley from Acolhuacan about AD 780, and founded the towns of Tollan, Colhuacan, and Mexico itself. The Acolhuans were pure Nahua, and may well have been the much-disputed Toltecs, for the Nahua people always insisted on the fact that the Toltecs were of the same stock as themselves, and spoke an older and purer form of the Nahua tongue. From the Acolhuans sprang the Tlascalans, the inveterate enemies of the Aztecs, who so heartily assisted Cortés in his invasion of the Aztec capital, Tenochtitlan, or Mexico.

The Tecpanecs

The Tecpanecs were a confederacy of purely Nahua tribes dwelling in towns situated upon the Lake of Tezcuco, the principal of which were Tlacopan and Azcapozalco. The name Tecpanec signifies that each settlement possessed its own chief's house, or *tecpan*. This tribe were almost certainly later Nahua immigrants who arrived in Mexico after the Acolhuans, and were great rivals to the Chichimec branch of the race.

The Aztecs

The Aztecâ, or Aztecs, were a nomad tribe of doubtful origin, but probably of Nahua blood. Wandering over the Mexican plateau for generations, they at length settled in the marshlands near the Lake of Tezcuco, hard by Tlacopan. The name Aztecâ means 'Crane People,' and was bestowed upon the tribe by the Tecpanecs, probably because of the fact that, like cranes, they dwelt in a marshy neighbourhood. They founded the town of Tenochtitlan, or Mexico, and for a while paid tribute to the Tecpanecs. But later they became the most powerful allies of that people, whom they finally surpassed entirely in power and splendour.

The features of the Aztecs as represented in the various Mexican paintings are typically Indian, and argue a northern origin. The race was, and is, of average height, and the skin is of a dark brown hue. The Mexican is grave, taciturn, and melancholic, with a deeply rooted love of the mysterious, slow to anger, yet almost inhuman in the violence of his passions when aroused. He is usually gifted with a logical mind, quickness of apprehension, and an ability to regard the subtle side of things with great nicety. Patient and imitative, the ancient Mexican excelled in those arts which demanded such qualities in their execution. He had a real affection for the beautiful in nature and a passion for flowers, but the Aztec music lacked gaiety, and the national amusements were too often of a gloomy and ferocious character. The women are more vivacious than the men, but were in the days before the conquest very subservient to the wills of their husbands. We have already very briefly outlined the trend of Nahua civilization, but it will be advisable to examine it a little more closely, for if the myths of this people are to be understood some knowledge of its life and general culture is essential.

Legends of the Foundation of Mexico

At the period of the conquest of Mexico by Cortés the city presented an imposing appearance. Led to its neighbourhood by Huitzilopochtli, a traditional chief, afterwards deified as the god of war, there are several legends which account for the choice of its site by the Mexicans. The most popular of these relates how the nomadic Nahua beheld perched upon a cactus plant an eagle of great size and majesty, grasping in its talons a huge serpent, and spreading its wings to catch the rays of the rising sun. The soothsayers or medicine men of the tribe, reading a good omen in the spectacle, advised the leaders of the people to settle on the spot, and, hearkening to the voice of what they considered divine authority, they proceeded to drive piles into the marshy ground, and thus laid the foundation of the great city of Mexico.

An elaboration of this legend tells how the Aztecs had about the year 1325 sought refuge upon the western shore of the Lake of Tezcuco, in an island among the marshes on which they found a stone on which forty years before one of their priests had sacrificed a prince of the name of Copal, whom they had made prisoner. A nopal plant had sprung from an earth-filled crevice in this rude altar, and upon this the royal eagle alluded to in the former account had alighted, grasping the serpent in his talons. Beholding in this a good omen, and urged by a supernatural impulse which he could not explain, a priest of high rank dived into a pool close at hand, where he found himself face to face with Tlaloc, the god of waters. After an interview with the deity the priest obtained permission from him to found a city on the site, from the humble beginnings of which arose the metropolis of Mexico-Tenochtitlan.

Mexico at the Conquest

At the period of the conquest the city of Mexico had a circumference of no less than twelve miles, or nearly that of modern Berlin without its suburbs. It contained 60,000 houses, and its inhabitants were computed to number 300,000. Many other towns, most of them nearly half as large, were grouped on the islands or on the margin of Lake Tezcuco, so that the population of what might almost be called 'Greater Mexico' must have amounted to several millions. The city was intersected by four great roadways or avenues built at right angles to one another, and laid four-square with the cardinal points. Situated as it was in the midst of a lake, it was traversed by numerous canals, which were used as thoroughfares for traffic. The four principal ways described above were extended across the lake as dykes or viaducts until they met its shores. The dwellings of the poorer classes were chiefly composed of adobes, but those of the nobility were built of a red porous stone quarried close by. They were usually of one story only, but occupied a goodly piece of ground and had flat roofs, many of which were covered with flowers. In general they were coated with a hard, white cement, which gave them an added resemblance to the Oriental type of building.

Towering high among these, and a little apart from the vast squares and market-places, were the *teocallis*, or temples. These were in reality not temples or covered-in buildings, but 'high places,' great pyramids of stone, built platform on platform, around which a staircase led to the summit, on which was usually erected a small shrine containing the tutelar deity to whom the *teocalli* had been raised. The great temple of Huitzilopochtli, the war-god, built by King Ahuizotl, was, besides being typical of all, by far the greatest of these votive piles. The enclosing walls of the building were 4800 feet in circumference, and strikingly decorated by carvings representing festoons of intertwined reptiles, from which circumstance they were called *coetpantli* (walls of serpents). A kind of gate-house on each side gave access to the enclosure. The *teocalli*, or great temple, inside the court was in the shape of a parallelogram, measuring 375 feet by 300 feet, and was built in six platforms, growing smaller in area as they descended. The mass of this structure was composed of a mixture of rubble, clay, and earth, covered with carefully worked stone slabs, cemented together with infinite care, and coated with a hard gypsum. A flight of 340 steps circled round the terraces and led to the upper platform, on which were raised two three-storied towers 56 feet in height, in which stood the great statues of the tutelar deities and the jasper stones of sacrifice. These sanctuaries, say the old Conquistadores who entered them, had the appearance and odour of shambles, and human blood was bespattered everywhere. In this weird chapel of horrors burned a fire, the extinction of which it was supposed would have brought about the end of the Nahua power. It was tended with a care as scrupulous as that with which the Roman Vestals guarded their sacred flame. No less than 600 of these sacred braziers were kept alight in the city of Mexico alone.

A Pyramid of Skulls

The principal fane of Huitzilopochtli was surrounded by upwards of forty inferior *teocallis* and shrines. In the Tzompantli (Pyramid of Skulls) were collected the grisly relics of the countless victims to the implacable war-god of the Aztecs, and in this horrid structure the Spanish conquerors counted no less than 136,000 human skulls. In the court or *teopan* which surrounded the temple were the dwellings of thousands of priests, whose duties included the scrupulous care of the temple precincts, and whose labours were minutely apportioned.

Nahua Architecture and Ruins

As we shall see later, Mexico is by no means so rich in architectural antiquities as Guatemala or Yucatan, the reason being that the growth of tropical forests has to a great extent protected ancient stone edifices in the latter countries from destruction. The ruins discovered in the northern regions of the republic are of a ruder type than those which approach more nearly to the sphere of Maya influence, as, for example, those of Mitla, built by the Zapotecs, which exhibit such unmistakable signs of Maya influence that we prefer to describe them when dealing with the antiquities of that people.

Cyclopean Remains

In the mountains of Chihuahua, one of the most northerly provinces, is a celebrated group called the Casas Grandes (Large Houses), the walls of which are still about 30 feet in height. These approximate in general appearance to the buildings of more modern tribes in New Mexico and Arizona, and may be referred to such peoples rather than to the Nahua. At Quemada, in Zacatecas, massive ruins of Cyclopean appearance have been discovered. These consist of extensive terraces and broad stone causeways, *teocallis* which have weathered many centuries, and gigantic pillars, 18 feet in height and 17 feet in circumference. Walls 12 feet in thickness rise above the heaps of rubbish which litter the ground. These remains exhibit little connection with Nahua architecture to the north or south of them. They are more massive than either, and must have been constructed by some race which had made considerable strides in the art of building.

Teotihuacan

In the district of the Totonacs, to the north of Vera Cruz, we find many architectural remains of a highly interesting character. Here the *teocalli* or pyramidal type of building is occasionally crowned by a covered-in temple with the massive roof characteristic of Maya architecture. The most striking examples found in this region are the remains of Teotihuacan and Xochicalco. The former was the religious Mecca of the Nahua races, and in its proximity are still to be seen the *teocallis* of the sun and moon, surrounded by extensive burying-grounds where the devout of Anahuac were laid in the sure hope that if interred they would find entrance into the paradise of the sun. The *teocalli* of the moon has a base covering 426 feet and a height of 137 feet. That of the sun is of greater dimensions, with a base of 735 feet and a height of 203 feet. These pyramids were divided into four stories, three of which remain. On the summit of that of the sun stood a temple containing a great image of that luminary carved from a rough block of stone. In the breast was inlaid a star of the purest gold, seized afterwards as loot by the insatiable followers of Cortés. From the *teocalli* of the moon a path runs to where a little rivulet flanks the 'Citadel.' This path is known as 'The Path of the Dead,' from the circumstance that it is surrounded by some nine square miles of tombs and tumuli, and, indeed, forms a road through the great cemetery. The Citadel, thinks Charnay, was a vast tennis or *tlachtli* court, where thousands flocked to gaze at the national sport of the Nahua with a zest equal to that of the modern devotees of football. Teotihuacan was a flourishing centre contemporary with Tollan. It was destroyed, but was rebuilt by the Chichimec king Xolotl, and preserved thenceforth its traditional sway as the focus of the Nahua national religion. Charnay identifies the architectural types discovered there with those of Tollan. The result of his labours in the vicinity included the unearthing of richly decorated pottery, vases, masks, and terra-cotta figures. He also excavated several large houses or palaces, some with chambers more than 730 feet in circumference, with walls over 7½ feet thick, into which were built rings and slabs to support torches and candles. The floors were tessellated in various rich designs, "like an Aubusson carpet." Charnay concluded that the monuments of Teotihuacan were partly standing at the time of the conquest.

The Hill of Flowers

Near Tezcuco is Xochicalco (The Hill of Flowers), a *teocalli* the sculpture of which is both beautiful and luxuriant in design. The porphyry quarries from which the great blocks, 12 feet in length, were cut lie many miles away. As late as 1755 the structure towered to a height of five stories, but the vandal has done his work only too well, and a few fragmentary carvings of exquisite design are all that today remain of one of Mexico's most magnificent pyramids.

Tollan

We have already indicated that on the site of the 'Toltec' city of Tollan ruins have been discovered which prove that it was the centre of a civilization of a type distinctly advanced. Charnay unearthed there gigantic fragments of caryatides, each some 7 feet high. He also found columns of two pieces, which were fitted together by means of mortise and tenon, bas-reliefs of archaic figures of undoubted Nahua type, and many fragments of great antiquity. On the hill of Palpan, above Tollan, he found the ground-plans of several houses with numerous apartments, frescoed, columned, and having benches and cisterns recalling the *impluvium* of a Roman villa. Water-pipes were also actually unearthed, and a wealth of pottery, many pieces of which were like old Japanese china. The ground-plan or foundations of the houses unearthed at Palpan showed that they had been designed by practical architects, and had not been built in any merely haphazard fashion. The cement which covered the walls and floors was of excellent quality, and recalled that discovered in ancient Italian excavations. The roofs had been of wood, supported by pillars.

Picture-Writing

The Aztecs, and indeed the entire Nahua race, employed a system of writing of the type scientifically described as 'pictographic,' in which events, persons, and ideas were recorded by means of drawings and coloured sketches. These were executed on paper made from the agave plant, or were painted on the skins of animals. By these means not only history and the principles of the Nahua mythology were communicated from generation to generation, but the transactions of daily life, the accountings of merchants, and the purchase and ownership of land were placed on record. That a phonetic system was rapidly being approached is manifest from the method by which the Nahua scribes depicted the names of individuals or cities. These were represented by means of several objects, the names of which resembled that of the person for which they stood. The name of King Ixcoatl, for example, is represented by the drawing of a serpent (*coatl*) pierced by flint knives (*iztli*), and that of Motequauhzoma (Montezuma) by a mouse-trap (*montli*), an eagle (*quauhtli*), a lancet (*zo*), and a hand (*maitl*). The phonetic values employed by the scribes varied exceedingly, so that at times an entire syllable would be expressed by the painting of an object the name of which commenced with it. At other times only a letter would be represented by the same drawing. But the general intention of the scribes was undoubtedly more ideographic than phonetic; that is, they desired to convey their thoughts more by sketch than by sound.

Interpretation of the Hieroglyphs

These *pinturas*, as the Spanish conquerors designated them, offer no very great difficulty in their elucidation to modern experts, at least so far as the general trend of their contents is concerned. In this they are unlike the manuscripts of the Maya of Central America with which we shall make acquaintance further on. Their interpretation was largely traditional, and was learned by rote, being passed on by one generation of *amamatini* (readers) to another, and was by no means capable of elucidation by all and sundry.

Native Manuscripts

The *pinturas* or native manuscripts which remain to us are but few in number. Priestly fanaticism, which ordained their wholesale destruction, and the still more potent passage of time have so reduced them that each separate example is known to bibliophiles and Americanists the world over. In such as still exist we can observe great fullness of detail, representing for the most part festivals, sacrifices, tributes, and natural phenomena, such as eclipses and floods, and the death and accession of monarchs. These events, and the supernatural beings who were supposed to control them, were depicted in brilliant colours, executed by means of a brush of feathers.

The Interpretative Codices

Luckily for future students of Mexican history, the blind zeal which destroyed the majority of the Mexican manuscripts was frustrated by the enlightenment of certain European scholars, who regarded the wholesale destruction of the native records as little short of a calamity, and who took steps to seek out the few remaining native artists, from whom they procured copies of the more important paintings, the details of which were, of course, quite familiar to them. To those were added interpretations taken down from the lips of the native scribes themselves, so that no doubt might remain regarding the contents of the manuscripts. These are known as the 'Interpretative Codices,' and are of considerable assistance to the student of Mexican history and customs. Three only are in existence. The Oxford Codex, treasured in the Bodleian Library, is of a historical nature, and contains a full list of the lesser cities which were subservient to Mexico in its palmy days. The Paris or Tellerio-Remensis Codex, so called from having once been the property of Le Tellier, Archbishop of Rheims, embodies many facts concerning the early settlement of the various Nahua city-states. The Vatican MSS. deal chiefly with mythology and the intricacies of the Mexican calendar system. Such Mexican paintings as were unassisted by an interpretation are naturally of less value to present-day students of the lore of the Nahua. They are principally concerned with calendric matter, ritualistic data, and astrological computations or horoscopes.

The Mexican 'Book of the Dead'

Perhaps the most remarkable and interesting manuscript in the Vatican collection is one the last pages of which represent the journey of the soul after death through the gloomy dangers of the Other-world. This has been called the Mexican 'Book of the Dead.' The corpse is depicted dressed for burial, the soul escaping from its earthly tenement by way of the mouth. The spirit is ushered into the presence of Tezcatlipoca, the Jupiter of the Aztec pantheon, by an attendant dressed in an ocelot skin, and stands naked with a wooden yoke round the neck before the deity, to receive sentence. The dead person is given over to the tests which precede entrance to the abode of the dead, the realm of Mictlan, and so that he may not have to meet the perils of the journey in a defenceless condition a sheaf of javelins is bestowed upon him. He first passes between two lofty peaks, which may fall and crush him if he cannot skilfully escape them. A terrible serpent then intercepts his path, and, if he succeeds in defeating this monster, the fierce alligator Xochitonal awaits him. Eight deserts and a corresponding number of mountains have then to be negotiated by the hapless spirit, and a whirlwind sharp as a sword, which cuts even through solid rocks, must be withstood. Accompanied by the shade of his favourite dog, the harassed ghost at length encounters the fierce Izpuzteque, a demon with the backward-bent legs of a cock, the evil Nextepehua, the fiend who scatters clouds of ashes, and many another grisly foe, until at last he wins to the gates of the Lord of Hell, before whom he does reverence, after which he is free to greet his friends who have gone before.

The Calendar System

As has been said, the calendar system was the source of all Mexican science, and regulated the recurrence of all religious rites and festivals. In fact, the entire mechanism of Nahua life was resident in its provisions. The type of time-division and computation exemplified in the Nahua calendar was also found among the Maya peoples of Yucatan and Guatemala and the Zapotec people of the boundary between the Nahua and Maya races. By which of these races it was first employed is unknown. But the Zapotec calendar exhibits signs of both Nahua and Maya influence, and from this it has been inferred that the calendar systems of these races have been evolved from it. It might with equal probability be argued that both Nahua and Maya art were offshoots of Zapotec art, because the characteristics of both are discovered in it, whereas the circumstance merely illustrates the very natural acceptance by a border people, who settled down to civilization at a relatively later date, of the artistic tenets of the two greater peoples who environed them. The Nahua and Maya calendars were in all likelihood evolved from the calendar system of that civilized race which undoubtedly existed on the Mexican plateau prior to the coming of the later Nahua swarms, and which in general is loosely alluded to as the 'Toltec.'

The Mexican Year

The Mexican year was a cycle of 365 days, without any intercalary addition or other correction. In course of time it almost lost its seasonal significance because of the omission of the extra hours included in the solar year, and furthermore many of its festivals and occasions were altered by high-priests and rulers to suit their convenience.

The Mexican *nexiuhilpililztli* (binding of years) contained fifty-two years, and ran in two separate cycles – one of fifty-two years of 365 days each, and another of seventy-three groups of 260 days each. The first was of course the solar year, and embraced eighteen periods of twenty days each, called 'months' by the old Spanish chroniclers, with five *nemontemi* (unlucky days) over and above. These days were not intercalated, but were included in the year, and merely overflowed the division of the year into periods of twenty days. The cycle of seventy-three groups of 260 days, subdivided into groups of thirteen days, was called the 'birth-cycle.'

Lunar Reckoning

People in a barbarous condition almost invariably reckon time by the period between the waxing and waning of the moon as distinct from the entire passage of a lunar revolution, and this period of twenty days will be found to be the basis in the time-reckoning of the Mexicans, who designated it *cempohualli*. Each day included in it was denoted by a sign, as 'house,' 'snake,' 'wind,' and so forth. Each *cempohualli* was subdivided into four periods of five days each, sometimes alluded to as 'weeks' by the early Spanish writers, and these were known by the sign of their middle or third day. These day-names ran on without reference to the length of the year. The year itself was designated by the name of the middle day of the week in which it began. Out of twenty day-names in the Mexican 'month' it was inevitable that the four *calli* (house), *tochtli* (rabbit), *acatl* (reed), and *tecpatl* (flint) should always recur in sequence because of the incidence of these days in the Mexican solar year. Four years made up a year of the sun. During the *nemontemi* (unlucky days) no work was done, as they were regarded as ominous and unwholesome.

We have seen that the civil year permitted the day-names to run on continuously from one year to another. The ecclesiastical authorities, however, had a reckoning of their own, and made the year begin always on the first day of their calendar, no matter what sign denominated that day in the civil system.

Groups of Years

As has been indicated, the years were formed into groups. Thirteen years constituted a *xiumalpilli* (bundle), and four of these a *nexiuhilpilitztli* (complete binding of the years). Each year had thus a double aspect, first as an individual period of time, and secondly as a portion of the 'year of the sun,' and these were so numbered and named that each year in the series of fifty-two possessed a different description.

The Dread of the Last Day

With the conclusion of each period of fifty-two years a terrible dread came upon the Mexicans that the world would come to an end. A stated period of time had expired, a period which was regarded as fixed by divine command, and it had been ordained that on the completion of one of those series of fifty-two years earthly time would cease and the universe be demolished. For some time before the ceremony of *toxilmolpilia* (the binding up of the years) the Mexicans abandoned themselves to the utmost prostration, and the wicked went about in terrible fear. As the first day of the fifty-third year dawned the people narrowly observed the Pleiades, for if they passed the zenith time would proceed and the world would be respited. The gods were placated or refreshed by the slaughter of the human victim, on whose still living breast a fire of wood was kindled by friction, the heart and body being consumed by the flames so lighted. As the planets of hope crossed the zenith loud acclamations resounded from the people, and the domestic hearths, which had been left cold and dead, were rekindled from the sacred fire which had consumed the sacrifice. Mankind was safe for another period.

The Birth-Cycle

The birth-cycle, as we have said, consisted of 260 days. It had originally been a lunar cycle of thirteen days, and once bore the names of thirteen moons. It formed part of the civil calendar, with which, however, it had nothing in common, as it was used for ecclesiastical purposes only. The lunar names were abandoned later, and the numbers one to thirteen adopted in their places.

Language of the Nahua

The Nahua language represented a very low state of culture. Speech is the general measure of the standard of thought of a people, and if we judged the civilization of the Nahua by theirs, we should be justified in concluding that they had not yet emerged from barbarism. But we must recollect that the Nahua of the conquest period had speedily adopted the older civilization which they had found awaiting them on their entrance to Mexico, and had retained their own primitive tongue. The older and more cultured people who had preceded them probably spoke a more polished dialect of the same language, but its influence had evidently but little effect upon the rude Chichimecs and Aztecs. The Mexican tongue, like most American languages, belongs to the 'incorporative' type, the genius of which is to unite all the related words in a sentence into one conglomerate term or word, merging the separate words of which it is composed one into another by altering their forms, and so welding them together as to express the whole in one word. It will be at once apparent that such a system was clumsy in the extreme, and led to the creation of words and names of the most barbarous appearance and sound. In a narrative of the Spanish discovery written by Chimalpahin, the native chronicler of Chalco, born in 1579, we have, for example, such a passage as the following: *Oc chiucnauhxihuitl inic onen quilantimanca España camo niman ic yuh ca omacoc ihuelitiliztli inic niman ye chiuhcnauhxiuhtica, in oncan ohualla*. This passage is chosen quite at random, and is an average specimen of literary Mexican of the sixteenth century. Its purport is, freely translated: "For nine years he [Columbus] remained in vain in Spain. Yea, for nine years there he waited for influence." The clumsy and cumbrous nature of the language could scarcely be better illustrated than by pointing out that *chiucnauhxihuitl* signifies "nine years"; *quilantimanca*, "he below remained"; and *omacoc ihuelitiliztli*, "he has got his powerfulness." It must be recollected that this specimen of Mexican was composed by a person who had had the benefit of a Spanish education, and is cast in literary form. What the spoken Mexican of pre-conquest times was like can be contemplated with misgiving in the grammars of the old Spanish missionaries, whose greatest glory is that they mastered such a language in the interests of their faith.

Aztec Science

The science of the Aztecs was, perhaps, one of the most picturesque sides of their civilization. As with all peoples in a semi-barbarous state, it consisted chiefly in astrology and divination. Of the former the wonderful calendar system was the basis, and by its aid the priests, or those of them who were set apart for the study of the heavenly bodies, pretended to be able to tell the future of new-born infants and the progress of the dead in the other world. This they accomplished by weighing the influence of the planets and other luminaries one against another, and extracting the net result. Their art of divination consisted in drawing omens from the song and flight of birds, the appearance of grains of seed, feathers, and the entrails of animals, by which means they confidently predicted both public and private events.

Nahua Government

The limits of the Aztec Empire may be defined, if its tributary states are included, as extending over the territory comprised in the modern states of Mexico, Southern Vera Cruz, and Guerrero. Among the civilized peoples of this extensive tract the prevailing form of government was an absolute monarchy, although several of the smaller communities were republics. The law of succession, as with the Celts of Scotland, prescribed that the eldest surviving brother of the deceased monarch should be elected to his throne, and, failing him, the eldest nephew. But incompetent persons were almost invariably ignored by the elective body, although the choice was limited to one family. The ruler was generally selected both because of his military prowess and his ecclesiastical and political knowledge. Indeed, a Mexican monarch was nearly always a man of the highest culture and artistic refinement, and the ill-fated Montezuma was an example of the true type of Nahua sovereign. The council of the monarch was composed of the electors and other personages of importance in the realm. It undertook the government of the provinces, the financial affairs of the country, and other matters of national import. The nobility held all the highest military, judicial, and ecclesiastical offices. To each city and province judges were delegated who exercised criminal and civil jurisdiction, and whose opinion superseded even that of the Crown itself. Petty cases were settled by lesser officials, and a still inferior grade of officers acted as a species of police in the supervision of families.

Domestic Life

The domestic life of the Nahua was a peculiar admixture of simplicity and display. The mass of the people led a life of strenuous labour in the fields, and in the cities they wrought hard at many trades, among which may be specified building, metal-working, making robes and other articles of bright featherwork and quilted suits of armour, jewellery, and small wares. Vendors of flowers, fruit, fish, and vegetables swarmed in the markets. The use of tobacco was general among the men of all classes. At banquets the women attended, although they were seated at separate tables. The entertainments of the upper class were marked by much magnificence, and the variety of dishes was considerable, including venison, turkey, many smaller birds, fish, a profusion of vegetables, and pastry, accompanied by sauces of delicate flavour. These were served in dishes of gold and silver. *Pulque*, a fermented drink brewed from the agave, was the universal beverage. Cannibalism was indulged in usually on ceremonial occasions, and was surrounded by such refinements of the table as served only to render it the more repulsive in the eyes of Europeans. It has been stated that this revolting practice was engaged in owing solely to the tenets of the Nahua religion, which enjoined the slaughter of slaves or captives in the name of a deity, and their consumption with the idea that the consumers attained unity with that deity in the flesh. But there is good reason to suspect that the Nahua, deprived of the flesh of the larger domestic animals, practised deliberate cannibalism. It would appear that the older race which preceded them in the country were innocent of these horrible repasts.

A Mysterious Toltec Book

A piece of Nahua literature, the disappearance of which is surrounded by circumstances of the deepest mystery, is the *Teo-Amoxtli* (Divine Book), which is alleged by certain chroniclers to have been the work of the ancient Toltecs. Ixtlilxochitl, a native Mexican author, states that it was written by a Tezcucan wise man, one Huematzin, about the end of the seventh century, and that it described the pilgrimage of the Nahua from Asia, their laws, manners, and customs, and their religious tenets, science, and arts. In 1838 the Baron de Waldeck stated in his *Voyage Pittoresque* that he had it in his possession, and the Abbé Brasseur de Bourbourg identified it with the Maya Dresden Codex and other native manuscripts. Bustamante also states that the *amamatini* (chroniclers) of Tezcuco had a copy in their possession at the time of the taking of their city. But these appear to be mere surmises, and if the *Teo-Amoxtli* ever existed, which on the whole is not unlikely, it has probably never been seen by a European.

A Native Historian

One of the most interesting of the Mexican historians is Don Fernando de Alva Ixtlilxochitl, a half-breed of royal Tezcucan descent. He was responsible for two notable works, entitled *Historia Chichimeca* (The History of the Chichimecs) and the *Relaciones*, a compilation of historical and semi-historical incidents. He was cursed, or blessed, however, by a strong leaning toward the marvellous, and has coloured his narratives so highly that he would have us regard the Toltec or ancient Nahua civilizations as by far the most splendid and magnificent that ever existed. His descriptions of Tezcuco, if picturesque in the extreme, are manifestly the outpourings of a romantic and idealistic mind, which in its patriotic enthusiasm desired to vindicate the country of his birth from the stigma of savagery and to prove its equality with the great nations of antiquity. For this we have not the heart to quarrel with him. But we must be on our guard against accepting any of his statements unless we find strong corroboration of it in the pages of a more trustworthy and less biased author.

Nahua Topography

The geography of Mexico is by no means as familiar to Europeans as is that of the various countries of our own continent, and it is extremely easy for the reader who is unacquainted with Mexico and the puzzling orthography of its place-names to flounder among them, and during the perusal of such a volume as this to find himself in a hopeless maze of surmise as to the exact locality of the more famous centres of Mexican history. A few moments' study of this paragraph will enlighten him in this respect, and will save him much confusion further on. The city of Mexico, or Tenochtitlan, its native name, was situated upon an island in the Lake of Tezcuco. This lake has now partially dried up, and the modern city of Mexico is situated at a considerable distance from it. Tezcuco, the city second in importance, lies to the north-east of the lake, and is somewhat more isolated, the other pueblo*s* (towns) clustering round the southern or western shores. To the north of Tezcuco is Teotihuacan, the sacred city of the gods. To the south-east of Mexico is Tlaxcallan, or Tlascala, the city which assisted Cortés against the Mexicans, and the inhabitants of which were the deadliest foes of the central Nahua power. To the north lie the sacred city of Cholula and Tula, or Tollan.

Nahua History

A brief historical sketch or epitome of what is known of Nahua history as apart from mere tradition will further assist the reader in the comprehension of Mexican mythology. From the period of the settlement of the Nahua on an agricultural basis a system of feudal government had evolved, and at various epochs in the history of the country certain cities or groups of cities held a paramount sway. Subsequent to the 'Toltec' period, which we have already described and discussed, we find the Acolhuans in supreme power, and ruling from their cities of Tollantzinco and Cholula a considerable tract of country. Later Cholula maintained an alliance with Tlascala and Huexotzinco.

Bloodless Battles

The maxim "Other climes, other manners" is nowhere better exemplified than by the curious annual strife betwixt the warriors of Mexico and Tlascala. Once a year they met on a prearranged battle-ground and engaged in combat, not with the intention of killing one another, but with the object of taking prisoners for sacrifice on the altars of their respective war-gods. The warrior seized his opponent and attempted to bear him off, the various groups pulling and tugging desperately at each other in the endeavour to seize the limbs of the unfortunate who had been first struck down, with the object of dragging him into durance or effecting his rescue. Once secured, the Tlascaltec warrior was brought to Mexico in a cage, and first placed upon a stone slab, to which one of his feet was secured by a chain or thong. He was then given light weapons, more like playthings than warrior's gear, and confronted by one of the most celebrated Mexican warriors. Should he succeed in defeating six of these formidable antagonists, he was set free. But no sooner was he wounded than he was hurried to the altar of sacrifice, and his heart was torn out and offered to Huitzilopochtli, the implacable god of war.

The Tlascaltecs, having finally secured their position by a defeat of the Tecpanecs of Huexotzinco about AD 1384, sank into comparative obscurity save for their annual bout with the Mexicans.

The Lake Cities

The communities grouped round the various lakes in the valley of Mexico now command our attention. More than two score of these thriving communities flourished at the time of the conquest of Mexico, the most notable being those which occupied the borders of the Lake of Tezcuco. These cities grouped themselves round two nuclei, Azcapozalco and Tezcuco, between whom a fierce rivalry sprang up, which finally ended in the entire discomfiture of Azcapozalco. From this event the real history of Mexico may be said to commence. Those cities which had allied themselves to Tezcuco finally overran the entire territory of Mexico from the Mexican Gulf to the Pacific.

Tezcuco

If, as some authorities declare, Tezcuco was originally Otomi in affinity, it was in later years the most typically Nahuan of all the lacustrine powers. But several other communities, the power of which was very nearly as great as that of Tezcuco, had assisted that city to supremacy. Among these was Xaltocan, a city-state of unquestionable Otomi origin, situated at the northern extremity of the lake. As we have seen from the statements of Ixtlilxochitl, a Tezcucan writer, his native city was in the forefront of Nahua civilization at the time of the coming of the Spaniards, and if it was practically subservient to Mexico (Tenochtitlan) at that period it was by no means its inferior in the arts.

The Tecpanecs

The Tecpanecs, who dwelt in Tlacopan, Coyohuacan, and Huitzilopocho, were also typical Nahua. The name, as we have already explained, indicates that each settlement possessed its own *tecpan* (chief's house), and has no racial significance. Their state was probably founded about the twelfth century, although a chronology of no less than fifteen hundred years was claimed for it. This people composed a sort of buffer-state betwixt the Otomi on the north and other Nahua on the south.

The Aztecs

The menace of these northern Otomi had become acute when the Tecpanecs received reinforcements in the shape of the Aztecâ, or Aztecs, a people of Nahua blood, who came, according to their own accounts, from Aztlan (Crane Land). The name Aztecâ signifies 'Crane People,' and this has led to the assumption that they came from Chihuahua, where cranes abound. Doubts have been cast upon the Nahua origin of the Aztecâ. But these are by no means well founded, as the names of the early Aztec chieftains and kings are unquestionably Nahuan. This people on their arrival in Mexico were in a very inferior state of culture, and were probably little better than savages. We have already outlined some of the legends concerning the coming of the Aztecs to the land of Anahuac, or the valley of Mexico, but their true origin is uncertain, and it is likely that they wandered down from the north as other Nahua immigrants did before them, and as the Apache Indians still do to this day. By their own showing they had sojourned at several points *en route*, and were reduced to slavery by the chiefs of Colhuacan. They proved so truculent in their bondage, however, that they were released, and journeyed to Chapoultepec, which they quitted because of their dissensions with the Xaltocanecs. On their arrival in the district inhabited by the Tecpanecs a tribute was levied upon them, but nevertheless they flourished so exceedingly that the swamp villages which the Tecpanecs had permitted them to raise on the borders of the lake soon grew into thriving communities, and chiefs were provided for them from among the nobility of the Tecpanecs.

The Aztecs as Allies

By the aid of the Aztecs the Tecpanecs greatly extended their territorial possessions. City after city was added to their empire, and the allies finally invaded the Otomi country, which they speedily subdued. Those cities which had been founded by the Acolhuans on the fringes of Tezcuco also allied themselves with the Tecpanecs with the intention of freeing themselves from the yoke of the Chichimecs, whose hand was heavy upon them. The Chichimecs or Tezcucans made a stern resistance, and for a time the sovereignty of the Tecpanecs hung in the balance. But eventually they conquered, and Tezcuco was overthrown and given as a spoil to the Aztecs.

New Powers

Up to this time the Aztecs had paid a tribute to Azcapozalco, but now, strengthened by the successes of the late conflict, they withheld it, and requested permission to build an aqueduct from the shore for the purpose of carrying a supply of water into their city. This was refused by the Tecpanecs, and a policy of isolation was brought to bear upon Mexico, an embargo being placed upon its goods and intercourse with its people being forbidden. War followed, in which the Tecpanecs were defeated with great slaughter. After this event, which may be placed about the year 1428, the Aztecs gained ground rapidly, and their march to the supremacy of the entire Mexican valley was almost undisputed. Allying themselves with Tezcuco and Tlacopan, the Mexicans overran many states far beyond the confines of the valley, and by the time of Montezuma I had extended their boundaries almost to the limits of the present republic. The Mexican merchant followed in the footsteps of the Mexican warrior, and the commercial expansion of the Aztecs rivalled their military fame. Clever traders, they were merciless in their exactions of tribute from the states they conquered, manufacturing the raw material paid to them by the subject cities into goods which they afterwards sold again to the tribes under their sway. Mexico became the chief market of the empire, as well as its political nucleus. Such was the condition of affairs when the Spaniards arrived in Anahuac. Their coming has been deplored by certain historians as hastening the destruction of a Western Eden. But bad as was their rule, it was probably mild when compared with the cruel and insatiable sway of the Aztecs over their unhappy dependents. The Spaniards found a tyrannical despotism in the conquered provinces, and a faith the accessories of which were so fiendish that it cast a gloom over the entire national life. These they replaced by a milder vassalage and the earnest ministrations of a more enlightened priesthood.

Mexican Mythology

Nahua Religion

THE RELIGION OF THE ANCIENT MEXICANS was a polytheism or worship of a pantheon of deities, the general aspect of which presented similarities to the systems of Greece and Egypt. Original influences, however, were strong, and they are especially discernible in the institutions of ritualistic cannibalism and human sacrifice. Strange resemblances to Christian practice were observed in the Aztec mythology by the Spanish Conquistadores, who piously condemned the native customs of baptism, consubstantiation, and confession as frauds founded and perpetuated by diabolic agency.

However, the Nahua displayed a theological advancement greatly superior to that of the Greeks or Romans, and quite on a level with that expressed by the Egyptians and Assyrians. Toward the period of the Spanish occupation the Mexican priesthood was undoubtedly advancing to the contemplation of the exaltation of one god, whose worship was fast excluding that of similar deities, and if our data are too imperfect to allow us to speak very fully in regard to this phase of religious advancement, we know at least that much of the Nahua ritual and many of the prayers preserved by the labours of the Spanish fathers are unquestionably genuine, and display the attainment of a high religious level.

Cosmology

Aztec theology postulated an eternity which, however, was not without its epochs. It was thought to be broken up into a number of aeons, each of which depended upon the period of duration of a separate 'sun.' No agreement is noticeable among authorities on Mexican mythology as to the number of these 'suns,' but it would appear as probable that the favourite tradition stipulated for four 'suns' or epochs, each of which concluded with a national disaster – flood, famine, tempest, or fire. The present aeon, they feared, might conclude upon the completion of every 'sheaf' of fifty-two years, the 'sheaf' being a merely arbitrary portion of an aeon. The period of time from the first creation to the current aeon was variously computed as 15,228, 2386, or 1404 solar years, the discrepancy and doubt arising because of the equivocal nature of the numeral signs expressing the period in the *pinturas* or native paintings. As regards the sequence of 'suns' there is no more agreement than there is regarding their number. The Codex Vaticanus states it to have been water, wind, fire, and famine. Humboldt gives it as hunger, fire, wind, and water; Boturini as water, famine, wind, and fire; and Gama as hunger, wind, fire, and water.

In all likelihood the adoption of four ages arose from the sacred nature of that number. The myth doubtless shaped itself upon the *tonalamatl* (Mexican native calendar), the great repository of the wisdom of the Nahua race, which the priestly class regarded as its *vade mecum*, and which was closely consulted by it on every occasion, civil or religious.

The Sources of Mexican Mythology

Our knowledge of the mythology of the Mexicans is chiefly gained through the works of those Spaniards, lay and cleric, who entered the country along with or immediately subsequent to the Spanish Conquistadores. From several of these we have what might be called first-hand accounts of the theogony and ritual of the Nahua people. The most valuable compendium is that of Father Bernardino Sahagun, entitled *A General History of the Affairs of New Spain*, which was published from manuscript only in the middle of last century, though written in the first half of the sixteenth century. Sahagun arrived in Mexico eight years after the country had been reduced by the Spaniards to a condition of servitude. He obtained a thorough mastery of the Nahuatl tongue, and conceived a warm admiration for the native mind and a deep interest in the antiquities of the conquered people. His method of collecting facts concerning their mythology and history was as effective as it was ingenious. He held daily conferences with reliable Indians, and placed questions before them, to which they replied by symbolical paintings detailing the answers which he required. These he submitted to scholars who had been trained under his own supervision, and who, after consultation among themselves, rendered him a criticism in Nahuatl of the hieroglyphical paintings he had placed at their disposal. Not content with this process, he subjected these replies to the criticism of a third body, after which the matter was included in his work. But ecclesiastical intolerance was destined to keep the work from publication for a couple of centuries. Afraid that such a volume would be successful in keeping alight the fires of paganism in Mexico, Sahagun's brethren refused him the assistance he required for its publication. But on his appealing to the Council of the Indies in Spain he was met with encouragement, and was ordered to translate his great work into Spanish, a task he undertook when over eighty years of age. He transmitted the work to Spain, and for three hundred years nothing more was heard of it.

The Romance of the Lost 'Sahagun'

For generations antiquarians interested in the lore of ancient Mexico bemoaned its loss, until at length one Muñoz, more indefatigable than the rest, chanced to visit the crumbling library of the ancient convent of Tolosi, in Navarre. There, among time-worn manuscripts and tomes relating to the early fathers and the intricacies of canon law, he discovered the lost Sahagun! It was printed separately by Bustamante at Mexico and by Lord Kingsborough in his collection in 1830, and has been translated into French by M. Jourdanet. Thus the manuscript commenced in or after 1530 was given to the public after a lapse of no less than three hundred years!

Torquemada

Father Torquemada arrived in the New World about the middle of the sixteenth century, at which period he was still enabled to take from the lips of such of the Conquistadores as remained much curious information regarding the circumstances of their advent. His *Monarchia Indiana* was first published at Seville in 1615, and in it he made much use of the manuscript of Sahagun, not then published. At the same time his observations upon matters pertaining to the native religion are often illuminating and exhaustive.

In his *Storia Antica del Messico* the Abbé Clavigero, who published his work in 1780, did much to disperse the clouds of tradition which hung over Mexican history and mythology. The clarity of his style and the exactness of his information render his work exceedingly useful.

Antonio Gama, in his *Descripcion Historica y Cronologica de las dos Piedras*, poured a flood of light on Mexican antiquities. His work was published in 1832. With him may be said to have ceased the line of Mexican archaeologists of the older school. Others worthy of being mentioned among the older writers on Mexican mythology (we are not here concerned with history) are Boturini, who, in his *Idea de una Nueva Historia General de la America Septentrional*, gives a vivid picture of native life and tradition, culled from first-hand communication with the people; Ixtlilxochitl, a half-breed, whose mendacious works, the *Relaciones* and *Historia Chichimeca*, are yet valuable repositories of tradition; José de Acosta, whose *Historia Natural y Moral de las Yndias* was published at Seville in 1580; and Gomara, who, in his *Historia General de las Indias* (Madrid, 1749), rested upon the authority of the Conquistadores. Tezozomoc's *Chronica Mexicana*, reproduced in Lord Kingsborough's great work, is valuable as giving unique facts regarding the Aztec mythology, as is the *Teatro Mexicana* of Vetancurt, published at Mexico in 1697–98.

The Worship of One God

The ritual of this dead faith of another hemisphere abounds in expressions concerning the unity of the deity approaching very nearly to many of those we ourselves employ regarding God's attributes. The various classes of the priesthood were in the habit of addressing the several gods to whom they ministered as 'omnipotent,' 'endless,' 'invisible,' 'the one god complete in perfection and unity,' and 'the Maker and Moulder of All.' These appellations they applied not to one supreme being, but to the individual deities to whose service they were attached. It may be thought that such a practice would be fatal to the evolution of a single and universal god. But there is every reason to believe that Tezcatlipoca, the great god of the air, like the Hebrew Jahveh, also an air-god, was fast gaining precedence of all other deities, when the coming of the white man put an end to his chances of sovereignty.

Tezcatlipoca

Tezcatlipoca (Fiery Mirror) was undoubtedly the Jupiter of the Nahua pantheon. He carried a mirror or shield, from which he took his name, and in which he was supposed to see reflected the actions and deeds of mankind. The evolution of this god from the status of a spirit of wind or air to that of the supreme deity of the Aztec people presents many points of deep interest to students of mythology. Originally the personification of the air, the source both of the breath of life and of the tempest, Tezcatlipoca possessed all the attributes of a god who presided over these phenomena. As the tribal god of the Tezcucans who had led them into the Land of Promise, and had been instrumental in the defeat of both the gods and men of the elder race they dispossessed, Tezcatlipoca naturally advanced so speedily in popularity and public honour that it was little wonder that within a comparatively short space of time he came to be regarded as a god of fate and fortune, and as inseparably connected with the national destinies. Thus, from being the peculiar deity of a small band of Nahua immigrants, the prestige accruing from the rapid conquest made under his tutelary direction and the speedily disseminated tales of the prowess of those who worshipped him seemed to render him at once the most popular and the best feared god in Anahuac, therefore the one whose cult quickly overshadowed that of other and similar gods.

Tezcatlipoca and Quetzalcoatl

We find Tezcatlipoca intimately associated with the legends which recount the overthrow of Tollan, the capital of the Toltecs. His chief adversary on the Toltec side is the god-king Quetzalcoatl, whose nature and reign we will consider later, but whom we will now merely regard as the enemy of Tezcatlipoca. The rivalry between these gods symbolizes that which existed between the civilized Toltecs and the barbarian Nahua, and is well exemplified in the myths on pages 202–206 [PAGE REFS!!]. It is obvious that these legends bear some resemblance to those of Ixtlilxochitl which recount the fall of the Toltecs. They are taken from Sahagun's work, *Historia General de Nueva España*, and are included as well for the sake of comparison as for their own intrinsic value.

Tezcatlipoca as Doomster

Tezcatlipoca was much more than a mere personification of wind, and if he was regarded as a life-giver he had also the power of destroying existence. In fact on occasion he appears as an inexorable death-dealer, and as such was styled Nezahualpilli (The Hungry Chief) and Yaotzin (The Enemy). Perhaps one of the names by which he was best known was Telpochtli (The Youthful Warrior), from the fact that his reserve of strength, his vital force, never diminished, and that his youthful and boisterous vigour was apparent in the tempest.

Tezcatlipoca was usually depicted as holding in his right hand a dart placed in an *atlatl* (spear-thrower), and his mirror-shield with four spare darts in his left. This shield is the symbol of his power as judge of mankind and upholder of human justice.

The Aztecs pictured Tezcatlipoca as rioting along the highways in search of persons on whom to wreak his vengeance, as the wind of night rushes along the deserted roads with more seeming violence than it does by day. Indeed one of his names, Yoalli Ehecatl, signifies 'Night Wind.' Benches of stone, shaped like those made for the dignitaries of the Mexican towns, were distributed along the highways for his especial use, that on these he might rest after his boisterous journeyings. These seats were concealed by green boughs, beneath which the god was supposed to lurk in wait for his victims. But if one of the persons he seized overcame him in the struggle he might ask whatever boon he desired, secure in the promise of the deity that it should be granted forthwith.

It was supposed that Tezcatlipoca had guided the Nahua, and especially the people of Tezcuco, from a more northerly clime to the valley of Mexico. But he was not a mere local deity of Tezcuco, his worship being widely celebrated throughout the country. His exalted position in the Mexican pantheon seems to have won for him especial reverence as a god of fate and fortune. The place he took as the head of the Nahua pantheon brought him many attributes which were quite foreign to his original character. Fear and a desire to exalt their tutelar deity will impel the devotees of a powerful god to credit him with any or every quality, so that there is nothing remarkable in the spectacle of the heaping of every possible attribute, human or divine, upon Tezcatlipoca when we recall the supreme position he occupied in Mexican mythology. His priestly caste far surpassed in power and in the breadth and activity of its propaganda the priesthoods of the other Mexican deities. To it is credited the invention of many of the usages of civilization, and that it all but succeeded in making his worship universal is pretty clear, as has been shown. The other gods were worshipped for some special purpose, but the worship of Tezcatlipoca was regarded as compulsory, and to some extent as a safeguard against the destruction of the universe, a calamity the Nahua had been led to believe might occur through his agency. He was known as Moneneque (The Claimer of Prayer), and in some of the representations of him an ear of gold was shown suspended from his hair, toward which small tongues of gold strained upward in appeal of prayer. In times of national danger, plague, or famine universal prayer was made to Tezcatlipoca. The heads of the community repaired to his *teocalli* (temple) accompanied by the people *en masse*, and all prayed earnestly together for his speedy intervention. The prayers to Tezcatlipoca still extant prove that the ancient Mexicans fully believed that he possessed the power of life and death, and many of them are couched in the most piteous terms.

The Teotleco Festival

The supreme position occupied by Tezcatlipoca in the Mexican religion is well exemplified in the festival of the Teotleco (Coming of the Gods), which is fully described in Sahagun's account of the Mexican festivals. Another peculiarity connected with his worship was that he was one of the few Mexican deities who had any relation to the expiation of sin. Sin was symbolized by the Nahua as excrement, and in various manuscripts Tezcatlipoca is represented as a turkey-cock to which ordure is being offered up.

Of the festival of the Teotleco Sahagun says: "In the twelfth month a festival was celebrated in honour of all the gods, who were said to have gone to some country I know not where. On the last day of the month a greater one was held, because the gods had returned. On the fifteenth day of this month the young boys and the servitors decked all the altars or oratories of the gods with boughs, as well as those which were in the houses, and the images which were set up by the wayside and at the cross-roads. This work was paid for in maize. Some received a basketful, and others only a few ears. On the eighteenth day the ever-youthful god Tlamatzincatl or Titlacahuan arrived. It was said that he marched better and arrived the first because he was strong and young. Food was offered him in his temple on that night. Everyone drank, ate, and made merry. The old people especially celebrated the arrival of the god by drinking wine, and it was alleged that his feet were washed by these rejoicings. The last day of the month was marked by a great festival, on account of the belief that the whole of the gods arrived at that time. On the preceding night a quantity of flour was kneaded on a carpet into the shape of a cheese, it being supposed that the gods would leave a footprint thereon as a sign of their return. The chief attendant watched all night, going to and fro to see if the impression appeared. When he at last saw it he called out, 'The master has arrived,' and at once the priests of the temple began to sound the horns, trumpets, and other musical instruments used by them. Upon hearing this noise everyone set forth to offer food in all the temples." The next day the aged gods were supposed to arrive, and young men disguised as monsters hurled victims into a huge sacrificial fire.

The Toxcatl Festival

The most remarkable festival in connection with Tezcatlipoca was the Toxcatl, held in the fifth month. On the day of this festival a youth was slain who for an entire year previously had been carefully instructed in the *rôle* of victim. He was selected from among the best war captives of the year, and must be without spot or blemish. He assumed the name, garb, and attributes of Tezcatlipoca himself, and was regarded with awe by the entire populace, who imagined him to be the earthly representative of the deity. He rested during the day, and ventured forth at night only, armed with the dart and shield of the god, to scour the roads. This practice was, of course, symbolical of the wind-god's progress over the night-bound highways. He carried also the whistle symbolical of the deity, and made with it a noise such as the weird wind of night makes when it hurries through the streets. To his arms and legs small bells were attached. He was followed by a retinue of pages, and at intervals rested upon the stone seats which were placed upon the highways for the convenience of Tezcatlipoca. Later in the year he was mated to four beautiful maidens of high birth, with whom he passed the time in amusement of every description. He was entertained at the tables of the nobility as the earthly representative of Tezcatlipoca, and his latter days were one constant round of feasting and excitement. At last the fatal day upon which he must be sacrificed arrived. He took a tearful farewell of the maidens whom he had espoused, and was carried to the *teocalli* of sacrifice, upon the sides of which he broke the musical instruments with which he had beguiled the time of his captivity. When he reached the summit he was received by the high-priest, who speedily made him one with the god whom he represented by tearing his heart out on the stone of sacrifice.

Huitzilopochtli, the War-God

Huitzilopochtli occupied in the Aztec pantheon a place similar to that of Mars in the Roman. His origin is obscure, but the myth relating to it is distinctly original in character (see page 207). It recounts how Huitzilopochtli defeated Coyolxauhqui as the latter attempted to kill their mother Coatlicue.

The name Huitzilopochtli signifies 'Humming-bird to the left,' from the circumstance that the god wore the feathers of the humming-bird, or *colibri*, on his left leg. From this it has been inferred that he was a humming-bird totem. The explanation of Huitzilopochtli's origin is a little deeper than this, however. Among the American tribes, especially those of the northern continent, the serpent is regarded with the deepest veneration as the symbol of wisdom and magic. From these sources come success in war. The serpent also typifies the lightning, the symbol of the divine spear, the apotheosis of warlike might. Fragments of serpents are regarded as powerful war-physic among many tribes. Atatarho, a mythical wizard-king of the Iroquois, was clothed with living serpents as with arobe, and his myth throws light on one of the names of Huitzilopochtli's mother, Coatlantona (Robe of Serpents). Huitzilopochtli's image was surrounded by serpents, and rested on serpent-shaped supporters. His sceptre was a single snake, and his great drum was of serpent-skin.

In American mythology the serpent is closely associated with the bird. Thus the name of the god Quetzalcoatl is translatable as 'Feathered Serpent,' and many similar cases where the conception of bird and serpent have been unified could be adduced.

Huitzilopochtli is undoubtedly one of these. We may regard him as a god the primary conception of whom arose from the idea of the serpent, the symbol of warlike wisdom and might, the symbol of the warrior's dart or spear, and the humming-bird, the harbinger of summer, type of the season when the snake or lightning god has power over the crops.

Huitzilopochtli was usually represented as wearing on his head a waving panache or plume of humming-birds' feathers. His face and limbs were striped with bars of blue, and in his right hand he carried four spears. His left hand bore his shield, on the surface of which were displayed five tufts of down, arranged in the form of a quincunx. The shield was made with reeds, covered with eagle's down. The spear he brandished was also tipped with tufts of down instead of flint. These weapons were placed in the hands of those who as captives engaged in the sacrificial fight, for in the Aztec mind Huitzilopochtli symbolized the warrior's death on the gladiatorial stone of combat. As has been said, Huitzilopochtli was war-god of the Aztecs, and was supposed to have led them to the site of Mexico from their original home in the north. The city of Mexico took its name from one of its districts, which was designated by a title of Huitzilopochtli's, Mexitli (Hare of the Aloes).

The War-God as Fertilizer

But Huitzilopochtli was not a war-god alone. As the serpent-god of lightning he had a connection with summer, the season of lightning, and therefore had dominion to some extent over the crops and fruits of the earth. The Algonquian Indians of North America believed that the rattlesnake could raise ruinous storms or grant favourable breezes. They alluded to it also as the symbol of life, for the serpent has a phallic significance because of its similarity to the symbol of generation and fructification. With some American tribes also, notably the Pueblo Indians of Arizona, the serpent has a solar significance, and with tail in mouth symbolizes the annual round of the sun. The Nahua believed that Huitzilopochtli could grant them fair weather for the fructification of their crops, and they placed an image of Tlaloc, the rain-god, near him, so that, if necessary, the war-god could compel the rain-maker to exert his pluvial powers or to abstain from the creation of floods. We must, in considering the nature of this deity, bear well in mind the connection in the Nahua consciousness between the pantheon, war, and the food-supply. If war was not waged annually the gods must go without flesh food and perish, and if the gods succumbed the crops would fail, and famine would destroy the race. So it was small wonder that Huitzilopochtli was one of the chief gods of Mexico.

Huitzilopochtli's principal festival was the Toxcatl, celebrated immediately after the Toxcatl festival of Tezcatlipoca, to which it bore a strong resemblance. Festivals of the god were held in May and December, at the latter of which an image of him, moulded in dough kneaded with the blood of sacrificed children, was pierced by the presiding priest with an arrow – an act significant of the death of Huitzilopochtli until his resurrection in the next year.

Strangely enough, when the absolute supremacy of Tezcatlipoca is remembered, the high-priest of Huitzilopochtli, the Mexicatl Teohuatzin, was considered to be the religious head of the Mexican priesthood. The priests of Huitzilopochtli held office by right of descent, and their primate exacted absolute obedience from the priesthoods of all the other deities, being regarded as next to the monarch himself in power and dominion.

Tlaloc, the Rain-God

Tlaloc was the god of rain and moisture. In a country such as Mexico, where the success or failure of the crops depends entirely upon the plentiful nature or otherwise of the rainfall, he was, it will be readily granted, a deity of high importance. It was believed that he made his home in the mountains which surround the valley of Mexico, as these were the source of the local rainfall, and his popularity is vouched for by the fact that sculptured representations of him occur more often than those of any other of the Mexican deities. He is generally represented in a semi-recumbent attitude, with the upper part of the body raised upon the elbows, and the knees half drawn up, probably to represent the mountainous character of the country whence comes the rain. He was espoused to Chalchihuitlicue (Emerald Lady), who bore him a numerous progeny, the Tlalocs (Clouds). Many of the figures which represented him were carved from the green stone called *chalchiuitl* (jadeite), to typify the colour of water, and in some of these he was shown holding a serpent of gold to typify the lightning, for water-gods are often closely identified with the thunder, which hangs over the hills and accompanies heavy rains. Tlaloc, like his prototype, the Kiche god Hurakan, manifested himself in three forms, as the lightning-flash, the thunderbolt, and the thunder. Although his image faced the east, where he was supposed to have originated, he was worshipped as inhabiting the four cardinal points and every mountain-top. The colours of the four points of the compass, yellow, green, red, and blue, whence came the rain-bearing winds, entered into the composition of his costume, which was further crossed with streaks of silver, typifying the mountain torrents. A vase containing every description of grain was usually placed before his idol, an offering of the growth which it was hoped he would fructify. He dwelt in a many-watered paradise called Tlalocan (The Country of Tlaloc), a place of plenty and fruitfulness, where those who had been drowned or struck by lightning or had died from dropsical diseases enjoyed eternal bliss. Those of the common people who did not die such deaths went to the dark abode of Mictlan, the all-devouring and gloomy Lord of Death.

In the native manuscripts Tlaloc is usually portrayed as having a dark complexion, a large round eye, a row of tusks, and over the lips an angular blue stripe curved downward and rolled up at the ends. The latter character is supposed to have been evolved originally from the coils of two snakes, their mouths with long fangs in the upper jaw meeting in the middle of the upper lip. The snake, besides being symbolized by lightning in many American mythologies, is also symbolical of water, which is well typified in its sinuous movements.

Many maidens and children were annually sacrificed to Tlaloc. If the children wept it was regarded as a happy omen for a rainy season. The Etzalqualiztli (When they eat Bean Food) was his chief festival, and was held on a day approximating to May 13, about which date the rainy season usually commenced. Another festival in his honour, the Quauitleua, commenced the Mexican year on February 2. At the former festival the priests of Tlaloc plunged into a lake, imitating the sounds and movements of frogs, which, as denizens of water, were under the special protection of the god. Chalchihuitlicue, his wife, was often symbolized by the small image of a frog.

Sacrifices to Tlaloc

Human sacrifices also took place at certain points in the mountains where artificial ponds were consecrated to Tlaloc. Cemeteries were situated in their vicinity, and offerings to the god interred near the burial-place of the bodies of the victims slain in his service. His statue was placed on the highest mountain of Tezcuco, and an old writer mentions that five or six young children were annually offered to the god at various points, their hearts torn out, and their remains interred. The mountains Popocatepetl and Teocuinani were regarded as his special high places, and on the heights of the latter was built his temple, in which stood his image carved in green stone.

The Nahua believed that the constant production of food and rain induced a condition of senility in those deities whose duty it was to provide them. This they attempted to stave off, fearing that if they failed in so doing the gods would perish. They afforded them, accordingly, a period of rest and recuperation, and once in eight years a festival called the Atamalqualiztli (Fast of Porridge-balls and Water) was held, during which everyone in the Nahua community returned for the time being to the conditions of savage life. Dressed in costumes representing all forms of animal and bird life, and mimicking the sounds made by the various creatures they typified, the people danced round the *teocalli* of Tlaloc for the purpose of diverting and entertaining him after his labours in producing the fertilizing rains of the past eight years. A lake was filled with water-snakes and frogs, and into this the people plunged, catching the reptiles in their mouths and devouring them alive. The only grain food which might be partaken during this season of rest was thin water-porridge of maize.

Should one of the more prosperous peasants or yeomen deem a rainfall necessary to the growth of his crops, or should he fear a drought, he sought out one of the professional makers of dough or paste idols, whom he desired to mould one of Tlaloc. To this image offerings of maize-porridge and *pulque* were made. Throughout the night the farmer and his neighbours danced, shrieking and howling round the figure for the purpose of rousing Tlaloc from his drought-bringing slumbers. Next day was spent in quaffing huge libations of *pulque*, and in much-needed rest from the exertions of the previous night.

In Tlaloc it is easy to trace resemblances to a mythological conception widely prevalent among the indigenous American peoples. He is similar to such deities as the Hurakan of the Kiche of Guatemala, the Pillan of the aborigines of Chile, and Con, the thunder-god of the Collao of Peru. Only his thunderous powers are not so apparent as his rain-making abilities, and in this he differs somewhat from the gods alluded to.

Quetzalcoatl

It is highly probable that Quetzalcoatl was a deity of the pre-Nahua people of Mexico. He was regarded by the Aztec race as a god of somewhat alien character, and had but a limited following in Mexico, the city of Huitzilopochtli. In Cholula, however, and others of the older towns his worship flourished exceedingly. He was regarded as 'The Father of the Toltecs,' and, legend says, was the seventh and youngest son of the Toltec Abraham, Iztacmixcohuatl. Quetzalcoatl (whose name means 'Feathered Serpent' or 'Feathered Staff') became, at a relatively early period, ruler of Tollan, and by his enlightened sway and his encouragement of the liberal arts did much to further the advancement of his people. His reign had lasted for a period sufficient to permit of his placing the cultivated arts upon a satisfactory basis when the country was visited by the cunning magicians Tezcatlipoca and Coyotlinaual, god of the Amantecas. Disentangled from its terms of myth, this statement may be taken to imply that bands of invading Nahua first began to appear within the Toltec territories. Tezcatlipoca, descending from the sky in the shape of a spider by way of a fine web, proffered him a draught of *pulque*, which so intoxicated him that the curse of lust descended upon him, and he forgot his chastity with Quetzalpetlatl. The doom pronounced upon him was the hard one of banishment, and he was compelled to forsake Anahuac. His exile wrought peculiar changes upon the face of the country. He secreted his treasures of gold and silver, burned his palaces, transformed the cacao-trees into mezquites, and banished all the birds from the neighbourhood of Tollan. The magicians, nonplussed at these unexpected happenings, begged him to return, but he refused on the ground that the sun required his presence. He proceeded to Tabasco, the fabled land of Tlapallan, and, embarking upon a raft made of serpents, floated away to the east. A slightly different version of this myth has already been given. Other accounts state that the king cast himself upon a funeral pyre and was consumed, and that the ashes arising from the conflagration flew upward, and were changed into birds of brilliant plumage. His heart also soared into the sky, and became the morning star. The Mexicans averred that Quetzalcoatl died when the star became visible, and thus they bestowed upon him the title 'Lord of the Dawn.' They further said that when he died he was invisible for four days, and that for eight days he wandered in the underworld, after which time the morning star appeared, when he achieved resurrection, and ascended his throne as a god.

It is the contention of some authorities that the myth of Quetzalcoatl points to his status as god of the sun. That luminary, they say, begins his diurnal journey in the east, whence Quetzalcoatl returned as to his native home. It will be recalled that Montezuma and his subjects imagined that Cortés was no other than Quetzalcoatl, returned to his dominions, as an old prophecy declared he would do. But that he stood for the sun itself is highly improbable, as will be shown. First of all, however, it will be well to pay some attention to other theories concerning his origin.

Perhaps the most important of these is that which regards Quetzalcoatl as a god of the air. He is connected, say some, with the cardinal points, and wears the insignia of the cross, which symbolizes them. Dr Seler says of him: "He has a protruding, trumpet-like mouth, for the wind-god blows.... His figure suggests whirls and circles. Hence his temples were built in circular form.... The head of the wind-god stands for the second of the twenty day signs, which was called Ehecatl (Wind)." The same authority, however, in his essay on Mexican chronology, gives to Quetzalcoatl a dual nature, "the dual nature which seems to belong to the wind-god Quetzalcoatl, who now appears simply a wind-god, and again seems to show the true characters of the old god of fire and light."

Dr Brinton perceived in Quetzalcoatl a similar dual nature. "He is both lord of the eastern light and of the winds," he writes (*Myths of the New World*, page 214). "Like all the dawn heroes, he too was represented as of white complexion, clothed in long, white robes, and, as many of the Aztec gods, with a full and flowing beard.... He had been overcome by Tezcatlipoca, the wind or spirit of night, who had descended from heaven by a spider's web, and presented his rival with a draught supposed to confer immortality, but in fact producing an intolerable longing for home. For the wind and the light both depart when the gloaming draws near, or when the clouds spread their dark and shadowy webs along the mountains, and pour the vivifying rain upon the fields."

The theory which derives Quetzalcoatl from a 'culture-hero' who once actually existed is scarcely reconcilable with probability. It is more than likely that, as in the case of other mythical paladins, the legend of a mighty hero arose from the somewhat weakened idea of a great deity. Some of the early Spanish missionaries professed to see in Quetzalcoatl the Apostle St Thomas, who had journeyed to America to effect its conversion!

The Man of the Sun

A more probable explanation of the origin of Quetzalcoatl and a more likely elucidation of his nature is that which would regard him as the Man of the Sun, who has quitted his abode for a season for the purpose of inculcating in mankind those arts which represent the first steps in civilization, who fulfils his mission, and who, at a late period, is displaced by the deities of an invading race. Quetzalcoatl was represented as a traveller with staff in hand, and this is proof of his solar character, as is the statement that under his rule the fruits of the earth flourished more abundantly than at any subsequent period. The abundance of gold said to have been accumulated in his reign assists the theory, the precious metal being invariably associated with the sun by most barbarous peoples. In the native *pinturas* it is noticeable that the solar disc and semi-disc are almost invariably found in connection with the feathered serpent as the symbolical attributes of Quetzalcoatl. The Hopi Indians of Mexico at the present day symbolize the sun as a serpent, tail in mouth, and the ancient Mexicans introduced the solar disc in connection with small images of Quetzalcoatl, which they attached to the head-dress. In still other examples Quetzalcoatl is pictured as if emerging or stepping from the luminary, which is represented as his dwelling-place.

Several tribes tributary to the Aztecs were in the habit of imploring Quetzalcoatl in prayer to return and free them from the intolerable bondage of the conqueror. Notable among them were the Totonacs, who passionately believed that the sun, their father, would send a god who would free them from the Aztec yoke. On the coming of the Spaniards the European conquerors were hailed as the servants of Quetzalcoatl, thus in the eyes of the natives fulfilling the tradition that he would return.

Various Forms of Quetzalcoatl

Various conceptions of Quetzalcoatl are noticeable in the mythology of the territories which extended from the north of Mexico to the marshes of Nicaragua. In Guatemala the Kiches recognized him as Gucumatz, and in Yucatan proper he was worshipped as Kukulcan, both of which names are but literal translations of his Mexican title of 'Feathered Serpent' into Kiche and Mayan. That the three deities are one and the same there can be no shadow of doubt. Several authorities have seen in Kukulcan a 'serpent-and-rain god.' He can only be such in so far as he is a solar god also. The cult of the feathered snake in Yucatan was unquestionably a branch of sun-worship. In tropical latitudes the sun draws the clouds round him at noon. The rain falls from the clouds accompanied by thunder and lightning – the symbols of the divine serpent. Therefore the manifestations of the heavenly serpent were directly associated with the sun, and no statement that Kukulcan is a mere serpent-and-water god satisfactorily elucidates his characteristics.

Quetzalcoatl's Northern Origin

It is by no means improbable that Quetzalcoatl was of northern origin, and that on his adoption by southern peoples and tribes dwelling in tropical countries his characteristics were gradually and unconsciously altered in order to meet the exigencies of his environment. The mythology of the Indians of British Columbia, whence in all likelihood the Nahua originally came, is possessed of a central figure bearing a strong resemblance to Quetzalcoatl. Thus the Thlingit tribe worship Yetl; the Quaquiutl Indians, Kanikilak; the Salish people of the coast, Kumsnöotl, Quäaqua, or Släalekam. It is noticeable that these divine beings are worshipped as the Man of the Sun, and totally apart from the luminary himself, as was Quetzalcoatl in Mexico. The Quaquiutl believe that before his settlement among them for the purpose of inculcating in the tribe the arts of life, the sun descended as a bird, and assumed a human shape. Kanikilak is his son, who, as his emissary, spreads the arts of civilization over the world. So the Mexicans believed that Quetzalcoatl descended first of all in the form of a bird, and was ensnared in the fowler's net of the Toltec hero Hueymatzin.

The titles bestowed upon Quetzalcoatl by the Nahua show that in his solar significance he was god of the vault of the heavens, as well as merely son of the sun. He was alluded to as Ehecatl (The Air), Yolcuat (The Rattlesnake), Tohil (The Rumbler), Nanihehecatl (Lord of the Four Winds), Tlauizcalpantecutli (Lord of the Light of the Dawn). The whole heavenly vault was his, together with all its phenomena. This would seem to be in direct opposition to the theory that Tezcatlipoca was the supreme god of the Mexicans. But it must be borne in mind that Tezcatlipoca was the god of a later age, and of a fresh body of Nahua immigrants, and as such inimical to Quetzalcoatl, who was probably in a similar state of opposition to Itzamna, a Maya deity of Yucatan.

The Worship of Quetzalcoatl

The worship of Quetzalcoatl was in some degree antipathetic to that of the other Mexican deities, and his priests were a separate caste. Although human sacrifice was by no means so prevalent among his devotees, it is a mistake to aver, as some authorities have done, that it did not exist in connection with his worship. A more acceptable sacrifice to Quetzalcoatl appears to have been the blood of the celebrant or worshipper, shed by himself. When we come to consider the mythology of the Zapotecs, a people whose customs and beliefs appear to have formed a species of link between the Mexican and Mayan civilizations, we shall find that their high-priests occasionally enacted the legend of Quetzalcoatl in their own persons, and that their worship, which appears to have been based upon that of Quetzalcoatl, had as one of its most pronounced characteristics the shedding of blood. The celebrant or devotee drew blood from the vessels lying under the tongue or behind the ear by drawing across those tender parts a cord made from the thorn-covered fibres of the agave. The blood was smeared over the mouths of the idols. In this practice we can perceive an act analogous to the sacrificial substitution of the part for the whole, as obtaining in early Palestine and many other countries – a certain sign that tribal or racial opinion has contracted a disgust for human sacrifice, and has sought to evade the anger of the gods by yielding to them a portion of the blood of each worshipper, instead of sacrificing the life of one for the general weal.

The Maize-Gods of Mexico

A special group of deities called Centeotl presided over the agriculture of Mexico, each of whom personified one or other of the various aspects of the maize plant. The chief goddess of maize, however, was Chicomecohuatl (Seven-serpent), her name being an allusion to the fertilizing power of water, which element the Mexicans symbolized by the serpent. As Xilonen she typified the *xilote*, or green ear of the maize. But it is probable that Chicomecohuatl was the creation of an older race, and that the Nahua new-comers adopted or brought with them another growth-spirit, the 'Earth-mother,' Teteoinnan (Mother of the Gods), or Tocitzin (Our Grandmother). This goddess had a son, Centeotl, a male maize-spirit. Sometimes the mother was also known as Centeotl, the generic name for the entire group, and this fact has led to some confusion in the minds of Americanists. But this does not mean that Chicomecohuatl was by any means neglected. Her spring festival, held on April 5, was known as Hueytozoztli (The Great Watch), and was accompanied by a general fast, when the dwellings of the Mexicans were decorated with bulrushes which had been sprinkled with blood drawn from the extremities of the inmates. The statues of the little *tepitoton* (household gods) were also decorated. The worshippers then proceeded to the maize-fields, where they pulled the tender stalks of the growing maize, and, having decorated them with flowers, placed them in the *calpulli* (the common house of the village). A mock combat then took place before the altar of Chicomecohuatl. The girls of the village presented the goddess with bundles of maize of the previous season's harvesting, later restoring them to the granaries in order that they might be utilized for seed for the coming year. Chicomecohuatl was always represented among the household deities of the Mexicans, and on the occasion of her festival the family placed before the image a basket of provisions surmounted by a cooked frog, bearing on its back a piece of cornstalk stuffed with pounded maize and vegetables. This frog was symbolic of Chalchihuitlicue, wife of Tlaloc, the rain-god, who assisted Chicomecohuatl in providing a bountiful harvest. In order that the soil might further benefit, a frog, the symbol of water, was sacrificed, so that its vitality should recuperate that of the weary and much-burdened earth.

The Sacrifice of the Dancer

A more important festival of Chicomecohuatl, however, was the Xalaquia, which lasted from June 28 to July 14, commencing when the maize plant had attained its full growth. The women of the pueblo (village) wore their hair unbound, and shook and tossed it so that by sympathetic magic the maize might take the hint and grow correspondingly long. *Chian pinolli* was consumed in immense quantities, and maize-porridge was eaten. Hilarious dances were nightly performed in the *teopan* (temple), the central figure in which was the Xalaquia, a female captive or slave, with face painted red and yellow to represent the colours of the maize plant. She had previously undergone a long course of training in the dancing-school, and now, all unaware of the horrible fate awaiting her, she danced and pirouetted gaily among the rest. Throughout the duration of the festival she danced, and on its expiring night she was accompanied in the dance by the women of the community, who circled round her, chanting the deeds of Chicomecohuatl. When daybreak appeared the company was joined by the chiefs and headmen, who, along with the exhausted and half-fainting victim, danced the solemn death-dance. The entire community then approached the *teocalli* (pyramid of sacrifice), and, its summit reached, the victim was stripped to a nude condition, the priest plunged a knife of flint into her bosom, and, tearing out the still palpitating heart, offered it up to Chicomecohuatl. In this manner the venerable goddess, weary with the labours of inducing growth in the maize plant, was supposed to be revivified and refreshed. Hence the name Xalaquia, which signifies 'She who is clothed with the Sand.' Until the death of the victim it was not lawful to partake of the new corn.

The general appearance of Chicomecohuatl was none too pleasing. Her image rests in the National Museum in Mexico, and is girdled with snakes. On the underside the symbolic frog is carved. The Americanists of the eighteenth and early nineteenth centuries were unequal to the task of elucidating the origin of the figure, which they designated Teoyaominqui. The first to point out the error was Payne, in his *History of the New World called America*, vol. i. page 424. The passage in which he announces his discovery is of such real interest that it is worth transcribing fully:

An Antiquarian Mare's-Nest

"All the great idols of Mexico were thought to have been destroyed until this was disinterred among other relics in the course of making new drains in the Plaza Mayor of Mexico in August 1790. The discovery produced an immense sensation. The idol was dragged to the court of the University, and there set up; the Indians began to worship it and deck it with flowers; the antiquaries, with about the same degree of intelligence, to speculate about it. What most puzzled them was that the face and some other parts of the goddess are found in duplicate at the back of the figure; hence they concluded it to represent two gods in one, the principal of whom they further concluded to be a female, the other, indicated by the back, a male. The standard author on Mexican antiquities at that time was the Italian *dilettante* Boturini, of whom it may be said that he is better, but not much better, than nothing at all. From page 27 of his work the antiquaries learned that Huitzilopochtli was accompanied by the goddess Teoyaominqui, who was charged with collecting the souls of those slain in war and sacrifice. This was enough. The figure was at once named Teoyaominqui or Huitzilopochtli (The One plus the Other), and has been so called ever since. The antiquaries next elevated this imaginary goddess to the rank of the war-god's wife. 'A soldier,' says Bardolph, 'is better accommodated than with a wife': *a fortiori*, so is a war-god. Besides, as Torquemada (vol. ii. page 47) says with perfect truth, the Mexicans did not think so grossly of the divinity as to have married gods or goddesses at all. The figure is undoubtedly a female. It has no vestige of any weapon about it, nor has it any limbs. It differs in every particular from the war-god Huitzilopochtli, every detail of which is perfectly well known. There never was any goddess called Teoyaominqui. This may be plausibly inferred from the fact that such a goddess is unknown not merely to Sahagun, Torquemada, Acosta, Tezozomoc, Duran, and Clavigero, but to all other writers except Boturini. The blunder of the last-named writer is easily explained. Antonio Leon y Gama, a Mexican astronomer, wrote an account of the discoveries of 1790, in which, evidently puzzled by the name of Teoyaominqui, he quotes a manuscript in Mexican, said to have been written by an Indian of Tezcuco, who was born in 1528, to the effect that Teoyaotlatohua and Teoyaominqui were spirits who presided over the fifteenth of the twenty signs of the fortune-tellers' calendar, and that those born in this sign would be brave warriors, but would soon die. (As the fifteenth sign was *quauhtli*, this is likely enough.) When their hour had come the former spirit scented them out, the latter killed them. The rubbish printed about Huitzilopochtli, Teoyaominqui, and Mictlantecutli in connection with this statue would fill a respectable volume. The reason why the features were duplicated is obvious. The figure was carried in the midst of a large crowd. Probably it was considered to be an evil omen if the idol turned away its face from its worshippers; this the duplicate obviated. So when the dance was performed round the figure (*cf.* Janus). This duplication of the features, a characteristic of the very oldest gods, appears to be indicated when the numeral *ome* (two) is prefixed to the title of the deity. Thus the two ancestors and preservers of the race were called Ometecuhtli and Omecihuatl (two-chief, two-woman), ancient Toltec gods, who at the conquest become less prominent in the theology of Mexico, and who are best represented in that of the Mexican colony of Nicaragua."

The Offering to Centeotl

During her last hours the victim sacrificed at the Xalaquia wore a ritual dress made from the fibres of the aloe, and with this garment the maize-god Centeotl was clothed. Robed in this he temporarily represented the earth-goddess, so that he might receive her sacrifice. The blood of victims was offered up to him in a vessel decorated with that brilliant and artistic feather-work which excited such admiration in the breasts of the connoisseurs and aesthetes of the Europe of the sixteenth century. Upon partaking of this blood-offering the deity emitted a groan so intense and terrifying that it has been left on record that such Spaniards as were present became panic-stricken. This ceremony was followed by another, the *nitiçapoloa* (tasting of the soil), which consisted in raising a little earth on one finger to the mouth and eating it.

As has been said, Centeotl the son has been confounded with Centeotl the mother, who is in reality the earth-mother Teteoinnan. Each of these deities had a *teopan* (temple) of his or her own, but they were closely allied as parent and child. But of the two, Centeotl the son was the more important. On the death of the sacrificed victim her skin was conveyed to the temple of Centeotl the son, and worn there in the succeeding ritual by the officiating priests. This gruesome dress is frequently depicted in the Aztec *pinturas*, where the skin of the hands, and in some instances the feet, of the victims can be seen dangling from the wrists and ankles of the priest.

Importance of the Food-Gods

To the Mexicans the deities of most importance to the community as a whole were undoubtedly the food-gods. In their emergence from the hunting to the agricultural state of life, when they began to exist almost solely upon the fruits of the earth, the Mexicans were quick to recognize that the old deities of the chase, such as Mixcoatl, could not now avail them or succour them in the same manner as the guardians of the crops and fertilizers of the soil. Gradually we see these gods, then, advance in power and influence until at the time of the Spanish invasion we find them paramount. Even the terrible war-god himself had an agricultural significance, as we have pointed out. A distinct bargain with the food-gods can be clearly traced, and is none the less obvious because it was never written or codified. The covenant was as binding to the native mind as any made betwixt god and man in ancient Palestine, and included mutual assistance as well as provision for mere alimentary supply. In no mythology is the understanding between god and man so clearly defined as in the Nahuan, and in none is its operation better exemplified.

Xipe

Xipe (The Flayed) was widely worshipped throughout Mexico, and is usually depicted in the *pinturas* as being attired in a flayed human skin. At his special festival, the 'Man-flaying,' the skins were removed from the victims and worn by the devotees of the god for the succeeding twenty days. He is usually represented as of a red colour. In the later days of the Aztec monarchy the kings and leaders of Mexico assumed the dress or classical garments of Xipe. This dress consisted of a crown made of feathers of the roseate spoonbill, the gilt timbrel, the jacket of spoonbill feathers, and an apron of green feathers lapping over one another in a tile-like pattern. In the Cozcatzin Codex we see a picture of King Axayacatl dressed as Xipe in a feather skirt, and having a tiger-skin scabbard to his sword. The hands of a flayed human skin also dangle over the monarch's wrists, and the feet fall over his feet like gaiters.

Xipe's shield is a round target covered with the rose-coloured feathers of the spoonbill, with concentric circles of a darker hue on the surface. There are examples of it divided into an upper and lower part, the former showing an emerald on a blue field, and the latter a tiger-skin design. Xipe was imagined as possessing three forms, the first that of the roseate spoonbill, the second that of the blue cotinga, and the last that of a tiger, the three shapes perhaps corresponding to the regions of heaven, earth, and hell, or to the three elements, fire, earth, and water. The deities of many North American Indian tribes show similar variations in form and colour, which are supposed to follow as the divinity changes his dwelling to north, south, east, or west. But Xipe is seldom depicted in the *pinturas* in any other form but that of the red god, the form in which the Mexicans adopted him from the Yopi tribe of the Pacific slope. He is the god of human sacrifice *par excellence*, and may be regarded as a Yopi equivalent of Tezcatlipoca.

Nanahuatl, or Nanauatzin

Nanahuatl (Poor Leper) presided over skin diseases, such as leprosy. It was thought that persons afflicted with these complaints were set apart by the moon for his service. In the Nahua tongue the words for 'leprous' and 'eczematous' also mean 'divine.' The myth of Nanahuatl tells how before the sun was created humanity dwelt in sable and horrid gloom. Only a human sacrifice could hasten the appearance of the luminary. Metztli (The Moon) led forth Nanahuatl as a sacrifice, and he was cast upon a funeral pyre, in the flames of which he was consumed. Metztli also cast herself upon the mass of flame, and with her death the sun rose above the horizon. There can be no doubt that the myth refers to the consuming of the starry or spotted night, and incidentally to the nightly death of the moon at the flaming hour of dawn.

Xolotl

Xolotl is of southern, possibly Zapotec, origin. He represents either fire rushing down from the heavens or light flaming upward. It is noticeable that in the *pinturas* the picture of the setting sun being devoured by the earth is nearly always placed opposite his image. He is probably identical with Nanahuatl, and appears as the representative of human sacrifice. He has also affinities with Xipe. On the whole Xolotl may be best described as a sun-god of the more southerly tribes. His head (*quaxolotl*) was one of the most famous devices for warriors' use, as sacrifice among the Nahua was, as we have seen, closely associated with warfare.

Xolotl was a mythical figure quite foreign to the peoples of Anahuac or Mexico, who regarded him as something strange and monstrous. He is alluded to as the 'God of Monstrosities,' and, thinks Dr Seler, the word 'monstrosity' may suitably translate his name. He is depicted with empty eye-sockets, which circumstance is explained by the myth that when the gods determined to sacrifice themselves in order to give life and strength to the newly created sun, Xolotl withdrew, and wept so much that his eyes fell out of their sockets. This was the Mexican explanation of a Zapotec attribute. Xolotl was originally the 'Lightning Beast' of the Maya or some other southern folk, and was represented by them as a dog, since that animal appeared to them to be the creature which he most resembled. But he was by no means a 'natural' dog, hence their conception of him as unnatural. Dr Seler is inclined to identify him with the tapir, and indeed Sahagun speaks of a strange animal-being, *tlaca-xolotl*, which has "a large snout, large teeth, hoofs like an ox, a thick hide, and reddish hair" – not a bad description of the tapir of Central America. Of course to the Mexicans the god Xolotl was no longer an animal, although he had evolved from one.

The Fire-God

This deity was known in Mexico under various names, notably Tata (Our Father), Huehueteotl (Oldest of Gods), and Xiuhtecutli (Lord of the Year). He was represented as of the colour of fire, with a black face, a headdress of green feathers, and bearing on his back a yellow serpent, to typify the serpentine nature of fire. He also bore a mirror of gold to show his connection with the sun, from which all heat emanates. On rising in the morning all Mexican families made Xiuhtecutli an offering of a piece of bread and a drink. He was thus not only, like Vulcan, the god of thunderbolts and conflagrations, but also the milder deity of the domestic hearth. Once a year the fire in every Mexican house was extinguished, and rekindled by friction before the idol of Xiuhtecutli. When a Mexican baby was born it passed through a baptism of fire on the fourth day, up to which time a fire, lighted at the time of its birth, was kept burning in order to nourish its existence.

Mictlan

Mictlantecutli (Lord of Hades) was God of the Dead and of the grim and shadowy realm to which the souls of men repair after their mortal sojourn. He is represented in the *pinturas* as a grisly monster with capacious mouth, into which fall the spirits of the dead. His terrible abode was sometimes alluded to as Tlalxicco (Navel of the Earth), but the

Mexicans in general seem to have thought that it was situated in the far north, which they regarded as a place of famine, desolation, and death. Here those who by the circumstances of their demise were unfitted to enter the paradise of Tlaloc – namely, those who had not been drowned or had not died a warrior's death, or, in the case of women, had not died in childbed – passed a dreary and meaningless existence. Mictlan was surrounded by a species of demons called *tzitzimimes*, and had a spouse, Mictecaciuatl. When we come to discuss the analogous deity of the Maya we shall see that in all probability Mictlan was represented by the bat, the animal typical of the underworld. In a preceding paragraph dealing with the funerary customs we have described the journey of the soul to the abode of Mictlan, and the ordeals through which the spirit of the defunct had to pass ere entering his realm (*see* page 32, The Mexican 'Book of the Dead').

Worship of the Planet Venus

The Mexicans designated the planet Venus Citlalpol (The Great Star) and Tlauizcalpantecutli (Lord of the Dawn). It seems to have been the only star worshipped by them, and was regarded with considerable veneration. Upon its rising they stopped up the chimneys of their houses, so that no harm of any kind might enter with its light. A column called Ilhuicatlan, meaning 'In the Sky,' stood in the court of the great temple of Mexico, and upon this a symbol of the planet was painted. On its reappearance during its usual circuit, captives were taken before this representation and sacrificed to it. It will be remembered that the myth of Quetzalcoatl states that the heart of that deity flew upward from the funeral pyre on which he was consumed and became the planet Venus. It is not easy to say whether or not this myth is anterior to the adoption of the worship of the planet by the Nahua, for it may be a tale of pre- or post-Nahuan growth. In the *tonalamatl* Tlauizcalpantecutli is represented as lord of the ninth division of thirteen days, beginning with Ce Coatl (the sign of 'One Serpent'). In several of the *pinturas* he is represented as having a white body with long red stripes, while round his eyes is a deep black painting like a domino mask, bordered with small white circles. His lips are a bright vermilion. The red stripes are probably introduced to accentuate the whiteness of his body, which is understood to symbolize the peculiar half-light which emanates from the planet. The black paint on the face, surrounding the eye, typifies the dark sky of night. In Mexican and Central American symbolizm the eye often represents light, and here, surrounded by blackness as it is, it is perhaps almost hieroglyphic. As the star of evening, Tlauizcalpantecutli is sometimes shown with the face of a skull, to signify his descent into the underworld, whither he follows the sun. That the Mexicans and Maya carefully and accurately observed his periods of revolution is witnessed by the *pinturas*.

Sun-Worship

The sun was regarded by the Nahua, and indeed by all the Mexican and Central American peoples, as the supreme deity, or rather the principal source of subsistence and life. He was always alluded to as *the teotl*, *the* god, and his worship formed as it were a background to that of all the other gods. His Mexican name, Ipalnemohuani (He by whom Men Live) shows that the Mexicans regarded him as the primal source of being, and the heart, the symbol of life, was looked upon as his special sacrifice. Those who rose at sunrise to prepare food for the day held up to him on his appearance the hearts of animals they had slain for cooking, and even the hearts of the victims to Tezcatlipoca and Huitzilopochtli were first held up to the sun, as if he had a primary right to the sacrifice, before being cast into the bowl of copal which lay at the feet of the idol. It was supposed that the luminary rejoiced in offerings of blood, and that it constituted the only food which would render him sufficiently vigorous to undertake his daily journey through the heavens. He is often depicted in the *pinturas* as licking up the gore of the sacrificial victims with his long tongue-like rays. The sun must fare well if he was to continue to give life, light, and heat to mankind.

The Mexicans, as we have already seen, believed that the luminary they knew had been preceded by others, each of which had been quenched by some awful cataclysm of nature. Eternity had, in fact, been broken up into epochs, marked by the destruction of successive suns. In the period preceding that in which they lived, a mighty deluge had deprived the sun of life, and some such catastrophe was apprehended at the end of every 'sheaf' of fifty-two years. The old suns were dead, and the current sun was no more immortal than they. At the end of one of the 'sheaves' he too would succumb.

Sustaining the Sun

It was therefore necessary to sustain the sun by the daily food of human sacrifice, for by a tithe of human life alone would he be satisfied. Naturally a people holding such a belief would look elsewhere than within their own borders for the material wherewith to placate their deity. This could be most suitably found among the inhabitants of a neighbouring state. It thus became the business of the warrior class in the Aztec state to furnish forth the altars of the gods with human victims. The most suitable district of supply was the pueblo of Tlaxcallan, or Tlascala, the people of which were of cognate origin to the Aztecs. The communities had, although related, been separated for so many generations that they had begun to regard each other as traditional enemies, and on a given day in the year their forces met at an appointed spot for the purpose of engaging in a strife which should furnish one side or the other with a sufficiency of victims for the purpose of sacrifice. The warrior who captured the largest number of opponents alive was regarded as the champion of the day, and was awarded the chief honours of the combat. The sun was therefore the god of warriors, as he would give them victory in battle in order that they might supply him with food. The rites of this military worship of the luminary were held in the Quauhquauhtinchan (House of the Eagles), an armoury set apart for the regiment of that name. On March 17 and December 1 and 2, at the ceremonies known as Nauhollin (The Four Motions – alluding to the quivering appearance of the sun's rays), the warriors gathered in this hall for the purpose of despatching a messenger to their lord the sun. High up on the wall of the principal court was a great symbolic representation of the orb, painted upon a brightly coloured cotton hanging. Before this copal and other fragrant gums and spices were burned four times a day. The victim, a war-captive, was placed at the foot of a long staircase leading up to the Quauhxicalli (Cup of the Eagles), the name of the stone on which he was to be sacrificed. He was clothed in red striped with white and wore white plumes in his hair – colours symbolical of the sun – while he bore a staff decorated with feathers and a shield covered with tufts of cotton. He also carried a bundle of eagle's feathers and some paint on his shoulders, to enable the sun, to whom he was the emissary, to paint his face. He was then addressed by the officiating priest in the following terms: "Sir, we pray you go to our god the sun, and greet him on our behalf; tell him that his sons and warriors and chiefs and those who remain here beg of him to remember them and to favour them from that place where he is, and to receive this small offering which we send him. Give him this staff to help him on his journey, and this shield for his defence, and all the rest that you have in this bundle." The victim, having undertaken to carry the message to the sun-god, was then despatched upon his long journey.

A Quauhxicalli is preserved in the National Museum of Mexico. It consists of a basaltic mass, circular in form, on which are shown in sculpture a series of groups representing Mexican warriors receiving the submission of war-captives. The prisoner tenders a flower to his captor, symbolical of the life he is about to offer up, for lives were the 'flowers' offered to the gods, and the campaign in which these 'blossoms' were captured was called Xochiyayotl (The War of Flowers). The warriors who receive the submission of the captives are represented in the act of tearing the plumes from their heads. These bas-reliefs occupy the sides of the stone. The face of it is covered by a great solar disc having eight rays, and the surface is hollowed out in the middle to form a receptacle for blood – the 'cup' alluded to in the name of the stone. The Quauhxicalli must not be confounded with the *temalacatl* (spindle stone), to which the alien warrior who received a chance of life was secured. The gladiatorial combat gave the war-captive an opportunity to escape through superior address in arms. The *temalacatl* was somewhat higher than a man, and was provided with a platform at the top, in the middle of which was placed a great stone with a hole in it through which a rope was passed. To this the war-captive was secured, and if he could vanquish seven of his captors he was released. If he failed to do so he was at once sacrificed.

A Mexican Valhalla

The Mexican warriors believed that they continued in the service of the sun after death, and, like the Scandinavian heroes in Valhalla, that they were admitted to the dwelling of the god, where they shared all the delights of his diurnal round. The Mexican warrior dreaded to die in his bed, and craved an end on the field of battle. This explains the desperate nature of their resistance to the Spaniards under Cortés, whose officers stated that the Mexicans seemed to desire to die fighting. After death they believed that they would partake of the cannibal feasts offered up to the sun and imbibe the juice of flowers.

The Feast of Totec

The chief of the festivals to the sun was that held in spring at the vernal equinox, before the representation of a deity known as Totec (Our Great Chief). Although Totec was a solar deity he had been adopted from the people of an alien state, the Zapotecs of Zalisco, and is therefore scarcely to be regarded as the principal sun-god. His festival was celebrated by the symbolical slaughter of all the other gods for the purpose of providing sustenance to the sun, each of the gods being figuratively slain in the person of a victim. Totec was attired in the same manner as the warrior despatched twice a year to assure the sun of the loyalty of the Mexicans. The festival appears to have been primarily a seasonal one, as bunches of dried maize were offered to Totec. But its larger meaning is obvious. It was, indeed, a commemoration of the creation of the sun. This is proved by the description of the image of Totec, which was robed and equipped as the solar traveller, by the solar disc and tables of the sun's progress carved on the altar employed in the ceremony, and by the robes of the victims, who were dressed to represent dwellers in the sun-god's halls. Perhaps Totec, although of alien origin, was the only deity possessed by the Mexicans who directly represented the sun. As a borrowed god he would have but a minor position in the Mexican pantheon, but again as the only sun-god whom it was necessary to bring into prominence during a strictly solar festival he would be for the time, of course, a very important deity indeed.

Tepeyollotl

Tepeyollotl means Heart of the Mountain, and evidently alludes to a deity whom the Nahua connected with seismic disturbances and earthquakes. By the interpreter of the Codex Telleriano-Remensis he is called Tepeolotlec, an obvious distortion of his real name. The interpreter of the codex states that his name "refers to the condition of the earth after the flood. The sacrifices of these thirteen days were not good, and the literal translation of their name is 'dirt sacrifices.' They caused palsy and bad humours.... This Tepeolotlec was lord of these thirteen days. In them were celebrated the feast to the jaguar, and the last four preceding days were days of fasting.... Tepeolotlec means the 'Lord of Beasts.' The four feast days were in honour of the Suchiquezal, who was the man that remained behind on the earth upon which we now live. This Tepeolotlec was the same as the echo of the voice when it re-echoes in a valley from one mountain to another. This name 'jaguar' is given to the earth because the jaguar is the boldest animal, and the echo which the voice awakens in the mountains is a survival of the flood, it is said."

From this we can see that Tepeyollotl is a deity of the earth pure and simple, a god of desert places. It is certain that he was not a Mexican god, or at least was not of Nahua origin, as he is mentioned by none of those writers who deal with Nahua traditions, and we must look for him among the Mixtecs and Zapotecs.

Macuilxochitl, or Xochipilli

This deity, whose names mean Five-Flower and Source of Flowers, was regarded as the patron of luck in gaming. He may have been adopted by the Nahua from the Zapotecs, but the converse may be equally true. The Zapotecs represented him with a design resembling a butterfly about the mouth, and a many-coloured face which looks out of the open jaws of a bird with a tall and erect crest. The worship of this god appears to have been very widespread. Sahagun says of him that a fête was held in his honour, which was preceded by a rigorous fast. The people covered themselves with ornaments and jewels symbolic of the deity, as if they desired to represent him, and dancing and singing proceeded gaily to the sound of the drum. Offerings of the blood of various animals followed, and specially prepared cakes were submitted to the god. This simple fare, however, was later followed by human sacrifices, rendered by the notables, who brought certain of their slaves for immolation. This completed the festival.

Father and Mother Gods

The Nahua believed that Ometecutli and Omeciuatl were the father and mother of the human species. The names signify Lords of Duality or Lords of the Two Sexes. They were also called Tonacatecutli and Tonacaciuatl (Lord and Lady of Our Flesh, or of Subsistence). They were in fact regarded as the sexual essence of the creative deity, or perhaps more correctly of deity in general. They occupied the first place in the Nahua calendar, to signify that they had existed from the beginning, and they are usually represented as being clothed in rich attire. Ometecutli (a literal translation of his name is Two-Lord) is sometimes identified with the sky and the fire-god, the female deity representing the earth or water – conceptions similar to those respecting Kronos and Gaea. We refer again to these supreme divinities later on.

The Pulque-Gods

When a man was intoxicated with the native Mexican drink of *pulque*, a liquor made from the juice of the *Agave Americana*, he was believed to be under the influence of a god or spirit. The commonest form under which the drink-god was worshipped was the rabbit, that animal being considered to be utterly devoid of sense. This particular divinity was known as Ometochtli. The scale of debauchery which it was desired to reach was indicated by the number of rabbits worshipped, the highest number, four hundred, representing the most extreme degree of intoxication. The chief *pulque*-gods apart from these were Patecatl and Tequechmecauiani. If the drunkard desired to escape the perils of accidental hanging during intoxication, it was necessary to sacrifice to the latter, but if death by drowning was apprehended Teatlahuiani, the deity who harried drunkards to a watery grave, was placated. If the debauchee wished his punishment not to exceed a headache, Quatlapanqui (The Head-splitter) was sacrificed to, or else Papaztac (The Nerveless). Each trade or profession had its own Ometochtli, but for the aristocracy there was only one of these gods, Cohuatzincatl, a name signifying 'He who has Grandparents.' Several of these drink-gods had names which connected them with various localities; for example, Tepoxtecatl was the *pulque*-god of Tepoztlan. The calendar day Ometochtli, which means 'Two-Rabbit,' because of the symbol which accompanied it, was under the special protection of these gods, and the Mexicans believed that any one born on that day was almost inevitably doomed to become a drunkard. All the *pulque*-gods were closely associated with the soil, and with the earth-goddess. They wore the golden Huaxtec nose-ornament, the *yaca-metztli*, of crescent shape, which characterized the latter, and indeed this ornament was inscribed upon all articles sacred to the pulque-gods. Their faces were painted red and black, as were objects consecrated to them, their blankets and shields. After the Indians had harvested their maize they drank to intoxication, and invoked one or other of these gods. On the whole it is safe to infer that they were originally deities of local husbandry who imparted virtue to the soil as *pulque* imparted strength and courage to the warrior.

It is of course clear that the drink-gods were of the same class as the food-gods – patrons of the fruitful soil – but it is strange that they should be male whilst the food-gods are mostly female.

The Goddesses of Mexico

Metztli

Metztli, or Yohualticitl (The Lady of Night), was the Mexican goddess of the moon. She had in reality two phases, one that of a beneficent protectress of harvests and promoter of growth in general, and the other that of a bringer of dampness, cold, and miasmic airs, ghosts, mysterious shapes of the dim half-light of night and its oppressive silence.

To a people in the agricultural stage of civilization the moon appears as the great recorder of harvests. But she has also supremacy over water, which is always connected by primitive peoples with the moon. Citatli (Moon) and Atl (Water) are constantly confounded in Nahua myth, and in many ways their characteristics were blended. It was Metztli who led forth Nanahuatl the Leprous to the pyre whereon he perished – a reference to the dawn, in which the starry sky of night is consumed in the fires of the rising sun.

Tlazolteotl

Tlazolteotl (God of Ordure), or Tlaelquani (Filth-eater), was called by the Mexicans the earth-goddess because she was the eradicator of sins, to whose priests the people went to make confession so that they might be absolved from their misdeeds. Sin was symbolized by the Mexicans as excrement. Confession covered only the sins of immorality. But if Tlazolteotl was the goddess of confession, she was also the patroness of desire and luxury. It was, however, as a deity whose chief office was the eradication of human sin that she was pre-eminent. The process by which this was supposed to be effected is quaintly described by Sahagun in the twelfth chapter of his first book. The penitent addressed the confessor as follows: "Sir, I desire to approach that most powerful god, the protector of all, that is to say, Tezcatlipoca. I desire to tell him my sins in secret." The confessor replied: "Be happy, my son: that which thou wishest to do will be to thy good and advantage." The confessor then opened the divinatory book known as the Tonalamatl (that is, the Book of the Calendar) and acquainted the applicant with the day which appeared the most suitable for his confession. The day having arrived, the penitent provided himself with a mat, copal gum to burn as incense, and wood whereon to burn it. If he was a person high in office the priest repaired to his house, but in the case of lesser people the confession took place in the dwelling of the priest. Having lighted the fire and burned the incense, the penitent addressed the fire in the following terms: "Thou, lord, who art the father and mother of the gods, and the most ancient of them all, thy servant, thy slave bows before thee. Weeping, he approaches thee in great distress. He comes plunged in grief, because he has been buried in sin, having backslidden, and partaken of those vices and evil delights which merit death. O master most compassionate, who art the upholder and defence of all, receive the penitence and anguish of thy slave and vassal."

This prayer having concluded, the confessor then turned to the penitent and thus addressed him: "My son, thou art come into the presence of that god who is the protector and upholder of all; thou art come to him to confess thy evil vices and thy hidden uncleannesses; thou art come to him to unbosom the secrets of thy heart. Take care that thou omit nothing from the catalogue of thy sins in the presence of our lord who is called

Tezcatlipoca. It is certain that thou art before him who is invisible and impalpable, thou who art not worthy to be seen before him, or to speak with him…."

The allusions to Tezcatlipoca are, of course, to him in the shape of Tlazolteotl. Having listened to a sermon by the confessor, the penitent then confessed his misdeeds, after which the confessor said: "My son, thou hast before our lord god confessed in his presence thy evil actions. I wish to say in his name that thou hast an obligation to make. At the time when the goddesses called Ciuapipiltin descend to earth during the celebration of the feast of the goddesses of carnal things, whom they name Ixcuiname, thou shalt fast during four days, punishing thy stomach and thy mouth. When the day of the feast of the Ixcuiname arrives thou shalt scarify thy tongue with the small thorns of the osier [called *teocalcacatl* or *tlazotl*], and if that is not sufficient thou shalt do likewise to thine ears, the whole for penitence, for the remission of thy sin, and as a meritorious act. Thou wilt apply to thy tongue the middle of a spine of maguey, and thou wilt scarify thy shoulders…. That done, thy sins will be pardoned."

If the sins of the penitent were not very grave the priest would enjoin upon him a fast of a more or less prolonged nature. Only old men confessed crimes *in veneribus*, as the punishment for such was death, and younger men had no desire to risk the penalty involved, although the priests were enjoined to strict secrecy.

Father Burgoa describes very fully a ceremony of this kind which came under his notice in 1652 in the Zapotec village of San Francisco de Cajonos. He encountered on a tour of inspection an old native *cacique*, or chief, of great refinement of manners and of a stately presence, who dressed in costly garments after the Spanish fashion, and who was regarded by the Indians with much veneration. This man came to the priest for the purpose of reporting upon the progress in things spiritual and temporal in his village. Burgoa recognized his urbanity and wonderful command of the Spanish language, but perceived by certain signs that he had been taught to look for by long experience that the man was a pagan. He communicated his suspicions to the vicar of the village, but met with such assurances of the *cacique's* soundness of faith that he believed himself to be in error for once. Shortly afterwards, however, a wandering Spaniard perceived the chief in a retired place in the mountains performing idolatrous ceremonies, and aroused the monks, two of whom accompanied him to the spot where the *cacique* had been seen indulging in his heathenish practices. They found on the altar "feathers of many colours, sprinkled with blood which the Indians had drawn from the veins under their tongues and behind their ears, incense spoons and remains of copal, and in the middle a horrible stone figure, which was the god to whom they had offered this sacrifice in expiation of their sins, while they made their confessions to the blasphemous priests, and cast off their sins in the following manner: they had woven a kind of dish out of a strong herb, specially gathered for this purpose, and casting this before the priest, said to him that they came to beg mercy of their god, and pardon for their sins that they had committed during that year, and that they brought them all carefully enumerated. They then drew out of a cloth pairs of thin threads made of dry maize husks, that they had tied two by two in the middle with a knot, by which they represented their sins. They laid these threads on the dishes of grass, and over them pierced their veins, and let the blood trickle upon them, and the priest took these offerings to the idol, and in a long speech he begged the god to forgive these, his sons, their sins which were brought to him, and to permit them to be joyful and hold feasts to him as their god and lord. Then the priest came back to those who had confessed, delivered a long discourse on the ceremonies they had still to perform, and told them that the god had pardoned them and that they might be glad again and sin anew."

Chalchihuitlicue

This goddess was the wife of Tlaloc, the god of rain and moisture. The name means Lady of the Emerald Robe, in allusion to the colour of the element over which the deity partly presided. She was specially worshipped by the water-carriers of Mexico, and all those whose avocation brought them into contact with water. Her costume was peculiar and interesting. Round her neck she wore a wonderful collar of precious stones, from which hung a gold pendant. She was crowned with a coronet of blue paper, decorated with green feathers. Her eyebrows were of turquoise, set in as mosaic, and her garment was a nebulous blue-green in hue, recalling the tint of sea-water in the tropics. The resemblance was heightened by a border of sea-flowers or water-plants, one of which she also carried in her left hand, whilst in her right she bore a vase surmounted by a cross, emblematic of the four points of the compass whence comes the rain.

Mixcoatl

Mixcoatl was the Aztec god of the chase, and was probably a deity of the Otomi aborigines of Mexico. The name means Cloud Serpent, and this originated the idea that Mixcoatl was a representation of the tropical whirlwind. This is scarcely correct, however, as the hunter-god is identified with the tempest and thunder-cloud, and the lightning is supposed to represent his arrows. Like many other gods of the chase, he is figured as having the characteristics of a deer or rabbit. He is usually depicted as carrying a sheaf of arrows, to typify thunderbolts. It may be that Mixcoatl was an air and thunder deity of the Otomi, older in origin than either Quetzalcoatl or Tezcatlipoca, and that his inclusion in the Nahua pantheon becoming necessary in order to quieten Nahua susceptibilities, he received the status of god of the chase. But, on the other hand, the Mexicans, unlike the Peruvians, who adopted many foreign gods for political purposes, had little regard for the feelings of other races, and only accepted an alien deity into the native circle for some good reason, most probably because they noted the omission of the figure in their own divine system. Or, again, dread of a certain foreign god might force them to adopt him as their own in the hope of placating him. Their worship of Quetzalcoatl is perhaps an instance of this.

Camaxtli

This deity was the war-god of the Tlascalans, who were constantly in opposition to the Aztecs of Mexico. He was to the warriors of Tlascala practically what Huitzilopochtli was to those of Mexico. He was closely identified with Mixcoatl, and with the god of the morning star, whose colours are depicted on his face and body. But in all probability Camaxtli was a god of the chase, who in later times was adopted as a god of war because of his possession of the lightning dart, the symbol of divine warlike prowess. In the mythologies of North America we find similar hunter-gods, who sometimes evolve into gods of war for a like reason, and again gods of the chase who have all the appearance and attributes of the creatures hunted.

Iztlilton

Ixtlilton (The Little Black One) was the Mexican god of medicine and healing, and therefore was often alluded to as the brother of Macuilxochitl, the god of well-being or good luck. From the account of the general appearance of his temple – an edifice of painted boards – it would seem to have evolved from the primitive tent or lodge of the medicine man, or *shaman*. It contained several water-jars called *tlilatl* (black water), the contents of which were administered to children in bad health. The parents of children who benefited from the treatment bestowed a feast on the deity, whose idol was carried to the residence of the grateful father, where ceremonial dances and oblations were made before it. It was then thought that Ixtlilton descended to the courtyard to open fresh jars of *pulque* liquor provided for the feasters, and the entertainment concluded by an examination by the Aztec Aesculapius of such of the *pulque* jars dedicated to his service as stood in the courtyard for everyday use. Should these be found in an unclean condition, it was understood that the master of the house was a man of evil life, and he was presented by the priest with a mask to hide his face from his scoffing friends.

Omacatl

Omacatl was the Mexican god of festivity and joy. The name signifies Two Reeds. He was worshipped chiefly by bon-vivants and the rich, who celebrated him in splendid feasts and orgies. The idol of the deity was invariably placed in the chamber where these functions were to take place, and the Aztecs were known to regard it as a heinous offence if anything derogatory to the god were performed during the convivial ceremony, or if any omission were made from the prescribed form which these gatherings usually took. It was thought that if the host had been in any way remiss Omacatl would appear to the startled guests, and in tones of great severity upbraid him who had given the feast, intimating that he would regard him no longer as a worshipper and would henceforth abandon him. A terrible malady, the symptoms of which were akin to those of falling-sickness, would shortly afterwards seize the guests; but as such symptoms are not unlike those connected with acute indigestion and other gastric troubles, it is probable that the gourmets who paid homage to the god of good cheer may have been suffering from a too strenuous instead of a lukewarm worship of him. But the idea of communion which underlay so many of the Mexican rites undoubtedly entered into the worship of Omacatl, for prior to a banquet in his honour those who took part in it formed a great bone out of maize paste, pretending that it was one of the bones of the deity whose merry rites they were about to engage in. This they devoured, washing it down with great draughts of *pulque*. The idol of Omacatl was provided with a recess in the region of the stomach, and into this provisions were stuffed. He was represented as a squatting figure, painted black and white, crowned with a paper coronet, and hung with coloured paper. A flower-fringed cloak and sceptre were the other symbols of royalty worn by this Mexican Dionysus.

Opochtli

Opochtli (The Left-handed) was the god sacred to fishers and bird-catchers. At one period of Aztec history he must have been a deity of considerable consequence, since for generations the Aztecs were marsh-dwellers and depended for their daily food on the fish netted in the lakes and the birds snared in the reeds. They credited the god with the invention of the harpoon or trident for spearing fish and the fishing-rod and bird-net. The fishermen and bird-catchers of Mexico held on occasion a special feast in honour of Opochtli, at which a certain liquor called *octli* was consumed. A procession was afterwards formed, in which marched old people who had dedicated themselves to the worship of the god, probably because they could obtain no other means of subsistence than that afforded by the vocation of which he was tutelar and patron. He was represented as a man painted black, his head decorated with the plumes of native wild birds, and crowned by a paper coronet in the shape of a rose. He was clad in green paper which fell to the knee, and was shod with white sandals. In his left hand he held a shield painted red, having in the centre a white flower with four petals placed crosswise, and in his right hand he held a sceptre in the form of a cup.

Yacatecutli

Yacatecutli was the patron of travellers of the merchant class, who worshipped him by piling their staves together and sprinkling on the heap blood from their noses and ears. The staff of the traveller was his symbol, to which prayer was made and offerings of flowers and incense tendered.

The Aztec Priesthood

The Aztec priesthood was a hierarchy in whose hands resided a goodly portion of the power of the upper classes, especially that connected with education and endowment. The mere fact that its members possessed the power of selecting victims for sacrifice must have been sufficient to place them in an almost unassailable position, and their prophetic utterances, founded upon the art of divination – so great a feature in the life of the Aztec people, who depended upon it from the cradle to the grave – probably assisted them in maintaining their hold upon the popular imagination. But withal the evidence of unbiased Spanish ecclesiastics, such as Sahagun, tends to show that they utilized their influence for good, and soundly instructed the people under their charge in the cardinal virtues; "in short," says the venerable friar, "to perform the duties plainly pointed out by natural religion."

Priestly Revenues

The establishment of the national religion was, as in the case of the mediaeval Church in Europe, based upon a land tenure from which the priestly class derived a substantial though, considering their numbers, by no means inordinate revenue. The principal temples possessed lands which sufficed for the maintenance of the priests attached to them. There was, besides, a system of first-fruits fixed by law for the priesthood, the surplusage therefrom being distributed among the poor.

Education

Education was entirely conducted by the priesthood, which undertook the task in a manner highly creditable to it, when consideration is given to surrounding conditions. Education was, indeed, highly organized. It was divided into primary and secondary grades. Boys were instructed by priests, girls by holy women or 'nuns.' The secondary schools were called calmecac, and were devoted to the higher branches of education, the curriculum including the deciphering of the *pinturas*, or manuscripts, astrology and divination, with a wealth of religious instruction.

Orders of the Priesthood

At the head of the Aztec priesthood stood the Mexicatl Teohuatzin (Mexican Lord of Divine Matters). He had a seat on the emperor's council, and possessed power which was second only to the royal authority. Next in rank to him was the high-priest of Quetzalcoatl, who dwelt in almost entire seclusion, and who had authority over his own caste only. This office was in all probability a relic from 'Toltec' times. The priests of Quetzalcoatl were called by name after their tutelar deity. The lesser grades included the Tlenamacac (Ordinary Priests), who were habited in black, and wore their hair long, covering it with a kind of mantilla. The lowest order was that of the Lamacazton (Little Priests), youths who were graduating in the priestly office.

An Exacting Ritual

The priesthood enjoyed no easy existence, but led an austere life of fasting, penance, and prayer, with constant observance of an arduous and exacting ritual, which embraced sacrifice, the upkeep of perpetual fires, the chanting of holy songs to the gods, dances, and the superintendence of the ever-recurring festivals. They were required to rise during the night to render praise, and to maintain themselves in a condition of absolute cleanliness by means of constant ablutions. We have seen that blood-offering – the substitution of the part for the whole – was a common method of sacrifice, and in this the priests engaged personally on frequent occasions. If the caste did not spare the people it certainly did not spare itself, and its outlook was perhaps only a shade more gloomy and fanatical than that of the Spanish hierarchy which succeeded it in the land.

The Maya Civilization

An Original Culture

IT WAS TO THE MAYA – the people who occupied the territory between the isthmus of Tehuantepec and Nicaragua – that the civilization of Central America owed most. The language they spoke was quite distinct from the Nahuatl spoken by the Nahua of Mexico, and in many respects their customs and habits were widely different from those of the people of Anahuac. The latter were the heirs of an older civilization; indeed, they had entered the valley of Mexico as savages, and practically all they knew of the arts of culture was taught them by the remnants of the people whom they dispossessed. It was not thus with the Maya. Their arts and industries were of their own invention, and bore the stamp of an origin of considerable antiquity. They were, indeed, the supreme intellectual race of America.

It has already been stated that many antiquarians see in the Maya those Toltecs who because of the inroads of barbarous tribes quitted their native land of Anahuac and journeyed southward to seek a new home in Chiapas and Yucatan. However, the architectural remains of the older race of Anahuac do not bear any striking likeness to Maya forms, and if the mythologies of the two peoples are in some particulars alike, that may well be accounted for by their mutual adoption of deities and religious customs. It is, though, distinctly noteworthy that the cult of the god Quetzalcoatl, regarded in Mexico as of alien origin, had a considerable vogue among the Maya and their allied races.

The Maya Kingdom

On the arrival of the Spaniards (after the celebrated march of Cortés from Mexico to Central America) the Maya were divided into a number of subsidiary states. That these had hived off from an original and considerably greater state there is good evidence to show, but internal dissension had played havoc with the polity of the central government of this empire, the disintegration of which had occurred at a remote period. In the semi-historical legends of this people we catch glimpses of a great kingdom, occasionally alluded to as the 'Kingdom of the Great Snake,' or the empire of Xibalba, realms which have been identified with the ruined city-centres of Palenque and Mitla. The sphere of Maya civilization and influence is pretty well marked, and embraces the peninsula of Yucatan, Chiapas, to the isthmus of Tehuantepec on the north, and the whole of Guatemala to the boundaries of the present republic of San Salvador. The true nucleus of Maya civilization, however, must be looked for in that part of Chiapas which skirts the banks of the Usumacinta river and in the valleys of its tributaries. Here Maya art and architecture reached a height of splendour unknown elsewhere, and in this district, too, the strange Maya system of writing had its most skilful exponents. Although the arts and industries of the several districts inhabited by people of Maya race exhibited many superficial differences, these are so small as to make us certain of the fact that the various areas inhabited by Maya stock had all drawn their inspiration toward civilization from one common nucleus, and had equally passed through a uniform civilization and drawn sap from an original culture-centre.

The Maya Dialects

Perhaps the most effectual method of distinguishing the various branches of the Maya people from one another consists in dividing them into linguistic groups. The various dialects spoken by the folk of Maya origin, although they exhibit some considerable difference, yet display strongly that affinity of construction and resemblance in root which go to prove that they all emanate from one common mother-tongue. In Chiapas the Maya tongue itself is the current dialect, whilst in Guatemala no less than twenty-four dialects are in use, the principal of which are the Quiche, or Kiche, the Kakchiquel, the Zutugil, Coxoh Chol, and Pipil. These dialects and the folk who speak them are sufficient to engage our attention, as in them are enshrined the most remarkable myths and legends of the race, and by the men who used them were the greatest acts in Maya history achieved.

Whence Came the Maya?

Whence came these folk, then, who raised a civilization by no means inferior to that of ancient Egypt, which, if it had had scope, would have rivalled in its achievements the glory of old Assyria? We cannot tell. The mystery of its entrance into the land is as deep as the mystery of the ancient forests which now bury the remnants of its mighty monuments and enclose its temples in impenetrable gloom. Generations of antiquarians have attempted to trace the origin of this race to Egypt, Phœnicia, China, Burma. But the manifest traces of indigenous American origin are present in all its works, and the writers who have beheld in these likenesses to the art of Asiatic or African peoples have been grievously misled by superficial resemblances which could not have betrayed any one who had studied Maya affinities deeply.

Civilization of the Maya

At the risk of repetition it is essential to point out that civilization, which was a newly acquired thing with the Nahua peoples, was not so with the Maya. They were indisputably an older race, possessing institutions which bore the marks of generations of use, whereas the Nahua had only too obviously just entered into their heritage of law and order. When we first catch sight of the Maya kingdoms they are in the process of disintegration. Such strong young blood as the virile folk of Anahuac possessed did not flow in the veins of the people of Yucatan and Guatemala. They were to the Nahua much as the ancient Assyrians were to the hosts of Israel at the entrance of the latter into national existence. That there was a substratum of ethnical and cultural relationship, however, it would be impossible to deny. The institutions, architecture, habits, even the racial cast of thought of the two peoples, bore such a general resemblance as to show that many affinities of blood and cultural relationship existed between them. But it will not do to insist too strongly upon these. It may be argued with great probability that these relationships and likenesses exist because of the influence of Maya civilization upon Mexican alone, or from the inheritance by both Mexican and Maya people of a still older culture of which we are ignorant, and the proofs of which lie buried below the forests of Guatemala or the sands of Yucatan.

The Zapotecs

The influence of the Maya upon the Nahua was a process of exceeding slowness. The peoples who divided them one from another were themselves benefited by carrying Maya culture into Anahuac, or rather it might be said that they constituted a sort of filter through which the southern civilization reached the northern. These peoples were the Zapotecs, the Mixtecs, and the Kuikatecs, by far the most important of whom were the first-mentioned. They partook of the nature and civilization of both races, and were in effect a border people who took from and gave to both Maya and Nahua, much as the Jews absorbed and disseminated the cultures of Egypt and Assyria. They were, however, of Nahua race, but their speech bears the strongest marks of having borrowed extensively from the Maya vocabulary. For many generations these people wandered in a nomadic condition from Maya to Nahua territory, thus absorbing the customs, speech, and mythology of each.

The Huasteca

But we should be wrong if we thought that the Maya had never attempted to expand, and had never sought new homes for their surplus population. That they had is proved by an outlying tribe of Maya, the Huasteca, having settled at the mouth of the Panuco river, on the north coast of Mexico. The presence of this curious ethnological island has of course given rise to all sorts of queer theories concerning Toltec relationship, whereas it simply intimates that before the era of Nahua expansion the Maya had attempted to colonize the country to the north of their territories, but that their efforts in this direction had been cut short by the influx of savage Nahua, against whom they found themselves unable to contend.

The Type of Maya Civilization

Did the civilization of the Maya differ, then, in type from that of the Nahua, or was it merely a larger expression of that in vogue in Anahuac? We may take it that the Nahua civilization characterized the culture of Central America in its youth, whilst that of the Maya displayed it in its bloom, and perhaps in its senility. The difference was neither essential nor radical, but may be said to have arisen for the most part from climatic and kindred causes. The climate of Anahuac is dry and temperate, that of Yucatan and Guatemala is tropical, and we shall find even such religious conceptions of the two peoples as were drawn from a common source varying from this very cause, and coloured by differences in temperature and rainfall.

Maya History

Before entering upon a consideration of the art, architecture, or mythology of this strange and highly interesting people it will be necessary to provide the reader with a brief sketch of their history. Such notices of this as exist in English are few, and their value doubtful. For the earlier history of the people of Maya stock we depend almost wholly upon tradition and architectural remains. The net result of the evidence wrung from these is that the Maya civilization was one and homogeneous, and that all the separate states must have at one period passed through a uniform condition of culture, to which they were all equally debtors, and that this is sufficient ground for the belief that all were at one time beneath the sway of one central power. For the later history we possess the writings of the Spanish fathers, but not in such profusion as in the case of Mexico. In fact the trustworthy original authors who deal with Maya history can almost be counted on the fingers of one hand. We are further confused in perusing these, and, indeed, throughout the study of Maya history, by discovering that many of the sites of Maya cities are designated by Nahua names. This is due to the fact that the Spanish conquerors were guided in their conquest of the Maya territories by Nahua, who naturally applied Nahuatlac designations to those sites of which the Spaniards asked the names.

The Nucleus of Maya Power

As has been said, the nucleus of Maya power and culture is probably to be found in that part of Chiapas which slopes down from the steep Cordilleras. Here the ruined sites of Palenque, Piedras Negras, and Ocosingo are eloquent of that opulence of imagination and loftiness of conception which go hand in hand with an advanced culture. The temples and palaces of this region bear the stamp of a dignity and consciousness of metropolitan power which are scarcely to be mistaken, so broad, so free is their architectural conception, so full to overflowing the display of the desire to surpass. But upon the necessities of religion and central organization alone was this architectural artistry lavished. Its dignities were not profaned by its application to mere domestic uses, for, unless what were obviously palaces are excepted, not a single example of Maya domestic building has survived. This is of course accounted for by the circumstance that the people were sharply divided into the aristocratic and labouring classes, the first of which was closely identified with religion or kingship, and was housed in the ecclesiastical or royal buildings, whilst those of less exalted rank were perforce content with the shelter afforded by a hut built of perishable materials, the traces of which have long since passed away. The temples were, in fact, the nuclei of the towns, the centres round which the Maya communities were grouped, much in the same manner as the cities of Europe in the Middle Ages clustered and grew around the shadow of some vast cathedral or sheltering stronghold.

Early Race Movements

We shall leave the consideration of Maya tradition until we come to speak of Maya myth proper, and attempt to glean from the chaos of legend some veritable facts connected with Maya history. According to a manuscript of Kuikatec origin recently discovered, it is probable that a Nahua invasion of the Maya states of Chiapas and Tabasco took place about the ninth century of our era, and we must for the present regard that as the starting-point of Maya history. The south-western portions of the Maya territory were agitated about the same time by race movements, which turned northward toward Tehuantepec, and, flowing through Guatemala, came to rest in Acalan, on the borders of Yucatan, retarded, probably, by the inhospitable and waterless condition of that country. This Nahua invasion probably had the effect of driving the more peaceful Maya from their northerly settlements and forcing them farther south. Indeed, evidence is not wanting to show that the warlike Nahua pursued the pacific Maya into their new retreats, and for a space left them but little peace. This struggle it was which finally resulted in the breaking up of the Maya civilization, which even at that relatively remote period had reached its apogee, its several races separating into numerous city-states, which bore a close political resemblance to those of Italy on the downfall of Rome. At this period, probably, began the cleavage between the Maya of Yucatan and those of Guatemala, which finally resolved itself into such differences of speech, faith, and architecture as almost to constitute them different peoples.

The Settlement of Yucatan

As the Celts of Wales and Scotland were driven into the less hospitable regions of their respective countries by the inroads of the Saxons, so was one branch of the

Maya forced to seek shelter in the almost desert wastes of Yucatan. There can be no doubt that the Maya did not take to this barren and waterless land of their own accord. Thrifty and possessed of high agricultural attainments, this people would view with concern a removal to a sphere so forbidding after the rich and easily developed country they had inhabited for generations. But the inexorable Nahua were behind, and they were a peaceful folk, unused to the horrors of savage warfare. So, taking their courage in both hands, they wandered into the desert. Everything points to a late occupation of Yucatan by the Maya, and architectural effort exhibits deterioration, evidenced in a high conventionality of design and excess of ornamentation. Evidences of Nahua influence also are not wanting, a fact which is eloquent of the later period of contact which is known to have occurred between the peoples, and which alone is almost sufficient to fix the date of the settlement of the Maya in Yucatan. It must not be thought that the Maya in Yucatan formed one homogeneous state recognizing a central authority. On the contrary, as is often the case with colonists, the several Maya bands of immigrants formed themselves into different states or kingdoms, each having its own separate traditions. It is thus a matter of the highest difficulty to so collate and criticise these traditions as to construct a history of the Maya race in Yucatan. As may be supposed, we find the various city-sites founded by divine beings who play a more or less important part in the Maya pantheon. Kukulcan, for example, is the first king of Mayapan, whilst Itzamna figures as the founder of the state of Itzamal. The gods were the spiritual leaders of these bands of Maya, just as Jehovah was the spiritual leader and guide of the Israelites in the desert. One is therefore not surprised to find in the *Popol Vuh*, the saga of the Kiche-Maya of Guatemala, that the god Tohil (The Rumbler) guided them to the site of the first Kiche city. Some writers on the subject appear to think that the incidents in such migration myths, especially the tutelage and guidance of the tribes by gods and the descriptions of desert scenery which they contain, suffice to stamp them as mere native versions of the Book of Exodus, or at the best myths sophisticated by missionary influence. The truth is that the conditions of migration undergone by the Maya were similar to those described in the Scriptures, and by no means merely reflect the Bible story, as short-sighted collators of both aver.

The Septs of Yucatan

The priest-kings of Mayapan, who claimed descent from Kukulcan or Quetzalcoatl, soon raised their state into a position of prominence among the surrounding cities. Those who had founded Chichen-Itza, and who were known as Itzaes, were, on the other hand, a caste of warriors who do not appear to have cherished the priestly function with such assiduity. The rulers of the Itzaes, who were known as the Tutul Xius, seem to have come, according to their traditions, from the western Maya states, perhaps from Nonohualco in Tabasco. Arriving from thence at the southern extremity of Yucatan, they founded the city of Ziyan Caan, on Lake Bacalar, which had a period of prosperity for at least a couple of generations. At the expiry of that period for some unaccountable reason they migrated northward, perhaps because at that particular time the incidence of power was shifting toward Northern Yucatan, and took up their abode in Chichen-Itza, eventually the sacred city of the Maya, which they founded.

The Cocomes

But they were not destined to remain undisturbed in their new sphere. The Cocomes of Mayapan, when at the height of their power, viewed with disfavour the settlement of the Tutul Xius. After it had flourished for a period of about 120 years it was overthrown by the Cocomes, who resolved it into a dependency, permitting the governors and a certain number of the people to depart elsewhere.

Flight of the Tutul Xius

Thus expelled, the Tutul Xius fled southward, whence they had originally come, and settled in Potonchan or Champoton, where they reigned for nearly 300 years. From this new centre, with the aid of Nahua mercenaries, they commenced an extension of territory northward, and entered into diplomatic relations with the heads of the other Maya states. It was at this time that they built Uxmal, and their power became so extensive that they reconquered the territory they had lost to the Cocomes. This on the whole appears to have been a period when the arts flourished under an enlightened policy, which knew how to make and keep friendly relations with surrounding states, and the splendid network of roads with which the country was covered and the many evidences of architectural excellence go to prove that the race had had leisure to achieve much in art and works of utility. Thus the city of Chichen-Itza was linked up with the island of Cozumel by a highway whereon thousands of pilgrims plodded to the temples of the gods of wind and moisture. From Itzamal, too, roads branched in every direction, in order that the people should have every facility for reaching the chief shrine of the country situated there. But the hand of the Cocomes was heavy upon the other Maya states which were tributary to them. As in the Yucatan of today, where the wretched henequen-picker leads the life of a veritable slave, a crushing system of helotage obtained. The Cocomes made heavy demands upon the Tutul Xius, who in their turn sweated the hapless folk under their sway past the bounds of human endurance. As in all tottering civilizations, the feeling of responsibility among the upper classes became dormant, and they abandoned themselves to the pleasures of life without thought of the morrow. Morality ceased to be regarded as a virtue, and rottenness was at the core of Maya life. Discontent quickly spread on every hand.

The Revolution in Mayapan

The sequel was, naturally, revolution. Ground down by the tyranny of a dissolute oligarchy, the subject states rose in revolt. The Cocomes surrounded themselves by Nahua mercenaries, who succeeded in beating off the first wave of revolt, led by the king or regulus of Uxmal, who was defeated, and whose people in their turn rose against him, a circumstance which ended in the abandonment of the city of Uxmal. Once more were the Tutul Xius forced to go on pilgrimage, and this time they founded the city of Mani, a mere shadow of the splendour of Uxmal and Chichen.

Hunac Eel

If the aristocracy of the Cocomes was composed of weaklings, its ruler was made of sterner stuff. Hunac Eel, who exercised royal sway over this people, and held in subjection the lesser principalities of Yucatan, was not only a tyrant of harsh and vindictive temperament, but a statesman of judgement and experience, who courted the assistance of the neighbouring Nahua, whom he employed in his campaign against the new assailant of his absolutism, the ruler of Chichen-Itza. Mustering a mighty host of his vassals, Hunac Eel marched against the devoted city whose prince had dared to challenge his supremacy, and succeeded in inflicting a crushing defeat upon its inhabitants. But apparently the state was permitted to remain under the sovereignty of its native princes. The revolt, however, merely smouldered, and in the kingdom of Mayapan itself, the territory of the Cocomes, the fires of revolution began to blaze. This state of things continued for nearly a century. Then the crash came. The enemies of the Cocomes effected a junction. The people of Chichen-Itza joined hands with the Tutul Xius, who had sought refuge in the central highlands of Yucatan and those city-states which clustered around the mother-city of Mayapan. A fierce concerted attack was made, beneath which the power of the Cocomes crumpled up completely. Not one stone was left standing upon another by the exasperated allies, who thus avenged the helotage of nearly 300 years. To this event the date 1436 is assigned, but, like most dates in Maya history, considerable uncertainty must be attached to it.

The Last of the Cocomes

Only a remnant of the Cocomes survived. They had been absent in Nahua territory, attempting to raise fresh troops for the defence of Mayapan. These the victors spared, and they finally settled in Zotuta, in the centre of Yucatan, a region of almost impenetrable forest.

It would not appear that the city of Chichen-Itza, the prince of which was ever the head and front of the rebellion against the Cocomes, profited in any way from the fall of the suzerain power. On the contrary, tradition has it that the town was abandoned by its inhabitants, and left to crumble into the ruinous state in which the Spaniards found it on their entrance into the country. The probability is that its people quitted it because of the repeated attacks made upon it by the Cocomes, who saw in it the chief obstacle to their universal sway; and this is supported by tradition, which tells that a prince of Chichen-Itza, worn out with conflict and internecine strife, left it to seek the cradle of the Maya race in the land of the setting sun. Indeed, it is further stated that this prince founded the city of Peten-Itza, on the lake of Peten, in Guatemala.

The Maya Peoples of Guatemala

When the Maya peoples of Guatemala, the Kiches and the Kakchiquels, first made their way into that territory, they probably found there a race of Maya origin of a type more advanced and possessed of more ancient traditions than themselves. By their connection with this folk they greatly benefited in the direction of artistic achievement as well as in the industrial arts. Concerning these people we have a large body of tradition in the *Popol Vuh*, a native chronicle, the contents of which will be fully dealt with in the chapter relating to the Maya myths and legendary matter. We cannot deal with it as a veritable historical document, but there is little doubt that a basis of fact exists behind the tradition it contains. The difference between the language of these people and that of their brethren in Yucatan was, as has been said, one of dialect only, and a like slight distinction is found in their mythology, caused, doubtless, by the incidence of local conditions, and resulting in part from the difference between a level and comparatively waterless land and one of a semi-mountainous character covered with thick forests. We shall note further differences when we come to examine the art and architecture of the Maya race, and to compare those of its two most distinctive branches.

The Maya Tulan

It was to the city of Tulan, probably in Tabasco, that the Maya of Guatemala referred as being the starting-point of all their migrations. We must not confound this place with the Tollan of the Mexican traditions. It is possible that the name may in both cases be derived from a root meaning a place from which a tribe set forth, a starting-place, but geographical connection there is none. From here Nima-Kiche, the great Kiche, started on his migration to the mountains, accompanied by his three brothers. Tulan, says the *Popol Vuh*, had been a place of misfortune to man, for he had suffered much from cold and hunger, and, as at the building of Babel, his speech was so confounded that the first four Kiches and their wives were unable to comprehend one another. Of course this is a native myth created to account for the difference in dialect between the various branches of the Maya folk, and can scarcely have any foundation in fact, as the change in dialect would be a very gradual process. The brothers, we are told, divided the land so that one received the districts of Mames and Pocomams, another Verapaz, and the third Chiapas, while Nima-Kiche obtained the country of the Kiches, Kakchiquels, and Tzutuhils. It would be extremely difficult to say whether or not this tradition rests on any veritable historical basis. If so, it refers to a period anterior to the Nahua irruption, for the districts alluded to as occupied by these tribes were not so divided among them at the coming of the Spaniards.

Doubtful Dynasties

As with the earlier dynasties of Egypt, considerable doubt surrounds the history of the early Kiche monarchs. Indeed, a period of such uncertainty occurs that even the number of kings who reigned is lost in the hopeless confusion of varying estimates. From this chaos emerge the facts that the Kiche monarchs held the supreme power among the peoples of Guatemala, that they were the contemporaries of the rulers of Mexico city, and that they were often elected from among the princes of the subject states. Acxopil, the successor of Nima-Kiche, invested his second son with the government of the Kakchiquels, and placed his youngest son over the Tzutuhils, whilst to his eldest son he left the throne of the Kiches. Icutemal, his eldest son, on succeeding his father, gifted the kingdom of Kakchiquel to his eldest son, displacing his own brother and thus mortally affronting him. The struggle which ensued lasted for generations, embittered the relations between these two branches of the Maya in Guatemala, and undermined their joint strength. Nahua mercenaries were employed in the struggle on both sides, and these introduced many of the uglinesses of Nahua life into Maya existence.

The Coming of the Spaniards

This condition of things lasted up to the time of the coming of the Spaniards. The Kakchiquels dated the commencement of a new chronology from the episode of the defeat of Cay Hun-Apu by them in 1492. They may have saved themselves the trouble; for the time was at hand when the calendars of their race were to be closed, and its records written in another script by another people. One by one, and chiefly by reason of their insane policy of allying themselves with the invader against their own kin, the old kingdoms of Guatemala fell as spoil to the daring Conquistadores, and their people passed beneath the yoke of Spain – bondsmen who were to beget countless generations of slaves.

The Riddle of Ancient Maya Writing

What may possibly be the most valuable sources of Maya history are, alas! sealed to us at present. We allude to the native Maya manuscripts and inscriptions, the writing of which cannot be deciphered by present-day scholars. Some of the old Spanish friars who lived in the times which directly succeeded the settlement of the country by the white man were able to read and even to write this script, but unfortunately they regarded it either as an invention of the Father of Evil or, as it was a native system, as a thing of no value. In a few generations all knowledge of how to decipher it was totally lost, and it remains to the modern world almost as a sealed book, although science has lavished all its wonderful machinery of logic and deduction upon it, and men of unquestioned ability have dedicated their lives to the problem of unravelling what must be regarded as one of the greatest and most mysterious riddles of which mankind ever attempted the solution.

The romance of the discovery of the key to the Egyptian hieroglyphic system of writing is well known. For centuries the symbols displayed upon the temples and monuments of the Nile country were so many meaningless pictures and signs to the learned folk of Europe, until the discovery of the Rosetta stone a hundred years ago made their elucidation possible. This stone bore the same inscription in Greek, demotic, and hieroglyphics, and so the discovery of the 'alphabet' of the hidden script became a comparatively easy task. But Central America has no Rosetta stone, nor is it possible that such an aid to research can ever be found. Indeed, such 'keys' as have been discovered or brought forward by scientists have proved for the most part unavailing.

The Maya Manuscripts

The principal Maya manuscripts which have escaped the ravages of time are the codices in the libraries of Dresden, Paris, and Madrid. These are known as the Codex Perezianus, preserved in the Bibliothèque Nationale at Paris, the Dresden Codex, long regarded as an Aztec manuscript, and the Troano Codex, so called from one of its owners, Señor Tro y Ortolano, found at Madrid in 1865. These manuscripts deal principally with Maya mythology, but as they cannot be deciphered with any degree of accuracy they do not greatly assist our knowledge of the subject.

The System of the Writing

The 'Tablet of the Cross' gives a good idea of the general appearance of the writing system of the ancient peoples of Central America. The style varies somewhat in most of the manuscripts and inscriptions, but it is generally admitted that all of the systems employed sprang originally from one common source. The square figures which appear as a tangle of faces and objects are said to be 'calculiform,' or pebble-shaped, a not inappropriate description, and it is known from ancient Spanish manuscripts that they were read from top to bottom, and two columns at a time. The Maya tongue, like all native American languages, was one which, in order to express an idea, gathered a whole phrase into a single word, and it has been thought that the several symbols or parts in each square or sketch go to make up such a compound expression.

The first key (so called) to the hieroglyphs of Central America was that of Bishop Landa, who about 1575 attempted to set down the Maya alphabet from native sources. He was highly unpopular with the natives, whose literary treasures he had almost completely destroyed, and who in revenge deliberately misled him as to the true significance of the various symbols.

The first real step toward reading the Maya writing was made in 1876 by Léon de Rosny, a French student of American antiquities, who succeeded in interpreting the signs which denote the four cardinal points. As has been the case in so many discoveries of importance, the significance of these signs was simultaneously discovered by Professor Cyrus Thomas in America. In two of these four signs was found the symbol which meant 'sun,' almost, as de Rosny acknowledged, as a matter of course. However, the Maya word for 'sun' (kin) also denotes 'day,' and it was later proved that this sign was also used with the latter meaning. The discovery of the sign stimulated further research to a great degree, and from the material now at their disposal Drs. Förstemann and Schellhas of Berlin were successful in discovering the sign for the moon and that for the Maya month of twenty days.

Clever Elucidations

In 1887 Dr Seler discovered the sign for night (*akbal*), and in 1894 Förstemann unriddled the symbols for 'beginning' and 'end.' These are two heads, the first of which has the sign *akbal*, just mentioned, for an eye. Now *akbal* means, as well as 'night,' 'the beginning of the month,' and below the face which contains it can be seen footsteps, or spots which resemble their outline, signifying a forward movement. The sign in the second head means 'seventh,' which in Maya also signifies 'the end.' From the frequent contrast of these terms there can be little doubt that their meaning is as stated.

'Union' is denoted by the sting of a rattlesnake, the coils of that reptile signifying to the Maya the idea of tying together. In contrast to this sign is the figure next to it, which represents a knife, and means 'division' or 'cutting.' An important 'letter' is the hand, which often occurs in both manuscripts and inscriptions. It is drawn sometimes in the act of grasping, with the thumb bent forward, and sometimes as pointing in a certain direction. The first seems to denote a tying together or joining, like the rattlesnake symbol, and the second Förstemann believes to represent a lapse of time. That it may represent futurity occurs as a more likely conjecture to the present writer.

The figure denoting the spring equinox was traced because of its obvious representation of a cloud from which three streams of water are falling upon the earth. The square at the top represents heaven. The obsidian knife underneath denotes a division or period of time cut off, as it were, from other periods of the year. That the sign means 'spring' is verified by its position among the other signs of the seasons.

The sign for 'week' was discovered by reason of its almost constant accompaniment of the sign for the number thirteen, the number of days in the Maya sacred week. The symbol of the bird's feather indicates the plural, and when affixed to certain signs signifies that the object indicated is multiplied. A bird's feather, when one thinks of it, is one of the most fitting symbols provided by nature to designate the plural, if the number of shoots on both sides of the stem are taken as meaning 'many' or 'two.'

Water is depicted by the figure of a serpent, which reptile typifies the undulating nature of the element. The sign entitled 'the sacrificial victim' is of deep human interest. The first portion of the symbol is the death-bird, and the second shows a crouching and beaten captive, ready to be immolated to one of the terrible Maya deities whose sanguinary religion demanded human sacrifice. The drawing which means 'the day of the new year,' in the month Ceh, was unriddled by the following means: The sign in the upper left-hand corner denotes the word 'sun' or 'day,' that in the upper right-hand corner is the sign for 'year.' In the lower right-hand corner is the sign for 'division,' and in the lower left-hand the sign for the Maya month Ceh, already known from the native calendars.

From its accompaniment of a figure known to be a deity of the four cardinal points, whence all American tribes believed the wind to come, the symbol entitled 'wind' has been determined.

Methods of Study

The method employed by those engaged in the elucidation of these hieroglyphs is typical of modern science. The various signs and symbols are literally 'worn out' by a process of indefatigable examination. For hours the student sits staring at a symbol, drinking in every detail, however infinitesimal, until the drawing and all its parts are wholly and separately photographed upon the tablets of his memory. He then compares the several portions of the symbol with similar portions in other signs the value of which is known. From these he may obtain a clue to the meaning of the whole. Thus proceeding from the known to the unknown, he advances logically toward a complete elucidation of all the hieroglyphs depicted in the various manuscripts and inscriptions.

The method by which Dr Seler discovered the hieroglyphs or symbols relating to the various gods of the Maya was both simple and ingenious. He says: "The way in which this was accomplished is strikingly simple. It amounts essentially to that which in ordinary life we call 'memory of persons,' and follows almost naturally from a careful study of the manuscripts. For, by frequently looking tentatively at the representations, one learns by degrees to recognize promptly similar and familiar figures of gods by the characteristic impression they make as a whole or by certain details, and the same is true of the accompanying hieroglyphs."

The Maya Numeral System

If Bishop Landa was badly hoaxed regarding the alphabet of the Maya, he was successful in discovering and handing down their numeral system, which was on a very much higher basis than that of many civilized peoples, being, for example, more practical and more fully evolved than that of ancient Rome. This system employed four signs altogether, the point for unity, a horizontal stroke for the number 5, and two signs for 20 and 0. Yet from these simple elements the Maya produced a method of computation which is perhaps as ingenious as anything which has ever been accomplished in the history of mathematics. In the Maya arithmetical system, as in ours, it is the position of the sign that gives it its value. The figures were placed in a vertical line, and one of them was employed as a decimal multiplier. The lowest figure of the column had the arithmetical value which it represented. The figures which appeared in the second, fourth, and each following place had twenty times the value of the preceding figures, while figures in the third place had eighteen times the value of those in the second place. This system admits of computation up to millions, and is one of the surest signs of Maya culture.

Much controversy has raged round the exact nature of the Maya hieroglyphs. Were they understood by the Indians themselves as representing ideas or merely pictures, or did they convey a given sound to the reader, as does our alphabet? To some extent controversy upon the point is futile, as those of the Spanish clergy who were able to learn the writing from the native Maya have confirmed its phonetic character, so that in reality each symbol must have conveyed a sound or sounds to the reader, not merely an idea or a picture. Recent research has amply proved this, so that the full elucidation of the long and painful puzzle on which so much learning and patience have been lavished may perhaps be at hand.

Maya Architecture

It was in the wonderful architectural system which it developed without outside aid that the Maya people most individually expressed itself. As has been said, those buildings which still remain, and which have excited the admiration of generations of archaeologists, are principally confined to examples of ecclesiastical and governmental architecture, the dwellings of the common people consisting merely of the flimsiest of wattle-and-daub structures, which would fall to pieces shortly after they were abandoned.

Buried in dense forests or mouldering on the sun-exposed plains of Yucatan, Honduras, and Guatemala, the cities which boasted these edifices are for the most part situated away from modern trade routes, and are not a little difficult to come at. It is in Yucatan, the old home of the Cocomes and Tutul Xius, that the most perfect specimens of Maya architecture are to be found, especially as regards its later development, and here, too, it may be witnessed in its decadent phase.

Methods of Building

The Maya buildings were almost always erected upon a mound or *ku*, either natural or artificial, generally the latter. In this we discover affinities with the Mexican *teocalli* type. Often these *kus* stood alone, without any superincumbent building save a small altar to prove their relation to the temple type of Anahuac. The typical Maya temple was built on a series of earth terraces arranged in exact parallel order, the buildings themselves forming the sides of a square. The mounds are generally concealed by plaster or faced with stone, the variety employed being usually a hard sandstone, of which the Maya had a good supply in the quarries of Chiapas and Honduras. Moderate in weight, the difficulty of transport was easily overcome, whilst large blocks could be readily quarried. It will thus be seen that the Maya had no substantial difficulties to surmount in connection with building the large edifices and temples they raised, except, perhaps, the lack of metal tools to shape and carve and quarry the stone which they used. And although they exhibit considerable ingenuity in such architectural methods as they employed, they were still surprisingly ignorant of some of the first essentials and principles of the art.

No Knowledge of the Arch

For example, they were totally ignorant of the principles upon which the arch is constructed. This difficulty they overcame by making each course of masonry overhang the one beneath it, after the method employed by a boy with a box of bricks, who finds that he can only make 'doorways' by this means, or by the simple expedient – also employed by the Maya – of placing a slab horizontally upon two upright pillars. In consequence it will readily be seen that the superimposition of a second story upon such an insecure foundation was scarcely to be thought of, and that such support for the roof as towered above the doorway would necessarily require to be of the most substantial description. Indeed, this portion of the building often appears to be more than half the size of the rest of the edifice. This space gave the Maya builders a splendid chance for mural decoration, and it must be said they readily seized it and made the most of it, ornamental façades being perhaps the most typical features in the relics of Maya architecture.

Pyramidal Structures

But the Maya possessed another type of building which permitted of their raising more than one story. This was the pyramidal type, of which many examples remain. The first story was built in the usual manner, and the second was raised by increasing the height of the mound at the back of the building until it was upon a level with the roof – another device well known to the boy with the box of bricks. In the centre of the space thus made another story could be erected, which was entered by a staircase outside the building. Hampered by their inability to build to any appreciable height, the Maya architects made up for the deficiency by constructing edifices of considerable length and breadth, the squat appearance of which is counterbalanced by the beautiful mural decoration of the sides and façade.

Definiteness of Design

He would be a merely superficial observer who would form the conclusion that these specimens of an architecture spontaneously evolved were put together without survey, design, or previous calculation. That as much thought entered into their construction as is lavished upon his work by a modern architect is proved by the manner in which the carved stones fit into one another. It would be absurd to suppose that these tremendous façades bristling with scores of intricate designs could have been first placed in position and subsequently laden with the bas-reliefs they exhibit. It is plain that they were previously worked apart and separately from one entire design. Thus we see that the highest capabilities of the architect were essential in a measure to the erection of these imposing structures.

Architectural Districts

Although the mason-craft of the Maya peoples was essentially similar in all the regions populated by its various tribes and offshoots, there existed in the several localities occupied by them certain differences in construction and ornamentation which would almost justify us in dividing them into separate architectural spheres. In Chiapas, for example, we find the bas-relief predominant, whether in stone or stucco. In Honduras we find a stiffness of design which implies an older type of architecture, along with caryatides and memorial pillars of human shape. In Guatemala, again, we find traces of the employment of wood. As the civilization of the Maya cannot be well comprehended without some knowledge of their architecture, and as that art was unquestionably their national *forte* and the thing which most sharply distinguished them from the semi-savage peoples that surrounded them, it will be well to consider it for a space as regards its better-known individual examples.

Fascination of the Subject

He would indeed be dull of imagination and of spirit who could enter into the consideration of such a subject as this without experiencing some thrill from the mystery which surrounds it. Although familiarized with the study of the Maya antiquities by reason of many years of close acquaintance with it, the author cannot approach the theme without a feeling of the most intense awe. We are considering the memorials of a race isolated for countless thousands of years from the rest of humanity – a race which by itself evolved a civilization in every respect capable of comparison with those of ancient Egypt or Assyria. In these impenetrable forests and sun-baked plains mighty works were raised which tell of a culture of a lofty type. We are aware that the people who reared them entered into religious and perhaps philosophical considerations their interpretations of which place them upon a level with the most enlightened races of antiquity; but we have only stepped upon the margin of Maya history. What dread secrets, what scenes of orgic splendour have those carven walls witnessed? What solemn priestly conclave, what magnificence of rite, what marvels of initiation, have these forest temples known? These things we shall never learn. They are hidden from us in a gloom as palpable as that of the tree-encircled depths in which we find these shattered works of a once powerful hierarchy.

Mysterious Palenque

One of the most famous of the ancient centres of priestly domination is Palenque, situated in the modern state of Chiapas. This city was first brought into notice by Don José Calderon in 1774, when he discovered no less than eighteen palaces, twenty great buildings, and a hundred and sixty houses, which proves that in his day the primeval forest had not made such inroads upon the remaining buildings as it has during the past few generations. There is good evidence besides this that Palenque was standing at the time of Cortés' conquest of Yucatan. And here it will be well at once to dispel any conception the reader may have formed concerning the vast antiquity of these cities and the structures they contain. The very oldest of them cannot be of a date anterior to the thirteenth century, and few Americanists of repute would admit such an antiquity for them. There may be remains of a fragmentary nature here and there in Central America which are relatively more ancient. But no temple or edifice which remains standing can claim a greater antiquity.

Palenque is built in the form of an amphitheatre, and nestles on the lowest slopes of the Cordilleras. Standing on the central pyramid, the eye is met by a ring of ruined palaces and temples raised upon artificial terraces. Of these the principal and most imposing is the Palace, a pile reared upon a single platform, forming an irregular quadrilateral, with a double gallery on the east, north, and west sides, surrounding an inner structure with a similar gallery and two courtyards. It is evident that there was little system or plan observed in the construction of this edifice, an unusual circumstance in Maya architecture. The dwelling apartments were situated on the southern side of the structure, and here there is absolute confusion, for buildings of all sorts and sizes jostle each other, and are reared on different levels.

Our interest is perhaps at first excited by three subterraneous apartments down a flight of gloomy steps. Here are to be found three great stone tables, the edges of which are fretted with sculptured symbols. That these were altars admits of little doubt, although some visitors have not hesitated to call them dining-tables! These constitute only one of the many puzzles in this building of 228 feet frontage, with a depth of 180 feet, which at the same time is only about 25 feet high!

On the north side of the Palace pyramid the façade of the Palace has crumbled into complete ruin, but some evidences of an entrance are still noticeable. There were probably fourteen doorways in all in the frontage, with a width of about nine feet each, the piers of which were covered with figures in bas-relief. The inside of the galleries is also covered at intervals with similar designs, or medallions, many of which are probably representations of priests or priestesses who once dwelt within the classic shades and practised strange rites in the worship of gods long since forgotten. One of these is of a woman with delicate features and high-bred countenance, and the frame or rim surrounding it is decorated in a manner recalling the Louis XV style.

The east gallery is 114 feet long, the north 185 feet, and the west 102 feet, so that, as remarked above, a lack of symmetry is apparent. The great court is reached by a Mayan arch which leads on to a staircase, on each side of which grotesque human figures of the Maya type are sculptured. Whom they are intended to portray or what rite they are engaged in it would indeed be difficult to say. That they are priests may be hazarded, for they appear to be dressed in the ecclesiastical *maxtli* (girdle), and one seems to be decorated with the beads seen in the pictures of the death-god. Moreover, they are mitred.

The courtyard is exceedingly irregular in shape. To the south side is a small building which has assisted our knowledge of Maya mural decoration; especially valuable is the handsome frieze with which it is adorned, on which we observe the rather familiar feathered serpent (Kukulcan or Quetzalcoatl). Everywhere we notice the flat Maya head – a racial type, perhaps brought about by deformation of the cranium in youth. One of the most important parts of the Palace from an architectural point of view is the east front of the inner wing, which is perhaps the best preserved, and exhibits the most luxurious ornamentation. Two roofed galleries supported by six pillars covered with bas-reliefs are reached by a staircase on which hieroglyphic signs still remain. The reliefs in cement are still faintly to be discerned on the pillars, and must have been of great beauty. They represent mythological characters in various attitudes. Above, seven enormous heads frown on the explorer in grim menace. The effect of the entire façade is rich in the extreme, even in ruin, and from it we can obtain a faint idea of the splendours of this wonderful civilization.

An Architectural Curiosity

One of the few towers to be seen among the ruins of Maya architecture stands at Palenque. It is square in shape and three stories in height, with sloping roof, and is not unlike the belfry of some little English village church.

The building we have been describing, although traditionally known as a 'palace,' was undoubtedly a great monastery or ecclesiastical habitation. Indeed, the entire city of Palenque was solely a priestly centre, a place of pilgrimage. The bas-reliefs with their representations of priests and acolytes prove this, as does the absence of warlike or monarchical subjects.

The Temple of Inscriptions

The Temple of Inscriptions, perched on an eminence some 40 feet high, is the largest edifice in Palenque. It has a façade 74 feet long by 25 feet deep, composed of a great gallery which runs along the entire front of the fane. The building has been named from the inscriptions with which certain flagstones in the central apartment are covered. Three other temples occupy a piece of rising ground close by. These are the Temple of the Sun, closely akin in type to many Japanese temple buildings; the Temple of the Cross, in which a wonderful altar-piece was discovered; and the Temple of the Cross No. II. In the Temple of the Cross the inscribed altar gave its name to the building. In the central slab is a cross of the American pattern, its roots springing from the hideous head of the goddess Chicomecohuatl, the Earth-mother, or her Maya equivalent. Its branches stretch to where on the right and left stand two figures, evidently those of a priest and acolyte, performing some mysterious rite. On the apex of the tree is placed the sacred turkey, or 'Emerald Fowl,' to which offerings of maize paste are made. The whole is surrounded by inscriptions.

Aké and Itzamal

Thirty miles east of Merida lies Aké, the colossal and primeval ruins of which speak of early Maya occupation. Here are pyramids, tennis-courts, and gigantic pillars which once supported immense galleries, all in a state of advanced ruin. Chief among these is the great pyramid and gallery, a mighty staircase rising toward lofty pillars, and somewhat reminiscent of Stonehenge. For what purpose it was constructed is quite unknown.

The House of Darkness

One ruin, tradition calls 'The House of Darkness.' Here no light enters save that which filters in by the open doorway. The vaulted roof is lost in a lofty gloom. So truly have the huge blocks of which the building is composed been laid that not even a needle could be inserted between them. The whole is coated with a hard plaster or cement.

The Palace of Owls

The Knuc (Palace of Owls), where a beautiful frieze of diamond-shaped stones intermingling with spheres may be observed, is noteworthy. All here is undoubtedly of the first Yucatec era, the time when the Maya first overran the country.

At Itzamal the chief object of interest is the great pyramid of Kinich-Kakmo (The Sun's Face with Fiery Rays), the base of which covers an area of nearly 650 square feet. To this shrine thousands were wont to come in times of panic or famine, and from the summit, where was housed the glittering idol, the smoke of sacrifice ascended to the cloudless sky, whilst a multitude of white-robed priests and augurs chanted and prophesied. To the south of this mighty pile stand the ruins of the Ppapp-Hol-Chac (The House of Heads and Lightnings), the abode of the chief priest.

Itzamna's Fane

At Itzamal, too, stood one of the chief temples of the great god Itzamna, the legendary founder of the Maya Empire. Standing on a lofty pyramid, four roads radiated from it, leading to Tabasco, Guatemala, and Chiapas; and here they brought the halt, the maimed, and the blind, aye, even the dead, for succour and resurrection, such faith had they in the mighty power of Kab-ul (The Miraculous Hand), as they designated the deity. The fourth road ran to the sacred isle of Cozumel, where first the men of Spain found the Maya cross, and supposed it to prove that St Thomas had discovered the American continent in early times, and had converted the natives to a Christianity which had become debased.

Bearded Gods

To the west arose another pyramid, on the summit of which was built the palace of Hunpictok (The Commander-in-chief of Eight Thousand Flints), in allusion, probably, to the god of lightning, Hurakan, whose gigantic face, once dominating the basement wall, has now disappeared. This face possessed huge mustachios, appendages unknown to the Maya race; and, indeed, we are struck with the frequency with which Mexican and Mayan gods and heroes are adorned with beards and other hirsute ornaments both on the monuments and in the manuscripts. Was the original governing class a bearded race? It is scarcely probable. Whence, then, the ever-recurring beard and moustache? These may have been developed in the priestly class by constant ceremonial shaving, which often produces a thin beard in the Mongolians – as witness the modern Japanese, who in imitating a custom of the West often succeed in producing quite respectable beards.

A Colossal Head

Not far away is to be found a gigantic head, probably that of the god Itzamna. It is 13 feet in height, and the features were formed by first roughly tracing them in rubble, and afterwards coating the whole with plaster. The figure is surrounded by spirals, symbols of wind or speech. On the opposite side of the pyramid alluded to above is found a wonderful bas-relief representing a tiger couchant, with a human head of the Maya type, probably depicting one of the early ancestors of the Maya, Balam-Quitze (Tiger with the Sweet Smile), of whom we read in the *Popol Vuh*.

Chichen-Itza

At Chichen-Itza (*see also* pages 112–125), in Yucatan, the chief wonder is the gigantic pyramid-temple known as El Castillo. It is reached by a steep flight of steps, and from it the vast ruins of Chichen radiate in a circular manner. To the east is the market-place, to the north a mighty temple, and a tennis-court, perhaps the best example of its kind in Yucatan, whilst to the west stand the Nunnery and the Chichan-Chob, or prison. Concerning Chichen-Itza Cogolludo tells the following story: "A king of Chichen called Canek fell desperately in love with a young princess, who, whether she did not return his affection or whether she was compelled to obey a parental mandate, married a more powerful Yucatec *cacique*. The discarded lover, unable to bear his loss, and moved by love and despair, armed his dependents and suddenly fell upon his successful rival. Then the gaiety of the feast was exchanged for the din of war, and amidst the confusion the Chichen prince disappeared, carrying off the beautiful bride. But conscious that his power was less than his rival's, and fearing his vengeance, he fled the country with most of his vassals." It is a historical fact that the inhabitants of Chichen abandoned their city, but whether for the reason given in this story or not cannot be discovered.

The Nunnery

The Nunnery at Chichen is a building of great beauty of outline and decoration, the frieze above the doorway and the fretted ornamentation of the upper story exciting the admiration of most writers on the subject. Here dwelt the sacred women, the chief of whom, like their male prototypes, were dedicated to Kukulcan and regarded with much reverence. The base of the building is occupied by eight large figures, and over the door is the representation of a priest with a *panache*, whilst a row of gigantic heads crowns the north façade. Here, too, are figures of the wind-god, with projecting lips, which many generations of antiquarians took for heads of elephants with waving trunks! The entire building is one of the gems of Central American architecture, and delights the eye of archaeologist and artist alike. In El Castillo are found wonderful bas-reliefs depicting bearded men, evidently the priests of Quetzalcoatl, himself bearded, and to the practised eye one of these would appear to be wearing a false hirsute appendage, as kings were wont to do in ancient Egypt. Were these beards artificial and symbolical?

The 'Writing in the Dark'

The Akab-sib (Writing in the Dark) is a bas-relief found on the lintel of an inner door at the extremity of the building. It represents a figure seated before a vase, with outstretched forefinger, and whence it got its traditional appellation it would be hard to say, unless the person represented is supposed to be in the act of writing. The figure is surrounded by inscriptions. At Chichen were found a statue of Tlaloc, the god of rain or moisture, and immense torsos representing Kukulcan. There also was a terrible well into which men were cast in time of drought as a propitiation to the rain-god.

Kabah

At Kabah there is a marvellous frontage which strikingly recalls that of a North American Indian totem-house in its fantastic wealth of detail. The ruins are scattered over a large area, and must all have been at one time painted in brilliant colours. Here two horses' heads in stone were unearthed, showing that the natives had copied faithfully the steeds of the conquering Spaniards. Nothing is known of the history of Kabah, but its neighbour, Uxmal, fifteen miles distant, is much more famous.

Uxmal

The imposing pile of the Casa del Gobernador (Governor's Palace, so called) at Uxmal is perhaps the best known and described of all the aboriginal buildings of Central America. It occupies three successive colossal terraces, and its frieze runs in a line of 325 feet, and is divided into panels, each of which frames a gigantic head of priest or deity. The striking thing concerning this edifice is that although it has been abandoned for over three hundred years it is still almost as fresh architecturally as when it left the builder's hands. Here and there a lintel has fallen, or stones have been removed in a spirit of vandalism to assist in the erection of a neighbouring *hacienda*, but on the whole we possess in it the most unspoiled piece of Yucatec building in existence. On the side of the palace where stands the main entrance, directly over the gateway, is the most wonderful fretwork and ornamentation, carried out in high relief, above which soar three eagles in hewn stone, surmounted by a plumed human head. In the plinth are three heads, which in type recall the Roman, surrounded by inscriptions. A clear proof of the comparative lateness of the period in which Uxmal was built is found in the circumstance that all the lintels over the doorways are of wood, of which much still exists in a good state of preservation. Many of the joists of the roofs were also of timber, and were fitted into the stonework by means of specially carved ends.

The Dwarf's House

There is also a nunnery which forcibly recalls that at Chichen, and is quite as elaborate and flamboyant in its architectural design. But the real mystery at Uxmal is the Casa del Adivino (The Prophet's House), also locally known as 'The Dwarf's House.' It consists of two portions, one of which is on the summit of an artificial pyramid, whilst the other, a small but beautifully finished chapel, is situated lower down facing the town. The loftier building is reached by an exceedingly steep staircase, and bears every evidence of having been used as a sanctuary, for here were discovered cacao and copal, recently burnt, by Cogolludo as late as 1656, which is good evidence that the Yucatecs did not all at once abandon their ancient faith at the promptings of the Spanish fathers. In his *Travels in Yucatan* Stephens has a legend relating to this house which may well be given in his own words (*see* page 295). The interpretation of this myth is by no means difficult. The old woman is undoubtedly the rain-goddess, the dwarf the Man of the Sun who emerges from the cosmic egg. In Yucatan dwarfs were sacred to the sun-god, and were occasionally sacrificed to him, for reasons which appear obscure.

The Mound of Sacrifice

Another building at Uxmal the associations of which render it of more than passing interest is the Pyramid of Sacrifice, an edifice built on the plan of the Mexican *teocalli*. Indeed, it is probably of Aztec origin, and may even have been erected by the mercenaries who during the fifteenth century swarmed from Mexico into Yucatan and Guatemala to take service with the rival chieftains who carried on civil war in those states. Beside this is another mound which was crowned by a very beautiful temple, now in an advanced state of ruin. The 'Pigeon House' is an ornate pile with pinnacles pierced by large openings which probably served as dovecotes. The entire architecture of Uxmal displays a type more primitive than that met elsewhere in Yucatan. There is documentary evidence to prove that so late as 1673 the Indians still worshipped in the ruins of Uxmal, where they burnt copal, and performed "other detestable sacrifices." So that even a hundred and fifty years of Spanish rule had not sufficed to wean the natives from the worship of the older gods to whom their fathers had for generations bowed down. This would also seem conclusive evidence that the ruins of Uxmal at least were the work of the existing race.

The Phantom City

In his *Travels in Central America* Stephens recounts a fascinating story told him by a priest of Santa Cruz del Quiche, to the effect that four days' journey from that place a great Indian city was to be seen, densely populated, and preserving the ancient civilization of the natives. He had, indeed, beheld it from the summit of a cliff, shining in glorious whiteness many leagues away. This was perhaps Lorillard City, discovered by Suarez, and afterwards by Charnay. In general type Lorillard closely resembles Palenque. Here was found a wonderfully executed stone idol, which Charnay thought represented a different racial type from that seen in the other Central American cities. The chief finds of interest in this ancient city were the intricate bas-reliefs, one over the central door of a temple, probably a symbolic representation of Quetzalcoatl, who holds the rain-cross, in both hands, and is seen *vis-à-vis* with an acolyte, also holding the symbol, though it is possible that the individual represented may have been the high-priest of Quetzalcoatl or Kukulcan. Another bas-relief represents a priest sacrificing to Kukulcan by passing a rope of maguey fibre over his tongue for the purpose of drawing blood – an instance of the substitution in sacrifice of the part for the whole.

The Horse-God

At Peten-Itza, Cortés left his horse, which had fallen sick, to the care of the Indians. The animal died under their mismanagement and because of the food offered it, and the terrified natives, fancying it a divine being, raised an image of it, and called it Izimin Chac (Thunder and Lightning), because they had seen its rider discharge a firearm, and they imagined that the flash and the report had proceeded from the creature. The sight of the idol aroused such wrath in the zealous bosom of a certain Spanish monk that he broke it with a huge stone – and, but for the interference of the *cacique*, would have suffered death for his temerity. Peten was a city "filled with idols," as was Tayasal, close at hand, where in the seventeenth century no less than nine new temples were built, which goes to prove that the native religion was by no means extinct. One of these new temples, according to Villagutierre, had a Spanish balcony of hewn stone! In the Temple of the Sun at Tikal, an adjoining city, is a wonderful altar panel, representing an unknown deity, and here also are many of those marvellously carved idols of which Stephens gives such capital illustrations in his fascinating book.

Copan

Copan, one of the most interesting of these wondrous city-centres, the name of which has, indeed, become almost a household word, is in the same district as the towns just described, and abounds chiefly in monolithic images. It yielded after a desperate struggle to Hernandez de Chaves, one of Alvarado's lieutenants, in 1530. The monolithic images so abundantly represented here are evolved from the stelae and the bas-relief, and are not statues in the proper sense of the term, as they are not completely cut away from the stone background out of which they were carved. An altar found at Copan exhibits real skill in sculpture, the head-dresses, ornaments, and expressions of the eight figures carved on its sides being elaborate in the extreme and exceedingly lifelike. Here again we notice a fresh racial type, which goes to prove that one race alone cannot have been responsible for these marvellous ruined cities and all that they contain and signify. We have to imagine a shifting of races and a fluctuation of peoples in Central America such as we know took place in Europe and Asia before we can rightly understand the ethnological problems of the civilized sphere of the New World, and any theory which does not take due account of such conditions is doomed to failure.

Mitla

We now come to the last of these stupendous remnants of a vanished civilization – Mitla, by no means the least of the works of civilized man in Central America. At the period of the conquest the city occupied a wide area, but at the present time only six palaces and three ruined pyramids are left standing. The great palace is a vast edifice in the shape of the letter 'T,' and measures 130 feet in its greater dimension, with an apartment of a like size. Six monolithic columns which supported the roof still stand in gigantic isolation, but the roof itself has long fallen in. A dark passage leads to the inner court, and the walls of this are covered with mosaic work in panels which recalls somewhat the pattern known as the 'Greek fret.' The lintels over the doorways are of huge blocks of stone nearly eighteen feet long. Of this building Viollet-le-Duc says: "The monuments of Greece and Rome in their best time can alone compare with the splendour of this great edifice."

A Place of Sepulture

The ruins at Mitla bear no resemblance to those of Mexico or Yucatan, either as regards architecture or ornamentation, for whereas the Yucatec buildings possess overlapping walls, the palaces of Mitla consist of perpendicular walls intended to support flat roofs. Of these structures the second and fourth palaces alone are in such a state of preservation as to permit of general description. The second palace shows by its sculptured lintel and two inner columns that the same arrangement was observed in its construction as in the great palace just described. The fourth palace has on its southern façade oblong panels and interesting caryatides or pillars in the shape of human figures. These palaces consisted of four upper apartments, finely sculptured, and a like number of rooms on the lower story, which was occupied by the high-priest, and to which the king came to mourn on the demise of a relative. Here, too, the priests were entombed, and in an adjoining room the idols were kept. Into a huge underground chamber the bodies of eminent warriors and sacrificial victims were cast. Attempts have been made to identify Mitla with

Mictlan, the Mexican Hades, and there is every reason to suppose that the identification is correct. It must be borne in mind that Mictlan was as much a place of the dead as a place of punishment, as was the Greek Hades, and therefore might reasonably signify a place of sepulture, such as Mitla undoubtedly was. The following passages from the old historians of Mitla, Torquemada and Burgoa, throw much light on this aspect of the city, and besides are full of the most intense interest and curious information, so that they may be given *in extenso*. But before passing on to them we should for a moment glance at Seler's suggestion that the American race imagined that their ancestors had originally issued from the underworld through certain caverns into the light of day, and that this was the reason why Mitla was not only a burial-place but a sanctuary.

An Old Description of Mitla

Of Mitla Father Torquemada writes:

"When some monks of my order, the Franciscan, passed, preaching and shriving, through the province of Zapoteca, whose capital city is Tehuantepec, they came to a village which was called Mictlan, that is, Underworld [Hell]. Besides mentioning the large number of people in the village they told of buildings which were prouder and more magnificent than any which they had hitherto seen in New Spain. Among them was a temple of the evil spirit and living-rooms for his demoniacal servants, and among other fine things there was a hall with ornamented panels, which were constructed of stone in a variety of arabesques and other very remarkable designs. There were doorways there, each one of which was built of but three stones, two upright at the sides and one across them, in such a manner that, although these doorways were very high and broad, the stones sufficed for their entire construction. They were so thick and broad that we were assured there were few like them. There was another hall in these buildings, or rectangular temples, which was erected entirely on round stone pillars, very high and very thick, so thick that two grown men could scarcely encircle them with their arms, nor could one of them reach the finger-tips of the other. These pillars were all in one piece, and, it was said, the whole shaft of a pillar measured 5 ells from top to bottom, and they were very much like those of the Church of Santa Maria Maggiore in Rome, very skilfully made and polished."

Father Burgoa gives a more exact description. He says:

"The Palace of the Living and of the Dead was built for the use of this person [the high-priest of the Zapotecs].... They built this magnificent house or pantheon in the shape of a rectangle, with portions rising above the earth and portions built down into the earth, the latter in the hole or cavity which was found below the surface of the earth, and ingeniously made the chambers of equal size by the manner of joining them, leaving a spacious court in the middle; and in order to secure four equal chambers they accomplished what barbarian heathen (as they were) could only achieve by the powers and skill of an architect. It is not known in what stone-pit they quarried the pillars, which are so thick that two men can scarcely encircle them with their arms. These are, to be sure, mere shafts without capital or pedestal, but they are wonderfully regular and smooth, and they are about 5 ells high and in one piece. These served to support the roof, which consists of stone slabs instead of beams. The slabs are about two ells long, one ell broad, and half an ell thick, extending from pillar to pillar. The pillars stand in a row, one behind the other, in order to receive the weight. The stone slabs are so regular and so exactly fitted that, without any mortar or cement, at the joints they resemble mortised beams. The four rooms, which are very spacious, are arranged in exactly the same way and covered with the same kind of roofing. But in the construction of the walls the greatest architects of the earth have been surpassed, as I have not found this kind of architecture described either among the Egyptians or among the Greeks, for they begin at the base with a narrow outline and, as the structure rises in height, spread out in wide copings at the top, so that the upper part exceeds the base in breadth and looks as if it would fall over. The inner side of the walls consists of a mortar or stucco of such hardness that no one knows with what kind of liquid it could have been mixed. The outside is of such extraordinary workmanship that on a masonry wall about an ell in height there are placed stone slabs with a projecting edge, which form the support for an endless number of small white stones, the smallest of which are a sixth of an ell long, half as broad, and a quarter as thick, and which are as smooth and regular as if they had all come from one mould. They had so many of these stones that, setting them in, one beside the other, they formed with them a large number of different beautiful geometric designs, each an ell broad and running the whole length of the wall, each varying in pattern up to the crowning piece, which was the finest of all. And what has always seemed inexplicable to the greatest architects is the adjustment of these little stones without a single handful of mortar, and the fact that without tools, with nothing but hard stones and sand, they could achieve such solid work that, though the whole structure is very old and no one knows who made it, it has been preserved until the present day.

Human Sacrifice at Mitla

"I carefully examined these monuments some thirty years ago in the chambers above ground, which are constructed of the same size and in the same way as those below ground, and, though single pieces were in ruins because some stones had become loosened, there was still much to admire. The doorways were very large, the sides of each being of single stones of the same thickness as the wall, and the lintel was made out of another stone which held the two lower ones together at the top. There were four chambers above ground and four below. The latter were arranged according to their purpose in such a way that one front chamber served as chapel and sanctuary for the idols, which were placed on a great stone which served as an altar. And for the more important feasts which they celebrated with sacrifices, or at the burial of a king or great lord, the high-priest instructed the lesser priests or the subordinate temple officials who served him to prepare the chapel and his vestments and a large quantity of the incense used by them. And then he descended with a great retinue, while none of the common people saw him or dared to look in his face, convinced that if they did so they would fall dead to the earth as a punishment for their boldness. And when he entered the chapel they put on him a long white cotton garment made like an alb, and over that a garment shaped like a dalmatic, which was embroidered with pictures of wild beasts and birds; and they put a cap on his head, and on his feet a kind of shoe woven of many coloured feathers. And when he had put on these garments he walked with solemn mien and measured step to the altar, bowed low before the idols, renewed the incense, and then in quite unintelligible murmurs he began to converse with these images, these depositories of infernal spirits, and continued in this sort of prayer with hideous grimaces and writhings, uttering inarticulate sounds, which filled all present with fear and terror, till he came out of that diabolical trance and told those standing around the lies and fabrications which the spirit had imparted to him or which he had invented himself. When human beings were sacrificed the ceremonies were multiplied, and the assistants of the high-priest stretched the victim out upon a large stone, baring his breast, which they tore open with a great stone knife, while the body writhed in fearful convulsions, and they laid the heart bare, ripping it out, and with it the soul, which the devil took, while they carried the heart to the high-priest that he might offer it to the idols by holding it to their mouths, among other ceremonies; and the body was thrown into the burial-place of their 'blessed,' as they called them. And if after the sacrifice he felt inclined to detain those who begged any favour he sent them word by the subordinate priests not to leave their houses till their gods were appeased, and he commanded them to do penance meanwhile, to fast and to speak with no woman, so that, until this father of sin had interceded for the absolution of the penitents and had declared the gods appeased, they did not dare to cross their thresholds.

"The second (underground) chamber was the burial-place of these high-priests, the third that of the kings of Theozapotlan, whom they brought hither richly dressed in their best attire, feathers, jewels, golden necklaces, and precious stones, placing a shield in the left hand and a javelin in the right, just as they used them in war. And at their burial rites great mourning prevailed; the instruments which were played made mournful sounds; and with loud wailing and continuous sobbing they chanted the life and exploits of their lord until they laid him on the structure which they had prepared for this purpose.

Living Sacrifices

"The last (underground) chamber had a second door at the rear, which led to a dark and gruesome room. This was closed with a stone slab, which occupied the whole entrance. Through this door they threw the bodies of the victims and of the great lords and chieftains who had fallen in battle, and they brought them from the spot where they fell, even when it was very far off, to this burial-place; and so great was the barbarous infatuation of those Indians that, in the belief of the happy life which awaited them, many who were oppressed by diseases or hardships begged this infamous priest to accept them as living sacrifices and allow them to enter through that portal and roam about in the dark interior of the mountain, to seek the feasting-places of their forefathers. And when any one obtained this favour the servants of the high-priest led him thither with special ceremonies, and after they allowed him to enter through the small door they rolled the stone before it again and took leave of him, and the unhappy man, wandering in that abyss of darkness, died of hunger and thirst, beginning already in life the pain of his damnation, and on account of this horrible abyss they called this village Liyobaa.

The Cavern of Death

"When later there fell upon these people the light of the Gospel, its servants took much trouble to instruct them, and to find out whether this error, common to all these nations, still prevailed; and they learned from the stories which had been handed down that all were convinced that this damp cavern extended more than thirty leagues underground, and that its roof was supported by pillars. And there were people, zealous prelates anxious for knowledge, who, in order to convince these ignorant people of their error, went into this cave accompanied by a large number of people bearing lighted torches and firebrands, and descended several large steps. And they soon came upon many great buttresses which formed a kind of street. They had prudently brought a quantity of rope with them to use as guiding-lines, that they might not lose themselves in this confusing labyrinth. And the putrefaction and the bad odour and the dampness of the earth were very great, and there was also a cold wind which blew out their torches. And after they had gone a short distance, fearing to be overpowered by the stench, or to step on poisonous reptiles, of which some had been seen, they resolved to go out again, and to completely wall up this back door of hell. The four buildings above ground were the only ones which still remained open, and they had a court and chambers like those underground; and the ruins of these have lasted even to the present day.

Palace of the High-Priest

"One of the rooms above ground was the palace of the high-priest, where he sat and slept, for the apartment offered room and opportunity for everything. The throne was like a high cushion, with a high back to lean against, all of tiger-skin, stuffed entirely with delicate feathers, or with fine grass which was used for this purpose. The other seats were smaller, even when the king came to visit him. The authority of this devilish priest was so great that there was no one who dared to cross the court, and to avoid this the other three chambers had doors in the rear, through which even the kings entered. For this purpose they had alleys and passage-ways on the outside above and below, by which people could enter and go out when they came to see the high-priest....

"The second chamber above ground was that of the priests and the assistants of the high-priest. The third was that of the king when he came. The fourth was that of the other chieftains and captains, and though the space was small for so great a number, and for so many different families, yet they accommodated themselves to each other out of respect for the place, and avoided dissensions and factions. Furthermore, there was no other administration of justice in this place than that of the high-priest, to whose unlimited power all bowed.

Furniture of the Temples

"All the rooms were clean, and well furnished with mats. It was not the custom to sleep on bedsteads, however great a lord might be. They used very tastefully braided mats, which were spread on the floor, and soft skins of animals and delicate fabrics for coverings. Their food consisted usually of animals killed in the hunt – deer, rabbits, armadillos, &c., and also birds, which they killed with snares or arrows. The bread, made of their maize, was white and well kneaded. Their drinks were always cold, made of ground chocolate, which was mixed with water and pounded maize. Other drinks were made of pulpy and of crushed fruits, which were then mixed with the intoxicating drink prepared from the agave; for since the common people were forbidden the use of intoxicating drinks, there was always an abundance of these on hand."

Mythology of the Maya

Affinities with the Nahua?

THE MAYA PANTHEON, although it bears a strong resemblance to that of the Nahua, differs from it in so many respects that it is easy to observe that at one period it must have been absolutely free from all Nahua influence. We may, then, provisionally accept the theory that at some relatively distant period the mythologies of the Nahua and Maya were influenced from one common centre, if they were not originally identical, but that later the inclusion in the cognate but divided systems of local deities and the superimposition of the deities and rites of immigrant peoples had caused such differentiation as to render somewhat vague the original likeness between them.

In the Mexican mythology we have as a key-note the custom of human sacrifice. It has often been stated as exhibiting the superior status in civilization of the Maya that their religion was free from the revolting practices which characterized the Nahua faith. This, however, is totally erroneous. Although the Maya were not nearly so prone to the practice of human sacrifice as were the Nahua, they frequently engaged in it, and the pictures which have been drawn of their bloodless offerings must not lead us to believe that they never indulged in this rite. It is known, for example, that they sacrificed maidens to the water-god at the period of the spring florescence, by casting them into a deep pool, where they were drowned.

Quetzalcoatl among the Maya

One of the most obvious of the mythological relationships between the Maya and Nahua is exhibited in the Maya cult of the god Quetzalcoatl. It seems to have been a general belief in Mexico that Quetzalcoatl was a god foreign to the soil; or at least relatively aboriginal to his rival Tezcatlipoca, if not to the Nahua themselves. It is amusing to see it stated by authorities of the highest standing that his worship was free from bloodshed. But it does not appear whether the sanguinary rites connected with the name of Quetzalcoatl in Mexico were undertaken by his priests of their own accord or at the instigation and pressure of the pontiff of Huitzilopochtli, under whose jurisdiction they were. The designation by which Quetzalcoatl was known to the Maya was Kukulcan, which signifies 'Feathered Serpent,' and is exactly translated by his Mexican name. In Guatemala he was called Gucumatz, which word is also identical in Kiche with his other native appellations. But the Kukulcan of the Maya appears to be dissimilar from Quetzalcoatl in several of his attributes. The difference in climate would probably account for most of these. In Mexico Quetzalcoatl, as we have seen, was not only the Man of the Sun, but the original wind-god of the country. The Kukulcan of the Maya has more the attributes of a thunder-god. In the tropical climate of Yucatan and Guatemala the sun at midday appears to draw the clouds around it in serpentine shapes. From these emanate thunder and lightning and the fertilizing rain, so that Kukulcan would appear to have appealed to the Maya more as a god of the sky who wielded the thunderbolts than a god of the atmosphere proper like Quetzalcoatl, though several of the stelae in Yucatan represent Kukulcan as he is portrayed in Mexico, with wind issuing from his mouth.

An Alphabet of Gods

The principal sources of our knowledge of the Maya deities are the Dresden, Madrid, and Paris codices alluded to previously, all of which contain many pictorial representations of the various members of the Maya pantheon. Of the very names of some of these gods we are so ignorant, and so difficult is the process of affixing to them the traditional names which are left to us as those of the Maya gods, that Dr Paul Schellhas, a German student of Maya antiquities, has proposed that the figures of deities appearing in the Maya codices or manuscripts should be provisionally indicated by the letters of the alphabet. The figures of gods which thus occur are fifteen in number, and therefore take the letters of the alphabet from A to P, the letter J being omitted.

Difficulties of Comparison

Unluckily the accounts of Spanish authors concerning Maya mythology do not agree with the representations of the gods delineated in the codices. That the three codices have a mythology in common is certain. Again, great difficulty is found in comparing the deities of the codices with those represented by the carved and stucco bas-reliefs of the Maya region. It will thus be seen that very considerable difficulties beset the student in this mythological sphere. So few data have yet been collected regarding the Maya mythology that to dogmatise upon any subject connected with it would indeed be rash. But much has been accomplished in the past few decades, and evidence is slowly but surely accumulating from which sound conclusions can be drawn.

The Conflict between Light and Darkness

We witness in the Maya mythology a dualism almost as complete as that of ancient Persia – the conflict between light and darkness. Opposing each other we behold on the one hand the deities of the sun, the gods of warmth and light, of civilization and the joy of life, and on the other the deities of darksome death, of night, gloom, and fear. From these primal conceptions of light and darkness all the mythologic forms of the Maya are evolved. When we catch the first recorded glimpses of Maya belief we recognize that at the period when it came under the purview of Europeans the gods of darkness were in the ascendant and a deep pessimism had spread over Maya thought and theology. Its joyful side was subordinated to the worship of gloomy beings, the deities of death and hell, and if the cult of light was attended with such touching fidelity it was because the benign agencies who were worshipped in connection with it had promised not to desert mankind altogether, but to return at some future indefinite period and resume their sway of radiance and peace.

The Calendar

Like that of the Nahua, the Maya mythology was based almost entirely upon the calendar, which in its astronomic significance and duration was identical with that of the Mexicans. The ritual year of twenty 'weeks' of thirteen days each was divided into four quarters, each of these being under the auspices of a different quarter of the heavens. Each 'week' was under the supervision of a particular deity, as will be seen when we come to deal separately with the various gods.

Traditional Knowledge of the Gods

The heavenly bodies had important representation in the Maya pantheon. In Yucatan the sun-god was known as Kinich-ahau (Lord of the Face of the Sun). He was identified with the Fire-bird, or Arara, and was thus called Kinich-Kakmo (Fire-bird; lit. Sun-bird). He was also the presiding genius of the north.

Itzamna, one of the most important of the Maya deities, was a moon-god, the father of gods and men. In him was typified the decay and recurrence of life in nature. His name was derived from the words he was supposed to have given to men regarding himself: "Itz en caan, itz en muyal" ("I am the dew of the heaven, I am the dew of the clouds"). He was tutelar deity of the west.

Chac, the rain-god, is the possessor of an elongated nose, not unlike the proboscis of a tapir, which of course is the spout whence comes the rain which he blows over the earth. He is one of the best represented gods on both manuscripts and monuments, and presides over the east. The black god Ekchuah was the god of merchants and cacao-planters. He is represented in the manuscripts several times.

Ix ch'el was the goddess of medicine, and Ix chebel yax was identified by the priest Hernandez with the Virgin Mary. There were also several deities, or rather genii, called Bacabs, who were the upholders of the heavens in the four quarters of the sky. The names of these were Kan, Muluc, Ix, and Cauac, representing the east, north, west, and south. Their symbolic colours were yellow, white, black, and red respectively. They corresponded in some degree to the four variants of the Mexican rain-god Tlaloc, for many of the American races believed that rain, the fertilizer of the soil, emanated from the four points of the compass. We shall find still other deities when we come to discuss the *Popol Vuh*, the saga-book of the Kiche, but it is difficult to say how far these were connected with the deities of the Maya of Yucatan, concerning whom we have little traditional knowledge, and it is better to deal with them separately, pointing out resemblances where these appear to exist.

Maya Polytheism

On the whole the Maya do not seem to have been burdened with an extensive pantheon, as were the Nahua, and their polytheism appears to have been of a limited character. Although they possessed a number of divinities, these were in a great measure only different forms of one and the same divine power – probably localised forms of it. The various Maya tribes worshipped similar gods under different names. They recognized divine unity in the god Hunabku, who was invisible and supreme, but he does not bulk largely in their mythology, any more than does the universal

All-Father in other early faiths. The sun is the great deity in Maya religion, and the myths which tell of the origin of the Maya people are purely solar. As the sun comes from the east, so the hero-gods who bring with them culture and enlightenment have an oriental origin. As Votan, as Kabil, the 'Red Hand' who initiates the people into the arts of writing and architecture, these gods are civilizing men of the sun as surely as is Quetzalcoatl.

The Bat-God

A sinister figure, the prince of the Maya legions of darkness, is the bat-god, Zotzilaha Chimalman, who dwelt in the 'House of Bats,' a gruesome cavern on the way to the abodes of darkness and death. He is undoubtedly a relic of cave-worship pure and simple. "The Maya," says an old chronicler, "have an immoderate fear of death, and they seem to have given it a figure peculiarly repulsive." We shall find this deity alluded to in the *Popol Vuh*, under the name Camazotz, in close proximity to the Lords of Death and Hell, attempting to bar the journey of the hero-gods across these dreary realms. He is frequently met with on the Copan reliefs, and a Maya clan, the Ah-zotzils, were called by his name. They were of Kakchiquel origin, and he was probably their totem.

Modern Research – The Alphabet Gods

We must now turn to the question of what modern research has done to elucidate the character of the various Maya deities. We have already seen that they have been provisionally named by the letters of the alphabet until such proof is forthcoming as will identify them with the traditional gods of the Maya, and we will now briefly examine what is known concerning them under their temporary designations.

God A

In the Dresden and other codices god A is represented as a figure with exposed vertebrae and skull-like countenance, with the marks of corruption on his body, and displaying every sign of mortality. On his head he wears a snail-symbol, the Aztec sign of birth, perhaps to typify the connection between birth and death. He also wears a pair of cross-bones. The hieroglyph which accompanies his figure represents a corpse's head with closed eyes, a skull, and a sacrificial knife. His symbol is that for the calendar day Cimi, which means death. He presides over the west, the home of the dead, the region toward which they invariably depart with the setting sun. That he is a death-god there can be no doubt, but of his name we are ignorant. He is probably identical with the Aztec god of death and hell, Mictlan, and is perhaps one of those Lords of Death and Hell who invite the heroes to the celebrated game of ball in the Kiche *Popol Vuh*, and hold them prisoners in their gloomy realm.

God B is the deity who appears most frequently in the manuscripts. He has a long, truncated nose, like that of a tapir, and we find in him every sign of a god of the elements. He walks the waters, wields fiery torches, and seats himself on the cruciform tree of the four winds which appears so frequently in American myth. He is evidently a culture-god or hero, as he is seen planting maize, carrying tools, and going on a journey, a fact which establishes his solar connection. He is, in fact, Kukulcan or Quetzalcoatl, and on examining him we feel that at least there can be no doubt concerning his identity.

Concerning god C matter is lacking, but he is evidently a god of the pole-star, as in one of the codices he is surrounded by planetary signs and wears a nimbus of rays.

God D is almost certainly a moon-god. He is represented as an aged man, with sunken cheeks and wrinkled forehead on which hangs the sign for night. His hieroglyph is surrounded by dots, to represent a starry sky, and is followed by the number 20, to show the duration of the moon. Like most moon deities he is connected with birth, for occasionally he wears the snail, symbol of parturition, on his head. It is probable that he is Itzamna, one of the greatest of Maya gods, who was regarded as the universal life-giver, and was probably of very ancient origin.

The Maize-God

God E is another deity whom we have no difficulty in identifying. He wears the leafed ear of maize as his head-dress. In fact, his head has been evolved out of the conventional drawings of the ear of maize, so we may say at once without any difficulty that he is a maize-god pure and simple, and a parallel with the Aztec maize-god Centeotl. Brinton calls this god Ghanan, and Schellhas thinks he may be identical with a deity Yum Kaax, whose name means 'Lord of the Harvest Fields.'

A close resemblance can be noticed between gods F and A, and it is thought that the latter resembles the Aztec Xipe, the god of human sacrifice. He is adorned with the same black lines running over the face and body, typifying gaping death-wounds.

The Sun-God

In G we may be sure that we have found a sun-god *par excellence*. His hieroglyph is the sun-sign, *kin*. But we must be careful not to confound him with deities like Quetzalcoatl or Kukulcan. He is, like the Mexican Totec, the sun itself, and not the Man of the Sun, the civilizing agent, who leaves his bright abode to dwell with man and introduce him to the arts of cultured existence. He is the luminary himself, whose only acceptable food is human blood, and who must be fed full with this terrible fare or perish, dragging the world of men with him into a fathomless abyss of gloom. We need not be surprised, therefore, to see god G occasionally wearing the symbols of death.

God H would seem to have some relationship to the serpent, but what it may be is obscure, and no certain identification can be made.

I is a water-goddess, an old woman with wrinkled brown body and claw-like feet, wearing on her head a grisly snake twisted into a knot, to typify the serpent-like nature of water. She holds in her hands an earthenware pot from which water flows. We cannot say that she resembles the Mexican water-goddess, Chalchihuitlicue, wife of Tlaloc, who was in most respects a deity of a beneficent character. I seems a personification of water in its more dreadful aspect of floods and water-spouts, as it must inevitably have appeared to the people of the more torrid regions of Central America, and that she was regarded as an agent of death is shown from her occasionally wearing the cross-bones of the death-god.

'The God with the Ornamented Nose'

God K is scientifically known as 'the god with the ornamented nose,' and is probably closely related to god B. Concerning him no two authorities are at one, some regarding him as a storm-god, whose proboscis, like that of Kukulcan, is intended to represent the blast of the tempest. But we observe certain stellar signs in connection with K which would go to prove that he is, indeed, one of the Quetzalcoatl group. His features are constantly to be met with on the gateways and corners of the ruined shrines of Central America, and have led many 'antiquarians' to believe in the existence of an elephant-headed god, whereas his trunk-like snout is merely a funnel through which he emitted the gales over which he had dominion, as a careful study of the *pinturas* shows, the wind being depicted issuing from the snout in question. At the same time, the snout may have been modelled on that of the tapir. "If the rain-god Chac is distinguished in the Maya manuscript by a peculiarly long nose curving over the mouth, and if in the other forms of the rain-god, to which, as it seems, the name of Balon Zacab belongs, the nose widens out and sends out shoots, I believe that the tapir which was employed identically with Chac, the Maya rain-god, furnished the model," says Dr Seler. Is K, then, the same as Chac? Chac bears every sign of affinity with the Mexican rain-god Tlaloc, whose face was evolved from the coils of two snakes, and also some resemblance to the snouted features of B and K. But, again, the Mexican pictures of Quetzalcoatl are not at all like those of Tlaloc, so that there can be no affinity between Tlaloc and K. Therefore if the Mexican Tlaloc and the Maya Chac be identical, and Tlaloc differs from Quetzalcoatl, who in turn is identical with B and K, it is clear that Chac has nothing to do with K.

The Old Black God

God L Dr Schellhas has designated 'the Old Black God,' from the circumstance that he is depicted as an old man with sunken face and toothless gums, the upper, or sometimes the lower, part of his features being covered with black paint. He is represented in the Dresden MS. only. Professor Cyrus Thomas, of New York, thinks that he is the god Ekchuah, who is traditionally described as black, but Schellhas fits this designation to god M. The more probable theory is that of Förstemann, who sees in L the god Votan, who is identical with the Aztec earth-god, Tepeyollotl. Both deities have similar face markings, and their dark hue is perhaps symbolical of the subterranean places where they were supposed to dwell.

The Travellers' God

God M is a veritable black god, with reddish lips. On his head he bears a roped package resembling the loads carried by the Maya porter class, and he is found in violent opposition with F, the enemy of all who wander into the unknown wastes. A god of this description has been handed down by tradition under the name of Ekchuah, and his blackness is probably symbolical of the black or deeply bronzed skin of the porter class among the natives of Central America, who are constantly exposed to the sun. He would appear to be a parallel to the Aztec Yacatecutli, god of travelling merchants or chapmen.

The God of Unlucky Days

God N is identified by Schellhas with the demon Uayayab, who presided over the five unlucky days which it will be recollected came at the end of the Mexican and Maya year. He was known to the Maya as 'He by whom the year is poisoned.' After modelling his image in clay they carried it out of their villages, so that his baneful influence might not dwell therein.

Goddess O is represented as an old woman engaged in the avocation of spinning, and is probably a goddess of the domestic virtues, the tutelar of married females.

The Frog-God

God P is shown with the body and fins of a frog on a blue background, evidently intended to represent water. Like all other frog-gods he is, of course, a deity of water, probably in its agricultural significance. We find him sowing seed and making furrows, and when we remember the important part played by frog deities in the agriculture of Anahuac we should have no difficulty in classing him with these. Seler asserts his identity with Kukulcan, but no reason except the circumstance of his being a rain-god can be advanced to establish the identity. He wears the year-sign on his head, probably with a seasonal reference.

The Popol Vuh

THERE IS NO DOCUMENT OF GREATER IMPORTANCE to the study of the pre-Columbian mythology of America than the *Popol Vuh*. It is the chief source of our knowledge of the mythology of the Kiché people of Central America, and it is further of considerable comparative value when studied in conjunction with the mythology of the Nahuatlacâ, or Mexican peoples. This interesting text, the recovery of which forms one of the most romantic episodes in the history of American bibliography, was written by a Christianised native of Guatemala some time in the seventeenth century, and was copied in the Kiché language, in which it was originally written, by a monk of the Order of Predicadores, one Francisco Ximenes, who also added a Spanish translation and scholia.

The Abbé Brasseur de Bourbourg, a profound student of American archæology and languages (whose euhemeristic interpretations of the Mexican myths are as worthless as the priceless materials he unearthed are valuable) deplored, in a letter to the Duc de Valmy, the supposed loss of the *Popol Vuh*, which he was aware had been made use of early in the nineteenth century by a certain Don Felix Cabrera. Dr. C. Scherzer, an Austrian scholar, thus made aware of its value, paid a visit to the Republic of Guatemala in 1854 or 1855, and was successful in tracing the missing manuscript in the library of the University of San Carlos in the city of Guatemala. It was afterwards ascertained that its scholiast, Ximenes, had deposited it in the library of his convent at Chichicastenango, whence it passed to the San Carlos library in 1830.

Scherzer at once made a copy of the Spanish translation of the manuscript, which he published at Vienna in 1856 under the title of *Las Historias del origen de los Indios de Guatemala, par el R. P. F. Francisco Ximenes*. The Abbé Brasseur also took a copy of the original, which he published at Paris in 1861, with the title *Vuh Popol: Le Livre Sacré de Quichés, et les Mythes de l'Antiquité Américaine*. In this work the Kiché original and the Abbe's French translation are set forth side by side. Unfortunately both the Spanish and the French translations leave much to be desired so far as their accuracy is concerned, and they are rendered of little use by reason of the misleading notes which accompany them.

The name *Popol Vuh* signifies 'Record of the Community,' and its literal translation is 'Book of the Mat,' from the Kiché word 'pop' or 'popol,' a mat or rug of woven rushes or bark on which the entire family sat, and 'vuh' or 'uuh,' paper or book, from 'uoch' to write. The *Popol Vuh* is an example of a world-wide genre – a type of annals of which the first portion is pure mythology, which gradually shades off into pure history, evolving from the hero-myths of saga to the recital of the deeds of authentic personages. It may, in fact, be classed with the Heimskringla of Snorre, the Danish History of Saxo-Grammaticus, the Chinese History in the Five Books, the Japanese *Nihongi*, and, so far as its fourth book is concerned, it somewhat resembles the Pictish Chronicle.

The language in which the *Popol Vuh* was written, was, as has been said, the Kiché, a dialect of the great Maya-Kiché tongue spoken at the time of the Conquest from the borders of Mexico on the north to those of the present State of Nicaragua on the south; but whereas the Mayan was spoken in Yucatan proper, and the State of Chiapas, the Kiché was the tongue of the peoples of that part of Central America now occupied by the States of Guatemala, Honduras and San Salvador, where it is still used by the natives. It is totally different to the Nahuatl, the language of the people of Anahuac or Mexico, both as regards its origin and structure, and its affinities with other American tongues are even less distinct than the those between the Slavonic and Teutonic groups. Of this tongue the *Popol Vuh* is practically the only monument; at all events the only work by a native of the district in which it was used. A cognate dialect, the Cakchiquel, produced the 'Annals' of that people, otherwise known as *The Book of Chilan Balam*, a work purely of genealogical interest, which may be consulted in the admirable translation of the late Daniel G. Brinton.

The Kiché people at the time of their discovery, which was immediately subsequent to the fall of Mexico, had in part lost that culture which was characteristic of the Mayan race, the remnants of which have excited universal wonder in the ruins of the vast desert cities of Central America. At a period not far distant from the Conquest the once centralised Government of the Mayan peoples had been broken up into petty States and Confederacies, which in their character recall the city-states of mediæval Italy. In all probability the civilization possessed by these peoples had been brought them by a race from Mexico called the Toltecs, who taught them the arts of building in stone and writing in hieroglyphics, and who probably influenced their mythology most profoundly. The Toltecs were not, however, in any way cognate with the Mayans, and were in all likelihood rapidly absorbed by them. The Mayans were notably an agricultural people, and it is not impossible that in their country the maize-plant was first cultivated with the object of obtaining a regular cereal supply.

Such, then, were the people whose mythology produced the body of tradition and mythi-history known as the *Popol Vuh*; and you can read the tales from the first three books in the section on Mayan Myths (*see* page 280).

The Fourth Book

The Fourth Book brings us down to what is presumably history. We say 'presumably,' because we have only the bare testimony of the *Popol Vuh* to go upon. We can note therein the evolution of the Kiché people from a comparatively simple and pastoral state of society to a political condition of considerable complexity. This account of the later periods is extremely confused, and as the names of many of the Kiché monarchs are the same as those of the gods, it is often difficult to discriminate between saga and history. Interminable conflicts are the subject of most of this book, and by the time the transcriber reached the twelfth chapter he seems to have tired of his labours and to have made up his mind to conclude with a genealogical list of the Kiché kings. He here traces the genealogies of the three royal houses of Cavek, Nihaib, and Ahau-Kiché. The state of transition and turmoil in which the country was for many years after the conquest must have tended to the disappearance of native records of any kind, and our author does not appear to have been as well versed in the history of his country which immediately preceded his own time as he was in her mythology and legends. According to a tradition recited by Don Domingo Juarros in his *History of the Kingdom of Guatemala*, the Toltecs emigrated from the neighbourhood of Tula in Mexico by direction of an oracle, in consequence of the great increase of population in the reign of Nimaquiché, fifth King of the Toltecs. "In performing this journey they expended many years and suffered extraordinary hardships." Nimaquiché was succeeded by his son Aexopil, from whom was descended Kicab Tanub, the contemporary of Montezuma II. This does not at all agree with the *Popol Vuh* account.

Cosmogony of the Popol Vuh

The cosmogony of the *Popol Vuh* exhibits many signs of Christian influence, but it would be quite erroneous to infer that such influence was of a direct nature; that is, that the native compiler deliberately infused into the original narrative those outstanding features of the Christian cosmogony, which were undoubtedly quite familiar to him. The resemblance which is apparent between the first few chapters of the *Popol Vuh* and the creation-myth in Genesis is no more the result of design than was the metamorphosis of King Arthur's Brythonic warriors into Norman knights by the jongleurs. The inclusion of obviously Christian elements was undoubtedly unconscious. A native Guatemalan, nurtured in the Christian faith, could, in fact, quite be expected to produce an incongruous blending of Christian and pagan cosmogony such as is here dealt with.

But another and more important question arises in connection with the initial chapters of the *Popol Vuh* – those which give an account of the Kiché creation-myth. Under the veneer of Biblical cosmogony the original myth would appear to be the sum of more than one native creation-story. We have here a number of beings, each of whom appear in some manner to exercise the function of a creator, and it might be gathered from this that the account now before us was produced by the fusion and reconciliation of more than one legend connected with the creation – a reconciliation of early rival faiths. We have to guide us in this the proved facts of a composite Peruvian cosmogony. The ruling Inca caste skilfully welded together no less than four early creation-myths, reserving for their own divine ancestors the headship of the heavens. And it is not unreasonable to believe that the diverse ethnological elements of which the Maya-Kiché people were undoubtedly composed possessed divergent cosmogonies, which were reconciled to one another in the later traditional versions of the *Popol Vuh.*

This would lead to the further supposition that the *Popol Vuh* is a monument of very considerable antiquity. The fusion of religious beliefs is, even with savages, a work of many generations. It would be rash to attempt to discover any approximate date for the original conception of the *Popol Vuh.* The only version which we possess is that now under review, and as the lack of an earlier version makes comparison impossible, we are thus without the guidance with which the criteria of philology would undoubtedly furnish us. That the Mayan civilization was of very considerable antiquity is possible, although no adequate proof exists for the assumption. This much is certain: that at the period of the Conquest written language was still in a state of transition from the pictographic to the phonetic-ideographic stage, and that therefore no version of the *Popol Vuh* which had been fixed by its receiving literary form could have long existed. It is much more probable that it existed for many generations by being handed down from mouth to mouth – a manner of literary preservation exceedingly common with the American peoples. The memories of the natives of America were and still are matter for astonishment for all who come into contact with them. The Conquistadores were astounded at the ease with which the Mexicans could recite poems and orations of stupendous length, and numerous instances of Indian feats of mnemonics are on record.

It is worthy of notice that the Kiché myth embodies the general aboriginal idea of creation which prevailed in the New World. In many of them the central idea of creation is supplied by the brooding of a great bird over the dark primeval waste of waters. Thus the Athapascans thought that a mighty raven, with eyes of fire and wings whose clapping was as the thunder, descended to the ocean and raised the earth to its surface. The Muscokis believed that a couple of pigeons, skimming the surface of the deep, espied a blade of grass upon its surface, which slowly evolved into the dry land. The Zuñis imagined that Awonawilona, the All-father, so impregnated the waters that a scum appeared upon their surface which became the earth and sky. The Iroquois said that their female ancestor, expelled from heaven by her angry spouse, landed upon the sea, from which mud at once arose. The Mixtecs imagined that two winds – those of the Nine Serpents and the Nine Caverns – under the guise of a bird and a winged serpent respectively, caused the waters to subside and the land to appear. The Costa Rican Guaymis related, according to Melendez, that Noncomala waded into the water and met the water-nymph Rutbe, who bore him twins, the sun and moon. In all these accounts, from widely divergent nations, it is surprising to note such unanimity of belief; and when the tenacity of legend is borne in mind, it is perhaps not too rash to state a belief in an original American creation-myth, which seems none the less possible when the fact of the ethnological unity among the American tribes is remembered.

It is by no means difficult to satisfactorily prove the genuine American character of the *Popol Vuh.* In its case reading is believing. Macpherson, in his preface to the first edition of the poems of Ossian, says of an 'ingenious gentleman' that ere he had read the poems he thought and remarked that a man diffident of his abilities might well ascribe these compositions to a person living in a remote antiquity; but when he had perused them his sentiments were changed. He found they abounded too much with those ideas that only belong to an early state of society to be the work of a modern poet. However this may apply to the reputed compositions of the Goidelic bard, there can be no doubt that it can be used with justice as regards the *Popol Vuh.* To any one who has given it a careful examination it must be abundantly evident that it is a composition that has passed through several stages of development; that it is unquestionably of aboriginal origin; and that it has only been influenced by European thought in a secondary and unessential manner. The very fact that it was composed in the Kiché tongue is almost sufficient proof of its genuine American character. The scholarship of the nineteenth century was unequal to the adequate translation of the *Popol Vuh*; the twentieth century has as yet shown no signs of being able to accomplish the task. It is, therefore, not difficult to credit that if modern scholarship is unable to properly translate the work, that of the eighteenth century was unable to create it; no European of that epoch was sufficiently versed in Kiché theology and history to compose in faultless Kiché such a work as the *Popol Vuh,* breathing as it does in every line an intimate and natural acquaintance with the antiquities of Guatemala.

The *Popol Vuh* is not the only mythi-historical work composed by an aboriginal American. In Mexico Ixtlilxochitl, and in Peru Garcilasso de la Vega, wrote exhaustive treatises upon the history and customs of their native countrymen shortly after the conquests of Mexico and Peru, and hieroglyphic records, such as the *Wallam Olum*, are not unknown among the North American Indians. In fact, the intelligence which fails to regard the *Popol Vuh* as a genuine aboriginal production must be more sceptical than critical.

Kiché and Mexican Mythology

The connection of Kiché and Mayan mythology with that of Mexico is obvious, but not altogether proven. It is possible that the main lines of the three systems were similar; that certain great deities like Gucumatz were common to all, but that the inclusion of local gods lent a very different complexion to the three mythologies. It also seems not unreasonable to suppose that the Kiché people must have been more liable to influence from the south, that is, from the north of South America. The inclusion of an Antillean deity (Hurakan) in their pantheon practically proves that they were, and their relative proximity to the Caribs – the great maritime race of America – leads to the assumption that they may have been influenced by those roving merchants and sailors more or less profoundly. This, however, can only be matter for surmise, and, however strong the probabilities seem in favour of such a theory, proof is wanting to strengthen it.

The Pantheon of the Popol Vuh

It must be remembered that we are dealing with Kiché and not with Mayan mythology. Although the two had much in common, it would be most unsafe in the present state of knowledge to attempt to identify Kiché with Mayan deities; such an attempt would, indeed, assume the bulk of a formidable treatise. Scholarship at the present time hesitates to designate the representations of Mayan gods on the walls of 'buried' cities otherwise than by a letter of the alphabet, and it is therefore wise to thoroughly ignore the question of Mayan affinities in dealing with myths purely Kiché. This does not apply to the Kiché-Mexican affinities. Mexican and Kiché deities are mostly known quantities, but this cannot be said of their Mayan congenors. The reason for this is that until Mayan myth is reconciled with the evidence of the Mayan monuments no certitude can be arrived at. This cannot well be achieved until the Mayan hieroglyphs give up their secret, a contingency of which there is no immediate likelihood. Bearing this in mind, we may proceed to a brief consideration of the Kiché pantheon and its probable Mexican affinities.

Almost at the beginning we encounter a pair of masculine-feminine beings of a type nearly hermaphroditic, named Xpiyacoc and Xmucane, who are credited with a considerable share of the creation of organic life in the Kiché cosmogony. These, we will remember, appeared in the myth of Vukub-Cakix and elsewhere. The first appears to apply to the paternal function, whilst the name Xmucane is derived from words signifying 'feminine vigour.' The Mexican equivalents of these gods were probably Cipactonatl and Oxomoco, the 'father and mother gods.'

Deities who early arrest our attention are Tepeu, Gucumatz and Hurakan. The name of the first signifies 'king.' According to Brinton this in Kiché applies to rulership chiefly, inasmuch as the conjugal prowess often ascribed to monarchs by savage people is concerned. A creative faculty is obviously indicated in the name, but Brinton assumes that this Kiché generic name for king can also be rendered 'syphilitic,' especially as the name of the Mexican sun-god Nanahuatl has a similar significance.

That Tepeu was a generative force, a creative deity, there can be no doubt, but strangely enough in certain passages of the *Popol Vuh* we find him praying to and rendering homage to Hurakan, the 'Heart of Heaven.' We also find the latter along with Xpiyacoc, Xmucane and Tepeu jointly and severally responsible for the creation of the mannikins, if not for the whole cosmological scheme. This, of course, bears out the assumption of a composite origin of the creation-myth in the *Popol Vuh,* but it is nevertheless strange to find Hurakan, whom we must reckon an alien deity, at the head of these Olympic councils.

Cucumatz is one and the same with the Nahuatlacan – or, more properly speaking, Toltecan Quetzalcohuatl. The name is compounded from two Kiché words signifying 'Feathered Serpent,' and its meaning in the Nahuatl is precisely the same. Concerning the nature of this deity, there is probably more difference of opinion than in the case of any other known to comparative mythology. Strangely enough, although unquestionably an alien in the mythology of the Aztecan branch of the Nahuatlacâ, he bulks more largely in the myths of that people than in the legends of the Kichés. To the Aztecâ he seems to have appeared as a half-friendly Baal, to worship or revile according to the opportunism of national fortune. If he were here to be dealt with as his importance demands the limits of this monograph would speedily be surpassed. Although unquestionably the same god to both Mexicans and Kichés, he had acquired a significance in Aztecan eyes quite out of all proportion to his Kiché or Mayan importance. To the Aztecan mind he was a culture-hero, unalterably associated with the sun, and with the origins of their civilization. To the Toltecs he was the 'Man of the Sun,' the traveller, who, with staff in hand, symbolized the daily journey of the Sun-god. In all likelihood Quetzalcohuatl was evolved upon Mexican soil by the Toltecs, perhaps adopted from some older cultus by them. He was at least worshipped sedulously by aboriginal or pre-Aztecan tribes in Anahuac. Mr. Payne writes: "The fact that the worship of Quetzalcohuatl under the name of Cuculcan or Gucumatz was extensively prevalent in Yucatan and Central America, while no trace is found of the worship of Tezcatlipoca, strongly suggests that the founders of the Central American pueblos (the Toltecs) were, in fact, devotees of Quetzalcohuatl, who preferred exile and adventure in strange lands to accepting a religious innovation which was intolerable to them."

That Quetzalcohuatl was not an aboriginal Maya-Kiché deity is proved by the relative importance granted him by a people – the Aztecâ – to whom he was alien; and that they regarded him as the aboriginal god of Anahuac par excellence is indisputable. Hurakan, the winged creative power, is the wind of the tempest. In the *Popol Vuh* he is designated 'The Heart of Heaven.' He is parallel with if not identical to the Aztecan deity Tezcatlipoca, who in his variant of Yoalli-ehecatl (the Wind of Night) was supplicated by the Aztecâ as the life-breath. Elsewhere we have hinted that Tezcatlipoca may have been an ice-god. Mr. Payne sees in him an elaboration of the vision of death in a polished 'scrying'-stone, which seems possible but scarcely probable. Hurakan was in all likelihood derived from an original deity of the Antilles. The term 'hurricane' is said to have originated from the name of this god, and although the direct evidence for this is scanty, other circumstances place the connection beyond reasonable doubt. Hurakan is also alluded to in the *Popol Vuh,* as 'The Strong Serpent,' and 'He who hurls below,' referring to his presence in the lightning. Brinton is of opinion that the name Hurakan signifies 'giant,' but the sequence of proof is not altogether convincing. Hurakan had the assistance of three demiurges, named respectively Cakulha-Hurakan (lightning), Chipi-Cakulha (lightning-flash), and Raxa-Cakulha (track-of-the-lightning). Hun-Ahpu and Xbalanque, who appear in the first myth proper – that of the destruction of Vukub-Cakix, are certainly 'of the gods,' but seem to be only demi-gods. They are constantly alluded to as 'young men.' Brasseur de Bourbourg, who saw in the Vukub-Cakix myth the struggle between the Toltecs and the invading Nahuatlacâ, believed these hero-gods to be equivalents of Tezcatlipoca and Nanahuatl, but the resemblance appears to exist merely in the martial character of the deities, and is hardly noticeable in other details. Hun-Ahpu would appear to signify 'The Master,' but Brinton translates the name as 'Magician.' It may have a reconciliatory translation as 'Adept.' A variant is the name of his father Hun-Hun-Ahpu, 'Each-one-a-Magician,' and some confusion is apparent in the Vukub-Cakix myth between the two names; but as the Abbé Brasseur de Bourbourg so justly observes, "these names are so symbolic in character that their absolute elucidation is impossible." Xbalanque signifies 'Little Tiger.'

"The gods of the Kichés were legion," but the foregoing list embraces practically all the deities proper with whom we have to deal in the *Popol Vuh.*

The Vukub-Cakix Myth

The outstanding point of interest in the myth of Vukub-Cakix and his two sons is its terrestrial significance. That they were of the earth as truly as were the Jotuns of Scandinavian mythology there can be no doubt. Like the Jotuns or the Titans, Vukub-Cakix and his progeny are made from the earth, and the parent giant is a living representation of its surface. Xpiyacoc and Xmucane remove his emerald teeth, and replace them with maize grains – surely a mythical interpretation or allegory of the removal of the green virgin turf of the earth, and its replacement by the maize seed. It is further worthy of notice that the maize is placed in Vukub-Cakix's mouth by divine beings. In the third book of the *Popol Vuh* it is stated that the gods gave maize to man. It was, indeed, brought to earth from heaven by the sacred animals.

Book II Commented Upon

The Second Book of the *Popol Vuh* is the most interesting of the four from a mythological point of view. That it treats of the dealings of the Kichés with the aboriginal people of the district they afterwards inhabited is not unlikely. Although the opinion of Brasseur that Xibalba was a prehistoric state which had Palenque for its capital is an exaggeration of whatsoever kernel of fact may be contained in the myth, yet it is not unlikely that the Abbé, who so often astonishes without illuminating, has in this instance come near the truth. The cliff-dwellings of Mexico and Colorado have of late years aroused speculation as to the aboriginal or directly prehistoric peoples of these regions. The *Popol Vuh* definitely describes Xibalba as the metropolis of an 'Underworld'; and with such examples as that of the Cliff Palace Cañon in Colorado before us, it is difficult to think that allusion is not made to some such semi-underground abode. There the living rock has been excavated to a considerable distance, advantage being taken of a huge natural recess to secure greater depth than could possibly have been attained by human agency, and in this immense alcove the ruins of a veritable city may still be seen, almost as well preserved as in the days of its evacuation, its towers, battlements and houses being as well marked and as plainly discernible as are the ruins of Philæ. It is then not unreasonable to suppose that in a more northerly home the Kichés may have warred with a race which dwelt in some such subterranean locality. A people's idea of an 'otherworld' is often coloured by the configuration of their own country.

One thing is certain: a hell, an abode of bad spirits as distinguished from beneficent gods, Xibalba was *not*. The American Indian was innocent of the idea of maleficent deities pitted in everlasting warfare against good and life-giving gods until contact with the whites coloured his mythology with their idea of the dual nature of supernatural beings. The transcriber of the *Popol Vuh* makes this clear so far as Kiché belief went. Dimly conscious that the *Popol Vuh* was coloured by his agency with the opinions of a lately adopted Christianity, he says of the Lords of Xibalba, Hun-Came and Vukub-Came: "In the old times they did not have much power. They were but annoyers and opposers of men, and, in truth, *they were not regarded as gods*." If not regarded as gods, then, what were they?

"The devil," says Cogolludo of the Mayas, "is called by them Xibilba, which means he who disappears or vanishes." The derivation of Xibalba is from a root meaning "to fear" from which comes the name for a ghost or phantom. Xibalba was, then, the Place of Phantoms. But it was not the Place of Torment, the abode of a devil who presided over punishment. The idea of sin is weak in the savage mind; and the idea of punishment for sin in a future state is unknown in pre-Christian American mythology.

"Under the influence of Christian catechising," says Brinton, "the Quiché legends portray this really as a place of torment, and its rulers as malignant and powerful; but as I have before pointed out they do so protesting that such was not the ancient belief, and they let fall no word that shows that it was regarded as the destination of the morally bad. The original meaning of the name given by Cogolludo points unmistakably to the simple fact of disappearance from among men, and corresponds in harmlessness to the true sense of those words of fear, Scheol, Hades, Hell, all signifying hidden from sight, and only endowed with more grim associations by the imaginations of later generations."

The idea of consigning elder peoples, who have been displaced in the land to an underworld, is not uncommon in mythology. The Xibalbans, or aborigines, were perhaps cave- or earth-dwellers like the Picts of Scottish folk-lore, gnomeish, and full of elvish tricks, as such folk usually are. Vanished people are, too, often classed with the dead, or as lords of the dead. It is well known, also, that legend speedily crystallises around the name of a dispossessed race, to whom is attributed every description of magic art. This is sometimes accounted for by the fact that the displaced people possessed a higher culture than their invaders, and sometimes, probably, by the dread which all barbarian peoples have of a religion in any way differing from their own. Thus the Norwegians credited the Finns – their predecessors in Norway – with tremendous magical powers, and similar instances of respectful timidity shown by invading races towards the original inhabitants of the country they had conquered could readily be multiplied. To be tricked the barbarian regards as a mortal indignity, as witness the wrath of Thor in Jotunheim, comparable with the sensitiveness of Hun-Ahpu and Xbalanque lest they should be outwitted by the Xibalbans.

The Harrying of Xibalba

The doings of Hun-Ahpu and Xbalanque, in Xibalba, may be regarded either as the Kiché account of the adventures of two veritable heroes in a new land, or as the visitation of divine beings to Hades for the express purpose of conquering death. But by the period of the formation of the myth it is probable that Xibalba had become confounded with the Place of the Dead, and was regarded as a fit theatre for the prodigies of craft and valour of the young hero-gods. The Kiché Hades had, in fact, evolved from the old northern home, exactly as had the Mexican Mictlan, which, although a subterranean locality, was also, and separately, a northern country. A complete Place of the Dead had been established, and the gods, to show their contempt of death, must descend thereto and emerge triumphant. The idea of metempsychosis was known to the American aboriginal mind. "We Indians shall not for ever die; even the grains of corn we put under the earth grow up and become living things," is the noble and touching reply of a chief to the interrogation of a Moravian Brother, regarding the native belief in immortality. Man must have the example of the gods, if he wishes to live in peace and quiet assurance of immortality. And just as we believe that our God descended into Hell and vanquished Sin and Death, so did these simple people gain strength to face Eternity from the thought that they had been preceded in the dark journey by the Immortals.

It is evident that the divine brothers feared ridicule, and profiting from the disasters of their father and uncle made sure of knowing the names of the chief Xibalbans ere they set out. In like manner they avoided making an obeisance to the dummy figures to which their predecessors had bowed so profoundly. The American savage, grave and reserved, cannot abide ridicule. He shrinks from it in a manner which a less self-regarding or a more self-assured people cannot comprehend. The other tests – the 'House of Tigers,' and the 'House of Cold,' and the various torments mentioned in the Second Book are much what might be expected from a barbarian idea of death – no more horrible, perhaps, than the European idea of Hell in the Middle Ages, certainly not more fear-compelling than the picture of Dante.

The American peoples are at one in their belief in a Paradise, a Place of Joy, if not of Reward. Their Hades appears to have been reserved almost entirely for the unillustrious. Paradise in some American mythologies, notably in that of Mexico, and perhaps in that of Peru, is nothing more than a preserve of the great; the poor might not enter therein, no more than might the coward pass the gates of the Norse Valhalla. It was to Mictlan or Supay, then, that the popular mind turned. How did the American peoples regard this drear abode? To enter it one must cross a deep and swift river by means of a bridge formed of a slender tree, said the Hurons and Iroquois to the first missionaries. On this frail passage the soul must defend itself from the attacks of a savage dog. The Chepewayan Athapascans told of a great water which the soul must cross in a stone canoe; the Chilians, of a western sea, where toll must be given to an evil hag, who plucked out an eye if payment were not forthcoming; the Algonquins, of a stream bridged by an enormous snake. The Aztecs called this river Chicunoapa, the Nine Rivers, where the departed must pay toll to a dog and a dragon. It will be recollected that the brothers in the *Popol Vuh,* cross a river of blood. This almost certainly alludes to the ocean under the red beams of the setting sun, towards which all these voyages are made.

The hero-gods in the myth voluntarily succumb to the power of the Lords of Death, and after being burned their bones are ground in a mill and thrown into the waters. The belief was almost universal in America that the soul resided in the bones. The bones were the basis of the man. Flesh would readily perish, but would return to clothe this more lasting foundation. So in many tribes the bones of the dead were carefully preserved. In all Central American countries the bones of distinguished persons were preserved in temples or council-houses in the small chests made of cane mentioned by the chroniclers of De Soto's expedition. This, too, may possibly have been the origin of mummification in Peru. In Egypt all the members and intestines must be preserved, in Peru only the bones. The state of comparative desiccation in which most Peruvian mummies are discovered proves that the preservation of the flesh or organs was not regarded as a necessity.

The game of ball figures very largely throughout the Third Book. The father and uncle of the young hero-gods were worsted in their favourite sport by the Xibalbans, but Hun-Ahpu and Xbalanque in their turn vanquish the Lords of the Underworld. This may have resembled the Mexican game of tlachtli, which was played in an enclosed court with a rubber ball between two opposite sides, each of two or three players. It was, in fact, not unlike hockey. This game of ball between the Powers of Light and the Powers of Darkness is somewhat reminiscent of that between Ormuzd and Ahriman in Persian myth. The game of tlachtli had a symbolic reference to stellar motions.

Book III Commented Upon

We are here engaged with the problem which the origin of man presented to the Kiché mind, and we shall find that its solution bears a remarkable likeness to that of similar American myths. We seldom hear of one first-created being. In the creation-myths of the New World four brothers are usually the progenitors of the human race. Man in these myths is nearly always earth-born. He and his fellows emerge from some cavern or subterranean place, fully grown and fully armed. Thus the Blackfoot Indians emerged from Nina-stahu, a peak in the Rockies. In the centre of Nunne Chaha, the High Hill, was a cavern, the house of the Master of Breath, whence came the Choctaws. The Peruvians come from Pacari Tambu, the House of the Dawn, near Cuzco, and an ancient legend of the Aztecâ states that they came from Chicomoztoc, the Seven Caverns, to the north of Mexico.

We find the first Mayan men speedily engaged in migration. Such must always be the life of the unsettled and unagricultural savage. He multiplies. Gods are given to each tribe. These he bears to a new country. In fact we have a complete migration myth in the Third Book of the *Popol Vuh,* and there are not wanting signs to show that this migration took place from the cold north to the warm south. The principal item of proof in favour of such a theory is, of course, the statement that the sun was 'not at first born,' and that at a later stage of the journey, when his beams appeared upon the horizon, it was as a weaker and dimmer luminary that he seemed to the wanderers than in after years. The allusion to 'shining sand,' by the aid of which they crossed rivers, may mean that they forded them when covered with ice. The whole myth is so strikingly akin to the Aztecân migration-myth given in the Mexican MS. in the Boturini Collection (No. 14, sec. viii.) that we cannot refrain from appending a short passage from the latter:

"This is the beginning of the record of the coming of the Mexicans from the place called Aztlan. It is by means of the water that they came this way, being four tribes, and in coming they rowed in boats. They built their huts on piles at the place called the Grotto of Quinevayan. It is there from which the eight tribes issued. The first tribe is that of the Huexotzincos, the second tribe the Chalcas, the third the Xochimilcas, the fourth the Cuitlavacas, the fifth the Mallinalcas, the sixth the Chicimecas, the seventh the Tepanecas, the eighth the Matlatzincas. It is there where they were founded in Colhuacan. They were the colonists of it since they landed there, coming from Aztlan.... It is there that they soon afterwards went away from, carrying before them the god Vitzillopochtli, which they had adopted for their god.... They came out of four places, when they went forward travelling this way.... There the eight tribes opened up our road *by water*."

We find a similar myth in the Wallam Olum, or painted records of the Lenape Indians. "After the flood," says this record, "the Lenape with the manly turtle beings dwelt close together at the cave house and dwelling of Talli.... They saw that the snake land was bright and wealthy. Having all agreed, they went over the *water of the frozen sea* to possess the land. It was wonderful when they all went over the smooth deep water of the frozen sea at the gap of snake sea in the great ocean."

We thus see that the Third Book of the *Popol Vuh* is a migration saga of a type not uncommon in America. Asiatic tribes may have come down from the Chi-Pixab of the *Popol Vuh* to British Columbia, and thence by easy stages to Central America. And the Third Book of the *Popol Vuh* may be the distant echo of a mighty wave of colonization, whose sound swept the entire surface of the New World.

Construction of the Houses of Yucatan

And: Obedience and Respect of the Indians for their Chiefs; Headgear and Wearing of Garments

IN BUILDING THEIR HOUSES their method was to cover them with an excellent thatch they have in abundance. or with the leaves of a palm well adapted to that purpose, the roof being very steep to prevent its raining through. They then run a wall lengthways of the whole house, leaving certain doorways into the half which they call the back of the house, where they have their beds. The other half they whiten with a very fine whitewash, and the chiefs also have beautiful frescos there.

This part serves for the reception and lodging of guests, and has no doorway but is open along the whole length of the house. The roof drops very low in front as a protection against sun and rain; also, they say, the better to defend the interior from enemies in case of necessity.

The common people build the chiefs' dwellings at their own expense. The houses having no doors, it is held a grave offense to do any wrong to another's house; in the back, however, they have a small door for household uses. They sleep on beds made of small rods, covered with mats, and with their mantles of cotton as covering. In the summer they sleep in the front part of the house on the mats, especially the men. Away from the house the entire village sows the fields of the chief, cares for them, and harvests what is required for him and his household; and whenever they hunt and fish, or at the salt gathering time, they always give a part to the chief; in these matters everything is always in common.

If the chief should die his eldest son would succeed him, but the others would always be much respected, favoured and held as lords. The leading men, lower than the chief, are favoured in all these matters according to who they are, or the favour shown them by the chief. The priests live upon their benefices and offerings. The chiefs govern the town, settling suits, ordering and adjusting the affairs of the commonwealths, doing all through the hands of the leading men. These latter are much honoured and obeyed, especially the wealthy, the chiefs visiting them and holding court at their houses for the settlement of affairs and business, this being done principally at night.

Whenever the chiefs leave the town they have a great company in attendance, and the same when they leave their houses.

The Indians of Yucatan are people of good physique, tall, robust and of great strength, and commonly are all bow-legged from having in their infancy been carried astride the mother's hip when they are taken somewhere. It was held as a grace to be cross-eyed, and this was artificially brought about by the mothers, who in infancy suspended a small plaster from the hair down between the eyebrows and reaching the eyes; this constantly binding, they finally became cross-eyed. They also had their heads and foreheads flattened from infancy by their mothers. Their ears were pierced for earrings and much scarified from the sacrifices. They did not grow beards and say that their mothers were used to burn their faces with hot cloths to prevent the growth. Nowaday beards are grown, although they are very rough, like hogs' bristles.

They allowed their hair to grow like the women; on top they ringed it, making a, good tonsure. Thus it grew long below but short on the crown; it was braided and wound around the head, with an end left behind like a queue. All the men used mirrors, and the women not; and to call a man a cuckold they said his wife had put the mirror in his hair behind his head. They bathed a great deal, not troubling to cover themselves before the women, except such as they might do with the hand. They were devoted to perfumes, having bouquets of flowers and odorous plants, arranged with much care and art. They painted their faces and bodies red, disfiguring themselves, though to them it seemed handsome.

Their clothing was a strip of cloth a hand broad that served for breeches and leggings, and which they wrapped several times about the waist, leaving one end hang in front and one behind. These ends were embroidered by their wives with much care and with featherwork. They wore large square mantles, which they threw over the shoulders. They wore sandals of hemp or deerskin tanned dry, and then no other garments.

Food and Drink of the Indians of Yucatan

THEIR PRINCIPAL SUSTENANCE IS MAIZE, of which they prepare various dishes and drinks; and even drunk as they do it, it serves as their food and drink. The Indian women put the maize to soak the night before in lime and water, and in the morning it is soft and half-cooked, having in the process lost the husk and nib. They next grind it on stones, and when half ground make it into great balls and loads for the use of labourers, travellers and sailors. In that shape it keeps for several months, except for souring. Of this they then take a lump and dissolve it in a vessel or gourd formed by the rind of a fruit that grows on a tree, whereby God has provided them with vessels; out of this they drink the liquor and then eat the rest, it being of excellent taste and very nourishing. From the maize that is more fully ground they take away the milk and thicken it at the fire, making a sort of curd for morning use; and this they drink hot. Upon what is left from the morning they put water for drinking through the day, since they are not accustomed to drink water alone. They also toast the maize and then grind and mix it with water into a very refreshing drink, putting into it a little Indian pepper or cacao.

Out of maize and ground cacao they make a sort of froth that is very delicious, and with which they celebrate their festivals. From the cacao they extract a grease that is much like butter, and from this together with maize, they prepare another agreeable and much esteemed drink. Still another is made from the substance of the ground maize, raw, which is also fresh and tasty. They prepare many kinds of bread, good and healthful, except that it is not good to eat when cold; so that the Indian women are kept busy with making it twice a day. They have not learned how to make flour that can be kneaded like wheat flour, and when they do make it as one makes wheat bread, it is good for nothing. They make ragouts of vegetables and venison, and of wild and domestic fowls of which there are plenty, and of fish of which there are plenty. Thus they have good provisions, especially since they are raising Spanish pigs and fowls.

In the mornings they take their hot drink with pepper, as we have said: through the day the cold drinks and in the evening the ragouts. When they have no meat they make their sauces of pepper and vegetables. The men and women do not eat together, but eat apart, on the ground; or if there is much, with a mat for a table. They live well when they have it, and endure hunger equally well when they have not, getting along on very little. After eating they wash their hands and mouth.

Painting and Tattooing of the Indians

And: Their Orgies, Wines and Banquests; Their Comedies, Music and Dances

THEY TATTOO THEIR BODIES and are accounted valiant and brave in proportion to its amount, for the process is very painful. In doing it the craftsman first covers the part he wishes with colour, and then delicately pierces the pictures in the skin, so that the blood and colour leaves the outlines on the body. This they do a little at a time, on account of the pain and because of the disorders that ensue; for the places fester and form matter. But for all this they ridicule those who are not tattooed. They set much store on amiability and the showing of graces and natural accomplishments; today they eat and drink as we do.

The Indians are very dissolute in drinking and becoming intoxicated, and many ills follow their excesses in this way. They kill each other; violate their beds, the poor women thinking they are receiving their own husbands; they treat their own fathers and mothers as if they were in the houses of enemies; they set fire to their houses, and so destroy themselves in their drunkenness. When the carouse is general, and for the sacrifices, all contribute to it; when private, the cost is borne by the entertainer, with the aid of his parents. Their wine they make of honey and water and the root of a certain tree they grow for the purpose, and which gives the wine strength and a very disagreeable odour. At their dances and merry-makings they eat seated two by two, or in fours. After the eating the cup-bearers, who have had to remain sober, help themselves from great jars until they are overcome, and their wives have great trouble in getting their drunken husbands home.

They often spend on one banquet all they have made by many days of trading or scheming. They have two methods of making these feasts; the first of these (that of the chiefs and leading men) obliges each guest to return an invitation to his host; to each guest the host must give a roast fowl and cacao and drinks in abundance, and after the banquet it is the custom to present each with a mantle to wear, with a small stand and a cup, as fine as the host can afford. If one of the guests has died, the obligation to give the return invitation lies on his house or parents.

The other kind is between kinsfolk, when they marry their children or celebrate the deeds of their ancestors. This does not have to be returned, except that if a hundred Indians have invited one to a feast, all are invited by him when he makes a feast or marries his children.

They think much of friendship and remember these invitations even when separated far from each other. At the banquets the drink is passed by beautiful women, who, after handing the goblet, turn the back until it is emptied.

The Indians have delightful ways of entertainment; particularly they have actors who perform with great skill, to such an extent as that they hire themselves to the Spaniards for nothing other than to observe the jests the Spaniards pass with their servants, their wives, and on themselves over their good or bad serving; all of this they act later with as much art as attentive Spaniards could.

They have small drums which they strike with the hand, and another drum of hollow wood that gives a deep, mournful sound. This they hit with a longish stick at the end of which is a ball of a certain gum that exudes from a tree. They have long, thin trumpets of hollow wood, the end of which is formed of a large twisted gourd. They have another instrument made of a whole tortoise with its shells, from which the flesh has been removed; this they strike with the palm of the hand, giving a mournful, sad sound.

They have whistles of cane and of deer hones, also large conchs and reed flutes; with these instruments they accompany the dancers. Two of their dances are especially virile and worth seeing; one is a game of reeds, whence they call it *colomché*, the word having that meaning [a 'palisade of sticks']. To perform it they make a large circle of dancers, whom the music accompanies, and in time with which two come into the circle; one of these dances erect, holding a handful of reeds, while the other dances squatting, both keeping time around the circle. The one with the reeds throws them with all his force at the other, who with great skill catches them with a small rod. When all are thrown they return, keeping time, into the circle, and others come out to do the same.

There is another dance in which 800 Indians, or more or less, dance with small flags in a great war measure, among all of them not one being out of time. They are heavy in their dances, since they do not cease dancing for the entire day, food and drink being brought to them. The men do not dance with the women.

Chichén Itzá

THE FIRST HISTORICAL NOTICE of the Maya Indians comes to us from Columbus, who did not get in touch with the more civilized races of America until the end of his career as an explorer, and then by an unlucky chance he failed to follow up the clue. During his fourth voyage Columbus landed on Bonacca, one of the Ruatan group of islands lying about thirty miles from the northern coast of Honduras, and the story of his meeting with the Maya Indians is well told by Washington Irving: –

"The Adelantado, with two launches full of people, landed on the principal island, which was extremely verdant and fertile. The inhabitants resembled those of other islands, excepting that their foreheads were narrower. While the Adelantado was on shore, he beheld a great canoe arriving, as from a distant and important voyage. He was struck with its magnitude and contents. It was eight feet wide, and as long as a galley, though formed of the trunk of a single tree. In the centre was a kind of awning or cabin of palm-leaves, after the manner of those in the gondolas of Venice, and sufficiently close to exclude both sun and rain. Under this sat a cacique with his wives and children. Twenty-five Indians rowed the canoe, and it was filled with all kinds of articles of the manufacture and natural production of the adjacent countries. It is supposed that this bark had come from the province of Yucatan, which is about forty leagues distant from this island.

"The Indians in the canoe appeared to have no fear of the Spaniards, and readily went alongside of the admiral's caravel. Columbus was overjoyed at thus having brought to him at once, without trouble or danger, a collection of specimens of all the important articles of this part of the New World. He examined, with great curiosity and interest, the contents of the canoe. Among various utensils and weapons similar to those already found among the natives, he perceived others of a much superior kind. There were hatchets for cutting wood, formed not of stone but copper; wooden swords, with channels on each side of the blade, in which sharp flints were firmly fixed by cords made of the intestines of fishes; being the same kind of weapon afterwards found among the Mexicans. There were copper bells, and other articles of the same metal, together with a rude kind of crucible in which to melt it; various vessels and utensils neatly formed of clay, of marble, and of hard wood; sheets and mantles of cotton, worked and dyed with various colours; great quantities of cacao, a fruit as yet unknown to the Spaniards, but which, as they soon found, the natives held in great estimation, using it both as food and money. There was a beverage also extracted from maize or Indian corn, resembling beer. Their provisions consisted of bread made of maize, and roots of various kinds, similar to those of Hispaniola. From among these articles, Columbus collected such as were important to send as specimens to Spain, giving the natives European trinkets in exchange, with which they were highly satisfied. They appeared to manifest neither astonishment nor alarm when on board of the vessels, and surrounded by people who must have been so strange and wonderful to them. The women wore mantles, with which they wrapped themselves, like the female Moors of Granada, and the men had cloths of cotton round their loins. Both sexes appeared more particular about these coverings, and to have a quicker sense of personal modesty than any Indians Columbus had yet discovered.

"These circumstances, together with the superiority of their implements and manufactures, were held by the admiral as indications that he was approaching more civilized nations. He endeavoured to gain particular information from these Indians about the surrounding countries; but as they spoke a different language from that of his interpreters, he could understand them but imperfectly. They informed him that they had just arrived from a country, rich, cultivated, and industrious, situated to the west. They endeavoured to impress him with an idea of the wealth and magnificence of the regions, and the people in that quarter, and urged him to steer in that direction. Well would it have been for Columbus had he followed their advice. Within a day or two he would have arrived at Yucatan; the discovery of Mexico and the other opulent countries of New Spain would have necessarily followed; the Southern Ocean would have been disclosed to him, and a succession of splendid discoveries would have shed fresh glory on his declining age, instead of its sinking amidst gloom, neglect, and disappointment."

Intent on discovering a strait by which he might gain the southern sea, Columbus ignored the advice of the Indians to travel towards the west, and thus the discovery of Yucatan and Mexico was left to others.

In the year 1517 an expedition was organized in Cuba under the command of Francisco Hernandez de Cordova, for the purpose of discovering new lands to the westward, and among the volunteers who joined the expedition was that perfect type of the Spanish 'conquistador,' Bernal Diaz del Castillo, who was the eye-witness of so many stirring events of those days, and whose delightful account of his adventures, dictated to his children in his old age, is one of the most valuable contributions to the history of the time. On leaving the west end of the island of Cuba the three vessels which carried the explorers were nearly lost in a severe storm, and it was not until the twenty-first day of the voyage that they made land near Cape Catoche, the north-east point of Yucatan. Here, for the first time, the Spaniards saw Indian houses built of stone; to quote Bernal Diaz, "From the ships we saw a great town about two leagues from the shore; as we had never seen in Cuba so great and populous a place we named it 'El Gran Cairo.'" The natives, who came off to the vessels in large dug-out canoes, made friendly overtures to the Spaniards and induced them to land and march towards the town, but as soon as the Spaniards got into broken ground a treacherous attack was made on them, and they were forced to retreat and take refuge in their ships. The expedition then coasted along the north and west shore of Yucatan, until it reached the town of Campeche, when again men were landed, and this time met with a somewhat better reception from the natives. "They led us," Bernal Diaz writes, "to some very large houses well built of stone and plaster, which were the sanctuaries of their Idols, where we saw figures of great serpents and other Idols carved and painted on the walls surrounding an altar which was drenched with blood still fresh."

The next landing was made a little further down the coast at Champoton, where the explorers received such a rough handling from the Indians that only one of them escaped unhurt, and Hernandez de Cordova himself died of his wounds on the return voyage when within a few days' sail of Cuba. Throughout the account of this expedition Bernal Diaz notes the bravery of the Indians, who fought the Spaniards hand to hand, and the excellence of their clothing, their arms, and their buildings. During the following year another expedition was despatched, under the command of Juan de Grijalva, who, also failing to make any headway against the natives of Yucatan, continued his voyage to the westward, discovered the coast of Mexico, and brought to light the riches of that country. The success of Grijalva's expedition fully aroused the interest of the Spaniards, and it was immediately followed up in February 1519 by the far-famed expedition under the command of Hernan Cortés, which resulted in the conquest of Mexico. Cortés, like his predecessors, on leaving Cuba made for the coast of Yucatan, but after a stay of some days' duration in the Island of Cozumel, he pushed on round the coast without delay to the mouth of the Tabasco River, where he fought a battle with the natives and took formal possession of the land in the name of the King of Spain. No attempt, however, was then made at colonization, and Cortés re-embarked his soldiers and pressed on to the rich prize of Mexico. Five years later, after Mexico had been conquered, Cortés returned to the province of Tabasco, and thence crossed the base of the peninsula of Yucatan in the course of his celebrated march to Honduras.

No effort was made to subdue the Mayas of Yucatan until the year 1528, when Francisco de Montejo, who had been appointed Adelantado of Yucatan, landed on the north-east coast with four hundred Spaniards and marched towards the interior. Unfortunately no contemporary record of this expedition is in existence, and we know little more than the fact that at the end of two years the Spaniards were driven from the country. It was not until the year 1540 that any further attempt was made at conquest; in that year Francisco de Montejo, the son of the Adelantado, marched inland from Campeche, and two years later founded the town of Merida, the present capital of the country, whilst his cousin, another Francisco de Montejo, marched to the eastward and founded a settlement at

Chuaca, which a few years later was moved to the present site of the town of Valladolid. From this time forward the dominion of the Spaniards over the northern and western portions of Yucatan remained undisturbed, but they never succeeded in subduing the natives in the central and eastern part of the province, and the Santa Cruz Indians maintain their independence of the Mexican Government to the present day.

The northern part of Yucatan is little better than a coral-reef raised a few feet above sea-level, covered with a thin coating of earth which supports a scrubby growth not worthy of the name of forest. The sea around the coast is everywhere shallow, and to the northward the great Bank of Yucatan extends for more than eighty miles from the shore before the line of fifty fathoms is reached. We had drifted over the edge of this bank in a steamer with a broken shaft on my return from Guatemala in 1885, and found an anchorage in forty-five fathoms of water at a distance of over fifty miles from the land. The most curious fact about this strange country is the total absence of rivers and even of streamlets. The heavy rainfall soaks through the porous limestone rock and oozes out again along the northern coast-line. The water-supply of the inhabitants is found in deep caves or openings in the limestone, known as *cenotes*, the Spanish form of a Maya word, which the reader will nearly approach by trying to pronounce *tznot* as a monosyllable.

With a low coast-line, a shallow sea, and an absence of rivers, follows a lack of good harbours; at Progreso there is merely an open roadstead, where the steamers anchor two miles from the shore, and at Campeche the conditions are much the same, only small vessels finding a little shelter by lying inside a raised coral bank.

On my voyages between Livingston and New Orleans I had frequently passed along the coast of Yucatan and had twice caught sight of the small ruined temple on the Island of Mugeres; but it was not until the winter of 1888-89 that I was able to set foot in the country with the purpose of examining some of the ruins, and I then chose Chichén Itzá as the site giving promise of the best results. There were disadvantages in thus breaking new ground, not the least of which was the absence of my faithful companions Gorgonio Lopez and his brothers, and I was well aware how greatly I should miss their assistance. Landing at Progreso on Christmas Eve I went on by rail, for a distance of about twenty-five miles, through a flat and uninteresting country to the city of Merida, and at once commenced preparations for the journey to Chichén.

I was soon to have experience of the inconvenience which may easily arise from the want of a good harbour, for the captain of the steamer carrying all my heavy baggage, encountering a heavy 'norther' as he approached the port of Progreso, preferred the open sea to anchorage on a lee shore, and passed on to make the round of the gulf ports before returning to land my cargo at Progreso a fortnight later.

Merida, as described by Stephens, was a charming, old-fashioned, out-of-the-world, sleepy city, with a cultivated and hospitable upper class of Spaniards and a picturesque population of Mestizos and Indians. Merida, as I found it, was a modernized Spanish-American town in the throes of a 'hemp' boom. The picturesqueness of the half-caste population remained, but there all the charm ended. There is only one product of the country which Europeans have found profit in cultivating for export, and that is the *Agave rigida*, a plant nearly related to the American aloe, which is known locally as 'Henequen,' and produces a fibre that has become of considerable commercial importance under the name of 'Sisal hemp.' It is to the increased demand for this fibre that at the time of my arrival the people of Yucatan owed a somewhat sudden access of riches. The rocky soil seems to suit the plant to perfection, the cultivation is simple and not very laborious, and cheap machinery had been devised for the extraction of the fibre from the leaves, so that for some time past it had been possible to sell the product at two cents a pound and leave a fair margin of profit. The henequen fibre is much inferior to that extracted from the stem of the banana and known as Manila hemp, but so small has the world become that a hurricane in Manila which destroyed the banana plants at once brought wealth to Yucatan. The loss of the Manila crop was accentuated by the increased demand for twine in North America for use in the reaping and binding machines which are so largely employed in harvesting the gigantic wheat-crop of the Western States, so that during my stay in Yucatan the price of henequen rose to thirteen cents a pound!

This was not a fortunate state of affairs for me, as I had need of many hands to help in clearing the ruins, and now that every proprietor was eager to increase the size of his henequen plantation, field-labourers were in great demand; I could only hope that as Chichén Itzá lay far from the centre of commercial activity, the villages in its neighbourhood might for some time yet escape the effects of the 'boom.' I had been accustomed in Guatemala and Honduras to depend to a great extent on the assistance of the local officials in engaging labourers; but although, through the kindness of the English Minister, I had come with ample recommendations from the Mexican Government to the local authorities, I found that I could not look for the same favourable result in Yucatan, as the Indians are less under the control of officials than they are under that of a small number of powerful Spanish families who are all large land-holders. Although the status of slavery does not legally exist, custom is slow in dying, and the greater number of Indian labourers are still tied to the soil.

After a month of weary waiting in Merida, during which time the only pleasant episodes were a short visit to Mr. E. Thompson, the United States Consul, who was at work exploring the ruins at Labná, and a day spent at the celebrated ruins of Uxmal, I was at last able to set out to the eastward, travelling the first day by rail, and then in a springless cart, known as a *volan coche*, to the town of Yzamal. This town occupies the site of an ancient Indian city, and the great pyramidal foundations which formerly supported the Maya temples are still the most prominent feature in the landscape.

At Yzamal I was most hospitably received by Dr. Gaumer, an American gentleman who has long been a collector of natural-history specimens for the Editors of the *Biologia Centrali-Americana*, and to him and to Mrs. Gaumer I was indebted for numerous acts of kindness during my stay in the country. Thence I pushed on to the town of Valladolid, which, with the exception of Comitan in Honduras, I may safely say is the most dead-alive town it has ever been my fate to enter. Here I presented letters from the Government to the local authorities, and made the best arrangements I could effect for a supply of labourers. I then returned by the main road as far as 'Citas, and on the 6th February rode by a bush track to Pisté, a small village about two miles distant from the ruins of Chichén Itzá.

When Stephens and Catherwood visited Chichén in 1842, a flourishing hacienda had been established among the ruins, and the ground was in part kept clear for pasturing cattle. A few years later, in 1847, the untamed Indians from the south made a raid into the settled portion of Yucatan, destroyed the hacienda at Chichén and the village of Pisté and carried their ravages, I believe, as far as Yzamal. At the time of my visit the village of Pisté had been partly re-occupied and some of the ruined houses had been rebuilt, but the large church was still roofless and the whole of the site of the ancient city, as well as the church and buildings of the Hacienda, was covered by a dense jungle.

For the first few days I put up in the house of Stephen, the village judge and far the most important person in the small community. He was a young man, well-built and athletic, with frank and pleasant manners, and a certain air of command about him which became him well; altogether he was a capital specimen of a half-caste yeoman. He was perhaps a little too fond of *aguardiente*, but he seemed to live a happy life in a somewhat patriarchal fashion. His legal wife (for there were some others in the background) was the mother of a most delightful boy, about four years old, a child who would have attracted attention in any part of the world for his robust beauty and his charming genial manners and fearless ways. The villagers adored this boy, and in return he lorded it over them royally; he never showed any shyness of me, and we became fast friends at once; he used to prattle away to me in Maya about all that was going on, although I could not understand a word of his language. I don't think I ever met a child who attracted me so much, and it was hard to believe that he was related to the people around him, for he seemed to belong to some superior race.

I was able to engage a few men in Pisté, and set them to work at once to clear the jungle around the principal buildings; at the end of a week I took up my quarters at the ruins themselves, in a building known as the Casa Colorada. Soon after my arrival in the country I had engaged a man named Pablo Parera as a general overseer, but he proved to be of very little use to me, and it was no great loss when, early in March, he begged a fortnight's leave of absence, saying that he had received news that his mother was dying in Merida. He was very circumstantial about the doctor's report on the lung trouble from which his mother was suffering, and at his earnest request I gave him the money for his journey and an order on my agent in Merida for a month's pay in advance, as he expressed himself most anxious to return to me. Early the next morning he set out on his journey. It so happened that the next day I had to ride into Yzamal, a distance of about forty miles, on business, where I chanced to hear that my friend Pablo had passed a cheerful evening the night before, apparently quite forgetful of his dying mother, and, moreover, that he had boasted that he well understood how to manage me, and was going on to Merida to have a good time at the Carnival. Luckily I was just in time to send a telegram to my agent in Merida, and when Pablo walked into his office the next morning he learnt that the order for his payment had been cancelled; he wisely made no protest and I never heard of him again. I then gave up all hopes of finding another overseer and chose the most intelligent amongst the workmen to take charge of the tools and act as 'caporal.' During the first few weeks all my labourers were men from Pisté, and as they returned to their homes before dark, I was left to sleep in the ruins alone. For a few nights I paid one of the Indians an extra 'real' to stop for the night; but as he could speak no Spanish, conversation was impossible, and the way he sat silently on the floor and followed my every movement with his eyes was worse than a nightmare, so I soon gave up the experiment, infinitely preferring the solitude of the ruins to his company.

In the beginning of March three local officials paid me a visit and stayed two days. They expressed great interest in the work I was doing and were most sympathetic over my troubles in engaging labourers; indeed, one of them, who was also editor of a newspaper, on his return home wrote a most flattering account of me. In a leading article he pointed out that my enterprise was one of national importance, in which every town and village in the neighbourhood should be proud to help. Unfortunately he failed to despatch the half-dozen soldiers whom he had been directed by his superior officer to send me from his own town; and I found that most of the alleged interest in my work and promises of assistance ended in the same way. However, by persistent application, by letter and in person, I managed for a time to worry a fair amount of assistance from the local officials, and secured the services of twenty or thirty Indian soldiers to clear bush, move the fallen stones, and dig away the earth which had accumulated round the base of the principal buildings.

As usual, I had been laughed at by my acquaintances in Merida for bringing with me wheelbarrows and spades, being assured by them that the Indians would never be persuaded to use them. They told me that an Indian's method of digging was to scrape a little earth together with his hands and, in a leisurely way, to ladle it into a small basket of plaited leaves or into his straw hat, if a basket were not at hand, and then to saunter off and empty the contents at a few yards distance. I must own that there was some difficulty in persuading newcomers that four men were not needed to take charge of one wheelbarrow, one to fill it half-full of earth and stones, and three to look on and see that the load was not unduly heavy, and then with a united effort to lift it by the wheel and two handles and carry it off bodily. I did once see an Indian load a wheelbarrow with a few stones, and (with the help of two friends to raise it up) carry off the loaded barrow on the top of his head. However, these vagaries were never indulged in for long, and as soon as they found that the wheels went round, and that their labour was lightened by the use of them, they always took kindly to the wheelbarrows. As the men went barefooted or wore thin sandals they could not work well with a spade, but they soon became skilful with a shovel. They are thoroughly accustomed to using hoes, and in handling a machete to clear jungle it would be difficult to find their equals.

Just before starting on my last journey to Yzamal, Stephen had come out to the ruins in a state of great distress to tell me that his boy had been ill for three or four days and that he feared that he was dying. I went in to see the poor little fellow as I passed through the village and found him in a pitiable state of fever and delirium. There was no doctor within forty miles, and there was nothing I could do for him beyond sending to my camp for a supply of beef-jelly and arrowroot in the hope of keeping up his strength; but I deeply regretted that I had not had earlier news of the child's illness, when perhaps simple remedies might have been efficacious. As I rode into the village on my return from Yzamal a few days later, my first inquiry was for the boy, and I learnt that he had never rallied and had been buried that morning. Stephen came to me, looking haggard and wretched, and asked me to put up for the night in another house in the village, as his house was being prepared for a religious service. The whole village was grief-stricken, and two of the elders called on me to say that on behalf of all the villagers they had a favour to ask of me. They said that it was a great grief to them all that they possessed no portrait of Stephen's son, and they proposed, if I was agreeable, to go at once and dig up the body so that I might take a photograph of it, and the appearance of one they loved so much would then never fade from their minds. Fortunately I could plead the excuse that I had no photographic plates ready for use, but it needed some tact to avoid hurting their feelings and a great deal of explanation before I could induce them to withdraw their ghastly request. Their distress was touching, and utterly unlike the usual callousness of the American native; but, as I have said, the child was possessed of exceptional beauty and charm of manner, and he had won his way to all their hearts.

Before dark I went over to Stephen's house to see the unhappy mother, and found the house clean and ready for the service. The small table at which I had been accustomed to write was turned into an altar and covered with a white cloth; above this was fixed a crucifix, flanked, incongruously enough, by two glaring oleographs, one of a very *décolletée* German damsel apparently singing the praises of lager-beer, whilst her companion on the other side of the crucifix was a sprightly Spanish girl who apparently preferred white wine. The altar itself was graced by half-a-dozen old beer-bottles with gaudy labels, filled with flowers. I was not bidden to the service, which Stephen must have conducted himself, as there was no priest within many miles, so, thinking they would prefer being left to themselves, I returned to my house. Stephen was clearly heart-broken over his loss, but I am sorry to say the proximate effect on him was a drinking-bout which lasted a fortnight.

In March Mr. Thompson paid me a short visit accompanied by Mr. H. Sweet, who had been assisting him in his work at Labná. Mr. Sweet was about to return home to Boston, but he was much attracted by the work to be done at Chichén, and I exerted my powers of persuasion to the utmost to induce him to stay on with me. At last he promised that should the letters he expected to receive on his return to Merida enable him to prolong his stay in Yucatan, he would come back to pay me another visit. Not many days later to my great delight he rode into camp, and I secured a charming companion for the remainder of my stay at the ruins.

By the time Sweet arrived a considerable amount of clearing had been done, and I had shifted my quarters from the Casa Colorada to the building known as the 'Casa de Monjas,' or the Nunnery. This is a fine structure, raised on a solid basement of masonry, 165 feet in length, 89 feet wide, and 35 feet high. A magnificent broad stairway of forty-nine steps leads to the level top of this basement, on which stands a house with eight chambers. One of the chambers had been filled in and sealed up so as to form a secure foundation to an upper story which is now in ruins; but the remainder were in good condition, and made a most comfortable lodging for us. The interior wall-surfaces had formerly been coated with plaster and covered with paintings; but of this decoration only a few fragments two or three inches square remained. The broad terrace around the house was on a level with the tree-tops, and our view extended over the forest-covered plain to the far horizon. To the southward, where no clearing had yet been made, the sea of verdure spread unbroken from our feet. During the lovely tropical nights, when a gentle breeze swayed the tree-tops, and the moonlight rippled over the foliage, it seemed to be a real sea in motion below us, and one almost expected to feel the pulsation of ocean waves against the walls. In the daytime the woods were alive with birds; the beautiful mot-mots were so tame that they flew fearlessly in and out of our rooms, and mocking-birds and scarlet cardinals poured forth a flood of melody such as I have never heard equalled.

The east wing of the Nunnery extends towards some detached buildings, one of which is known as *la iglesia*. Huge grotesque masks or faces with projecting snouts are the most prominent objects in the decoration of this building. On either side of the middle mask in the lower frieze is a panel holding two dilapidated figures of humanized animals: the figure on the right of the central mask is clearly intended for a turtle, and that on the left for an alligator.

Looking northwards from our high platform the ruins lay spread out before us. To the right we could see the front of the many-chambered *Ak at 'cib* ('the writing in the dark'), so called from the carved inscription on the doorway of an inner room. More immediately in front of us rose the strange circular building known as the 'Caracol,' from the small winding stairway hidden in the central mass of masonry. The circular form of this building, and the curiously unsymmetrical arrangement of the terraces, steps, and doorways, suggest the idea that it may have been used as an observatory, and that the direction of the lines of the terraces and the outlook from the doorways may have reference to the rising and setting of the heavenly bodies. To the left stands the Casa Colorada and the much-ruined buildings surrounding it. Beyond this, again, rises a pyramid which once had supported a temple of which nothing now remains but the two serpent columns which formed the doorway.

About three hundred yards to the N.E. of our house lay the cenote from which we drew our supply of water, its rocky and precipitous banks overhung by a thick growth of trees which afforded a grateful shade. The water was about sixty feet below the level of the ground, and could only be reached at one spot by a rough pathway, but we eased the labour of drawing water by rigging up a rope and pulley to an overhanging tree and hauling up the water in a bucket. Beyond the buildings I have already mentioned, we could see from our terrace the lofty Castillo and the top of the temple on the east wall of the Ball Court.

The Castillo is a stately building, even in its ruined condition, and must have been magnificent in the days of its splendour. The great pyramidal foundation, 195 feet square at its base, is ascended on each side by a grand stairway of over ninety steps, with a low, broad, stone edging. The sides of the foundation were terraced and faced with stone, and were probably at one time ornamented with mural paintings. The temple which stands on this magnificent foundation faces N.N.E., and is not set quite true to the lines of the base of the pyramid. At the foot of the northern stairway are two huge serpents' heads, and the porch of the temple is supported by two serpent columns. Both doorways and interior columns are rich in carving, but the design and execution of the ornament is poor in comparison with that found in some of the other temples.

Westward of the Castillo is a complicated group of colonnades and temples which had not been previously surveyed. We were able only to make a surface survey, and such excavations as were necessary to ascertain the ground-plan of the temples; there still remains in this direction a splendid field for investigation by the next explorer.

To the north-west of the Castillo stands the Great Ball Court, which is perhaps the most interesting building at Chichén. Two parallel walls, 272 feet long and 27 feet high, standing 119 feet apart, form the side boundaries of the court, which is open at either end. A terrace, five feet high and 10 feet broad, projects from the base of the walls as is shown in the section. From the middle of each wall, three feet from the top, projected a great stone ring, measuring four feet in diameter and 18 inches in aperture, carved from a single block of stone 11 inches in thickness, and ornamented with a design of entwined serpents. At each end of the Court stands the ruins of a detached temple profusely ornamented with carving.

The game which was played in this magnificent court was, no doubt, much the same as the Mexican Tlachtli, which is thus described by Herrera: – "The game was called *Tlachtli*, which is the same as *Trinquete* in Spanish. The ball was made of the gum from a tree which grows in the hot country. This tree, when tapped, exudes some large white drops, which soon congeal and when mixed and kneaded become as black as pitch; of this material the balls are made, and, although heavy and hard to the hand, they bound and rebound as lightly as footballs, and are indeed better, as there is no need to inflate them. They do not play for 'chases' (*al chaçar*), but to make a winning stroke (*al vencer*), as in the game of *Chueca* – that is, to strike the ball against or to hit it over the wall which the opposite party defend. The ball may be struck with any part of the body, either such part as is most convenient or such as each player is most skilful in using. Sometimes it is arranged that it should count against any player who touches the ball otherwise than with his hip, for this is considered by them to show the greatest skill, and on this account they would wear a piece of stiff raw hide over the hips, so that the ball might better rebound. The ball might be struck as long as it bounded, and it made many bounds one after the other, as though it were alive. They played in parties, so many on each side, and for such a stake as a parcel of cotton cloths (*una carga de mantas*), more or less, according to the wealth of the players. They also played for articles of gold and for feathers, and at times staked their own persons. The place where they played was a court on the level of the ground (*sala baja*), long, narrow, and high, but wider above than below, and higher at the sides than at the ends (*fronteras*). So that it should be better to play in, the court was well cemented, and the walls and floors made quite smooth. In the side walls were fixed two stones like millstones, with a hole pierced through the middle, through which there was just room for the ball to pass, and the player who hit the ball through the hole won the game; and as this was a rare victory, which few gained, by the ancient custom and law of the game, the victor had a right to the mantles of all the spectators; and when the ball passed through the hole it was an amusing sight to see all the onlookers take to flight with much merriment and laughter in the hope of saving their mantles, which others clutched at on behalf of the victor, who had to make certain sacrifices to the Idol of Trinquete and of the stone (ring) through which the ball had passed. To those who saw the feat performed for the first time it seemed like a miracle, and they said that a player who had such good luck would become a thief or an adulterer, or would die soon. And the memory of such a victory lasted many days, until it was followed by another, which put it out of mind. Every Trinquete court was a temple, and at midnight on a lucky day two Idols – one of the game and one of the ball – were placed on the top of the lower walls with certain ceremonies and witchcraft; and in the middle of the floor they sang songs and performed other ceremonies; then a priest from the great temple with other holy men came to bless the court. Certain words were said, the ball was thrown four times, as in the game, and after such ceremonies the court became consecrated and fit to play in, but not before."

I cannot help thinking that Tlachtli must have been a much more complicated game than that which Herrera describes. To a tennis-player the presence of the rings in the wall would suggest the use of a net to divide the court; but it is useless to speculate on the rules of the game, and our only hope is that some more detailed and accurate description of the manner in which it was played may yet come to light, possibly as the result of Señor Troncoso's researches into the manuscripts of Padre Sahagun which have recently been discovered in Florence.

On the top of the wall above the rings and at the boundaries of the court I discovered the remains of what were evidently the marker's boxes.

At the southern end of the eastern wall there is no marker's box, but its place is taken by what must have been a most beautiful little temple opening towards the court. A restoration of this temple is given on the opposite page. Unfortunately for us, the builders made use of wooden beams instead of stone lintels with which to span the porch, and, as the wood decayed, the strangely-shaped capitals over-balanced by the heavy projections in the form of the tail of a rattlesnake, fell forward and carried the front of the building with them. The shafts and base of each column with the huge snake's head attached are still in place, and the restoration has been effected in the drawing merely by replacing the rattle-snakes' tails, which were found amongst the debris at the foot of the wall and carefully measured, and by continuing the ornament on the sides and back of the building across the front, so that no new feature is introduced.

The wooden beams forming the lintel above the doorway leading to the inner chamber of this building are still perfectly sound, and the lower one is beautifully carved, as are also the stone door-jambs. The walls of the inner chamber are covered with mural paintings, alas! now woefully mutilated. Unluckily I had no tracing-paper with me, but by the use of thin sheets of letter-paper I was able to trace some of the better-preserved pictures and to transfer them to drawing-paper. Above the doorway is a picture which represents a human sacrifice. The serpent-priest stands over the body of the victim, which is stretched backwards over a sacrificial stone so as to expose the chest to the knife.

On the south side of the doorway the whole wall-surface is occupied by a battle-scene, where one party, apparently led by the serpent-priest, is attacking a town, while the women, standing on the roofs of the houses, cheer on their defenders and bewail their losses. The arms used are short spears hurled from a throwing-stick (the Mexican *atlatl*), and all the warriors carry shields, which in some cases are covered with feathered mantles. It is worth noting that although the use of bows and arrows is frequently mentioned by the Spanish writers, the bow is never figured on any of the Maya sculptures, and was probably a late introduction.

At the back of this temple, on the level of the ground, is another chamber which possesses features of great interest. The greater part of the roof had fallen in, carrying portions of the wall with it, and the floor of the chamber was closely packed with the debris to the height of four feet. When this was cleared away, we were rewarded by finding intact the lower part of the columns which had supported the doorway, and lying between them a curious altar in the shape of a grotesque tiger. Then we set to work to make paper moulds of the sculptured ornament, representing processions of armed men in quaint ceremonial costumes, which cover the whole of the surface of the interior walls and the four sides of the square columns. The time at our disposal was limited, as the moulding-paper had, for some unknown reason, been delayed in Havana, and when at last it did arrive it was found to be badly damaged with salt water, so that it was difficult to manipulate. The scene of our labours was about three-quarters of a mile from our house and nearly half a mile from the cenote, from which all the water had to be carried on men's backs. The heat was terrific, for the ruined chamber formed a sort of shallow cave facing E.S.E., into which the June sun poured its rays until past noon, raising it to the heat of an oven. We could not begin work until three o'clock in the afternoon, and even then the wall was so hot that the damp paper refused to adhere to it, and the precious water had to be freely used to cool it down; time after time a half-finished mould would fall away from the heated surface and the labour would have to be gone through again. All moulding had to be done with our own hands, as no native could be found competent to help us; and as I was still busy on the survey, the heavier share fell to Mr. Sweet, who stuck to his task manfully until the paper was all used up; I hope some day soon to show him the fine cast of the interior of the building which is now exhibited at the South Kensington Museum.

To the east of the Great Ball Court are two structures which Diego de Landa, Bishop of Yucatan, writing in 1566, describes as "two small theatres built of stone, with four stairways, and paved with flagstones at the top, on which they say they played farces and comedies for the solace of the public." He then goes on to describe the sacred cenote as follows: –

"There runs from the patio in front of these theatres a beautiful broad causeway to a pool about two stone throws off. In this pool they have had, and had at that time, the custom to throw into it live men as a sacrifice to the Gods in time of drought, and they hold that these men do not die although they are never more seen. They threw in also many things made of precious stones and other things which they prized, so that if this land has had gold in it, it would be in this pool that most of it would be, so greatly did the Indians revere it.

"This pool has a depth of fully seven fathoms to the surface of the water, and is more than a hundred feet across and is round in shape, and it is a wonder to look at, for it is clean cut rock down to the water, and the water appears to have a green colour, and I think this is caused by the trees which surround it – and it is very deep.

"There is on the top, near the opening, a small building where I found Idols made in honour of each of the principal buildings of the land, almost like the Pantheon of Rome. I do not know if this was a contrivance of the ancients or one of the people of to-day, so that they might meet with their Idols when they went to the pool with their offerings."

In the year 1579, in answer to a despatch from the Spanish Government, a report was drawn up by three of the founders of Valladolid describing the Indian towns in the neighbourhood, in which the following passage occurs: –

"Eight leagues from this town stand some buildings called Chicheniça, amongst them there is a *Cu* made by the hand (of man) of hewn stone and masonry, and this is the principal building.

"It has over ninety steps, and the steps go all round, so as to reach to the top of it, the height of each step a little over the third of a *vara* high. On the summit stands a sort of tower with rooms in it.

"This *Cu* stands between two *zenotes* of deep water – one of them is called the *Zenote of Sacrifice*. They call the place Chicheniça, after an Indian named Alquin Itzá, who was living at the foot of the *Zenote of Sacrifice*.

"At this *zenote* the Lords and Chiefs of all the provinces of Valladolid observed this custom. After having fasted for sixty days without raising their eyes during that time even to look at their wives, nor at those who brought them food, they came to the mouth of this *zenote* and, at the break of day, they threw into it some Indian women, some belonging to each of the Lords, and they told the women that they should beg for a good year in all those things which they thought fit, and thus they cast them in unbound, but as they were thrown headlong they fell into the water, giving a great blow on it; and exactly at midday she who was able to come out, cried out loud that they should throw her a rope to drag her out with, and she arrived at the top half dead, and they made great fires round her and incensed her with Copal; and when she came to herself she said that below there were many of her nation, both men and women, who received her, and that raising her head to look at some of them, they gave her heavy blows on the neck, making her put her head down, which was all under water, in which she fancied were many hollows and deeps; and in answer to the questions which the Indian girl put to them, they replied to her whether it should be a good or bad year, and whether the devil was angry with any of the Lords who had cast in the Indian girls, but these Lords already knew that if a girl did not beg to be taken out at midday it was because the devil was angry with them, and she never came out again. Then seeing that she did not come out, all the followers of that Lord and the Lord himself threw great stones into the water and with loud cries fled from the place."

I fear that this slight description of Chichén must wholly fail to convey to my readers the sensation of a ghostly grandeur and magnificence which becomes almost oppressive to one who wanders day after day amongst the ruined buildings. Although Chichén is not to be compared in picturesqueness with some of the ruined towns in Guatemala and Tabasco, there is a spaciousness about it which is strangely impressive, and the wide horizon, broken only here and there by a distant mound or lofty temple, is more suggestive of the easy access and free movement of a large population than the narrow valley of Copan or the terraced hillsides of Palenque. It is difficult to estimate accurately the actual size of the ancient city, for we were not able to carry our clearings beyond the neighbourhood of the principal buildings still left standing; but it is almost impossible to penetrate the surrounding jungle in any direction without coming across artificial mounds and terraces and other signs of human handiwork.

Had Chichén Itzá been fully peopled in the year 1528, it is almost incredible that Montejo could have held it for two years with a force which numbered only four hundred men, and during a great part of the time must have been reduced to less than half that number. It seems more reasonable to suppose either that the historians were at fault in describing Chichén Itzá as the site of Montejo's camp, or that the city was in a state of decadence and had already been partly abandoned by its population. The latter supposition is strengthened by the passage quoted above from the Valladolid document, in which no mention is made of a great population, and no word occurs which would lead one to suppose that in 1542 Chichén Itzá was still a great living city, although it was undoubtedly still looked on as a sacred place where certain time-honoured ceremonies were performed.

In comparing the ruins of Chichén with those of Copan and Quirigua, one notices at Chichén the greater size of the buildings, the free use of columns, the absence of sculptured *stelæ*, the scarcity of hieroglyphic inscriptions, and, most important of all, the fact that every man is shown as a warrior with *atlatl* and spears in his hand; the only representation of a woman depicts her watching a battle from the roof of a house in a beleagured town, whereas at Copan and Quirigua there are no representations of weapons of war, and at Copan a woman was deemed worthy of a fine statue in the Great Plaza. I am inclined to think that it must have been the stress of war that drove the peaceable inhabitants of the fertile valleys of the Motagua and Usumacinta and the highlands of the Vera Paz to the loss hospitable plains of Yucatan, where, having learnt the arts of war, they re-established their power. Then again they passed through evil times: intertribal feuds and Nahua invasions may account for the destruction or abandonment of their great cities, such as Chichén Itzá and Mayapan, and in these latter contests they may have learned the use of the bows and arrows with which they fought the Spaniards.

This view is somewhat strengthened by the result of a very careful examination of the caves and *cenotes* of Yucatan made in 1895 by Mr. Henry Mercer, who records the conclusions he has come to in the following words: – Firstly, that no earlier inhabitant had preceded the builders of the ruined cities of Yucatan; secondly, that the people revealed in the caves had reached the country in geologically recent times; thirdly, that these people, substantially the ancestors of the present Maya Indians, had not developed their culture in Yucatan, but had brought it with them from somewhere else.

It was not until the 2nd July that we left the ruins and set out for Merida, and even then we were reluctant to depart and leave unexamined so much that is of interest; but our store of food had run out and we found the greatest difficulty in getting supplies in the neighbourhood. Moreover, the heavy showers and great heat made such work as we were engaged on almost impossible. During the month of May we had both suffered from malarious fever. Fortunately our attacks occurred on alternate days, so that we could each tend the other in turn, and we both made complete recovery. The difficulty in engaging labourers was never smoothed away, and was the occasion of much vexatious waste of time. During the time we were ill with fever we were altogether bereft of labourers for about a fortnight, and found the greatest difficulty in supplying ourselves with firewood and water. After this matters mended, and we were better served; but towards the end of our stay, I had again to depend solely on the villagers from Pisté, some of whom would condescend to do a short day's work for me at about three times the current rate of wages.

To Sweet's arrival at the most critical moment the success of my expedition was very largely due. He was keenly interested in his work, and, in spite of attacks of fever, we spent a very happy three months together. Sweet undertook all the photography, and was also of the greatest assistance in the survey; and with his ever-ready help and cheery companionship, I could make light of the numberless petty annoyances and delays which were so hard to bear when I was alone; moreover he supplied that invaluable stimulus to work which came from discussing with an intelligent companion the various problems which presented themselves for solution as the clearings widened out and the remains of the ancient city were disclosed to our view.

Tikál and Menché

BEFORE CLOSING THE NOTES ON MY WANDERINGS a few words must be said about two other ruins, Tikál, which I visited both in 1881 and 1882, and Menché, which I visited in the latter year only. On both occasions I started from Coban and travelled northward for ten days through the then almost uninhabited forest to the Paso Real on the Rio de la Pasion, where the Government maintains a ferryman and serviceable canoes for the passage of the river, and thence to Sacluc, a village standing in the savannah land about fifteen miles north of the river.

Sacluc, which had risen into notice as the headquarters of the mahogany-cutters, had only recently become the residence of the Jefe Político of the department of Peten, and had been euphemistically renamed *La Libertad*, possibly to hide the fact that a condition not very far removed from slavery was more noticeable there than in other parts of the Republic. All labourers' wages are paid in advance, and as the wood-cutters are a thriftless folk, any cash they may receive is soon dissipated, and then before returning to work an additional charge must be incurred for tools and the necessary stores for sustenance during many months' absence in the forest. In theory the long score against a workman in the patron's books will be wiped out by the product of a season's work, but in practice it only increases until the debt has reached the limit of value which is placed on the man's services. Then, if the patron is in luck, he may find a purchaser for his workman; that is to say, he may sell the debt to another employer and the man's services pass with it, for the law compels him to serve his new master until the debt is paid. Of course it is vastly immoral, but the system does not seem to work so badly after all; for if the patrones are too harsh, which did not seem to be the case, the frontiers of Mexico and British Honduras are not far distant, and a man could always take a few days' walk through the forest and leave his debts behind him. Such migrations are not at all uncommon, and many Mexicans from Tabasco, Campeche, and Yucatan, as well as some runaway negroes from the British West India regiments, were numbered in the population of Sacluc. As a last resort, if a man has made Mexico, Guatemala, and Belize all too hot to hold him there is yet left a refuge in the no-man's land held by the Santa Cruz Indians, and he may add to the mongrel and turbulent population of Xaxe Venic or some of the other frontier villages. Naturally such a mixed community as that which inhabits the isolated province of Peten would be likely sometimes to give trouble to the officials sent to rule over it; the last Jefe Político had paid with his life for some effort to enforce the orders of the Central Government, and a custom-house officer had been murdered shortly before my arrival and his murderer was confined in the room next to that in which I slept. But although the Peteneros resent too much interference on the part of Government officials, and have a natural prejudice against a high customs tariff, I don't think they can be called a disorderly people, and I have never heard of them causing any annoyance to travellers.

A woodcutter is indeed to be pitied who has to seek recreation in such a hot, dull, dreary place as Sacluc; the condition of the water alone would justify his preference for *aguardiente*, as all the drinking water for the supply of the village is brought from small shallow unfenced ponds in the savannah, in which the women wash clothes, and where horses, cattle, and pigs wallow in the mud.

Soon after my arrival I received a visit from an elderly Englishman, who told me he resided there 'because the climate suited him'; he was an eccentric waif who had at one time served with the British army, in what capacity I could not discover, although he gave me many unavailing hints that it was as a commissioned officer, and he was fond of talking about his 'little place' in Somersetshire. The poor fellow earned an occasional dollar by taking very imperfect photographs, and his visit to me was in order to learn my intentions, as he had heard that I also was a *retratista* and was sadly afraid I would cut him out of his business. He told me that some years earlier when on the road to Peten he had lost his way in the forest and nearly died of starvation, and that some Peteneros who found him had carried him to their village and treated him with the greatest kindness during the illness which followed from the hardships he had gone through, although they knew he had nothing with which to repay them. His long residence in Peten had not enabled him to speak Spanish; but this did not interfere with his efforts to increase his income by giving lessons in English, and I greatly regret that I have lost the copy of a notice to that effect which he had written in Spanish and nailed on his door; it was certainly a masterpiece of 'Spanish as she is spoke.' As he put it to me "Spanish is a very curious language; you may know lots of words, but somehow or other they won't go together." I met the poor old fellow another year when he was in broken health and almost penniless, and was able to help him on his way to Guatemala, where the foreign residents got him into the Infirmary and he passed quietly away.

A day's ride to the north-east of Sacluc brings one to the lake of Peten-Itzá with its island town of Flores, known in ancient times as Tayasal. Flores is a small island not more than a third of a mile across, lying close to the southern shore of the lake, and its population (probably including some hamlets on the neighbouring mainland) is said to number twelve hundred. After a day passed in hunting up a crew, we spent the night, when the wind usually falls light, in paddling up to El Remate, at the other end of the lake, whence a walk of about thirty miles through the forest brought us to the ruins of Tikál.

The whole site of the ancient town was so completely covered over with forest that it took us some time to discover the position of the more important buildings and clear away the trees which covered them. There were five great pyramidal temple mounds. The lintels over the doorways of the houses had apparently in all cases been formed of three or four squared beams of hard wood, probably the wood of the chico-sapote tree, and some of them are still in a perfectly sound condition; the greater number, however, have slowly rotted away, and buildings can be seen in every state of decay, many of them reduced to shapeless masses of hewn stone. The lofty foundation mounds of the principal temples are terraced and faced with well-wrought stone arranged in panels, somewhat in the same manner as in the Castillo at Chichén Itzá. At Tikál, however, access to the temple is gained by a single stairway only, instead of by four stairways, one on each side of the mound, as is usual at Chichén. The base of the oblong foundation mound of one of the larger temples (Temple C) measures 184 feet by 168 feet, and the stairway is 38 feet across. The height of the front slope (measured on the slope, which is very steep) is 112 feet. The base of the temple itself measures roughly 41 feet by 28 feet, and the height must be over 50 feet, but I was not able to measure it. The temples are all built on much the same plan; the thickness of the walls is very remarkable, as is also the method by which the length of axis is secured, by cutting across the parallel stone vaulted chambers and connecting them by square-headed doorways with wooden lintels, the thickness of the walls through which the doorways pass far exceeding the width of the vaulted chambers. Of the Temple D I took no measurements and have merely guessed at the size.

Temple E is by far the largest, the foundation mound measuring 280 feet in length and 160 feet on the slope from the door of the temple to the ground, with extraordinarily thick walls. One might almost suppose that the people had originally worshipped in caves in the natural hills, and had in process of time learnt how to build their caves in artificial hills, but, unfortunately for any such theory, no Maya cave temples are known to have existed.

There is, however, no other group of temples in Central America which offers such support to the theory that the position and form of the buildings is due to astronomical considerations. The lofty elevation so as to secure a clear view, the evident desire to gain length of axis, and the fact that all the temples may be roughly said to face the cardinal points favour this theory, and it may be that we can trace the sequence of the structures by their position. For instance, the temples B, C, and E, facing the rising sun, would follow one another in order of time, C would have been built when the erection of A had impeded the fairway of B, and E would have been built when the fairway of C had been obscured by the large group of buildings to the east of it; and it will be observed that this sequence follows the order of size, C being larger than B, and E than C. The fairway of A, which faces the setting sun, is still unimpeded, and there is therefore no larger temple facing in that direction. Unfortunately at the time of my visits to these ruins I did not pay any particular attention to the orientation of the temples beyond what was sufficient to fix their positions in the general sketch-plan; indeed I was not provided with instruments for an accurate survey, even if I had had time to use them. I now especially regret that I did not more carefully examine the smaller mounds in the neighbourhood of A and B, for I am inclined to think that we might trace an earlier northern temple in the mound marked f, which, when its fairway was interrupted, was superseded by the large temple D, whose foundation mound stands on higher ground and still commands a clear view.

Tikál is not rich in carved stone monuments; there are a few small monoliths and circular altars in the plaza between temples A and B ornamented with figures and inscriptions, but they are all much weather-worn. The most important inscriptions, and they are amongst the best examples of Maya art, were found in the carved wooden beams which spanned the doorways of the temples. Many of these beams have decayed, but the best specimens were removed at the instance of Dr. Bernoulli, who visited the ruins about 1877, and are now preserved in the museum at Basle, and two small fragments are to be seen in the British Museum.

The greatest discomfort in exploring the ruins of Tikál is due to the want of a good supply of water. Every drop of water we used had to be brought the distance of a mile and a half from an overgrown muddy lagoon not more than 150 yards wide, and it was so thick and dirty that I never dared to drink it until it had first been boiled and then filtered, and my Indian workmen who refused to take any precautions suffered considerably from fever. The Indians seldom drink cold water when they are at work, and during a journey they will make frequent halts by the roadside to light fires and prepare warm drinks; but notwithstanding this prevalent habit, when we were encamped in places where the water was indubitably bad, I was never able to persuade my *mozos* that any advantage would be gained by actually bringing the water to the boil and then allowing it to stand and cool.

A few years before the date of my visit to Tikál a party of Indians from the borders of the lake had attempted to form a settlement in the neighbourhood of the ruins. The solitary survivor of this party accompanied me as a guide, all the others having died of fever. This man told me that the small lagoon was the only source of water-supply, and that the nearest running stream was a branch of the Rio Hondo some miles distant. The ancient inhabitants probably stored water in *chaltunes*, the underground cisterns which are found in such large numbers amongst the ruins in the north of Yucatan; I discovered two such cisterns beneath the floor of the plaza, but had not time to clear them out.

I must now ask my reader to return with me, by way of Flores and Sacluc, to the Paso Real, on the Rio de la Pasion, whence, on the 14th of March, 1882, I started, in company with Mr. Schulte, the manager of Jamet & Sastre's mahogany cuttings, on an expedition down the river, my object being to explore the ruins of Menché. I had heard of these ruins from Professor Rockstroh, of the Instituto Nacional in Guatemala, who had visited them the year before, and was, I believe, the first European to write any description of them. At the Paso Real I was fortunately able to secure as guide one of the canoemen who had accompanied Prof. Rockstroh on his expedition.

Three days later I parted company with Mr. Schulte near the mouth of the Rio Lacandon, where he was about to establish a new *Monteria*. The banks of the river here begin to lose their monotonous appearance, and for the first time since leaving the Paso Real we caught sight of some hills in the distance. At midday we entered a gorge about a league in length, where the river flows between high rocky and wooded banks and in some places the stream narrowed to a width of forty feet. The current was not very swift, but the surface of the water moved in great oily-looking swirls which seemed to indicate a great depth. Below the narrows the river widens very considerably and the current becomes much more rapid, and great care had to be taken in guiding the canoes so as to avoid the numerous rocks and snags. This day we travelled about thirty miles below the Boca del Cerro and then camped for the night. Several times during the day we had seen traces of the Lacandones, *Jicaques* or *Caribes* as my men called them (the untamed Indians who inhabit the forests between Chiapas and Peten), and while stopping to examine one of their canoes, which we found hauled up on a sand-spit, its owner, accompanied by a woman and child, came out of the forest to meet us. The man was an uncouth-looking fellow, with sturdy limbs, long black hair, very strongly-marked features, prominent nose, thick lips, and complexion about the tint of that of my half-caste canoemen. He was clothed in a single long brown garment of roughly-woven material, which looked like sacking, splashed over with blots of some red dye. The man showed no signs of fear and readily entered into conversation with one of my men who spoke the Maya language; but the woman kept at a distance, and I could not get a good look at her.

Later in the day we landed to visit a *caribal*, or Indian village, which my guide told me stood somewhere near the river-bank. There was no trace of it, however, near the river, so we followed a narrow path into the forest marked by two jaguars' skulls stuck on poles, and here and there by some sticks laid across the track, over which the Indians had probably dragged their small canoes. About two miles distant from the river we found three houses standing in a clearing near the bank of a small stream. A woman came out to meet us, and received us most courteously, asking us to rest in a small shed. Her dress was a single sack-like garment similar to that worn by the man whom we had met earlier in the day; her straight black hair fell loose over her shoulders, and round her neck hung strings of brown seeds interspersed with beads and silver coins, dollars and half-dollars, which she said were obtained in Tabasco. Two other women came out of their houses to greet us, and they told us that all the men were away hunting for wild cacao in the forest and would not return for five days. The walls of the houses were very low, but in other respects they resembled the ordinary ranchos of the civilized Indians. I asked if I might look into one of them, but my *mozos* strongly advised me not to make the attempt, as the numerous howling dogs shut up inside were very savage, and were sure to attack me.

The clearing round the houses was planted with maize, plantains, chillies, tobacco, gourds, tomatoes, calabash-trees, and cotton. We exchanged a little salt for some plantains, yams, and tomatoes without any haggling, and the women agreed to make me some *totoposte*, which I was to send for in a few days, and one of them, pointing to a silver dollar on her necklace, said that they wanted a coin like that in payment. I was surprised to find the women so pleasant-mannered and free from the dull shyness which characterizes the civilized Indians. On my return up the river some days later I again visited this *caribal*, and was received with equal courtesy by the men, who had then returned from the forest, to whom I repeated my request to see the inside of one of their houses; however, a very rapid glance was sufficient to satisfy my curiosity, for as soon as I showed myself at the half-open door seven or eight dogs tied to the wall-posts nearly brought down the house in their efforts to get at me, and two of them were with difficulty prevented by the women from breaking the cords which held them. Some especial significance must attach to the wearing of the brown-seed necklaces, for no offers which

I could make would induce either man or woman to part with one of them. I was much impressed by the striking likeness which the features of the elder man, who appeared to be the leader of the village, bore to those carved in stone at Palenque and Menché. The extremely sloping forehead was not quite so noticeable in the younger men, and it may be that the custom of binding back the forehead in infancy, which undoubtedly obtained amongst the ancients, is being now abandoned. These people still use bows and stone-tipped arrows, which they carry with them wrapped in a sheet of bark.

To return to my journey to Menché. After visiting the *caribal* we continued our course down-stream and camped for the night on the right bank of the river; the next morning an hour's paddle with the very rapid current brought us in sight of a mound of stones piled up on the left bank of the river, which we had been told marked the site of the ruins. On the 18th March, the day of my arrival, the water in the river was so low that the mound stood high and dry; but from the colour and marks on the stones it appears as though the average height of the water were two or three feet from the top of the mound. We soon scrambled up the rough river-bank, and began to cut our way through the undergrowth in search of the ancient buildings, which we found to be raised on a succession of terraces to a height of over 250 feet, with slopes faced with well-laid masonry or formed into flights of steps. Some buildings are still in a fair state of preservation, but others have fallen and become mere heaps of broken masonry. My plan drawing was no more than a rough sketch, as I had no instrument with me for measuring vertical angles, and the distances were judged by pacing, and checked by the occasional use of a tape measure.

The house or temple which I chose for a dwelling-place is a long narrow structure, measuring on the outside 73 feet long by 17 feet broad. There are three doorways giving access to the single chamber, which is divided up into a number of recesses by interior buttress-walls. In the middle recess we found a cross-legged figure of heroic size, reminding me of the seated figure on the great Turtle of Quirigua; the head with its headdress of grotesque masks and feather-work was broken off and lying beside it. There appears to have been some sort of canopy of ornamental plaster-work above the recess, which had fallen down and lay in a confused heap of dust and fragments around the figure. When I first entered the house there must have been over a hundred pieces of rough pottery, similar to those here figured, strewn on the floor and clustered around the stone figure. Many of these pots contained half-burnt copal, and from the positions in which we found them it is evident that they must have been placed in the house within recent years, probably by the Lacandones, who still, I am told, hold the place in reverence. In this house, and in most of the other buildings still standing, stone lintels span the doorways, many of them elaborately carved on the underside.

On the outside of the house the lower wall surface is flat, and it seems probable that it had formerly been decorated in colours, as slight traces of colour can still be found where the plaster coating has adhered to the underside of the lower cornice. Between the lower and upper cornice is a broad frieze marked with three large and eight small niches; these niches have held seated figures and other ornaments modelled in stucco, of which only a few small fragments now remain in position. Above the upper cornice rises a light stone superstructure similar to that on the Temple of the Cross at Palenque, but here also all the ornament which it was built to support has fallen away. However, in the middle is a large niche in which a sort of skeleton of a seated figure of giant proportions can still be traced. The bulk of the body, the bench on which it was seated, and one long stone representing a leg can be made out in the photograph, and a close inspection enables one to trace the outline of the head and to note the prominent stone which marks the position of the nose; but the stucco which clothed this skeleton and made it a work of art has been pierced with the thousand roots of the clinging vegetation and washed away with hundreds of years of tropical rains.

Many if not all of the other houses and temples had been similarly decorated, and, although the area covered by them is not of great extent, there can be little doubt the groups of highly ornamented and richly-coloured buildings raised above the rushing waters of the river on gleaming slopes of stucco-covered masonry must have formed a picture both beautiful and strikingly impressive.

When we had been some days at work at the ruins I sent three of my men in a canoe up-stream to the *caribal* to get the supply of *totoposte* I had ordered from the Lacandones; they returned the next day without much food, but handed me something they had brought with them, carefully wrapped up in paper, which, much to my surprise, proved to be a card from M. Desiré Charnay, the head of a Franco-American scientific exploring expedition, who for two years had been at work examining the antiquities of Mexico and Yucatan. M. Charnay had come up the Usumacinta from Frontera to the head of the navigable water at Tenosique, and had thence ridden through the forest to a spot on the river-bank within a short distance of the *caribal* described earlier in this chapter, known to the canoemen as the Paso de Yalchilan. Having no canoes in which to convey his party down the river he had been brought to a halt and was making arrangements for the passage of himself and his secretary in two small cayucos borrowed from the Lacandones, when to his great surprise my canoe appeared on the scene. The next day I sent my canoes back for him, and leaving his men camped at Yalchilán, he arrived with his secretary at the ruins and occupied a house which had been cleared for him, and he very kindly added his ample supply of provisions to my somewhat meagre stock.

M. Charnay has published an interesting account of his journeys in a book entitled *Les Anciennes Villes du Nouveau Monde*, and the collection of casts made from moulds taken during his two years' wanderings, which is now exhibited at the Trocadero Museum in Paris, and in other museums in Europe and America, has formed the basis of much modern research.

In one of the half-ruined buildings we found a beautifully carved lintel, fallen from its place and resting face downwards against the side of the doorway.

This excellent example of Maya art I determined to carry home with me, and at once set my men to work to reduce the weight of the stone, which must have exceeded half a ton, by cutting off the undecorated ends of the slab and reducing it in thickness. This was no easy matter, as we had not come provided with tools for such work, but shift was made with the end of a broken pickaxe and some carpenter's chisels; by keeping *mozos* at work at it, three at a time, in continual rotation, at the end of a week the weight of the stone had been reduced by half, and we were able to move it to the river-bank and pack it in the bottom of our largest canoe.

On the 26th March we struck our camp and all started up the river together, and on the following day, at the Paso de Yalchilan, I lost the pleasant companionship of M. Charnay, who here rejoined his men and returned direct to Tenosique. It was very hard work hauling the canoe, heavily laden with the stone lintel, against the swift current of the river, and we were four days getting as far as the mouth of the Rio Lacandon. On the 30th March we reached the first inhabited rancho at Santa Rosa, and next day I met Mr. Schulte at the mouth of the Rio Salinas and accepted a passage in his canoe to the Paso Real, leaving the mozos and my heavily-laden canoes to follow more slowly. On the way upstream we landed on the left bank of the river not far from the mouth of the Rio Salinas, and passed a few hours in examining the ruins of a town of considerable extent. I could find no stone houses standing, but there were several fragments of sculptured stones bearing hieroglyphic inscriptions lying amongst the numerous foundation mounds, and the whole site would probably repay careful exploration.

From the Paso Real the stone lintel was carried by Indians to Sacluc, where I purchased a saw from one of the wood-cutters and was again able slightly to reduce the weight of the stone. From Sacluc it was hauled across the savannah to the neighbourhood of Flores on a solid-wheeled ox-cart, the solitary wheeled vehicle then existing in the province of Peten; then it was again slung on a strong pole and carried by sixteen Indian *mozos* through the forest to the British frontier village of El Cayo, where it was again packed in the bottom of a canoe and sent down the river to Belize; it now rests at Bloomsbury in the British Museum.

At the time of my visit Menché was supposed to lie within the Guatemalan frontier, and a few years later leave was obtained for me from the Government of that Republic to remove some other carved lintels from the ruins. Gorgonio Lopez and his brothers were sent down the river for this purpose, and after making careful moulds of all the carved lintels still in position in the houses, they removed some others from those houses which had fallen into ruin; these they packed in the canoes and hauled up the Usumacinta to the mouth of the Rio Salinas. That stream was then ascended to a point above the Nueve Cerros where canoe-navigation ceases, and the stones were thence carried overland to Coban, where they were carefully packed and sent in carts to the port of Panzos, on the Rio Polichic, for shipment to England. I presented these sculptures also to the National Collection, and they are now to be seen at the British Museum. By a recent treaty Menché and the valley of the Lacandon River have passed into the possession of Mexico. Since the date of my visit a party of mahogany-cutters formed a camp on the site of the ruins, but at the end of two years the *monteria* was abandoned, and the ancient city is again left in the solitude of the forest.

Myths of the Chibcha

FRAY PEDRO SIMON WROTE HIS *Noticias Historiales* in 1623, some four score years from the conquest, giving in his fourth Noticia an account of the myths and rites of the Chibcha (the Muisca people) which is our primary source for the beliefs of these tribes. Like other American peoples the Chibcha recognized a Creator, apparently the Heaven Father, but like most others their active cults centred about lesser powers: the Sun (to whom human sacrifices were made), the Moon, the Rainbow, spirits of lakes and other ***genii locorum***, culture deities, male and female, and the manes of ancestors. Idols of gold and copper, of wood and clay and cotton, represented gods and fetishes, and to them offerings were made, especially of emeralds and golden ornaments. Fray Pedro says that the Pijaos aborigines and some of those of Tunja had in their sanctuaries images having three heads or three faces on a single body which, the natives said, represented three persons with one heart; and he also records their use of crosses to mark the graves of those dead of snake-bite, as well as their belief that the souls of the dead fared to the centre of the earth, crossing the Stygian river on ***balsas*** made of spiders' webs, for which reason spiders were never killed. Like the Aztec they held that the lot of men slain in battle and of women dying in child-birth was especially delectable in the other world.

The worship of mountains, serpents, and lakes was implied in many of the Chibcha rites. Slaves were sacrificed, and their bodies were buried on hill-tops; children, who were the particular offering to the Sun, were sometimes taken to mountain-tops to be slain, their bodies being supposed to be consumed by the Sun; and an interesting case of the surrogate for human victims was the practice of sacrificing parrots which had been taught to speak. In masked dances, addressed to the Sun, tears were represented on the masks as a supplication for pity; and another curious rite, apparently solar, was performed at Tunja, where twelve men in red, presumably typifying the moons of the year, danced about a blue man, who was doubtless the sky-god. The ceremony of El Dorado is only one of many rites in which the divinities of the sacred lakes were propitiated; and it is probable that these water-spirits were conceived in the form of snakes, as when, at Lake Guatavita, a huge serpent was supposed to issue from the depths to secure offerings left upon the bank.

The same concept of serpentiform water-deities appears in the curious and novel creation-myth of the Chibcha, briefly told by Fray Simon. In the beginning all was darkness, for light was imprisoned in a great house in charge of a being called Chiminigagua, whom the friar names as the Supreme God, omnipotent, ever good, and lord of all things. After creating huge black birds, to whom he gave the light, commanding them to carry it in their beaks until all the world was illumined and resplendent, Chiminigagua formed the Sun, the Moon (to be the Sun's wife and companion), and the rest of the universe. The human race was of another origin, for shortly after the creation of light, from Lake Iguaque, not far from Tunja, emerged a woman named Bachue or Turachogue ('the Good Woman'), bearing with her a boy just out of infancy. When he was grown, Bachue married him; and their prolific offspring – she brought forth four or six children at a birth – peopled the earth; but finally the two returned beneath the waters, Bachue enjoining upon the people to keep the peace, to obey the laws which she had given them, and in particular to preserve the cult of the gods; while the pair assumed the form of serpents, in which they were supposed sometimes to reappear to their worshippers.

The belief that the ancestors of men issued from a lake or spring was common to many Andean tribes, being found far to the south, where the Indians of Cuzco pointed to Lake Titicaca as the place whence they had come. The myth is easy to explain for the obvious reason that lakesides are desirable abodes and that migrating tribes would hark back to abandoned lakeside homes as their primal sites; however, another suggestion is made plausible by various fragments of origin-myths which have been preserved, namely, that the Andean legends belong to the great cycle of American tales which make men immigrants to the upper world from an under-earth realm whence they have been driven by the malevolence of the water-monster, a serpent or a dragon. There are many striking parallels between the Colombian tales and those of the Pueblo tribes of North America – the great underworld-goddess, the serpent and the spider as subaqueous and subterranean powers, the return of the dead to the realm below, the importance of birds in cosmogony, the cult of the rainbow; and along with these there are tales of a culture hero and of a pair of divine brothers such as are common to nearly all American peoples.

Other Colombian legends of the origin of men include the Pijaos belief, recorded by Fray Simon, that their ancestors had issued from a mountain, and the tradition of the Muzo – western neighbours of the Chibcha – that a shadow, Aré, formed faces from sand, which became men and women when he sprinkled them with water. A true creation-story (as distinguished from tales of origin through generation) was told also by the people of Tunja. In the beginning all was darkness and fog, wherein dwelt the caciques of Ramiriqui and of Sogamozo, nephew and uncle. From yellow clay they fashioned men, and from an herb they created women; but since the world was still unillumined, after enjoining worship upon their creatures, they ascended to the sky, the uncle to become the Sun, the nephew the Moon. It was at Sogamozo that the dance of the twelve red men – each garlanded and carrying a cross, and each with a young bird borne as a crest above his head – was danced about the blue sky-man, while all sang how human beings are mortal and must change their bodies into dust without knowing what shall be the fate of their souls.

Fray Simon relates an episode of these same Indians which is enlightening both as to the missionary and as to the aboriginal conception of the powers that be. After the first missionary had laboured among the natives of Tunja and Sogamozo, "the Demon there began to give contrary doctrines; and among other matters he sought to discredit the teaching of the Incarnation, telling them that such a thing had not yet taken place. Nevertheless, it should happen that the Sun, assuming human flesh in the body of a virgin of the pueblo of Guacheta, should cause her to bring forth that which she should conceive from the rays of the sun, although remaining virgin. This was bruited throughout the provinces, and the cacique of the pueblo named, wishing to prove the miracle, took two virgins, and leading them forth from his house every dawn, caused them to dispose themselves upon a neighbouring hill, where the first rays of the sun would shine upon them. Continuing this for some days, it was granted to the Demon by Divine permission (whose judgements are incomprehensible) that the event should issue according to his desire: in such manner that in a few days one of the damsels became pregnant, as she said, by the Sun." At the end of nine months the girl brought forth a *hacuata*, a large and beautiful emerald, which was treated as an infant, and after being carried for several days, became a living creature – "all by the order of the Demon." The child was called Goranchacha, and when he was grown he became cacique, with the title of 'Child of the Sun.' It is to be suspected that the story of the virgin-born son of the Sun was older than the first preaching of the Incarnation, and that Spanish ears had too eagerly misheard some tale of rites or myths which must have been analogous to the Inca legends of descent from the Sun and to their consecration of virgins to his worship.

Like the other civilized American nations the Chibcha preserved the tradition of a bearded old man, clothed in long robes who came from the east to instruct them in the arts of life and to raise them from primeval barbarism; and like other churchly writers Fray Pedro Simon regarded this as evidence of the preaching of the Gospel by an apostle. Nempterequeteva, or Nemquetheba, and Xue, or Zuhé, are two of the names of this culture hero, worshipped as the god Bochica. He taught the weaving of cotton, the cultivation of fruits, the building of houses, the adoration of the gods; and then he passed on his mysterious way, leaving as proof of his mission designs of crosses and serpents, and the custom of erecting crosses over the graves of the victims of snake-bite – to Fray Pedro an obvious reminiscence of the brazen serpent raised on a cross by Moses in the Wilderness. One of the epithets of this greybeard was Chiminizagagua, or 'Messenger of Chiminigagua,' the supreme god; and when the Spaniards appeared they were called Gagua, after the light-giver; but later, when their cruelties had set them in a different context, the aborigines changed the name to Suegagua ('Demon with Light') after their principal devil, Suetiva, "and this they give today to the Spaniards." Piedrahíta says the Spaniards were termed *Zuhá*, but he identifies the name as belonging to the hero Bochica.

A curious episode follows the departure of the culture hero. Among the people appeared a woman, beautiful and resplendent – "or, better to say, a devil in her figure" – who taught doctrines wholly opposed to the injunctions of Chiminizagagua. Dancing and carousal were the tenets of her evangel; and in displeasure at this, Chiminizagagua transformed the woman (variously known as Chie, Huytaca, or Xubchasgagua) into an owl, condemning her to walk the night. Humboldt says that Bochica changed his wife Chia into the Moon (*chia* signifies 'moon' in the Chibchan tongue, says Acosta de Samper); and it seems altogether likely that in the culture hero, Messenger of Light, and the festal heroine, with their opposite doctrines, we have a myth of sun and moon.

The Chibcha, of course, had their deluge-legend. In the version given by Fray Pedro Simon it is associated with the appearance of the rainbow as the symbol of hope; and since the rainbow cult was important throughout the Andean region, it may everywhere have been associated with some such myth as the friar recounts. Chibchachum, the tutelary of the natives of Bogotá, being offended by the people, who murmured against him and indeed openly offended, sent a flood to punish them, whereupon they, in their peril, appealed to Bochica, who appeared to them upon a rainbow, and, striking the mountains with his staff, opened a conduit for the waters. Chibchachum was punished, as Zeus punished the Titans, by being thrust beneath the earth to take the place of the lignum-vitae-trees which had hitherto upheld it, and his weary restlessness is the cause of earthquakes; while the rainbow, Chuchaviva, was thenceforth honoured as a deity, though not without fear; for Chibchachum, in revenge for his disgrace, announced that when it appeared, many would die. In the version of this tale given by Piedrahíta, Huytaca plays a part, for it is as a result of her artifices that the waters rise; but Bochica is again the deliverer, and the place opened for the issuance of the waters was shown at the cataract of Téquendama – "one of the wonders of the world."

The myth of Chibchachum, shaking the world which he supports, has its analogue not only in the tale of Atlas but also in the Tlingit legend of the Old Woman Below who jars the post that upholds the world. It would seem, however, not impossible that the story is an etymological myth, for Fray Pedro Simon says that Chibchachum means 'Staff of the Chibcha,' a name which might easily lend itself to the mythopoesy of the deluge-tale; nor is it unreasonable from the point of view of cultural advancement, for the Chibcha were beyond the stage in which it is profitable to refer all deifications to natural phenomena. Chibchachum, says the friar, was god of commerce and industries – a complex divinity, not a mere hero of myth – and Bochica, the most universally venerated of Chibchan deities, was revered as a law-giver, divinity of caciques and captains; served with sacrifices of gold and tobacco, he was worshipped with fasts and hymns, and his image was that of a man with the golden staff of authority. There was a fox-god and a bear-god, but Nemcatacoa, the bear-god, was patron of weavers and dyers, and, oddly, of drunkards; in his bear's form he was supposed to sing and dance with his followers. Chukem, deity of boundaries and foot-races, must have been an American Hermes, and Bachue, goddess of agriculture and of the springs of life, was, no doubt, a personification of the earth itself, a Ge or Demeter. Chuchaviva, the Rainbow, aided women in child-birth and those sick with a fever – and we think of the images of the rainbow goddess on the sweat lodges of the Navaho far to the north, and of the rainbow insignia of the royal Incas in the imperial south. Certain it is that here we have to do with a pantheon that reflects the complexity of a life developed beyond the primitive needs of those whom we call nature-folk.

The Civilization & History of Old Peru

Topography Influencing Civilization

IF THE CIVILIZATION OF ANCIENT PERU did not achieve the standard of general culture reached by the Mexicans and Maya, it did not fall far short of the attainment of these peoples. But the brutal and sanguinary tyranny of the Apu-Ccapac Incas makes the rulers of Mexico at their worst appear as enlightened. The Quichua-Aymara race which inhabited Peru was inferior to the Mexican in general mental culture, if not in mental capacity, as is proved by its inability to invent any method of written communication or any adequate time-reckoning. In imitative art, too, the Peruvians were weak, save in pottery and rude modelling, and their religion savoured much more of the materialistic.

It is probable that in no country in the world has the configuration of the land so modified the events in the life of the people dwelling within its borders. The chain of the Andes divides into two branches near the boundary between Bolivia and Chili, and, with the Cordillera de la Costa, encloses at a height of over 3000 feet the Desaguadero, a vast tableland with an area equal to France. To the north of this is Cuzco, the ancient capital of the Incas, to the south Potosi, the most elevated town in the world, whilst between them lies Lake Titicaca, the largest body of fresh water in South America. Cereals cannot ripen, and animals are rare. Yet it was in these desolate regions that the powerful and highly organized empire of Peru arose – an empire extending over an area 3000 miles long by 400 broad.

The Andeans

The prehistoric natives of the Andean region had evolved a civilization long before the days of the Inca dynasties, and the cyclopean ruins of their edifices are to be found at intervals scattered over a wide field on the slopes of the range under the shadow of which they dwelt. Their most extraordinary achievement was probably the city of Tiahuanaco, on the southern shore of Lake Titicaca, built at a level 13,000 feet above the sea, occupying nearly half an acre in extent, and constructed of enormous megalithic blocks of trachytic rock. The great doorway, carved out of a single block of rock, is 7 feet in height by 13½ feet wide, and 1½ feet thick. The upper portion of this massive portal is carved with symbolic figures. In the centre is a figure in high relief, the head surrounded by solar rays, and in each hand a sceptre, the end of which terminates in the head of a condor. This figure is flanked on either side by three tiers of kneeling suppliants, each of whom is winged and bears a sceptre similar in design to the central ones. Elsewhere are mighty blocks of stone, some 36 feet long, remains of enormous walls, standing monoliths, and in earlier times colossal statues were seen on the site. When the Spanish conquerors arrived no tradition remained regarding the founders of these structures, and their origin still remains a mystery; but that they represent the remains of the capital of some mighty prehistoric kingdom is practically admitted.

A Strange Site

The greatest mystery of all regarding the ruins at Tiahuanaco is the selection of the site. For what reason did the prehistoric rulers of Peru build here? The surroundings are totally unsuitable for the raising of such edifices, and the tableland upon which they are placed is at once desolate and difficult of access. The snow-line is contiguous, and breathing at such a height is no easy matter. There is no reason to suppose that climatic conditions in the day of these colossal builders were different from those which obtain at the present time. In face of these facts the position of Tiahuanaco remains an insoluble riddle.

Sacsahuaman and Ollantay

Other remains of these prehistoric people are found in various parts of Peru. At Sacsahuaman, perched on a hill above the city of Cuzco, is an immense fortified work six hundred yards long, built in three lines of wall consisting of enormous stones, some of which are twenty-seven feet in length. Pissac is also the site of wonderful ruined masonry and an ancient observatory. At Ollantay-tampu, forty-five miles to the north of Cuzco, is another of these gigantic fortresses, built to defend the valley of the Yucay. This stronghold is constructed for the most part of red porphyry, and its walls average twenty-five feet in height. The great cliff on which Ollantay is perched is covered from end to end with stupendous walls which zigzag from point to point of it like the salient angles of some modern fortalice. At intervals are placed round towers of stone provided with loopholes, from which doubtless arrows were discharged at the enemy. This outwork embraces a series of terraces, world-famous because of their gigantic outline and the problem of the use to which they were put. It is now practically agreed that these terraces were employed for the production of maize, in order that during a prolonged investment the beleaguered troops and country-folk might not want for a sufficiency of provender. The stone of which this fortress was built was quarried at a distance of seven miles, in a spot upwards of three thousand feet above the valley, and was dragged up the steep declivity of Ollantay by sheer human strength. The nicety with which the stones were fitted is marvellous.

The Drama-Legend of Ollantay

Among the dramatic works with which the ancient Incas were credited is that of *Apu-Ollanta*, which may recount the veritable story of a chieftain after whom the great stronghold of Ollantay was named. It was probably divided into scenes and supplied with stage directions at a later period, but the dialogue and songs are truly aboriginal. The period is that of the reign of the Inca Yupanqui Pachacutic, one of the most celebrated of the Peruvian monarchs. The central figure of the drama is a chieftain named Ollanta, who conceived a violent passion for a daughter of the Inca named Curi-Coyllur (Joyful Star). This passion was deemed unlawful, as no mere subject who was not of the blood-royal might aspire to the hand of a daughter of the Inca. As the play opens we overhear a dialogue between Ollanta and his man-servant Piqui-Chaqui (Flea-footed), who supplies what modern stage-managers would designate the 'comic relief.' They are talking of Ollanta's love for the princess, when they are confronted by the high-priest of the Sun, who tries to dissuade the rash chieftain from the dangerous course he is taking by means of a miracle. In the next scene Curi-Coyllur is seen in company with her mother, sorrowing over the absence of her lover. A harvest song is here followed by a love ditty of undoubtedly ancient origin. The third scene represents Ollanta's interview with the Inca in which he pleads his suit and is slighted by the scornful monarch. Ollanta defies the king in a resounding speech, with which the first act concludes. In the first scene of the second act we are informed that the disappointed chieftain has raised the standard of rebellion, and the second scene is taken up with the military preparations consequent upon the announcement of a general rising. In the third scene Rumi-ñaui as general of the royal forces admits defeat by the rebels.

The Love-Story of Curi-Coyllur

Curi-Coyllur gives birth to a daughter, and is imprisoned in the darksome Convent of Virgins. Her child, Yma Sumac (How Beautiful), is brought up in the same building, but is ignorant of the near presence of her mother. The little girl tells her guardian of groans and lamentations which she has heard in the convent garden, and of the tumultuous emotions with which these sad sounds fill her heart. The Inca Pachacutic's death is announced, and the accession of his son, Yupanqui. Rebellion breaks out once more, and the suppression of the malcontents is again entrusted to Rumi-ñaui. That leader, having tasted defeat already, resorts to cunning. He conceals his men in a valley close by, and presents himself covered with blood before Ollanta, who is at the head of the rebels. He states that he has been barbarously used by the royal troops, and that he desires to join the rebels. He takes part with Ollanta and his men in a drunken frolic, in which he incites them to drink heavily, and when they are overcome with liquor he brings up his troops and makes them prisoners.

Mother and Child

Yma Sumac, the beautiful little daughter of Curi-Coyllur, requests her guardian, Pitu Salla, so pitifully to be allowed to visit her mother in her dungeon that the woman consents, and mother and child are united. Ollanta is brought as a prisoner before the new Inca, who pardons him. At that juncture Yma Sumac enters hurriedly, and begs the monarch to free her mother, Curi-Coyllur. The Inca proceeds to the prison, restores the princess to her lover, and the drama concludes with the Inca bestowing his blessing upon the pair.

The play was first put into written form in the seventeenth century, has often been printed, and is now recognized as a genuine aboriginal production.

The Races of Peru

Many races went to make up the Peruvian people as they existed when first discovered by the conquering Spaniards. From the south came a civilizing race which probably found a number of allied tribes, each existing separately in its own little valley, speaking a different dialect, or even language, from its neighbours, and in many instances employing different customs. Although tradition alleged that these invaders came from the north by sea within historical times, the more probable theory of their origin is one which states that they had followed the course of the affluents of the Amazon to the valleys where they dwelt when the more enlightened folk from the south came upon them. The remains of this aboriginal people – for, though they spoke diverse languages, the probability is that they were of one or not more than two stocks – are still found scattered over the coastal valleys in pyramidal mounds and adobe-built dwellings.

The Coming of the Incas

The arrival of the dominant race rudely broke in upon the peaceful existence of the aboriginal folk. This race, the Quichua-Aymara, probably had its place of origin in the Altaplanicie highlands of Bolivia, the eastern cordillera of the Andes. This they designated Tucuman (World's End), just as the Kiche of Guatemala were wont to describe the land of their origin as Ki Pixab (Corner of the Earth). The present republic of Argentina was at a remote period covered by a vast, partially land-locked sea, and beside the shores of this the ancestors of the Quichua-Aymara race may have settled as fishers and fowlers. They found a more permanent settlement on the shores of Lake Titicaca, where their traditions state that they made considerable advances in the arts of civilization. It was, indeed, from Titicaca that the sun emerged from the sacred rock where he had erstwhile hidden himself. Here, too, the llama and paco were domesticated and agricultural life initiated, or perfected. The arts of irrigation and terrace-building – so marked as features of Peruvian civilization – were also invented in this region, and the basis of a composite advancement laid.

The Quichua-Aymara

This people consisted of two groups, the Quichua and Aymara, so called from the two kindred tongues spoken by each respectively. These possess a common grammatical structure, and a great number of words are common to both. They are in reality varying forms of one speech. From the valley of Titicaca the Aymara spread from the source of the Amazon river to the higher parts of the Andes range, so that in course of time they exhibited those qualities which stamp the mountaineer in every age and clime. The Quichua, on the other hand, occupied the warm valleys beyond the river Apurimac, to the north-west of the Aymara-speaking people – a tract equal to the central portion of the modern republic of Peru. The name 'Quichua' implies a warm valley or sphere, in contradistinction to the 'Yunca,' or tropical districts of the coast and lowlands.

The Four Peoples

The metropolitan folk of Cuzco considered Peru to be divided into four sections – that of the Colla-suyu, with the valley of Titicaca as its centre, and stretching from the

Bolivian highlands to Cuzco; the Conti-suyu, between the Colla-suyu and the ocean; the Quichua Chinchay-suyu, of the north-west; and the Anti-suyu, of the *montaña* region. The Inca people, coming suddenly into these lands, annexed them with surprising rapidity, and, making the aboriginal tribes dependent upon their rule, spread themselves over the face of the country. Thus the ancient chroniclers. But it is obvious that such rapid conquest was a practical impossibility, and it is now understood that the Inca power was consolidated only some hundred years before the coming of Pizarro.

The Character of Inca Civilization

Apart from the treatment which they meted out to the subject races under their sway, the rule of the Inca monarchs was enlightened and contained the elements of high civilization. It is scarcely clear whether the Inca race arrived in the country at such a date as would have permitted them to profit by adopting the arts and sciences of the Andean people who preceded them. But it may be affirmed that their arrival considerably post-dated the fall of the megalithic empire of the Andeans, so that in reality their civilization was of their own manufacture. As architects they were by no means the inferiors of the prehistoric race, if the examples of their art did not bulk so massively, and the engineering skill with which they pushed long, straight tunnels through vast mountains and bridged seemingly impassable gorges still excites the wonder of modern experts. They also made long, straight roads after the most improved macadamised model. Their temples and palaces were adorned with gold and silver images and ornaments; sumptuous baths supplied with hot and cold water by means of pipes laid in the earth were to be found in the mansions of the nobility, and much luxury and real comfort prevailed.

An Absolute Theocracy

The empire of Peru was the most absolute theocracy the world has ever seen. The Inca was the direct representative of the sun upon earth, the head of a socio-religious edifice intricate and highly organized. This colossal bureaucracy had ramifications into the very homes of the people. The Inca was represented in the provinces by governors of the blood-royal. Officials were placed above ten thousand families, a thousand families, and even ten families, upon the principle that the rays of the sun enter everywhere, and that therefore the light of the Inca must penetrate to every corner of the empire. There was no such thing as personal freedom. Every man, woman, and child was numbered, branded, and under surveillance as much as were the llamas in the royal herds. Individual effort or enterprise was unheard of. Some writers have stated that a system of state socialism obtained in Peru. If so, then state surveillance in Central Russia might also be branded as socialism. A man's life was planned for him by the authorities from the age of five years, and even the woman whom he was to marry was selected for him by the Government officials. The age at which the people should marry was fixed at not earlier than twenty-four years for a man and eighteen for a woman. Coloured ribbons worn round the head indicated the place of a person's birth or the province to which he belonged.

A Golden Temple

One of the most remarkable monuments of the Peruvian civilization was the Coricancha (Town of Gold) at Cuzco, the principal fane of the sun-god. Its inner and outer walls were covered with plates of pure gold. Situated upon an eminence eighty feet high, the temple looked down upon gardens filled, according to the conquering Spaniards, with treasures of gold and silver. The animals, insects, the very trees, say the chroniclers, were of the precious metals, as were the spades, hoes, and other implements employed for keeping the ground in cultivation. Through the pleasances rippled the river Huatenay. Such was the glittering Intipampa (Field of the Sun). That the story is true, at least in part, is proved by the traveller Squier, who speaks of having seen in several houses in Cuzco sheets of gold preserved as relics which came from the Temple of the Sun. These, he says, were scarcely as thick as paper, and were stripped off the walls of the Coricancha by the exultant Spanish soldiery.

The Great Altar

But this house of gold had but a roof of thatch! The Peruvians were ignorant of the principle of the arch, or else considered the feature unsuitable, for some reason best known to their architects. The doorways were formed of huge monoliths, and the entire aspect of the building was cyclopean. The interior displayed an ornate richness which impressed even the Spaniards, who had seen the wealth of many lands and Oriental kingdoms, and the gold-lust must have swelled within their hearts at sight of the great altar, behind which was a huge plate of the shining metal engraved with the features of the sun-god. The surface of this plate was enriched by a thousand gems, the scintillation of which was, according to eye-witnesses, almost insupportable. Around this dazzling sphere were seated the mummified corpses of the Inca kings, each on his throne, with sceptre in hand.

Planetary Temples

Surrounding the Coricancha several lesser temples clustered, all of them dedicated to one or other of the planetary bodies – to the moon, to Cuycha, the rainbow, to Chasca, the planet Venus. In the temple of the moon, the mythic mother of the Inca dynasty, a great plate of silver, like the golden one which represented the face of the sun-god, depicted the features of the moon-goddess, and around this the mummies of the Inca queens sat in a semicircle, like their spouses in the greater neighbouring fane. In the rainbow temple of Cuycha the seven-hued arch of heaven was depicted by a great arc of gold skilfully tempered or painted in suitable colours. All the utensils in these temples were of gold or silver. In the principal building twelve large jars of silver held the sacred grain, and even the pipes which conducted the water-supply through the earth to the sanctuary were of silver. Pedro Pizarro himself, besides other credible eye-witnesses, vouched for these facts. The colossal representation of the sun became the property of a certain Mancio Serra de Leguicano, a reckless cavalier and noted gambler, who lost it on a single throw of the dice! Such was the spirit of the adventurers who conquered this golden realm for the crown of Spain. The walls of the Coricancha are still standing, and this marvellous shrine of the chief luminary of heaven, the great god of the Peruvians, is now a Christian church.

The Mummies of Peru

The fact that the ancient Peruvians had a method of mummification has tempted many 'antiquarians' to infer therefrom that they had some connection with ancient Egypt. These theories are so numerous as to give the unsophisticated reader the idea that a regular system of immigration was carried on between Egypt and America. As a matter of fact the method of mummification in vogue in Peru was entirely different from that employed by the ancient Egyptians. Peruvian mummies are met with at apparently all stages of the history of the native races. Megalithic tombs and monuments contain them in the doubled-up posture so common among early peoples all over the world. These megalithic tombs, or *chulpas*, as they are termed, are composed of a mass of rough stones and clay, faced with huge blocks of trachyte or basalt, so put together as to form a cist, in which the mummy was placed. The door invariably faces the east, so that it may catch the gleams of the rising sun – a proof of the prevalence of sun-worship. Squier alludes to one more than 24 feet high. An opening 18 inches square gave access to the sepulchral chamber, which was 11 feet square by 13 feet high. But the tomb had been entered before, and after getting in with much difficulty the explorer was forced to retreat empty-handed.

Many of these *chulpas* are circular, and painted in gay primary colours. They are very numerous in Bolivia, an old Peruvian province, and in the basin of Lake Titicaca they abound. The dead were wrapped in llama-skins, on which the outlines of the eyes and mouth were carefully marked. The corpse was then arrayed in other garments, and the door of the tomb walled up. In some parts of Peru the dead were mummified and placed in the dwelling-houses beside the living. In the rarefied air of the plateaus the bodies rapidly became innocuous, and the custom was not the insanitary one we might imagine it to be.

On the Pacific coast the method of mummification was somewhat different. The body was reduced to a complete state of desiccation, and was deposited in a tomb constructed of stone or adobe. Vases intended to hold maize or *chicha* liquor were placed beside the corpse, and copper hatchets, mirrors of polished stone, earrings, and bracelets have been discovered in these burial-places. Some of the remains are wrapped in rich cloth, and vases of gold and silver were placed beside them. Golden plaques are often discovered in the mouths, probably symbolic of the sun. The bodies exhibit no traces of embalming, and are usually in a sitting posture. Some of them have evidently been dried before inhumation, whilst others are covered with a resinous substance. They are generally accompanied by the various articles used during life; the men have their weapons and ornaments, women their household implements, and children their toys. The dryness of the climate, as in Egypt, keeps these relics in a wonderful state of preservation. In the grave of a woman were found not only vases of every shape, but also some cloth she had commenced to weave, which her death had perhaps prevented her from completing. Her light brown hair was carefully combed and plaited, and the legs from the ankle to the knee were painted red, after the fashion in vogue among Peruvian beauties, while little bladders of toilet-powder and gums were thoughtfully placed beside her for her use in the life to come.

Laws and Customs

The legal code of the Incas was severe in the extreme. Murderers and adulterers were punished by death, and the unpardonable sin appears to have been blasphemy against the sun, or his earthly representative, the Inca. The Virgin of the Sun (or nun) who broke her vow was buried alive, and the village from whence she came was razed to the ground. Flogging was administered for minor offences. A peculiar and very trying punishment must have been that of carrying a heavy stone for a certain time.

On marriage a home was apportioned to each couple, and land assigned to them sufficient for their support. When a child was born a separate allowance was given it – one *fanega* for a boy, and half that amount for a girl, the *fanega* being equal to the area which could be sown with a hundred pounds of maize. The outlook of the average native was limited in the extreme. The Inca class of priests and warriors retained every vestige of authority; and that they employed their power unmercifully to grind down the millions beneath them was a sufficient excuse for the Spanish Conquistadores in dispossessing them of the empire they had so harshly administered.

The public ground was divided afresh every year according to the number of the members of each family, and agrarian laws were strictly fixed. Private property did not exist among the people of the lower classes, who merely farmed the lot which each year was placed at their disposal. Besides this, the people had perforce to cultivate the lands sacred to the Inca, and only the aged and the sick could evade this duty.

The Peruvian Calendar

The standard chronology known to the Peru of the Incas was a simple lunar reckoning. But the four principal points in the sun's course were denoted by means of the *intihuatana*, a device consisting of a large rock surmounted by a small cone, the shadow of which, falling on certain notches on the stone below, marked the date of the great sun-festivals. The Peruvians, however, had no definite calendar. At Cuzco, the capital, the solstices were gauged by pillars called *pachacta unanchac*, or indicators of time, which were placed in four groups (two pillars to a group) on promontories, two in the direction of sunrise and two in that of sunset, to mark the extreme points of the sun's rising and setting. By this means they were enabled to distinguish the arrival and departure of the solstices, during which the sun never went beyond the middle pair of pillars. The Inca astronomer's approximation to the year was 360 days, which were divided into twelve moons of thirty days each. These moons were not calendar months in the correct sense, but simply a succession of lunations, which commenced with the winter solstice. This method, which must ultimately have proved confusing, does not seem to have been altered to co-ordinate with the reckoning of the succession of years. The names of the twelve moons, which had some reference to the daily life of the Peruvian, were as follows:

Huchuy Pucuy Quilla
(Small Growing Moon), approx. January

Hatun Pucuy Quilla
(Great Growing Moon), approx. February

Pancar Pucuy Quilla
(Flower-growing Moon), approx. March

Ayrihua Quilla
(Twin Ears Moon), approx. April

Aymuray Quilla
(Harvest Moon), approx. May

Auray Cusqui Quilla
(Breaking Soil), approx. June

Chahua Huarqui Quilla
(Irrigation Moon), approx. July

Tarpuy Quilla
(Sowing Moon), approx. August

Ccoya Raymi Quilla
(Moon of the Moon Feast), approx. September

Uma Raymi Quilla
(Moon of the Feast of the Province of Uma), approx. October

Ayamarca Raymi Quilla
(Moon of the Feast of the Province of Ayamarca), approx. November

Ccapac Raymi Quilla
(Moon of the Great Feast of the Sun), approx. December

The Festivals

That the Peruvian standard of time, as with all American people, was taken from the natural course of the moon is known chiefly from the fact that the principal religious festivals began on the new moon following a solstice or equinox. The ceremonies connected with the greatest festival, the Ccapac Raymi, were made to date near the lunar phases, the two stages commencing with the ninth day of the December moon and twenty-first day, or last quarter. But while these lunar phases indicated certain festivals, it very often happened that the civil authorities followed a reckoning of their own, in preference to accepting ecclesiastical rule. Considerable significance was attached to each month by the Peruvians regarding the nature of their festivals. The solstices and equinoxes were the occasions of established ceremonies. The arrival of the winter solstice, which in Peru occurs in June, was celebrated by the Intip Raymi (Great Feast of the Sun). The principal Peruvian feast, which took place at the summer solstice, when the new year was supposed to begin, was the national feast of the great god Pachacamac, and was called Ccapac Raymi. Molina, Fernandez, and Garcilasso, however, date the new year from the winter solstice. The third festival of the Inca year, the Ccapac Sitŭa, or Ccoya Raymi (Moon Feast), which is signalled by the beginning of the rainy season, occurred in September. In general character these festivals appear to have been simple, and even childlike. The sacrifice of animals taken from sacred herds of llamas was doubtless a principal feature of the ceremony, accompanied by the offering up of *maguey*, or maize spirit, and followed by the performance of symbolic dances.

The Llama

The llama was the chief domestic animal of Peru. All llamas were the property of the Inca. Like the camel, its distant relative, this creature can subsist for long periods upon little nourishment, and it is suitable for the carriage of moderate loads. Each year a certain amount of llama wool was given to the Peruvian family, according to the number of women it contained, and these wove it into garments, whatever was over being stored away in the public cloth-magazines for the general use. The large flocks of llamas and alpacas also afforded a supply of meat for the people such as the Mexicans never possessed. Naturally much attention was given to the breeding of these animals, and the alpaca was as carefully regarded by the Peruvian as the sheep by the farmer of today. The guanacos and vicuñas, wild animals of the llama or auchenia family, were also sources of food- and wool-supply.

Architecture of the Incas

The art in which the Incan Peruvians displayed the greatest advance was that of architecture. The earlier style of Inca building shows that it was closely modelled, as has already been pointed out, on that of the megalithic masons of the Tiahuanaco district, but the later style shows stones laid in regular courses, varying in length. No cement or mortar of any kind was employed, the structure depending for stability upon the accuracy with which the stones were fitted to each other. An enormous amount of labour must have been expended upon this part of the work, for in the monuments of Peruvian architecture which still exist it is impossible to insert even a needle between the stones of which they are composed. The palaces and temples were built around a courtyard, and most of the principal buildings had a hall of considerable dimensions attached to them, which, like the baronial halls of the England of the Middle Ages, served for feasting or ceremony. In this style is built the front of the palace on the Colcampata, overlooking the city of Cuzco, under the fortress which is supposed to have been the dwelling of Manco Capac, the first Inca. Palaces at Yucay and Chinchero are also of this type.

Unsurpassed Workmanship

In an illuminating passage upon Inca architecture Sir Clements Markham, the greatest authority upon matters Peruvian, says:

"In Cuzco the stone used is a dark trachyte, and the coarse grain secured greater adhesion between the blocks. The workmanship is unsurpassed, and the world has nothing to show in the way of stone-cutting and fitting to equal the skill and accuracy displayed in the Ynca structures of Cuzco. No cement is used, and the larger stones are in the lowest row, each ascending course being narrower, which presents a most pleasing effect. The edifices were built round a court, upon which the rooms opened, and some of the great halls were 200 paces long by 60 wide, the height being 35 to 40 feet, besides the spring of the roof. The roofs were thatch; and we are able to form an idea of their construction from one which is still preserved, after a lapse of three centuries. This is on a circular building called the Sondor-huasi, at Azangaro, and it shows that even thatch in the hands of tasteful builders will make a sightly roof for imposing edifices, and that the interior ornament of such a roof may be exceedingly beautiful."

The Temple of Viracocha

The temple of Viracocha, at Cacha, in the valley of the Vilcamayu, is built on a plan different from that of any other sacred building in Peru. Its ruins consist of a wall of adobe or clay 40 feet high and 330 long, built on stone foundations eight feet in height. The roof was supported on twenty-five columns, and the width of the structure was 87 feet. It was a place of pilgrimage, and the caravanserais where the Faithful were wont to be housed still stand around the ruined fane.

Titicaca

The most sacred of the Peruvian shrines, however, was Titicaca, an island on the lake of that name. The island of Coati, hard by, enjoyed an equal reverence. Terraced platforms on the former, reached by flights of steps, support two buildings provided for the use of pilgrims about to proceed to Coati. On Titicaca there are the ruins of an extensive palace which commands a splendid view of the surrounding barren country. A great bath or tank is situated half-way down a long range of terraces supported by cut stone masonry, and the pool, 40 feet long by 10, and five feet deep, has similar walls on three sides. Below this tank the water is made to irrigate terrace after terrace until it falls into the lake.

Coati

The island of Coati is about six miles distant. The principal building is on one of the loftiest of seven terraces, once radiant with flowers and shrubs, and filled with rich loam transported from a more fertile region. It is placed on three sides of a square, 183 feet long by 80, and is of stone laid in clay and coated with plaster. "It has," says Markham, "thirty-five chambers, only one of which is faced with hewn stones. The ornament on the façade consists of elaborate niches, which agreeably break the monotony of the wall, and above them runs a projecting cornice. The walls were painted yellow, and the niches red; and there was a high-pitched roof, broken here and there by gables. The two largest chambers are 20 long by 12, and loftier than the rest, each with a great niche in the wall facing the entrance. These were probably the holy places or shrines of the temple. The beautiful series of terraces falls off from the esplanade of the temple to the shores of the lake."

Mysterious Chimu

The coast folk, of a different race from the Incas, had their centre of civilization near the city of Truxillo, on the plain of Chimu. Here the ruins of a great city litter the plain for many acres. Arising from the mass of ruin, at intervals stand *huacas*, or artificial hills. The city was supplied with water by means of small canals, which also served to irrigate the gardens. The mounds alluded to were used for sepulture, and the largest, at Moche, is 800 feet long by 470 feet in breadth, and 200 feet in height. It is constructed of adobes. Besides serving the purpose of a cemetery, this mound probably supported a large temple on its summit.

The Palace

A vast palace occupied a commanding position. Its great hall was 100 feet long by 52 broad, and its walls were covered with a highly ornate series of arabesques in relief done in stucco, like the fretwork on the walls of Palenque. Another hall close at hand is ornamented in coloured stucco, and from it branch off many small rooms, which were evidently dormitories. From the first hall a long corridor leads to secret storehouses, where many vessels of gold and silver have been discovered hidden away, as if to secure them either from marauding bands or the gaze of the vulgar. All of these structures are hollowed out of a vast mound covering several acres, so that the entire building may be said to be partially subterranean in character. "About a hundred yards to the westward of this palace there was a sepulchral mound where many relics were discovered. The bodies were wrapped in cloths, woven in ornamental figures and patterns of different colours. On some of the cloths were sewn plates of silver, and they were edged with borders of feathers, the silver being occasionally cut in the shape of fishes. Among the ruins of the city there are great rectangular areas enclosed by massive walls, and containing courts, streets, dwellings, and reservoirs for water. The largest is about a mile south of the mound-palace, and is 550 yards long by 400. The outer wall is about 30 feet high, 10 feet thick at the base, with sides inclining toward each other. Some of the interior walls are highly ornamented in stuccoed patterns; and in one part there is an edifice containing forty-five chambers or cells, in five rows of nine each, which is supposed to have been a prison. The enclosure also contained a reservoir 450 feet long by 195 broad, and 60 feet deep."

The Civilization of Chimu

The ruins of Chimu are undoubtedly the outcome of a superior standard of civilization. The buildings are elaborate, as are their internal arrangements. The extent of the city is great, and the art displayed in the manufacture of the utensils discovered within it and the taste evinced in the numerous wall-patterns show that a people of advanced culture inhabited it. The jeweller's work is in high relief, and the pottery and plaques found exhibit much artistic excellence.

Pachacamac

The famous ruins of the temple and city of Pachacamac, near the valley of Lurin, to the south of Lima, overlook the Pacific Ocean from a height of 500 feet. Four vast terraces still bear mighty perpendicular walls, at one time painted red. Here was found the only perfect Peruvian arch, built of large adobe bricks – a proof that the Peruvian mind did not stand still in matters architectural at least.

Irrigation Works

It was in works of irrigation, however, that the race exhibited its greatest engineering genius. In the valley of Nasca the Incas cut deep trenches to reinforce the irrigating power of a small river, and carried the system high up into the mountains, in order that the rainfall coming therefrom might be conducted into the needful channel. Lower down the valley the main watercourse is deflected into many branches, which irrigate each estate by feeding the small surface streams. This system adequately serves the fifteen estates of Nasca today! Another high-level canal for the irrigation of pasture-lands was led for more than a hundred and fifty miles along the eastern slope of the central cordillera.

A Singular Discovery

In Peru, as in Mexico, it is probable that the cross was employed as a symbol of the four winds. An account of the expedition of Fuentes to the valley of Chichas recounts the discovery of a wooden cross as follows:

"When the settlers who accompanied Fuentes in his glorious expedition approached the valley they found a wooden cross, hidden, as if purposely, in the most intricate part of the mountains. As there is not anything more flattering to the vanity of a credulous man than to be enabled to bring forward his testimony in the relation of a prodigy, the devotion of these good conquerors was kindled to such a degree by the discovery of this sacred memorial that they instantly hailed it as miraculous and divine. They accordingly carried it in procession to the town, and placed it in the church belonging to the convent of San Francisco, where it is still worshipped. It appears next to impossible that there should not, at that time, have been any individual among them sufficiently enlightened to combat such a persuasion, since, in reality, there was nothing miraculous in the finding of this cross, there having been other Christian settlers, before the arrival of Fuentes, in the same valley. The opinion, notwithstanding, that the discovery was altogether miraculous, instead of having been abandoned at the commencement, was confirmed still more and more with the progress of time. The Jesuits Antonio Ruiz and Pedro Lozano, in their respective histories of the missions of Paraguay, &c., undertook to demonstrate that the Apostle St. Thomas had been in America. This thesis, which was so novel, and so well calculated to draw the public attention, required, more than any other, the aid of the most powerful reasons, and of the most irrefragable documents, to be able to maintain itself, even in an hypothetical sense; but nothing of all this was brought forward. Certain miserable conjectures, prepossession, and personal interest, supplied the place of truth and criticism. The form of a human foot, which they fancied they saw imprinted on the rock, and the different fables of this description invented by ignorance at every step, were the sole foundations on which all the relations on this subject were made to repose. The one touching the peregrinations of St. Thomas from Brazil to Quito must be deemed apocryphal, when it is considered that the above reverend fathers describe the Apostle with the staff in the hand, the black cassock girt about the waist, and all the other trappings which distinguish the missionaries of the society. The credit which these histories obtained at the commencement was equal to that bestowed on the cross of Tarija, which remained in the predicament of being the one St. Thomas had planted in person, in the continent of America."

The Incas as Craftsmen

The Incan Peruvians had made some progress in the metallurgic, ceramic, and textile arts. By washing the sands of the rivers of Caravaya they obtained large quantities of gold, and they extracted silver from the ore by means of blast-furnaces. Copper also was abundant, and was employed to manufacture bronze, of which most of their implements were made. Although it is difficult to know at what period their mining operations were carried on, it is evident that they could only have learned the art through long experience. Many proofs are to be found of their skill in jewellery, and amongst these are wonderful statuettes which they made from an amalgam of gold and mercury, afterwards exposed to great heat. A number of curious little ornaments made of various substances, with a little hole bored through them, were frequently found under the *huacas* – probably talismans. The finest handiwork of the Incas was undoubtedly in jewellery; but unfortunately most of the examples of their work in this craft were melted down to assuage the insatiable avarice of the Spanish conquerors, and are therefore forever lost to us. The spade and chisel employed in olden times by the Peruvians are much the same as the people use now, but some of their tools were clumsy. Their javelins, tomahawks, and other military arms were very futile weapons. Some found near the mines of Pasco were made of stone.

The spinning, weaving, and dyeing of the Peruvians were unequalled in aboriginal America, their cloths and tapestries being both graceful in design and strong in texture.

Stamps of bark or earthenware were employed to fix designs upon their woollen stuffs, and feathers were added to the garments made from these, the combination producing a gay effect much admired by the Spaniards. The British Museum possesses some good specimens of these manufactures.

Pottery

The Peruvians excelled in the potter's art. The pottery was baked in a kiln, and was varied in colour, red, black, and grey being the favourite shades. It was varnished outside, and the vases were moulded in two pieces and joined before heating. Much of the work is of great grace and elegance, and the shapes of animals were very skilfully imitated. Many drinking-cups of elegant design have been discovered, and some vases are of considerable size, measuring over three feet in height. A simple geometric pattern is usually employed for decoration, but sometimes rows of birds and insects figure in the ceramics. The pottery of the coast people is more rich and varied than that of the Inca race proper, and among its types we find vases moulded in the form of human faces, many of them exhibiting so much character that we are forced to conclude that they are veritable portraits. Fine stone dishes are often found, as well as platters of wood, and these frequently bear as ornament tasteful carvings representing serpents. On several cups and vases are painted representations of battles between the Inca forces and the savages of the eastern forests using bows and arrows; below wander the animals of the forest region, a brightly painted group.

The Archaeological Museum of Madrid gives a representation of very varied kinds of Peruvian pottery, including some specimens modelled upon a series of plants, interesting to botanists. The Louvre collections have one or two interesting examples of earthenware, as well as the Ethnographical Museum of St Petersburg, and in all these collections there are types which are believed to be peculiar to the Old World.

The Trocadero Museum has a very curious specimen with two necks called the 'Salvador.' A drawing on the vase represents a man with a tomahawk. The Peruvians, like the Mexicans, also made musical instruments out of earthenware, and heavy ornaments, principally for the ear.

Historical Sketch of the Incan Peruvians

The Inca dominion, as the Spaniards found it, was instituted only about a century before the coming of the white man. Before that time Inca sway held good over scattered portions of the country, but had not extended over the entire territory which in later times was connected with the Inca name. That it was founded on the wreck of a more ancient power which once existed in the district of Chinchay-suyu there can be little doubt. This power was wielded over a space bounded by the lake of Chinchay-cocha on the north and Abancay on the south, and extended to the Pacific at the valley of Chincha. It was constituted by an alliance of tribes under the leadership of the chief of Pucara, in the Huanca country. A branch of this confederacy, the Chanca, pushing southward in a general movement, encountered the Inca people of Colla-suyu, who, under their leader, Pachacutic, a young but determined chieftain, defeated the invaders in a decisive battle near Cuzco. In consequence of this defeat the Chanca deserted their former allies and made common cause with their victors. Together the armies made a determined attack on the Huanca alliance, which they broke up, and conquered the northern districts of the Chinchay-suyu. Thus Central Peru fell to the Inca arms.

The Inca Monarchs

Inca history, or rather tradition, as we must call it in the light of an unparalleled lack of original documentary evidence, spoke of a series of eleven monarchs from Manco Capac to Huaina Ccapac, who died shortly before the Spanish conquest. These had reigned for a collective period of nearly 350 years. The evidence that these chiefs had reigned was of the best, for their mummified bodies were preserved in the great Temple of the Sun at Cuzco, already described. There they received the same daily service as when in the flesh. Their private herds of llamas and slaves were still understood to belong to them, and food and drink were placed before them at stated intervals. Clothes were made for them, and they were carried about in palanquins as if for daily exercise. The descendants of each at periodical intervals feasted on the produce of their ancestor's private estate, and his mummy was set in the centre of the diners and treated as the principal guest.

The First Incas

After Manco Capac and his immediate successor, Sinchi Roca (Wise Chief), Lloque Yupanqui comes third in the series. He died while his son was still a child. Concerning Mayta Ccapac, who commenced his reign while yet a minor, but little is known. He was followed by Ccapac Yupanqui, who defeated the Conti-suyu, who had grown alarmed at the great power recently attained by Cuzco. The Inca and his men were attacked whilst about to offer sacrifice. A second attempt to sack Cuzco and divide its spoil and the women attached to the great Temple of the Sun likewise ended in the total discomfiture of the jealous invaders. With Inca Roca, the next Inca, a new dynasty commences, but it is well-nigh impossible to trace the connection between it and the preceding one. Of the origin of Inca Roca nothing is related save that he claimed descent from Manco Capac. Roca, instead of waiting to be attacked in his own dominions, boldly confronted the Conti-suyu in their own territory, defeated them decisively at Pumatampu, and compelled them to yield him tribute. His successor, Yahuarhuaccac, initiated a similar campaign against the

Colla-suyu people, against whom he had the assistance of the conquered Conti-suyu. But at a feast which he held in Cuzco before setting out he was attacked by his allies, and fled to the Coricancha, or Golden Temple of the Sun, for refuge, along with his wives. Resistance was unavailing, and the Inca and many of his favourites were slaughtered. The allied tribes which had overrun Central Peru now threatened Cuzco, and had they advanced with promptitude the Inca dynasty would have been wiped out and the city reduced to ruins. A strong man was at hand, however, who was capable of dealing with the extremely dangerous situation which had arisen. This was Viracocha, a chieftain chosen by the vote of the assembled warriors of Cuzco. By a prudent conciliation of the Conti-suyu and Colla-suyu he established a confederation which not only put an end to all threats of invasion, but so menaced the invaders that they were glad to return to their own territory and place it in a suitable state of defence.

Viracocha the Great

With Viracocha the Great, or 'Godlike' [he titled himself 'Viracocha' after the god], the period of true Inca ascendancy commences. He was the real founder of the enlarged Inca dominion. He was elected Inca on his personal merits, and during a vigorous reign succeeded in making the influence of Cuzco felt in the contiguous southern regions. In his old age he retired to his country seats at Yucay and Xaquixahuana, and left the conduct of the realm to his son and successor, Urco-Inca, a weak-minded voluptuary, who neglected his royal duties, and was superseded by his younger brother, Pachacutic, a famous character in Inca history.

The Plain of Blood

The commencement of Pachacutic's reign witnessed one of the most sanguinary battles in the history of Peru. Hastu-huaraca, chief of the Antahuayllas, in the Chanca country, invaded the Inca territory, and encamped on the hills of Carmenca, which overlooks Cuzco. Pachacutic held a parley with him, but all to no purpose, for the powerful invader was determined to humble the Inca dynasty to the dust. Battle was speedily joined. The first day's fight was indecisive, but on the succeeding day Pachacutic won a great victory, the larger part of the invading force being left dead on the field of battle, and Hastu-huaraca retreating with five hundred followers only. The battle of Yahuar-pampa (Plain of Blood) was the turning-point in Peruvian history. The young Inca, formerly known as Yupanqui, was now called Pachacutic (He who changes the World). The warriors of the south made full submission to him, and came in crowds to offer him their services and seek his alliance and friendship, and he shortly found himself supreme in the territories over which his predecessors had exercised merely a nominal control.

The Conquest of Middle Peru

Hastu-huaraca, who had been commissioned by the allied tribesmen of Chinchay-suyu to reduce the Incas, now threw in his lot with them, and together conqueror and conquered proceeded to the liberation of the district of Chinchay-suyu from the tyranny of the Huanca alliance. The reduction of the southern portion of that territory was speedily accomplished. In the valley of Xauxa the invaders came upon the army of the Huanca, on which they inflicted a final defeat. The Inca spared and liberated the prisoners of war, who were numerous. Once more, at Tarma, were the Huanca beaten, after which all resistance appears to have been overcome. The city-state of Cuzco was now the dominant power throughout the whole of Central Peru, a territory 300 miles in length, whilst it exercised a kind of suzerainty over a district of equal extent toward the south-east, which it shortly converted into actual dominion.

Fusion of Races

This conquest of Central Peru led to the fusing of the Quichua-speaking tribes on the left bank of the Apurimac with the Aymara-speaking folk on the right bank, with the result that the more numerous Quichua speedily gained linguistic ascendancy over their brethren the Aymara. Subsequently to this the peoples of Southern and Central Peru, led by Inca headmen, swept in a great wave of migration over Cerro de Pasco, where they met with little or no resistance, and Pachacutic lived to be lord over a dominion extending for a thousand miles to the northward, and founder of a great Inca colony south of the equator almost identical in outline with the republic of Ecuador.

Two Branches of the Incas

These conquests, or rather race-movements, split up the Inca people into two separate portions, the respective centres of which were well-nigh a thousand miles apart. The centre of the northern district was at Tumipampa, Riopampa, and Quito at different periods. The political separation of these areas was only a question of time. Geographical conditions almost totally divided the two portions of the empire, a sparsely populated stretch of country 400 miles in extent lying between them.

The Laws of Pachacutic

Pachacutic united to his fame as a warrior the reputation of a wise and liberal ruler. He built the great Temple of the Sun at Cuzco, probably on the site of a still older building, and established in its walls the convent in which five hundred maidens were set apart for the service of the god. He also, it is said, instituted the great rite of the Ccapac-cocha, at which maize, cloth, llamas, and children were sacrificed in honour of the sun-god. He devised a kind of census, by which governors were compelled periodically to render an account of the population under their rule. This statement was made by means of *quipos*. Agriculture was his peculiar care, and he was stringent in the enforcement of laws regarding the tilling of the soil, the foundation and upkeep of stores and granaries, and the regulation of labour in general. As an architect he took upon himself the task of personally designing the principal buildings of the city of Cuzco, which were rebuilt under his instructions and in accordance with models moulded from clay by his own hands. He appears to have had a passion for order, and to him we may be justified in tracing the rigorous and almost grandmotherly system under which the Peruvians were living at the time of the arrival of their Spanish conquerors. To Pachacutic, too, is assigned the raising of the immense fortress of Sacsahuaman, already described. He further instituted the order of knighthood known as Auqui, or 'Warrior,' entrance to which was granted to suitable applicants at the great feast of Ccapac Raymi, or Festival of the Sun. He also named the succession of moons, and erected the pillars on the hill of Carmenca by which the season of solstice was found. In short, all law and order which had a place in the Peruvian social economy were attributed to him, and we may designate him the Alfred of his race.

Tupac-Yupanqui

Pachacutic's son, Tupac-Yupanqui, for some time before his father's death acted as his lieutenant. His name signifies 'Bright' or 'Shining.' His activity extended to every portion of the Inca dominion, the borders of which he enlarged, suppressing revolts, subjugating tribes not wholly brought within the pale of Inca influence, and generally completing the work so ably begun by his father.

A spirit of cruelty and excess such as was unknown to Pachacutic marked the military exploits of Tupac. In the valley of Huarco, near the Pacific coast, for example, he was repulsed by the natives, who were well supplied with food and stores of all sorts, and whose town was well fortified and very strongly situated. Tupac constructed an immense camp, or rather town, the outlines of which recalled those of his capital of Cuzco, on a hill opposite the city, and here he calmly sat down to watch the gradual starvation of the enemy. This siege continued for three years, until the wretched defenders, driven to despair through want of food, capitulated, relying on the assurance of their conqueror that they should become a part of the Inca nation and that their daughters should become the wives of Inca youths. The submission of their chiefs having been made, Tupac ordered a general massacre of the warriors and principal civilians. At the conquest the Spaniards could still see the immense heaps of bones which littered the spot where this heartless holocaust took place, and the name Huarco (The Gibbet) became indissolubly associated with the district.

Huaina Ccapac

Tupac died in 1493, and was succeeded by his son Huaina Ccapac (The Young Chief). Huaina was about twenty-two years of age at the time of his father's death, and although the late Inca had named Ccapac-Huari, his son by another wife, as his successor, the claims of Huaina were recognized. His reign was peaceful, and was marked by wise administrative improvements and engineering effort. At the same time he was busily employed in holding the savage peoples who surrounded his empire in check. He favoured the northern colony, and rebuilt Tumipampa, but resided at Quito. Here he dwelt for some years with a favourite son by a wife of the lower class, named Tupac-atau-huallpa (The Sun makes Good Fortune). Huaina was the victim of an epidemic raging in Peru at the time. He was greatly feared by his subjects, and was the last Inca who held undisputed sway over the entire dominion. Like Nezahualcoyotl in Mexico, he attempted to set up the worship of one god in Peru, to the detriment of all other *huacas*, or sacred beings.

The Inca Civil War

On the death of Huaina his two sons, Huascar and Atauhuallpa, strove for the crown. Before his demise Huaina had divided his dominion between his two sons, but it was said that he had wrested Quito from a certain chieftain whose daughter he had married, and by whom he had Atauhuallpa, who was therefore rightful heir to that province. The other son, Huascar, or Tupac-cusi-huallpa (The Sun makes Joy), was born to his principal sister-wife – for, according to Inca custom, the monarchs of Peru, like those of certain Egyptian dynasties, filled with pride of race, and unwilling to mingle their blood with that of plebeians, took spouses from among their sisters. This is the story as given by many Spanish chroniclers, but it has no foundation in fact. Atauhuallpa was in reality the son of a woman of the people, and Huascar was not the son of Huaina's sister-wife, but of a wife of less intimate relationship. Therefore both sons were on an equality as regards descent. Huascar, however, was nearer the throne by virtue of his mother's status, which was that of a royal princess, whereas the mother of Atauhuallpa was not officially recognized. Huascar by his excesses and his outrages on religion and public decency aroused the people to revolt against his power, and Atauhuallpa, discerning his opportunity in this *émeute*, made a determined attack on the royal forces, and succeeded in driving them slowly back, until at last Tumipampa was razed to the ground, and shortly afterwards the important southerly fortress of Caxamarca fell into the hands of the rebels.

A Dramatic Situation

Atauhuallpa remained at Caxamarca, and despatched the bulk of his forces into the enemy's country. These drove the warriors of Huascar back until the upper courses of the Apurimac were reached. Huascar fled from Cuzco, but was captured, and carried a prisoner with his mother, wife, and children to Atauhuallpa. Not many days afterwards news of the landing of the Spaniards was received by the rebel Inca. The downfall of the Peruvian Empire was at hand.

A Worthless Despotism

If the blessings of a well-regulated government were dispensed by the Incas, these benefits were assuredly counterbalanced by the degrading despotism which accompanied them. The political organization of the Peruvian Empire was in every sense more complete than that of Mexico. But in a state where individual effort and liberty are entirely crushed even such an effective organization as the Peruvian can avail the people little, and is merely a device for the support of a calculated tyranny.

Manco Capac to Mayta Capac

HERE WE GIVE some extracts from descriptions of some of the Inca monarchs and their deeds, from Manco Capac, after the founding of Cuzco, to the fourth Inca Mayta Capac, from Pedro Sarmiento De Gamboa's sixteenth-century ***History of Peru***:

The Difference Between Manco Capac and the Alcabisas, Respecting the Arable Land

It has been said that one of the natural tribes of this valley of Cuzco was the Alcabisas. At the time when Manco Capac settled at Ynti-cancha and seized the goods of the Sauaseras and Huallas, the Alcabisas were settled half an arquebus shot from Ynti-canchi, towards the part where Santa Clara now stands. Manco Capac had a plan to spread out his forces that his tyrannical intentions might not be impeded, so he sent his people, as if loosely and idly, making free with the land. He took the lands without distinction, to support his companies. As he had taken those of the Huallas and Sauaseras, he wished also to take those of the Alcabisas. As these Alcabisas had given up some, Manco Capac wished and intended to take all or nearly all. When the Alcabisas saw that the new comers even entered their houses, they said: "These are men who are bellicose and unreasonable! they take our lands! Let us set up landmarks on the fields they have left to us." This they did, but Mama Huaco said to Manco Capac, "let us take all the water from the Alcabisas, and then they will be obliged to give us the rest of their land." This was done and they took away the water. Over this there were disputes; but as the followers of Manco Capac were more and more masterful, they forced the Alcabisas to give up their lands which they wanted, and to serve them as their lords, although the Alcabisas never voluntarily served Manco Capac nor looked upon him as their lord. On the contrary they always went about saying with loud voices-to those of Manco Capac: "Away! away! out of our territory." For this Manco Capac was more hard upon them, and oppressed them tyrannically.

Besides the Alcabisas there were other tribes, as we have mentioned before. These Manco Capac and Mama Huaco totally destroyed, and more especially one which lived near Ynti-cancha, in the nearest land, called Humanamean, between Ynti-cancha and Cayocachi, where there also lived another native Sinchi named Culunchima. Manco Capac entered the houses and lands of all the natives, especially of the Alcabisas, condemned their Sinchi to perpetual imprisonment, sending the others to banishment in Cayocachi, and forcing them to pay tribute. But they were always trying to free themselves from the tyranny, as the Alcabisas did later.

Having completed the yoke over the natives, their goods and persons, Manco Capac was now very old. Feeling the approach of death, and fearing that in leaving the sovereignty to his son, Sinchi Rocca, he and his successors might not be able to retain it owing to the bad things he had done and to the tyranny he had established, he ordered that the ten lineages or companies that had come with him from Tampu-tocco should form themselves into a garrison or guard, to be always on the watch over the persons of his son and of his other descendants to keep them safe. They were to elect the successor when he had been nominated by his father, or succeeded on the death of his father. For he would not trust the natives to nominate or elect, knowing the evil he had done, and the force he had used towards them. Manco Capac being now on the point of death, he left the bird *indi* enclosed in its cage, the *tupac-yauri* or sceptre, the *napa* and the *suntur-paucar* the insignia of a prince, [*though tyrant*,] to his son Sinchi Rocca that he might take his place, [*and this without the consent or election of any of the natives*].

Thus died Manco Capac, according to the accounts of those of his *ayllu* or lineage, at the age of 144 years, which were divided in the following manner. When he set out from Paccari-tampu or Tampu-tocco he was 36 years of age. From that time until he arrived at the valley of Cuzco, during which interval he was seeking for fertile lands, there were eight years. For in one place he stayed one, in another two years, in others more or less until he reached Cuzco, where he lived all the rest of the time, which was 100 years, as *Capac* or supreme and rich sovereign.

They say that he was a man of good stature, thin, rustic, cruel though frank, and that in dying he was converted into a stone of a height of a vara and a half. The stone was preserved with much veneration in the Ynti-cancha until the year 1559 when, the licentiate Polo Ondegardo being Corregidor of Cuzco, found it and took it away from where it was adored and venerated by all the Incas, in the village of Bimbilla near Cuzco.

From this Manco Capac were originated the ten ayllus mentioned above. From his time began the idols *huauquis*, which was an idol or demon chosen by each Inca for his companion and oracle which gave him answers. That of Manco Capac was the bird *indi* already mentioned. This Manco Capac ordered, for the preservation of his memory, the following: His eldest son by his legitimate wife, who was his sister, was to succeed to the sovereignty. If there was a second son his duty was to be to help all the other children and relations. They were to recognize him as the head in all their necessities, and he was to take charge of their interests, and for this duty estates were set aside. This party or lineage was called *ayllu* If there was no second son, or if there was one who was incapable, the duty was to be passed on to the nearest and ablest relation. And that those to come might have a precedent or example, Manco Capac made the first *ayllu* and called it *Chima Panaca Ayllu*, which means the lineage descending from Chima, because the first to whom he left his *ayllu* or lineage in charge was named *Chima*, and *Panaca* means «to descend.» It is to be noted that the members of this *ayllu* always adored the statue of Manco Capac, and not those of the other Incas, but the *ayllus* of the other Incas always worshipped that statue and the others also. It is not known what was done with the body, for there was only the statue. They carried it in their wars, thinking that it secured the victories they won. They also took it to Huanacauri, when they celebrated the *huarachicos* of the Incas. Huayna Capac took it with him to Quito and Cayambis, and afterwards it was brought back to Cuzco with the dead body of that Inca. There are still those of this *ayllu* in Cuzco who preserve the memory of the deeds of Manco Capac. The principal heads of the *ayllu* are now Don Diego Chaco, and Don Juan Huarhua Chima. They are Hurin-cuzcos. Manco Capac died in the year 665 of the nativity of Christ our Lord, Loyba the Goth reigning in Spain, Constantine IV being Emperor. He lived in the Ynti-cancha, House of the Sun.

Commences the Life of Sinchi Rocca, the Second Inca

It has been said that Manco Capac, the first Inca, who tyrannized over the natives of the valley of Cuzco, only subjugated the Huallas, Alcabisas, Sauaseras, Culunchima, Copalimayta and the others mentioned above, who were all within the circuit of what is now the city of Cuzco.

To this Manco Capac succeeded his son Sinchi Rocca, son also of Mama Occlo, his mother and aunt. He succeeded by nomination of his father, under the care of the *ayllus* who then all lived together, but not by election of the people, they were all either in flight, prisoners, wounded or banished, and were all his mortal enemies owing to the cruelties and robberies exercised upon them by his father Manco Capac. Sinchi Rocca was not a warlike person, and no feats of arms are recorded of him, nor did he sally forth from Cuzco, either himself or by his captains. He added nothing to what his father had subjugated, only holding by his *ayllus* those whom his father had crushed. He had for a wife Mama Cuca of the town of Saño by whom he had a son named Lloqui Yupanqui. Lloqui means left-handed, because he was so. He left his *ayllu* called *Raura Panaca Ayllu* of the Hurin-cuzco side. There are some of this *ayllu* living, the chiefs being Don Alonso Puscon and Don Diego Quispi. These have the duty of knowing and maintaining the things and memories of Sinchi Rocca. He lived in Ynti-cancha, the House of the Sun, and all his years were 127. He succeeded when 108, and reigned 19 years. He died in the year of the nativity of our Lord Jesus Christ 675, Wamba being King of Spain, Leo IV Emperor, and Donus Pope. He left an idol of stone shaped like a fish called *Huanachiri Amaru*, which during life was his idol or *guauqui*. Polo, being Corregidor of Cuzco, found this idol, with the body of Sinchi Rocca, in the village of Bimbilla, among some bars of copper. The idol had attendants and cultivated lands for its service.

The Life of Lloqui Yupanqui, the Third Inca

On the death of Sinchi Rocca the Incaship was occupied by Lloqui Yupanqui, son of Sinchi Rocca by Mama Cuca his wife. It is to be noted that, although Manco Capac had ordered that the eldest son should succeed, this Inca broke the rule of his grandfather, for he had an elder brother named Manco Sapaca, as it is said, who did not consent, and the Indians do not declare whether he was nominated by his father. From this I think that Lloqui Yupanqui was not nominated, but Manco Sapaca as the eldest, for so little regard for the natives or their approval was shown. This being so, it was tyranny against the natives and infidelity to relations with connivance of the *ayllus* legionaries; and with the Inca›s favour they could do what they liked, by supporting him. So Lloqui Yupanqui lived in Ynti-cancha like his father. He never left Cuzco on a warlike expedition nor performed any memorable deed, but merely lived like his father, having communication with some provinces and chiefs. These were Huaman Samo, chief of Huaro, Pachaculla Viracocha, the Ayamarcas of Tampu-cunca, and the Quilliscachis.

One day Lloqui Yupanqui being very sad and afflicted, the Sun appeared to him in the form of a person and consoled him by saying: "Do not be sorrowful, Lloqui Yupanqui, for from you shall descend great Lords," also, that he might hold it for certain that he would have male issue. For Lloqui Yupanqui was then very old, and neither had a son nor expected to have one. This having been made known, and what the Sun had announced to Lloqui Yupanqui having been published to the people, his relations determined to seek a wife for him. His brother Manco Sapaca, understanding the fraternal disposition, sought for a woman who was suitable for it. He found her in a town called Oma, two leagues from Cuzco, asked for her from her guardians, and, with their consent, brought her to Cuzco. She was then married to Lloqui Yupanqui. Her name was Mama Cava, and by her the Inca had a son named Mayta Capac.

This Lloqui did nothing worthy of remembrance. He carried with him an idol, which was his *guauqui* called *Apu Mayta*. His *ayllu* is *Avayni Panaca Ayllu*, because the first who had the charge of this *ayllu* was named Avayni. This Inca lived and died in Ynti-cancha. He was 132 years of age, having succeeded at the age of 21, so that he was sovereign or 'Capac' for 111 years. He died in 786, Alfonso el Casto being King of Spain and Leo IV Supreme Pontiff. Some of this *ayllu* still live at Cuzco. The chiefs are Putisuc Titu Avcaylli, Titu Rimachi, Don Felipe Titu Cunti Mayta, Don Agustin Cunti Mayta, Juan Bautista Quispi Cunti Mayta. They are Hurin-cuzcos. The Licentiate Polo found the body of this Inca with the rest.

The Life of Mayta Capac, the Fourth Inca

Mayta Capac, the fourth Inca, son of Lloqui Yupanqui and his wife Mama Cava, is to those Indians what Hercules is to us, as regards his birth and acts, for they relate strange things of him. At the very first the Indians of his lineage, and all the others in general, say that his father, when he was begotten, was so old and weak that every one believed he was useless, so that they thought the conception was a miracle. The second wonder was that his mother bore him three months after conception, and that he was born strong and with teeth. All affirm this, and that he grew at such a rate that in one year he had as much strength and was as big as a boy of eight years or more. At two years he fought with very big boys, knocked them about and hurt them seriously. This all looks as if it might be counted with the other fables, but I write what the natives believe respecting their ancestors, and they hold this to be so true that they would kill anyone who asserted the contrary.

They say of this Mayta that when he was of very tender years, he was playing with some boys of the Alcabisas and Culunchimas, natives of Cuzco, when he hurt many of them and killed some. And one day, drinking or taking water from a fountain, he broke the leg of the son of a Sinchi of the Alcabisas, and hunted the rest until they shut themselves up in their houses, where the Alcabisas lived without injuring the Incas.

But now the Alcabisas, unable to endure longer the naughtiness of Mayta Capac, which he practised under the protection of Lloqui Yupanqui, and the *ayllus* who watched over him, determined to regain their liberty and to venture their lives for it. So they selected ten resolute Indians to go to the House of the Sun where Lloqui Yupanqui and his son Mayta Capac lived, and enter it with the intention of killing them. At the time Mayta Capac was in the court yard of the house, playing at ball with some other boys. When he saw enemies entering the house with arms, he threw one of the balls he was playing with, and killed one. He did the same to another, and, attacking the rest, they all fled. Though the rest escaped, they had received many wounds, and in this state they went back to their Sinchis of Calunchima and Alcabasa.

The Chiefs, considering the harm Mayta Capac had done to the natives when a child, feared that when he was grown up he would destroy them all, and for this reason they resolved to die for their liberty. All the inhabitants of the valley of Cuzco, that had been spared by Manco Capac, united to make war on the Incas. This very seriously alarmed Lloqui Yupanqui. He thought he was lost, and reprehended his son Mayta Capac, saying, "Son! why hast thou been so harmful to the natives of this valley, so that in my old age I shall die at the hands of our enemies?" As the *ayllus*, who were in garrison with the Incas, rejoiced more in rapine and disturbances than in quiet, they took the part of Mayta Capac and told the old Inca to hold his peace, leaving the matter to his son, so Lloqui Yupanqui took no further steps in reprehending Mayta Capac. The Alcabisas and Culunchimas assembled their forces and Mayta Capac marshalled his *ayllus*. There was a battle between the two armies and although it was doubtful for some time, both sides fighting desperately for victory, the Alcabisas and Calunchimas were finally defeated by the troops of Mayta Capac.

But not for this did the Alcabisas give up the attempt to free themselves and avenge their wrongs. Again they challenged Mayta Capac to battle, which he accepted. As they advanced they say that such a hail storm fell over the Alcabisas that they were defeated a third time, and entirely broken up. Mayta Capac imprisoned their Sinchi for the remainder of his life.

Mayta Capac married Mama Tacucaray, native of the town of Tacucaray, and by her he had a legitimate son named Capac Yupanqui, besides four others named Tarco Huaman, Apu Cunti Mayta, Queco Avcaylli, and Rocca Yupanqui.

This Mayta Capac was warlike, and the Inca who first distinguished himself in arms after the time of Mama Huaco and Manco Capac. They relate of him that he dared to open the hamper containing the bird *indi*. This bird, brought by Manco Capac from Tampu-tocco, had been inherited by his successors, the predecessors of Mayta Capac, who had always kept it shut up in a hamper or box of straw, such was the fear they had of it. But Mayta Capac was bolder than any of them. Desirous of seeing what his predecessors had guarded so carefully, he opened the hamper, saw the bird *indi* and had some conversation with it. They say that it gave him oracles, and that after the interview with the bird he was wiser, and knew better what he should do, and what would happen.

With all this he did not go forth from the valley of Cuzco, although chiefs from some distant nations came to visit him. He lived in Ynti-cancha, the House of the Sun. He left a lineage called *Usca Mayta Panaca Ayllu*, and some members of it are still living in Cuzco. The heads are named Don Juan Tambo Usca Mayta, and Don Baltasar Quiso Mayta. They are Hurin-cuzcos. Mayta Capac died at the age of 112 years, in the year 890 of the nativity of our Lord Jesus Christ. The Licentiate Polo found his body and idol *guauqui* with the rest.

The Life of Capac Yupanqui, the Fifth Inca

At the time of his death, Mayta Capac named Capac Yupanqui as his successor, his son by his wife Mama Tacucaray. This Capac Yupanqui, as soon as he succeeded to the Incaship, made his brothers swear allegiance to him, and that they desired that he should be Capac. They complied from fear, for he was proud and cruel. At first he lived very quietly in the Ynti-cancha. It is to be noted that although Capac Yupanqui succeeded his father, he was not the eldest son. Cunti Mayta, who was older, had an ugly face. His father had, therefore, disinherited him and named Capac Yupanqui as successor to the sovereignty, and Cunti Mayta as high priest. For this reason Capac Yupanqui was not the legitimate heir, although he tyrannically forced his brothers to swear allegiance to him.

This Inca, it is said, was the first to make conquests beyond the valley of Cuzco. He forcibly subjugated the people of Cuyumarca and Ancasmarca, four leagues from Cuzco. A wealthy Sinchi of Ayamarca, from fear, presented his daughter, named Ccuri-hilpay to the Inca. Others say that she was a native of Cuzco. The Inca received her as his wife, and had a son by her named Inca Rocca, besides five other sons by various women. These sons were named Apu Calla, Humpi, Apu Saca, Apu Chima-chaui, and Uchun-cuna-ascalla-rando. Apu Saca had a son named Apu Mayta, a very valiant and famous captain, who greatly distinguished himself in the time of Inca Rocca and Viracocha Inca, in company with Vicaquirau, another esteemed captain. Besides these Capac Yupanqui had another son named Apu Urco Huaranca. This Capac Yupanqui lived 104 years, and was Capac for 89 years. He succeeded at the age of 15, and died in the year 980 of the nativity of our redeemer Jesus Christ. His *ayllu* or lineage was and is called *Apu Mayta Panaca Ayllu*. Several of this lineage are now living, the principal heads being four in number, namely, Don Cristobal Cusi-hualpa, Don Antonio Piçuy, Don Francisco

Cocasaca, and Don Alonso Rupaca. They are Hurin-cuzcos. The Licentiate Polo found the idol or *guaoqui* of this Inca with the body. They were hidden with the rest, to conceal the idolatrous ceremonies of heathen times.

The Legacy of Pachacuti Inca Yupanqui

THE YNCA PACHACUTEC (Pachacutic or Pachacuti Inca Yupanqui, the ninth Inca), being now old, resolved to rest and not to make further conquests; for he had increased his empire until it was more than one hundred and thirty leagues from north to south, and in width from the snowy chain of the Andes to the sea, being sixty leagues from east to west in some places, and seventy in others, more or less. He now devoted himself to the confirmation of the laws of his ancestors, and to the enactment of new laws for the common good.

He founded many towns in those lands which by industry and by means of the numerous irrigation channels he caused to be made, were converted from sterile and uncultivated wilds into fruitful and rich districts.

He built many temples of the Sun in imitation of that of Cuzco, and many convents of virgins. He ordered many store-houses on the royal roads to be repaired, and houses to be built where the Yncas might lodge when travelling.

He also caused store-houses to be built in all villages, large or small, where supplies might be kept for succouring the people in time of scarcity, and he ordered these depots to be filled from the crops of the Ynca and of the Sun. In short, it may be said that he completely reformed the empire, as well as regards their vain religion, which he provided with new rites and ceremonies, destroying the numerous idols of his vassals, as by enacting new laws and regulations for the daily and moral life of the people, forbidding the abuses and barbarous customs to which the Indians were addicted before they were brought under his rule.

He also reformed the army in such fashion as proved him to be as great a captain as he was a king and a ruler; and he increased the honours and favours shown to those who distinguished themselves in war. He especially favoured and enlarged the great city of Cuzco, enriching it with new edifices and a larger population. He ordered a palace to be built for himself near the schools founded by his great grandfather Ynca Rocca. On account of these deeds, as well as for his amiable disposition and benignant government, he was loved and worshipped as another Jupiter. He reigned, according to the accounts of the Indians, more than fifty years, and some say more than sixty years. He lived in much peace and tranquillity, being alike beloved and obeyed, and at the end of this long time he died. He was universally lamented by all his vassals, and was placed among the number of their gods, as were the other Kings Yncas, his ancestors. He was embalmed, according to their custom, and the mourning, sacrifices and burial ceremonies lasted for a year.

He left as his heir the Ynca Yupanqui, who was his son by the Ccoya Anahuarque, his legitimate wife and sister. He left more than three hundred other sons and daughters, and some even say that, judging from his long life and the number of his wives, he must have had four hundred either legitimate or illegitimate children; and though this is a great many, the Indians say that it was few for such a father.

The Spanish historians confuse these two Kings, father and son, giving the names of both to one. The father was named Pachacutec. The name Ynca was common to all, for it was their title from the days of the first Ynca, called Manco Ccapac. In our account of the life of Lloque Yupanqui we described the meaning of the word Yupanqui, which word was also the name of this King, and combining the two names, they formed Ynca Yupanqui, which title was applied to all the Kings Yncas, so that Yupanqui ceased to be a special name. These two names are equivalent to the names Caesar Augustus, given to all the Emperors. Thus the Indians, in recounting the deeds of their Kings, and calling them by their names, would say, Pachacutec Ynca Yupanqui. The Spaniards understood that this was one King, and they do not admit the son and successor of Pachacutec, who was called Ynca Yupanqui, taking the two titles as his special name, and giving the same name to his own eldest son. But the Indians, to distinguish him from his father, called the latter Tupac (which means 'He who shines') Ynca Yupanqui. He was father of Huayna Ccapac Ynca Yupanqui, and grandfather of Huascar Ynca Yupanqui; and so all the other Yncas may be called by these titles. I have said this much to enable those who read this history to avoid confusion.

The Father Blas Valera, speaking of this Ynca, says as follows: "The Ynca Huiraccocha being dead and worshipped among the Indians as a god, his son, the great Titu, with surname of Manco Ccapac, succeeded him. This was his name until his father gave him that of Pachacutec, which means 'Reformer of the World.' That title was confirmed afterwards by his distinguished acts and sayings, insomuch that his first name was entirely forgotten. He governed his empire with so much industry, prudence and resolution, as well in peace as in war, that not only did he increase the boundaries of all the four quarters, called *Ttahua-ntin suyu*, but also he enacted many laws, all which have been confirmed by our Catholic Kings, except those relating to idolatry and to forbidden degrees of marriage. This Ynca above all things ennobled and increased, with great privileges, the schools that were founded in Cuzco by the King Ynca Rocca. He added to the number of the masters, and ordered that all the lords of vassals and captains and their sons, and all the Indians who held any office, should speak the language of Cuzco; and that no one should receive any office or lordship who was not well acquainted with it. In order that this useful law might have full effect, he appointed very learned masters for the sons of the princes and nobles, not only for those in Cuzco, but also for those throughout the provinces, in which he stationed masters that they might teach the language of Cuzco to all who were employed in the service of the state. Thus it was that in the whole empire of Peru one language was spoken, although now (owing to negligence) many provinces, where it was understood, have entirely lost it, not without great injury to the preaching of the gospel. All the Indians who, by obeying this law, still retain a knowledge of the language of Cuzco, are more civilized and more intelligent than the others.

"This Pachacutec prohibited any one, except princes and their sons, from wearing gold, silver, precious stones, plumes of feathers of different colours, nor the wool of the vicuña, which they weave with admirable skill. He permitted the people to be moderately ornamented on the first days of the month, and on some other festivals. The tributary

Indians still observe this law, and content themselves with ordinary clothes, by which they avoid much vice which gay clothing is apt to cause. But the Indians, who are servants to Spaniards, and those who live in Spanish cities, are very extravagant in this particular, and do much harm alike to their pockets and consciences. This Ynca also ordered that great frugality should be observed in eating, although in drinking more freedom was allowed, both among the princes and the common people. He ordained that there should be special judges to try the idle, and desired that all should be engaged in work of some kind, either in serving their parents or masters, or in the service of the state; so much so, that even boys and girls of from five to seven years of age were given something to do suitable to their years. The blind, lame, and dumb, who could use their hands, were employed in some kind of work, and the aged were sent to scare the birds from the crops, and were supplied with food and clothing from the public store-houses. In order that labour might not be so continuous as to become oppressive, the Ynca ordained that there should be three holidays every month, in which the people should divert themselves with various games. He also commanded that there should be three fairs every month, when the labourers in the field should come to the market and hear anything that the Ynca or his Council might have ordained. They called these assemblies *Catu*, and they took place on the holidays.

"The Ynca also made a law that every province should have a fixed boundary enclosing the forests, pastures, rivers, lakes, mountains, and lands for tillage; all which should belong to that province and be within its jurisdiction in perpetuity. No Governor or Curaca could diminish or divide or appropriate to his own use any portion; but the land was divided according to a fixed rule which was defined by the same law for the common good, and the special benefit of the inhabitants of the province. The royal estates and those of the Sun were set apart, and the Indians had to plough, sow, and reap the crops, as well on their own lands as on those of the State. Hence it will be seen that it is false, what many have asserted, that the Indians had no proprietary right in the land. For this division was not made with reference to proprietary right, but for the common and special work to be expended upon the land. It was a very ancient custom among the Indians to work together not only on public lands, but also on their own, and with this view they measured the land, that each might complete such portion as he was able. The whole population assembled, and first worked their own lands in common, each one helping his neighbours, and then they began upon the royal estates; and the same practice was followed in sowing and in reaping. Almost in the same way they built their houses. The Indian who required a house went to the Council to appoint a day when it should be built, the inhabitants with one accord assembled to assist their neighbour, and thus the house was completed. The Ynca approved of this custom, and confirmed it by law. To this day many villages of Indians observe this law, and help each other with Christian charity; but avaricious men, who think only of themselves, do themselves harm and their neighbours no good.

"In fine, this King, with the advice of his Council, made many laws, rules, ordinances, and customs for the good of the people in numerous provinces. He also abolished many others which were detrimental either to the public peace or to his sovereignty. He also enacted many statutes against blasphemy, patricide, fratricide, homicide, treason, adultery, child-stealing, seduction, theft, arson; as well as regulations for the ceremonies of the temple. He confirmed many more that had been enacted by the Yncas his ancestors; such as that sons should obey and serve their fathers until they reached the age of twenty-five, that none should marry without the consent of the parents, and of the parents of the girl;

that a marriage without this consent was invalid and the children illegitimate; but that if the consent was obtained afterwards the children then became legitimate. This Ynca also confirmed the laws of inheritance to lordships according to the ancient customs of each province; and he forbade the judges from receiving bribes from litigants. This Ynca made many other laws of less importance, which I omit, to avoid prolixity. Further on I shall relate what laws he made for the guidance of judges, for the contracting of marriages, for making wills, and for the army, as well as for reckoning the years. In our time the Viceroy, Don Francisco de Toledo, changed or revoked many laws and regulations made by this Ynca; and the Indians, admiring his absolute power, called him the second Pachacutec, for they said he was the Reformer of the first Reformer. Their reverence and veneration for this Ynca was so great that to this day they cannot forget him."

Down to this point is from what I found amongst the torn papers of Father Blas Valera. That which he promises to write further on, touching the judges, marriages, wills, the army, and the reckoning of the year, is lost, which is a great pity. On another leaf I found part of the sententious sayings of this Ynca Pachacutec, which are as follows: –

"When subjects, captains and Curacas, cordially obey the King, then the kingdom enjoys perfect peace and quiet.

"Envy is a worm that gnaws and consumes the entrails of the envious.

"He that envies and is envied, has a double torment.

"It is better that others should envy you for being good, than that you should envy others, you yourself being evil.

"He that envies another, injures himself.

"He that envies the good, draws evil from them for himself, as does the spider in taking poison from flowers.

"Drunkenness, anger and madness go together; only the first two are voluntary and to be removed, while the last is perpetual.

"He that kills another without authority or just cause, condemns himself to death.

"He that kills his neighbour must of necessity die; and for this reason the ancient Kings, our ancestors, ordained that all homicides should be punished by a violent death, a law which we confirm afresh.

"Under no circumstances should thieves be tolerated, who, being able to gain a livelihood by honest labour and to possess it by a just right, wish to have more by robbing and stealing. It is very just that he who is a thief should be put to death.

"Adulterers, who destroy the peace and happiness of others, ought to be declared thieves, and condemned to death without mercy.

"The noble and generous man is known by the patience he shows in adversity.

"Impatience is the sign of a vile and base mind, badly taught and worse accustomed.

"When subjects do their best to obey without any hesitation, kings and governors ought to treat them with liberality and kindness; but when they act otherwise, with rigour and strict justice, though always with prudence.

"Judges who secretly receive gifts from suitors ought to be looked upon as thieves, and punished with death as such.

"Governors ought to attend to two things with much attention. The first is, that they and their subjects keep and comply exactly with the laws of their king. The second, that they consult with much vigilance and care, touching the common and special affairs of their provinces. The man who knows not how to govern his house and family, will know much less how to rule the state. Such a man should not be preferred above others.

"The physician herbalist that is ignorant of the virtues of herbs, or who, knowing the uses of some, has not attained a knowledge of all, understands little or nothing. He ought to work until he knows all, as well the useful as the injurious plants, in order to deserve the name he pretends to.

"He who attempts to count the stars, not even knowing how to count the marks and knots of the '*quipus*,' ought to be held in derision."

These are the sayings of Ynca Pachacutec. He speaks of the marks and knots of the accounts because, as they had neither letters for writing nor figures for ciphering, they kept their accounts by means of marks and knots.

The Mythology & Religion of Ancient Peru

THE RELIGION OF THE ANCIENT PERUVIANS had obviously developed in a much shorter time than that of the Mexicans. The more ancient character inherent in it was displayed in the presence of deities many of which were little better than mere totems, and although a definite monotheism or worship of one god appears to have been reached, it was not by the efforts of the priestly caste that this was achieved, but rather by the will of the Inca Pachacutic, who seems to have been a monarch gifted with rare insight and ability – a man much after the type of the Mexican Nezahualcoyotl.

In Inca times the religion of the people was solely directed by the state, and regulated in such a manner that independent theological thought was permitted no outlet. But it must not be inferred from this that no change had ever come over the spirit of Peruvian religion. As a matter of fact, sweeping changes had been effected, but these had been solely the work of the Inca race, the leaders of which had amalgamated the various faiths of the peoples whom they had conquered into one official belief.

Totemism

Garcilasso el Inca de la Vega, an early Spanish writer on matters Peruvian, states that tradition ran that in ante-Inca times every district, family, and village possessed its own god, each different from the others. These gods were usually such objects as trees, mountains, flowers, herbs, caves, large stones, pieces of jasper, and animals. The jaguar, puma, and bear were worshipped for their strength and fierceness, the monkey and fox for their cunning, the condor for its size and because several tribes believed themselves to be descended from it. The screech-owl was worshipped for its beauty, and the common owl for its power of seeing in the dark. Serpents, particularly the larger and more dangerous varieties, were especially regarded with reverence.

Although Payne classes all these gods together as totems, it is plain that those of the first class – the flowers, herbs, caves, and pieces of jasper – are merely fetishes. A fetish is an object in which is believed to be resident a spirit which, by its magic, will assist one in one's undertakings. A totem is an object or an animal, usually the latter, with which the people of a tribe believe themselves to be connected by ties of blood and from which they are descended. It later becomes the type or symbol of the tribe.

Paccariscas

Lakes, springs, rocks, mountains, precipices, and caves were all regarded by the various Peruvian tribes as *paccariscas* – places whence their ancestors had originally issued to the upper world. The *paccarisca* was usually saluted with the cry, "Thou art my birthplace, thou art my life-spring. Guard me from evil, O Paccarisca!" In the holy spot a spirit was supposed to dwell which served the tribe as a kind of oracle. Naturally the *paccarisca* was looked upon with extreme reverence.

Worship of Stones

The worship of stones appears to have been almost as universal in ancient Peru as it was in ancient Palestine. Man in his primitive state believes stones to be the framework of the earth, its bony structure. He considers himself to have emerged from some cave – in fact, from the entrails of the earth. Nearly all American creation myths regard man as thus emanating from the bowels of the great terrestrial mother. Rocks which were thus chosen as *paccariscas* are found, among many other places, at Callca, in the valley of the Yucay, and at Titicaca there is a great mass of red sandstone on the top of a high ridge with almost inaccessible slopes and dark, gloomy recesses where the sun was thought to have hidden himself at the time of the great deluge which covered all the earth. The rock of Titicaca was, in fact, the great *paccarisca* of the sun itself.

We are thus not surprised to find that many standing stones were worshipped in Peru in aboriginal times. Thus Arriaga states that rocks of great size which bore some resemblance to the human figure were imagined to have been at one time gigantic men or spirits who, because they disobeyed the creative power, were turned into stone. According to another account they were said to have suffered this punishment for refusing to listen to the words of Thonapa, the son of the creator, who, like Quetzalcoatl or Manco Capac, had taken upon himself the guise of a wandering Indian, so that he might have an opportunity of bringing the arts of civilization to the aborigines. At Tiahuanaco a certain group of stones was said to represent all that remained of the villagers of that place, who, instead of paying fitting attention to the wise counsel which Thonapa the Civilizer bestowed upon them, continued to dance and drink in scorn of the teachings he had brought to them.

Again, some stones were said to have become men. In the legend of Ccapac Inca Pachacutic, when Cuzco was attacked in force by the Chancas an Indian erected stones to which he attached shields and weapons so that they should appear to represent so many warriors in hiding. Pachacutic, in great need of assistance, cried to them with such vehemence to come to his help that they became men, and rendered him splendid service.

Huacas

Whatever was sacred, of sacred origin, or of the nature of a relic the Peruvians designated a *huaca*, from the root *huacan*, to howl, native worship invariably taking the form of a kind of howl, or weird, dirge-like wailing. All objects of reverence were known as *huacas*, although those of a higher class were also alluded to as *viracochas*. The Peruvians had, naturally, many forms of *huaca*, the most popular of which were those of the fetish class which could be carried about by the individual. These were usually stones or pebbles, many of which were carved and painted, and some made to represent human beings. The llama and the ear of maize were perhaps the most usual forms of these sacred objects. Some of them had an agricultural significance. In order that irrigation might proceed favourably a *huaca* was placed at intervals in proximity to the *acequias*, or irrigation canals, which was supposed to prevent them leaking or otherwise failing to supply a sufficiency of moisture to the parched maize-fields. *Huacas* of this sort were known as *ccompas*, and were regarded as deities of great importance, as the food-supply of the community was thought to be wholly dependent upon their assistance. Other *huacas* of a similar kind were called *chichics* and *huancas*, and these presided over the fortunes of the maize, and ensured that a sufficient supply of rain should be forthcoming. Great numbers of these agricultural fetishes were destroyed by the zealous commissary Hernandez de Avendaño.

The Mamas

Spirits which were supposed to be instrumental in forcing the growth of the maize or other plants were the *mamas*. We find a similar conception among many Brazilian tribes today, so that the idea appears to have been a widely accepted one in South American countries. The Peruvians called such agencies 'mothers,' adding to the generic name that of the plant or herb with which they were specially associated. Thus *acsumama* was the potato-mother, *quinuamama* the quinua-mother, *saramama* the maize-mother, and *cocamama* the mother of the coca-shrub. Of these the *saramama* was naturally the most important, governing as it did the principal source of the food-supply of the community. Sometimes an image of the *saramama* was carved in stone, in the shape of an ear of maize. The *saramama* was also worshipped in the form of a doll, or *huantaysara*, made out of stalks of maize, renewed at each harvest, much as the idols of the great corn-mother of Mexico were manufactured at each harvest-season. After having been made, the image was watched over for three nights, and then sacrifice was done to it. The priest or medicine man of the tribe would then inquire of it whether or not it was capable of existing until that time in the next year. If its spirit replied in the affirmative it was permitted to remain where it was until the following harvest. If not it was removed, burnt, and another figure took its place, to which similar questions were put.

The Huamantantac

Connected with agriculture in some degree was the Huamantantac (He who causes the Cormorants to gather themselves together). This was the agency responsible for the gathering of sea birds, resulting in the deposits of guano to be found along the Peruvian coast which are so valuable in the cultivation of the maize plant. He was regarded as a most beneficent spirit, and was sacrificed to with exceeding fervour.

Huaris

The *huaris*, or 'great ones,' were the ancestors of the aristocrats of a tribe, and were regarded as specially favourable toward agricultural effort, possibly because the land had at one time belonged to them personally. They were sometimes alluded to as the 'gods of strength,' and were sacrificed to by libations of *chicha*. Ancestors in general were deeply revered, and had an agricultural significance, in that considerable tracts of land were tilled in order that they might be supplied with suitable food and drink offerings. As the number of ancestors increased more and more land was brought into cultivation, and the hapless people had their toil added to immeasurably by these constant demands upon them.

Huillcas

The *huillcas* were *huacas* which partook of the nature of oracles. Many of these were serpents, trees, and rivers, the noises made by which appeared to the primitive Peruvians – as, indeed, they do to primitive folk all over the world – to be of the quality of articulate speech. Both the Huillcamayu and the Apurimac rivers at Cuzco were *huillca* oracles of this kind, as their names, 'Huillca-river' and 'Great Speaker,' denote. These oracles often set the mandate of the Inca himself at defiance, occasionally supporting popular opinion against his policy.

The Oracles of the Andes

The Peruvian Indians of the Andes range within recent generations continued to adhere to the superstitions they had inherited from their fathers. A rare and interesting account of these says that they "admit an evil being, the inhabitant of the centre of the earth, whom they consider as the author of their misfortunes, and at the mention of whose name they tremble. The most shrewd among them take advantage of this belief to obtain respect, and represent themselves as his delegates. Under the denomination of *mohanes*, or *agoreros*, they are consulted even on the most trivial occasions. They preside over the intrigues of love, the health of the community, and the taking of the field. Whatever repeatedly occurs to defeat their prognostics, falls on themselves; and they are wont to pay for their deceptions very dearly. They chew a species of vegetable called *piripiri*, and throw it into the air, accompanying this act by certain recitals and incantations, to injure some, to benefit others, to procure rain and the inundation of the rivers, or, on the other hand, to occasion settled weather, and a plentiful store of agricultural productions. Any such result, having been casually verified on a single occasion, suffices to confirm the Indians in their faith, although they may have been cheated a thousand times. Fully persuaded that they cannot resist the influence of the *piripiri*, as soon as they know that they have been solicited in love by its means, they fix their eyes on the impassioned object, and discover a thousand amiable traits, either real or fanciful, which indifference had before concealed from their view. But the principal power, efficacy, and it may be said misfortune of the *mohanes* consist in the cure of the sick. Every malady is ascribed to their enchantments, and means are instantly taken to ascertain by whom the mischief may have been wrought. For this purpose, the nearest relative takes a quantity of the juice of *floripondium*, and suddenly falls intoxicated by the violence of the plant. He is placed in a fit posture to prevent suffocation, and on his coming to himself, at the end of three days, the *mohane* who has the greatest resemblance to the sorcerer he saw in his visions is to undertake the cure, or if, in the interim, the sick man has perished, it is customary to subject him to the same fate. When not any sorcerer occurs in the visions, the first *mohane* they encounter has the misfortune to represent his image."

Lake-Worship in Peru

At Lake Titicaca the Peruvians believed the inhabitants of the earth, animals as well as men, to have been fashioned by the creator, and the district was thus sacrosanct in their eyes. The people of the Collao called it Mamacota (Mother-water), because it furnished them with supplies of food. Two great idols were connected with this worship. One called Copacahuana was made of a bluish-green stone shaped like a fish with a human head, and was placed in a commanding position on the shores of the lake. On the arrival of the Spaniards so deeply rooted was the worship of this goddess that they could only suppress it by raising an image of the Virgin in place of the idol. The Christian emblem remains to this day. Mamacota was venerated as the giver of fish, with which the lake abounded. The other image, Copacati (Serpent-stone), represented the element of water as embodied in the lake itself in the form of an image wreathed in serpents, which in America are nearly always symbolical of water.

The Lost Island

A strange legend is recounted of this lake-goddess. She was chiefly worshipped as the giver of rain, but Huaina Ccapac, who had modern ideas and journeyed through the country casting down *huacas*, had determined to raise on an island of Lake Titicaca a temple to Yatiri (The Ruler), the Aymara name of the god Pachacamac in his form of Pachayachachic. He commenced by raising the new shrine on the island of Titicaca itself. But the deity when called upon refused to vouchsafe any reply to his worshippers or priests. Huaina then commanded that the shrine should be transferred to the island of Apinguela. But the same thing happened there. He then inaugurated a temple on the island of Paapiti, and lavished upon it many sacrifices of llamas, children, and precious metals. But the offended tutelary goddess of the lake, irritated beyond endurance by this invasion of her ancient domain, lashed the watery waste into such a frenzy of storm that the island and the shrine which covered it disappeared beneath the waves and were never thereafter beheld by mortal eye.

The Thunder-God of Peru

The rain-and-thunder god of Peru was worshipped in various parts of the country under various names. Among the Collao he was known as Con, and in that part of the Inca dominions now known as Bolivia he was called Churoquella. Near the cordilleras of the coast he was probably known as Pariacaca, who expelled the *huaca* of the district by dreadful tempests, hurling rain and hail at him for three days and nights in such quantities as to form the great lake of Pariacaca. Burnt llamas were offered to him. But the Incas, discontented with this local worship, which by no means suited their system of central government, determined to create one thunder-deity to whom all the tribes in the empire must bow as the only god of his class. We are not aware what his name was, but we know from mythological evidence that he was a mixture of all the other gods of thunder in the Peruvian Empire, first because he invariably occupied the third place in the triad of greater deities, the creator, sun, and thunder, all of whom were more or less amalgamations of provincial and metropolitan gods, and secondly because a great image of him was erected in the Coricancha at Cuzco, in which he was represented in human form, wearing a headdress which concealed his face, symbolic of the clouds, which ever veil the thunder-god's head. He had a special temple of his own, moreover, and was assigned a share in the sacred lands by the Inca Pachacutic. He was accompanied by a figure of his sister, who carried jars of water. An unknown Quichuan poet composed on the myth the following graceful little poem, which was translated by the late Daniel Garrison Brinton:

Bounteous Princess,
Lo, thy brother
Breaks thy vessel
Now in fragments.
From the blow come
Thunder, lightning,
Strokes of lightning;
And thou, Princess,
Tak'st the water,
With it rainest,
And the hail or
Snow dispensest,
Viracocha,
World-constructor.

It will be observed that the translator here employs the name Viracocha as if it were that of the deity. But it was merely a general expression in use for a more than usually sacred being. Brinton, commenting upon the legend, says: "In this pretty waif that has floated down to us from the wreck of a literature now forever lost there is more than one point to attract the notice of the antiquary. He may find in it a hint to decipher those names of divinities so common in Peruvian legends, Contici and Illatici. Both mean 'the Thunder Vase,' and both doubtless refer to the conception here displayed of the phenomena of the thunderstorm." Alluding to Peruvian thunder-myth elsewhere, he says in an illuminating passage: "Throughout the realms of the Incas the Peruvians venerated as maker of all things and ruler of the firmament the god Ataguju. The legend was that from him proceeded the first of mortals, the man Guamansuri, who descended to the earth and there wedded the sister of certain Guachimines, rayless ones or Darklings, who then possessed it. They destroyed him, but their sister gave birth to twin sons, Apocatequil and Piguerao. The former was the more powerful. By touching the corpse of his mother he brought her to life, he drove off and slew the Guachimines, and, directed by Ataguju, released the race of Indians from the soil by turning it up with a spade of gold. For this reason they adored him as their maker. He it was, they thought, who produced the thunder and the lightning by hurling stones with his sling. And the thunderbolts that fall, said they, are his children. Few villages were willing to be without one or more of these. They were in appearance small, round stones, but had the admirable properties of securing fertility to the fields, protecting from lightning, and, by a transition easy to understand, were also adored as gods of fire as well material as of the passions, and were capable of kindling the dangerous flames of desire in the most frigid bosoms. Therefore they were in great esteem as love-charms. Apocatequil's statue was erected on the mountains, with that of his mother on one hand and his brother on the other. 'He was Prince of Evil, and the most respected god of the Peruvians. From Quito to Cuzco not an Indian but would give all he possessed to conciliate him. Five priests, two stewards, and a crowd of slaves served his image. And his chief temple was surrounded by a very considerable village, whose inhabitants had no other occupation but to wait on him.'" In memory of these brothers twins in Peru were always deemed sacred to the lightning.

There is an instance on record of how the *huillca* could refuse on occasion to recognize even royalty itself. Manco, the Inca who had been given the kingly power by Pizarro, offered a sacrifice to one of these oracular shrines. The oracle refused to recognize him, through the medium of its guardian priest, stating that Manco was not the rightful Inca. Manco therefore caused the oracle, which was in the shape of a rock, to be thrown down, whereupon its guardian spirit emerged in the form of a parrot and flew away. It is probable that the bird thus liberated had been taught by the priests to answer to the questions of those who came to consult the shrine. But we learn that on Manco commanding that the parrot should be pursued it sought another rock, which opened to receive it, and the spirit of the *huillca* was transferred to this new abode.

The Great God Pachacamac

Later Peruvian mythology recognized only three gods of the first rank, the earth, the thunder, and the creative agency. Pachacamac, the great spirit of earth, derived his name from a word *pacha*, which may be best translated as 'things.' In its sense of visible things it is equivalent to 'world,' applied to things which happen in succession it denotes 'time,' and to things connected with persons 'property,' especially clothes. The world of visible things is thus Mamapacha (Earth-Mother), under which name the ancient Peruvians worshipped the earth. Pachacamac, on the other hand, is not the earth itself, the soil, but the spirit which animates all things that emerge therefrom. From him proceed the spirits of the plants and animals which come from the earth. Pachamama is the mother-spirit of the mountains, rocks, and plains, Pachacamac the father-spirit of the grain-bearing plants, animals, birds, and man. In some localities Pachacamac and Pachamama were worshipped as divine mates. Possibly this practice was universal in early times, gradually lapsing into desuetude in later days. Pachamama was in another phase intended to denote the land immediately contiguous to a settlement, on which the inhabitants depended for their food-supply.

Viracocha

The name Viracocha was, besides being the specific appellation of a certain deity, a generic name for divine beings. It signifies 'Foam of the Water,' thus alluding to the legend that the god had arisen out of the depths of Lake Titicaca. On his appearance from the sacred waters Viracocha created the sun, moon, and stars, and mapped out for them the courses which they were to hold in the heavens. He then created men carved out of stone statues made by himself, and bade them follow him to Cuzco. Arrived there he collected the inhabitants, and placed over them one, Allca Vica, who subsequently became the ancestor of the Incas. He then returned into Lake Titicaca, into the waters of which he disappeared.

It is evident that this legend clashes strongly with that of the solar origin of the Incas, and it would seem to have been put forward by a rival priesthood which had survived the introduction of solar worship, but which was not powerful enough to combat it.

Viracocha was usually represented as a god bearded with water-rushes, and this hirsute adornment is so far significant in that it may have some connection with the older legends of the Peruvians which tell of a white and bearded race which advanced to Cuzco, the centre of civilization, from the regions of Lake Titicaca. He is also spoken of as being without flesh or bone, yet swift in movement, and this description does not leave us long in doubt as to his real nature. He was the water-god, the fertiliser of all plant life. In the somewhat arid country surrounding Lake Titicaca that great body of water would undoubtedly come to be regarded as the generator of all fertility to be found in its vicinity. Hence Viracocha's origin. His consort was his sister Cocha, the lake itself. He, like Tlaloc among the Mexicans, had a penchant for human sacrifice, but his worship was by no means so sanguinary as was that of his Mexican prototype.

We must then regard Viracocha as the god of a faith anterior to the sun-worship which obtained in Peru at the time of the Spanish conquest. But we shall also be forced to admit that Pachacamac, although a member of the Peruvian pantheon and a great god, was but there on sufferance. The name Pachacamac signifies 'earth-generator,' and the primitive centres of the worship of this deity were in the valleys of Lurin and Rimac, near the city of Lima. In the latter once stood a great temple to Pachacamac, the ruins of which, alone, now remain. Pachacamac would seem to have borne the reputation of a great civilizer, and to some extent he usurped the claims of Viracocha to this honour. Viracocha, so runs the legend, was defeated by him in combat, and fled, whereupon the victor created a new world more to his liking by the simple expedient of transferring the race of men then upon earth into wild animals, and creating a new and higher humanity. He was also a god of fertility, as on the remains of his temples fishes are to be found evidently symbolising this attribute.

The hostility of Pachacamac and Viracocha has a mythical significance. Pachacamac was the god of volcanoes, earthquakes, and subterranean fire, and was therefore hostile to water. His worship was much more mysterious than that of Viracocha. The Peruvians, in fact, regarded Pachacamac as a dreaded and unseen deity, at whose mutterings in the centre of the earth they prostrated themselves in dread. Rimac, indeed, where the worship of this god had its focus, means 'the speaker,' 'the murmurer,' and a kind of oracular character appears ultimately to have been associated with the name of this terrible deity, who on occasion demanded to be appeased by human sacrifice.

Peruvian Creation Myths

A number of variations on several origin and creation tales native to Peru can be fond on pages 298–343, but here are some initial descriptions and summaries:

The Coming of Manco Capac

Peruvian myth has its Quetzalcoatl in Manco Capac, a veritable son of the sun. The Life-giver, observing the deplorable condition of mankind, who seemed to exist for war and feasting alone, despatched his son, Manco Capac (a figure who has some basis in history as well as myth – *see* pages 150 and 154), and his sister-wife, Mama Oullo Huaca, to earth for the purpose of instructing the degraded peoples in the arts of civilized life. The heavenly pair came to earth in the neighbourhood of Lake Titicaca, and were provided with a golden wedge which they were assured would sink into the earth at the precise spot on which they should commence their missionary labours. This phenomenon occurred at Cuzco, where the wedge disappeared. The derivation of the name Cuzco, which means 'Navel,' or, in more modern terms, 'Hub of the Universe,' proves that it was regarded as a great culture-centre. On this spot the civilizing agents pitched their camp, gathering the uncultured folk of the country around them. Whilst Manco taught the men the arts of agriculture, Mama Oullo instructed the women in those of weaving and spinning. Great numbers gathered in the vicinity of Cuzco, and the foundations of a city were laid. Under the mild rule of the heavenly pair the land of Peru abounded in every desirable thing, like the Eden of Genesis. The legend of Manco Capac as we have it from an old Spanish source is worth giving. It is as follows: "There [in Tiahuanaco] the creator began to raise up the people and nations that are in that region, making one of each nation in clay, and painting the dresses that each one was to wear; those that were to wear their hair, with hair, and those that were to be shorn, with hair cut. And to each nation was given the language that was to be spoken, and the songs to be sung, and the seeds and food that they were to sow. When the creator had finished painting and making the said nations and figures of clay, he gave life and soul to each one, as well man as woman, and ordered that they should pass under the earth. Thence each nation came up in the places to which he ordered them to go. Thus they say that some came out of caves, others issued from hills, others from fountains, others from the trunks of trees. From this cause and others, and owing to having come forth and multiplied from those places, and to having had the beginning of their lineage in them, they made *huacas* and places of worship of them, in memory of the origin of their lineage. Thus each nation uses the dress with which they invest their *huaca*; and they say that the first that was born in that place was there turned into stone. Others say that they were turned into falcons, condors, and other animals and birds. Hence the *huacas* they use are in different shapes."

The Peruvian Creation Story

The Incan Peruvians believed that all things emanated from Pachacamac, the all-pervading spirit, who provided the plants and animals (which they believed to be produced from the earth) with 'souls.' The earth itself they designated Pachacamama (Earth-Mother). Here we observe that Pachacamac was more the maker and moulder than the originator of matter, a view common to many American mythologies. Pachacamac it was who breathed the breath of life into man, but the Peruvian conception of him was only evolved in later Inca times, and by no means existed in the early days of Inca rule, although he was probably worshipped before this under another and less exalted shape. The mere exercise of will or thought was sufficient, according to the Peruvians, to accomplish the creative act. In the prayers to the creator, and in other portions of Inca rite, we read such expressions as "Let a man be," "Let a woman be," and "The creative word," which go to prove that the Peruvian consciousness had fully grasped the idea of a creator capable of evolving matter out of nothingness. Occasionally we find the sun acting as a kind of demiurge or sub-creator. He it is who in later legend founds the city of Cuzco, and sends thither three eggs composed of gold, silver, and copper, from which spring the three classes of Peruvians, kings, priests, and slaves. The inevitable deluge occurs, after which we find the prehistoric town of Tiahuanaco regarded as the theatre of a new creation of man. Here the creator made man, and separated him into nations, making one of each nation out of the clay of the earth, painting the dresses that each was to wear, and endowing them with national songs, languages, seeds to sow suitable to the environment of each, and food such as they would require. Then he gave the peoples life and soul, and commanded them to enter the bowels of the earth, whence they came upward in the places where he ordered them to go. Perhaps this is one of the most complete ('wholesale' would be a better word) creation myths in existence, and we can glean from its very completeness that it is by no means of simple origin, but of great complexity. It is obviously an attempt to harmonize several conflicting creation-stories, notably those in which the people are spoken of as emanating from caves, and the later one of the creation of men at Tiahuanaco, probably suggested to the Incas by the immense ruins at that place, for which they could not otherwise account.

Local Creation myths

In some of the more isolated valleys of Peru we discover local creation myths. For example, in the coastal valley of Irma, Pachacamac was not considered to be the creator of the sun, but to be himself a descendant of it. The first human beings created by him were speedily separated, as the man died of hunger, but the woman supported herself by living on roots. The sun took compassion upon her and gave her a son, whom Pachacamac slew and buried. But from his teeth there grew maize, from his ribs the long white roots of the manioc plant, and from his flesh various esculent plants.

Peruvian Creation Stories – Pachacamac or Viracocha?

It is easy to see how such a conception as Pachacamac, the spirit of animated nature, would become one with the idea of a universal or even a partial creator. That there was a pre-existing conception of a creative agency can be proved from the existence of the Peruvian name Conticsi-viracocha (He who gives Origin, or Beginning). This conception and that of Pachacamac must at some comparatively early period have clashed, and been amalgamated probably with ease when it was seen how nearly akin were the two ideas. Indeed, Pachacamac was alternatively known as Pacharurac, the 'maker' of all things – sure proof of his amalgamation with the conception of the creative agency. As such he had his symbol in the great Coricancha at Cuzco, an oval plate of gold, suspended between those of the sun and the moon, and placed vertically, it may be hazarded with some probability, to represent in symbol that universal matrix from which emanated all things. Elsewhere in Cuzco the creator was represented by a stone statue in human form.

Pachayachachic

In later Inca days this idea of a creator assumed that of a direct ruler of the universe, known as Pachayachachic. This change was probably due to the influence of the Inca Pachacutic, who is known to have made several other doctrinal innovations in Peruvian theology. He commanded a great new temple to the creator-god to be built at the north angle of the city of Cuzco, in which he placed a statue of pure gold, of the size of a boy of ten years of age. The small size was to facilitate its removal, as Peruvian worship was nearly always carried out in the open air. In form it represented a man with his right arm elevated, the hand partially closed and the forefinger and thumb raised, as if in the act of uttering the creative word. To this god large possessions and revenues were assigned, for previously service rendered to him had been voluntary only.

Ideas of Creation

It is from aboriginal sources as preserved by the first Spanish colonists that we glean our knowledge of what the Incas believed the creative process to consist. By means of his word (*ñisca*) the creator, a spirit, powerful and opulent, made all things. We are provided with the formulae of his very words by the Peruvian prayers still extant: "Let earth and heaven be," "Let a man be; let a woman be," "Let there be day," "Let there be night," "Let the light shine." The sun is here regarded as the creative agency, and the ruling caste as the objects of a special act of creation.

Pacari Tampu

Pacari Tampu (House of the Dawn) was the place of origin, according to the later Inca theology, of four brothers and sisters who initiated the four Peruvian systems of worship. The eldest climbed a neighbouring mountain, and cast stones to the four points of the compass, thus indicating that he claimed all the land within sight. But his youngest brother succeeded in enticing him into a cave, which he sealed up with a great stone, thus imprisoning him forever. He next persuaded his second brother to ascend a lofty mountain, from which he cast him, changing him into a stone in his descent. On beholding the fate of his brethren the third member of the quartette fled. It is obvious that we have here a legend concocted by the later Inca priesthood to account for the evolution of Peruvian religion in its different stages. The first brother would appear to represent the oldest religion in Peru, that of the *paccariscas*, the second that of a fetishistic stone-worship, the third perhaps that of Viracocha, and the last sun-worship pure and simple. There was, however, an 'official' legend, which stated that the sun had three sons, Viracocha, Pachacamac, and Manco Capac. To the last the dominion of mankind was given, whilst the others were concerned with the workings of the universe. This politic arrangement placed all the power, temporal and spiritual, in the hands of the reputed descendants of Manco Capac – the Incas.

The Aymara-Quichua and Viracocha

The Aymara-Quichua race worshipped Viracocha as a great culture hero. They did not offer him sacrifices or tribute, as they thought that he, being creator and possessor of all things, needed nothing from men, so they only gave him worship. After him they idolized the sun. They believed, indeed, that Viracocha had made both sun and moon, after emerging from Lake Titicaca, and that then he made the earth and peopled it. On his travels westward from the lake he was sometimes assailed by men, but he revenged himself by sending terrible storms upon them and destroying their property, so they humbled themselves and acknowledged him as their lord. He forgave them and taught them everything, obtaining from them the name of Pachayachachic. In the end he disappeared in the western ocean. He either created or there were born with him four beings who, according to mythical beliefs, civilized Peru. To them he assigned the four quarters of the earth, and they are thus known as the four winds, north, south, east, and west. One legend avers they came from the cave Pacari, the Lodging of the Dawn.

Worship of the Sea

The ancient Peruvians worshipped the sea as well as the earth, the folk inland regarding it as a menacing deity, whilst the people of the coast reverenced it as a god of benevolence, calling it Mama-cocha, or Mother-sea, as it yielded them subsistence in the form of fish, on which they chiefly lived. They worshipped the whale, fairly common on that coast, because of its enormous size, and various districts regarded with adoration the species of fish most abundant there. This worship can have partaken in no sense of the nature of totemism, as the system forbade that the totem animal should be eaten. It was imagined that the prototype of each variety of fish dwelt in the upper world, just as many tribes of North American Indians believe that the eponymous ancestors of certain animals dwell at the four points of the compass or in the sky above them. This great fish-god engendered the others of his species, and sent them into the waters of the deep that they might exist there until taken for the use of man. Birds, too, had their eponymous counterparts among the stars, as had animals. Indeed, among many of the South American races, ancient and modern, the constellations were called after certain beasts and birds.

Sun-Worship in Peru

The name 'Inca' means 'People of the Sun,' which luminary the Incas regarded as their creator. But they did not worship him totemically – that is, they did not claim him as a progenitor, although they regarded him as possessing the attributes of a man. And here we may observe a difference between Mexican and Peruvian sun-worship. For whereas the Nahua primarily regarded the orb as the abode of the Man of the Sun, who came to earth in the shape of Quetzalcoatl, the Peruvians looked upon the sun itself as the deity. The Inca race did not identify their ancestors as children of the sun until a comparatively late date. Sun-worship was introduced by the Inca Pachacutic, who averred that the sun appeared to him in a dream and addressed him as his child. Until that time the worship of the sun had always been strictly subordinated to that of the creator, and the deity appeared only as second in the trinity of creator, sun, and thunder. But permanent provision was made for sacrifices to the sun before the other deities were so recognized, and as the conquests of the Incas grew wider and that provision extended to the new territories they came to be known as 'the Lands of the Sun,' the natives observing the dedication of a part of the country to the luminary, and concluding therefrom that it applied to the whole. The material reality of the sun would enormously assist his cult among a people who were too barbarous to appreciate an unseen god, and this colonial conception reacting upon the mother-land would undoubtedly inspire the military class with a resolve to strengthen a worship so popular in the conquered provinces, and of which they were in great measure the protagonists and missionaries.

The Sun's Possessions

In every Peruvian village the sun had considerable possessions. His estates resembled those of a territorial chieftain, and consisted of a dwelling-house, a *chacra*, or portion of land, flocks of llamas and pacos, and a number of women dedicated to his service. The cultivation of the soil within the solar enclosure devolved upon the inhabitants of the neighbouring village, the produce of their toil being stored in the *inti-huasi*, or sun's house. The Women of the Sun prepared the daily food and drink of the luminary, which consisted of maize and *chicha*. They also spun wool and wove it into fine stuff, which was burned in order that it might ascend to the celestial regions, where the deity could make use of it. Each village reserved a portion of its solar produce for the great festival at Cuzco, and it was carried thither on the backs of llamas which were destined for sacrifice.

Inca Occupation of Titicaca

The Rock of Titicaca, the renowned place of the sun's origin, naturally became an important centre of his worship. The date at which the worship of the sun originated at this famous rock is extremely remote, but we may safely assume that it was long before the conquest of the Collao by the Apu-Ccapac-Inca Pachacutic, and that reverence for the luminary as a war-god by the Colla chiefs was noticed by Tupac, who in suppressing the revolt concluded that the local observance at the rock had some relationship to the disturbance. It is, however, certain that Tupac proceeded after the reconquest to establish at this natural centre of sun-worship solar rites on a new basis, with the evident intention of securing on behalf of the Incas of Cuzco such exclusive benefit as might accrue from the complete possession of the sun's *paccarisca*. According to a native account, a venerable *colla* (or hermit), consecrated to the service of the sun, had proceeded on foot from Titicaca to Cuzco for the purpose of commending this ancient seat of sun-worship to the notice of Tupac. The consequence was that Apu-Ccapac-Inca, after visiting the island and inquiring into the ancient local customs, re-established them in a more regular form. His accounts can hardly be accepted in face of the facts which have been gathered. Rather did it naturally follow that Titicaca became subservient to Tupac after the revolt of the Collao had been quelled. Henceforth the worship of the sun at the place of his origin was entrusted to Incas resident in the place, and was celebrated with Inca rites. The island was converted into a solar estate and the aboriginal inhabitants removed. The land was cultivated and the slopes of the hills levelled, maize was sown and the soil consecrated, the grain being regarded as the gift of the sun. This work produced considerable change in the island. Where once was waste and idleness there was now fertility and industry. The harvests were skilfully apportioned, so much being reserved for sacrificial purposes, the remainder being sent to Cuzco, partly to be sown in the *chacras*, or estates of the sun, throughout Peru, partly to be preserved in the granary of the Inca and the *huacas* as a symbol that there would be abundant crops in the future and that the grain already stored would be preserved. A building of the Women of the

Sun was erected about a mile from the rock, so that the produce might be available for sacrifices. For their maintenance, tribute of potatoes, ocas, and quinua was levied upon the inhabitants of the villages on the shores of the lake, and of maize upon the people of the neighbouring valleys.

Pilgrimages to Titicaca

Titicaca at the time of the conquest was probably more frequented than Pachacamac itself. These two places were held to be the cardinal shrines of the two great *huacas*, the creator and the sun respectively. A special reason for pilgrimage to Titicaca was to sacrifice to the sun, as the source of physical energy and the giver of long life; and he was especially worshipped by the aged, who believed he had preserved their lives, Then followed the migration of pilgrims to Titicaca, for whose shelter houses were built at Capacahuana, and large stores of maize were provided for their use. The ceremonial connected with the sacred rites of the rock was rigorously observed. The pilgrim ere embarking on the raft which conveyed him to the island must first confess his sins to a *huillac* (a speaker to an object of worship); then further confessions were required at each of the three sculptured doors which had successively to be passed before reaching the sacred rock. The first door (Puma-puncu) was surmounted by the figure of a puma; the others (Quenti-puncu and Pillco-puncu) were ornamented with feathers of the different species of birds commonly sacrificed to the sun. Having passed the last portal, the traveller beheld at a distance of two hundred paces the sacred rock itself, the summit glittering with gold-leaf. He was permitted to proceed no further, for only the officials were allowed entry into it. The pilgrim on departing received a few grains of the sacred maize grown on the island. These he kept with care and placed with his own store, believing they would preserve his stock, The confidence the Indian placed in the virtue of the Titicaca maize may be judged from the prevalent belief that the possessor of a single grain would not suffer from starvation during the whole of his life.

Sacrifices to the New Sun

The Intip-Raymi, or Great Festival of the Sun, was celebrated by the Incas at Cuzco at the winter solstice (see also a more in-depth look at this festival on pages 186–92). In connection with it the Tarpuntaita-cuma, or sacrificing Incas, were charged with a remarkable duty, the worshippers journeying eastward to meet one of these functionaries on his way. On the principal hill tops between Cuzco and Huillcanuta, on the road to the rock of Titicaca, burnt offerings of llamas, coca, and maize were made at the feast to greet the arrival of the young sun from his ancient birthplace. Molina has enumerated more than twenty of these places of sacrifice. The striking picture of the celebration of the solar sacrifice on these bleak mountains in the depth of the Peruvian winter has, it seems, no parallel in the religious rites of the ancient Americans. Quitting their thatched houses at early dawn, the worshippers left the valley below, carrying the sacrificial knife and brazier, and conducting the white llama, heavily laden with fuel, maize, and coca leaves, wrapped in fine cloth, to the spot where the sacrifice was to be made. When sunrise appeared the pile was lighted. The victim was slain and thrown upon it. The scene then presented a striking contrast to the bleak surrounding wilderness. As the flames grew in strength and the smoke rose higher and thicker the clear atmosphere was gradually illuminated from the east. When the sun advanced above the horizon the sacrifice was at its height. But for the crackling of the flames and the murmur of a babbling stream on its way down the hill to join the river below, the silence had hitherto been unbroken. As the sun rose the Incas marched slowly round the burning mass, plucking the wool from the scorched carcase, and chanting monotonously: "O Creator, Sun and Thunder, be forever young! Multiply the people; let them ever be in peace!"

The Citoc Raymi

The most picturesque if not the most important solar festival was that of the Citoc Raymi (Gradually Increasing Sun), held in June, when nine days were given up to the ceremonial. A rigorous fast was observed for three days previous to the event, during which no fire must be kindled. On the fourth day the Inca, accompanied by the people *en masse*, proceeded to the great square of Cuzco to hail the rising sun, which they awaited in silence. On its appearance they greeted it with a joyous tumult, and, joining in procession, marched to the Golden Temple of the Sun, where llamas were sacrificed, and a new fire was kindled by means of an arched mirror, followed by sacrificial offerings of grain, flowers, animals, and aromatic gums. This festival may be taken as typical of all the seasonal celebrations. The Inca calendar was purely agricultural in its basis, and marked in its great festivals the renewal or abandonment of the labours of the field. Its astronomical observations were not more advanced than those of the calendars of many American races otherwise inferior in civilization.

Human Sacrifice in Peru

Writers ignorant of their subject have often dwelt upon the absence of human sacrifice in ancient Peru, and have not hesitated to draw comparisons between Mexico and the empire of the Incas in this respect, usually not complimentary to the former. Such statements are contradicted by the clearest evidence. Human sacrifice was certainly not nearly so prevalent in Peru, but that it was regular and by no means rare is well authenticated. Female victims to the sun were taken from the great class of Acllacuna (Selected Ones), a general tribute of female children regularly levied throughout the Inca Empire. Beautiful girls were taken from their parents at the age of eight by the Inca officials, and were handed over to certain female trainers called *mamacuna* (mothers). These matrons systematically trained their *protégées* in housewifery and ritual. Residences or convents called *aclla-huasi* (houses of the Selected) were provided for them in the principal cities.

Minor Deities and Animals

We will now pass to a consideration of the minor deities of the Peruvian mythology. These were numerous, and had been mostly evolved from nature forces and natural phenomena. Among the more important was Chasca, the planet Venus, the 'long-haired,' the 'Page of the Sun.' Cuycha, the rainbow, was the servant of the sun and moon. He was represented in a private chapel of his own, contiguous to that of the Sun, by large plates of gold so fired as to represent the various colours in the prismatic hues of the rainbow. Fire, also, was an object of profound veneration with the Peruvians, derived, as it was believed to be, from the sun. Its preservation was scrupulously attended to in the Temple of the Sun and in the House of the Virgins of the Sun, of which an account will be found in the next chapter.

We now descend gradually and almost insensibly in the scale of deism, until little by little we reach a condition of gross idolatry, not far removed from that still practised by many African tribes. Here we find even vegetables adored as symbols of sustenance. The potato was glorified under the appellation of acsumama, and the maize as saramama. Trees partook of divine attributes, and we seem to see in this condition of things a state analogous to the reverence paid by the early Greeks and Romans to Sylvanus and his train, and the vivification of trees by the presence within them of dryads.

Certain animals were treated with much reverence by the Peruvians. Thus we find the serpent, especially Urcaguay, the keeper of subterranean gold, an object of great veneration. The condor or vulture of the Andes Mountains was the messenger or Mercury of the Sun, and he held the same place on the sceptre of the Incas as the eagle on the sceptre of the Emperor of Germany or Russia. Whales and sharks were also worshipped by the people who lived near the sea.

But in all this nature and animal worship it is difficult to detect a totemic origin. The basis of totemism is the idea of blood-kinship with an animal or plant, which idea in the course of generations evolves into an exaggerated respect, and finally (under conditions favourable for development) into a full-blown mythology. At first it would appear as if the perfect organization of the Peruvian state and its peculiar marriage laws had originated in a condition of totemism; but had totemism ever entered into the constitution of the Peruvian religion at any period of its development, it would have left as deep an impression upon it as it did in the case of the Egyptian religion – that is, some of the more important deities would have betrayed a totemic origin. That they betray an origin wholly naturalistic there is no room for doubt. And here the root difference between the Mexican and Peruvian mythologies may be pointed out – that although both systems had grown up from various constituents grouping themselves around the central worship of the Sun, the constituents of the Aztec religion were almost wholly totemic, whereas those of the Peruvian religion were naturalistic.

But the factor of fetishism was not wanting in the construction of the Peruvian religion. All that was sacred, from the sun himself to the tomb of a righteous person, was Huaca, or sacred. The chief priest of Cuzco was designated Huacapvillac, or 'he who speaks with sacred beings,' but the principal use to which the term Huaca was put was in reference to objects of metal, wood, and stone, which cannot be better described than as closely resembling those African fetishes so common in our museums. These differed considerably in size. The reverence for them was probably of prehistoric origin, and in this cultus we have the second brother whom Pirrhua Manca changed into a stone. They were believed by the Peruvians to be the veritable dwelling-places of spirits. Many of these Huacas were public property, and had gifts of flocks of llamas dedicated to them. The majority, however, were private property.

It will be necessary to mention one more deity. This is Supay, god of the dead, who dwelt in a dreary underworld. He was the Pluto of Peruvian mythology, and is usually portrayed as an open-mouthed monster of voracious appetite, into whose maw are thrown the souls of the departed.

For the study of the worship of old Peru the materials are less plentiful than in the case of the Mexican mythology. Stratum upon stratum of belief is discovered, like those in the ruins of some ancient city where each yard of earth holds the story of a dynasty. To the student of comparative religion an exhaustive study of the complex mythology of the ancient Peruvians offers an almost unparalleled opportunity for comparison with and elucidation of other mythologies, since in it the process of its evolution is exhibited with greater clearness than in the case of any other belief, ancient or modern.

Methods of Medicine Men

A quaint account of the methods of the medicine men of the Indians of the Peruvian Andes probably illustrates the manner in which the superstitions of a barbarian people evolve into a more stately ritual.

"It cannot be denied," it states, "that the *mohanes* [priests] have, by practice and tradition, acquired a knowledge of many plants and poisons, with which they effect surprising cures on the one hand, and do much mischief on the other, but the mania of ascribing the whole to a preternatural virtue occasions them to blend with their practice a thousand charms and superstitions. The most customary method of cure is to place two hammocks close to each other, either in the dwelling, or in the open air: in one of them the patient lies extended, and in the other the *mohane*, or *agorero*. The latter, in contact with the sick man, begins by rocking himself, and then proceeds, by a strain in falsetto, to call on the birds, quadrupeds, and fishes to give health to the patient. From time to time he rises on his seat, and makes a thousand extravagant gestures over the sick man, to whom he applies his powders and herbs, or sucks the wounded or diseased parts. If the malady augments, the *agorero*, having been joined by many of the people, chants a short hymn, addressed to the soul of the patient, with this burden: 'Thou must not go, thou must not go.' In repeating this he is joined by the people, until at length a terrible clamour is raised, and augmented in proportion as the sick man becomes still fainter and fainter, to the end that it may reach his ears. When all the charms are unavailing, and death approaches, the *mohane* leaps from his hammock, and betakes himself to flight, amid the multitude of sticks, stones, and clods of earth which are showered on him. Successively all those who belong to the nation assemble, and, dividing themselves into bands, each of them (if he who is in his last agonies is a warrior) approaches him, saying: 'Whither goest thou? Why dost thou leave us? With whom shall we proceed to the *aucas* [the enemies]?' They then relate to him the heroical deeds he has performed, the number of those he has slain, and the pleasures he leaves behind him. This is practised in different tones: while some raise the voice, it is lowered by others; and the poor sick man is obliged to support these importunities without a murmur, until the first symptoms of approaching dissolution manifest themselves. Then it is that he is surrounded by a multitude of females, some of whom forcibly close the mouth and eyes, others envelop him in the hammock, oppressing him with the whole of their weight, and causing him to expire before his time, and others, lastly, run to extinguish the candle, and dissipate the smoke, that the soul, not being able to perceive the hole through which it may escape, may remain entangled in the structure of the roof. That this may be speedily effected, and to prevent its return to the interior of the dwelling, they surround the entrances with filth, by the stench of which it may be expelled.

Death by Suffocation

"As soon as the dying man is suffocated by the closing of the mouth, nostrils, &c., and wrapt up in the covering of his bed, the most circumspect Indian, whether male or female, takes him in the arms in the best manner possible, and gives a *gentle* shriek, which echoes to the bitter lamentations of the immediate relatives, and to the cries of a thousand old women collected for the occasion. As long as this dismal howl subsists, the latter are subjected to a constant fatigue, raising the palm of the hand to wipe away the tears, and lowering it to dry it on the ground. The result of this alternate action is, that a circle of earth, which gives them a most hideous appearance, is collected about the eyelids and brows, and they do not wash themselves until the mourning is over. These first clamours conclude by several good pots of *masato*, to assuage the thirst of sorrow, and the company next proceed to make a great clatter among the utensils of the deceased: some break the kettles, and others the earthen pots, while others, again, burn the apparel, to the end that his memory may be the sooner forgotten. If the defunct has been a *cacique*, or powerful warrior, his exequies are performed after the manner of the Romans: they last for many days, all the people weeping in concert for a considerable space of time, at daybreak, at noon, in the evening, and at midnight. When the appointed hour arrives, the mournful music begins in front of the house of the wife and relatives, the heroical deeds of the deceased being chanted to the sound of instruments. All the inhabitants of the vicinity unite in chorus from within their houses, some chirping like birds, others howling like tigers, and the greater part of them chattering like monkeys, or croaking like frogs. They constantly leave off by having recourse to the *masato*, and by the destruction of whatever the deceased may have left behind him, the burning of his dwelling being that which concludes the ceremonies. Among some of the Indians, the nearest relatives cut off their hair as a token of their grief, agreeably to the practice of the Moabites, and other nations....

The Obsequies of a Chief

"On the day of decease, they put the body, with its insignia, into a large earthen vessel, or painted jar, which they bury in one of the angles of the quarter, laying over it a covering of potter's clay, and throwing in earth until the grave is on a level with the surface of the ground. When the obsequies are over, they forbear to pay a visit to it, and lose every recollection of the name of the warrior. The Roamaynas disenter their dead, as soon as they think that the fleshy parts have been consumed, and having washed the bones from the skeleton, which they place in a coffin of potter's clay, adorned with various symbols of death, like the hieroglyphics on the wrappers of the Egyptian mummies. In this state the skeleton is carried home, to the end that the survivors may bear the deceased in respectful memory, and not in imitation of those extraordinary voluptuaries of antiquity, who introduced into their most splendid festivals a spectacle of this nature, which, by reminding them of their dissolution, might stimulate them to taste, before it should overtake them, all the impure pleasures the human passions could afford them. A space of time of about a year being elapsed, the bones are once more inhumed, and the individual to whom they belonged forgotten forever."

Priests, Temples & Further Rituals of Peru

WITH THE PERUVIANS, as with the Mexicans, paradise was a preserve of the aristocrats. The poor might languish in the gloomy shades of the Hades presided over by Supay, Lord of the Dead, but for the Incas and their immediate relatives, by whom was embraced the entire nobility, the Mansions of the Sun were retained, where they might dwell with the Sun, their father, in undisturbed felicity. In a community where everything was ordered with military exactitude, sin meant disobedience, and consequently death. Indeed it took the form of direct blasphemy against the Inca, and was thus stripped of the purely ethical sense it holds for a free population. The sinner expiated his crime at once, and was consigned to the grey shades of the underworld, there to pass the same nebulous existence as his more meritorious companions. Some writers upon Peru refer to a belief on the part of the people in a place of retribution where the wicked would expiate their offences by ages of arduous toil. But there is little ground for the acceptance of these statements.

Strictly speaking, there was no priesthood in Peru. The ecclesiastical caste consisted of the Inca and his relatives, who were also known as Incas. These assumed all the principal positions in the national religion, but were unable, of course, to fill all the lesser provincial posts. These were undertaken by the priests of the local deities, who were at the same time priests of the imperial deities, a policy which permitted the conquered peoples to retain their own form of worship, and at the same time led them to recognize the paramountcy of the religion of the Incas. Nothing could be more intense than the devotion shown by all ranks of the population to the person of the Inca. He was the sun incarnate upon earth, and his presence must be entered with humble mien and beggarly apparel, and a further show of humility must also be made by carrying a bundle upon the back.

The High Priest, who has been already alluded to as holding the title of Huacapvillac, or 'He who converses with divine beings!' also held the more general one of Villac Oumau, or 'Chief Sacrificer.' He derived his position solely from the Inca, but made all inferior appointments, and was answerable to the monarch alone. He was invariably an Inca of exalted rank, as were all the priests who officiated at Cuzco, the capital. Only those ecclesiastics of the higher grades wore any distinguishing garb, the lower order dressing in the same manner as the people.

The existence of a Peruvian priest was an arduous one. It was necessary for him to master a ritual as complex as any ever evolved by a hierarchy. At regular intervals he was relieved by his fellow-priests, who were organized in companies, each of which took duty for a specified period of the day or night. The duties of the Peruvian priesthood, whilst even more exacting than that of the Mexican, did not appear to have been lightened in a similar manner by the acquirement of knowledge, or by mental exercise of any description, and this may be partly accounted for by the fact that the art of writing was discouraged among them, probably on the assumption that the whole duty of man culminated in unfailing obedience to the Inca and his representatives, and that the acquirement of further knowledge was the work of supererogation.

The Evolution of the Temple

It is deeply interesting to notice (isolated as was everything Peruvian) that it was in this far corner of America that the native evolution of the temple took place, as distinguished from the altar or teocalli. Originally the Peruvian priesthood had adopted that pyramidal form of structure now familiar to us as that in use by the Mexicans, but as time went on they began to roof over these high altars, and this practice at length culminated in the erection of huge temples like that at Cuzco.

The great temple of Cuzco, known as *Coricancha*, or 'The Place of Gold,' was the greatest and most magnificent example of Peruvian ecclesiastical architecture. The exterior gave an impression of massiveness and solidity rather than of grace. Round the outer circumference of the building ran a frieze of the purest gold, and the interior was profusely ornamented with plates of the same metal. The doorways were formed from huge monoliths, and the whole aspect of the building was Cyclopean. In the dressing of stone and the fitting of masonry the Peruvians were expert, and the placing of immense blocks of stone appears to have had no difficulties for them. So accurately indeed were these fitted that the blade of a knife could not be inserted between them. Inside the Temple of the Sun was placed a great plate of gold, upon which was engraved the features of the god of the luminary, and this was so placed that the rays of the rising sun fell full upon it, and bathed it in a flood of radiance. The scintillations from a thousand gems, with which its surface was enriched, lent to it a brilliance which eye-witnesses declare to have been almost insupportable. Enthroned around this dazzling object were the mummified bodies of the monarchs of the Inca dynasty, giving to the place an air of holy mystery which must have deeply impressed the pious and simple people. The roof was composed of rafters of choice woods, but was merely covered in by a thatching of maize straw. The principle of the arch had never been thoroughly grasped by the Peruvians, and that of adequate roofing appears to have been equally unknown to them.

Surrounding this, the principal temple, were others dedicated to the moon; Cuycha, the rainbow; Chasca, the planet Venus; the Pleiades; and Catequil, the thunder-god. In that of the moon, the mother of the Incas, a plate of silver, similar to that which represented the face of the sun in his own sanctuary, was placed, and was surrounded by the mummified forms of the dead queens of the Incas. In that of Cuycha, the rainbow, as already explained, a golden representation of the arch of heaven was to be found, and the remaining buildings in the precincts of the great temple were set apart for the residences of the priests.

The most ancient of the temples of Peru was that on the island of Titicaca, to which extraordinary veneration was paid. Everything in connection with it was sacred in the extreme, and in the surrounding maize-fields was annually raised a crop which was distributed among the various public granaries, in order to leaven the entire crop of the country with sanctity.

All the utensils in use in these temples were of solid gold and silver. In that of Cuzco twelve large jars of silver held the sacred grain, and censers, ewers, and even the pipes which conducted the water-supply through the earth to the temple, were of silver. In the surrounding gardens, the hoes, spades, and other implements in use were also of silver, and hundreds of representations of plants and animals executed in the precious metals were to be found in them. These facts are vouched for by numerous eye-witnesses, among whom was Pedro Pizarro himself, and subsequent historians have seen no reason to regard their descriptions as in any way untrustworthy.

Similarities with Catholicism

As in Mexico, so in Peru, the Spanish conquerors were astonished to find among the religious customs of the people practices which appeared to them identical with some of the sacraments of the Roman Catholic faith. Among these were confession, communion, and baptism. Confession appears to have been practised in a somewhat loose and irregular manner, but penance for ill-doing was apportioned, and absolution granted. At the festival of Raymi (*see* pages 177 and 186–92), bread and wine were distributed in much the same manner as that prescribed in Christian communities. Baptism also was practised. Some three months after birth the child was plunged into water after having received its name. The ceremony, however, appears to have partaken more of the nature of an exorcism of evil spirits than of a cleansing from original sin.

Preservation of the Dead

Like the ancient Egyptians, the Peruvians practised the art of embalming the dead, but it does not appear that they did so with any idea in view of corporeal resurrection as did the former. As to the method by which they preserved the remains of the dead, authorities are not agreed, some believing that the cold of the mountains to which the corpses were subjected was sufficient to produce a state of mummification, and others that a process akin to that of the Ancient Egyptians was gone through.

Dances

As with the Mexicans, the sacred dance was a striking feature of the Peruvian religion. These choral dances were brought to a very high state of perfection, and in the case of the common people were often wild and full of the fire of abandoned fanaticism. The Incas, however, possessed a dance of their own, which was sufficiently grave and stately. At great festivals two choral dances and hymns were rendered to the sun, each strophe of which ended with the cry of *Hailly*, or 'triumph.' Some of those Peruvian hymns were preserved in the work of a Spanish composer, who in 1555 wrote a mass, into the body of which he introduced these curious waifs of American melody. That choral dances are still in favour with the aborigines of Peru is proved by the evidence of Baron Eland Nordenskjöld, who arrived (August 1907) from an eight months' ethnological expedition to some of the Andes tribes. He states that the 'so-called civilised Indians – the Quichuas and Aymaras – living around Titicaca … have retained many customs unaltered or but slightly modified since the time of the Incas…. Thus it was found that the Indians often worship Christ and the Virgin Mary by dances, in which the sun is used as the symbol for Christ, and the moon for the Virgin Mary.'

Further Festivals

With the Peruvians each month had its appropriate festival. The solstices and equinoxes were of course the occasions of the most remarkable of these, and four times a year the feast of Raymi was celebrated. We have already touched upon the Intip-Raymi and the Citoc Raymi (*see* pages 177 and 186–92), but here is a little on three more festivals:

The Citua Raymi was the festival of the spring, and fell in September. It was known as the Feast of Purification. The country must be purified from pestilence, and to secure this, round cakes, kneaded in the blood of children, were eaten. To secure this blood the children were merely bled above the nose, and not slaughtered, as with the more ferocious Aztecs – almost an example of the substitution of the part for the whole. These cakes were also rubbed upon the doorways, and the people smeared them all over their bodies as a preventive against disease. The circuit of the state of Cuzco was then made by relays of armed Incas, who planted their spears on the boundaries as talismans against evil. A torchlight procession followed, after which the torches were cast into the river as symbolic of the destruction of evil spirits.

The festival of the Aymorai, or harvest, fell in May, when a statue made of corn was worshipped under the name of Pirrhua, who seems to be an admixture of Manco Capac and Viracocha in his rôle of fertiliser. The fourth great festival, Capac Raymi, fell in December, when the thunder-god shared the honours paid to the Sun. It was then that the younger generation of Incas after a vigorous training received an honour equivalent to that of knighthood.

A Conventual System

The Peruvians possessed a fully developed conventual system. A number of maidens, selected for their beauty and their birth, were dedicated to the deity as 'Virgins of the Sun.' Under the guidance of *mamacones*, or matrons, these maidens were instructed in the nature of their religious duties, which chiefly consisted in the weaving of priestly garments and temple-hangings. They also watched over the sacred fire which had been kindled at the feast of Raymi. No communication with the outside world was permitted to them, and detection in a love-affair meant living burial, the execution of the lover, and the entire destruction of the place of his birth. In the convent of Cuzco were lodged between one and two thousand maidens of the royal blood, and at a marriageable age these became brides of the Sun in his incarnate shape of the Inca, the most beautiful being selected for the harem of the monarch.

Divination and Morality

Sorcery and divination were frequently employed by the Peruvians, and the *Huacarimachi*, 'They who make the gods speak,' were held in great veneration by the ignorant masses. The oracles in the valleys of Lima and Rimac were much resorted to, and auguries of all descriptions were in popular favour.

The Peruvians were ignorant of morality as we appreciate the term. That they were, however, a most moral people there is every evidence. But as has been before pointed out, all crime was a direct offence against the majesty of the Inca, who, as viceroy of the Sun on earth, had been blasphemed by the breaking of his law. Under such a régime the true significance of sin was bound to be obscured, if not altogether lost. Terror took the place of conscience, and the necessity for implicit obedience gave no scope to the true moral sense – probably to the detriment of the entire community.

The political and religious history of Peru is unique in the annals of mankind, and its study offers a startling instance of what prolonged isolation may work in the mind of man. That the Peruvian mind, isolated in a remote part of the world as it was, was never wholly blind to the existence of a great and beneficent creative Power, the degradation of a cramping theocracy notwithstanding, is triumphant proof that the knowledge of that Power is a thing inalienable from the mind of man.

More on The Festival of the Sun

The Principal Festival of the Sun, and How They Prepared Themselves for It

THE WORD RAYMI is equivalent to our word Easter. Among the four festivals which the Kings celebrated in the city of Cuzco, the most solemn was that in honour of the Sun, during the month of June. It was called *Yntip Raymi*, which means the 'Solemn Feast of the Sun.' They called this feast especially *Raymi*, and though the word was also used for other festivals, this was the Raymi, and took place in the June solstice.

They celebrated this festival of the Sun in acknowledgment that they held and adored Him as the sole and universal God who, by his light and power, creates and sustains all things on earth; and that He was the natural father of the first Ynca Manco Ccapac and of his wife Mama Ocllo Huaco, and of all their descendants, who were sent to this earth for the benefit of all people. For these reasons, as they themselves say, this was their most solemn feast.

There were present at it all the chief captains not then employed in war, and all the Curacas, lords of vassals, from all parts of the empire, not because they were ordered to be present, but because they rejoiced to take part in the solemnities of so great a festival. For, as the ceremonies included the worship of the Sun God and of the Ynca their king, there was no one who did not desire to take part in it. When the Curacas were prevented, by old age or sickness, from being present, or by the public service or the long distance, they sent their sons and brothers, accompanied by the noblest of their kindred, to be at the festival in their place. The Ynca was there in person, if not prevented by absence at the wars or while inspecting the provinces.

The opening ceremonies were performed by the king himself as High Priest; for, although there was always a High Priest of the blood royal, who was legitimate uncle or brother of the Ynca, yet the Ynca himself officiated at this great festival, as first-born of the Sun.

The Curacas came in all the splendour they could afford. Some wore dresses adorned with bezants of gold and silver, and with the same fastened as a circlet round their headdresses. Others came in a costume neither more nor less than that in which Hercules is painted, wrapped in the skins of lions, with the heads fixed over their own. These were the Indians who claimed descent from a lion. Others came attired in the fashion that they paint angels, with great wings of the bird called *Cuntur*. These wings are black and white, and so long that the Spaniards have often killed birds measuring fourteen feet between the tips of the wings. These are the Indians who declare that they are descended from a *Cuntur*. The Yuncas came attired in the most hideous masks that can be imagined, and they appeared at the feasts making all sorts of grimaces, like fools and simpletons; and for this purpose they brought instruments in their hands, such as badly-made flutes and tambourines, and pieces of skin, to assist them in their fooleries. Other Curacas wore various costumes to distinguish them, and each different tribe came with the arms with which they fought in war. Some had bows and arrows; others lances, darts, javelins, clubs, slings, axes with short handles, and two-handed axes with long handles.

They brought with them paintings of the deeds they had performed in the service of the Sun and of the Yncas, and also great drums and trumpets, with many musicians to play them. In short, they all came in the best attire they could procure, and attended by the grandest and most imposing retinue their means would admit of.

All prepared themselves for the Raymi of the Sun by a rigorous fast; for, in three days they ate nothing but a little unripe maize, and a few herbs called Chucam, with plain water. During this time no fire was lighted throughout the city, and all men abstained from sleeping with their wives.

After the fast, in the evening before the festival, the Ynca sacrificial Priests prepared the sheep and lambs for sacrifice, and got ready the other offerings of food and drink that were to be offered to the Sun. All these offerings had been provided by the people who came to the feast, not only the Curacas and envoys, but also all their relations, vassals, and servants.

The Women of the Sun were engaged, during the night, in preparing an immense quantity of maize pudding called *Canca*. This was made up into small round cakes, about the size of an apple. It must be understood that the Indians never ate their corn kneaded and made into bread, except at this feast and at another called *Situa*, and they did not eat this bread during the whole meal, but only two or three mouthfuls of it at the beginning. Their usual food, in place of bread, was maize toasted or boiled in the grain.

The flour for this bread, especially for what was intended for the Ynca and those of the blood royal, was ground by the chosen virgins of the Sun, who cooked all the other food for this feast; that it might appear to be given rather by the Sun to his children than by his sons to him; and it was therefore prepared by the virgins, as women of the Sun.

Another vast assemblage of women ground the corn and cooked the food for the common people. And though the bread was intended for the people, it was yet prepared with care, because this bread was looked upon as sacred, and was only allowed to be eaten once during the year, on occasion of this feast, which was, among the people, the festival of their festivals.

In Worshipping the Sun, They Went to the Temple, and Sacrificed a Lamb

The necessary preparations having been made, the Ynca came forth at dawn, on the day of the festival, accompanied by all his relations, marching according to their age and dignity. They proceeded to the great square, which was called Huacay-pata. Here they waited for sunrise, all of them being barefooted, and all watching the east with great attention. As soon as the sun appeared, they all bent down resting on their elbows (which, among these Indians, is the same as going down on the knees), with the arms apart and the hands raised. Thus they worshipped, and kissed the air (which with them is the equivalent to kissing the hand or the dress of a Prince in Spain); and they adored with much fervour and devotion, looking upon the Sun as their god and natural father.

The Curacas, not being of the blood royal, assembled in an adjoining square, called the Casi-pata, where they used the same forms of adoration as the Yncas.

Presently the King rose to his feet, the rest being still prostrate, and took two great cups of gold, called aquilla, full of the beverage that they drink. He performed this ceremony as the first-born, in the name of his father, the Sun, and, with the cup in his right hand, invited all his relations to drink. This custom of inviting each other to drink was the usual mode by which superiors showed favour and complacency to inferiors, and by which one friend saluted another.

Having given the invitation to drink, the Ynca emptied the vase in his right hand, which was dedicated to the Sun, into a jar of gold, whence the liquor flowed down a stone conduit of very beautiful masonry from the great square to the temple of the Sun, thus being looked upon as drunk by the deity. From the vase in his left hand the Ynca himself drank, that being his share, and then divided what remained among the other Yncas, pouring it into smaller cups of gold and silver. Gradually the principal vase, which the Ynca held, was emptied; and the partakers thus received such virtue from it as was imparted by its having been sanctified by the Sun or the Ynca, or rather by both together. Each member of the blood royal drank of this liquor. The Curacas in the other square received drinks of the beverage made by the chosen virgins, but not that which had also been sanctified by the Ynca.

This ceremony having been performed, which was but a foretaste of what would have to be drunk afterwards, all went in procession to the temple of the Sun. All took off their shoes, except the King, at two hundred paces before reaching the doors; but the King remained with his shoes on, until he came to the doors. The Ynca and his relations then entered the temple as legitimate children of the deity, and there worshipped the image of the Sun. But the Curacas, being unworthy of so great an honour, remained outside in a large square before the temple doors.

The Ynca offered to the Sun the golden vases with which he had performed the ceremony, and the other members of his family gave their cups to the Ynca priests, who were set apart for that office; for persons who were not priests, even if they were of the royal blood, were not allowed to perform the priestly office. Having offered up the cups of the Yncas, the priests came to the doors to receive those of the Curacas, who took their places according to their seniority as vassals, and presented the gold and silver articles which they had brought from their provinces as offerings to the Sun. These offerings were in the form of sheep, lambs, lizards, toads, serpents, foxes, tigers, lions, and many sorts of birds, in short, of all the animals in the provinces, each imitated from nature in gold and silver, though the size of each article was not great.

As soon as the offerings were made, the chiefs returned to their places in procession; and presently the priests came out with many lambs, ewes, and rams of all colours, for the native sheep of that country are of different colours, like the horses in Spain. All this flock was the property of the Sun. They took a black lamb, for among the Indians this colour was preferred for the sacrifices, as more sacred. For they said that a black beast was black all over, while a white one, though its body might be white, always had a black nose, which was a defect, and caused it to be less perfect than a black beast. For this reason also, the Kings generally dressed in black, and their mourning was the natural colour of the wool, which they call grey.

This first sacrifice of a black lamb was made to prognosticate the omens of the festival. For they almost always sacrificed a lamb before undertaking any act either of peace or war, in order to see, by examining the heart and lungs, whether it was acceptable to the Sun, that is to say, whether it would be successful or the reverse. In order to seek an omen to tell them whether a harvest would be good; for some crops they used a lamb, for others a ram, for others a sterile ewe; but they never killed a fruitful sheep even to eat, until it was past bearing.

They took the lamb or sheep, and placed it with the head towards the east. They did not tie its feet, but three or four Indians held it, and it was cut open on the left side while still alive. They then forced their hands in, and pulled out the heart with the lungs and gullet up to the mouth, and the whole had to be taken out entire, without being cut.

Of the Omens in Their Sacrifices, and the Fires for Them

If the lungs were palpitating, or had not ceased to live as they call it, the augury was looked upon as most fortunate. If this omen appeared, they took no note of others that might appear of an opposite character. For they said that the excellence of this lucky omen would overcome the evil of all contrary signs. They then took the entrails, blew air into them, and fastened up the mouth, or held it tight with their hands. Presently they began to watch the ways by which the air entered and distended the veins and arteries. If they were very full of air, it was looked upon as a good omen. They had other ways of seeking auguries of which I took no note, but I remember having seen these two methods practised on two occasions when I was a child. I went into a yard on one occasion, where some old unbaptised Indians were performing a sacrifice, not of the Raymi, for that festival had been abolished before I was born, but for some special purpose, in order to watch the omens. With this object they sacrificed lambs and sheep, as on the feast of Raymi, for their special sacrifices were performed in imitation of those at the great festivals.

It was considered a very bad omen if the beast rose on its feet while they were opening its side, in spite of those who held it; or if the entrails broke and did not come out whole. It was also an evil sign if the lungs or heart were torn or bruised in being pulled out; and there were other signs which, as I have said, I neither inquired about nor took note of. I remember this because I heard the Indians, who made the sacrifice, asking each other concerning the bad or evil omens, and they did not mind me because I was but a child.

To return to the solemnities of the Raymi. If the sacrifice of the lamb did not furnish good auguries, they made another sacrifice of a sheep, and if this was also unpropitious they offered up another. But, even if the third sacrifice was unlucky, they did not desist from celebrating the festival, though they did so with inward sorrow and misgiving, believing that their father, the Sun, was enraged against them for some fault or negligence that they must have unintentionally committed against his service.

They feared that cruel wars, failure of crops, diseases in their flocks, and other misfortunes might befall them. But when the omens were propitious, their joy was very great with which they celebrated the festival, as they looked forward to future good fortune.

After the sacrifice of the lamb, they brought a great quantity of lambs and sheep for a general sacrifice, and they did not cut these open while they were alive, but beheaded them first. The blood and hearts of all these, as well as of the first lamb, were preserved and offered to the Sun, and the bodies were burnt until they were converted to ashes.

It was necessary that the fire for the sacrifice should be new, and given by the hand of the Sun, as they expressed it. For this purpose they took a large bracelet, called *chipana* (like those they usually wear on the left thumb). This was held by the high priest. It was larger than usual, and had on it a highly polished concave plate, about the diameter of an orange. They put this towards the Sun, at an angle, so that the reflected rays might concentrate on one point, where they had placed a little cotton well pulled out, for they did not know how to make tinder; but the cotton was soon lighted in the natural way. With this fire, thus obtained from the hands of the Sun, they consumed the sacrifice, and roasted all the meat on that day. Portions of the fire were then conveyed to the temple of the Sun, and to the convent of virgins, where they were kept in all the year, and it was an evil omen if they were allowed to go out. If on the eve of the festival, which was the time when they made the preparations for the sacrifice, there was no sun wherewith to light the new fire, they obtained it by means of two thin cylindrical sticks, about the girth of a man's finger, and half a *vara* long, which they rubbed together. They give the name of *Vyaca* both to the sticks and to the act of obtaining fire from them, the same word serving both for a noun and a verb. The Indians use these sticks instead of flint and steel, and they travel with them, so as to have the means of making a fire at their sleeping places, when in an uninhabited region. I have often seen this when I have made a journey with the Indians, and the shepherds make use of sticks for the same purpose.

They looked upon it as a bad omen to light the fire for the festival in this way, saying that, as the Sun refused to kindle the flame with his own hand, he must be angry with them. All the meat for the feast was roasted in public, in the two squares, and it was distributed amongst all those who were present at the feast, whether Yncas, Curacas, or common people. And each received a piece of the bread called *Canca* with the meat. This was the first dish in their grand and solemn banquet. Afterwards they received a great quantity of eatables, which were eaten without drinking; for it was the universal custom of the Indians of Peru not to drink while they were eating.

From what has been related, the assertion made by some Spaniards may have arisen that the Yncas and their vassals communicated like Christians. We have described the custom of the Indians, and each reader can make out the similitude as he pleases.

After the eating was over, they brought liquor in great quantity, for this was one of the most prevalent vices among the Indians. But at the present day, through the mercy of God and the good example which has been set them in this particular by the Spaniards, no Indian can get drunk without being despised and reviled by his fellows. If the Spaniards had set a like example as regards other vices, they would have been apostolic preachers of the gospel.

How They Drank to Each Other and in What Order

The Ynca, seated in his golden chair, which was placed on a platform of the same metal, sent to the members of the tribes called Hanan Cuzco and Hurin Cuzco, desiring them to drink, in his name, with the most distinguished Indians belonging to other nations.

First, they invited the captains who had shown valour in war, who, even when they were not lords of vassals, were for their bravery preferred to Curacas. But if a Curaca, besides being a lord of vassals, was also a captain in the wars, they did him honour both on the one account and on the other. Next the Ynca ordered the Curacas living in the vicinity of Cuzco, to be invited to drink, being those whose ancestors the first Ynca Manco Ccapac had reduced to his service. These chiefs, owing to the great privilege of bearing the name of Ynca, which that Prince had granted them, were looked upon as nobles of the highest rank next to the Yncas of the blood royal, and before all the chiefs of other tribes. For those kings never thought of diminishing in the smallest degree any privilege or favour that their ancestors had granted to any of their vassals, but on the contrary confirmed and increased them.

In these drinking bouts that the Indians had with each other, it must be understood that they all held their cups touching each other, two and two, and whether large or small, they were always of the same size and shape, and of the same metal, whether gold, silver or wood. This custom was enforced that each might drink the same quantity. He who gave an invitation to drink carried the two cups in his hands, and if the invited person was of lower rank he was given the cup in the left hand, if of equal or higher rank, the cup in the right; and with more or less ceremony according to the position in life of one and the other. Then they both drank together, and, the person inviting to drink, having received back his cup, returned to his place. On these occasions the first invitation was from a superior to his inferior, in token of favour and kindness. Afterwards the inferior invited his superior, as an acknowledgment of his vassalage and duty.

In observing this custom, the Ynca first sent an invitation to his vassals, in each nation preferring the captains before those who were not warriors. The Ynca who took the invitation said to the invited person: – "The sole Ynca sends me to invite you to drink, and I come to drink with you in his name." The captain or Curaca then took the cup with much reverence, raised his eyes to the Sun, as though he would give thanks for so undeserved a favour conferred by his son, and having drunk, he returned the cup to the Ynca without another word, only making signs of adoration with his hands and kissing the air with his lips.

And it must be understood that the Ynca did not send invitations to drink to all the Curacas (though he did so to all captains) but only to a select number, who were most worthy and who were most devoted to the public good. For this was the mark at which they all shot, as well the Ynca as the Curacas and the ministers of peace and war. The rest of the Curacas were invited to drink by the same Yncas who brought the cups, but in their own names and not in that of the Ynca, which satisfied them, because the invitation came from one who was a child of the Sun, like their king.

After the first invitation to drink, the captains and Curacas of all the nations returned the challenges in the order that they had received them, some to the Ynca himself, and the others to his relations, according as the first invitation had been received. The Ynca was approached without a word, and merely with the signs of adoration I have already described. He received them with much condescension, and took the cups they presented, but as he could not, nor was it lawful for him to drink of them all, he merely put them to his lips, drinking a little from all of them, from some more, from others less, according to the favour he wished to show to their owners, which was regulated by their rank and merit. And he ordered the attendants, who were all Yncas by privilege, to drink for him with those captains and Curacas; who having done so, returned the cups.

The Curacas held these cups in great veneration as sacred things, because the sole Ynca had touched them with his hands and lips. They never drank out of them again, nor touched them, but looked upon them as idols fit to be worshipped, in memory of their having been touched by the Ynca. Certainly nothing can show more than this how great was the love and veneration, both internal and outward, that these Indians felt for their kings.

The invitation and the return challenge to drink having been observed, all returned to their places. Presently the dances and songs began, in different fashions, and with the several insignia, masks, and dresses used by each nation. While the singing and dancing continued they did not leave off drinking, the Yncas and Curacas inviting each other, according to their special friendships, or to the nearness of their places of residence.

The celebration of the feast of Raymi lasted for nine days, during which time there was abundance of eating and drinking, and such rejoicing as each person could show. But the sacrifices for observing omens were only made on the first day. As soon as the nine days were over the Curacas returned to their lands with the permission of the King, very joyful and contented at having celebrated the principal feast of their god the Sun. When the King was occupied in war or in visiting his dominions, he celebrated the feast in the place where he happened to be, but not with so much solemnity as when he was at Cuzco; while the Ynca governor, the High Priest, and others of the blood royal who remained behind, took care to celebrate it in the capital. On those occasions the Curacas assembled in the provinces, each one going to the feast which was held nearest to the place of his abode.

Ttahua-Ntin-Suyu

A Deeper Account of the Expansion of the Inca Empire

I
Cunti-suyu

THE OFFICIAL NAME OF THE EMPIRE OF THE INCAS was *Ttahua-ntin-suyu*, the word *ttahua* meaning four, *ntin* a collective plural, and *suyu* province. 'The four combined provinces' with reference to the dominions west, north, south, and east of the central land of the Incas. The western division was called *Cunti-suyu*, and included the country from the Apurimac to the maritime Cordillera and the coast. *Chinchay-suyu* was the northern division including Huamanca, the valley of the Jauja, Haunuco, Caxamarca, as far as Quito, with the coast valleys. The *Colla-suyu*, or southern division, was the basin of Lake Titicaca, and Charcas, as far as Tucuman, Chile, and the valleys of

Arequipa, Moquegua, and Tacna. The country to the east of the land of the Incas and all that was known of the Amazonian forests was ***Anti-suyu***.

From a geographical point of view the *Cunti-suyu* division is formed of three regions west of the Apurimac, within the meridians of 70° and 76° W., all watered by tributaries of the Apurimac. The first lies between the Apurimac and the Pachachaca rivers, the second between the Pachachaca and the Pampas, and the third includes the maritime Cordillera between those meridians. They may be called, after their chief *ayllus* or tribes, the Quichua, Chanca, and Lucana regions.

The Quichuas occupied the beautiful valley of Apancay, and some valleys in the mountains as far as the fortress of Curamba, beyond the Pachachaca. Their position is partly defined in the account of Tupac's first campaign, when he occupied the Quichua strongholds of Tuyara, Cayara, and Curampa. The Quichuas were very closely allied to the Inca people in race, and their language was the same. Indeed, the first Spanish grammarian of the general language of the Incas called it Quichua, probably from having studied it in their country. Mossi gives a definition of the word from the passive participle of *quehuini* (I twist), which is *quehuisca* (twisted) and *ichu* (grass), that is *quehuisca-ychu* (twisted grass), by syncope *quichua*. It came to mean a temperate region, neither too hot nor too cold.

The Apancay valley presents scenes of great beauty. On the mountain to the south the products of almost every clime may be seen at one glance. The rapid little river flows along at its base, amongst waving maize crops and fruit trees. On the steep slopes immediately above there are crops of potatoes and other edible roots, then pastures on the steep mountain side with rocks cropping out, and higher the peaks shooting up into the sky. On the other side of Apancay there are terraced slopes, and cultivated tracts sloping down to the banks of the Pachachaca. Higher up the Pachachaca and other tributaries of the Apurimac, the mountain gorges and lofty punas were inhabited by four ayllus of hardy mountaineers closely allied to the Quichuas. These were the *Chumpi-uilcas*, *Cotapampas*, *Umasayus*, and *Aymaras*.

The beauty of the scenery between the rivers Pachachaca and Pampas is most striking as the summit ridges are reached, and the eye ranges over such valleys and gorges as are presented by Angamos, Pincos,and Huancarama. On a grassy plateau, commanding the road, is the ancient fortress of Curamba, a stronghold of the Quichuas. It consists of three terraces, one above the other with stone revetments, and a ramp on the east side forming a sloping way to each terrace. There were no doubt stockaded defences when it was used for operations of war. The great feature of this Chanca region is the extensive and fertile valley of Andahuaylas, capable of sustaining a very large population. There are other fertile valleys between Andahuaylas and the river Pampas which, like the Apurimac, flows through a gorge so profound that the vegetation on the river banks is quite tropical.

Beyond the Pampas, in the valleys formed by its tributaries flowing from the maritime Cordillera, and on the Pacific slopes, there dwelt two powerful mountain tribes called Soras and Lucanas. They seem to have been more advanced in civilization than their neighbours, for there are ruins of important edifices in the Sora country, called Vilcas-huaman. This was a palace of the Incas and their principal station in Cunti-suyu, but it existed before the annexation, for Montesinos mentions a king of Vilcas, and the Soras did not submit without making some resistance. Their neighbours, the Lucanas, occupied both slopes of the Cordillera. On the Pacific side there is a large alpine lake frequented by flamingoes called Parihuana-cocha, round the banks of which their principal seat appears to have been. Below is the lovely coast valley of *Nasca*, owing its fertility to the most remarkable system of irrigation in Peru, which I believe to have been due to the skill, intelligence, and industry of the Lucanas. These mountaineers were remarkable for their strength, as well as for their skill and industry. In later times it was their special privilege to carry the imperial litter.

The Nasca valley is one of the most striking monuments of Andean civilization. The fertilizing water is led from the mountains of Lucanas by subterraneous channels, built of stone and the height of a man. Their origin in the mountains is now unknown. The water flows down them perennially, and is eventually spread over the valley by smaller channels, converting a coast desert into an earthly paradise. Pottery of a peculiar design, and believed to be of great antiquity, has recently been found in the valley of Nasca.

II
Chinchay-suyu

Chinchay-suyu, the northern division of the empire, includes the two great ranges of the Andes, and the rich and fertile valleys between them. The direction becomes nearly north and south, following the trend of the coast, not east and west as in Cunti-suyu. The valleys supported very large populations, and the mountains were inhabited by tribes of hardy mountaineers.

When the Inca Pachacuti sent the first army for the conquest of Chinchay-suyu, it included a large contingent of the conquered Chancas, led by one of their own chiefs named Anco-ayllu. They fought well for the Incas, but their leader chafed at his subjection, and incited his men to desert. A plot was arranged, and on a day settled beforehand the Chanca contingent left the camp and, led by Anco-ayllu, they proceeded by forced marches into the Amazonian forests. This exodus was commenced at a place called Huarac-tampu, near Huanuco. They were soon beyond the reach of pursuit, and it is believed that they settled in valleys along the lower course of the Huallaga. They were found there by a Spanish expedition in 1556, and a recent traveller has suggested that the half-civilized Lamistas, or Motilones, on the Huallaga, are their descendants. This event made a deep impression on the Inca recorders, for it is mentioned by several Spanish writers who received their information from the native Amautas.

On marching north from Vilcas-huaman, after crossing the deep gorge of the Pampas by a bridge of aloe cables, the Inca army entered upon the basin of the Jauja river, another tributary of the Apurimac. The various streams flowing to the Jauja are in the bottoms of deep ravines, while the intervening higher lands are fertile and produced large crops. To the west the splendid maritime cordillera rises abruptly, and in this part the fierce and warlike Morochucos sought for pastures and raised edible roots among the giddy heights. To the east were the equally imposing mountains of Cuntur-cunca, in the rear of which the Iquichanos defied invasion. The intervening plains and ravines were inhabited by the numerous tribe of Pocras, who made a desperate fight for independence.

The final stand of the Pocras and Morochucos was on a slope between two ravines, at the foot of the Cuntur-cunca heights. There was a terrible slaughter, and the place was ever afterwards called the *Ayacucho*, or 'corner of death.' The remnant of Morochucos fled westward to their own mountains, followed closely by the Inca general, who finally encamped on a grassy slope at the foot of the first steep ascent. As he sat with his officers around him at their evening meal, a falcon soared in circles round his head. He threw up a piece of llama flesh to it, crying out "*Huaman-ca*" ("take it, falcon!") The tradition was never forgotten, and the natives tell it to this day. The place, afterwards the site of a Spanish city, was called *Huamanca* (Guamanga), in memory of the Inca's supper guest.

Advancing northwards up the Jauja valley, the Incas next defeated and brought under subjection the Huanca nation, which cultivated and inhabited that fertile region. In the mountains to the westward there were two remarkable tribes, the Yauyos and Huarochiris, who appear to have descended into the adjacent coast valleys, and to have greatly increased their well-being by exchanges of products raised in different climes. The Yauyos seem to have spread over the valleys of Pisco, Chincha, Huarcu (Cañete), and Mala; and in a ravine leading up from the Huarcu valley, called Runa-huana, there are some interesting ruins. According to Garcilasso the inhabitants of Huarcu made a very desperate resistance to the Inca arms, and this seems to be confirmed by the fact that the ruins of an extensive Incarial fortress and palace, called Hervay, exist on a defensive hill close to the sea, flanked by a rapid river on one side and the desert on the other.

The Yauyos spoke a peculiar dialect of their own, called *Cauqui*. Much reduced in numbers and living in small villages high up in the mountains, there are now not more than 1500 people who still speak this dialect. Like the Rucanas and Moro-chucos, the Yauyos are an intelligent race, and make excellent artificers when any of them have opportunities of learning trades in the coast valleys which once belonged to them.

The Huarochiris lived in lofty gorges of the maritime cordilleras to the north of the Yauyos, with terrible passes over the snowy heights. But the descent on either side gradually led down to fairer scenes, on one side to the fertile vale of the Jauja, on the other to the coast valleys of Chilca, Lurin, and Rimac. The imposing grandeur of some of this scenery, contrasted with the peaceful beauty of the rest, seems to have been impressed on the imaginations of the Huarochiri, and to have given rise to a mythology full of quaint legends and fables. The temple to the fish god at Pachacamac attracted pilgrims from far and near as a famous oracle, as well as the oracle which gave its name to the Rimac valley. Both appear to have been due to the highly imaginative tendencies of those of the Huarochiris who settled on the coast. It was a little further north, at Pativilca, on the coast, that the more northern dominions of the Grand Chimu found its southern frontier. But this coast region, between Pativilca and the Rimac, seems to have been long in an unsettled state. The dwellings of the chiefs who occupied the Rimac valley were built on immense mounds of great extent, and strongly fortified. The mountain tribes of the maritime Cordillera are quite exceptionally interesting, because the advances they had made in civilization were due largely to their occupation of valleys on the coast.

The Incas received the submission of the mountaineers without invading their fastnesses, and pressed onwards in their northern conquests. They were now an immense distance from their base, but their generalship was carefully thought out and so sound that they advanced with confidence to the great lake of Chinchay-cocha and the mountain knot of Cerro Pasco, which, like that of Vilcañota, connects the eastern

Andes with the maritime cordillera. The march, be it remembered, was not a matter of months, but of years.

The conquerors now entered another region, the basin of the Marañon, and the very remarkable formation known as the 'Callejon de Huaras.' At Huanuco a great palace was projected and afterwards built by Tupac Inca Yupanqui, forming eventually the chief seat of Inca government in Chinchay-suyu. Among the Conchucos they met with a people who had made marked progress in the arts, and had taken their own line in the conception of a religious belief. The Incas passed on and, after slight opposition, occupied Caxamarca. In another campaign Tupac Inca conquered the Paltas, and the turbulent tribe of Cañaris, while the territories of the great Chimu, in the coast valleys, were reduced to subjection. Quito also became part of the empire after one decisive battle.

The greatest proof of the genius of these Inca generals is the way in which they changed their tactics and methods of warfare as soon as they encountered circumstances of which they had previously no experience. Tupac Inca was at the palace he had caused to be built at Tumipampa, in the country of the Canaris, when he heard of the riches of Manta, the land of emeralds, and of other coast regions. He resolved to explore, and to add these countries to the empire. He led his army down through the dense forests to the country of the Chonos (the modern Guayaquil), constructing a road as he advanced. With a hostile country, difficulties in arranging for supplies, and the extraordinary obstacles caused by the dense vegetation, the enterprise seemed almost hopeless. On reaching the banks of the Guayaquil, where it is navigable, he found the enemy in a large fleet of canoes, while he was without any means of attacking. But with Tupac Inca there was no such word as impossible. Having a very excellent system of road-making, and efficient commissariat arrangements, he was without anxiety about supplies. The more insuperable appeared the difficulties the more determined he was to overcome them. He proceeded to build canoes, and to exercise his soldiers as canoe-men until they were fairly expert. This occupied several months. He then attacked the enemy's fleet, and the manoeuvres continued for several days, sometimes one side and sometimes the other having command of the river. The Incarial soldiers were more accustomed to the use of the lance than to naval warfare, so their very able general gave orders to grapple and fight at close quarters. The result was then no longer doubtful, and the Chonos submitted. The Inca landed where now stands the city of Guayaquil, and after a sojourn of a year he resolved upon the conquest of the island of Pirna, in the Gulf of Guayaquil, assisted by the chiefs of the Chonos, who had become his allies. Many canoes were got ready, and good pilots were engaged. Here seamanlike skill was needed rather than reliance upon numbers. But nothing could resist Tupac's superior strategy, and the island was conquered. Most generous terms were granted, and a cordial friendship, cemented by a marriage, was established between the Inca and the Puna chiefs. The coast provinces of Manta and Esmeraldas, to the north, sent in their submission, and the port of Tumbez, to the south of the Gulf of Guayaquil, was fixed upon as a military station.

While the Tupac Inca Yupanqui was at Tumbez, he received information that, far out in the ocean, there were islands called *Hahua-chumpi* and *Nina-chumpi*, the outer and the fire islands. The Inca was a man of lofty ideals, and, as Sarmiento says, "he resolved to challenge a happy fortune, and try if it would favour him by sea." This was a wonderful expedition, but Sarmiento's account is corroborated by Balboa, and I have come to the conclusion that the story of the voyage is historically true.

The Incas caused an immense number of balsas to be constructed, consisting of inflated seal-skins fastened together, and some rafts. He then embarked with a large detachment of his army, leaving the main body to await his return at Tumbez.

Tupac Inca sailed away on this memorable voyage of discovery, disappearing below the horizon of those who gazed from the hills round Tumbez. To them it must have seemed an enterprise as appalling as it was unprecedented. If the Inca ever returned, his people would be convinced that there was nothing he might not do. It is said that he reached the islands, and that he was absent for nine months. Sarmiento believed that he reached the Solomon Islands, but there can be little doubt that it was two of the Galapagos Islands that the Inca discovered and explored. Sarmiento says that he brought back gold, a chair of brass, and the skin and jawbone of a horse, which were preserved in the fortress at Cuzco. It is more likely that the nature of these curiosities was not understood, and that they were really specimens of the large terrapins and other products of the Galapagos Islands.

The conquest and settlement of Chinchay-suyu by the Incas must be looked upon as the greatest of their military achievements. It occupied several years, and there were a number of campaigns. Still, when the immense distances from their base, the care and forethought needed to keep the army properly supplied, the inaccessible character of a great part of the country, and the necessity for adapting the troops to very different kinds of warfare, often in the face of the enemy, are considered, it must be acknowledged that the genius and ability of this remarkable race is very striking. The voyage of discovery to the Galapagos Islands is marvellous. These statesmen and warriors were no ordinary conquerors, and they were well fitted to rule the vast empire they brought together with such extraordinarv skill and determination.

III
Colla-suyu

After the disruption of the ancient empire there was a long period of centuries of barbarism. The tribes which came to inhabit the country round Lake Titicaca may have been partly descendants of subjects of the megalithic kings and partly descendants of invaders. They were a hardy race of mountaineers, strong and thick-set, and capable of enduring great fatigue. Like the Incas and Quichuas, they spoke dialects of the same original language.

Of these tribes the *Canas* were on the crest of the water-parting between the Titicaca drainage and the Vilcamayu. The *Collas* occupied the whole of the northern half of the Titicaca basin. They were the most numerous and powerful of the tribes in the Titicaca region. Along the western shores of the lake were the *Lupacas*. The *Pacasas* occupied the eastern side, and to the south were the *Pacajes* and *Quillaguas*. There was also an almost amphibious tribe living among the reeds in the south-west angle of Lake Titicaca, called *Urus*. They spoke a language of their own. Another language, called Puquina, was spoken in part of Colla-suyu. Great invasions from the south are recorded, even from Chile, and the tribes of the lake basin were practised in mountain fighting.

The Collas had acquired predominance over the other tribes, and early writers give the generic name of Collas to them all. It was probably a confederacy, with the Colla chief at its head. He was becoming very powerful, extending his sway over Arequipa and Tacna towards the Pacific, and into some of the eastern valleys where coca is grown. His chief seat was at Hatun-cola, a few miles north-west of the north-western angle of Lake Titicaca. Here there are figures carved on stones, and some few other vestiges of the former greatness of the Colla chief. Just above are the towers or *chulpas* of Sillustani, overlooking a mountain lake.

The Collas buried their dead in cromlechs consisting of huge blocks of stone, many of which are still extant. Later they built circular towers of fine ashlar masonry, vaulted above with a coping round the upper part. Some are square. The best examples are at Sillustani, near Hatun-colla, the probable burial-place of the Colla chiefs.

Chuchi Ccapac was the name of the great chief who haughtily refused to submit to the Inca. He had a large force of hardy mountaineers around him, inured to hardships, brave, and of fine physique. They were concentrated for the defence of Hatun-colla, led by Chuchi Ccapac and all the chiefs of his confederacy.

The Collas were constantly making incursions down the valley of the Vilcamayu, and were as constantly driven back over the pass. At last the Inca built a wall from the snows of Vilcañota across the road to the snows on the western side. The Collas agreed that this should be their boundary. But they broke the treaty and continued their raids. The Inca, therefore, resolved to conquer them. Lizarraga says that the remains of the wall were still visible in his time, at the point on the summit of the pass called La Raya by the Spaniards.

The Inca Pachacuti assembled a great army, crossed the pass of Vilcañota, and advanced across the Collao without opposition until he came in sight of the enemy's forces drawn up in front of Hatun-colla. The proud chief was called upon either to serve and obey the Inca or to try his fortunes in battle. The reply was that Chuchi Ccapac expected the Inca to submit to him, like the chiefs of other nations he had conquered. The answer concluded with a savage threat.

The two armies then encountered each other in desperate hand-to-hand combats, and the issue was for a long time doubtful. The Inca was in every part, giving orders, fighting, and animating his troops. For a moment there was a pause. The slightest thing might have turned the scale. At this momentous crisis the Inca shouted a few words of encouragement and dashed into the thickest of the fight, closely followed by his Orejones. With renewed vigour all his troops rallied, and at length the gallant enemy turned and fled. Chuchi Ccapac was taken prisoner, and Pachacuti entered Hatun-colla in triumph. There he remained until all the confederate tribes were reduced to submission. An Inca viceroy was appointed to govern the Collao, with the necessary garrisons, and Pachacuti returned to Cuzco.

Colla-suyu was not, however, to be subdued in one campaign. A few years afterwards the sons of Chuchi Ccapac escaped, and raised the standard of revolt. The confederate tribes rallied round them. This time the battle took place further north, and the Collas were again defeated with great slaughter, near Lampa. Pachacuti returned to Cuzco, but two of his very able sons, Tupac Ayar Manco and Apu Paucar Usnu, remained to pacify the country, and to extend the conquest southwards over the countries of the Charcas and Chichas.

After the accession of Inca Tupac Yupanqui, the Collas rebelled once more to secure their freedom. They had constructed four strong places, all in the Colla country, to the north of Lake Titicaca, at Llallahua, Asillo, Arapa (on a small lake), and Pucara, an isolated rocky mountain rising out of the plain to a great height. The Inca generals were occupied for several years in reducing these fortresses. The final stand was at Pucara, where the Collas sustained a crushing defeat. All thoughts of further resistance were abandoned.

The Inca proceeded to include Tucuman and Chile in his conquests. A story is told by Monte-sinos respecting the Chilian annexation which seems quite probable.

It appears that two Chilian chiefs, who had come with a contingent to help the Collas, were taken prisoners and sent to Cuzco. They were received with great kindness by the Inca, who gave them two *Pallas*, his half-sisters, for their wives. They returned to Chile, and had two sons by the Inca princesses. In course of time the Inca's Chilian nephews proposed a visit to their imperial uncle, and arrived at Cuzco with a large retinue. They were received by the Inca with much love and great rejoicings. They entreated their uncle to visit their country, where all desired to see him. He consented to do so in the following year, and his nephews returned to Chile with many Orejones and several Amautas to teach them the art of government. But a number of Chilian chiefs thought that this friendship with the Inca boded no good to them, and they took up arms. The nephews, however, defeated them, even before the Inca could arrive in Chile, which he did with a great army. All the chiefs submitted to him and, after two years, he left his nephews in peaceful possession as his viceroys. His dominions extended to the river Maulé in the south of Chile. Thus the empire was more than 2000 miles in length, from the river Maulé to Pasto.

From that time the Collas and Chilians furnished valuable contingents to the Inca armies.

The Inca Tupac Yupanqui saw the necessity for establishing permanent tranquillity in the Collao by a system of colonization. Great numbers of Collas and Lupacas were sent to colonize the charming valleys of Arequipa, Moquegua, and Tacna on the west side of the maritime cordillera. Others were sent down into the Amazonian valleys to the eastward, to cultivate coca and wash for gold. Traditions are preserved even now, which tell from which district in the Collao the exiles were taken, and whither sent. The conquest of the Collao was of immense importance, because it was the only source of tin for their bronze weapons and tools, and the principal source of gold from Caravaya.

Tupac Inca was deeply impressed by the vast ruins at Tiahuanacu, of unknown origin, by the beauties of the great lake, and of the sun rising over the snowy peaks of Illimani and Illampu. He caused a palace to be built on the island of Coati, in the lake, with baths and gardens. number of Orejones remained in the Collao to carry on the administration, and emigrants arrived to take the places of the exiled Collas and Lupacas.

These emigrants were chiefly Quichuas various tribes from Cunti-suyu. A number of Aymaras, from the head-waters of the Pachachaca, were settled among the remaining Lupacas at Juli on the west coast of the lake, where the languages of the two races appear to have got considerably mixed. In 1576 the Jesuits settled at Juli, and had a printing-press there, and here they learnt the language of the Lupacas from the Aymara emigrants, who gave them many Quichua words, for they seem to have used words of both languages in their conversations. This explains the reason why the first priests who acquired the Colla language and afterwards the Jesuits gave the name of 'Aymara' to the language of the Collao. Ludovico Bertonio was at Juli from 1590 to 1612, and before he arrived the Jesuits had adopted the name of 'Aymara' to what Bertonio calls *esta lengua Lupaca*. He published his 'Arte y Gramatica' of 'Aymara' at Rome in 1603, and a second edition, with a dictionary, at Juli in July 1612. Torres Rubio followed with a grammar and vocabulary of 'Aymara' in 1616. The word 'Aymara' is now generally, but very erroneously, applied to the language and people of the basin of Lake Titicaca.

IV
Anti-suyu

The chain of the eastern Andes is penetrated by five great rivers, which unite to form the 'mighty Orellana.' They flow northwards until they unite, and then flow eastward in one majestic stream to the Atlantic. The Amazonian basin which they traverse consists of millions of square miles of virgin forest. The first river is the Marañon, and being the most western and distant its source in the Andean lake of Lauricocha is considered to be the source of the Amazon. Next is the river Huallaga, flowing north until it joins the Marañon. Further to the east the great Ucayali tributary is formed by the Perene, Apurimac, and Vilcamayu, which all force away through the Andes. Furthers outh the Tono, Arasa, Inambari, Tambopata, and Beni rise on the eastern slopes of the Andes and do not penetrate the range. With the Mamoré and Itenez they form the great Madeira tributary. The rivers which have part of their courses within the Andean system, all have formidable rapids when they force their way through the mountains and enter the great Amazonian plains. These mountain rapids were called *puncu*, or doors, which the rivers had opened by their irresistible force. That of the Maranon is called the Puncu de Manseriche. On the Huallaga the rapid is known as the Salto de Aguirre, respecting which there is an interesting tradition: then the river is navigable for 160 miles. The Ucayali, a broad stream navigable for 1400 miles, breaks through the mountains at Cancha-guayo. The Vilcamayu, navigable for 100 miles, enters the primeval forests by the Puncu de Mainique.

The vast Amazonian forests are approached by the descent of the eastern side of the Andes, down gorges and ravines which present magnificent scenery, the long spurs being covered with the richest tropical vegetation to their summits. Here are seen the lovely chinchona trees with their red-veined glossy leaves, and panicles of white flowers with pink laciniæ, emitting a delicious fragrance. Here, too, are many species of Melastomas, especially the Lasiandra with its purple flowers and triple-veined leaves. But the flowering trees and bushes are innumerable, and above the thick foliage are seen the feathery fronds of palm trees. From the loftier mountains waterfalls may be seen in rapid descent until they are lost to view behind the dense vegetation; some in sheets of spray, others like films of lace, but most in a solid volume of moving water, all glittering when the clouds open and the sun throws its rays upon them. These are scenes of unsurpassed loveliness. But in the plains below the view is obstructed by the vegetation growing in dense masses beneath the lofty trees. Only on the river banks there are beautiful views formed by long vistas of tropical vegetation.

It was to the forests eastward of Cuzco that the Incas first turned their attention. To the east of the valley of the Vilcamayu the range of the Andes is cut laterally by the Yanatilde valley, and further east by the long valley through which the river Paucartampu flows. Both the Yanatilde and Paucartampu flow north to join the Vilcamayu, though their previously unknown courses were only traced, for the first time, a very few years ago. From the last range of the Andes, on the east side of the Paucartampu river, the descent is rapid into the *montaña*, as the tropical forests are called by the Spaniards. The forests were very scantily inhabited by wild Indians who wandered about, some in canoes as fishermen, some hunting with bows and arrows or the pucuna (blowpipe). A few had some affinity with the people of the Andes, but the great majority of the Amazonian tribes were of a different race.

The subjugation of the parts of the *montaña* nearest to the foot of the Andes was a matter of great importance to the Incas. In the tropical valleys the coca plantations were formed and every Peruvian chewed coca. From the *montaña* also came supplies of bamboo, of wood of the chonta palm for their weapons, other timber for building, plumes for head-dresses, and the principal supplies of gold.

The campaign of Tupac Inca Yupanqui for the conquest of Anti-suyu was, like all his warlike operations, masterly in design and bold in execution. The long valley of Paucartambo, at the foot of the last ridge of the Andes, formed a convenient base where the three columns, forming the army of Anti-suyu, was to assemble. The Inca himself started from a place in the valley called Ahua-tuna, descending into the forest by the lovely ravine of the Chiri-mayu. The central column under Prince Uturuncu Achachi, the Inca's brother, was at a place called Amaru, the modern town of Paucartampu. It was to enter by the route now called 'Tres Cruces.' A captain named Chalco Yupanqui led the right column from the Pilcopata or 'garland hill.' At the same time the *montaña* of Marcapata, to the south, was to be invaded by Apu-ccuri-machi with a fourth column.

The three columns in the Paucartambo valley were to start at the same time on converging lines, to form a junction at Opotari in the forest, about twelve miles from the foot of the mountains. The inhabitants, who belonged to the tribe called Campas or Antis, submitted at once, and the settlement called Abisca, for the cultivation of coca, was formed near the river Tono. The Inca then began to make a road through the dense forest in order to reach the settlements of the next tribe. Tall trees were climbed to seek out the positions of inhabited places by the smoke rising over the trees. The troops suffered from the change of climate, and from the toil of hewing out the road. There was much sickness and many died. At one time the Inca, with a third of the troops, lost his way and wandered about for many days until, at last, they fell in with the column of Uturuncu, who put them on the route. The combined forces then descended the river Tono.

The final result of the campaign was that three branches of the Campas, a tribe of fine muscular men and beautiful women, submitted and became subjects of the Inca. These were the Opataris, the Mañaris, called also Yana-simis or 'black mouths,' and the Chunchos. The submission included a vast tract of forest, yielding valuable timber, and with land suitable for coca plantations. The Mañaris were also met with on the lower reaches of the river Vilcamayu, and in the *montaña* beyond the Vilcapampa mountains, and they always remained friendly to the Incas. Further north there was a fierce and hostile tribe called Pilcosones.

The Marcapata column led by Apu-ccuri-machi marched eastward to the Inambari, and advanced as far as a river called Paytiti, where their leader set up the frontier pillars of the Inca. Uturuncu was left to complete the conquest, aided by detachments of colonists who made clearings for coca plantations, and collected chonta poles and other products. Most of the settlements were round Abisca, and in the basin of the river Tono; but there were others on the banks of the Vilcamayu and in Marcapata.

After the conquest of Colla-suyu the forests of the province of Caravaya also became a great source of wealth to the Incas. Large numbers of Collas were sent down into the beautiful valleys to grow fruit trees and cultivate the coca plant, as well as to work and wash for gold. Indeed, it was principally from Caravaya that the immense quantities of gold came which were used for vases and other utensils, for adorning the temples and idols, for the imperial thrones and litters, for ornamenting the rich dresses, and for many other purposes. Much gold also came from the rich valleys whose rivers unite to form the Beni.

Further south there were some fierce and savage tribes in the forests of the 'Gran Chacu,' or great hunting ground. Among these the most troublesome were the Chirihuanas, who were said to have been cannibals. They were always hostile, and even had the audacity to make incursions into the higher lands of Charcas.

On the river Huallaga the remnant of the Chancas took refuge, and the ancestors of the existing Amazonian tribe of Mayorunas are said to have fled before the Chancas to settle lower down the course of the great river. The present Huallaga tribes of Cholones and Motilones, or Lamistas, may be descendants of the Chancas. The Incas occupied Chachapoyas in the basin of the Marañon. An expedition is recorded, sent by the Inca Huayna Ccapac to the country of the Cofanes, a tribe in the forests of the river Napo to the east of Quito. A story is also told by Montesinos of some Orejones having found their way thence by the waterways and through the dense forests to Cuzco, a voyage which occupied several years. It was certainly a most remarkable achievement if true, and considering the energy and intelligence of these people I can see no sufficient reason for doubting the truth of the story.

The wisdom of the Incas is well shown in their policy with regard to the region of Amazonian forests. They made no useless raids or expeditions, but worked with the distinct object of securing advantages for the empire. From their *montaña* settlements, quite sufficiently supplied with labour, they received gold in large quantities, coca which was almost a necessary of life for their people, timber for building, wood of the chonta palm for lances and other weapons, bamboos, plumes of feathers, fruit, and medicinal herbs, gums, and resins. In return the colonists received meat and potatoes, maize, clothing, salt and other condiments. The forests of the *montaña* formed a part, and no unimportant part, of the great system of Incarial administration.

Amazons of America

European Rumours Only?

WHEN CHRISTOPHER COLUMBUS was returning from his first voyage of discovery, he was told by the Indians of Hispaniola of another island, called Mantinino, which was inhabited solely by women. They employed themselves in labour not suited to their sex, using the bow and arrow, hunting, and going to war. Once a year they received

Caribs from other islands among them, the men only staying a short time, and on their next annual visit taking away with them the male infants that had been born, the girls remaining with their mothers. These women, besides using bows and arrows, had defensive armour of brass plates. This intelligence added to the admiral's conviction that he was on the coast of the Indies, for the ancients had spoken of islands where the Themysciran Amazons had taken refuge, and one of his own countrymen, a great traveller by land, the Venetian, Marco Polo, as we know, had given an account of what was considered by many as their last abode. But although Columbus constantly heard rumours of the mysterious island, which often seemed to be in the immediate neighbourhood, yet ever receded, he was not destined to see it or any of its inhabitants. No one, indeed, succeeded in identifying the particular island of which the natives of the Caribbean Sea seemed to give such explicit details. Other Spanish adventurers, however, had different tales to tell.

In 1540, some forty years after Allonzo Pinzon had discovered the great Marañon, Francesco de Orellana, making his way from far-off Peru to the Atlantic through the Brazils, explored the magnificent river, he and his companions meeting with many difficulties. They were told of a race of pigmies, of men whose heads grew out of their backs, of others whose feet were turned the wrong way round, so that if any one attempted to follow in their tracks, the pursuers were misled, actually receding from those they desired to catch up. There were also men with tails, and stories of the Ozacoulets, a tribe of warriors with white skins, blue eyes, and long light-coloured beards; but most persistent of all were the rumours of warrior women who lived apart from men. The grandeur and novelty of the scenes they were passing through, the weirdness of the stories they heard, all prepared the Spanish adventurers to accept the marvellous, so that when they had accomplished rather more than half of their journey, and were approaching the Trombetus River in the neighbourhood of the great, densely wooded island of Tumpinambaranas, formed by the junction of the Madera with the Marañon, they found themselves opposed by warlike natives gathered on the banks, and among them noticed women seemingly acting as leaders of the men, they readily fell into the notion that here they had stumbled upon the renowned Amazons. In this belief they were confirmed by the natives whom they cross-examined, and de Orellana, duly impressed with this wonderful discovery, and some say actuated by a desire to magnify his own exploits, renamed the Marañon River the Amazon, a name subsequently given to a whole vast province.

Garcilaso Inca de la Vega, in his account of the expedition of Gonzalo Pizarro and his lieutenants, quotes Father Carbajal, who was in the train of de Orellana. The good father says that the Indians attacked the small but well-armed party of Spaniards so fiercely because they were tributaries to the Amazons, which betrays a certain confusion of ideas with Asiatic traditions. However, he and others of his Spanish companions saw some ten or twelve Amazons who were fighting in the front ranks of the Indians, acting as though they were in command, and with such vigour that the Indians did not dare to turn their backs, and those who fled before the enemy were killed with sticks by their own party. These women appeared to be very tall, robust, fair of complexion, with long hair twisted over their heads, skins of wild beasts wound round their loins, and carried bows and arrows in their hands, with which they killed many of the explorer's party.

These rumours of the Amazonian nation were plentiful, but no one ever came across the country, at least no one of sufficient standing to give accurate geographical indications. The country was supposed to be buried in the gloomy forests, though it was said to possess rich cities. Some time after the adventure of de Orellana and Carbajal, another missionary, Father Cristobal de Acuña, who had long dwelt in the Brazils, gave, in his *New Discovery of the Great River of the Amazons*, considerably more details. "These man-like women," he writes, "have their abodes in the extensive forests and lofty hills, among which that which rises above the rest, and is therefore beaten by the winds for its pride with most violence, so that it is bare and clear of vegetation, is called Yacamiaba. The Amazons are women of great valour, and they have always preserved themselves without the ordinary intercourse with men; and even when these, by agreement, come every year to their land, they receive them with arms in their hands, such as bows and arrows, which they brandish about for a time, until they are satisfied that the Indians come with peaceful intentions. They then drop their arms and go down to the canoes of their guests, where each one chooses a hammock, the nearest at hand, which they take to their own houses, and, hanging them in a place where their owners could recognize them, they receive the Indians as guests for a few days. After this the Indians return to their own country, repeating their visits every year at the same season. The daughters who are born from this intercourse are preserved and brought up by the Amazons themselves, as they are destined to inherit their valour and the customs of the nation; but it is not so certain what they do with the sons. An Indian who had gone with his father to this country when very young stated that the boys were given to their fathers when they returned the following year. But others – and they appear most probable, as it is most general – say that when the Amazons find that a baby is a male, they kill it. Time will discover the truth; and if these are the Amazons made famous by historians, there are treasures shut up in their territory which would enrich the whole world." This is much the same story that was gathered by Columbus, though the admiral's will-o'-the-wisp tribe are supposed to be on an island of the Caribbean Sea, while those brought before de Orellana were on the mainland, some said hidden in the forests, others safe on an island formed by the sweep of two rivers, an island like Tumpinambaranas, which is 210 miles long and contains 950 square miles, or, again, on an island in one of the great lakes.

Alas for the good father! time exploded the legend, at least as he understood the matter. Neither Amazon nation nor their fabulous treasures have ever been found. Yet it was not from any want of willingness or energy on the part of the Spaniards. Animated by stories such as those recorded by Acosta and Herrera and sworn to by wandering whites and natives before the Royal Audienza at Quito, there was real enthusiasm and emulation displayed in furthering exploration for this constantly receding country "where women alone are." Nuño de Gusman, writing in July 1530 from Omittan to the Emperor Charles V. (Charles I. of Spain), says, with cheerful anticipation of what was in store for a lucky and enterprising Don, "I shall go to find the Amazons, which some say dwell in the sea, some in an arm of the sea, and that they are rich and accounted of the people for goodness, and whiter than other women. They use bows and arrows and targets; have many great treasures." We find, among others, Hernando de Ribera conducting a search party. He came across many natives who reported to him that beyond the Mansion of the Sun – that is to say, westward of a great lake wherein the sun sank daily to rest – there would be found that much-sought-after country "where women alone dwelt." This might allude even to Peru, where, among the Cordilleras of the Andes, temples of the sun had been built on high mountains, such as Intihuatana, "the Seat of the Sun," a fortress temple on a high hill near Cuzco, in the vicinity of Lake Titikaka, some 1300 feet above sea-level. There was, however, no record of women warriors on that side of the Andes, at all events in the days of the Incas. To return to Brazil, Ribera was told that the women possessed both white and yellow metal (silver and gold) in such abundance that they made their seats and household utensils out of them. Close neighbours of theirs, so it was said, were the pigmies, who formed a nation by themselves. About forty-seven years later Anthony Knivet, who went with Thomas Candish on his second voyage to the South Seas, was captured by the Portuguese, escaped, and wandered through Brazil. He heard of the Amazons, and, indeed, claimed that his Indian companions said that they traversed the mysterious country; but when Knivet urged an attack on the women, the natives "durst not, for they said, We know that the country is very populous, and we shall all be killed."

On the other hand, we hear rumours of the Amazons in quite another direction. Sir Walter Raleigh, in his *Discovery of Guiana*, says that he spoke to a cacique who had been to the Amazon River and beyond. This chief reported that "the nations of these women are on the south side of the river, in the province of Topago, and their chiefest strength and retreats are in the lands situate on the south side of the entrance, some sixty leagues within the mouth of the same river. The memories of the like women," adds the gallant knight, "very ancient as well in Africa as in Asia, in many histories they are verified to have been in divers ages and provinces, but they which are not far from Guiana do accompany with men but once a year, and for the time of one month, which I gather by their relations to be April. At that time all the kings of the borders assemble and the queens of the Amazons; and after the queens have chosen, the rest cast lots for their valentines. This one month they feast, dance, and drink of their wines in abundance; and the moon being done, they all depart to their own provinces. If they conceive and be delivered of a son, they return him to the father; if of a daughter, they nourish it and retain it. And as many as have daughters send unto the begetter presents, all being desirous to increase their own sex and kind; but that they cut off the right breast I do not find to be true. It was further told me that if in the wars they took any prisoners that they would accompany with those also at what time soever, but in the end for certain they put them to death; for they are said to be very cruel and bloodthirsty, especially to such as offer to invade their country. These Amazons have likewise great store of these plates of gold, which they recover in exchange chiefly for a kind of green stones, which the Spaniards call *piedras hijadas*, and we use for spleen stones: and for the disease of the stone we also esteem them. Of these I saw divers in Guiana, and commonly every cacique has one, which their wives for the most part wear, and they esteem them as great jewels."

Then the direction again changes, and we hear of the women on the north side of the great river, retreating up the Rio Negro, ultimately hiding successfully in Guiana. Raleigh says: "On the south side of the main mouth of the Orinoco are the Arwacas, and beyond them the cannibals [Caribs], and to the south of them the Amazons." Many years after this Father Gili, writing of the Orinoco and its neighbourhood, said he closely questioned an Indian as to the surrounding tribes. Several were mentioned, and among them were the Aikeambenanoes: "Well acquainted with the Tanamac tongue," the priest declares, "I instantly comprehended the sense of the last word, which is a compound and signifies 'women living alone.'" The Indian at once confirmed his interrogator's conjecture, and giving certain details of these near yet unapproachable women, alleged that their chief industry was the making of blowpipes for the discharge of poisoned arrows in war and in the chase. When de la Condamine went through Brazil in 1745 he also questioned the natives closely as to the Amazons, and he heard of an old Indian whose father had actually conversed with "the women without husbands." On reaching the village, it was found that the old man was dead, but his son, aged apparently seventy, said that his grandfather had spoken to four Amazons, one of whom was suckling an infant at her breast, as they passed from the south side of the river to go up the valley of the Rio Negro. Another Indian living near Para actually offered to show a river farther up which (beyond the falls in the mountain fastness) the Amazons were to be found to that day. Unfortunately, this offer does not seem to have been accepted. The upper regions of Guiana appeared to be the centre most spoken of in these days as the home of the women. Although he says, "I know that all or the greater part of the Indians of South America are liars, credulous, and enamoured of the marvellous," still de la Condamine saw no reason for scepticism, even as regards the more elaborate details of the tribe and the manner of its maintenance.

Of the origin of the "women who live without husbands" a very significant legend appears to have been current along the middle and lower reaches of the Amazon. We are told that in some far-off indeterminate age the women rebelled against their husbands and retired to the hills accompanied by only one old man. They lived by their own industry, quite isolated. All daughters born to this lopsided community were carefully reared, while all boys were killed. Then one luckless male baby, coming into the world deformed and covered with scars, called forth maternal pity. In secrecy the mother lavished all her tenderness and art in the endeavour to cure her child, but without effect until she placed him in a strongly woven bag and squeezed him into a lovely shape. Thereafter he grew apace in seclusion, day by day becoming more charming in form and character. Eventually his retreat was discovered. Then began a long and tender persecution from the women, though the boy remained unmoved. Mother and son consulted together, and to escape his tormentors the youth was thrown into the lake, where he assumed the shape of a fish. Whenever the mother called, the fish swam ashore and was instantly transformed into his beautiful human form, taking food from the hands of his mother. Jealously guarded though the secret was, feminine curiosity soon ferreted it out; and then the other women, imitating the calls, clasped the deceived young man in their arms. It was next the turn of the old man to grow uneasy, for he noticed that he was being neglected. So he set himself to watch, and the spy was driven to fierce anger by the scene of magic enacted before his eyes. His own calls to the fish were of no avail, so he made strong nets. None was stout enough, however, for always the boy-fish escaped, breaking through the meshes. The old man sat down and thought deeply, and decided upon a plan. Going to each woman of the tribe, he craftily begged them for tresses of their hair. Therewith he made a net so strong and entangling that he promptly caught and killed the fish. After this the women finally abandoned the slayer; but while he was away in his fields, his hut was always put in order by some unknown agency, and his meals prepared for him by unseen hands. So again he hid and set himself to spy. And then he saw a pet parrot fly down, put off her feathers, and swiftly change into a beautiful girl, who at once set about her duties with painstaking industry. To rush forward and fling the feathers into the fire was the work of an instant, then the watcher turned and demanded, "Who are you?" "I am," replied the mysterious squaw, "the only woman who ever loved you. Now you have broken the spell I was under, and I am glad."

A variant of this is given by Barboza Rodriguez. He records a legend which shows the women as rebels against their husbands, flying to the woods, and protected in their flight by the elements and wild beasts. The men found their passage barred by flood and tempest; fierce animals fought them; monkeys gathered in the trees and pelted them with deadly missiles. So the women retired and led their own lives. Then they repented, and admitted the men to their presence once a year, giving up the boys to them, but retaining the girls. And so matters went on, until one day the whole tribe of women disappeared down a hole in the earth, led to their last resting-place by an armadillo.

It would take us too long and certainly carry us too far from our present inquiry to fully analyse each clause of these exceedingly picturesque and pregnant stories. Some points, however, may be briefly noted. In these accounts of the Amazons we have a motive for their existence introduced which is quite distinct from anything suggested by the Greeks in the case of those of Asia. In the first story, the women retiring to the hills accompanied by one old man have all the appearance of a religious guard surrounding a priest-king. There is more than one hint of sacrifice, pre-eminently so in the case of the boy-fish, here introduced as a symbol of fertility; and finally in the most instructive version of the fable of net-entanglements – magic and woman's wiles. Hair is woman's delight and glory, but also a great means of offence. In certain cities of Asia Minor, Ashtoreth demanded the shaven head as the lesser of two personal sacrifices from her female worshippers. The Talmudists say that Lilith, the semi-human, semi-demon first wife of Adam, would, when she could, strangle the sons of men with tresses of her golden hair, out of revenge for the disinheritance of her own offspring, the Jinns. For this reason the amulet 'childbirth tablets' hung on the walls of lying-in rooms of Jews both in the East and Eastern Europe always bore a representation of Lilith with an invocation for protection. But to return to our Brazilian legends. In the second, far less complicated, there is yet much that is suggestive, for here too we see the women set apart, protected supernaturally, and ending by sacrifice. For the descent into the earth means death, and its collective form and the leadership of the armadillo hints if not at the inhumation of the living, at least sacrificial burial on the death of some semi-divine chief.

It will be observed that in these two fables we are not asked to look upon the women as of a bellicose disposition-apart from their initiatory quarrel with their husbands – or as belonging to a war organization. As a rule, however, the stories all laid stress upon their fighting, qualities, and this was very persistent among the Caribs, themselves a most warlike people.

Sir Robert Schomburgk, who knew Guiana and Venezuela so well, declaring that the "Caribs are most versed in wonderful tales," disbelieved all these rumours. Of course it was impossible altogether to ignore the positive assertions of eye-witnessing Spaniards, and so, to explain these away, Sir Robert suggested that they had mistaken young men with flowing hair, and wearing necklaces and ear-rings, for women; an opinion backed up by several other authors. This is not convincing, for we must remember that Father Carbajal expressly states that the fighting women he and his companions saw had their hair twisted round their heads. A recent writer, Mr. C.R. Enoch, in his book *The Andes and the Amazon*, quotes an official Peruvian report on the native tribes inhabiting the forest regions and eastern slope of the Andes, in which the following passage occurs: "The Nahumedes are an almost extinct tribe, on the river of the same name. They are those who attacked the explorer de Orellana, who believed that these savages, with their chemises and skirts and long hair, were women warriors, or Amazons, and which name was given to the river. This must be the explanation of the supposed existence of women warriors in these regions, for no legend or history among the Indians can be found relating to any empire of women." This is an example of doubt carried to extreme limits. If the Nahumedes are the people who attacked de Orellana, they have shifted their ground considerably, which, of course, is quite possible; but it is too much to say that the Indians possess no traditions of a tribe of fighting women, in face of the legends and rumours gathered not only by such men as Father de Acuña and those more or less his contemporaries, but by such travellers as de la Condamine and others.

We do not find among early writers any claim that the female warriors were called by any local name remotely approaching that of Amazons, although these writers had always clearly in their minds the Asiatic and African stories. A recent authority, Dr. D. G. Brinton, however, has made the curious discovery that the word *amazunu* is used by the natives at the mouth of the mighty river to describe "a torrent of roaring water," and as especially applied to a bore at the outfall of the Marañon. Thereupon he suggests that the Spaniards heard this term used in reference to something wild, impetuous, and dangerous in connection with the river, and straightway evolved a non-existent tribe. It is only fair to say that there is no evidence of this in Carbajal's account or that of de Acuña. Still, it would be interesting to trace the origin of such a compound word. It is certain that the river and province was named by the Spaniards from "the Amazons made famous by historians," descendants of whom they imagined they had stumbled upon, and not from any chance name uttered by the Indians. Is it possible that the compound word is, after all, of later date than the Spanish Conquest and the renaming of the river? Such tricks of philology are by no means uncommon.

As late as 1743, when de la Condamine was travelling through the country, rumours about the Amazons still persisted, but, like de Acuña, de Ribera, Gili, and many more, this worthy explorer never caught a glimpse of them or the mysterious Manoa. He could only meet people who said they had seen them in some remote, ill-defined region, and who knew others who had years before visited the women and country, which, however, could never be located. When de la Condamine was making his inquiries, it was said that the Amazons had moved off up the Rio Negro, and they continued to retreat before the inquisitive whites into the unmapped forest regions of Guiana. Humboldt, like de la Condamine, was a strong believer in the tales, though his investigations were as little conclusive. Sceptics were equally numerous, and some had made their voices heard even in the days of the conquistadors. There were those ready to insist that the legend grew from the crafty designs of de Orellana, who wished by these devious means to wipe out the memory of his gross treachery to his chief Pizarro, thinking that by marvellous accounts of his own exploits he would wrest applause and rewards from those at home. It is scarcely necessary to attribute wilful intention to mislead on the part of Father Carbajal and other explorers on this head. That women did appear in arms in America as well as in Asia, and for the matter of that in Europe too, there is no reason to doubt. Many instances may be cited.

Juan de lo Cosa reported that when he sailed with Rodrigo de Bastides in 1501 he landed with a party far north of the Orinoco on the site now occupied by Cartagena, and he and his party were boldly attacked by men and women who mingled in the fight, both sexes wielding most dexterously the long dart, or azagay, and bow with poisoned arrows. Hulderick Schnirdel, who travelled in company with Spaniards through the country of the River Plate and the Amazon between the years 1534 and 1554, heard much of the fighting Amazons, who were said to live in an island, to have no silver or gold, which they left with their husbands on the mainland – altogether a novel account. Schnirdel went in search of the island, but fruitlessly. He doubted that a nation existed, though he attests that the fighting of women in the ranks with their menkind was common enough. A little later, in 1587, Lopez Vaz recounts the adventures of Lopez de Agira. This de Agira was the rebel and renegade who murdered Don Fernando de Gusman, who had proclaimed himself Emperor of Peru. After the murder, de Agira, accompanied by a few soldiers and natives, started down the Amazon *en route* for the Atlantic. They met with some opposition, and found it was true that Amazons existed – "that is to say, women who fight in the wars with bows and arrows; but these women fight to aid their husbands, and not by themselves alone without companies of men, as de Orellana reports. There were of these women upon divers parts of the river, who, seeing Spaniards fighting with their husbands, came in to succour them, and showed themselves more valiant than their husbands." But the comparative rarity of the phenomena would be sufficient to stir the imagination of the Spaniards, whose minds, as we have said, were stored with stories of the classic period and tales of the East.

The early Spanish critics accepted the story of the fighting women, as evidence to this effect accumulated, while more or less politely disbelieving the story of Amazon 'nations,' and their arguments are based on the very fact that women fight side by side with their husbands, and that such-like warrior women were well known both in ancient and modern history. It must also be remembered that America was still part of the Indies to most of the early explorers, and to them it seemed quite natural that the famous Themysciran nation should have migrated farther afield. It followed that these explorers should find that these warrior women were white, for so the fitness of things demanded, though there is a possible explanation for a light-coloured band of women if we suppose them to have belonged to a semi-religious caste. Then there was another school, holding that this nation of women was the remnant of those who had escaped from Asia through Africa by way of Hesperides or the lost Atlantis. To most of the travellers, as with Father de Acuña, the "Amazons made famous by historians," or, in other words, the Asiatic dames, could not be forgotten, and the stories of fabulous wealth could only contribute to their belief.

Down to quite recent times there were persistent rumours of wonderful cities hidden away in almost impenetrable forests, stored with great treasures of gold, and often said to be guarded by women, though we see from Schnirdel's report that the office of treasure-guardianship might be reversed. The typical examples were the phantom cities of Dobayba, where there existed a golden temple to a Nature goddess, and Manoa del Dorado, so constantly talked about as near at hand, but never seen: the latter a city with houses roofed with gold, bathed by a crystal-clear lake, the waters rippling over sands of gold. Now, in justification of this, we may point out that when the Spaniards came to Peru for the second time, and made the unfortunate Emperor Atahualpa prisoner in his own castle of Cajamarca, the Inca offered as a ransom to fill a room, said to be 22 feet by 27 feet, as high as he could reach, say 6 feet, with gold. This, it has been estimated, would have amounted to a value of a hundred million sterling. But the Spaniards were impatient, and slaughtered their prisoner, a proceeding indefensible on moral grounds, and as a matter of policy less sensible than killing the goose that laid the golden eggs. The treasure was never forthcoming. Yet at Cuzco, the true capital of the Inca power, and at Pachacamac, the Spaniards found the palace walls covered with plates of gold. Offerings of gold chains and flowers of golden plates also seem to have been thrown into lakes. At the birth of the last undoubted heir of the Incas, who received the symbolic name of Huasca, 'The Chain,' or 'The Cable,' a commemorative chain said to be 233 yards long and composed of heavy links of gold was made and cast into Lake Orcos, no doubt as a thanksoffering.

That the sands of lakes and rivers abounded in alluvial deposits of finely powdered gold is true to this day as it was of old. Stories of such richly endowed cities were not confined to Brazil and Peru, but were common to Guiana, Honduras, and so on. The grounds for these legends were perfectly natural, as we have just shown. Besides, many of the most wonderful buildings of the Incas, Aztecs, and others were placed either in most difficultly accessible mountains, or on islands in big lakes, or in dense forests. Von Hassell in 1905 explored much of the upper reaches of the Amazon on the Atlantic side of the Cordilleras, and he visited the great fluvial island of Tumpinambaranas, where he found stupendous ruins, reminding him of the civilization of the Incas. He says that the Amazon plain must have been visited by repeated waves of emigrants, having civilization as advanced as that of the Incas, but who had disappeared, leaving faint traces behind them. Baron Nordenskold, on his travels in Chaco, in Argentina, "found large places in the primeval forests beyond the real Calchaqui territory, in districts at present very sparsely inhabited."

The Toltec city of Quiché, capital of Utatlan, Central America, apparently had a population of 3,000,000, and the Spaniards' description of the Royal Palace reads like an account of the Alhambra in its days of glory. Experience taught that it was customary for people threatened with invasion to remove their treasures to as inaccessible retreats as possible, where, also, the womenfolk would be gathered, and these, in default of men, would as occasion demanded take part in the defence of their lares and penates. Villages, too, were often occupied by women, old men, and young children alone for many weeks together, while the men and youths were away on the war-path or some great hunting expedition. Moreover, in this part of the American continent, where moon-worship prevailed, there were certain ceremonies connected with womanhood and child-bearing involving the separation of women from all males, and apparently elaborate dances in the moonlight. Upon these solid enough foundations the Spaniards, by frequently injudicious questioning of the natives, built up a rickety superstructure of many strange fables. The evil practice of our own Counsels learned in the law have taught us the very real danger of putting leading questions, even when addressed to educated people able to grasp their meaning. But when you have a credulous cross-examiner, bewildered by the novelty of his surroundings, his head stuffed full with the stories from Quintus Curtius and Diodorus the Sicilian, and on the other hand a horde of naked savages, or even of semi-barbarians, catching most imperfectly at the meaning of their questioners, it will be readily seen that the answers easily took the form that the interlocutor more or less unconsciously desired.

That women did fight on occasion – and this would be particularly true of the hill and forest tribes – we have already seen by various travellers' accounts. That they were occasionally for a length of several moons a tribe, as it were, by themselves, and guardians of tribal treasures, there is no reason to disbelieve. Ample material here for a very robust and circumstantial legend, without either party to the making thereof being, liars of malice aforethought.

An extraordinary fact, which should be mentioned in this place, as it may have some bearing on the subject, is that the Lenâpé tribe of North American Indians were called 'Women.' They were a branch of the great Algonkin nation, but found themselves down in Delaware, surrounded by the warlike Iroquois. That they could boast of an honourable origin is proved by the fact that the three Delaware sub-tribes had as their totems the tortoise (above all honoured as the servant of the All-Powerful Creator, and on whose back the earth was built up), the wolf, and the turkey. Moreover, Dr. Brinton informs us that Lenâpé means 'men of our nation,' or 'our men.' Yet it appears that for a lengthy period this tribe never went to war, and although in later years apparently not held in high esteem, unquestionably filled an important office as a kind of buffer nation of peacemakers. Among most American tribes there existed a Council of Women, composed of the old matrons, whose privilege it was to meet in war-time and discuss matters affecting the tribe. If they advocated peace, it was no disgrace for the 'braves' to listen to them and consider the advisability of offering terms to the enemy. It was in some such position as this that the whole tribe of Delaware Algonkins were placed. According to their own statements, the Lenâpés became the peacemaking tribe at the special request of the Iroquois, who saw that the nations were eating each other up. So they approached the Lenâpés with an honourable proposition, and in the presence of the other assembled tribes gave the Delawares the long robe and ear-rings of women, so that they should not bear arms or mingle in strife; the calabash of oil and medicine, to the end that they might become the nurses; the corn pestle and hoe, so that they might cultivate the land; and, in order to emphasise the whole solemnity, bestowed on the chiefs of the 'Women' tribe a belt of wampum, the greatest of symbols of peace and fraternity within their gift, as each division of the strange ceremony was reached. That the Lenâpés fulfilled their mission seems certain, although as time went on the Iroquois began to treat them as a conquered tribe, and used the term 'Women' as applied to them with some contumely. This buffer tribe, with its claims to a high mission and its equivocal position and attributes, appears to be unique in American Indian social economy; on the other hand, at all events in the southern part of the continent, there were classes of men in the barbarian nations dressed and treated as women. The whole problem of the 'Women' tribe, however, is far from being cleared up. Was it cajoled into its curious place as the result of some dim recollection of a once-powerful women-priest caste? Or was it merely a clever device suggested by pressing needs when it began to be recognized that there must be occasional cessation from the interminable intertribal slaughter? It is a mystery full of suggestion.

To most, if not to all, of the tales that the Spaniards gave a willing credence there was a solid substratum of truth. The splendid build of the Caribs, the abnormal proportions of the men down in the terrible Tierra del Fuego, and the dwarfish tribes of the forest regions and of the degenerate Aztecs, would account for the giants and pigmies of whom so much was heard. In such matters the terms are essentially comparative to both questioner and questioned, and, moreover, the 'little men' term may be relative not only to their stature but to moral qualities also. To the hard-fighting, hungry Carib the man of peace was unquestionably a 'little man' no matter how tall or broad-shouldered he might be, just as to-day in the East the mass of people without influence are 'little men' to the rulers and their satellites. Even the men with their toes pointing the wrong way (of whom the world had heard before from the early Greek writers on India) existed, for the reversing of moccasins or other feet-covering is a natural dodge adopted to bewilder, and the attempted explanation of such a trick would be quite sufficient to make confusion worse confounded.

Nor need we have a moment's hesitation in crediting the existence of tailed tribes, for totemism and the respect that comes of fear inspired by wild horned beasts was quite sufficient to make man proud of caudal appendages and to supply his own deficiencies in this matter. Even Hercules so managed the draping of the lion's skin about his own body as to secure a very fine tail. Dionysus also treated his panther's skin in the same way, while his Seleni sported the tails of giddy goats with waggish effrontery. In most parts of Africa the buffalo's tail is an emblem of power, as the horse's tail is in Northern Africa and Arabia, whether carried in the hand or worn pendant behind from the waist, the latter method of personal adornment applying to the buffalo's tail, and is found to prevail in the south, east, and west.

Lord Hindlip, writing of the Kavirondo tribes in British East Africa, says the women are fond of a certain amount of adornment, and that "a peculiar ornament is a grass tail tied round the waist generally by a string of beads. I believe," he adds, "that this is an emblem of marriage, and to touch one of those tails is a breach of good manners, the offender being liable to a fine of five goats." Bruce and Baker also mention women in the far Sudan and in the Upper Nile Valley wearing tails of plaited skin or of string. In North America certain ceremonials include the Buffalo Dance, when every 'brave' carries horns on his head and a tail waggles fiercely in the rear during the saltatory performance. Both the men and women of the Aymara Indians of Peru and Bolivia wear their hair long and plaited into tails, hence it was supposed that they had originally emigrated from China, or at least been influenced by a Chinese invasion prior to the Inca era. To all these, tails are of no small importance, and would be looked upon by their neighbours with awe or contempt according to tribal relations.

It is in this spirit that most of the Amazon stories must be treated. At the same time, we must not omit to quote some weighty opinions pointing to a more direct acceptation. De la Condamine, who was a thoroughgoing believer in the American Amazon nation, argued that its evolution was quite natural and a development for which we might have looked with confidence. He held that the women leading migratory lives, often following their husbands to war, were usually compelled to submit to very harsh domestic conditions. But the very conditions imposed upon them by their mode of life afforded ample opportunities for them to escape from the tyranny by simply detaching themselves from the tribe and forming a community wherein, if they did not exactly gain independence, they would no longer be slaves and beasts of burden. This method of establishing new communities was, he pointed out, going on in every colony where slave-holding was tolerated; the slaves growing tired of ill-treatment escaped to the forests or swamps, setting up their own camps and villages. Robert Southey re-echoed this opinion that "the lot of women is usually dreadful among savages … Had we never heard of the Amazons of antiquity, I should, without hesitation, believe in those of America." To him the terrible hardships of the Indian women's lives demanded some such relief, and he looked upon the existence of such communities as redounding to the credit of humanity, showing that there was hope for its regeneration. A recent writer of deep philosophic tendencies, Mr. E.J. Payne, follows on the same lines. He regards the whole phenomena of Amazonian states as a perfectly legitimate and understandable outcome of the transition from savagery to barbarism, a period when life is peculiarly harsh to womankind. But, as he says, such communities always carry within themselves the seeds of decay, for they cannot extend, cannot indeed exist for long, without the tolerance of man. A day comes when he grows tired of a complacent attitude, and the women then have nothing to do but surrender on his own terms. These are undoubtedly both interesting and plausible theories, which do not really enter into conflict with the opinions that we have ventured to advance on the whole subject.

Aztec & Mexican Myths

Introduction

ANCIENT MESOAMERICANS in general believed the habitable globe to have been created from the slime which arose above the primeval waters, and there can be no doubt that the Nahua shared this belief. We encounter in Nahua myth two beings of a bisexual nature, known to the Aztecs as Ometecutli-Omeciuatl (Lords of Duality), who were represented as the deities dominating the genesis of things, the beginning of the world. These beings, whose individual names were Tonacatecutli and Tonacaciuatl (Lord and Lady of our Flesh), occupy the first place in the calendar, a circumstance which makes it plain that they were regarded as responsible for the origin of all created things.

Most of this culture's myths deal with creation and stories of origin of one kind or another, as you will see from the following selection, whether it is the cosmological fundamentals of the sun and the passage of time or the genesis of the first people. Other Aztec myths deal with the birth of their gods, such as Huitzilopochtli, pseudo-historical narratives like that dealing with the rise and fall of the Toltecs, or gruesome tales of murderous princesses (Chachiuhnenetzin).

This section also includes folkloric tales from the indigenous Yaqui people of the Sonoran desert in Mexico and are thus a mixture of ancient folklore combined with Mexican Catholic themes.

The Creation Story of the Five Suns

TONACATECUTLI AND TONACACIUATL dwelt from the beginning in the thirteenth heaven. To them were born, as to an elder generation, four gods – the ruddy Camaxtli (chief divinity of the Tlascalans); the black Tezcatlipoca, wizard of the night; Quetzalcoatl, the wind-god; and the grim Huitzilopochtli, of whom it was said that he was born without flesh, a skeleton.

For six hundred years these deities lived in idleness; then the four brethren assembled, creating first the fire (hearth of the universe) and afterward a half-sun. They formed also Oxomoco and Cipactonal, the first man and first woman, commanding that the former should till the ground, and the latter spin and weave; while to the woman they gave powers of divination and grains of maize that she might work cures. They also divided time into days and inaugurated a year of eighteen twenty-day periods, or three hundred and sixty days. Mictlantecutli and Mictlanciuatl they created to be Lord and Lady of Hell, and they formed the heavens that are below the thirteenth storey of the celestial regions, and the waters of the sea, making in the sea a monster Cipactli, from which they shaped the earth. The gods of the waters, Tlaloctecutli and his wife Chalchiuhtlicue, they created, giving them dominion over the Quarters.

The son of the first pair married a woman formed from a hair of the goddess Xochiquetzal; and the gods, noticing how little was the light given forth by the half-sun, resolved to make another half-sun, whereupon Tezcatlipoca became the sun-bearer – for what we behold traversing the daily heavens is not the sun itself, but only its brightness; the true sun is invisible. The other gods created huge giants, who could uproot trees by brute force, and whose food was acorns. For thirteen times fifty-two years, altogether six hundred and seventy-six, this period lasted – as long as its Sun endured; and it is from this first Sun that time began to be counted, for during the six hundred years of the idleness of the gods, while Huitzilopochtli was in his bones, time was not reckoned.

This Sun came to an end when Quetzalcoatl struck down Tezcatlipoca and became Sun in his place. Tezcatlipoca was metamorphosed into a jaguar (Ursa Major) which is seen by night in the skies wheeling down into the waters whither Quetzalcoatl cast him; and this jaguar devoured the giants of that period.

At the end of six hundred and seventy-six years Quetzalcoatl was treated by his brothers as he had treated Tezcatlipoca, and his Sun came to an end with a great wind which carried away most of the people of that time or transformed them into monkeys.

Then for seven times fifty-two years Tlaloc was Sun; but at the end of this three hundred and sixty-four years Quetzalcoatl rained fire from heaven and made Chalchiuhtlicue Sun in place of her husband, a dignity which she held for three hundred and twelve years (six times fifty-two); and it was in these days that maize began to be used.

Now two thousand six hundred and twenty-eight years had passed since the birth of the gods, and in this year it rained so heavily that the heavens themselves fell, while the people of that time were transformed into fish. When the gods saw this, they created four men, with whose aid Tezcatlipoca and Quetzalcoatl again upreared the heavens, even as they are today; and these two gods becoming lords of the heavens and of the stars, walked therein.

After the deluge and the restoration of the heavens, Tezcatlipoca discovered the art of making fire from sticks and of drawing it from the heart of flint. The first man, Piltzintecutli, and his wife, who had been made of a hair of Xochiquetzal, did not perish in the flood, because they were divine. A son was born to them, and the gods created other people just as they had formerly existed.

But since, except for the fires, all was in darkness, the gods resolved to create a new Sun. This was done by Quetzalcoatl, who cast his own son, by Chalchiuhtlicue, into a great fire, whence he issued as the Sun of our own time; Tlaloc hurled his son into the cinders of the fire, and thence rose the Moon, ever following after the Sun. This Sun, said the gods, should eat hearts and drink blood, and so they established wars that there might be sacrifices of captives to nourish the orbs of light.

Creation Story of the Mixtecs

WHEN THE EARTH HAD ARISEN from the primeval waters, one day the deer-god, who bore the surname Puma-Snake, and the beautiful deer-goddess, or Jaguar-Snake, appeared. They had human form, and with their great knowledge (that is, with their magic) they raised a high cliff over the water, and built on it fine palaces for their dwelling. On the summit of this cliff they laid a copper axe with the edge upward, and on this edge the heavens rested. The palaces stood in Upper Mixteca, close to Apoala, and the cliff was called Place where the Heavens Stood. The gods lived happily together for many centuries, when it chanced that two little boys were born to them, beautiful of form and skilled and experienced in the arts. From the days of their birth they were named Wind-Nine-Snake (Viento de Neuve Culebras) and Wind-Nine-Cave (Viento de Neuve Cavernas). Much care was given to their education, and they possessed the knowledge of how to change themselves into an eagle or a snake, to make themselves invisible, and even to pass through solid bodies.

After a time these youthful gods decided to make an offering and a sacrifice to their ancestors. Taking incense vessels made of clay, they filled them with tobacco, to which they set fire, allowing it to smoulder. The smoke rose heavenward, and that was the first offering (to the gods). Then they made a garden with shrubs and flowers, trees and fruit-bearing plants, and sweet-scented herbs. Adjoining this they made a grass-grown level place (*un prado*), and equipped it with everything necessary for sacrifice. The pious brothers lived contentedly on this piece of ground, tilled it, burned tobacco, and with prayers, vows, and promises they supplicated their ancestors to let the light appear, to let the water collect in certain places and the earth be freed from its covering (water), for they had no more than that little garden for their subsistence. In order to strengthen their prayer they pierced their ears and their tongues with pointed knives of flint, and sprinkled the blood on the trees and plants with a brush of willow twigs.

The deer-gods had more sons and daughters, but there came a flood in which many of these perished. After the catastrophe was over the god who is called the Creator of All Things formed the heavens and the earth, and restored the human race.

The Mexican Noah

AND THIS YEAR was that of Ce-calli, and on the first day all was lost. The mountain itself was submerged in the water, and the water remained tranquil for fifty-two springs.

Now toward the close of the year Titlacahuan had forewarned the man named Nata and his wife Nena, saying, "Make no more *pulque*, but straightway hollow out a large cypress, and enter it when in the month Tozoztli the water shall approach the sky." They entered it, and when Titlacahuan had closed the door he said, "Thou shalt eat but a single ear of maize, and thy wife but one also."

As soon as they had finished eating, they went forth, and the water was tranquil; for the log did not move any more; and opening it they saw many fish.

Then they built a fire, rubbing together pieces of wood, and they roasted fish. The gods Citallinicue and Citallatonac, looking below, exclaimed, "Divine Lord, what means that fire below? Why do they thus smoke the heavens?"

Straightway descended Titlacahuan-Tezcatlipoca, and commenced to scold, saying, "What is this fire doing here?" And seizing the fishes (or in other versions, Nata and Nena themselves) he moulded their hinder parts and changed their heads, and they were at once transformed into dogs.

Xolotl Creates the Parents of Mankind

ALL PROVINCES WERE AGREED that in heaven were a god and goddess, Citlallatonac and Citlalicue, and that the goddess gave birth to a stone knife (*tecpatl*), to the amazement and horror of her other sons which were in heaven. The stone hurled forth by these outraged sons and falling to Chicomoxtoc ('Seven Caves'), was shattered, and from its fragments arose sixteen hundred earth-godlings. These sent Tlotli, the Hawk, heavenward to demand of their mother the privilege of creating men to be their servants;

and she replied that they should send to Mictlantecutli, Lord of Hell, for a bone or ashes of the dead, from which a man and woman would be born.

Xolotl was dispatched as messenger, secured the bone, and fled with it; but being pursued by the Lord of Hell, he stumbled, and the bone broke. With such fragments as he could secure he reached the earth, and the bones, placed in a vessel, were sprinkled with blood drawn from the bodies of the gods. On the fourth day a boy emerged from the mixture; on the eighth, a girl; and these were reared by Xolotl to become parents of mankind. Men differ in size because the bone broke into unequal fragments; and as human beings multiplied, they were assigned as servants to the several gods.

Now, the Sun had not been shining for a long time, and the deities assembled at Teotiuacan to consider the matter. Having built a great fire, they announced that that one among their devotees who should first hurl himself into it should have the honour of becoming the Sun, and when one had courageously entered the flames, they awaited the sunrise, wagering as to the quarter in which he would appear; but they guessed wrong, and for this they were condemned to be sacrificed, as they were soon to learn.

When the Sun appeared, he remained ominously motionless; and although Tlotli was sent to demand that he continue his journey, he refused, saying that he should remain where he was until they were all destroyed. Citli ('Hare') in anger shot the Sun with an arrow, but the latter hurled it back, piercing the forehead of his antagonist. The gods then recognized their inferiority and allowed themselves to be sacrificed, their hearts being torn out by Xolotl, who slew himself last of all. Before departing, however, each divinity gave to his followers, as a sacred bundle, his vesture wrapped about a green gem which was to serve as a heart. Tezcatlipoca was one of the departed deities, but one day he appeared to a mourning follower whom he commanded to journey to the House of the Sun beyond the waters and to bring thence singers and musical instruments to make a feast for him. This the messenger did, singing as he went. The Sun warned his people not to harken to the stranger, but the music was irresistible, and some of them were lured to follow him back to earth, where they instituted the musical rites.

A Story of the Rise and Fall of the Toltecs

THE TOLTECS, IXTLILXOCHITL SAYS, founded the magnificent city of Tollan in the year 566 of the Incarnation. This city, the site of which is now occupied by the modern town of Tula, was situated north-west of the mountains which bound the Mexican valley. Thither were the Toltecs guided by the powerful necromancer Hueymatzin (Great Hand), and under his direction they decided to build a city upon the site of what had been their place of bivouac.

For six years they toiled at the building of Tollan, and magnificent edifices, palaces, and temples arose, the whole forming a capital of a splendour unparalleled in the New

World. The valley wherein it stood was known as the 'Place of Fruits,' in allusion to its great fertility. The surrounding rivers teemed with fish, and the hills which encircled this delectable site sheltered large herds of game. But as yet the Toltecs were without a ruler, and in the seventh year of their occupation of the city the assembled chieftains took counsel together, and resolved to surrender their power into the hands of a monarch whom the people might elect. The choice fell upon Chalchiuh Tlatonac (Shining Precious Stone), who reigned for fifty-two years.

Legends of Toltec Artistry

Happily settled in their new country, and ruled over by a king whom they could regard with reverence, the Toltecs made rapid progress in the various arts, and their city began to be celebrated far and wide for the excellence of its craftsmen and the beauty of its architecture and pottery. The name of 'Toltec,' in fact, came to be regarded by the surrounding peoples as synonymous with 'artist,' and as a kind of hall-mark which guaranteed the superiority of any article of Toltec workmanship. Everything in and about the city was eloquent of the taste and artistry of its founders. The very walls were encrusted with rare stones, and their masonry was so beautifully chiselled and laid as to resemble the choicest mosaic. One of the edifices of which the inhabitants of Tollan were most justly proud was the temple wherein their high-priest officiated. This building was a very gem of architectural art and mural decoration. It contained four apartments. The walls of the first were inlaid with gold, the second with precious stones of every description, the third with beautiful sea-shells of all conceivable hues and of the most brilliant and tender shades encrusted in bricks of silver, which sparkled in the sun in such a manner as to dazzle the eyes of beholders. The fourth apartment was formed of a brilliant red stone, ornamented with shells.

The House of Feathers

Still more fantastic and weirdly beautiful was another edifice, 'The House of Feathers.' This also possessed four apartments, one decorated with feathers of a brilliant yellow, another with the radiant and sparkling hues of the Blue Bird. These were woven into a kind of tapestry, and placed against the walls in graceful hangings. An apartment described as of entrancing beauty was that in which the decorative scheme consisted of plumage of the purest and most dazzling white. The remaining chamber was hung with feathers of a brilliant red.

Huemac the Wicked

A succession of more or less able kings succeeded the founder of the Toltec monarchy, until in 994 CE Huemac II ascended the throne of Tollan. He ruled first with wisdom, and paid great attention to the duties of the state and religion. But later he fell from the high place he had made for himself in the regard of the people by his faithless deception of them and his intemperate and licentious habits. The provinces rose in revolt, and many signs and gloomy omens foretold the downfall of the city. Toveyo, a cunning sorcerer, collected a great concourse of people near Tollan, and by dint of beating upon a magic drum until the darkest hours of the night, forced them to dance to its sound until, exhausted by their efforts, they fell headlong over a dizzy precipice into a deep ravine, where they were turned into stone. Toveyo also maliciously destroyed a stone bridge, so that thousands of people fell into the river beneath and were drowned. The neighbouring volcanoes burst into eruption, presenting a frightful aspect, and grisly apparitions could be seen among the flames threatening the city with terrible gestures of menace.

The rulers of Tollan resolved to lose no time in placating the gods, whom they decided from the portents must have conceived the most violent wrath against their capital. They therefore ordained a great sacrifice of war-captives. But upon the first of the victims being placed upon the altar a still more terrible catastrophe occurred. In the method of sacrifice common to the Nahua race the breast of a youth was opened for the purpose of extracting the heart, but no such organ could the officiating priest perceive. Moreover the veins of the victim were bloodless. Such a deadly odour was exhaled from the corpse that a terrible pestilence arose, which caused the death of thousands of Toltecs. Huemac, the unrighteous monarch who had brought all this suffering upon his folk, was confronted in the forest by the Tlalocs, or gods of moisture, and humbly petitioned these deities to spare him, and not to take from him his wealth and rank. But the gods were disgusted at the callous selfishness displayed in his desires, and departed, threatening the Toltec race with six years of plagues.

The Plagues of the Toltecs

In the next winter such a severe frost visited the land that all crops and plants were killed. A summer of torrid heat followed, so intense in its suffocating fierceness that the streams were dried up and the very rocks were melted. Then heavy rain-storms descended, which flooded the streets and ways, and terrible tempests swept through the land. Vast numbers of loathsome toads invaded the valley, consuming the refuse left by the destructive frost and heat, and entering the very houses of the people. In the following year a terrible drought caused the death of thousands from starvation, and the ensuing winter was again a marvel of severity. Locusts descended in cloud-like swarms, and hail- and thunder-storms completed the wreck. During these visitations nine-tenths of the people perished, and all artistic endeavour ceased because of the awful struggle for food.

King Acxitl

With the cessation of these inflictions the wicked Huemac resolved upon a more upright course of life, and became most assiduous for the welfare and proper government of his people. But he had announced that Acxitl, his illegitimate son, should succeed him, and had further resolved to abdicate at once in favour of this youth. With the Toltecs, as with most primitive peoples, the early kings were regarded as divine, and the attempt to place on the throne one who was not of the royal blood was looked upon as a serious offence against the gods. A revolt ensued, but its two principal leaders were bought over by promises of preferment. Acxitl ascended the throne, and for a time ruled wisely. But he soon, like his father, gave way to a life of dissipation, and succeeded in setting a bad example to the members of his court and to the priesthood, the vicious spirit communicating itself to all classes of his subjects and permeating every rank of society. The iniquities of the people of the capital and the enormities practised by the royal favourites caused such scandal in the outlying provinces that at length they broke into open revolt, and Huehuetzin, chief of an eastern viceroyalty, joined to himself two other malcontent lords and marched upon the city of Tollan at the head of a strong force. Acxitl could not muster an army sufficiently powerful to repel the rebels, and was forced to resort to the expedient of buying them off with rich presents, thus patching up a truce. But the fate of Tollan was in the balance. Hordes of rude Chichimec savages, profiting by the civil broils in the Toltec state, invaded the lake region of Anahuac, or Mexico, and settled upon its fruitful soil. The end was in sight!

A Terrible Visitation

The wrath of the gods increased instead of diminishing, and in order to appease them a great convention of the wise men of the realm met at Teotihuacan, the sacred city of the Toltecs. But during their deliberations a giant of immense proportions rushed into their midst, and, seizing upon them by scores with his bony hands, hurled them to the ground, dashing their brains out. In this manner he slew great numbers, and when the panic-stricken folk imagined themselves delivered from him he returned in a different guise and slew many more. Again the grisly monster appeared, this time taking the form of a beautiful child. The people, fascinated by its loveliness, ran to observe it more closely, only to discover that its head was a mass of corruption, the stench from which was so fatal that many were killed outright. The fiend who had thus plagued the Toltecs at length deigned to inform them that the gods would listen no longer to their prayers, but had fully resolved to destroy them root and branch, and he further counselled them to seek safety in flight.

Fall of the Toltec State

By this time the principal families of Tollan had deserted the country, taking refuge in neighbouring states. Once more Huehuetzin menaced Tollan, and by dint of almost superhuman efforts old King Huemac, who had left his retirement, raised a force sufficient to face the enemy. Acxitl's mother enlisted the services of the women of the city, and formed them into a regiment of Amazons. At the head of all was Acxitl, who divided his forces, despatching one portion to the front under his commander-in-chief, and forming the other into a reserve under his own leadership. During three years the king defended Tollan against the combined forces of the rebels and the semi-savage Chichimecs. At length the Toltecs, almost decimated, fled after a final desperate battle into the marshes of Lake Tezcuco and the fastnesses of the mountains. Their other cities were given over to destruction, and the Toltec empire was at an end.

The Chichimec Exodus

Meanwhile the rude Chichimecs of the north, who had for many years carried on a constant warfare with the Toltecs, were surprised that their enemies sought their borders no more, a practice which they had engaged in principally for the purpose of obtaining captives for sacrifice. In order to discover the reason for this suspicious quiet they sent out spies into Toltec territory, who returned with the amazing news that the Toltec domain for a distance of six hundred miles from the Chichimec frontier was a desert, the towns ruined and empty and their inhabitants scattered. Xolotl, the Chichimec king, summoned his chieftains to his capital, and, acquainting them with what the spies had said, proposed an expedition for the purpose of annexing the abandoned land. No less than 3,202,000 people composed this migration, and only 1,600,000 remained in the Chichimec territory.

The Chichimecs occupied most of the ruined cities, many of which they rebuilt. Those Toltecs who remained became peaceful subjects, and through their knowledge of commerce and handicrafts amassed considerable wealth. A tribute was, however, demanded from them, which was peremptorily refused by Nauhyotl, the Toltec ruler of Colhuacan; but he was defeated and slain, and the Chichimec rule was at last supreme.

The Disappearance of the Toltecs

The transmitters of this legendary account give it as their belief, which is shared by some authorities of standing, that the Toltecs, fleeing from the civil broils of their city and the inroads of the Chichimecs, passed into Central America, where they became the founders of the civilization of that country, and the architects of the many wonderful cities the ruins of which now litter its plains and are encountered in its forests.

Tezcatlipoca, Overthrower of the Toltecs

IN THE DAYS OF QUETZALCOATL there was abundance of everything necessary for subsistence. The maize was plentiful, the calabashes were as thick as one's arm, and cotton grew in all colours without having to be dyed. A variety of birds of rich plumage filled the air with their songs, and gold, silver, and precious stones were abundant. In the reign of Quetzalcoatl there was peace and plenty for all men.

But this blissful state was too fortunate, too happy to endure. Envious of the calm enjoyment of the god and his people the Toltecs, three wicked 'necromancers' plotted their downfall. The reference is of course to the gods of the invading Nahua tribes, the deities Huitzilopochtli, Titlacahuan or Tezcatlipoca, and Tlacahuepan. These laid evil enchantments upon the city of Tollan, and Tezcatlipoca in particular took the lead in these envious conspiracies. Disguised as an aged man with white hair, he presented himself at the palace of Quetzalcoatl, where he said to the pages-in-waiting: "Pray present me to your master the king. I desire to speak with him."

The pages advised him to retire, as Quetzalcoatl was indisposed and could see no one. He requested them, however, to tell the god that he was waiting outside. They did so, and procured his admittance.

On entering the chamber of Quetzalcoatl the wily Tezcatlipoca simulated much sympathy with the suffering god-king. "How are you, my son?" he asked. "I have brought you a drug which you should drink, and which will put an end to the course of your malady."

"You are welcome, old man," replied Quetzalcoatl. "I have known for many days that you would come. I am exceedingly indisposed. The malady affects my entire system, and I can use neither my hands nor feet."

Tezcatlipoca assured him that if he partook of the medicine which he had brought him he would immediately experience a great improvement in health. Quetzalcoatl drank the potion, and at once felt much revived. The cunning Tezcatlipoca pressed another and still another cup of the potion upon him, and as it was nothing but *pulque*, the wine of the country, he speedily became intoxicated, and was as wax in the hands of his adversary.

Tezcatlipoca Deceives the Toltecs

TEZCATLIPOCA, IN PURSUANCE OF HIS POLICY inimical to the Toltec state, took the form of an Indian of the name of Toueyo (Toveyo), and bent his steps to the palace of Uemac, chief of the Toltecs in temporal matters. This worthy had a daughter so fair that she was desired in marriage by many of the Toltecs, but all to no purpose, as her father refused her hand to one and all. The princess, beholding the false Toueyo passing her father's palace, fell deeply in love with him, and so tumultuous was her passion that she became seriously ill because of her longing for him. Uemac, hearing of her indisposition, bent his steps to her apartments, and inquired of her women the cause of her illness. They told him that it was occasioned by the sudden passion which had seized her for the Indian who had recently come that way. Uemac at once gave orders for the arrest of Toueyo, and he was haled before the temporal chief of Tollan.

"Whence come you?" inquired Uemac of his prisoner, who was very scantily attired.

"Lord, I am a stranger, and I have come to these parts to sell green paint," replied Tezcatlipoca.

"Why are you dressed in this fashion? Why do you not wear a cloak?" asked the chief.

"My lord, I follow the custom of my country," replied Tezcatlipoca.

"You have inspired a passion in the breast of my daughter," said Uemac. "What should be done to you for thus disgracing me?"

"Slay me; I care not," said the cunning Tezcatlipoca.

"Nay," replied Uemac, "for if I slay you my daughter will perish. Go to her and say that she may wed you and be happy."

Now the marriage of Toueyo to the daughter of Uemac aroused much discontent among the Toltecs; and they murmured among themselves, and said: "Wherefore did Uemac give his daughter to this Toueyo?" Uemac, having got wind of these murmurings, resolved to distract the attention of the Toltecs by making war upon the neighbouring state of Coatepec. The Toltecs assembled armed for the fray, and having arrived at the country of the men of Coatepec they placed Toueyo in ambush with his body-servants, hoping that he would be slain by their adversaries. But Toueyo and his men killed a large number of the enemy and put them to flight. His triumph was celebrated by Uemac with much pomp. The knightly plumes were placed upon his head, and his body was painted with red and yellow – an honour reserved for those who distinguished themselves in battle.

Tezcatlipoca's next step was to announce a great feast in Tollan, to which all the people for miles around were invited. Great crowds assembled, and danced and sang in the city to the sound of the drum. Tezcatlipoca sang to them and forced them to accompany the rhythm of his song with their feet. Faster and faster the people danced, until the pace became so furious that they were driven to madness, lost their footing, and tumbled pell-mell down a deep ravine, where they were changed into rocks. Others in attempting to cross a stone bridge precipitated themselves into the water below, and were changed into stones.

On another occasion Tezcatlipoca presented himself as a valiant warrior named Tequiua, and invited all the inhabitants of Tollan and its environs to come to the flower-garden called Xochitla. When assembled there he attacked them with a hoe, and slew a great number, and others in panic crushed their comrades to death.

Tezcatlipoca and Tlacahuepan on another occasion repaired to the market-place of Tollan, the former displaying upon the palm of his hand a small infant whom he caused to dance and to cut the most amusing capers. This infant was in reality Huitzilopochtli, the Nahua god of war. At this sight the Toltecs crowded upon one another for the purpose of getting a better view, and their eagerness resulted in many being crushed to death. So enraged were the Toltecs at this that upon the advice of Tlacahuepan they slew both Tezcatlipoca and Huitzilopochtli. When this had been done the bodies of the slain gods gave forth such a pernicious effluvia that thousands of the Toltecs died of the pestilence. The god Tlacahuepan then advised them to cast out the bodies lest worse befell them, but on their attempting to do so they discovered their weight to be so great that they could not move them. Hundreds wound cords round the corpses, but the strands broke, and those who pulled upon them fell and died suddenly, tumbling one upon the other, and suffocating those upon whom they collapsed.

The Toltecs were so tormented by the enchantments of Tezcatlipoca that it was soon apparent to them that their fortunes were on the wane and that the end of their empire was at hand. Quetzalcoatl, chagrined at the turn things had taken, resolved to quit Tollan and go to the country of Tlapallan, whence he had come on his civilizing mission to Mexico. He burned all the houses which he had built, and buried his treasure of gold and precious stones in the deep valleys between the mountains. He changed the cacao-trees into mezquites, and he ordered all the birds of rich plumage and song to quit the valley of Anahuac and to follow him to a distance of more than a hundred leagues. On the road from Tollan he discovered a great tree at a point called Quauhtitlan. There he rested, and requested his pages to hand him a mirror. Regarding himself in the polished surface, he exclaimed, "I am old," and from that circumstance the spot was named Huehuequauhtitlan (Old Quauhtitlan). Proceeding on his way accompanied by musicians who played the flute, he walked until fatigue arrested his steps, and he seated himself upon a stone, on which he left the imprint of his hands. This place is called Temacpalco (The Impress of the Hands). At Coaapan he was met by the Nahua gods, who were inimical to him and to the Toltecs.

"Where do you go?" they asked him. "Why do you leave your capital?"

"I go to Tlapallan," replied Quetzalcoatl, "whence I came."

"For what reason?" persisted the enchanters.

"My father the Sun has called me thence," replied Quetzalcoatl.

"Go, then, happily," they said, "but leave us the secret of your art, the secret of founding in silver, of working in precious stones and woods, of painting, and of feather-working, and other matters."

But Quetzalcoatl refused, and cast all his treasures into the fountain of Cozcaapa (Water of Precious Stones). At Cochtan he was met by another enchanter, who asked him whither he was bound, and on learning his destination proffered him a draught of wine. On tasting the vintage Quetzalcoatl was overcome with sleep. Continuing his journey in the morning, the god passed between a volcano and the Sierra Nevada (Mountain of Snow), where all the pages who accompanied him died of cold. He regretted this misfortune exceedingly, and wept, lamenting their fate with most bitter tears and mournful songs. On reaching the summit of Mount Poyauhtecatl he slid to the base. Arriving at the sea-shore, he embarked upon a raft of serpents, and was wafted away toward the land of Tlapallan.

Huitzilopochtli and Coyolxauhqui

UNDER THE SHADOW OF THE MOUNTAIN of Coatepec, near the Toltec city of Tollan, there dwelt a pious widow called Coatlicue, the mother of a tribe of Indians called Centzonuitznaua, who had a daughter called Coyolxauhqui, and who daily repaired to a small hill with the intention of offering up prayers to the gods in a penitent spirit of piety. Whilst occupied in her devotions one day she was surprised by a small ball of brilliantly coloured feathers falling upon her from on high. She was pleased by the bright variety of its hues, and placed it in her bosom, intending to offer it up to the sun-god. Some time afterwards she learnt that she was to become the mother of another child. Her sons, hearing of this, rained abuse upon her, being incited to humiliate her in every possible way by their sister Coyolxauhqui.

Coatlicue went about in fear and anxiety; but the spirit of her unborn infant came and spoke to her and gave her words of encouragement, soothing her troubled heart. Her sons, however, were resolved to wipe out what they considered an insult to their race by the death of their mother, and took counsel with one another to slay her. They attired themselves in their war-gear, and arranged their hair after the manner of warriors going to battle. But one of their number, Quauitlicac, relented, and confessed the perfidy of his brothers to the still unborn Huitzilopochtli, who replied to him: "O brother, hearken attentively to what I have to say to you. I am fully informed of what is about to happen." With the intention of slaying their mother, the Indians went in search of her. At their head marched their sister, Coyolxauhqui. They were armed to the teeth, and carried bundles of darts with which they intended to kill the luckless Coatlicue.

Quauitlicac climbed the mountain to acquaint Huitzilopochtli with the news that his brothers were approaching to kill their mother.

"Mark well where they are at," replied the infant god. "To what place have they advanced?"

"To Tzompantitlan," responded Quauitlicac.

Later on Huitzilopochtli asked: "Where may they be now?"

"At Coaxalco," was the reply.

Once more Huitzilopochtli asked to what point his enemies had advanced.

"They are now at Petlac," Quauitlicac replied.

After a little while Quauitlicac informed Huitzilopochtli that the Centzonuitznaua were at hand under the leadership of Coyolxauhqui. At the moment of the enemy's arrival Huitzilopochtli was born, flourishing a shield and spear of a blue colour. He was painted, his head was surmounted by a panache, and his left leg was covered with feathers. He shattered Coyolxauhqui with a flash of serpentine lightning, and then gave chase to the Centzonuitznaua, whom he pursued four times round the mountain. They did not attempt to defend themselves, but fled incontinently. Many perished in the waters of the adjoining lake, to which they had rushed in their despair. All were slain save a few who escaped to a place called Uitzlampa, where they surrendered to Huitzilopochtli and gave up their arms.

The Fugitive Prince

THE TECPANECS OVERCAME the Acolhuans of Tezcuco and slew their king about the year 1418. Nezahualcoyotl (Fasting Coyote), the heir to the Tezcucan throne, beheld the butchery of his royal father from the shelter of a tree close by, and succeeded in making his escape from the invaders. He had not enjoyed many days of freedom when he was captured by those who had set out in pursuit of him, and, being haled back to his native city, was cast into prison. He found a friend in the governor of the place, who owed his position to the prince's late father, and by means of his assistance he succeeded in once more escaping from the hostile Tecpanecs.

For aiding Nezahualcoyotl, however, the governor promptly paid the penalty of death. The royal family of Mexico interceded for the hunted youth, and he was permitted to find an asylum at the Aztec court, whence he later proceeded to his own city of Tezcuco, occupying apartments in the palace where his father had once dwelt. For eight years he remained there, existing unnoticed on the bounty of the Tecpanec chief who had usurped the throne of his ancestors.

Maxtla the Fierce

In course of time the original Tecpanec conqueror was gathered to his fathers, and was succeeded by his son Maxtla, a ruler who could ill brook the studious prince, who had journeyed to the capital of the Tecpanecs to do him homage. He refused Nezahualcoyotl's advances of friendship, and the latter was warned by a favourably disposed courtier to take refuge in flight. This advice he adopted, and returned to Tezcuco, where, however, Maxtla set a snare for his life. A function which took place in the evening afforded the tyrant his chance. But the prince's preceptor frustrated the conspiracy, by means of substituting for his charge a youth who strikingly resembled him. This second failure exasperated Maxtla so much that he sent a military force to Tezcuco, with orders to despatch Nezahualcoyotl without delay. But the same vigilant person who had guarded the prince so well before became apprised of his danger and advised him to fly. To this advice, however, Nezahualcoyotl refused to listen, and resolved to await the approach of his enemies.

A Romantic Escape

When they arrived he was engaged in the Mexican ball-game of *tlachtli*. With great politeness he requested them to enter and to partake of food. Whilst they refreshed themselves he betook himself to another room, but his action excited no surprise, as he could be seen through the open doorway by which the apartments communicated with each other. A huge censer, however, stood in the vestibule, and the clouds of incense which arose from it hid his movements from those who had been sent to slay him. Thus obscured, he succeeded in entering a subterranean passage which led to a large disused water-pipe, through which he crawled and made his escape.

A Thrilling Pursuit

For a season Nezahualcoyotl evaded capture by hiding in the hut of a zealous adherent. The hut was searched, but the pursuers neglected to look below a heap of maguey fibre used for making cloth, under which he lay concealed. Furious at his enemy's escape, Maxtla now ordered a rigorous search, and a regular battue of the country round Tezcuco was arranged. A large reward was offered for the capture of Nezahualcoyotl dead or alive, along with a fair estate and the hand of a noble lady, and the unhappy prince was forced to seek safety in the mountainous country between Tezcuco and Tlascala. He became a wretched outcast, a pariah lurking in caves and woods, prowling about after nightfall in order to satisfy his hunger, and seldom having a whole night's rest, because of the vigilance of his enemies. Hotly pursued by them, he was compelled to seek some curious places of concealment in order to save himself. On one occasion he was hidden by some friendly soldiers inside a large drum, and on another he was concealed beneath some *chia* stalks by a girl who was engaged in reaping them. The loyalty of the Tezcucan peasantry to their hunted prince was extraordinary, and rather than betray his whereabouts to the creatures of Maxtla they on many occasions suffered torture, and even death itself. At a time when his affairs appeared most gloomy, however, Nezahualcoyotl experienced a change of fortune. The tyrannous Maxtla had rendered himself highly unpopular by his many oppressions, and the people in the territories he had annexed were by no means contented under his rule.

The Defeat of Maxtla

These malcontents decided to band themselves together to defy the tyrant, and offered the command of the force thus raised to Nezahualcoyotl. This he accepted, and the Tecpanec usurper was totally defeated in a general engagement. Restored to the throne of his fathers, Nezahualcoyotl allied himself with Mexico, and with the assistance of its monarch completely routed the remaining force of Maxtla, who was seized in the baths of Azcapozalco, haled forth and sacrificed, and his city destroyed.

The Solon of Anahuac

Nezahualcoyotl profited by the hard experiences he had undergone, and proved a wise and just ruler. The code of laws framed by him was an exceedingly drastic one, but so wise and enlightened was his rule that on the whole he deserves the title which has been conferred upon him of 'the Solon of Anahuac.' He generously encouraged the arts, and established a Council of Music, the purpose of which was to supervise artistic endeavour of every description. In Nezahualcoyotl Mexico found, in all probability, her greatest native poet.

The Poet Prince

We find Nezahualcoyotl's later days stained by an act which was unworthy of such a great monarch and wise man. His eldest son, the heir to the crown, entered into an intrigue with one of his father's wives, and dedicated many passionate poems to her, to which she replied with equal ardour. The poetical correspondence was brought before the king, who prized the lady highly because of her beauty. Outraged in his most sacred feelings, Nezahualcoyotl had the youth arraigned before the High Court, which passed sentence of death upon him – a sentence which his father permitted to be carried out. After his son's execution he shut himself up in his palace for some months, and gave orders that the doors and windows of the unhappy young man's residence should be built up so that never again might its walls echo to the sound of a human voice.

The Queen with a Hundred Lovers

WHEN AXAIACATZIN, KING OF MEXICO, and other lords sent their daughters to King Nezahualpilli, for him to choose one to be his queen and lawful wife, whose son might succeed to the inheritance, she who had the highest claims among them, for nobility of birth and rank, was Chachiuhnenetzin, the young daughter of the Mexican king. She had been brought up by the monarch in a separate palace, with great pomp, and with numerous attendants, as became the daughter of so great a monarch. The number of servants attached to her household exceeded two thousand.

Young as she was, she was exceedingly artful and vicious; so that, finding herself alone, and seeing that her people feared her on account of her rank and importance, she began to give way to an unlimited indulgence of her power. Whenever she saw a young man who pleased her fancy she gave secret orders that he should be brought to her, and shortly afterwards he would be put to death. She would then order a statue or effigy of his person to be made, and, adorning it with rich clothing, gold, and jewellery, place it in the apartment in which she lived. The number of statues of those whom she thus sacrificed was so great as to almost fill the room. When the king came to visit her, and inquired respecting these statues, she answered that they were her gods; and he, knowing how strict the Mexicans were in the worship of their false deities, believed her.

But, as no iniquity can be long committed with entire secrecy, she was finally found out in this manner: Three of the young men, for some reason or other, she had left alive. Their names were Chicuhcoatl, Huitzilimitzin, and Maxtla, one of whom was lord of Tesoyucan and one of the grandees of the kingdom, and the other two nobles of high rank. It happened that one day the king recognized on the apparel of one of these a very precious jewel which he had given to the queen; and although he had no fear of treason on her part it gave him some uneasiness. Proceeding to visit her that night, her attendants told him she was asleep, supposing that the king would then return, as he had done at other times. But the affair of the jewel made him insist on entering the chamber in which she slept; and, going to wake her, he found only a statue in the bed, adorned with her hair, and closely resembling her. Seeing this, and noticing that the attendants around were in much trepidation and alarm, the king called his guards, and, assembling all the people of the house, made a general search for the queen, who was shortly found at an entertainment with the three young lords, who were arrested with her.

The king referred the case to the judges of his court, in order that they might make an inquiry into the matter and examine the parties implicated. These discovered many individuals, servants of the queen, who had in some way or other been accessory to her crimes – workmen who had been engaged in making and adorning the statues, others who had aided in introducing the young men into the palace, and others, again, who had put them to death and concealed their bodies. The case having been sufficiently investigated, the king despatched ambassadors to the rulers of Mexico and Tlacopan, giving them information of the event, and signifying the day on which the punishment of the queen and her accomplices was to take place; and he likewise sent through the empire to summon all the lords to bring their wives and their daughters, however young they might be, to be witnesses of a punishment which he designed for a great example. He also made a truce with all the enemies of the empire, in order that they might come freely to see it.

The time having arrived, the number of people gathered together was so great that, large as was the city of Tezcuco, they could scarcely all find room in it. The execution took place publicly, in sight of the whole city. The queen was put to the garrotte (a method of strangling by means of a rope twisted round a stick), as well as her three gallants; and, from their being persons of high birth, their bodies were burned, together with the effigies before mentioned. The other parties who had been accessory to the crimes, who numbered more than two thousand persons, were also put to the garrotte, and burned in a pit made for the purpose in a ravine near a temple of the Idol of Adulterers. All applauded so severe and exemplary a punishment, except the Mexican lords, the relatives of the queen, who were much incensed at so public an example, and, although for the time they concealed their resentment, meditated future revenge. It was not without reason, says the chronicler, that the king experienced this disgrace in his household, since he was thus punished for an unworthy subterfuge made use of by his father to obtain his mother as a wife!

The Noble Tlascalan

LESS THAN A YEAR BEFORE THE SPANIARDS ARRIVED in Mexico war broke out between the Huexotzincans and the Tlascalans, to the former of whom the Aztecs acted as allies. On the battlefield there was captured by guile a very valiant Tlascalan leader called Tlalhuicole, so renowned for his prowess that the mere mention of his name was generally sufficient to deter any Mexican hero from attempting his capture. He was brought to Mexico in a cage, and presented to the Emperor Montezuma, who, on learning of his name and renown, gave him his liberty and overwhelmed him with honours. He further granted him permission to return to his own country, a boon he had never before extended to any captive.

But Tlalhuicole refused his freedom, and replied that he would prefer to be sacrificed to the gods, according to the usual custom. Montezuma, who had the highest regard for him, and prized his life more than any sacrifice, would not consent to his immolation. At this juncture war broke out between Mexico and the Tarascans, and Montezuma announced the appointment of Tlalhuicole as chief of the expeditionary force. He accepted the command, marched against the Tarascans, and, having totally defeated them, returned to Mexico laden with an enormous booty and crowds of slaves. The city rang with his triumph. The emperor begged him to become a Mexican citizen, but he replied that on no account would he prove a traitor to his country.

Montezuma then once more offered him his liberty, but he strenuously refused to return to Tlascala, having undergone the disgrace of defeat and capture. He begged Montezuma to terminate his unhappy existence by sacrificing him to the gods, thus ending the dishonour he felt in living on after having undergone defeat, and at the same time fulfilling the highest aspiration of his life – to die the death of a warrior on the stone of combat. Montezuma, himself the noblest pattern of Aztec chivalry, touched at his request, could not but agree with him that he had chosen the most fitting fate for a hero, and ordered him to be chained to the stone of combat, the blood-stained *temalacatl*. The most renowned of the Aztec warriors were pitted against him, and the emperor himself graced the sanguinary tournament with his presence. Tlalhuicole bore himself in the combat like a lion, slew eight warriors of renown, and wounded more than twenty. But at last he fell, covered with wounds, and was haled by the exulting priests to the altar of the terrible war-god Huitzilopochtli, to whom his heart was offered up.

The Return of Papantzin

ON TAKING UP THE REINS OF GOVERNMENT, Montezuma had married his sister Papantzin to one of his most illustrious servants, the governor of Tlatelulco, and after his death it would appear that she continued to exercise his almost viceregal functions and to reside in his palace.

In course of time she died, and her obsequies were attended by the emperor in person, accompanied by the greatest personages of his court and kingdom. The body was interred in a subterranean vault of his own palace, in close proximity to the royal baths, which stood in a sequestered part of the extensive grounds surrounding the royal residence. The entrance to the vault was secured by a stone slab of moderate weight, and when the numerous ceremonies prescribed for the interment of a royal personage had been completed the emperor and his suite retired.

At daylight next morning one of the royal children, a little girl of some six years of age, having gone into the garden to seek her governess, espied the Princess Papan standing near the baths. The princess, who was her aunt, called to her, and requested her to bring her governess to her. The child did as she was bid, but her governess, thinking that imagination had played her a trick, paid little attention to what she said. As the child persisted in her statement, the governess at last followed her into the garden, where she saw Papan sitting on one of the steps of the baths. The sight of the supposed dead princess filled the woman with such terror that she fell down in a swoon. The child then went to her mother's apartment, and detailed to her what had happened. She at once proceeded to the baths with two of her attendants, and at sight of Papan was also seized with affright. But the princess reassured her, and asked to be allowed to accompany her to her apartments, and that the entire affair should for the present be kept absolutely secret.

Later in the day she sent for Tiçotzicatzin, her major-domo, and requested him to inform the emperor that she desired to speak with him immediately on matters of the greatest importance. The man, terrified, begged to be excused from the mission, and Papan then gave orders that her uncle Nezahualpilli, King of Tezcuco, should be communicated with. That monarch, on receiving her request that he should come to her, hastened to the palace. The princess begged him to see the emperor without loss of time and to entreat him to come to her at once. Montezuma heard his story with surprise mingled with doubt. Hastening to his sister, he cried as he approached her: "Is it indeed you, my sister, or some evil demon who has taken your likeness?" "It is I indeed, your Majesty," she replied. Montezuma and the exalted personages who accompanied him then seated themselves, and a hush of expectation fell upon all as they were addressed by the princess in the following words:

"Listen attentively to what I am about to relate to you. You have seen me dead, buried, and now behold me alive again. By the authority of our ancestors, my brother, I am returned from the dwellings of the dead to prophesy to you certain things of prime importance.

"At the moment after death I found myself in a spacious valley, which appeared to have neither commencement nor end, and was surrounded by lofty mountains. Near the middle I came upon a road with many branching paths. By the side of the valley there flowed a river of considerable size, the waters of which ran with a loud noise. By the borders of this I saw a young man clothed in a long robe, fastened with a diamond, and shining like the sun, his visage bright as a star. On his forehead was a sign in the figure of a cross. He had wings, the feathers of which gave forth the most wonderful and glowing reflections and colours. His eyes were as emeralds, and his glance was modest. He was fair, of beautiful aspect and imposing presence. He took me by the hand and said: 'Come hither. It is not yet time for you to cross the river. You possess the love of God, which is greater than you know or can comprehend.' He then conducted me through the valley, where I espied many heads and bones of dead men. I then beheld a number of black folk, horned, and with the feet of deer. They were engaged in building a house, which was nearly completed. Turning toward the east for a space, I beheld on the waters of the river a vast number of ships manned by a great host of men dressed differently from ourselves. Their eyes were of a clear grey, their complexions ruddy, they carried banners and ensigns in their hands and wore helmets on their heads. They called themselves 'Sons of the Sun.' The youth who conducted me and caused me to see all these things said that it was not yet the will of the gods that I should cross the river, but that I was to be reserved to behold the future with my own eyes, and to enjoy the benefits of the faith which these strangers brought with them; that the bones I beheld on the plain were those of my countrymen who had died in ignorance of that faith, and had consequently suffered great torments; that the house being builded by the black folk was an edifice prepared for those who would fall in battle with the seafaring strangers whom I had seen; and that I was destined to return to my compatriots to tell them of the true faith, and to announce to them what I had seen that they might profit thereby."

Montezuma hearkened to these matters in silence, and felt greatly troubled. He left his sister's presence without a word, and, regaining his own apartments, plunged into melancholy thoughts.

The Twin Heroes and the Lords of Xibalba

IN XIBALBA, the land that the sun goes down into, the land whose Lords are the Lords of the Dead, there grew a tree which was a forbidden tree – none were permitted to approach it. The leaves of that tree were wide and dark; the fruits of it were round and heavy, and they grew like gourds along the branches. A princess of Xibalba said, "Why should I not go to this tree? The fruits of it must be precious." Then she made her way to the tree.

Now amongst the fruits that hung from the branches was the head of a man. And when the princess (Xquiq was her name) stood before the tree and said to herself, "Should I die if I pluck a fruit?" a voice said to her, "Draw nearer." It was from the head that was amongst the wide, dark leaves. And the voice said, "The round lumps upon the branches and amongst the leaves are but skulls and death's-heads. Not as they are am I yet. Do you stretch forth your hand."

The princess stretched her hand forth amongst the branches and through the leaves. Then that head, striving greatly, spat into her hand. "This that I give thee is my posterity," said the head. "Now I shall cease to speak. As for thee, flee from this place into the Upperworld, and go where I shall tell thee." The princess sank down beneath the tree, and the voice told her what man the head had been upon, and told her, too, what place to go to upon the earth.

There had been two brothers whose names were Hunhun-Ahpu and Vukub-Hunapu; they were adepts at ball-playing. The Lords of Xibalba heard of their playing and sent their Owl-men to challenge the brothers to play a game in the Underworld. The brothers agreed to go. They went down a steep descent; they crossed a river in a deep gorge; they crossed a boiling river and a river of blood; they came to four roads that were red, black, white, and yellow. "I am the road to the king," said the black road, and it led the brothers to where two figures were seated on thrones. The brothers saluted them; they received no answer to their salutations, and they heard the scornful laughter of the Lords of Xibalba. Then they knew that the figures were of wood, and they were made ashamed. The game began; angrily the brothers played against the Lords of Xibalba. When that day's game was over they were brought to where they might seat themselves. But the seats they took were heated stones, and the brothers sprang up in pain and went away from them.

Then the Lords of Xibalba conducted them to the House of Gloom: there they were to take their night's rest. Torches were put into their hands, and they were commanded to keep them so that the sticks would not be black when the brothers appeared before the Lords of Xibalba the next day. The brothers did not know what to do to keep this command. They were but a short time in the House of Gloom when the torches burned out, and they were left with the blackened sticks in their hands.

When the brothers appeared before them next day, the Lords of Xibalba said to them, "Your torches are not as we said they were to be." "Lords," the brothers said, "the torches burned themselves out." But the Lords of Xibalba had the brothers sacrificed; their heads were put upon the branches of the tree that it was forbidden to approach. The head of Hunhun-Ahpu had life still in it when Xquiq came to the tree.

She, being found there, was doomed to be sacrificed. The Owl-men were sent to slay her. Xquiq beguiled them. The Owl-men took back to the Lords of the Underworld the thickened sap of a weed as her heart; its smell was the smell of blood, and the Lords of Xibalba were made content.

The princess then journeyed towards the world from which the brothers had come – the Upperworld. She was long upon the way, and she was near to the time of her delivery when she came to the house of Hunhun-Ahpu's mother. She was not well treated for a time; the woman would not receive her as her daughter-in-law, and the woman's two sons who were in the house mocked at her. The woman, Hunhun-Ahpu's mother, told her that before she would be given shelter in the house she would have to gather maize in a field. Xquiq went into the field. The maize had all been cut, and it was left in one heap in the field. She was told that she would have to get maize without touching any that was in the heap. Maize sprang up as she went through the field, and she gathered what was wanted. Then, seeing that the Gods had helped her, Hunhun-Ahpu's mother took Xquiq into the house.

Children were born to her; they were twins, and they were wise from their birth. Their grandmother knew that they would become great heroes and great magicians. But their uncles mocked at them and strove to destroy them. Their uncles were Hunbatz and Hunchouen; they knew all the arts that were then in the world, for they were singers and flute-players, painters and sculptors, jewel-workers and smiths; also they were blow-gun shooters. But to the children of Xquiq they were cruel and envious uncles.

They would not have the youths grow up into men; they would not have them become heroes and magicians whose deeds would be greater than their own. They took the twins into a forest, and they would have sacrificed them there. But the youths transformed them into monkeys: in the trees they stayed. But even as monkeys, Hunbatz and Hunchouen are prayed to by the singers and flute-players, by the painters and sculptors, by the jewel-workers, smiths, and blow-gun shooters to this day.

After this the twins (Hunahpu and Xbalanque were their names) fashioned magic tools for themselves, and with these tools they cleared a field, pulling up the trees and cutting the vines away. The tools worked by themselves while the twins went hunting in the forest. When they came back at the end of the day they found the field ready for sowing. But when they went out of their house the next day they saw the trees growing and the vines flourishing as before. Again they set their magic tools to clear the field, and again they went hunting. And when they came back the field was once more cleared and ready for sowing. They did not sleep that night; they stayed outside their house and watched the field to see what would happen in it. And they saw that when darkness fell all the animals came into the field: the puma came and the jaguar; the hare, the rat, and the opossum; the deer, the coyote, the porcupine, and the peccary; also the birds came into the field. They called upon the felled trees and the cut vines to grow and flourish again. They lifted the tree-trunks and put them back upon their stumps, and they joined the cut vines together. This they did going through the whole of the field, and when the dawn came the twins found their field with trees and vines growing and flourishing in it.

Then they gave chase to the birds and the animals. The birds flew high above their heads. The animals fled swiftly away from them. They caught the deer and the rabbit by their tails. The deer and the rabbit pulled away from them leaving their tails in the brothers' hands. To this day these animals are without their tails. The rat was the only creature the brothers were able to catch and hold. The rat begged mercy from them. It declared that it would reveal a great secret to the brothers if they would spare it its life.

They spared the rat its life, and the rat told them where their grandmother had hidden the ball, the gloves, and the ring which their father and their uncle had used in the days when they played ball. Their grandmother had hidden these things away, fearing that the twins should find them, and become players, and be led to their destruction as their father and their uncle had been led to destruction. Now when they found the ball, the gloves, and the ring, the twins began to play the game; every day they played ball, and soon they forgot everything else except this game.

Now as they went over the world playing games against all sorts of people, they heard of the Earth Giants. There were three of them, and the three were proud and boastful. They gave no reverence to the Gods, for one of them would say, "It is I who am the sun," and another would say, "It is I who move the earth," and the third would say, "I can shake the sky and overturn the ground." The twins when they heard of this insolence resolved that they would leave off playing their game of ball until they had rid the earth of these Giants.

Vukub-Cakix was the first of them. Every day he would say to the whole of creation, "I am above all created beings; I am their sun; I am their dawn; I am their moon. Of silver are the balls of my eyes, and my teeth shine like the sky at noon. My nostrils are like the moon. Of silver is my throne, and the earth lives when I step upon it. I am the sun, I am the moon, I am the bringer of all pleasantness." All this he would say when he came to the tree on which grew the fruit that nourished him; at dawn he used to come to it. Wonderful was the tree that Vukub-Cakix owned.

The brothers came to the tree. They hid themselves in the branches. When the Giant came to the tree, Hunahpu blew a dart at him with his blow-gun. It pierced his jaw. Then the Giant raised up his arms and caught Hunahpu in the tree. He tore his arm off. Then carrying the arm, and roaring in pain, the Giant went back to his house.

Now the twins had to get back the arm that had been torn off one of their bodies. Also they had to destroy Vukub-Cakix. So they changed their appearance and they went to the Giant's house as physicians. They saw where Hunahpu's arm was being held before a fire; the Giant's wife was holding it there, and she was chanting spells over it, so that the arm might become withered and never join with the shoulder again. And they heard Vukub-Cakix crying because of the pain in his jaw.

They told him they could cure his pain. "It is not because of the dart shot through your jaw that you suffer," they said, "but it is because there are worms in your teeth. We will take your teeth out, and your jaw will be well again." "It is by my teeth alone that I am king," the Giant said. "All my beauty comes from my shining teeth and my shining eyeballs." "We will give you more shining teeth in their place," the brothers said. The Giant then consented, and he let the brothers tie him to the roots of trees. They drew his teeth out. They took away the gleam of his eyes. And then the Giant, Vukub-Cakix, died where he was tied.

They snatched Hunahpu's arm from the Giant's wife as she was still uttering spells over it. It was unwithered yet, and they joined it to Hunahpu's shoulder. And then they went forth to destroy the second of the Earth Giants.

This was Zipacna. He shook the earth, making men's houses fall down. The twins came upon him when they had with them a great host of youths. They beguiled Zipacna so that he went down into a great and a deep pit. Then Hunahpu and Xbalanque and all who were with them hurled trees down upon him. After a while the Giant ceased to stir in the pit. They filled it up with stones; they built a great house on it; they went within the house and made merry over the death of Zipacna, the Giant who made the earth shake. But as they were making merry Zipacna rose beneath the house; he flung it down; he took the hundreds of young men who had been the brothers' helpers and he flung them up into the sky. There they stayed; they have become the Four Hundred Stars.

But Hunahpu and Xbalanque the Giant was not able to catch. And when he went away they followed on his tracks, and once again they planned his destruction. Zipacna loved to gorge himself with great crabs that came up from the sea. The brothers formed a crab out of wood – the greatest crab that had ever been seen in the world – and they placed it in a deep ravine. They came to where the Giant was, and, saying that they were hunters, told him of a crab so great that they had been frightened by the sight of it. The Giant went to where he could see it. Deep down in the ravine he saw what seemed to him to be the world's greatest crab, and he climbed down the face of a cliff to come to it. And when he was down in the ravine the brothers hurled mountains upon him-mountains of such weight that not even he could get from under them. And so Zipacna, he who shook the earth, was destroyed by Hunahpu and Xbalanque.

Then, as the twins went through the world, playing the game of ball and challenging others to play against them, they came upon the last of the Earth Giants. This was Cabrakan. He tore through the forests and he made the skies shake. They came upon him as he was wallowing in his lair on the ground. "How strong art thou, O Cabrakan?" said the brothers to him. "We have heard it said that thou couldst shift a mountain as great as this one." "I will shift it while you watch me," said Cabrakan. "Eat first, O Cabrakan," said the brothers, "We will kill and cook a bird for thine eating." So they killed a great bird, and they put the bird in the earth to bake. But they put poison in the mud they encrusted the bird with. The Giant watched their cooking; he ate of the great bird greedily, and when he had licked up the scraps of flesh and crunched all the bones, he started to shift the mountain. But no sooner had he grasped the top of it than he fell down dead into the ravine that was near the mountain.

And so the Earth Giants who had disturbed the world, Vukub-Cakix, Zipacna, and Cabrakan, were destroyed by the hero twins, Hunahpu and Xbalanque. But the Lords of the Underworld had heard their movements as they went up and down on the earth, playing their game of ball. "Who are these who make such play with the ball?" they said to one another. "Do not the withered heads of Hunhun-Ahpu and Vukub-Hunahpu hang amongst the branches of our tree? Who, then, are these who play on the earth as they once played?" Then the Lords of the Underworld sent their Owl-men to challenge the brothers to play a game of ball in Xibalba.

They went down into Xibalba. They went down a long descent; they crossed a river in a deep gorge; they crossed a boiling torrent; they crossed a river of blood; beyond the fourth river they came upon the four roadways-the black, white, red, and yellow roadways.

They had heard from their mother and their grandmother how the Lords of Xibalba had received their father and their uncle, and the brothers resolved to use all the craft they had against them. So when the black road said, "I am the way to the king," they did not go upon it at first: they took an insect named Xan and sent it upon the road. And Xan came first to the images that were seated upon thrones: it pricked each of them; they did not move. Then Xan went where others stood: it pricked a leg of each and each gave a cry. "What is it, Hun-Came?" one was asked. "What is it, Vukub-Came?" All the names of the Lords of Xibalba were uttered – Xiquipat, Ahalpuh, Cuchumaquiq, Chamiabak, Abalcana, Chamiaholom, Patan, Quiqxic, Quiqrixgag, and Quiqurc. And having heard the names, Xan went back to the brothers, told them the names it had heard, and described where the images of wood were seated.

Then the twins went on the black roadway and came to where the Lords of Xibalba stood beside the images of wood. The images they did not salute. They saluted the Lords of Xibalba, each according to his own name. Then were the Lords alarmed; they knew not what sort of men they had to deal with. They motioned the brothers towards the seats that were heated stones; but they would not seat themselves. "These are not our seats," they said.

Then they began to play the game of ball against the Lords of the Underworld. The night came before the game was finished. Then the brothers were brought to the House of Gloom in which they were to rest until the next day when the game would be played again. Torches were put into their hands, and they were commanded to appear before the Lords of Xibalba next day with torches that were not blackened.

When they went within the House of Gloom they quenched their torches. They covered them with red paint. When they came out of the House of Gloom their torches were unblackened. "Who are you?" cried the Lords of Xibalba. "Whence do you come?" "Who can say who we are, or whence we come?" the brothers answered. "We ourselves do not know." Again the game was started, and the brothers played against the Lords of Xibalba. And now the game was coming to its end, and they of the Underworld were becoming more and more anxious about ways of bringing to destruction the two who had come to them from the world above.

They sent them to the House of Cold; there the brothers kept the warmth of life in them by burning knots of pine which they found under the dust. They sent them into the House of the Jaguars, and there they fought off for the whole of the night the fierce beasts that snarled all round them. They sent them to get flowers from Vukub-Came's garden, a garden that was guarded by poisonous snakes; the ants aided them, for all creatures were ready to help the brothers in the game they were playing against the Lords of the Underworld; the ants brought the flowers to them; the brothers filled four vases with flowers and presented them to the Lords of Xibalba.

The game was begun again, and at the end of the day Hunahpu and Xbalanque were sent to the most dread place of all; they were sent into the House of the Bats. All night they lay in the cave, the bats hovering over them. They lay flat upon their faces. But Hunahpu lifted his head. Then a great bat swept down and sheared his head off. And Hunahpu would have bled to death if a tortoise had not come and fixed himself to where the head had been. The tortoise held to his neck, giving him something like a head. Next morning the Lords of Xibalba came crowding around the cave, demanding that the brothers come forth and play the finish of the game. As they stood before the cave-mouth a rabbit sprang up at their feet. The Lords of Xibalba, thinking that this was the ball that the brothers had thrown, ran after the rabbit. Then Xbalanque looked around the cave that now was lighted. And on a ledge he found Hunahpu's head. He took the tortoise off and put the head upon Hunahpu's neck. It fastened itself there, and when the Lords of Xibalba came back from their chase of the rabbit, the brothers were ready to play the finish of the game with them.

They played; they won over the Lords of Xibalba. Then the brothers told them that they would show themselves to them as wonder-workers. They had themselves killed and their bones ground to powder. Then they transformed themselves into fishes and swam away. They came back as beggars and stood once more before the Lords of the Underworld. They burned down houses, and immediately they built them up again. They killed a dog belonging to one of the Lords and immediately restored it to life and movement. They killed each other, and brought each other back to life again. The Lords of Xibalba cried, "Do the like with us. Make us, too, know death, and life after death." "Can death exist for you, Lords of Xibalba?" the brothers cried. "Let us know death, and life afterwards," they continued to cry.

They had consented to death. The brothers slew them, but they did not bring them back to life again. They left them lying under the branches of their own forbidden tree. Then Hunahpu and Xbalanque declared who they were. "We are the avengers of the deaths of our father and our uncle," they cried. They took their withered heads from amongst the dark leaves, and they buried them with honours. Then to all who were left in Xibalba they said, "Your state and your power are gone from you. No more will you rule over any creatures. Go forth from where you ruled, and make things of clay; make pots and maize-grinders. The beasts that live in the wilderness shall be your prey and your helpers, but all that is pleasant, all that is cultivated, shall be far from you. Only the bees shall be yours to care for and to rule over. O ye wicked, cruel, dismal ones, go forth and fulfill your dooms." So the Twin Heroes said, and they who had lorded it in the Underworld went forth and took up their menial tasks.

Quetzalcoatl

IN TOLLAN DWELT QUETZALCOATL. And in Tollan all the arts and crafts that we know of were first practised, for Quetzalcoatl taught them to the people there. He taught them the smelting of silver and the clearing and setting of precious stones; he taught the craft of building with stones; he taught them how to make statues, and paint signs in books, and keep count of the moons and suns. All crafts except the craft of war

Quetzalcoatl taught the people of Tollan. And they made sacrifice to him with bread, and flowers, and perfumes, and not as other peoples made sacrifice to the other gods – by tearing the hearts out of the opened breasts of men and women.

He lived in a house that was made of silver: four chambers that house had: the chamber to the east was of gold, the chamber to the west was set with stones of precious green – emeralds and turquoises and nephrite stones, the chamber to the south was set with coloured sea-shells, and the chamber to the north was set with jasper. The house was thatched with the feathers of bright-plumaged birds. All the birds of rich plumage and sweet song were gathered in that place. In the fields the maize grew so big that a man could not carry more than one stalk in his arms; pumpkins were great in their round as a man is high; cotton grew in the fields red and yellow, blue, and black, and white, and men did not have to dye it. All who lived where Quetzalcoatl was had everything to make them prosperous and happy.

There was a time when they did not have maize, when they lived upon roots and on what they gained in the chase. Maize there was, but it was hidden within a mountain, and no one could come to where it was. Different gods had tried to rend the mountain apart that they might come to where the maize was; but this could not be done. Then Quetzalcoatl took the form of a black ant; with a red ant to guide him he went within the mountain Tonacatepetl, and he came to where the maize was: he took the grain, and laboriously he bore it back to men. Then men planted fields with maize; they had crops for the first time; they built cities, and they lived settled lives, and Quetzalcoatl showed them all the crafts that they could learn from him. They honoured him who dwelt in the shining house. And Quetzalcoatl had many servants; some of them were dwarfs, and all were swift of foot.

Then it came to pass that Tezcatlipoca, he who can go into all places, he who wanders over the earth stirring up strife and war amongst men, descended upon Tollan by means of spider-webs. And from the mountain he came down on a blast of wind of such coldness that it killed all the flowers in Quetzalcoatl's bright garden. And Quetzalcoatl, feeling that coldness, said to his servants, "One has come who will drive me hence; perhaps it were better that I went before he drives me, and drank from a fountain in the Land of the Sun, whence I may return, young as a boy." So he said, and his servants saw him burn down his house of silver with its green precious stones and its thatch of bright plumage, and its door-posts of white and red shells. And they saw him call upon his birds of sweet song and rich plumage, and they heard him bidding them to fly into the land of Anahuac.

Then Tezcatlipoca, that god and that sorcerer, went to where Quetzalcoatl stood, and took him into the ball-court that the two might play a game together. All the people of the city stood round to watch that game. The ball had to be cast through a ring that was high upon the wall. Quetzalcoatl took up the ball to cast it. As he did Tezcatlipoca changed himself into a jaguar and sprang upon him. Then Quetzalcoatl fled. And Tezcatlipoca chased him, driving him through the streets of the city, and out into the highways of the country.

His dwarfs fled after him and joined themselves to him. With them he crossed the mountains and came to a hill on which a great tree grew. Under it he rested. As he rested he looked into a mirror and he said, "I am grown to be an old man." Then he threw the mirror down and took up stones and cast them at the tree.

He went on, and his dwarfs made music for him, playing on flutes as they went before him. Once again he became weary, and he rested on a stone by the wayside;

there, looking back towards Tollan, he wept, and his tears pitted the stone on which he sat, and his hands left their imprints upon it where he grasped the stone. The stone is there to this day with the pits and the imprints upon it. He rose up, and once again he went on his way. And men from Tollan met him, and he instructed them in crafts that he had not shown them before.

But he did not give them the treasure of jewels that his dwarfs and humpbacked servants carried for him. He flung this treasure into the fountain Cozcaapan; there it stays to this day – Quetzalcoatl's treasure. On his way he passed over a Fire-mountain and over a mountain of snow. On the mountain of snow his dwarfs and humpbacked servants all died from the cold. Bitterly he bewailed them in a song he made in that place.

Then Quetzalcoatl went down the other side of the mountain, and he came to the sea-shore. He made a raft of snakes, and on that raft he sailed out on the sea. Or so some say, telling Quetzalcoatl's story. And those who tell this say that he came to the land of Tlappallan in the Country of the Sun, and there he drank of the Water of Immortality They say that he will one day return from that land young as a boy. But others say that when he reached the sea-shore he divested himself of his robe with its bright feathers, of his snake-skin mask of the colour of turquoise, and that, leaving these vestments upon the shore, he cast himself into a fire and was consumed to ashes. And they say that Quetzalcoatl's ashes changed into bright-coloured and sweet-singing birds, and that his heart went up into the sky and became the Morning Star. After he had been dead for eight days that star became visible to men, and thereafter Quetzalcoatl was named the Lord of the Dawn.

Quetzalcoatl's Enemy

QUETZALCOATL'S ENEMY DID NOT LEAVE TOLLAN. Naked he went into the market-place and stayed there; where he sat was under the palace of the king. The king had but one daughter, and this girl, looking out upon the market-place, saw Tezcatlipoca. He pretended to be selling peppers. The girl, straightway, was smitten with love for him; she sickened and was like to die. When the king inquired about her the women told him that his daughter was like to die because of her love for a man whom she had seen in the market-place, a foreigner and a naked man.

The king sought out this foreigner. And when Quetzalcoatl's enemy was brought before him, the king said, "Thou must heal my daughter of her sickness." Then they clothed him, and dyed his body, and cut his hair, and brought him in to the king's daughter. And the girl was delighted with his company, and the cunning Tezcatlipoca made her sound and well.

After this Tezcatlipoca adorned himself, and he sent a crier from the king's palace to tell the youths and girls of Tollan of a feast he had prepared for them. They all gathered together in the market-place. Tezcatlipoca led them, playing upon his flute; the youths and girls followed him, singing and dancing. Up the mountain Texcalapa he led them. There he had them dance. He sang songs to them; they sang the same songs after him, verse for verse, although they had not known before the songs he sang. Then he beat upon a drum and a panic came upon the youths and girls; they ran, and their way was across a bridge. But Tezcatlipoca crossed the bridge before them, and he broke the bridge down, and the youths and girls, as they came to the place, pushed each other down. Those who fell from that place were turned into rocks and stones.

He changed himself again and he went into the garden that Quetzalcoatl had made. He called on the men and women of Tollan to come into it, that they might repair the waste of that garden. And when they came into it he fell upon them with a digging-tool, and left them lying dead amongst the blasted flowers in Quetzalcoatl's garden.

Another evil he did to the people of Tollan. Changing himself again he came into the market-place, and he showed the people a manikin that he had, a manikin the size of his finger who danced upon the palm of his hand. All crowded round him to see the wonder, and many of the people were trampled down. Then they heard a voice – it was Tezcatlipoca's voice, but he made it come from afar – that said, "Do not be befooled, people of Tollan. Take stones and slay this sorcerer and his manikin." They took up stones and flung them at the man and the manikin, and they left them on the ground, covered with heaps of stones. Then the odour from their bodies infected the place, and many people died of sickness that came from that odour. A voice was heard by them; it said, "Cast the bodies of the man and the manikin outside the town so that no more will die from the disease that comes from them." Then the people of Tollan fastened ropes to the man and the manikin and pulled at them. But such was the weight that was in the bodies that the people by no effort could move them. More ropes were fastened to the bodies and more people pulled at the ropes. But the ropes broke with sudden snaps, and those who were pulling were killed when they broke.

Then a voice came to the people, saying, "O people of Tollan, a verse of a song will do it." The corpse of the man and the corpse of the manikin sang, and the people took up the song, and pulled at the bodies. This time they dragged them outside the city. They cast the bodies down a steep place, and they returned to the city of Tollan.

They went back as if they were all drunken, and none amongst them could remember what they had been doing. As they went back they saw that the mountain that was beside Tollan was all on fire. They saw a white bird transfixed with an arrow flying over the city. And then stones rained down upon them, and their city was left waste and uninhabitable.

The Gods of the Azteca

QUETZALCOATL TOLD THE PEOPLE ABOUT THE GODS and about the creation of men and women.... At first there was Citlalatonac and Citlalicue, the Sky-father and the Earth-mother. Then Citlalicue gave birth to a knife of flint, and when this knife of flint was flung down it became the sixteen hundred Earth-gods. They had to live as men and women of to-day have to live – by labouring and searching for their food. But after a while they began to think that it was unfitting that they should have to do this – they, the children of the Sky-father and the Earth-mother. They sent Tlotli the Hawk to their mother, asking that men be made who would serve them, the sixteen hundred Earth-gods.

Now there had been an earth before the earth they lived on, and men and women had been upon it, and the earth and the men and women on it had been destroyed, not once, but many times. Once the earth and all that was on it had been destroyed by floods. Once all had been destroyed by the force of great winds, and once all had been destroyed by fire. Now when the sixteen hundred Earth-gods asked that a race of men and women be created who would serve them, the Earth-mother told them what they should do to bring about this creation.

They were to send one of their number down to Mictlampa, the place where there is no light, and the one who went down was to ask the Lord of that place for a bone the bone of a man of the last race that had perished. The Earth-gods chose Xolotl for their messenger; they sent him down to Mictlampa, the place where there is no light.

Xolotl went where they sent him; he came before Mictlantecutli, the Lord of Mictlampa, and found him pouring fire into a vessel of blood. And Mictlantecutli, he whose head is a bare skull, thinking that he might beguile one of the Earth-gods and keep him for ever in that place where there is no light, spoke fairly to him. He would give the Earth-gods a bone, he said, a bone of one of the giants who had dwelt upon the earth; this bone should be put into a vessel when it was brought into the Upperworld, and each of the Earth-gods was to put a drop of his blood into the vessel with the bone; out of what would brew in the vessel two who would make the new race of men and women would come.

Xolotl knew that Mictlantecutli intended evil to him. He stole the bone and bore it away through that place of darkness. The bone was a great one, for it was a bone of one who belonged to the giant race. Yet the messenger of the Earth-gods was able to go swiftly with it through the darkness. But when he came near to the Upperworld the great owls that guard Mictlantecutli's realm flew at him and tore at his eyes. Xolotl stumbled and the great bone fell and broke into fragments. He gathered up the fragments and carried them into the Upperworld where the rest of the Earth-gods waited for him.

Then the sixteen hundred Earth-gods put the fragments of the great bone in a vessel, and each of them drew blood from his own body and dropped the blood into the vessel that held the fragments of the bone. For three days they watched over it, stirring what was in the vessel. Their labour, it seemed, was in vain. Then, on the fourth day, what was in the vessel simmered and bubbled. Out of the brew emerged a human child, a boy. The Earth-gods watched over the vessel for another four days. Then out of the brew emerged a human child, a girl. The Earth-gods took the children and nourished them on the juice of the maguey-plant; the children grew to be a man and a woman. They became man and wife, and from them come the men and women of our time.

The bone that Xolotl brought into the Upperworld was in fragments: for that reason the men and women whom it went to form are not great of stature like the giants who had lived on the earth before; the fragments were of different sizes, and for that reason the men and woman of to-day are not all of one size – some are very tall, and others are small, and there are dwarfs amongst them. The world that the first men and women of our race came into was without sun or moon. Then the great Gods held a council to decide how luminaries might be made for the sky.

At that council the gods declared that it was their will that luminaries should be formed by transformations of a pair of gods; they declared that the two who should enter a fire and allow themselves to be consumed should become the sun and the moon. They built two towers, one for each of the gods who would undertake to make a luminary for the day and for the night, and they strewed the ground with branches and flowers, and they made sacrifices. Two of the gods agreed to cast themselves down into the fires and make themselves into the sun and the moon. These two put on their crowns and their robes of bright feathers and they went up upon the towers. The rest of the gods sat around the fires that had been lighted for four days. Then the two who were upon the towers cast themselves into the fires beneath them; they were consumed.

Then the gods, at that sacred place, waited to witness the resurrection of the pair as the sun and the moon. Four days they waited beside the towers. Then they saw the sky grow red; they knew not what was going to come about; they were terrified. The sun appeared in the sky; it was very red, and none of the gods could look at it because of its blinding rays. Then the moon appeared at the other side of the sky; its light was no less great than the sun's. One of the gods took a rabbit and flung the rabbit in the face of the moon. The rabbit remained there to dim the moon's brightness. And so the moon was made more dim than the sun.

But the two luminaries stayed moveless in the sky. "Die, all of you," they cried down to the gods, "die all of you and create the stars." Then a great Wind came. It blew upon them until the gods were destroyed by the force of it. Their remains were carried up to the sky, and in the sky they stay, having become the stars. The wind blew upon the sun; it made it hurry across the sky. It did not blow upon the moon, and so the moon remains moveless in the sky. But the moon comes into the sky at a different time from the sun.

All this Quetzalcoatl told the dwellers in Tollan.

The Azteca

MANY TIMES SINCE THE AZTECA came into the valley had the years been tied into bundles, each bundle being fifty-two years. And many times at the Tying of the Years had the fires been quenched and a new fire lighted on the breast of a sacrificed man. Many times had that festival come round that is called the Knot of the Years, and many times had the king and the priests consulted about the portents that chow themselves when the fires are quenched and a new fire lighted.

Montezuma the Conqueror was king at that Tying of the Years. And the portent that showed itself was in a pair of great sandals that were found upon the floor of the Temple of Huizilopochtli, the War God of the Azteca. Montezuma the Conqueror said, "This is a sign from Huizilopochtli; it signifies that he will never leave the Azteca." And he said to the priests, "Bear these sandals to Coatlicue, the mother of our god. She dwells in Aztlan the White Place. Out of Aztlan the Azteca went in the old days, guided by Huizilopochtli. They made themselves possessors of the valley; they conquered the tribes of the valley and the uplands; they built the great city Tenochtitlan. Go, tell Coatlicue all this. And say that by my arms they have now subdued the people farthest away, and have taken captives for the sacrifices from them. Huizilopochtli will never leave a people who have proved themselves such conquerors. Go; bear these sandals in all reverence to the mother of Huizilopochtli; they will be a sign to her that her son will not return to Aztlan the White Place."

So the priests of Huizilopochtli searched in their books and found out the ways that led back to Aztlan the White Place. It was a mountain that waters surrounded. The waters were filled with fish; flocks of ducks swam around; birds delighted those who dwelt there with the sight of their green and yellow plumage and enchanted them with their songs. And there, in the caverns of the mountain, the Azteca had dwelt for unnumbered generations. All the good things they had had been brought from there – the maize, the beans, the fruits. For on the waters there were barges, and on the barges grew all nourishing things. And when the men and women of the Azteca went out of the caverns that were filled with precious stones they would go in canoes amongst the floating gardens, and watch the ducks swimming, the cormorants diving, the herons flying overhead; they would gather the bright flowers of the gardens and listen to the enchanting songs of the birds.

But Huizilopochtli roused up many to depart from that place; they left the mountain and their floating gardens, taking with them, however, many of the plants that grew in the gardens. They went upon the land. The herbs of the ground pricked them; the stones bruised their feet. Plains that were filled with thorns spread out before them. Jaguars lay in wait for them, and sprang upon stragglers and tore their flesh. But aroused by Huizilopochtli and guided by him the Azteca went on. They went through deserts where famine wasted them. Then they reached the Place of the Seven Caves where they rested and were at ease for a while. Then they came to where there was a tree broken by lightning, and there some stayed. Others went on, Huizilopochtli still guiding them. And at last they came to the Lake Tezcuco. They beheld a high rock with a cactus growing on it. Upon the cactus was an eagle. Up he rose; he flew towards the rising sun, and in his talons he held a serpent. The omen was good; the Azteca halted their march there. Many battles did they fight there; they subdued the tribes that dwelt in the valley, and they built Tenochtitlan, the greatest of cities.

And now the priests of Huizilopochtli, the ambassadors of Montezuma the Conqueror, travelled the ways back to Aztlan the White Place. In Tollan, which is the navel of the world, they found four magicians who guided them across the deserts. Then they beheld a mountain that rose out of the midst of waters. The priests went towards it, leaving the magicians behind them. The smell of flowers came to them on the airs of night; in the morning they heard the songs of birds. On they went, and they saw the gardens upon the water; they saw the flocks of ducks swimming around, and the cormorants diving from the juttings of the mountain, and the herons fishing or flying overhead. They saw the birds of green and yellow plumage flying from garden to garden, and they heard them singing from the branches of fruitful trees.

The people who were there spoke to them in a language that the priests knew, and asked them why they had come across deserts to them. The priests said that they had come back to the ancestral place. They brought to Coatlicue, they said, the sandals of her son Huizilopochtli.

But when the priests mentioned the name of Montezuma the Conqueror and mentioned the names of his lords, the people of the waters said that those who had gone from them in the old days had borne no such names. They named the lords who were with the Azteca when they went from Aztlan the White Place. Then the ambassadors of Montezuma said, "We know not these lords; we have never seen them; they are long since dead." Then the people of the waters were surprised, and they said, "We who knew them are living yet."

The priest of Coatlicue came to bring them into the presence of the Goddess. She lived on a peak of the mountain. As they went upward the feet of the men from Tenochtitlan sank in the ground, for the mountain became like a heap of loosened sand. "What makes you so heavy?" their guide asked them. He was an ancient, but he went lightly upon the ground. "What do you eat?" he asked them. "We eat flesh, and we drink pulque," the ambassadors of Montezuma answered him. "It is the meat and drink you have consumed that prevent your reaching the place where your fathers dwelt. Here we eat but fruits, and roots, and grain; we drink only water, and so there is no clog upon us when we walk." As he said this a swift wind came and brought him and brought the ambassadors up to the peak of the mountain and into the cavern where Coatlicue dwelt.

They saw her; her dress was of serpents, and they were terrified of her. When she looked upon the sandals they laid before her she lamented, saying, "When Huizilopochtli went from Aztlan he said to me, his mother, 'When my time is accomplished I shall return to your lap; until that time I shall know nought save weariness. Therefore, give me two pairs of sandals, one for going forth, and one for returning.' And now, you say, he will not return to this lap of mine." Then the Goddess put on a garment of mourning, and the ambassadors went from the cavern where she dwelt.

They did not think that they stayed long in Aztlan the White Place. But when they returned to Tenochtitlan they found that the years were again being tied into a bundle, that the fires of the land were quenched, and that a new fire was being lighted on the breast of a sacrificed man. A king who was called the Second Montezuma ruled over the Azteca. Many and dread portents showed themselves at that Tying of the Years. A fisherman caught a strange bird: a shining stone was in the head of that bird, and when that stone was brought to him, the Second Montezuma looked into it and he saw wars being waged against the Azteca in which strange and more death-dealing weapons than he had ever known were being used. And at the time of the quenching of the fires his sister had died; she had been buried, but now she was seen seated at a fountain in a garden of the palace. Montezuma and his lords went before her. She told them that she had been brought to the Eastern Sea. She had seen great ships upon the sea, and in the ships were fair-faced and bearded men who carried more death-dealing weapons than any that had ever been seen in the land of the Azteca. And after that a pillar of fire appeared in the east, and it seemed too cast fire upon the whole land. Rejoicings were heard amongst the captives, and lamentations were heard amongst the old men: it was thought that the pillar of fire in the east presaged the destruction of the Empire of the Azteca.

The Giant Pyramid-Builder

IF YOU TRAVEL THROUGH THAT BEAUTIFUL LAND of lakes and mountains north of the City of Mexico, you will hardly fail to visit the ancient sacred city of Cholula. Nor can you fail to marvel at the remains of that incredible Pyramid, four times as large as the famous Pyramid of Cheops in Egypt.

Cortes and his followers wondered at the fifty-acre structure nearly four centuries back. Humboldt measured it, studied it and speculated about it a hundred years ago. The general belief was that it had always been devoted to the worship of Quetzal, that Fair

God of old Mexico. But there were once wise ancients among the Acolhuan Indians who remembered the truth passed down by tradition from times immemorial.

This is the tale of the Pyramid-builder.

As everyone knows, for 4800 years after the creation of the world the land of Anahuac was inhabited by a race of vast giants. (Have not their mighty bones, dwarfing those of modern men, been dug up time and again through the centuries?)

These monsters were enemies both of gods and men. Fierce were the wars waged against them by the people of Tlascala, and many a giant was overcome by their multitudes, or driven forth into the wilderness to perish of starvation.

Always, however, there were enough of the dreadful race left to keep the land in an uproar; and particularly one Xelhua and his six brothers defied all attempts against them, holding themselves above laws, and doing only that which pleased their own ruthless cruelty. Very crafty as well as very strong they were, and the land of Anahuac groaned beneath their devastating tread. Finding there was none alive who might resist them, they waxed arrogant past belief, and scorned the very gods above, confident that there was no power in earth or heaven which could resist their will.

But at last the heavenly rulers grew wearied of this senseless tumult below. They determined to put an end to it all, and poured forth an overwhelming deluge on the earth. The clouds burst wide and precipitated their inexhaustible reservoirs; the irresistible ocean itself was loosed from its bounds; the underground rivers shot up from beneath the earth upon men and giants alike, and those who were not drowned were transformed into fishes.

All except crafty Xelhua and his six brothers: as the flood from above met the rising sea, they fled northward, climbed the lofty slopes of Mt. Tlaloc and hid themselves in seven caverns within its sides, rolling huge boulders in front of the openings to shut out the waters should they rise so high. Here they lay secure while the deluge raged unchecked throughout the universe.

When the appointed time came, the destroying waters withdrew to their stations above the clouds, beneath the earth, and in the ocean. Xelhua and his brothers came forth from their caves of refuge, the only living creatures, and by their arts peopled the earth with a new race, who were to be their servants.

They were now more arrogant than before – for had they not succeeded in evading the utmost wrath of the gods? So Xelhua, who was skilled in building, determined to erect a structure such as the world had not yet seen – to serve not only as a perpetual memorial of his triumph, but also as an easier means of escape from any future attempt made against him by the lords of the winds and waters.

On the plain of Cholula this edifice was staked out, four sided, in girth like some great hill, in height planned to pierce the very clouds aloft.

In far-away Tlamanalco, at the foot of the Sierra, a multitude of men were set to work at digging clay, shaping it in moulds, and burning it into bricks. Instead of having these heavy loads carried across the hills, Xelhua stationed a line of workmen all the way from the brickyard to Cholula: these passed the bricks from hand to hand continually, so that the builders never lacked a supply. Bitumen too was similarly brought from a great distance to plaster the bricks firmly in place.

Under the hands of these myriads of workers the foundation of the incredible Pyramid grew as if it were a living thing. Day by day it mounted upwards, and the heart of Xelhua waxed high with pride when even he had to climb laboriously to reach the dizzy level where the swarming ant-like labourers still built themselves aloft bodily. Looking upwards, he regretted that he had not planned an even larger base: for surely that was the only thing which in any way limited this monument to his power and guarantee of future security. There was one consolation: when this reached the apex of its sloping sides, he could build another, infinitely larger and loftier. Meanwhile, a future deluge must be worse than the former one to reach him upon the summit of this almost completed structure.

But the gods do not sleep, though they be long silent.

With rising wrath they beheld the growth of this presumptuous edifice and the increasing audacity of its builder. Still they bided their time, and the pyramid of Xelhua crept upwards till the low-hanging clouds often lay far beneath its upper courses.

The day came when a man might easily count the space of time still needed to complete the structure. Xelhua urged on his host of workers.

Then suddenly the heavens opened. A huge mass of flaming rock fell with irresistible force upon the proud pyramid and those that built it. The upper portion crashed down in ruins, carrying to destruction thousands of the labourers and the master-builder Xelhua himself.

Wherefore men doubted no longer that there were eternal powers on high. The fragment of the building which remained was dedicated thenceforth to the Fair God, Quetzal. And down to the time of that worthy Dominican, Pedro de los Rios, the priests showed to unbelievers a portion of the very thunderbolt, a stone shaped like a toad, which had confounded the mad presumption of Xelhua; while the dancing celebrants sang in their festival hymn the tale of these happenings, that reverence might no more perish among men.

Moreover, since that day the tribes have no longer spoken the same tongue, but each has a language of its own, unintelligible to the others.

The Walking Stone

THERE WAS A BEAUTIFUL YOUNG WOMAN by the name of Sawali Wiikit, or, 'Little Yellow Bird,' who had lovely, long hair, and eyes as shining as a star. But there was one thing about her that was bad. She was disobedient, and she liked to walk about with her friends at night without asking permission of either her father or her mother. She would walk about until dawn and then come home to sleep.

One day, very early in the morning, Sawali Wiikit came into the house to sleep. But before she could lie down her mother spoke to her, "Listen to me, Sawali Wiikit, I don't want you to walk about like this either in the nighttime or in the daytime. I want to you to help me with the things of the household. It would be well for you to stop walking about day and night."

Sawali Wiikit did not reply, but she planned in her heart to continue on her midnight walks in the company of men. She slept, and again at night she left the house. She went to the home of another woman who always went with her. This girl's name was Maso Hubi'aria. She didn't walk about at night, but she would serve Sawali Wiikit pitahaya wine there in her house. That night they drank and became intoxicated. By dawn, Sawali Wiikit was quite drunk on pitahaya wine. When she arrived home, her mother and her father spoke to her.

Her father said, "If you are not going to stop all of this vice and begin to respect your parents, then you will do me the favour of going away. Go anywhere you please."

"Yes, my father, I will go."

"Wait a moment," he said, and he went out of the house. The young girl waited, and her father soon returned carrying a long, flexible branch. With him came a maestro from the church of Rahum.

The maestro said to the girl, "So you think it better to leave your mother and father forever?"

"Yes," replied Sawali Wiikit.

Then the maestro said to her father, "Punish your daughter so that she will always remember you." So her father gave her three lashes. And he said, "Now you may go."

The maestro accompanied her out of Rahum to the north. Near a mesquite tree he said, "Here you may beg forgiveness of Dios for your sins and your disobedience. If Dios forgives you, you may return to your home."

"But I don't want to return."

"Well, then ask Dios for some penance."

So she knelt and said, "Dios, I do not want to return. I would rather become a tree or a stone or an animal. I do not want to be a good woman."

She had no more than finished speaking when she was changed into a stone.

The maestro went back to Rahum and told what had happened. All of the young people were frightened and were very good to their parents thereafter.

The stone of Sawali Wiikit walked from there to Rahum, to Guamuchil, to Potam, and toward Torim. Sometimes people would put it on top of a mesquite tree, but the next day they would find it somewhere else. Once they found it near Lencho, and they carried it to Torim and put it in front of the church. But it was not there at dawn. It is said that lately it has been seen in the vicinity of Vicam. This is the story of Sawali Wiikit, the walking stone. It ends here.

Five Friends of Takochai

THERE LIVED IN THE LAND OF THE YAQUI an Indian called Teta Hiapsi and he was very industrious. He enjoyed building good things. For this reason, he talked one day with a large group of Yaquis to see if they would work for him if he paid them a fair salary. In those days, there were no dollars, or half-dollars. Instead, the Yaquis used for money some silver discs, lacking any stamp, discs about four inches in diameter and an inch thick. They called them *te'okita*, which means pure silver. They also used similar discs of gold which they called *sawai tomi*, which is the same as saying yellow money.

All of the Indians wanted to work with Teta Hiapsi, so he put them to work cutting sticks and branches to make a *serco*, or fence. This *serco* was twenty-four kilometers in circumference and in its centre, a little creek ran all the time. In this corral there were lions, bears, tigers, and snakes of many sizes. In fact, Teta Hiapsi's *serco* surrounded an immense forest containing in it a number of water-holes.

Thus Teta Hiapsi considered himself very rich indeed. Also he had a cave, quite wide and deep, full of *te'okita* and *sawai tomi*. From it he paid his workers every Saturday.

One Saturday arrived and he paid all of his workers except one Yaqui whose name was Takochai. To Takochai he said, "You didn't get any money. So you may do anything you want to me to get even." Teta Hiapsi was a very curious man. He enjoyed jokes and pranks, and he knew that Takochai was a clever trickster. He knew that something would happen.

Well, Takochai went away to think of something to do to Teta Hiapsi to get even.

To a little stream which lies west of Cumuripa among some low hills, to a little valley fertile and picturesque, Takochai took his bow and arrows. In this place he met a big Indian. This Indian was so strong that to amuse himself he walked along tearing up mesquite trees by the roots as if they were onions. He would give one jerk and the tree with all its root would come up and he would toss it off into the distance. He did the same with sahuaros. This Yaqui was very strong.

Takochai came up to him and said, "What are you doing?"

"Oh, I'm just pulling up these little sticks," answered the Indian, Hoso Hoseli.

"May I go along with you?" asked Takochai.

"Why yes, it would give me pleasure," said Hoso Hoseli, and the two walked on a little distance together. It was late and they stopped to sleep under a tree.

The next day they took to the road again. They had only travelled a little distance when they met a Yaqui who was pointing an arrow at a mountain range which was so far away that it could hardly be seen.

"What are you doing?" asked Takochai.

"I wanted to kill a deer that was over there in those mountains, but you disturbed me and the deer has gone."

"Oh, but how distant are those mountains!" exclaimed Takochai. "They are barely visible."

"More distant deer have I killed," responded the hunter whose name was Mekkata'obia, which means 'Light that Illumines the Distance.' Takochai invited Mekkata'obia to come along with him and Hoso Hoseli, and the three adventurers went off.

They soon met a tall, thin Indian. He was standing on one foot holding a rope made of hide and tying the other leg which was doubled up. They saluted him and asked, "What are you doing, tying up your leg like that?"

He answered, "I am tying up this leg so I won't walk so fast. With two legs I run as fast as the wind, and with one tied I can walk about as fast as a light breeze." This Yaqui was called Yuku Beo'oti, or 'Lightning.' Takochai and Hoso Hoseli and Mekkata'obia invited Yuku Beo'oti to accompany them, and the four went on together. They went on until it was late and they stopped to sleep.

The next day they again took to the road. After walking only a short distance they met a very short little Yaqui who wore a skin cap. One side of this cap was decorated with red feathers and the other side with green ones. When he put it on with the red feathers to the right the weather became hot, and when he put it on with the green feathers to the right it became cold. He kept making this change every minute, never stopping. This little fellow was called Tasa'a Bali, which means 'Cool Summer.' He is called this because he made heat and cold by moving his headdress of two colours.

The four companions invited Tasa'a Bali to come along with them, and now there were five.

The next day they encountered a man on top of a little hill. He stood with his feet upon a rock and one hand against a tree. With the other hand he stopped up one of his nostrils. Through the other nostril he blew mightily, a volcano of air. The travellers came up to him and asked him what he was doing.

The man on the hill said that over on the other side of the green monte were many Yaquis milling earth and rock to take out the gold. "I make the mills run by blowing with this nostril. There are four mills for the stone and three to draw up water. When I stop blowing, those windmills stop. Right now while I am chatting, they are quiet."

His name was Hekkateni'a.

Takochai and his companions invited this great blower to come along with them.

So the six companions all went on to the *serco* of Teta Hiapsi.

Takochai greeted Teta Hiapsi and said, "I have come to bet with you, Teta Hiapsi, to win from you all that you own."

And Teta Hiapsi agreed to run a race.

Now, Teta Hiapsi had a daughter who was something of a witch woman. It was known that she knew how to fly like a bird. But Takochai was now the chief of five clever men.

Many Indians, men and women and boys, gathered to see the race between the witch and the swiftest of the companions, Yuku Beo'oti. Since Takochai had no money, he put up his life against this witch whose name was Sochik, meaning 'Bat.'

The race was to be from *ili bakam* to *bemela ba'am*, such a great distance that a man on a good horse travelling at a run does not arrive there in one long summer day.

The people gathered and the racers were ready. Someone gave the shout to start. Sochik flew off through the air as fast as she could, and Yuku Beo'oti disappeared like the wind. He soon arrived at *bemela ba'am*, filled his canteen with water and started back. This was the agreement. He who should arrive there and fill his canteen and be the first back in *ili bakam* was to win the race.

When Yuku Beo'oti was about half way back, he lay down to sleep, putting his head on a stump.

Sochik had hardly started for *bemela ba'am*. When she came upon Yuku Beo'oti and saw him sleeping, she threw the water out of his canteen and went on her way toward the waterhole. Then Mekkata'obia, from the great distance saw that the water had been thrown out and he shot an arrow into the tree trunk that served Yuku Beo'oti as a pillow. Yuku Beo'oti awoke and noticed that his water had been thrown out. Taking his canteen, he ran past Sochik to the waterhole, filled it, and returned to *ili bakam* with the water. Thus Yuku Beo'oti won the race and Sochik lost, for she arrived very late.

"I have lost," said Teta Hiapsi pleasantly. And he gave Takochai half of a cave full of silver and gold. "Now, in order for you to win from me all that I own, you and your men must sleep inside of that oven all night."

The oven was big and square. It was used to cook large animals in. There were no windows in it. It was on top of four big flat stones.

Takochai looked at the oven and said, "Very well, we shall all sleep there. And tomorrow you must give me all of your money and your well and your animals."

Takochai and his five companions entered the oven, and Teta Hiapsi, with the help of other Indians, covered it. They put firewood below and above and lit the fire and it burned all night.

When the men inside began to feel the heat, Tasa'a Bali put his cap on with the green side to the right and they felt no more heat.

Dawn came and Teta Hiapsi thought that they must be well cooked. But when he opened the door they all stepped out, alive and shivering from cold.

Thus Teta Hiapsi had to give all of the gold and silver in his cave to Takochai. The companions made a huge purse of many skins. In it they put the money and Hoso Hoseli tossed it up on his shoulders as if it were nothing. He was very strong, Hoso Hoseli, that man who pulls up mesquite trees.

"Now, let us go," said Takochai to his companions. "We will come back for the rest later." And they marched away in triumph.

Teta Hiapsi then gathered together some six hundred Yaquis to follow and kill Takochai and his men. But Mekkata'obia, who could see far, discovered them. The friends stopped at the foot of a little hill above a large plain.

When the Yaquis of Teta Hiapsi came across the plain, Takochai ordered Hekkateni'a, he of the great wind, to blow at them. Hekkateni'a covered one nostril and blew so strongly that the Yaquis were blown high into the air, very high. Then he stopped blowing and the Yaquis fell to the earth like stones. Here ends this tale.

The Snake People

LONG AGO THERE LIVED A YAQUI by the name of Habiel Mo'el. He was an orphan, but he had many relatives all over the Yaqui country. This man did not enjoy hunting as most young Yaqui men did. Instead, he liked lo travel from house to house and from pueblo to pueblo, attending fiestas and eating and chatting with his friends and relatives.

The only weapon he ever carried was a big, thick club. He lived at the foot of the hill, Mete'etomakame. One day he started out for Hekatakari where there was to be a little fiesta. When he came to Maata'ale, the monte became too thick for passage, and he turned around and went to Jori. From Jori, he cut across toward Bataconsica, where an arroyo empties into the Rio Yaqui. Travel there was very difficult, for the undergrowth was extremely dense. He crawled on his belly under branches, crawled over them, or pushed past them.

When he came upon a sort of clearing, a big snake appeared, crawling across his path. Habiel Mo'el hit the snake right in its middle, but it vanished into the underbrush before he could strike it again. So he continued on his path toward the ranchería at Hekatakari.

Suddenly, what had been nothing but thick monte stretching before him became a large Yaqui pueblo with many people in it, moving about their business. Habiel Mo'el felt very strange. As he walked between the houses, a *cabo* from the *guardia* came up to him. and greeted him.

He told Habiel Mo'el that his chief would like to see him at the *guardia*. So the two went over there. Inside, on the front bench was seated the head *kobanao*. On the next bench, Habiel Mo'el was told to seat himself. The other *kobanaom* were seated on the other benches. To one side a young girl was sitting. About her waist was a bandage of leaves.

The head kobanao spoke to Habiel Mo'el, "We have brought you here to ask you why you beat a girl this afternoon as you were travelling along between Jori and Bataconsica.

Habiel Mo'el was very surprised. He replied that from Jori to this place he had met no one on his journey. "I did not beat any girl," he said.

"You struck a girl this afternoon, and you are liable to punishment. Why did you do this?" insisted the *kobanaom*.

Habiel Mo'el could not remember having done so; and he repeated this. Then he explained where he had come from and his route, saying that he had seen no girl on the path. He respectfully asked their pardon, but insisted that he had done nothing at all.

The head kobanao turned to the girl, who was seated to one side, and asked her if this were the man who had beaten her.

"Yes," she answered. "'And he is still carrying the stick with which he beat me and almost killed me. That is the man."

Habiel Mo'el said that he had never seen the girl before and that he remembered nothing of it. He again asked their pardon, but disclaimed guilt. The *kobanaom* considered the matter among themselves.

Then the head *kobanao* said, "We will pardon you this once, since it is your first offense. But after this, when you are travelling, never harm anyone at all who may cross your path offering you no danger. You may go this time."

Habiel Mo'el thanked them and left the *guardia*. As he went out, he found himself in the middle of the *monte* with no sign of a village.

He travelled on toward his destination. It was dark when he arrived at Hekatakari and the house of his relative. He greeted the little old man whose name was Wete'epoi.

They sat down to a meal of pitahaya and Habiel Mo'el told Wete'epoi about his strange experience concerning the appearance and disappearance of the large Yaqui pueblo, and of his accusation.

The old man listened and then said, "You have done a great wrong. All animals, as well as people, have their authorities and their laws. You hurt a snake which crossed your path, doing you no harm. The authorities of that group took action against you. You must never again do that thing. The chiefs of the snakes met when the girl complained. They turned into people to punish you. I will give you some advice. Never hurt any snake, coyote, or any kind of animal, which is just crossing your path and offering no harm. If a snake lies coiled in the path, kill it. You are defending yourself then. But always kill it completely, never let it get away or it will complain and its chiefs will punish you."

Kaiman

DOWN ON THE YAQUI RIVER the waters of the sea once rose and reached far up into the *monte* where many things were growing, such as ***sinam***, ***choan***, and ***ono'em***. Among all these natural plants, the water came and carried with it the great turtle, Kaiman. Thus has it been said.

When the waters receded this great animal remained on the ground among the trees. And it could not raise itself.

After the flood, a Yaqui encountered this Kaiman stretched in the sun. When the Yaquis see such a thing, they always feel pity. This trait of the Yaquis is very stupid. The man placed the huge Kaiman on his shoulders. It was heavy. And he carried it to the river. Arriving at the bank, he entered the water up to his knees, and started to put the animal down into the water.

Kaiman then spoke, "There is very little water here. Would you be so kind as to carry me out a bit farther. I am very weak and hungry."

So the Yaqui carried him out until the water reached to his waist.

"Oh," said Kaiman, "farther than this, please, just a little farther."

"I can't walk very well," said the man, "but I will do what you ask." Until the water reached his neck, he carried the animal out and then put him down.

"I wish you might have carried me farther out," said Kaiman. "But this will do. Now I would like to ask the favour of eating you."

The man could not move. He said, "Are you not satisfied that I have done you a great favour? Why should you now want to eat me?"

"Don't you know that a good deed is always paid with evil?"

The man was very sad to hear this. He had no strength now. "Very well," he said, "But wait a minute. Over there comes someone who may know if it is right for you to eat me or not."

A dog appeared at the edge of the river to take a drink. The turtle spoke to the dog, saying, "Is it not certain that a good deed is always repaid with evil?"

"Why?" asked the dog.

"Because I should like to eat this man."

"Eat him, then. Man is bad. He beats us."

But the man said, "Wait. Here comes another friend of mine who might help me."

A horse came up. To him Kaiman said, "Is it not true that a good deed is paid with evil?"

"Why?" said the horse.

To him also, Kaiman said, "Because I wish to eat this man."

Said the horse, "Then eat him."

Then along came a goat, and other animals of the household. And every one of them answered, "Eat him."

Last of all came Coyote. Kaiman was getting restless and more and more hungry. But he said to Coyote, "It is true is it not, that a good deed is paid with evil?"

"What's that you say?" asked Coyote. "I am a bit deaf." Coyote had learned this trick from the Mexicans. "Come a little nearer. I can't hear a thing you say."

"Isn't it true that a good deed is paid with evil?" asked Kaiman, moving closer to Coyote. "I want to eat this man."

"What did this man do?" asks Coyote.

"He carried me into the deep water."

"Yes, I carried him here," said the man.

"And from where?" asks Coyote.

"From the *monte*."

"Well," says Coyote, "Let us go to the *monte*. There's where the trouble started." Then he asks, "And how did this man carry you?"

"Why, this way."

"Well, carry him that way, then," said Coyote to the man. So the man picked up Kaiman and carried him back to the *monte*.

"Here we are," says Kaiman.

"Well," says Coyote, "Put him down the way you found him." Then he asks, "Were you in that position?"

"Yes," replies Kaiman, "Like this."

"All right," says Coyote to the man, "leave him there. And don't ever pick up this kind of animal again."

And Coyote ate Kaiman.

The Big Bird

THIS IS Yaqui belief.

A great bird lived on the hill of Otam Kawi. Every morning he would fly out in search of food. He caught men, women and little children and carried them back to Otam Kawi to eat. In those days the people always were watchful. They couldn't have fiestas because when they had pascolas, always two or three of the people were carried away by the big bird. The Yaquis lived in *hu'ukis*, little houses made of mud and branches that looked like the house of a pack-rat, because they were afraid of the great bird.

There was an old man who earned his livelihood by hunting deer. He did nothing else. He had only one daughter. She was big with a child who was soon to be born, when the bird carried away her husband. The old hunter, his wife and the daughter only remained, and the daughter pregnant. The baby came in the afternoon.

It was a man child that the girl had. And the old grandfather continued hunting deer.

About a year later the grandmother went out early one morning to bring in water. The bird came by and carried her away. So the grandfather and the girl went on bringing up the child.

The next year the bird carried away the mother, and the grandfather brought the child up on cow's milk. There were cows in those days, but no animals of the claw.

When the little boy was old enough to walk, he went everywhere with his grandfather. He walked all over the *monte* hunting. This little boy never grew very big. When he was ten, he was still very small.

One afternoon he was seated outside of the house and he said, "I have no mother."

"Ah," said the grandfather, "The big bird carried her away. First he took your father, then your grandmother, then your mother."

"Where is that bird? I am going to grow up and kill that bird."

The old man laughed.

When the boy was older, his grandfather made him a bow and some arrows, and every day he went out practicing. He became very strong. But he was still small. When he was fifteen years old, he measured no more than three and a half feet in stature. He went everywhere with the old deer-hunter, his grandfather.

One day the boy said, "I am going to hunt out that bird. I am angry." When he was still not full-grown, he went about alone, walking through the *monte* and looking up into the sky.

There is a level plain east of Potam called *maretabo'oka'apo*. There the little boy walked. He had been hunting for three days. He carried many arrows in his quiver of javelina hide. Then he saw the bird. Quickly he jumped into a hole. The big bird sat down in a mesquite tree, waiting for him to come out of the hole. The boy stayed there all day long, watching the big bird in the mesquite tree. He saw everything; the size, the colours of the feathers, the big eyes, and all. At night he went farther back in the hole and fell asleep. Late at night he awoke. The bird had gone with the coming of night.

Three days later, the boy returned to his home, very late. His grandfather was not there. The boy carried two dark sticks on which he had placed many *pitahayas*. He hung them near the door where his grandfather would enter. The boy was inside cooking deer meat when the old man returned and saw the *pitahayas*.

As he entered he asked, "My son, where have you been?"

"Over in the hills."

"Weren't you afraid of the big bird?"

The little boy said, "I saw him. I saw all of his coloured feathers and his big eyes. I climbed into a hole. I return only to ask permission to kill the bird. This bow would never kill him. It is too little. I wish you would make me one of that wood called *kunwo*. And I need another kind of arrow, made of *wo'i baka*. I will go as soon as you make me these."

"But you are so little. That bird will kill you," said the old man.

Many Yaquis lived in the neighbourhood and they all came over that night to talk. They asked the little boy if he had really seen the big bird.

"Yes, I saw it. It has feathers of many colours, a big body, and long claws. I am going to make a lot of little animals out of that bird."

"This boy is crazy," said an old man. And many of the elders believed that he was. "But we'll see," said these older men. And they went back to their homes.

The old grandfather then made three kinds of *pinol*. The little boy had asked him to. He made *pinol* of corn, of wheat, and of garbanzas. When the little boy had this and his bow and arrows, he said, "Call the people together."

All of the people gathered, *kobanaom*, soldiers, women and children. Everybody came, from all of the eight pueblos. They said, "Are you the boy who is going to kill the big bird?"

"Are you the man?" laughed a kobanao.

"Yes," said the little boy.

Then an old man who lived near to Otam Kawi spoke. "Wait for this bird near Otam Kawi. He lives there. He only goes away to catch the people. He always comes back there. You will see there a great pile of bones."

The people bade the boy good-by that night, and he said to his grandfather, "Now I know I can kill that bird. I will be back in three days."

Everybody was content. "If you kill him, we can have *pascolas* again!"

The next day, before dawn, the boy and the grandfather left. At dawn, they saw the bird fly over. But they were safe below the mesquite trees. They walked through the *monte* toward Otam Kawi. "No farther than this," said the boy, Leave me here. I'm going to find out where the big bird roosts."

All day long the boy waited. At last he saw the bird come in and alight in a large tree. Night fell and the bird went to sleep. Then the boy softly approached the tree. There, he knelt and prayed for a long time. Then he began to measure. He measured twenty-five feet from the foot of the mesquite tree toward the west. There he made a deep hole, ten feet deep. When dawn came, he was still hunting poles and branches with which to cover it.

The bird saw him and was angry. The boy went down into the hole. He prepared his bow well. The bird came down from the mesquite tree and went to the cave. The boy was inside, looking out. He shot the big bird in the eye with an arrow.

The bird flew to the top of the mesquite tree. The boy shot three more arrows. The bird fell.

For a long time the boy did not come out of the cave. He waited to be sure that the bird was dead. When he was sure, he came out and went over to the big dead bird.

He pulled out a handful of its feathers and threw them into the air and the feathers became owls. With another handful of feathers he made smaller owls. With four handfuls of feathers, he made four classes of owls.

In the same way, with other handfuls of feathers, he made birds of every kind, crows and roadrunners. He threw the feathers and they became birds of different colours.

When he had finished all of the feathers, he cut off a piece of meat from the dead bird. He threw this and it became a mountain lion. He cut another piece and made another kind of lion, which is a little braver. With another he made the *topol*, and with another, a spotted cat. Thus, the boy made four classes of big cats. After that he made four smaller kinds of cats.

With more meat the boy made foxes and racoons and also four types of coyotes. He made snakes and all kinds of animals that have claws.

When all of the meat was gone, only bones remained. He dragged the bones under the mesquite tree and started home. He arrived there in two days. He came in very happily, dressed in a suit of feathers he had made from the bird, and he wore four feathers in his hat, two on either side.

He entered and his grandfather was frightened to see him covered with blood from the meat of the animal.

The old man was afraid, and he said, "What happened to you?"

"I killed the big bird. Now you may walk about the world."

The old man rushed out of the house. He talked with his neighbours who ran to advise those in other pueblos, and the people of those pueblos spread the news to others.

People came from all the eight pueblos. They still walked at night as before, because they didn't believe the big bird was dead. The governor came, and when all of the people were gathered the old men talked. "You really did kill it?" they asked.

"Yes, sirs. I made many little animals out of the feathers and the meat. I made owls of four kinds. I made four kinds of coyotes, four kinds of small cats, four kinds of lions, all animals of the claw."

"Well, let us see if this is true. We will send men from each pueblo, from Potam, from Vicam, from Torim, from Bacum, from Cocorit, Rajum, Juirivis and Belen to see the proof."

"The bones are there," said the little boy. "If they aren't you may cut my neck." And he led off on horseback. They all arrived and the boy showed them the hole he had dug. "From here I shot and hit him in the eye."

Along the road the people saw many animals, and little birds flying. The boy talked to the people, saying "These little birds don't do any harm to us. But those animals I made from the meat of the big bird, you must take care about those. From today on they are not going to be gentle. We no longer have danger from above. Now we must take care from below. These animals aren't much good for food, only for clothing. The birds are valuable only for their pretty feathers."

The men and the soldiers saw the bones of the big bird, and they went away contented, and in every pueblo began to make great fiestas.

The Death of Kutam Tawi

THERE LIVED in the pueblo of Potam a Yaqui captain named Tawachime'a. He had been a captain a long time when he married a very beautiful native girl with an enchanting appearance who was called Kuku Tosa, which means 'Dove Nest.' From this marriage a very handsome little Yaqui boy resulted.

As soon as this little boy was born, the captain Tawachime'a called together all of those men who were wise, those who knew how to divine certain things. He had them come to his hut, and he asked them to tell him what the destiny of his son would be, what luck was he to expect during his life. Above all, what was going to cause the boy's death and how long was he going to live. All of this, Tawachime'a desired to know.

Well, these intelligent men were united there for three days in order to divine. On the third day an ancient Yaqui named Chikul, which means 'Rat,' presented himself to the captain. "Do you truly wish to know?"

"Yes, Chikul," said the captain.

Then the old man, Chikul, seated himself on a log of cottonwood and he said, "Your son will be very intelligent but his destiny is bad. When he is fifteen years old, at midday, your son will die at the hands of a stranger."

Tawachime'a was studying in his mind how, in what manner, his only son might escape death. The son was called Kutam Tawi.

"However, continued Chikul, "this boy, if he is not dead at the age of fifteen, will live to the age of sixty-three."

The captain Tawachime'a gave credit to the ancient, for he knew that Chikul never told a lie. He brought out two bags. From one he took some native tobacco, *hiakbeibam*. He gave this to Chikul. From the other sack he took many discs of pure silver. And he said, "Chikul, take this little gift." And he gave Chikul the silver. Chikul took the gift and gave his thanks. Then the woman of Tawachime'a, Kuku Tosa, brought out an *olla* full of bee's honey and another full of wild seeds and a pair of tiger skins. She said to Chikul, "May Dios bless you."

"Many thanks," said the wise Chikul, and retired to his hut.

The young man, Kutam Tawi, grew. Eight days before he would be fifteen years of age, Tawachime'a and Kuku Tosa took him to the hill named Tohkobi 'iku. There they arrived, close to the foot of the sierra. Scratching the ground with his foot from side to side, Tawachime'a found a large flat stone. He took up the stone and they went down into a tunnel. An hour or so later Tawachime'a and Kuku Tosa came out again. They left Kutam Tawi there in order to save him from death.

But near-by a young Yaqui was hidden. He had just hidden there, filled with fear because of a struggle with some bad Yaquis. He had run away in order to escape sure death. The bad Yaquis were looking for him, saying, "Wherever you go, we'll get you out!" Thus the young Yaqui had come to hide close to the tunnel.

When Tawachime'a and Kuku Tosa had gone far away, the young man came out of his hiding place, opened the cave, entered and covered the entrance with the same stone. He presented himself to Kutam timidly, saying, "Please excuse me, brother, but I come here frightened. Some Yaquis want to kill me. Let me hide with you until I get over my fright and my enemies leave."

"Stay here with me," said Kutam Tawi. "My parents brought me here to stay until I am fifteen years old. It is foretold a stranger may kill me."

"And how many days until you are fifteen?"

"Six days," answered Kutam Tawi.

"Well, I must not stay here. I don't want to kill anyone."

"If you kill me, it would be the will of Dios. Stay here and be my companion until the day fixed for my death."

When the fatal day arrived, the boy Kutam Tawi was reposing on some lion skins. It was twelve minutes before twelve. He would die at twelve; thus was the prediction. Kutam Tawi, lying there, said to Kama Wiroa, "Will you bring me my spear.

The weapon was a piece of wood with a very fine point. Kama Wiroa picked up the spear. On coming up to Kutam Tawi, he tripped and fell. The weapon struck into the boy's heart, killing him instantly.

Kama Wiroa knelt on his knees and wept bitterly. He was weeping when Tawachime'a and Kuku Tosa arrived. They entered to find the young Yaqui kneeling and crying out loudly, "I have become a criminal without wishing it."

"Be it as Dios desires," they said.

They picked up the dead boy, and Kama Wiroa accompanied them to Potam where they buried him after a great fiesta and ceremony. Here ends this story.

The Bride of Huitzil

I

In Anahuac there reigned a king
Some fifty summers old,
The bloody darling of his gods,
Who sent him luck and gold

And captives from a thousand fights,
And victory in each war;
No mercy kept within his heart –
He trusted in his star.
But doubts began to sap his mind,
For he was growing old.
The gods he feared might turn unkind;
He gave them plundered gold
And hung their images with hearts
Like roses on a bride,
And all the young slaves from the marts
On Huitzil's altars died.
The priests got everything they sought.
They said the gods were wroth;
They had the rolls of tribute brought –
Chose bales of twisted cloth,
And cloaks of richest feather-work,
And opals set in gilt,
And many a keen obsidian knife
With carved and curious hilt,
And pearls for which their wives would quarrel,
And bags of cochineal,
And carefully matched and scarlet coral,
And chests of yellow meal,
And rainbow skins of quetzal birds,
Lip jewels, and each a ring;
And all they gave was doubtful words –
No comfort to the king.
Huitzil, they said, was sorely vexed;
Tlaloc would send no rain;
The more they kept the king perplexed
The more they had to gain.
"Gold I have given," said the king,
"And victims for the feasts;
What more is there that I can bring?"
"Bring beauty!" said the priests.
"Send runners swift to each cacique
With scrolls of your command;
In hut and palace bid them seek
Fair virgins through the land;
Then bring them here and choose the maid
Who most shall please your eyes,
And have her as your bride arrayed,
And led to sacrifice."
So buzzing rumor rose and spread
Like locusts through the land;
The king would choose a wife, men said:

And chiefs on every hand
Snatched maidens from the cotton-looms,
Girls, grinding maize for cakes,
Captives for Tenochtitlan,
The city 'mid five lakes.
Across the causeways, borne by slaves,
The trembling virgins came;
They saw the Smoking Hill that laves
Its molten sides in flame.
Canoes along the causeway's sides
Kept near; on rafts the throngs
Burned lamps to welcome home the brides;
Far rowers sang strange songs.
Now when the moon was fully grown,
The king left his abode
To sit upon the judgement throne
Set in the 'Place of God,'
Massive with polished seat of jade;
A skull was his footstool.
The arras on the wall was made
Of beasts' hair wove like wool.
There, while a scribe announced the dower,
The women came, so fair –
Young warriors whispered, and their plumes
Bent, nodding, as when air
Of summer stirs the fronded trees
Along a mountain wall,
Where pigeons' wooings lull the breeze
And snow-fed rivers fall.
And so they passed from morn till noon:
First came a princess in;
Like polished bronze beneath the moon
Was her smooth, olive skin;
But rumour in the market place
Told of a strangled lover,
Of silver masks made of his face;
The priests said, "Choose another!"
Then daughters of rich merchants came,
Dowered with silver T's.
With downcast eyes, they were too tame;
Huitzil would none of these.
And daughters of Tlascala's chiefs,
Bringing a precious dower –
Their fathers' friendship, with rich fiefs
Boasting a warlike power.
Pale girls from Huexotzinco's shades,
Where willows cool the air,

From far Tlaxcallan, sun-burned maids,
Bronzed in the cornfields there.
Girls from Cholula's pyramid,
Born by its terraced side –
The morning shadows waned and hid;
The king had found no bride!
Then came a maid straight as a spear,
Lithe as the bending maize
When only silk is in the ear;
Upon her eyes a haze.
She walked with all a panther's grace,
And like a pleasant tune
Her voice, and her round breasts were firm
As rosebuds in young June.
And as a cougar longs for meat,
The king desired the maid.
He cast an arrow at her feet –
A sign his choice was made.
The priests on twisted conch-shells blew,
Shouted the market place;
Hatred of Huitzil seized the king;
He loved the maiden's face.
She was a huntress, fair but poor,
Sleek puma skins her dower,
Traced through the jungle by their spoor
Past many a vine-closed bower,
Tracked to the hills and brought to bay,
Slain by the ice-green streams,
With the hissing arrow at break of day,
When the wakened eagle screams.
But when the high priest found the king
Had chosen her for bride,
He raged at heart to hear the thing –
"No dower" hurt his pride
And avarice; and straightway he sent
Down to the king's abode,
To say that sunset was the time
To bring her to the god.
The king's house rang with happiness
And sound of marriage gongs;
Ten maidens helped the bride to dress,
While slave girls sang old songs;
She was arrayed in cloaks of plumes
From birds of paradise,
Woven on feather-workers' looms,
More gorgeous than bright dyes,
Lined with the down of humming-birds,

Trimmed with the parrot's wing;
And compliments as smooth as curds
And jewels came from the king,
And gifts brought by his brother's wife
With well dissembled smile –
Wishes for children and long life
Whispered with subtle guile.
Meantime the king had gone aside,
His heart and brain at odds
Whether to keep his lovely bride
Or give her to the gods.
At sunset, in a silver litter
He brought her through the city,
Still doubtful, and his heart grew bitter
Struggling with fear and pity.
White flowers fell before the maiden –
He crushed them with his feet.
The air with garden scents was laden,
Mad dancers filled the street.
Before cruel Huitzil's pyramid
She waited for the king.
He loved her so, fear of the gods
Now seemed a foolish thing,
Something to laugh at and to scorn,
A sick thought he had dreamed,
Vaguely recalled at early morn –
So Huitzil's vengeance seemed.
Fresh courage flushed his veins, as spring
With new sap thrills an oak,
And he remembered he was king;
Never a word he spoke.
A grim smile sat upon his face;
He led her up the stair,
Up to the holy level space,
Where chanting smote the air.
Before the fire, priests knelt in lines.
A beast-mask was afoot:
Prayers droned like night-winds in the pines.
Painted with blood and soot,
The high priest cried, as though in prayer,
"Bring hither Huitzil's bride!
Be swift, point out the victim, king!"
And she smiled by his side.
Gazing about with narrowed eyes
Like puma's in the sun,
While priests prepared for sacrifice,
He saw his brother's son –

How merciful to send him death
And spare him life's sure pains –
Death's but a stupor at the worst,
A languor in the veins!
Straightway he pointed out the child,
Who instantly was hid
By the swift dancers – in a breath
Across the pyramid
They swept him to the waiting stone,
Bull-rattles drowned his cries;
Before he died, he saw his heart
Held up before his eyes.
The high priest raged behind his mask,
But yet he dared not falter.
He joined the king to Huitzil's bride
Before the god's own altar,
Knowing the king's cup must be full
And vengeance would abide.
That night the king laughed in his heart
And slept with Huitzil's bride.

II

The king held revels in the town
Next evening, and there came
Chieftains and minstrels of renown
To taste the roasted game
And drink strong mescal to the bride,
But there no priests were bid;
Scowling, the high priest hied him down
From Huitzil's pyramid
To the long palace in the town,
Where many litters fared,
And wrangling bearers set guests down,
And sputtering torches flared
With fluxing light along the walls,
And music's measured din
Sounded above the idlers' calls,
While rich guests hurried in.
The sentries talked before the doors,
But in a time of gloom
The priest sneaked in – down corridors –
Past many an empty room –
For all were at the king's repast;
Slaves near each darkened door
Slept by their earthen lamps. At last
He found upon the floor

The mother of the child he'd slain,
Pallid from many tears
Shed in her agony from pain
That scarcely dulls with years.
She knew him standing there.
Nothing was said.
Her face she covered with her hair
And lay as dead.
"Hail, mother," said the priest,
"Where is your little one,
The king's dead brother's son?
Does he sit with his uncle at the feast,
Whence they will bring him, sleepy, to your side?
Is he still smiling there
Where marriage torches flare,
And warriors drain the pulque to the bride?"
Then with a voice grown weak with many tears,
She spoke, as in a dream, and said,
"Yours was the hand that slew him on the stone –
You know that he is dead."
The far feasters shouted and he heard her moan.
"Yes," said the priest, "Mine was the hand,
But by the king's command, not mine he died.
He died in place of Huitzil's bride
And needs no funeral,
For now he serves the gods
In the high mountain glen
Where Huitzil sits at everlasting feast
And morning sunshine bathes the wall;
His spirit is at peace with them."
"It is his body that I want,"
The mother said, "His little feet –
Dear little feet, that I shall hear no more!
Each footfall was a stroke upon my heart;
His voice that called me 'mother' at the door;
What could the gods want with my child?
His shoes wait still and empty by the bed,
And his soft kisses I shall feel no more,
Oh, he is gone – is dead!"
And then the priest poured in her ear
How the high gods were wronged;
How he had slain the lad from fear,
And how the bride belonged
To Huitzil – and the ruthless king
Slept in a cursèd bed.
"He lives," she gasped – fire swept her brain –
"And my sweet son is dead!"

"Avenge yourself!" replied the priest,
"Arise, put gladness on,
Win near the king at his bad feast;
An hour before the dawn,
A priest will bring the holy dish,
The heart of your young son;
Persuade the king to grant this wish –
And your revenge is won:
Ask him to let you bless the sacrifice;
But you must choose
To taste the heart with him, lest otherwise,
Suspecting, he refuse;
But when you spread your hands to bless the dish,
Bless with your lips and curse within,
And pray to Huitzil for revenge,
And drop this in.
It is a subtle pearl of death;
No more by her soft side
In dalliance, with deep-taken breath,
The king shall seek his bride,
But sleep will lead him to the couch of death,
And death to strange abodes;
Then you will be revenged,
And I shall claim his loved one for the gods."
She rose, and washed away her tears.
And put bright colours on,
Long pendant ear-rings in her ears –
Meanwhile the priest had gone –
She clutched the poison in her hand,
Resolved to play her part,
And by the great door took her stand
While rage surged in her heart.
The room shone with a noonday glare –
Torches on silver urns –
Steam from hot dishes rose in air,
Wild songs were sung by turns;
Huge turkeys in their feathers dressed
Smoked down the crowded board;
From earthen jars behind each guest
Brown slaves the pulque poured.
She stood long by the entrance door
And listened to the feast,
Bronze spear-butts rang upon the floor
In honour to the priest
Who brought the king the holy meat,
Hot from the temple fires –
Huge dish to hide so small a heart!

"Silence!" proclaimed the criers.
The priest strode down the banquet hall,
The woman following after,
Chill silence fell upon them all.
The slave girls ceased their laughter.
He set the dish down, and they heard
The mumbled words of prayer.
The woman stood without a word;
No one could brave her stare.
Only a blind slave mouthed a bone.
A dog the silence broke –
Hunting in dreams, he gave a moan.
The king arose and spoke.
"Sister," he said, "what brings you here,
Where weeping has no place?
Have you no tears for your dead child?
I see none on your face."
"None;" said the woman, "I have wept,
But now I weep no more,
My tearful vigil has been kept.
Children have died before!
I come to show all Anahuac
No woman is above
Bearing her children for the gods.
Duty is more than love!
Therefore, give me the holy dish
To bless it to your use,
For that is all I ask – a wish
Custom can scarce refuse."
But the king tried the woman's soul,
Delayed, and shook his head,
And held aloft the steaming bowl,
Pondered awhile, and said,
"Sup with me from the holy dish.
If you but taste the heart,
Then you may bless it as you wish,
And afterward depart."
"Yea," said the woman, "I will taste
The heart of my own son
If I may bless it; but make haste,
The night is nearly done."
Smiling, he took away the cover.
She gave a cry and start,
Then spread her hands and held them over
The little smoking heart.
Trembling, she blessed with hands outspread,
But writhed and cursed within

And prayed for vengeance on his head –
And dropped the sleep-pearl in.
Then stifling horror in her soul,
She tasted of the heart.
And then the king supped from the bowl,
And let her straight depart.
She sought her lonely, shadowed room,
And there, with fluttering breath,
She blew the light out, and in gloom
Slept to a welcome death.
Then a slave struck upon a gong,
And each guest
Departed with much talk,
And some with song;
And the bride left with her maidens
To their rest.
But the king sat sleeping there alone.
The torches died away,
Glimmering to their sockets in the stone,
While far dogs bayed
The last belated revelers going home.
Only the blind slave sat behind the door,
Mumbling an endless tune,
Peering with eyeballs dim;
Outside there sank the moon,
But light and darkness were alike to him.

III

And no one dared awake the king –
He slept – to him it seemed
White vapour covered everything,
And through its rifts there gleamed
A figure striding through the mist;
Dimly he saw the head,
The white skull set with turquoise stones,
The goddess of the dead.
Now at the hour before the dawn,
When owlets cease to call,
He put a cloak of black skins on
And walked forth from the hall,
Across the terrace, down the stair,
Along an empty street,
Where the lone watchman felt his hair
Rise at the soundless feet.
But to the dying king it seemed
As though he moved with ease

Upon a journey he had dreamed –
No weight above his knees –
So from his house he passed away,
Down to the stony strand
Where the black water of the lake
Whimpered against the land.
And there he hailed a boatman dim
Who gave a toothless scream
And motioned to wade out to him;
Cold as a mountain stream
He felt the lake rise to his chin;
It seemed to strike him through
And freeze his heart – but he plunged in,
And clutched the black canoe.
And the blind boatman helped him up,
Gave him a drink of blood;
Far in the lake he tossed the cup,
And straight across the flood
They moved like stars across the night,
Passing a fisher's raft
Where, seated by a flickering light,
A brown child sat and laughed,
Kissing again her painted doll;
She screamed at the strange sight –
The shadowy boatman tall –
The boat as black as night.
And they passed fishermen's canoes,
Anchored in shallow spots
Where nets were staked – among the crews
Fires glowed in earthen pots –
And chinampas, where in tended rows
White, cherished orchids grew.
They saw far mountain snows
Glimmer against the blue
Of night that now turned faintly gray,
And the wide lake grew flushed
With the first scarlet of the day
As on they rushed.
But the king looked toward the shore,
And saw they left no wake.
The long streak gleamed that shows before
The sun bursts on the lake.
Vague lay the city and the land,
Veiled by a rain – or tears –
Where he had ruled with ruthless hand –
Dreams mirrored back dead years:
Childhood – and little shells brought to his mother.

On the beach at sunset when the lake grew dark;
Young faces of his playmates in old days,
And the first lusts of his strong youth.
The look of his first love, now long since dead;
And walks among the maize fields with his friend,
And that great day the high priest hailed him king –
Long lines of warriors charging home, with streaming feathers,
And the crash of shields,
The spurting arc of blood from one he smote
upon the neck in battle;
Houses and streets, and sights;
And cunning thoughts, and plans that
he had made in the dim city
There across the lake,
That he should see no more.
But now they neared a porphyry cliff
Where lingered blacker night,
And from the prow of the dark skiff
The king beheld a light
That burned upon a landing place
Where a stream cleft the land,
And the torch showed his nephew's face
Shaded by one small hand.
There the king leaped ashore,
And followed up the steep ravine.
The naked child went on before;
On pools there fell the sheen
Of his young body in the light,
And the king heard his echoed calls
And followed after through the night,
Up slippery waterfalls
On rough steps hollowed by the stream,
Up to the high plateaus
Where far across the valley gleam
Iztaccihuatl's snows.
Then they glowed ruddy in the dawn
And the valley, one huge cup,
Lay shining, city and lake and lawn;
The sun was coming up.
In the morning light they stood alone
Upon a spine-like crest,
And the child took a jagged stone
Out from his empty breast,
And said, "The gods have sent you this;
They bid you to their feast.
The place you will not miss:
It lies due east."

Then in the shadows of the place
He seemed to melt away
As a smile fades from the face –
And it was day.
But the king pressed on across the plain
Where in long, dusty lines
The sand blew, for there fell scant rain;
The lizard with sharp spines
Hid mid the myriad cactus thorns,
And swifts would dart and cling,
And the toad blinked beneath his horns,
And birds never sing.
Ever the king rose higher,
Where gila monsters slept by dens
And the slopes grew drier –
Into the huge and solitary glens,
Wounds of a lonely world,
About whose beetling cliffs
The little clouds lay curled.
Framed at the end of one long vale
Was cleft a narrow gate,
A rocky entrance to the dale,
The only break
In the black cliffs to left and right;
It looked into the sky
As one square window frames the light.
To this the king drew nigh.
Suddenly he heard
The sound of stricken metal,
Like a spoken word,
And loud ringing gongs,
The shivering clash
Of cymbals, and the crash
Of drums, and timbrels with the noise
Of piping, and shrill songs of gelded boys.
Around, around him swept a howling rout
Of dancers in the masks of beasts,
With toss of feet and arms about
Like crazy drinkers at wild feasts;
These swept him to the gate, and there
Back to the rock caves fled,
Leaving flat silence on the air
And a dumb dread.
But through the gate he made his way,
Cut in the hill's midriff,
And found the sun with whitest day
Beating upon a cliff

That fell sheer to the valley dim;
And when the clouds would lift,
He saw the far landscape swim
Glimmering through the rift.
Then, reeling from the gaping height,
Back through a lava alley,
Stumbling on rocks in the half-light,
He came into a valley,
The hollow of a cup-shaped hill,
Where the long clouds lay
And all was gray and still.
There at their everlasting feast,
Around a table carved about
With many a tigerish beast
And faces, heavy-lipped, that pout
In stone, the gods sat –
Totec, parrot-faced, with stony stare,
And the water goddess fat,
With writhing serpents in her hair;
Huitzil, with flickering plumes
Of waving fire above his head,
And white-skulled Coatlicue,
The goddess of the dead;
Tlaloc, god of rain, with beryl eyes,
Who gloats on children brought
And slain to him with dismal cries,
In withering times of draught;
And Tezcat, lord of sharp obsidian,
And Quetzalcoatl with his golden curls,
Worshipped at Tlacopan
With sacrifice at noontide hours
Of copal gum, while girls
Bring heaps of fruit and flowers.
In blue folds his snake was curled,
The holy snake with crest
Of feathers, lord of this green world,
Swathed in a rustling nest
Of maize leaves – the wise god,
That makes the rain, and harvest wave,
And the grain ripen in the pod.
Now a desperate courage seized the king;
He dropped his warrior's cloak
And threw away his plumes and ring,
Drew near, and spoke:
"Naked to judgement, Merciless Ones, I come,
Nor fear the tomb,
Knowing that what I did was done

By your own doom."
Then the gods counseled among themselves,
Muttering like summer thunder,
As when the distant earthquake delves
Beneath the hills, and wonder
Falls on the cities of the plain
At the vast, rocking rumble –
Then terror, and men flee in vain,
And the high towers tumble.
So spoke the gods, and a thick gloom
Came upon everything
While the serpent hissed their doom
Upon the king.
"One act of mercy spoils a life
Of fragrant slaughter full.
Since you are nothing –
Neither merciless nor merciful,
Your doom is this:
You shall be hurled
From a cliff
And this good world to nothingness."
So spoke the serpent in a hiss.
Then Huitzil seized a monster spear
And drove the king along the path.
His soul now first knew fear
At the beast laugh
The gods gave – once he looked back,
But following after,
Huge Huitzil strode upon his track,
Shaking with laughter.
Now the far valley burst upon his view
With rolling hill and plain,
Cloud-shadowed to the mountains blue.
He stood upon the cliff again –
Tottered – and heard an eagle scream –
Then suddenly he seemed to fall
As one falls in a dream.
Down in the palace in the town,
The king's body stirred and cried
A fearful cry, and startled slaves ran in;
And rumour spread that he had died.
Then came a loud uproar
And the priests raged outside,
And with stone hammers smote upon the door
And Huitzil claimed his bride.

Sacrifice of the Toltecs

CENTURIES AGO, when Toltec civilization had extended over Arizona, and perhaps over the whole West, the valleys were occupied by large towns – the towns whose ruins are now known as the City of Ovens, City of Stones, and City of the Dead. The people worked at trades and arts that had been practised by their ancestors before the pyramids were built in Egypt. Montezuma had come to the throne of Mexico, and the Aztecs were a subject people; Europe had discovered America and forgotten it, and in America the arrival of Europeans was recalled only in traditions. But, like other nations, the Toltecs became a prey to self-confidence, to luxury, to wastefulness, and to deadening superstitions. Already the fierce tribes of the North were lurking on the confines of their country in a faith of speedy conquest, and at times it seemed as if the elements were against them.

The villagers were returning from the fields, one day, when the entire region was smitten by an earthquake. Houses trembled, rumblings were heard, people fell in trying to reach the streets, and reservoirs burst, wasting their contents on the fevered soil. A sacrifice was offered. Then came a second shock, and another mortal was offered in oblation. As the earth still heaved and the earthquake demon muttered underground, the king gave his daughter to the priests, that his people might be spared, though he wrung his hands and beat his brow as he saw her led away and knew that in an hour her blood would stream from the altar.

The girl walked firmly to the cave where the altar was erected – a cave in Superstition Mountains. She knelt and closed her eyes as the officiating-priest uttered a prayer, and, gripping his knife of jade stone, plunged it into her heart. She fell without a struggle. And now, the end.

Hardly had the innocent blood drained out and the fires been lighted to consume the body, when a pall of cloud came sweeping across the heavens; a hot wind surged over the ground, laden with dust and smoke; the storm-struck earth writhed anew beneath pelting thunder-bolts; no tremor this time, but an upheaval that rent the rocks and flung the cities down. It was an hour of darkness and terror. Roars of thunder mingled with the more awful bellowing beneath; crash on crash told that houses and temples were falling in vast ruin; the mountainsides were loosened and the rush of avalanches added to the din; the air was thick, and through the clouds the people groped their way toward the fields; rivers broke from their confines and laid waste farms and gardens! The gods had indeed abandoned them, and the spirit of the king's daughter took its flight in company with thousands of souls in whose behalf she had suffered uselessly.

The king was crushed beneath his palace-roof and the sacerdotal executioner perished in a fall of rock. The survivors fled in panic and the Ishmaelite tribes on their frontier entered their kingdom and pillaged it of all abandoned wealth. The cities never were rebuilt and were rediscovered but a few years ago, when the maiden's skeleton was also found. Nor does any Indian cross Superstition Mountains without a sense of apprehension.

Aztec Hymns

THIS COLLECTION OF HYMNS comes from ***Rig Veda Americanus***, which Daniel G. Brinton (1837–99) named "after the similar cyclus of sacred hymns, which are the most venerable product of the Aryan mind" and took from sixteenth-century missionary and ethnographer Bernardino de Sahagún's ***Historia general de las cosas de la Nueva España***. They are "sacred songs of the ancient mexicans" translated from nahuatl. Brinton offers his translation "with the utmost reserve… All that I hope to have achieved is … to give a general idea of the sense and purport of the originals."

He goes on to point out that "the desirability of preserving and publishing these texts seems to me to be manifest. They reveal to us the undoubtedly authentic spirit of the ancient religion; they show us the language in its most archaic form; they preserve references to various mythical cycli of importance to the historian; and they illustrate the alterations in the spoken tongue adopted in the esoteric dialect of the priesthood. Such considerations will, I trust, attract the attention of scholars to these fragments of a lost literature."

The Hymn of Huitzilopochtli

Huitzilopochtli is first in rank, no one, no one
is like unto him: not vainly do I sing (his praises) coming
forth in the garb of our ancestors; I shine; I glitter.
He is a terror to the Mixteca; he alone destroyed the Picha-Huasteca, he conquered them.
The Dart-Hurler is an example to the city, as he sets to work. He who
commands in battle is called the representative of my God.
When he shouts aloud he inspires great terror, the divine hurler, the god turning
himself in the combat, the divine hurler, the god turning himself in the combat.
Amanteca, gather yourselves together with me in the house of war
against your enemies, gather yourselves together with me.
Pipiteca, gather yourselves together with me in the house of war
against your enemies, gather yourselves together with me.

The War Song of the Huitznahuac

What ho! my work is in the hall of arms, I listen to no mortal, nor can any put
me to shame, I know none such, I am the Terror, I know none other, I am where
war is, my work is said to be in the hall of arms, let no one curse my children.
Our adornment comes from out the south, it is varied in colour as the clothing of the eagle.
Ho! ho! abundance of youths doubly clothed, arrayed in feathers, are my
captives, I deliver them up, I deliver them up, my captives arrayed in feathers.
Ho! youths for the Huitznahuac, arrayed in feathers, these are my captives,
I deliver them up, I deliver them up, arrayed in feathers, my captives.
Youths from the south, arrayed in feathers, my captives, I deliver
them up, I deliver them up, arrayed in feathers, my captives.

The god enters, the Huitznahuac, he descends as an example, he
shines forth, he shines forth, descending as an example.
Adorned like us he enters as a god, he descends as an example,
he shines forth, he shines forth, descending as an example.

The Hymn of Tlaloc

In Mexico the god appears; thy banner is unfolded in all directions, and no one weeps.
I, the god, have returned again, I have turned again to the place of abundance
of blood-sacrifices; there when the day grows old, I am beheld as a god.
Thy work is that of a noble magician; truly thou hast made thyself to
be of our flesh; thou hast made thyself, and who dare affront thee?
Truly he who affronts me does not find himself well with me;
my fathers took by the head the tigers and the serpents.
In Tlalocan, in the verdant house, they play at ball, they cast the reeds.
Go forth, go forth to where the clouds are spread abundantly,
where the thick mist makes the cloudy house of Tlaloc.
There with strong voice I rise up and cry aloud.
Go ye forth to seek me, seek for the words which I have said, as I rise, a terrible one, and cry aloud.
After four years they shall go forth, not to be known, not to be numbered, they
shall descend to the beautiful house, to unite together and know the doctrine.
Go forth, go forth to where the clouds are spread abundantly,
where the thick mist makes the cloudy house of Tlaloc.

Hymn to the Mother of the Gods

Hail to our mother, who caused the yellow flowers to blossom, who
scattered the seeds of the maguey, as she came forth from Paradise.
Hail to our mother, who poured forth flowers in abundance, who
scattered the seeds of the maguey, as she came forth from Paradise.
Hail to our mother, who caused the yellow flowers to blossom, she who
scattered the seeds of the maguey, as she came forth from Paradise.
Hail to our mother, who poured forth white flowers in abundance, who
scattered the seeds of the maguey, as she came forth from Paradise.
Hail to the goddess who shines in the thorn bush like a bright butterfly.
Ho! she is our mother, goddess of the earth, she supplies food
in the desert to the wild beasts, and causes them to live.
Thus, thus, you see her to be an ever-fresh model of liberality toward all flesh.
And as you see the goddess of the earth do to the wild beasts,
so also does she toward the green herbs and the fishes.

Hymn to Chimalipan in Parturition

Chimalipan was a virgin when she brought forth the adviser of battles;
Chimalipan was a virgin when she brought forth the adviser of battles.
On the Coatepec was her labour; on the mountain he ripened into age; as
he became a man truly the earth was shaken, even as he became a man.

Hymn to Ixcoçauhqui

In the Hall of Flames let me not put to shame my ancestors;
descending there, let me not put you to shame.
I fasten a rope to the sacred tree, I twist it in eight folds, that
by it I, a magician, may descend to the magical house.
Begin your song in the Hall of Flames; begin your song in the Hall of
Flames; why does the magician not come forth? Why does he not rise up?
Let his subjects assist in the Hall of Flames; he appears, he appears, let his subjects assist.
Let the servants never cease the song in the Hall of Flames;
let them rejoice greatly, let them dance wonderfully.
Call ye for the woman with abundant hair, whose care is the mist and the rain, call ye for her.

Hymn of Mixcoatl

I come forth from Chicomoztoc, only to you, my friends, to you, honoured ones.
I come forth from Tziuactitlan, only to you my friends, only to you honoured ones.
I sought, I sought, in all directions I sought with my pack; in all directions I sought with my pack.
I sought, I sought, in all directions I sought with my travelling net.
I took them in hand, I took them in hand; yes, I took them in hand; yes, I took them in hand.
In the ball ground I sang well and strong, like to the quetzal bird; I answered back to the god.

Hymn to Xochipilli

O friends, the quetzal bird sings, it sings its song at midnight to Cinteotl.
The god will surely hear my song by night, he will hear my song as the day begins to break.
I send forth the priests to the house of Tlaloc.
The priests to the house of Tlaloc do I send forth.
I shall go forth, I shall join myself unto them, I shall go
where is Cinteotl, I shall follow the path to him.
The priests go forth to the house of Tlaloc, to the home of the gods of the plain.

Hymn to Amimitl

Join together your hands in the house, take hands in the sequent course,
let them spread forth, spread forth in the hall of arrows. Join hands,
join hands in the house, for this, for this have I come, have I come.
Yes, I have come, bringing four with me, yes I have come, four being with me.
Four noble ones, carefully selected, four noble ones, carefully selected, yes, four noble ones.
They personally appear before his face, they personally appear
before his face, they personally appear before his face.

Hymn of Olontecutli

At Nonoalco he rules, at Nonoalco, Oho! Oho!
In the pine woods he prepares your destruction at Nonoalco, in the
tuna woods, in the cacao woods he prepares your destruction.

I, dweller in the palace, shook them; I, Quetzalcoatl, shook them.
There was a splendour of spears, a splendour of spears.
With my captain, with my courage, with my skill, the Mexicans were
put to flight; even the Mexicans, with my courage, with my skill.
Go forth, ye shield bearers, put the Mexicans to flight
with my courage, with my skill.

Hymn to Ayopechcatl

Truly in whatever house there is a lying-in, Ayopechcatl takes charge of the child.
Truly in whatever house there is a lying-in, Ayopechcatl takes
charge of the child, there where it is weeping in the house.
Come along and cry out, cry out, cry out, you new comer, come along and cry out.
Come along and cry out, cry out, cry out, you little jewel, cry out.

Hymn to Cihuacoatl

Quilaztli, plumed with eagle feathers, with the crest of eagles, painted
with serpents' blood, comes with her hoe, beating her drum, from Colhuacan.
She alone, who is our flesh, goddess of the fields
and shrubs, is strong to support us.
With the hoe, with the hoe, with hands full, with the hoe, with
hands full, the goddess of the fields is strong to support us.
With a broom in her hands the goddess of the fields strongly supports us.
Our mother is as twelve eagles, goddess of drum-beating, filling
the fields of tzioac and maguey like our lord Mixcoatl.
She is our mother, a goddess of war, our mother, a goddess of war, an
example and a companion from the home of our ancestors (Colhuacan).
She comes forth, she appears when war is waged, she protects us
in war that we shall not be destroyed, an example and
companion from the home of our ancestors.
She comes adorned in the ancient manner with the eagle
crest, in the ancient manner with the eagle crest.

Hymn to Chicomecoatl

O noble Chicomolotl, arise, awake, leave us not unprotected
on the way, conduct us to the home of Tlaloc.
Arise, awake, leave us not unprotected on the way,
conduct us to the home of Tlaloc.

Hymn to Xochiquetzal

I, Xochiquetzal, go forth willingly to the dancing place by the
water, going forth to the houses in Tamoanchan.
Ye noble youths, ye priests who wept, seeking
Xochiquetzal, go forth there where I am going.

Hymn of the Eight-yearly Fasting on Bread and Water

The flower in my heart blossoms and spreads abroad in the middle of the night.
Tonan has satisfied her passion, the goddess Tlazolteotl has satisfied her passion.
I, Cinteotl, was born in Paradise, I come from the place of
flowers. I am the only flower, the new, the glorious one.
Cinteotl was born from the water; he came born as a mortal, as a
youth, from the cerulean home of the fishes, a new, a glorious god.
He shone forth as the sun; his mother dwelt in the house of the dawn,
varied in hue as the quechol bird, a new, a glorious flower.
I came forth on the earth, even to the market place like a
mortal, even I, Quetzalcoatl, great and glorious.
Be ye happy under the flower-bush varied in hue as the quetzal bird;
listen to the quechol singing to the gods; listen to the singing of the quechol
along the river; hear its flute along the river in the house of the reeds.
Alas! would that my flowers would cease from dying; our flesh
is as flowers, even as flowers in the place of flowers.
He plays at ball, he plays at ball, the servant of marvellous
skill; he plays at ball, the precious servant; look at him; even
the ruler of the nobles follows him to his house.
O youths! O youths! follow the example of your ancestors; make yourselves
equal to them in the ball count; establish yourselves in your houses.
She goes to the mart, they carry Xochiquetzal to the mart; she speaks
at Cholula; she startles my heart; she startles my heart; she has not
finished, the priest knows her; where the merchants sell green jade
earrings she is to be seen, in the place of wonders she is to be seen.
Sleep, sleep, sleep, I fold my hands to sleep, I, O woman, sleep.

Hymn of the High Priest of Xipe Totec

The nightly drinking, why should I oppose it? Go forth and array yourselves
in the golden garments, clothe yourselves in the glittering vestments.
My god descended upon the water, into the beautiful glistening
surface; he was as a lovely water cypress, as a beauteous
green serpent; now I have left behind me my suffering.
I go forth, I go forth about to destroy, I, Yoatzin; my soul is in the
cerulean water; I am seen in the golden water; I shall appear
unto mortals; I shall strengthen them for the words of war!
My god appears as a mortal; O Yoatzin, thou art seen upon the mountains;
I shall appear unto mortals; I shall strengthen them for the words of war.

Hymn to Yacatecutli

I know not what is said, I know not what is said, what is said
about Tzocotzontlan, I know not what
is said about Tzocotzontlan.

I know not what is said of Pipitlan, what is said of Pipitlan, nor
what is said of Chollollan, what of Pipitlan, of Pipitlan.
Now I seek our food, proceeding to eat it and to drink
of the water, going to where the sand begins.
Now I go to my beautiful house, there to eat my food, and to
drink of the water, going to where the sand begins.

The Hymn of Atlaua

I Chalmecatl, I Chalmecatl, I leave behind my sandles,
I leave my sandles and my helmet.
Go ye forth and follow the goddess Quilaztli, follow her
I shall call upon thee to arise when among the
shields, I shall call upon thee to arise.
I boast of my arrows, even my reed arrows, I
boast of my arrows, not to be broken.
Arrayed in priestly garb, take the arrow in thy hand, for even
now I shall arise and come forth like the quetzal bird.
Mighty is my god Atlaua; truly I shall arise and come forth like the quetzal bird.

Hymn to Macuilxochitl

Yes, I shall go there tonight, to the house of flowers; I
shall exercise the priestly office tonight.
We labour in thy house, our mother, from dawn unto night,
fulfilling the priestly office, labouring in the night.
A dreadful god is our god Tezcatlipoca, he is the only god, he will answer us.
His heart is in the Tezcatzontli; my god is not timid like a hare nor is he
peaceable; I shall overturn, I shall penetrate the Mixcoatepec in Colhuacan.
I sing, I play on an instrument, I am the noble instrument, the mirror; I am
he who lifts the mirror; I cry aloud, intoxicated with the wine of the tuna.

MAYAN MYTHS

Introduction

OUR KNOWLEDGE OF THE MYTHOLOGY of the Maya is by no means so full and comprehensive as in the case of Mexican mythology. Traditions are few and obscure, and the hieroglyphic matter is closed to us. But one great mine of Maya-Kiche mythology exists which furnishes us with much information regarding Kiche cosmogony and pseudo-history, with here and there an interesting allusion to the various deities of the Kiche pantheon. This is the *Popol Vuh*, a volume in which a little real history is mingled with much mythology. It was composed in the form in which we now possess it by a Christianised native of Guatemala in the seventeenth century, and copied in the original Kiche by one Francisco Ximenes, a monk, who also added to it a Spanish translation.

The entire work bears the stamp of being a purely native compilation, and has a flavour of great antiquity. The name *Popol Vuh* means 'The Collection of Written Leaves,' which proves that the book must have contained traditional matter reduced to writing at a very early period. It is, indeed, a compilation of mythological character, interspersed with pseudo-history, which, as the account reaches modern times, shades off into pure history and tells the deeds of authentic personages. The beginning of this interesting book is taken up with the Kiche story of the creation, and what occurred directly subsequent to that event. Here we will focus on the most captivating tales.

The Mayan Creation Story

WE ARE TOLD THAT THE GOD HURAKAN, the mighty wind, a deity in whom we can discern a Kiche (Mayan from Guatemala) equivalent to Tezcatlipoca, passed over the universe, still wrapped in gloom. He called out "Earth," and the solid land appeared.

Then the chief gods took counsel among themselves as to what should next be made. These were Hurakan, Gucumatz or Quetzalcoatl, and Xpiyacoc and Xmucane, the mother and father gods. They agreed that animals should be created. This was accomplished, and they next turned their attention to the framing of man. They made a number of mannikins carved out of wood. But these were irreverent and angered the gods, who resolved to bring about their downfall.

Then Hurakan (The Heart of Heaven) caused the waters to be swollen, and a mighty flood came upon the mannikins. Also a thick resinous rain descended upon them. The bird Xecotcovach tore out their eyes, the bird Camulatz cut off their heads, the bird Cotzbalam devoured their flesh, the bird Tecumbalam broke their bones and sinews and ground them into powder. Then all sorts of beings, great and small, abused the mannikins. The household utensils and domestic animals jeered at them, and made game of them in their plight. The dogs and hens said: "Very badly have you treated us and you have bitten us. Now we bite you in turn." The millstones said: "Very much were we tormented by you, and daily, daily, night and day, it was squeak, screech, screech, holi, holi, huqi, huqi, for your sake. Now you shall feel our strength, and we shall grind your flesh and make meal of your bodies." And the dogs growled at the unhappy images because they had not been fed, and tore them with their teeth. The cups and platters said: "Pain and misery you gave us, smoking our tops and sides, cooking us over the fire, burning and hurting us as if we had no feeling. Now it is your turn, and you shall burn."

The unfortunate mannikins ran hither and thither in their despair. They mounted upon the roofs of the houses, but the houses crumbled beneath their feet; they tried to climb to the tops of the trees, but the trees hurled them down; they were even repulsed by the caves, which closed before them. Thus this ill-starred race was finally destroyed and overthrown, and the only vestiges of them which remain are certain of their progeny, the little monkeys which dwell in the woods.

Vukub-Cakix, the Great Macaw

ERE THE EARTH WAS QUITE RECOVERED from the wrathful flood which had descended upon it there lived a being orgulous and full of pride, called Vukub-Cakix (Seven-times-the-colour-of-fire – the Kiche name for the great macaw bird). His teeth were of emerald, and other parts of him shone with the brilliance of gold and silver. In short, it is evident that he was a sun-and-moon god of prehistoric times. He boasted dreadfully, and his conduct so irritated the other gods that they resolved upon his destruction. His two sons, Zipacna and Cabrakan (Cockspur or Earth-heaper, and Earthquake), were earthquake-gods of the type of the Jötuns of Scandinavian myth or the Titans of Greek legend. These also were prideful and arrogant, and to cause their downfall the gods despatched the heavenly twins Hun-Apu and Xbalanque to earth, with instructions to chastise the trio.

Vukub-Cakix prided himself upon his possession of the wonderful nanze-tree, the tapal, bearing a fruit round, yellow, and aromatic, upon which he breakfasted every morning. One morning he mounted to its summit, whence he could best espy the choicest fruits, when he was surprised and infuriated to observe that two strangers had arrived there before him, and had almost denuded the tree of its produce. On seeing Vukub, Hun-Apu raised a blow-pipe to his mouth and blew a dart at the giant. It struck him on the mouth, and he fell from the top of the tree to the ground. Hun-Apu leapt down upon Vukub and grappled with him, but the giant in terrible anger seized the god by the arm and wrenched it from the body. He then returned to his house, where he was met by his wife, Chimalmat, who inquired for what reason he roared with pain. In reply he pointed to his mouth, and so full of anger was he against Hun-Apu that he took the arm he had wrenched from him and hung it over a blazing fire. He then threw himself down to bemoan his injuries, consoling himself, however, with the idea that he had avenged himself upon the disturbers of his peace.

Whilst Vukub-Cakix moaned and howled with the dreadful pain which he felt in his jaw and teeth (for the dart which had pierced him was probably poisoned) the arm of Hun-Apu hung over the fire, and was turned round and round and basted by Vukub's spouse, Chimalmat. The sun-god rained bitter imprecations upon the interlopers who had penetrated to his paradise and had caused him such woe, and he gave vent to dire threats of what would happen if he succeeded in getting them into his power.

But Hun-Apu and Xbalanque were not minded that Vukub-Cakix should escape so easily, and the recovery of Hun-Apu's arm must be made at all hazards. So they went to consult two great and wise magicians, Xpiyacoc and Xmucane, in whom we see two of the original Kiche creative deities, who advised them to proceed with them in disguise to the dwelling of Vukub, if they wished to recover the lost arm. The old magicians resolved to disguise themselves as doctors, and dressed Hun-Apu and Xbalanque in other garments to represent their sons.

Shortly they arrived at the mansion of Vukub, and while still some way off they could hear his groans and cries. Presenting themselves at the door, they accosted him. They told him that they had heard some one crying out in pain, and that as famous doctors they considered it their duty to ask who was suffering.

Vukub appeared quite satisfied, but closely questioned the old wizards concerning the two young men who accompanied them.

"They are our sons," they replied.

"Good," said Vukub. "Do you think you will be able to cure me?"

"We have no doubt whatever upon that head," answered Xpiyacoc. "You have sustained very bad injuries to your mouth and eyes."

"The demons who shot me with an arrow from their blow-pipe are the cause of my sufferings," said Vukub. "If you are able to cure me I shall reward you richly."

"Your Highness has many bad teeth, which must be removed," said the wily old magician. "Also the balls of your eyes appear to me to be diseased."

Vukub appeared highly alarmed, but the magicians speedily reassured him.

"It is necessary," said Xpiyacoc, "that we remove your teeth, but we will take care to replace them with grains of maize, which you will find much more agreeable in every way."

The unsuspicious giant agreed to the operation, and very quickly Xpiyacoc, with the help of Xmucane, removed his teeth of emerald, and replaced them by grains of white maize. A change quickly came over the Titan. His brilliancy speedily vanished, and when they removed the balls of his eyes he sank into insensibility and died.

All this time the wife of Vukub was turning Hun-Apu's arm over the fire, but Hun-Apu snatched the limb from above the brazier, and with the help of the magicians replaced it upon his shoulder. The discomfiture of Vukub was then complete. The party left his dwelling feeling that their mission had been accomplished.

The Earth-Giants

But in reality it was only partially accomplished, because Vukub's two sons, Zipacna and Cabrakan, still remained to be dealt with. Zipacna was daily employed in heaping up mountains, while Cabrakan, his brother, shook them in earthquake. The vengeance of Hun-Apu and Xbalanque was first directed against Zipacna, and they conspired with a band of young men to bring about his death.

The young men, four hundred in number, pretended to be engaged in building a house. They cut down a large tree, which they made believe was to be the roof-tree of their dwelling, and waited in a part of the forest through which they knew Zipacna must pass. After a while they could hear the giant crashing through the trees. He came into sight, and when he saw them standing round the giant tree-trunk, which they could not lift, he seemed very much amused.

"What have you there, O little ones?" he said laughing.

"Only a tree, your Highness, which we have felled for the roof-tree of a new house we are building."

"Cannot you carry it?" asked the giant disdainfully.

"No, your Highness," they made answer; "it is much too heavy to be lifted even by our united efforts."

With a good-natured laugh the Titan stooped and lifted the great trunk upon his shoulder. Then, bidding them lead the way, he trudged through the forest, evidently not disconcerted in the least by his great burden. Now the young men, incited by Hun-Apu and Xbalanque, had dug a great ditch, which they pretended was to serve for the foundation of their new house. Into this they requested Zipacna to descend, and, scenting no mischief, the giant readily complied. On his reaching the bottom his treacherous acquaintances cast huge trunks of trees upon him, but on hearing them coming down he quickly took refuge in a small side tunnel which the youths had constructed to serve as a cellar beneath their house.

Imagining the giant to be killed, they began at once to express their delight by singing and dancing, and to lend colour to his stratagem Zipacna despatched several friendly ants to the surface with strands of hair, which the young men concluded had been taken from his dead body. Assured by the seeming proof of his death, the youths proceeded to build their house upon the tree-trunks which they imagined covered Zipacna's body, and, producing a quantity of pulque, they began to make merry over the end of their enemy. For some hours their new dwelling rang with revelry.

All this time Zipacna, quietly hidden below, was listening to the hubbub and waiting his chance to revenge himself upon those who had entrapped him.

Suddenly arising in his giant might, he cast the house and all its inmates high in the air. The dwelling was utterly demolished, and the band of youths were hurled with such force into the sky that they remained there, and in the stars we call the Pleiades we can still discern them wearily waiting an opportunity to return to earth.

The Undoing of Zipacna

But Hun-Apu and Xbalanque, grieved that their comrades had so perished, resolved that Zipacna must not be permitted to escape so easily. He, carrying the mountains by night, sought his food by day on the shore of the river, where he wandered catching fish and crabs. The brothers made a large artificial crab, which they placed in a cavern at the bottom of a ravine. They then cunningly undermined a huge mountain, and awaited events. Very soon they saw Zipacna wandering along the side of the river, and asked him where he was going.

"Oh, I am only seeking my daily food," replied the giant.

"And what may that consist of?" asked the brothers.

"Only of fish and crabs," replied Zipacna.

"Oh, there is a crab down yonder," said the crafty brothers, pointing to the bottom of the ravine. "We espied it as we came along. Truly, it is a great crab, and will furnish you with a capital breakfast."

"Splendid!" cried Zipacna, with glistening eyes. "I must have it at once," and with one bound he leapt down to where the cunningly contrived crab lay in the cavern.

No sooner had he reached it than Hun-Apu and Xbalanque cast the mountain upon him; but so desperate were his efforts to get free that the brothers feared he might rid himself of the immense weight of earth under which he was buried, and to make sure of his fate they turned him into stone.

Thus at the foot of Mount Meahŭan, near Vera Paz, perished the proud Mountain-Maker.

The Discomfiture of Cabrakan

Now only the third of this family of boasters remained, and he was the most proud of any.

"I am the Overturner of Mountains!" said he.

But Hun-Apu and Xbalanque had made up their minds that not one of the race of Vukub should be left alive.

At the moment when they were plotting the overthrow of Cabrakan he was occupied in moving mountains. He seized the mountains by their bases and, exerting his mighty strength, cast them into the air; and of the smaller mountains he took no account at all. While he was so employed he met the brothers, who greeted him cordially.

"Good day, Cabrakan," said they. "What may you be doing?"

"Bah! nothing at all," replied the giant. "Cannot you see that I am throwing the mountains about, which is my usual occupation? And who may you be that ask such stupid questions? What are your names?"

"We have no names," replied they. "We are only hunters, and here we have our blow-pipes, with which we shoot the birds that live in these mountains. So you see that we do not require names, as we meet no one."

Cabrakan looked at the brothers disdainfully, and was about to depart when they said to him: "Stay; we should like to behold these mountain-throwing feats of yours."

This aroused the pride of Cabrakan.

"Well, since you wish it," said he, "I will show you how I can move a really great mountain. Now, choose the one you would like to see me destroy, and before you are aware of it I shall have reduced it to dust."

Hun-Apu looked around him, and espying a great peak pointed toward it. "Do you think you could overthrow that mountain?" he asked.

"Without the least difficulty," replied Cabrakan, with a great laugh. "Let us go toward it."

"But first you must eat," said Hun-Apu. "You have had no food since morning, and so great a feat can hardly be accomplished fasting."

The giant smacked his lips. "You are right," he said, with a hungry look. Cabrakan was one of those people who are always hungry. "But what have you to give me?"

"We have nothing with us," said Hun-Apu.

"Umph!" growled Cabrakan, "you are a pretty fellow. You ask me what I will have to eat, and then tell me you have nothing," and in his anger he seized one of the smaller mountains and threw it into the sea, so that the waves splashed up to the sky.

"Come," said Hun-Apu, "don't get angry. We have our blow-pipes with us, and will shoot a bird for your dinner."

On hearing this Cabrakan grew somewhat quieter.

"Why did you not say so at first?" he growled. "But be quick, because I am hungry."

Just at that moment a large bird passed overhead, and Hun-Apu and Xbalanque raised their blow-pipes to their mouths. The darts sped swiftly upward, and both of them struck the bird, which came tumbling down through the air, falling at the feet of Cabrakan.

"Wonderful, wonderful!" cried the giant. "You are clever fellows indeed," and, seizing the dead bird, he was going to eat it raw when Hun-Apu stopped him.

"Wait a moment," said he. "It will be much nicer when cooked," and, rubbing two sticks together, he ordered Xbalanque to gather some dry wood, so that a fire was soon blazing.

The bird was then suspended over the fire, and in a short time a savoury odour mounted to the nostrils of the giant, who stood watching the cooking with hungry eyes and watering lips.

Before placing the bird over the fire to cook, however, Hun-Apu had smeared its feathers with a thick coating of mud. The Indians in some parts of Central America still do this, so that when the mud dries with the heat of the fire the feathers will come off with it, leaving the flesh of the bird quite ready to eat. But Hun-Apu had done this with a purpose. The mud that he spread on the feathers was that of a poisoned earth, called *tizate*, the elements of which sank deeply into the flesh of the bird.

When the savoury mess was cooked, he handed it to Cabrakan, who speedily devoured it.

"Now," said Hun-Apu, "let us go toward that great mountain and see if you can lift it as you boast."

But already Cabrakan began to feel strange pangs.

"What is this?" said he, passing his hand across his brow. "I do not seem to see the mountain you mean."

"Nonsense," said Hun-Apu. "Yonder it is, see, to the east there."

"My eyes seem dim this morning," replied the giant.

"No, it is not that," said Hun-Apu. "You have boasted that you could lift this mountain, and now you are afraid to try."

"I tell you," said Cabrakan, "that I have difficulty in seeing. Will you lead me to the mountain?"

"Certainly," said Hun-Apu, giving him his hand, and with several strides they were at the foot of the eminence.

"Now," said Hun-Apu, "see what you can do, boaster."

Cabrakan gazed stupidly at the great mass in front of him. His knees shook together so that the sound was like the beating of a war-drum, and the sweat poured from his forehead and ran in a little stream down the side of the mountain.

"Come," cried Hun-Apu derisively, "are you going to lift the mountain or not?"

"He cannot," sneered Xbalanque. "I knew he could not."

Cabrakan shook himself into a final effort to regain his senses, but all to no purpose. The poison rushed through his blood, and with a groan he fell dead before the brothers.

Thus perished the last of the earth-giants of Guatemala, whom Hun-Apu and Xbalanque had been sent to destroy.

A Challenge from Hades

ON ONE OCCASION Hunhun-Apu and Vukub-Hunapu played a game of ball which in its progress took them into the vicinity of the realm of Xibalba (the Kiche Hades). The rulers of that drear abode, imagining that they had a chance of capturing the brothers, extended a challenge to them to play them at ball, and this challenge Hun-Came and Vukub-Came, the sovereigns of the Kiche Hell, despatched by four messengers in the shape of owls.

The brothers accepted the challenge, and, bidding farewell to their mother Xmucane and their respective sons and nephews, followed the feathered messengers down the long hill which led to the Underworld.

The Fooling of the Brethren

The American Indian is grave and taciturn. If there is one thing he fears and dislikes more than another it is ridicule. To his austere and haughty spirit it appears as something derogatory to his dignity, a slur upon his manhood. The hero-brothers had not been long in Xibalba when they discovered that it was the intention of the Lords of Hades to fool them and subject them to every species of indignity. After crossing a river of blood, they came to the palace of the Lords of Xibalba, where they espied two seated figures in front of them. Thinking that they recognized in them Hun-Came and Vukub-Came, they saluted them in a becoming manner, only to discover to their mortification that they were addressing figures of wood. This incident excited the ribald jeers of the Xibalbans, who scoffed at the brothers. Next they were invited to sit on the seat of honour, which they found to their dismay to be a red-hot stone, a circumstance which caused unbounded amusement to the inhabitants of the Underworld. Then they were imprisoned in the House of Gloom, where they were sacrificed and buried. The head of Hunhun-Apu was, however, suspended from a tree, upon the branches of which grew a crop of gourds so like the dreadful trophy as to be indistinguishable from it. The fiat went forth that no one in Xibalba must eat of the fruit of that tree. But the Lords of Xibalba had reckoned without feminine curiosity and its unconquerable love of the forbidden.

The Princess Xquiq

One day – if day ever penetrated to that gloomy and unwholesome place – a princess of Xibalba called Xquiq (Blood), daughter of Cuchumaquiq, a notability of Xibalba, passed under the tree, and, observing the desirable fruit with which it was covered, stretched out her hand to pluck one of the gourds. Into the outstretched palm the head of Hunhun-Apu spat, and told Xquiq that she would become a mother. Before she returned home, however, the hero-god assured her that no harm would come to her, and that she must not be afraid. In a few months' time the princess's father heard of her adventure, and she was doomed to be slain, the royal messengers of Xibalba, the owls, receiving commands to despatch her and to bring back her heart in a vase. But on the way she overcame the scruples of the owls by splendid promises, and they substituted for her heart the coagulated sap of the bloodwort plant.

The Birth of Hun-Apu and Xbalanque

Xmucane, left at home, looked after the welfare of the young Hunbatz and Hunchouen, and thither, at the instigation of the head of Hunhun-Apu, went Xquiq for protection. At first Xmucane would not credit her story, but upon Xquiq appealing to the gods a miracle was performed on her behalf, and she was permitted to gather a basket of maize where no maize grew to prove the authenticity of her claim. Shortly afterwards, when she had won the good graces of the aged Xmucane, her twin sons were born, the Hun-Apu and Xbalanque whom we have already met as the central figures of the preceding myths, which come from the first book of the *Popol Vuh*.

The Divine Children

But the divine children were both noisy and mischievous. They tormented their venerable grandmother with their shrill uproar and tricky behaviour. At last Xmucane, unable to put up with their habits, turned them out of doors. They took to an outdoor life with surprising ease, and soon became expert hunters and skilful in the use of the serbatana (blow-pipe), with which they shot birds and small animals. They were badly treated by their half-brothers Hunbatz and Hunchouen, who, jealous of their fame as hunters, annoyed them in every possible manner. But the divine children retaliated by turning their tormentors into hideous apes. The sudden change in the appearance of her grandsons caused Xmucane the most profound grief and dismay, and she begged that they who had brightened her home with their singing and flute-playing might not be condemned to such a dreadful fate. She was informed by the divine brothers that if she could behold their antics unmoved by mirth her wish would be granted. But the capers they cut and their grimaces caused her such merriment that on three separate occasions she was unable to restrain her laughter, and the men-monkeys took their leave.

The Magic Tools

THE CHILDHOOD OF HUN-APU AND XBALANQUE was full of such episodes as might be expected from these beings. We find, for example, that on attempting to clear a *milpa* (maize plantation) they employed magic tools which could be trusted to undertake a good day's work whilst they were absent at the chase. Returning at night, they smeared soil over their hands and faces, for the purpose of deluding Xmucane into the belief that they had been toiling all day in the fields.

But the wild beasts met in conclave during the night, and replaced all the roots and shrubs which the magic tools had cleared away. The twins recognized the work of the various animals, and placed a large net on the ground, so that if the creatures came to the spot on the following night they might be caught in its folds. They did come, but all made good their escape save the rat. The rabbit and deer lost their tails, however, and that is why these animals possess no caudal appendages! The rat, in gratitude for their sparing its life, told the brothers the history of their father and uncle, of their heroic efforts against the powers of Xibalba, and of the existence of a set of clubs and balls with which they might play *tlachtli* on the ball-ground at Ninxor-Carchah, where Hunhun-Apu and Vukub-Hunapu had played before them.

But the watchful Hun-Came and Vukub-Came soon heard that the sons and nephews of their first victims had adopted the game which had led these last into the clutches of the cunning Xibalbans, and they resolved to send a similar challenge to Hun-Apu and Xbalanque, thinking that the twins were unaware of the fate of Hunhun-Apu and Vukub-Hunapu. They therefore despatched messengers to the home of Xmucane with a challenge to play them at the ball-game, and Xmucane, alarmed by the nature of the message, sent a louse to warn her grandsons. The louse, unable to proceed as quickly as he wished, permitted himself to be swallowed by a toad, the toad by a serpent, and the serpent by the bird Voc, the messenger of Hurakan. At the end of the journey the other animals duly liberated each other, but the toad could not rid himself of the louse, who had in reality hidden himself in the toad's gums, and had not been swallowed at all. At last the message was delivered, and the twins returned to the abode of Xmucane, to bid farewell to their grandmother and mother. Before leaving they each planted a cane in the midst of the hut, saying that it would wither if any fatal accident befell them.

The Tricksters Tricked

They then proceeded to Xibalba, on the road trodden by Hunhun-Apu and Vukub-Hunapu, and passed the river of blood as the others had done. But they adopted the precaution of despatching ahead an animal called Xan as a sort of spy or scout. They commanded this animal to prick all the Xibalbans with a hair from Hun-Apu's leg, in order that they might discover which of them were made of wood, and incidentally learn the names of the others as they addressed one another when pricked by the hair. They were thus enabled to ignore the wooden images on their arrival at Xibalba, and they carefully avoided the red-hot stone. Nor did the ordeal of the House of Gloom affright them, and they passed through it scatheless. The inhabitants of the Underworld were both amazed and furious with disappointment. To add to their annoyance, they were badly beaten in the game of ball which followed. The Lords of Hell then requested the twins to bring them four bouquets of flowers from the royal garden of Xibalba, at the same time commanding the gardeners to keep good watch over the flowers so that none of them might be removed. But the brothers called to their aid a swarm of ants, who succeeded in returning with the flowers. The anger of the Xibalbans increased to a white fury, and they incarcerated Hun-Apu and Xbalanque in the House of Lances, a dread abode where demons armed with sharp spears thrust at them fiercely. But they bribed the lancers and escaped. The Xibalbans slit the beaks of the owls who guarded the royal gardens, and howled in fury.

The Houses of the Ordeals

They were next thrust into the House of Cold. Here they escaped a dreadful death from freezing by warming themselves with burning pine-cones. Into the House of Tigers and the House of Fire they were thrown for a night each, but escaped from both. But they were not so lucky in the House of Bats. As they threaded this place of terror, Camazotz, Ruler of the Bats, descended upon them with a whirring of leathern wings, and with one sweep of his sword-like claws cut off Hun-Apu's head. But a tortoise which chanced to pass the severed neck of the hero's prostrate body and came into contact with it was immediately turned into a head, and Hun-Apu arose from his terrible experience not a whit the worse.

With the object of proving their immortal nature to their adversaries, Hun-Apu and Xbalanque, first arranging for their resurrection with two sorcerers, Xulu and Pacaw, stretched themselves upon a bier and died. Their bones were ground to powder and thrown into the river. They then went through a kind of evolutionary process, appearing on the fifth day after their deaths as men-fishes and on the sixth as old men, ragged and tatterdemalion in appearance, killing and restoring each other to life. At the request of the princes of Xibalba, they burned the royal palace and restored it to its pristine splendour, killed and resuscitated the king's dog, and cut a man in pieces, bringing him to life again. The Lords of Hell were curious about the sensation of death, and asked to be killed and resuscitated. The first portion of their request the hero-brothers speedily granted, but did not deem it necessary to pay any regard to the second.

Throwing off all disguise, the brothers assembled the now thoroughly cowed princes of Xibalba, and announced their intention of punishing them for their animosity against themselves, their father and uncle. They were forbidden to partake in the noble and classic game of ball – a great indignity in the eyes of Maya of the higher caste – they were condemned to menial tasks, and they were to have sway over the beasts of the forest alone. After this their power rapidly waned. These princes of the Underworld are described as being owl-like, with faces painted black and white, as symbolical of their duplicity and faithless disposition.

As some reward for the dreadful indignities they had undergone, the souls of Hunhun-Apu and Vukub-Hunapu, the first adventurers into the darksome region of Xibalba, were translated to the skies, and became the sun and moon, and with this apotheosis the second book ends.

The Creation Story of the Third Book

THE OPENING OF THE THIRD BOOK of the *Popol Vuh* finds the gods once more deliberating as to the creation of man. Four men are evolved as the result of these deliberations. These beings were moulded from a paste of yellow and white maize, and were named Balam-Quitze (Tiger with the Sweet Smile), Balam-Agab (Tiger of the Night), Mahacutah (The Distinguished Name), and Iqi-Balam (Tiger of the Moon).

But the god Hurakan who had formed them was not overpleased with his handiwork, for these beings were too much like the gods themselves. The gods once more took counsel, and agreed that man must be less perfect and possess less knowledge than this new race. He must not become as a god. So Hurakan breathed a cloud over their eyes in order that they might only see a portion of the earth, whereas before they had been able to see the whole round sphere of the world. After this the four men were plunged into a deep sleep, and four women were created, who were given them as wives. These were Caha-Paluma (Falling Water), Choima (Beautiful Water), Tzununiha (House of the Water), and Cakixa (Water of Parrots, or Brilliant Water), who were espoused to the men in the respective order given above.

These eight persons were the ancestors of the Kiche only, after which were created the forerunners of the other peoples. At this time there was no sun, and comparative darkness lay over the face of the earth. Men knew not the art of worship, but blindly lifted their eyes to heaven and prayed the Creator to send them quiet lives and the light of day. But no sun came, and dispeace entered their hearts. So they journeyed to a place called Tulan-Zuiva (The Seven Caves) – practically the same as Chicomoztoc in the Aztec myth – and there gods were vouchsafed to them. The names of these were Tohil, whom Balam-Quitze received; Avilix, whom Balam-Agab received; and Hacavitz, granted to Mahacutah. Iqi-Balam received a god, but as he had no family his worship and knowledge died out.

The Granting of Fire

Grievously did the Kiche feel the want of fire in the sunless world they inhabited, but this the god Tohil (The Rumbler, the Fire-god) quickly provided them with. However, a mighty rain descended and extinguished all the fires in the land. These, however, were always supplied again by the thunder-god Tohil, who had only to strike his feet together to produce fire.

The Kiche Babel

Tulan-Zuiva was a place of great misfortune to the Kiche, for here the race suffered alienation in its different branches by reason of a confounding of their speech, which recalls the story of Babel. Owing to this the first four men were no longer able to comprehend each other, and determined to leave the place of their mischance and to seek the leadership of the god

Tohil into another and more fortunate sphere. In this journey they met with innumerable hardships. They had to cross many lofty mountains, and on one occasion had to make a long *detour* across the bed of the ocean, the waters of which were miraculously divided to permit of their passage. At last they arrived at a mountain which they called Hacavitz, after one of their deities, and here they remained, for it had been foretold that here they should see the sun. At last the luminary appeared. Men and beasts went wild with delight, although his beams were by no means strong, and he appeared more like a reflection in a mirror than the strong sun of later days whose fiery beams speedily sucked up the blood of victims on the altar. As he showed his face the three tribal gods of the Kiche were turned into stone, as were the gods or totems connected with the wild animals. Then arose the first Kiche town, or permanent dwelling-place.

The Last Days of the First Men

Time passed, and the first men of the Kiche race grew old. Visions came to them, in which they were exhorted by the gods to render human sacrifices, and in order to obey the divine injunctions they raided the neighbouring lands, the folk of which made a spirited resistance. But in a great battle the Kiche were miraculously assisted by a horde of wasps and hornets, which flew in the faces of their foes, stinging and blinding them, so that they could not wield weapon nor see to make any effective resistance. After this battle the surrounding races became tributary to them.

Death of the First Men

Now the first men felt that their death-day was nigh, and they called their kin and dependents around them to hear their dying words. In the grief of their souls they chanted the song 'Kamucu,' the song 'We see,' that they had sung so joyfully when they had first seen the light of day. Then they parted from their wives and sons one by one. And of a sudden they were not, and in their place was a great bundle, which was never opened. It was called the 'Majesty Enveloped.' So died the first men of the Kiche.

Queen Móo

ONE OF THE IDEAS OF AUGUSTUS LE PLONGEON, a nineteenth-century French-American archaeologist and antiquarian, was that a certain hall among the ruins of Chichen-Itza had been built by a Queen Móo, a Maya princess who after the tragic fate of her brother-husband and the catastrophe which ended in the sinking of the continent of Atlantis fled to Egypt, where she founded the ancient Egyptian civilization. It would be easy to refute this theory. But the tale as told by Dr Le Plongeon possesses a sufficiency of romantic interest to warrant its being rescued from the little-known volume in which he published it. His account runs as follows:

The Funeral Chamber

"As we are about to enter the funeral chamber hallowed by the love of the sister-wife, Queen Móo, the beauty of the carvings on the zapote beam that forms the lintel of the doorway calls our attention. Here is represented the antagonism of the brothers Aac and Coh, that led to the murder of the latter by the former. Carved on the lintel are the names of these personages, represented by their totems – a leopard head for Coh, and a boar head as well as a turtle for Aac, this word meaning both boar and turtle in Maya. Aac is pictured within the disk of the sun, his protective deity which he worshipped, according to mural inscriptions at Uxmal. Full of anger he faces his brother. In his right hand there is a badge ornamented with feathers and flowers. The threatening way in which this is held suggests a concealed weapon.... The face of Coh also expresses anger. With him is the feathered serpent, emblematic of royalty, thence of the country, more often represented as a winged serpent protecting Coh. In his left hand he holds his weapon down, whilst his right hand clasps his badge of authority, with which he covers his breasts as for protection, and demanding the respect due to his rank....

"Passing between the figures of armed chieftains sculptured on the jambs of the doorway, and seeming like sentinels guarding the entrance of the funeral chamber, we notice one wearing a headdress similar to the crown of Lower Egypt, which formed part of the *pshent* of the Egyptian monarchs.

The Frescoes

"The frescoes in the funeral chamber of Prince Coh's Memorial Hall, painted in water-colours taken from the vegetable kingdom, are divided into a series of *tableaux* separated by blue lines. The plinths, the angles of the room, and the edges of the ceiling, being likewise painted blue, indicate that this was intended for a funeral chamber.... The first scene represents Queen Móo while yet a child. She is seated on the back of a peccary, or American wild boar, under the royal umbrella of feathers, emblem of royalty in Mayach, as it was in India, Chaldea, and other places. She is consulting a *h-men*, or wise man; listening with profound attention to the decrees of fate as revealed by the cracking of the shell of an armadillo exposed to a slow fire on a brazier, the condensing on it of the vapour, and the various tints it assumes. This mode of divination is one of the customs of the Mayas....

The Soothsayers

"In front of the young Queen Móo, and facing her, is seated the soothsayer, evidently a priest of high rank, judging from the colours, blue and yellow, of the feathers of his ceremonial mantle. He reads the decrees of fate on the shell of the armadillo, and the scroll issuing from his throat says what they are. By him stands the winged serpent, emblem and protective genius of the Maya Empire. His head is turned towards the royal banner, which he seems to caress. His satisfaction is reflected in the mild and pleased expression of his face. Behind the priest, the position of whose hand is the same as that of Catholic priests in blessing their congregation, and the significance of which is well known to occultists, are the ladies-in-waiting of the young Queen.

The Royal Bride

"In another *tableau* we again see Queen Móo, no longer a child, but a comely young woman. She is not seated under the royal umbrella or banner, but she is once more in the presence of the *h-men*, whose face is concealed by a mask representing an owl's head. She, pretty and coquettish, has many admirers, who vie with each other for the honour of her hand. In company with one of her wooers she comes to consult the priest, accompanied by an old lady, her grandmother probably, and her female attendants. According to custom the old lady is the spokeswoman. She states to the priest that the young man, he who sits on a low stool between two female attendants, desires to marry the Queen. The priest's attendant, seated also on a stool, back of all, acts as crier, and repeats in a loud voice the speech of the old lady.

Móo's Refusal

"The young Queen refuses the offer. The refusal is indicated by the direction of the scroll issuing from her mouth. It is turned backward, instead of forward towards the priest, as would be the case if she assented to the marriage. The *h-men* explains that Móo, being a daughter of the royal family, by law and custom must marry one of her brothers. The youth listens to the decision with due respect to the priest, as shown by his arm being placed across his breast, the left hand resting on the right shoulder. He does not accept the refusal in a meek spirit, however. His clenched fist, his foot raised as in the act of stamping, betoken anger and disappointment, while the attendant behind him expostulates, counselling patience and resignation, judging by the position and expression of her left-hand palm upward.

The Rejected Suitor

"In another *tableau* we see the same individual whose offer of marriage was rejected by the young Queen in consultation with a *nubchi*, or prophet, a priest whose exalted rank is indicated by his headdress, and the triple breastplate he wears over his mantle of feathers. The consulter, evidently a person of importance, has come attended by his *hachetail*, or confidential friend, who sits behind him on a cushion. The expression on the face of the said consulter shows that he does not accept patiently the decrees of fate, although conveyed by the interpreter in as conciliatory a manner as possible. The adverse decision of the gods is manifested by the sharp projecting centre part of the scroll, but it is wrapped in words as persuasive and consoling, preceded by as smooth a preamble as the rich and beautiful Maya language permits and makes easy. His friend is addressing the prophet's assistant. Reflecting the thoughts of his lord, he declares that the *nubchi's* fine discourse and his pretended reading of the will of the gods are all nonsense, and exclaims 'Pshaw!' which contemptuous exclamation is pictured by the yellow scroll, pointed at both ends, escaping from his nose like a sneeze. The answer of the priest's assistant, evidenced by the gravity of his features, the assertive position of his hand, and the bluntness of his speech, is evidently 'It is so!'

Aac's Fierce Wooing

"Her brother Aac is madly in love with Móo. He is portrayed approaching the interpreter of the will of the gods, divested of his garments in token of humility in presence of their majesty and of submission to their decrees. He comes full of arrogance, arrayed in gorgeous attire, and with regal pomp. He comes not as a suppliant to ask and accept counsel, but haughty, he makes bold to dictate. He is angered at the refusal of the priest to accede to his demand for his sister Móo's hand, to whose totem, an armadillo on this occasion, he points imperiously. It was on an armadillo's shell that the fates wrote her destiny when consulted by the performance of the *Pou* ceremony. The yellow flames of wrath darting from all over his person, the sharp yellow scroll issuing from his mouth, symbolize Aac's feelings. The pontiff, however, is unmoved by them. In the name of the gods with serene mien he denies the request of the proud nobleman, as his speech indicates. The winged serpent, genius of the country, that stands erect and ireful by Aac, is also wroth at his pretensions, and shows in its features and by sending its dart through Aac's royal banner a decided opposition to them, expressed by the ends of his speech being turned backwards, some of them terminating abruptly, others in sharp points.

Prince Coh

"Prince Coh sits behind the priest as one of his attendants. He witnesses the scene, hears the calm negative answer, sees the anger of his brother and rival, smiles at his impotence, is happy at his discomfiture. Behind him, however, sits a spy who will repeat his words, report his actions to his enemy. He listens, he watches. The high-priest himself, Cay, their elder brother, sees the storm that is brewing behind the dissensions of Coh and Aac. He trembles at the thought of the misfortunes that will surely befall the dynasty of the Cans, of the ruin and misery of the country that will certainly follow. Divested of his priestly raiment, he comes nude and humble as it is proper for men in the presence of the gods, to ask their advice how best to avoid the impending calamities. The chief of the auspices is in the act of reading their decrees on the palpitating entrails of a fish. The sad expression on his face, that of humble resignation on that of the pontiff, of deferential astonishment on that of the assistant, speak of the inevitable misfortunes which are to come in the near future.

"We pass over interesting battle scenes … in which the defenders have been defeated by the Mayas. Coh will return to his queen loaded with spoils that he will lay at her feet with his glory, which is also hers.

The Murder of Coh

"We next see him in a terrible altercation with his brother Aac. The figures in that scene are nearly life-size, but so much disfigured and broken as to make it impossible to obtain good tracings. Coh is portrayed without weapons, his fists clenched, looking menacingly at his foe, who holds three spears, typical of the three wounds he inflicted in his brother's back when he killed him treacherously. Coh is now laid out, being prepared for cremation. His body has been opened at the ribs to extract the viscera and heart, which, after being charred, are to be preserved in a stone urn with cinnabar, where the writer found them in 1875. His sister-wife, Queen Móo, in sad contemplation of the remains of the beloved, … kneels at his feet…. The winged serpent, protective genius of the country, is pictured without a head. The ruler of the country has been slain. He is dead. The people are without a chief."

The Widowhood of Móo

The widowhood of Móo is then said to be portrayed in subsequent pictures. Other suitors, among them Aac, make their proposals to her, but she refuses them all. "Aac's pride being humiliated, his love turned to hatred. His only wish henceforth was to usurp the supreme power, to wage war against the friend of his childhood. He made religious disagreement the pretext. He proclaimed that the worship of the sun was to be superior to that of the winged serpent, the genius of the country; also to that of the worship of ancestors, typified by the feathered serpent, with horns and a flame or halo on the head.... Prompted by such evil passions, he put himself at the head of his own vassals, and attacked those who had remained faithful to Queen Móo and to Prince Coh's memory. At first Móo's adherents successfully opposed her foes. The contending parties, forgetting in the strife that they were children of the same soil, blinded by their prejudices, let their passions have the better of their reason. At last Queen Móo fell a prisoner in the hands of her enemy."

The Manuscript Troano

Dr. Le Plongeon here assumes that the story is taken up by the Manuscript Troano. As no one is able to decipher this manuscript completely, he is pretty safe in his assertion. Here is what the *pintura* alluded to says regarding Queen Móo, according to our author:

"The people of Mayach having been whipped into submission and cowed, no longer opposing much resistance, the lord seized her by the hair, and, in common with others, caused her to suffer from blows. This happened on the ninth day of the tenth month of the year Kan. Being completely routed, she passed to the opposite sea-coast in the southern parts of the country, which had already suffered much injury."

The Legend of the Dwarf

AN OLD WOMAN LIVED ALONE IN HER HUT, rarely leaving her chimney-corner. She was much distressed at having no children, and in her grief one day took an egg, wrapped it up carefully in cotton cloth, and put it in a corner of her hut. She looked every day in great anxiety, but no change in the egg was observable. One morning, however, she found the shell broken, and a lovely tiny creature was stretching out its arms to her.

The old woman was in raptures. She took it to her heart, gave it a nurse, and was so careful of it that at the end of a year the baby walked and talked as well as a grown-up man. But he stopped growing. The good old woman in her joy and delight exclaimed that the baby should be a great chief.

One day she told him to go to the king's palace and engage him in a trial of strength. The dwarf begged hard not to be sent on such an enterprise. But the old woman insisted on his going, and he was obliged to obey. When ushered into the presence of the sovereign he threw down his gauntlet. The latter smiled, and asked him to lift a stone of three *arobes* (75 lb). The child returned crying to his mother, who sent him back, saying, "If the king can lift the stone, you can lift it too." The king did take it up, but so did the dwarf. His strength was tried in many other ways, but all the king did was as easily done by the dwarf.

Wroth at being outdone by so puny a creature, the prince told the dwarf that unless he built a palace loftier than any in the city he should die. The affrighted dwarf returned to the old woman, who bade him not to despair, and the next morning they both awoke in the palace which is still standing. The king saw the palace with amazement. He instantly sent for the dwarf, and desired him to collect two bundles of *cogoiol* (a kind of hard wood), with one of which he would strike the dwarf on the head, and consent to be struck in return by his tiny adversary. The latter again returned to his mother moaning and lamenting. But the old woman cheered him up, and, placing a *tortilla* on his head, sent him back to the king. The trial took place in the presence of all the state grandees. The king broke the whole of his bundle on the dwarf's head without hurting him in the least, seeing which he wished to save his own head from the impending ordeal; but his word had been passed before his assembled court, and he could not well refuse. The dwarf struck, and at the second blow the king's skull was broken to pieces. The spectators immediately proclaimed the victorious dwarf their sovereign.

After this the old woman disappeared. But in the village of Mani, fifty miles distant, is a deep well leading to a subterraneous passage which extends as far as Merida. In this passage is an old woman sitting on the bank of a river shaded by a great tree, having a serpent by her side. She sells water in small quantities, accepting no money, for she must have human beings, innocent babies, which are devoured by the serpent. This old woman is the dwarf's mother.

Miss Pound-the-Stones

IN THE FORESTS OF YUCATAN, there once lived a maiden who surpassed all others in loveliness of face and form. And even as that one excelled all maidens in beauty, so also did she exceed them in the wickedness of her heart. She was called Miss Pound-the-Stones, because she would pound upon the stones to attract people to her. But woe be to that one who answered her call!

Once, it happened, that a youth travelling alone, toward the close of the day, saw a wonderfully beautiful maiden near him. He had never seen any one so lovely. He hastened his steps that he might be near her, but to his astonishment the maiden moved as quickly as he, and kept the same distance between them. Just as he was about to slacken his pace, and put the thought of her out of his mind, he heard from in front of him, the sound as of some one tapping upon stones.

"That must be Miss Pound-the-Stones," the youth thought. "Ah! but Miss Pound-the-Stones is a wicked fairy. She is not a beautiful maiden. One so evil as that wicked one could never be so innocent and alluring as this maiden is." He hurried after the maiden still more eagerly, because she had tapped upon the stones to attract him to her.

The maiden moved toward the forest, and the youth followed her as ardently as a hunter pursues his game. Far in the deep forest he overtook her and clasped her in his arms. But, even as the youth touched the maiden her beautiful body become transformed into a thorny bush, which pierced him with its poison needles. The dainty feet that had sped before him became sharp claws which rent the flesh from his body.

Torn and bleeding, the youth painfully journeyed homeward amazed that one so alluring could have been at heart a bush of poison thorns. And the youth betook himself to his bed, the victim of a deadly fever.

And thus it was that Miss Pound-the-Stones would lure to their death, thoughtless youths whose gaze pierced not through her loveliness.

Thus it was, in the long ago, in the forests of Yucatan.

Myths of the Incas & Peru

Introduction

PERU IS NOT SO RICH IN MYTHS as Mexico, but the following legends well illustrate the mythological ideas of the Inca race (inevitably the central body of Andean myth, as transmitted to us, is that of the Incas, who, having reached the position of a great imperial clan, naturally glorified both their own gods and their own legendary history).

Again, the mythology of these people most often was their way of explaining the origination of things, creatures and places – see the tale of Manco Capac's founding of Cuzco, or that of how the Cañari people are descended from macaws (*quacamayo*) – but they also tell of the exploits of their gods, such as those of the cunning Huathiacuri who benefited from the wisdom of his father to secure his bride and outdo his competitors.

You will discover that Viracocha, the great creator deity, crops up again and again, and it is interesting to see the variations in how the different tales treat of his acts.

Viracocha and the Coming of the Incas

THE NATIVES OF THIS LAND affirm that in the beginning, and before this world was created, there was a being called Viracocha. He created a dark world without sun, moon or stars. Owing to this creation he was named Viracocha Pachayachachi, which means 'Creator of all things.' And when he had created the world he formed a race of giants of disproportioned greatness painted and sculptured, to see whether it would be well to make real men of that size. He then created men in his likeness as they are now; and they lived in darkness.

Viracocha ordered these people that they should live without quarrelling, and that they should know and serve him. He gave them a certain precept which they were to observe on pain of being confounded if they should break it. They kept this precept for some time, but it is not mentioned what it was. But as there arose among them the vices of pride and covetousness, they transgressed the precept of Viracocha Pachayachachi and falling, through this sin, under his indignation, he confounded and cursed them. Then some were turned into stones, others into other things, some were swallowed up by the earth, others by the sea, and over all there came a general flood which they call *uñu pachacuti*, which means 'water that overturns the land.' They say that it rained 60 days and nights, that it drowned all created things, and that there alone remained some vestiges of those who were turned into stones, as a memorial of the event, and as an example to posterity, in the edifices of Pucara, which are 60 leagues from Cuzco.

Some of the nations, besides the Cuzcos, also say that a few were saved from this flood to leave descendants for a future age. Each nation has its special fable which is told by its people, of how their first ancestors were saved from the waters of the deluge. That the ideas they had in their blindness may be understood, I will insert only one, told by the nation of the Cañaris, a land of Quito and Tumibamba, 400 leagues from Cuzco and more.

They say that in the time of the deluge called *uñu pachacuti* there was a mountain named Guasano in the province of Quito and near a town called Tumipampa. The natives still point it out. Up this mountain went two of the Cañaris named Ataorupagui and Cusicayo. As the waters increased the mountain kept rising and keeping above them in such a way that it was never covered by the waters of the flood. In this way the two Cañaris escaped. These two, who were brothers, when the waters abated after the flood, began to sow. One day when they had been at work, on returning to their but, they found in it some small loaves of bread, and a jar of *chicha*, which is the beverage used in this country in place of wine, made of boiled maize. They did not know who had brought it, but they gave thanks to the Creator, eating and drinking of that provision. Next day the same thing happened. As they marvelled at this mystery, they were anxious to find out who brought the meals. So one day they hid themselves, to spy out the bringers of their food. While they were watching they saw two Cañari women preparing the victuals and putting them in the accustomed place. When about to depart the men tried to seize them, but they evaded their would-be captors and escaped. The Cañaris, seeing the mistake they had made in molesting those who had done them so much good, became sad and prayed to Viracocha for pardon for their sins, entreating him to let the women come back and give them the accustomed meals. The Creator granted their petition. The women came back and said to the Cañaris – "The Creator has thought it well that we should return to you, lest you should die of hunger." They brought them food. Then there was friendship between the women and the Cañari brothers, and one of the Cañari brothers had connexion with one of the women. Then, as the elder brother was drowned in a lake which was near, the survivor married one of the women, and had the other as a concubine. By them he had ten sons who formed two lineages of five each, and increasing in numbers they called one Hanansaya which is the same as to say the upper party, and the other Hurinsaya, or the lower party. From these all the Cañaris that now exist are descended.

In the same way the other nations have fables of how some of their people were saved, from whom they trace their origin and descent. But the Incas and most of those of Cuzco, those among them who are believed to know most, do not say that anyone escaped from the flood, but that Viracocha began to create men afresh, as will be related further on. One thing is believed among all the nations of these parts, for they all speak generally and as well known of the general flood which they call *uñu pachacuti*. From this we may clearly understand that if, in these parts they have a tradition of the great flood, this great mass of the floating islands which they afterwards called the Atlanticas, and now the Indies of Castille, or America, must have begun to receive a population immediately after the flood, although; by their account, the details are different from those which the true Scriptures teach us. This must have been done by divine Providence, through the first people coming over the land of the Atlantic Island, which was joined to this, as has been already said. For as the natives, though barbarous, give reasons for their very ancient settlement, by recording the flood, there is no necessity for setting aside the Scriptures by quoting authorities to establish this origin. We now come to those who relate the events of the second age after the flood, which is the subject of the next chapter.

Fable of the Second Age, and Creation of the Barbarous Indians According to their Account

It is related that everything was destroyed in the flood called *uñu pachacuti*. It must now be known that Viracocha Pachayachachi, when he destroyed that land as has been already recounted, preserved three men, one of them named Taguapaca, that they might serve and help him in the creation of new people who had to be made in the second age after the deluge, which was done in this manner. The flood being passed and the land dry, Viracocha determined to people it a second time, and, to make it more perfect, he decided upon creating luminaries to give it light. With this object he went, with his servants, to a great lake in the Collao, in which there is an island called Titicaca, the meaning being 'the rock of lead,' of which we shall treat in the first part. Viracocha went to this island, and presently ordered that the sun, moon, and stars should come forth, and be set in the heavens to give light to the world, and it was so. They say that the moon was created brighter than the sun, which made the sun jealous at the time when they rose into the sky. So the sun threw over the moon's face a handful of ashes, which gave it the shaded colour it now presents. This frontier lake of Chucuito, in the territory of the

Collao, is 57 leagues to the south of Cuzco. Viracocha gave various orders to his servants, but Taguapaca disobeyed the commands of Viracocha. So Viracocha was enraged against Taguapaca, and ordered the other two servants to take him, tie him hands and feet, and launch him in a balsa on the lake. This was done. Taguapaca was blaspheming against Viracocha for the way he was treated, and threatening that he would return and take vengeance, when he was carried by the water down the drain of the same lake, and was not seen again for a long time. This done, Viracocha made a sacred idol in that place, as a place for worship and as a sign of what he had there created.

Leaving the island, he passed by the lake to the main land, taking with him the two servants who survived. He went to a place now called Tiahuanacu in the province of Collasuyu, and in this place he sculptured and designed on a great piece of stone, all the nations that he intended to create. This done, he ordered his two servants to charge their memories with the names of all tribes that he had depicted, and of the valleys and provinces where they were to come forth, which were those of the whole land. He ordered that each one should go by a different road, naming the tribes, and ordering them all to go forth and people the country. His servants, obeying the command of Viracocha, set out on their journey and work. One went by the mountain range or chain which they call the heights over the plains on the South Sea. The other went by the heights which overlook the wonderful mountain ranges which we call the Andes, situated to the east of the said sea. By these roads they went, saying with a loud voice "Oh you tribes and nations, hear and obey the order of Ticci Viracocha Pachayachachi, which commands you to go forth, and multiply and settle the land." Viracocha himself did the same along the road between those taken by his two servants, naming all the tribes and places by which he passed. At the sound of his voice every place obeyed, and people came forth, some from lakes, others from fountains, valleys, caves, trees, rocks and hills, spreading over the land and multiplying to form the nations which are to-day in Peru.

Others affirm that this creation of Viracocha was made from the Titicaca site where, having originally formed some shapes of large strong men which seemed to him out of proportion, he made them again of his stature which was, as they say, the average height of men, and being made he gave them life. Thence they set out to people the land. As they spoke one language previous to starting, they built those edifices, the ruins of which may still be seen, before they set out. This was for the residence of Viracocha, their maker. After departing they varied their languages, noting the cries of wild beasts, insomuch that, coming across each other afterwards, those could not understand who had before been relations and neighbours.

Whether it was in one way or the other, all agree that Viracocha was the creator of these people. They have the tradition that he was a man of medium height, white and dressed in a white robe like an alb secured round the waist, and that he carried a staff and a book in his hands.

Besides this they tell of a strange event; how that Viracocha, after he had created all people, went on his road and came to a place where many men of his creation had congregated. This place is now called Cacha. When Viracocha arrived there, the inhabitants were estranged owing to his dress and bearing. They murmured at it and proposed to kill him from a hill that was near. They took their weapons there, and gathered together with evil intentions against Viracocha. He, falling on his knees on some plain ground, with his hands clasped, fire from above came down upon those on the hill, and covered all the place, burning up the earth and stones like straw. Those bad men were terrified at the fearful fire. They came down from the hill, and sought pardon from Viracocha for their sin. Viracocha was moved by compassion. He went to the flames and put them out with his staff. But the hill remained quite parched up, the stones being rendered so light by the burning that a very large stone which could not have been carried on a cart, could be raised easily by one man. This may be seen at this day, and it is a wonderful sight to behold this hill, which is a quarter of a league in extent, all burnt up. It is in the Collao.

After this Viracocha continued his journey and arrived at a place called Urcos, six leagues to the south of Cuzco. Remaining there some days he was well served by the natives of that neighbourhood. At the time of his departure, he made them a celebrated *huaca* or statue, for them to offer gifts to and worship; to which statue the Incas, in after times, offered many rich gifts of gold and other metals, and above all a golden bench. When the Spaniards entered Cuzco they found it, and appropriated it to themselves. It was worth $17,000. The Marquis Don Francisco Pizarro took it himself, as the share of the General.

Returning to the subject of the fable, Viracocha continued his journey, working his miracles and instructing his created beings. In this way he reached the territory on the equinoctial line, where are now Puerto Viejo and Manta. Here he was joined by his servants. Intending to leave the land of Peru, he made a speech to those he had created, apprising them of the things that would happen. He told them that people would come, who would say that they were Viracocha their creator, and that they were not to believe them; but that in the time to come he would send his messengers who would protect and teach them. Having said this he went to sea with his two servants, and went travelling over the water as if it was land, without sinking. For they appeared like foam over the water, and the people, therefore, gave them the name of Viracocha which is the same as to say the grease or foam of the sea. At the end of some years after Viracocha departed, they say that Taguapaca, whom Viracocha ordered to be thrown into the lake of Titicaca in the Collao, as has already been related, came back and began, with others, to preach that he was Viracocha. Although at first the people were doubtful, they finally saw that it was false, and ridiculed them.

This absurd fable of their creation is held by these barbarians and they affirm and believe it as if they had really seen it to happen and come to pass.

The Ancient Freedoms of These Kingdoms of Peru and Their Provinces

It is important to note that these barbarians could tell nothing more respecting what happened from the second creation by Viracocha down to the time of the Incas. But it may be assumed that, although the land was peopled and full of inhabitants before the Incas, it had no regular government, nor did it have natural lords elected by common consent to govern and rule, and who were respected by the people, so that they were obeyed and received tribute. On the contrary all the people were scattered and disorganized, living in complete liberty, and each man being sole lord of his house and estate. In each tribe there were two divisions. One was called Hanansaya, which means the upper division, and the other Hurinsaya, which is the lower division, a custom which continues to this day. These divisions do not mean anything more than a way to count each other, for their satisfaction; though afterwards it served a more useful purpose, as will be seen in its place.

As there were dissensions among them, a certain kind of militia was organized for defence, in the following way. When it became known to the people of one district that some from other parts were coming to make war, they chose one who was a native, or he might be a stranger, who was known to be a valiant warrior. Often such a man offered himself to aid and to fight for them against their enemies. Such a man was followed and his orders were obeyed during the war. When the war was over he became a private man as he had been before, like the rest of the people, nor did they pay him tribute either before or afterwards, nor any manner of tax whatever. To such a man they gave and still give the name of *Sinchi* which means valiant. They call such men *Sinchi-cuna* which means 'valiant now' as who should say – "now during the time the war lasts you shall be our valiant man, and afterwards no": or another meaning would be simply 'valiant men,' for *cuna* is an adverb of time, and also denotes the plural. In whichever meaning, it is very applicable to these temporary captains in the days of general liberty. So that from the general flood of which they have a tradition to the time when the Incas began to reign, which was 3519 years, all the natives of these kingdoms lived on their properties without acknowledging either a natural or an elected lord. They succeeded in preserving, as it is said, a simple state of liberty, living in huts or caves or humble little houses. This name of *Sinchi* for those who held sway only during war, lasted throughout the land until the time of Tupac Inca Yupanqui, the tenth Inca, who instituted *Curacas* and other officials in the order which will be fully described in the life of that Inca. Even at the present time they continue this use and custom in the provinces of Chile and in other parts of the forests of Peru to the east of Quito and Chachapoyas, where they only obey a chief during war time, not any special one, but he who is known to be most valiant, enterprising and daring in the wars. The reader should note that all the land was private property with reference to any dominion of chiefs, yet they had natural chiefs with special rights in each province, as for instance among the natives of the valley of Cuzco and in other parts, as we shall relate of each part in its place.

The First Settlers in the Valley of Cuzco

I have explained how the people of these lands preserved their inheritances and lived on them in ancient times, and that their proper and natural countries were known. There were many of these which I shall notice in their places, treating specially at present of the original settlers of the valley where stands the present city of Cuzco. For from there we have to trace the origin of the tyranny of the Incas, who always had their chief seat in the valley of Cuzco.

Before all things it must be understood that the valley of Cuzco is in 130° 15' from the equator on the side of the south pole. In this valley, owing to its being fertile for cultivation, there were three tribes settled from most ancient times, the first called Sauaseras, the second Antasayas, the third Huallas. They settled near each other, although their lands for sowing were distinct, which is the property they valued most in those days and even now. These natives of the valley lived there in peace for many years, cultivating their farms.

Some time before the arrival of the Incas, three *Sinchis*, strangers to this valley, the first named Alcabisa, the second Copalimayta, and the third Culunchima, collected certain companies and came to the valley of Cuzco, where, by consent of the natives, they settled and became brothers and companions of the original inhabitants. So they lived for a long time. There was concord between these six tribes, three native and three immigrant. They relate that the immigrants came out to where the Incas then resided, as we shall relate presently, and called them relations. This is an important point with reference to what happened afterwards.

Before entering upon the history of the Incas I wish to make known or, speaking more accurately, to answer a difficulty which may occur to those who have not been in these parts. Some may say that this history cannot be accepted as authentic being taken from the narratives of these barbarians, because, having no letters, they could not preserve such details as they give from so remote an antiquity. The answer is that, to supply the want of letters, these barbarians had a curious invention which was very good and accurate. This was that from one to the other, from fathers to sons, they handed down past events, repeating the story of them many times, just as lessons are repeated from a professor's chair, making the hearers say these historical lessons over and over again until they were fixed in the memory. Thus each one of the descendants continued to communicate the annals in the order described with a view to preserve their histories and deeds, their ancient traditions, the numbers of their tribes, towns, provinces, their days, months and years, their battles, deaths, destructions, fortresses and *Sinchis*. Finally they recorded, and they still record, the most notable things which may be expressed in numbers (or statistics), on certain cords called *quipu*, which is the same as to say reasoner or accountant. On these cords they make certain knots by which, and by differences of colour, they distinguish and record each thing as by letters. It is a thing to be admired to see what details may be recorded on these cords, for which there are masters like our writing masters.

Besides this they had, and still have, special historians in these nations, an hereditary office descending from father to son. The collection of these annals is due to the great diligence of Pachacuti Inca Yupanqui, the ninth Inca, who sent out a general summons to an the old historians in all the provinces he had subjugated, and even to many others throughout those kingdoms. He had them in Cuzco for a long time, examining them concerning their antiquities, origin, and the most notable events in their history. These were painted on great boards, and deposited in the temple of the Sun, in a great hall. There such boards, adorned with gold, were kept as in our libraries, and learned persons were appointed, who were well versed in the art of understanding and declaring their contents. No one was allowed to enter where these boards were kept, except the Inca and the historians, without a special order of the Inca.

In this way they took care to have all their past history investigated, and to have records respecting all kinds of people, so that at this day the Indians generally know and agree respecting details and important events, though, in some things, they hold different opinions on special points. By examining the oldest and most prudent among them, in all ranks of life, who had most credit, I collected and compiled the present history, referring the sayings and declarations of one party to their antagonists of another party, for they are divided into parties, and seeking from each one a memorial of its lineage and of that of the opposing party. These memorials, which are all in my possession, were compared and corrected, and ultimately verified in public, in presence of representatives of all the parties and lineages, under oaths in presence of a judge, and with expert and very faithful interpreters also on oath, and I thus finished what is now written. Such great diligence has been observed, because the facts which will be obvious on the true completion of such a great work – the establishment of the tyranny of the cruel Incas of this land – will make all the nations of the world understand the judicial and more than legitimate right that the King of Castille has to these Indies and to other lands adjacent, especially to these kingdoms of Peru. As all the histories of past events have been verified by proof, which in this case has been done so carefully and faithfully by order and owing to the industry of the most excellent Viceroy Don Francisco de Toledo, no one can doubt that everything in this volume is most sufficiently established and verified without any room being left for reply or contradiction. I have been desirous of making this digression because, in writing the history, I have heard that many entertain the doubts I have above referred to, and it seemed well to satisfy them once for all.

How the Incas Began to Tyrannize Over the Lands and Inheritances

Having explained that, in ancient times, all this land was owned by the people, it is necessary to state how the Incas began their tyranny. Although the tribes all lived in simple liberty without recognizing any lord, there were always some ambitious men among them, aspiring for mastery. They committed violence among their countrymen and among strangers to subject them and bring them to obedience under their command, so that they might serve them and pay tribute. Thus bands of men belonging to one region went to others to make war and to rob and kill, usurping the lands of others.

As these movements took place in many parts by many tribes, each one trying to subjugate his neighbour, it happened that six leagues from the valley of Cuzco, at a place called Paccari-tampu, there were four men with their four sisters, of fierce courage and evil intentions, although with lofty aims. These, being more able than the others, understood the pusillanimity of the natives of those districts and the ease with which they could be made to believe anything that was propounded with authority or with any force. So they conceived among themselves the idea of being able to subjugate many lands by force and deception. Thus all the eight brethren, four men and four women, consulted together how they could tyrannize over other tribes beyond the place where they lived, and they proposed to do this by violence. Considering that most of the natives were ignorant and could easily be made to believe what was said to them, particularly if they were addressed with some roughness, rigour and authority, against which they could make neither reply nor resistance because they are timid by nature, they sent abroad certain fables respecting their origin, that they might be respected and feared. They said that they were the sons of Viracocha Pachayachachi, the Creator, and that they had come forth out of certain windows to rule the rest of the people. As they were fierce, they made the people believe and fear them, and hold them to be more than men, even worshipping them as gods. Thus they introduced the religion that suited them. The order of the fable they told of their origin was as follows.

The Fable of the Origin of the Incas of Cuzco

All the native Indians of this land relate and affirm that the Incas Ccapac originated in this way. Six leagues S.S.W. of Cuzco by the road which the Incas made, there is a place called Paccari-tampu, at which there is a hill called Tampu-tocco, meaning 'the house of windows.' It is certain that in this hill there are three windows, one called

'Maras-tocco,' the other 'Sutic-tocco,' while that which is in the middle, between these two, was known as 'Ccapac-tocco,' which means 'the rich window,' because they say that it was ornamented with gold and other treasures. From the window called 'Maras-tocco' came forth, without parentage, a tribe of Indians called Maras. There are still some of them in Cuzco. From the 'Sutic-tocco' came Indians called Tampus, who settled round the same hill, and there are also men of this lineage still in Cuzco. From the chief window of 'Ccapac-tocco,' came four men and four women, called brethren. These knew no father nor mother, beyond the story they told that they were created and came out of the said window by order of Ticci Viracocha, and they declared that Viracocha created them to be lords. For this reason they took the name of Inca, which is the same as lord. They took 'Ccapac' as an additional name because they came out of the window 'Ccapac-tocco,' which means 'rich,' although afterwards they used this term to denote the chief lord over many.

The names of the eight brethren were as follows: The eldest of the men, and the one with the most authority was named Manco Ccapac, the second Ayar Auca, the third Ayar Cachi, the fourth Ayar Uchu. Of the women the eldest was called Mama Occlo, the second Mama Huaco, the third Mama Ipacura, or, as others say, Mama Cura, the fourth Mama Raua.

The eight brethren, called Incas, said – "We are born strong and wise, and with the people who will here join us, we shall be powerful. We will go forth from this place to seek fertile lands and when we find them we will subjugate the people and take the lands, making war on all those who do not receive us as their lords." This, as they relate, was said by Mama Huaco, one of the women, who was fierce and cruel. Manco Ccapac, her brother, was also cruel and atrocious. This being agreed upon between the eight, they began to move the people who lived near the hill, putting it to them that their reward would be to become rich and to receive the lands and estates of those who were conquered and subjugated. For these objects they moved ten tribes or ayllus, which means among these barbarians 'lineages' or 'parties'; the names of which are as follows:

I. Chauin Cuzco Ayllu of the lineage of Ayar Cachi, of which there are still some in Cuzco, the chiefs being Martin Chucumbi, and Don Diego Huaman Paucar.

II. Arayraca Ayllu Cuzco-Callan. At present there are of this ayllu Juan Pizarro Yupanqui, Don Francisco Quispi, Alonso Tarma Yupanqui of the lineage of Ayar Uchu.

III. Tarpuntay Ayllu. Of this there are now some in Cuzco.

IV. Huacaytaqui Ayllu. Some still living in Cuzco.

V. Sañoc Ayllu. Some still in Cuzco. The above five lineages are Hanan-Cuzco, which means the party of Upper Cuzco.

VI. Sutic-Tocco Ayllu is the lineage which came out of one of the windows called 'Sutic-Tocco,' as has been before explained. Of these there are still some in Cuzco, the chiefs being Don Francisco Avca Micho Avri Sutic, and Don Alonso Hualpa.

VII. Maras Ayllu. These are of the men who came forth from the window 'Maras-Tocco.' There are some of these now in Cuzco, the chiefs being Don Alonso Llama Oca, and Don Gonzalo Ampura Llama Oca.

VIII. Cuycusa Ayllu. Of these there are still some in Cuzco, the chief being Cristoval Acllari.

IX. Masca Ayllu. Of this there is in Cuzco, Juan Quispi.

X. Oro Ayllu. Of this lineage is Don Pedro Yucay.

I say that all these ayllus have preserved their records in such a way that the memory of them has not been lost. There are more of them than are given above, for I only insert the chiefs who are the protectors and heads of the lineages, under whose guidance they are preserved. Each chief has the duty and obligation to protect the rest, and to know the history of his ancestors. Although I say that these live in Cuzco, the truth is that they are in a suburb of the city which the Indians call Cayocache and which is known to us as Belem, from the church of that parish which is that of our Lady of Belem.

Returning to our subject, all these followers above-mentioned marched with Manco Ccapac and the other brethren to seek for land (and to tyrannize over those who did no harm to them, nor gave them any excuse for war, and without any right or title beyond what has been stated). To be prepared for war they chose for their leaders Manco Ccapac and Mama Huaco, and with this arrangement the companies of the hill of Tampu-tocco set out, to put their design into execution.

The Road Which These Companies of the Incas Took to the Valley of Cuzco, and of the Fables Which are Mixed with their History

The Incas and the rest of the companies or *ayllus* set out from their homes at Tampu-tocco, taking with them their property and arms, in sufficient numbers to form a good squadron, having for their chiefs the said Manco Ccapac and Mama Huaco.

Manco Ccapac took with him a bird like a falcon, called *indi*, which they all worshipped and feared as a sacred, or, as some say, an enchanted thing, for they thought that this bird made Manco Ccapac their lord and obliged the people to follow him. It was thus that Manco Ccapac gave them to understand, and it was always kept in a covered hamper of straw, like a box, with much care. He left it as an heirloom to his son, and the Incas had it down to the time of Inca Yupanqui. In his hand he carried with him a staff of gold, to test the lands which they would come to.

Marching together they came to a place called Huanacancha, four leagues from the valley of Cuzco, where they remained for some time, sowing and seeking for fertile land. Here Manco Ccapac had connection with his sister Mama Occlo, and she became pregnant by him. As this place did not appear able to sustain them, being barren, they advanced to another place called Tampu-quiro, where Mama Occlo begot a son named Sinchi Rocca. Having celebrated the natal feasts of the infant, they set out in search of fertile land, and came to another place called Pallata, which is almost contiguous to Tampu-quiro, and there they remained for some years.

Not content with this land, they came to another called Hays-quisro, a quarter of a league further on. Here they consulted together over what ought to be done respecting their journey, and over the best way of getting rid of Ayar Cachi, one of the four brothers. Ayar Cachi was fierce and strong, and very dexterous with the sling. He committed great cruelties and was oppressive both among the natives of the places they passed, and among his own people. The other brothers were afraid that the conduct of Ayar Cachi would cause their companies to disband and desert, and that they would be left alone. As Manco Ccapac was prudent, he concurred with the opinion of the others that they should secure their object by deceit. They called Ayar Cachi and said to him, "Brother! Know that in Ccapac-tocco we have forgotten the golden vases called *tupac-cusi*, and certain seeds, and the *napa*, which is our principal ensign of sovereignty." The *napa* is a sheep of the country, the colour white, with a red body cloth, on the top ear-rings of gold, and on the breast a plate with red badges such as was worn by rich Incas when they went abroad; carried in front of all on a pole with a cross of plumes of feathers. This was called *suntur-paucar*. They said that it would be for the good of all, if he would go back and fetch them. When Ayar Cachi refused to return, his sister Mama Huaco, raising her foot, rebuked him with furious words, saying, "How is it that there should be such cowardice in so strong a youth as you are? Get ready for the journey, and do not fail to go to Tampu-tocco, and do what you are ordered." Ayar Cachi was shamed by these words. He obeyed and started to carry out his orders. They gave him, as a companion, one of those who had come with them, named Tampu-chacay, to whom they gave secret orders to kill Ayar Cachi at Tampu-tocco, and not to return with him. With these orders they both arrived at Tampu-tocco. They had scarcely arrived when Ayar Cachi entered through the window Ccapac-tocco, to get the things for which he had been sent. He was no sooner inside than Tampu-chacay, with great celerity, put a rock against the opening of the window and sat upon it, that Ayar Cachi might remain inside and die there. When Ayar Cachi turned to the opening and found it closed he understood the treason of which the traitor Tampu-chacay had been guilty, and determined to get out if it was possible, to take vengeance. To force an opening he used such force and shouted so loud that he made the mountain tremble. With a loud voice he spoke these words to Tampu-chacay, "Thou traitor! thou who hast done me so much harm, thinkest thou to convey the news of my mortal imprisonment? That shall, never happen. For thy treason thou shalt remain outside, turned into a stone." So it was done, and to this day they show the stone on one side of the window Ccapac-tocco. Turn we now to the seven brethren who had remained at Hays-quisro. The death of Ayar Cachi being known, they were very sorry for what they had done, for, as he was valiant, they regretted much to be without him when the time came to make war on any one. So they mourned for him. This Ayar Cachi was so dexterous with a sling and so strong that with each shot he pulled down a mountain and filled up a ravine. They say that the ravines, which we now see on their line of march, were made by Ayar Cachi in hurling stones.

The seven Incas and their companions left this place, and came to another called Quirirmanta at the foot of a hill which was afterwards called Huanacauri. In this place they consulted together how they should divide the duties of the enterprise amongst themselves, so that there should be distinctions between them. They agreed that as Manco Ccapac had had a child by his sister, they should be married and have children to continue the lineage, and that he should be the leader. Ayar Uchu was to remain as a *huaca* for the sake of religion. Ayar Auca, from the position they should select, was to take possession of the land set apart for him to people.

Leaving this place they came to a hill at a distance of two leagues, a little more or less, from Cuzco. Ascending the hill they saw a rainbow, which the natives call *huanacauri*. Holding it to be a fortunate sign, Manco Ccapac said: "Take this for a sign that the world will not be destroyed by water. We shall arrive and from hence we shall select where we shall found our city." Then, first casting lots, they saw that the signs were good for doing so, and for exploring the land from that point and becoming lords of it. Before they got to the height where the rainbow was, they saw a *huaca* which was a place of worship in human shape, near the rainbow. They determined among themselves to seize it and take it away from there. Ayar Uchu offered himself to go to it, for they said that he was very like it. When Ayar Uchu came to the statue or *huaca*, with great courage he sat upon it, asking it what it did there. At these words the *huaca* turned its head to see who spoke, but, owing to the weight upon it, it could not see. Presently, when Ayar Uchu wanted to get off he was not able, for he found that the soles of his feet were fastened to the shoulders of the *huaca*. The six brethren, seeing that he was a prisoner, came to succour him. But Ayar Uchu, finding himself thus transformed, and that his brethren could not release him, said to them – "O Brothers, an evil work you have wrought for me. It was for your sakes that I came where I must remain for ever, apart from your company. Go! go! happy brethren. I announce to you that you will be great lords. I, therefore, pray that in recognition of the desire I have always had to please you, you will honour and venerate me in all your festivals and ceremonies, and that I shall be the first to whom you make offerings. For I remain here for your sakes. When you celebrate the *huarachico* (which is the arming of the sons as knights) you shall adore me as their father, for I shall remain here for ever." Manco Ccapac answered that he would do so, for that it was his will and that it should be so ordered. Ayar Uchu promised for the youths that he would bestow on them the gifts of valour, nobility, and knighthood, and with these last words he remained, turned into stone. They constituted him the *huaca* of the Incas, giving it the name of Ayar Uchu Huanacauri. And so it always was, until the arrival of the Spaniards, the most venerated *huaca*, and the one that received the most offerings of any in the kingdom. Here the Incas went to arm the young knights until about twenty years ago, when the Christians abolished this ceremony. It was religiously done, because there were many abuses and idolatrous practices, offensive and contrary to the ordinances of God our Lord.

Entry of the Incas into the Valley of Cuzco, and the Fables They Relate Concerning It

The six brethren were sad at the loss of Ayar Uchu, and at the loss of Ayar Cachi; and, owing to the death of Ayar Cachi, those of the lineage of the Incas, from that time to this day, always fear to go to Tampu-tocco, lest they should have to remain there like Ayar Cachi.

They went down to the foot of the hill, whence they began their entry into the valley of Cuzco, arriving at a place called Matahua, where they stopped and built huts, intending to remain there some time. Here they armed as knight the son of Manco Ccapac and of Mama Occlo, named Sinchi Rocca, and they bored his ears, a ceremony which is called *huarachico*, being the insignia of his knighthood and nobility, like the custom known among ourselves. On this occasion they indulged in great rejoicings, drinking for many days, and at intervals mourning for the loss of their brother Ayar Uchu. It was here that they invented the mourning sound for the dead, like the cooing of a dove. Then they performed the dance called *Ccapac Raymi*, a ceremony of the royal or great lords. It is danced, in long purple robes, at the ceremonies they call *quicochico*, which is when girls come to maturity, and the *huarachico*, when they pierce the ears of the Incas, and the *rutuchico*, when the Inca's hair is cut the first time, and the *ayuscay*, which is when a child is born, and they drink continuously for four or five days.

After this they were in Matahua for two years, waiting to pass on to the upper valley to seek good and fertile land. Mama Huaco, who was very strong and dexterous, took two wands of gold and hurled them towards the north. One fell, at two shots of an arquebus, into a ploughed field called Colcapampa and did not drive in well, the soil being loose and not terraced. By this they knew that the soil was not fertile. The other went further, to near Cuzco, and fixed well in the territory called Huanay-pata, where they knew the land to be fertile. Others say that this proof was made by Manco Ccapac with the staff of gold which he carried himself, and that thus they knew of the fertility of the land, when the staff sunk in the land called Huanay-pata, two shots of an arquebus from Cuzco. They knew the crust of the soil to be rich and close, so that it could only be broken by using much force.

Let it be by one way or the other, for all agree that they went trying the land with a pole or staff until they arrived at this Huanay-pata, when they were satisfied. They were sure of its fertility, because after sowing perpetually, it always yielded abundantly, giving more the more it was sown. They determined to usurp that land by force, in spite of the natural owners, and to do with it as they chose. So they returned to Matahua.

From that place Manco Ccapac saw a heap of stones near the site of the present monastery of Santo Domingo at Cuzco. Pointing it out to his brother Ayar Auca, he said, "Brother! you remember how it was arranged between us, that you should go to take possession of the land where we are to settle. Well! look at that stone." Pointing out the stone he continued, "Go thither flying," for they say that Ayar Auca had developed some wings, "and seating yourself there, take possession of land seen from that heap of stones. We will presently come to settle and reside." When Ayar Auca heard the words of his brother, he opened his wings and flew to that place which Manco Ccapac had pointed out. Seating himself there, he was presently turned into stone, and was made the stone of possession. In the ancient language of this valley the heap was called *cozco*, whence that site has had the name of Cuzco to this day. From this circumstance the Incas had a proverb which said, "Ayar Auca cuzco huanca," or, "Ayar Auca a heap of marble." Others say that Manco Ccapac gave the name of Cuzco because he wept in that place where he buried his brother Ayar Cachi. Owing to his sorrow and to the fertility, he gave that name which in the ancient language of that time signified sad as well as fertile. The first version must be the correct one because Ayar Cachi was not buried at Cuzco, having died at Ccapac-tocco as has been narrated before. And this is generally affirmed by Incas and natives.

Five brethren only remaining, namely Manco Ccapac, and the four sisters, and Manco Ccapac being the only surviving brother out of four, they presently resolved to advance to where Ayar Auca had taken possession. Manco Ccapac first gave to his son Sinchi Rocca a wife named Mama Cuca, of the lineage of Sañu, daughter of a Sinchi named Sitic-huaman, by whom he afterwards had a son named Sapaca. He also instituted the sacrifice called *capa cocha*, which is the immolation of two male and two female infants before the idol Huanacauri, at the time when the Incas were armed as knights. These things being arranged, he ordered the companies to follow him to the place where Ayar Auca was.

Arriving on the land of Huanay-pata, which is near where now stands the *Arco de la plata* leading to the Charcas road, he found settled there a nation of Indians named Huallas, already mentioned. Manco Ccapac and Mama Occlo began to settle and to take possession of the land and water, against the will of the Huallas. In this business they did many violent and unjust things. As the Huallas attempted to defend their lives and properties, many cruelties were committed by Manco Ccapac and Mama Occlo. They relate that Mama Occlo was so fierce that, having killed one of the Hualla Indians, she cut him up, took out the inside, carried the heart and lungs in her mouth, and with an *ayuinto*, which is a stone fastened to a rope, in her hand, she attacked the Huallas with diabolical resolution. When the Huallas beheld this horrible and inhuman spectacle, they feared that the same things would be done to them, being simple and timid, and they fled and abandoned their rights. Mama Occlo reflecting on her cruelty, and fearing that for it they would be branded as tyrants, resolved not to spare any Huallas, believing that the affair would thus be forgotten. So they killed all they could lay their hands upon, dragging infants from their mothers' wombs, that no memory might be left of these miserable Huallas.

Having done this Manco Ccapac advanced, and came within a mile of Cuzco to the S. E., where a Sinchi named Copalimayta came out to oppose him. We have mentioned this chief before and that, although he was a late comer, he settled with the consent of the natives of the valley, and had been incorporated in the nation of Sauaseray Panaca, natives of the site of Santo Domingo at Cuzco. Having seen the strangers invading their lands and tyrannizing over them, and knowing the cruelties inflicted on the Huallas, they had chosen Copalimayta as their *Sinchi*. He came forth to resist the invasion, saying that the strangers should not enter his lands or those of the natives. His resistance was such that Manco Ccapac and his companions were obliged to turn their backs. They returned to Huanay-pata, the land they had usurped from the Huallas. From the sowing they had made they derived a fine crop of maize, and for this reason they gave the place a name which means something precious.

After some months they returned to the attack on the natives of the valley, to tyrannize over them. They assaulted the settlement of the Sauaseras, and were so rapid in their attack that they captured Copalimayta, slaughtering many of the Sauaseras with great cruelty. Copalimayta, finding himself a prisoner and fearing death, fled out of desperation, leaving his estates, and was never seen again after he escaped. Mama Huaco and Manco Ccapac usurped his houses, lands and people. In this way Manco Ccapac, Mama Huaco, Sinchi Rocca, and Manco Sapaca settled on the site between the two rivers, and erected the House of the Sun, which they called Ynti-cancha. They divided all that position, from Santo Domingo to the junction of the rivers into four neighbourhoods or quarters which they call *cancha*. They called one Quinti-cancha, the second Chumpi-cancha, the third Sayri-cancha, and the fourth Yarampuy-cancha. They divided the sites among themselves, and thus the city was peopled, and, from the heap of stones of Ayar Auca it was called Cuzco.

Viracocha

IN OTHER DAYS we who are of the race of the Incas worshipped the Sun; we held that he was the greatest and most benignant of all beings, and we named ourselves the children of the Sun. We had traditions that told of the pitiable ways that we and the rest of the human race lived in before the Sun, having had compassion upon us, decided to lead us towards better ways of living … Lo, now! Our Lord, the Sun, put his two children, a son and a daughter, in a boat upon Lake Titicaca. He told them they were to float upon the water until they came to where men lived. He put his golden staff into the hands of his son. He told him he was to lead men into a place where that staff, dropped upon the earth, sank deep down into it.

So the children of our Lord the Sun went upon the waters of Lake Titicaca. They came to where our fathers lived in those far days.... Where we live now we see villages and cities; we see streams flowing down from the mountains, and being led this way and that way to water our crops and our trees; we see flocks of llamas feeding on good grass with their lambs – countless flocks. But in those days we lived where there were thickets and barren rocks; we had no llamas; we had no crops; we knew not how to make the waters flow this way and that way; we had no villages, no cities, no temples. We lived in clefts of the rocks and holes in the ground. The covering of our bodies was of bark or of leaves, or else we went naked in the day and without covering to put over us in the night. We ate roots that we pulled up out of the ground, or fought with the foxes for the dead things they were carrying away. No one bore rule amongst us, and we knew nothing of duty or kindness of one to another.

Out of their boat on Lake Titicaca came the children of our Lord to us. They brought us together; they had rule over us, and they showed us how to live as husband and wife and children, and how to know those who were leaders amongst us and how to obey those leaders. And having showed us these things they led us from the land they had found us in.

And often did he who was the son of our Lord the Sun drop the golden staff upon the ground as we went on. Sometimes the staff sank a little way into the earth, sometimes it sank to half its length in the earth. We came to a place where the golden staff, dropped by him who was the son of our Lord the Sun, sank into the earth until only its top was to be seen. And there we stayed, or, rather, there our fathers stayed, for we are many generations from the men and women who came into this place with the two who were the children of the Sun.

They showed us how to sow crops in that rich ground, and how to lead water down from the hills to water the crops and the trees. They showed us how to tame the llamas, and how to herd them and tend them as tamed beasts. They showed us how to take the wool from them and weave the wool into garments for ourselves; also, they showed us how to dye our garments so that we went brightly clad in the light of the sun. They showed us how to work in gold and silver, and how to make vessels of clay, and how to put shapes and figures upon these vessels. They showed us how to build houses, and how to build villages, and cities, and temples. And they showed us, too, how to obey the rule of those who were left to rule over us, the Incas.

Then the two who were the son and daughter of the Sun left us. Before they went from us they told us that the Sun, their father, would adopt us as his children. And so we of the Inca race became the children of the Sun. They said to us, too, "Our father, the Sun, does good to the whole world; he gives light that men may see and follow their pursuits; he makes men warm when they had been cold; he ripens their crops; he increases their flocks of llamas; he brings dew upon the ground. The Sun, our father, goes round the earth each day that he may know of man's necessities and help him to provide for them. Be like the Sun, then, far-seeing, regular in all your occupations. And bring the worship of the Sun amongst the tribes who live in darkness and ignorance."

And so these two, his son and daughter who were sent to us by the Sun, were seen no more by us. But we knew ourselves now as the children of the Sun. We subdued the tribes in his name, and brought the knowledge of his beneficence amongst them. We built a great temple to him. And the daughters of the Incas in hundreds served him as Virgins of the Sun.

Yes, but there were those amongst us who came to have other thoughts about Heaven and the ways of Heaven. "Does not the Sun go as another being directs him to go?" one of the Incas said to his councillors. "Is he not like an arrow shot onward by a man? Is he not like a llama tethered by the will of a man rather than like one who has freedom? Does he not let a little cloud obscure his splendour? Is it not plain that he may never take rest from his tasks?"

So men amongst us have said, and they who have said them have mentioned a name. Viracocha that name is. And then they would say words from rites that were known to the people of this land before the Incas came into it. They would say, "O conquering Viracocha! Thou gavest life and valour to men, saying, 'let this be a man,' and to women saying, 'let this be a woman.' Thou madest them and gavest them being! Watch over them that they may live in health and peace! Thou who art in the high heavens, and among the clouds of the tempest, grant this with long life, and accept this sacrifice, O Creator!" So those who were priests in the land before our fathers came into it prayed.

And they said that it was Viracocha who created the Sun, and created the Moon also. They said that at the beginning the Sun was not brighter than the Moon, and that in his jealousy he flung ashes upon the face of the Moon and dimmed the Moon's primal brightness. And they said that Viracocha could make great terraces of rock and clay rear themselves up with crops upon them, and that he could bring the water-courses to freshen terraces and gardens merely by striking with a hollow cane that he carried.

Now although Viracocha was so great, he obscured himself, and came back to live amongst the Gods in the guise of a beggar. None knew him for Viracocha, the Creator of all things. And he saw the Goddess Cavillaca as she sat amongst llama lambs under a lucma-tree, weaving the wool of the white llama. He saw her and he approached her. He left a ripe fruit beside her. She ate the fruit and she became with child by him.

And when her child was born her parents and her friends said to her, "You must find out who is the father of this child. Let all who live near come to this lucma-tree, and let the child crawl amongst them. The man he crawls to and touches with his hand we will know is his father."

So under the lucma-tree Cavillaca sat, and her child was with her. All who lived near came to that place, and amongst them came Viracocha, still in his beggar's dress. All came near to Cavillaca and her child. The child crawled where they stood. He came to Viracocha. He put his hand up and touched the man who was in the beggar's garb.

Then was Cavillaca made ashamed before all the Gods. She snatched up her child and held him to her. She fled away from that place. She fled towards the ocean with her child. Viracocha put on his robes of splendour and hastened after her. And as he went he cried out, "O Goddess, turn; look back at me! See how splendid I am!" But the Goddess, without turning, fled with her child from before him.

Viracocha went seeking them. As he crossed the peaks he met a condor, and the condor flew with him, and consoled him. Viracocha blessed the condor, and gave him long life and the power to traverse the wilderness and go over the highest peaks; also he gave him the right to prey upon creatures. Afterwards he met a fox; but the fox derided him, telling him that his quest was vain. He cursed the fox, saying to him that he would have to hunt at night, and that men would slay him. He met a puma, and the puma went with him and consoled him. He blessed the puma, saying that he would receive honour from men. As he went down the other side of the mountain, he came upon parrots flying from the trees of their forest. And the parrots cried out words that were of ill-omen. He cursed the parrots, saying that they would never have honour from men. But he blessed the falcon that flew with him down to the sea.

And when he came to the sea he found that Cavillaca and her child had plunged themselves into the water and had been transformed into rocks. Then Viracocha in his grief remained beside the sea.

Now beside the sea there were two virgins who were Urpihuachac's daughters. They were guarded by a serpent. Viracocha charmed the serpent with his wisdom, and the serpent permitted him to approach Urpihuachac's daughters. One flew away and became a dove. But the other lived there with Viracocha. And this Virgin of the Sea showed Viracocha where her mother kept all the fishes of the world. They were in a pond and they could not go through the waters of the world.

Viracocha broke down the walls of their pond, and let them go through the streams and the lakes and the sea. And thus he let men have fishes to eat.

He lived amongst men, and he taught them many arts. He it was, as the priests of those who were here before the Incas say, showed men how to bring streams of water to their crops, and taught them how to build terraces upon the mountains where crops would grow. He set up a great cross upon the mountain Caravay. And when the bird that cries out four times at dawn cried out, and the light came upon the cross he had set up, Viracocha went from amongst men. He went down to the sea, and he walked across it towards the west. But he told those whom he had left behind that he would send messengers back who would protect them and give them renewed knowledge of all he had taught them. He left them, but men still remember the chants that those whom he left on the mountain, by the cross, cried out their longing:

Oh, hear me! From the sky above, In which thou mayst be, From the sea beneath, In which thou mayst be, Creator of the world, Maker of all men; Lord of all Lords, My eyes fail me For longing to see thee; For the sole desire to know thee.

The Llama-Herder and the Virgin of the Sun

THERE WAS A LLAMA-HERDER, a young man who played a flute as he tended his flock; white llamas were in his flock, and many of them had their tender young lambs beside them. Near where he herded was the House of the Virgins of the Sun. Often those who were of that house walked abroad; there were two of them who often drew near and stood behind the rocks to listen to the music of that young man's flute.

One day the young herder whose name was Aroya-Napa looked up, and saw the two Virgins of the Sun standing beside two fountains that were there. And what else should that young man think but that these two most lovely Princesses were the embodiments of the two lovely fountains? He went on his knees to them. They gave him their hands to kiss. And then he knew that they were flesh and blood, albeit flesh and blood of the Inca, and that they were Virgins dedicated to the Sun.

He played upon his flute again, and one of the Princesses felt her heart torn with a love that came into it – a love for this young man who herded llamas. Her name was Chuquillantu, 'Shadow-of-a-lance.' And when her companion turned to go back to the House of the Virgins of the Sun she could hardly bring herself to turn back. Indeed she would not return until she had obtained something that belonged to Aroya-Napa. This was a silver plate that was on his forehead – a silver plate that had on it two figures eating a heart.

Then with her companion, Shadow-of-a-lance went back to the House of the Virgins. When they went within the doorway they were examined as was the custom; their clothes and all they carried were looked over, so that nothing that was unfitting might be brought into the House of the Virgins of the Sun.

In the place where Shadow-of-a-lance slept there were four fountains. Now she lay upon her bed and she thought upon the llama-herder, and she thought upon the silver plate that he had owned and that she now had upon her own forehead, and she thought that what it showed was her own condition, for her heart, too, was being eaten by two figures. She slept, and in her sleep she saw a bird flying between two trees and crying mournfully. In her dream she spoke to the bird – a checollo it was – and she told it that she, too, mourned for that for which there was no remedy – for a love that she, a Virgin of the Sun, had for a young man who herded llamas.

Then the bird told her that she was to arise and seat herself between the fountains, and there sing to herself what was most in her thought. If the fountains sang back the words that she sang to them, a remedy would come to her. Shadow-of-a-lance rose from her bed and sat between the fountains, and sang of the heart that was being eaten by two beings. The fountains sang her words back to her, but sang them in a way that lulled her. All night she sat singing and listening to the song that the fountains sang back to her.

Now he who herded the llamas had a mother who lived upon the mountain. She had skill and wisdom. She dreamed about her son, and when the dawn came she hurried down to where he kept his flock. He was sleeping when she came to where he lay; she saw that his face was covered with the marks of tears. He awakened; she asked him where was the silver plate that he wore upon his forehead; he told her he had given it away, and he told her to whom he had given it. Then the Woman of the Mountain knew that her son longed for a princess, and for a princess who had been dedicated a Virgin of the Sun.

She stood before the but, and she saw Shadow-of-a-lance and her companion coming towards the place where the llama-flock was pasturing. She bade her son lie in his sleeping-place, and she covered him with a cloak she had brought with her – a magic cloak. Then she went amongst the rocks. She gathered herbs; she dipped the herbs in the fountains, and then she cooked them. The two princesses came to where she was; she served them upon her knees – she served them with the dish of herbs she had cooked.

They asked permission to go into the hut; they looked around it, and they looked in places beside it. Shadow-of-a-lance desired to see the young man she had dreamed about, and her companion did as she did. But they did not see the young man. They saw a cloak spread over a sleeping-place, but they knew there was no one under the cloak. Through the magic of the Woman of the Mountain, her son had passed into and was now part of that cloak.

Shadow-of-a-lance admired the texture and the colours of the cloak. The Woman of the Mountain told her that it had been given to her by a woman who had been beloved by Pachacamac, the great God. Then Shadow-of-a-lance, thinking that never again would she look upon the young man who had played on the flute, asked that she might be given the cloak – she wanted to have something that had gone upon him.

The Woman of the Mountain gave her the cloak, and Shadow-of-a-lance and her companion carried it between them. They went into the House of the Virgins of the Sun. 'Me doorkeepers, as was the custom, stayed them and searched them so that nothing unfitting might be brought into that house. Then they went within, carrying the cloak.

Shadow-of-a-lance, as before, lay on her bed. She had laid the cloak beside her bed. In a while she rose, and she sat by the fountains, and she sang of the two beings who were eating her heart. The fountains did not sing her words back to her, and she wept, sitting there. Then she looked to where the cloak lay, and behold! the cloak filled out and became the youth whom she loved, the youth who loved her.

The two were together all through the night, and the fountains sang to them. In the morning they stole out together. But not all the guards were sleeping. One saw them and pursued them. Shadow-of-a-lance and her lover fled up the mountain. But now all the guards of the House of the Virgins of the Sun gave chase to them. They did not come to where there was safety; for the Sun turned the two of them into stones, and as stones they stand to this day between Calca and Huayllapampa.

The Bird Bride

THE CANARIS INDIANS are named from the province of Canaribamba, in Quito, and they have several myths regarding their origin. One recounts that at the deluge two brothers fled to a very high mountain called Huacaquan, and as the waters rose the hill ascended simultaneously, so that they escaped drowning.

When the flood was over they had to find food in the valleys, and they built a tiny house and lived on herbs and roots. They were surprised one day when they went home to find food already prepared for them and *chicha* to drink. This continued for ten days. Then the elder brother decided to hide himself and discover who brought the food.

Very soon two birds, one Aqua, the other Torito (otherwise *quacamayo* birds), appeared dressed as Canaris, and wearing their hair fastened in the same way. The larger bird removed the *llicella*, or mantle the Indians wear, and the man saw that they had beautiful faces and discovered that the bird-like beings were in reality women. When he came out the bird-women were very angry and flew away. When the younger brother came home and found no food he was annoyed, and determined to hide until the bird-women returned.

After ten days the *quacamayos* appeared again on their old mission, and while they were busy the watcher contrived to close the door, and so prevented the younger bird from escaping. She lived with the brothers for a long time, and became the mother of six sons and daughters, from whom all the Canaris proceed. Hence the tribe look upon the *quacamayo* birds with reverence, and use their feathers at their festivals.

The Vision of Yupanqui

THE INCA YUPANQUI before he succeeded to the sovereignty is said to have gone to visit his father, Viracocha Inca. On his way he arrived at a fountain called Susur-pugaio. There he saw a piece of crystal fall into the fountain, and in this crystal he saw the figure of an Indian, with three bright rays as of the sun coming from the back of his head. He wore a ***hautu***, or royal fringe, across the forehead like the Inca. Serpents wound round his arms and over his shoulders. He had ear-pieces in his ears like the Incas, and was also dressed like them. There was the head of a lion between his legs, and another lion was about his shoulders.

Inca Yupanqui took fright at this strange figure, and was running away when a voice called to him by name telling him not to be afraid, because it was his father, the sun, whom he beheld, and that he would conquer many nations, but he must remember his father in his sacrifices and raise revenues for him, and pay him great reverence. Then the figure vanished, but the crystal remained, and the Inca afterwards saw all he wished in it. When he became king he had a statue of the sun made, resembling the figure as closely as possible, and ordered all the tribes he had conquered to build splendid temples and worship the new deity instead of the creator.

Thonapa

SOME MYTHS TELL of a divine personage called Thonapa, who appears to have been a hero-god or civilizing agent like Quetzalcoatl. He seems to have devoted his life to preaching to the people in the various villages, beginning in the provinces of Colla-suya. When he came to Yamquisupa he was treated so badly that he would not remain there. He slept in the open air, clad only in a long shirt and a mantle, and carried a book. He cursed the village. It was soon immersed in water, and is now a lake.

There was an idol in the form of a woman to which the people offered sacrifice at the top of a high hill, Cachapucara. This idol Thonapa detested, so he burnt it, and also destroyed the hill. On another occasion Thonapa cursed a large assembly of people who were holding a great banquet to celebrate a wedding, because they refused to listen to his preaching. They were all changed into stones, which are visible to this day.

Wandering through Peru, Thonapa came to the mountain of Caravaya, and after raising a very large cross he put it on his shoulders and took it to the hill Carapucu, where he preached so fervently that he shed tears. A chief's daughter got some of the water on her head, and the Indians, imagining that he was washing his head (a ritual offence), took him prisoner near the Lake of Carapucu. Very early the next morning a beautiful youth appeared to Thonapa, and told him not to fear, for he was sent from the divine guardian who watched over him. He released Thonapa, who escaped, though he was well guarded. He went down into the lake, his mantle keeping him above the water as a boat would have done.

After Thonapa had escaped from the barbarians he remained on the rock of Titicaca, afterwards going to the town of Tiya-manacu, where again he cursed the people and turned them into stones. They were too bent upon amusement to listen to his preaching. He then followed the river Chacamarca till it reached the sea, and, like Quetzalcoatl, disappeared. This is good evidence that he was a solar deity, or 'man of the sun,' who, his civilizing labours completed, betook himself to the house of his father.

Manco Capac Founds Cuzco

WE ARE TOLD THAT TAMPU-TOCCO was a house on a hill, provided with three windows, named Maras, Sutic, and Capac. Through the first of these came the Maras tribe, through Sutic came the Tampu tribe, and through Capac, the regal window, came four Ayars with their four wives – Ayar Manco and Mama Ocllo; Ayar Auca (the 'joyous,' or 'fighting,' Ayar) and Mama Huaco (the 'warlike'); Ayar Cachi (the 'Salt' Ayar) and Mama Ipacura (the 'Elder Aunt'); Ayar Uchu (the 'Pepper' Ayar) and Mama Raua.

The four pairs knew no father nor mother, beyond the story they told that they came out of the said window by order of Ticci Viracocha; and they declared that Viracocha created them to be lords; but it was believed that by the counsel of the fierce Mama Huaco they decided to go forth and subjugate peoples and lands. Besides the Maras and Tampu peoples, eight other tribes were associated with the Ayars, as vassals, when they began their quest, taking with them their goods and their families. Manco Capac carrying with him, as a palladium, a falcon, called Indi, or Inti – the name of the Sun-god – bore also a golden rod which was to sink into the land at the site where they were to abide; and Salcamayhua says that, in setting out, the hero was wreathed in rainbows, this being regarded as an omen of success.

The journey was leisurely, and in course of it Sinchi Rocca, who was to be the second Inca, was born to Mama Ocllo and Manco Capac; but then came a series of magic transformations by which the three brothers disappeared, leaving the elder without a rival. Ayar Cachi, who had such great power that, with stones hurled from his sling, he split the hills and hurled them up to the clouds, was the first to excite the envy of his brothers; and on the pretext that certain royal treasures had been forgotten in a cave of Tampu-Tocco, he was sent back to secure them, accompanied by a follower who had secret instructions from the brothers to immure him in the cave, once he was inside. This was done, and though Ayar Cachi made the earth shake in his efforts to break through, he could not do so. Nevertheless, he appeared to his brothers, coming in the air with great wings of coloured feathers; and despite their terror, he commanded them to go on to their destiny, found Cuzco, and establish the empire. "I shall remain in the form and fashion that ye shall see on a hill not distant from here; and it will be for your descendants a place of sanctity and worship, and its name shall be Huanacauri. And in return for the good things that ye will have received from me, I pray that ye will always adore me as god and in that place will set up altars whereat to offer sacrifices. If ye do this, ye shall receive help from me in war; and as a sign that from henceforth ye are to be esteemed, honoured, and feared, your ears shall be bored in the manner that ye now behold mine." (It was from this custom of boring and enlarging the ears that the Spaniards called the ruling caste *Orejones* ('Big-Ears'); and it was at the hill of Huanacauri that the Ayar instructed the Incas in the rites by which they initiated youths into the warrior caste. At this mount, which became one of the great Inca shrines, both the Salt and the Pepper Ayars were reputed to have been transformed into stones, or idols, and it was here that the rainbow sign of promise was given.)

As they approached the hill, they saw near the rainbow what appeared to be a man-shaped idol; and Ayar Uchu offered himself to go to it, for they said that he was very like it. He did so, sat upon the stone, and himself became stone, crying: "O Brothers, an evil work ye have wrought for me. It was for your sakes that I came where I must remain forever, apart from your company. Go! go! happy brethren, I announce to you that ye shall be great lords. I therefore pray that, in recognition of the desire I have always had to please you, ye shall honour and venerate me in all your festivals and ceremonies, and that I shall be the first to whom ye make offerings, since I remain here for your sakes. When ye celebrate the *huarochico* (the arming of the sons as knights), ye shall adore me as their father, for I shall remain here forever."

Finally Manco Capac's staff sank into the ground and from their camp the hero pointed to a heap of stones on the site of Cuzco. Showing this to his brother, Ayar Auca, he said, "Brother! thou rememberest how it was arranged between us that thou shouldst go to take possession of the land where we are to settle. Well! behold that stone." Pointing it out, he continued, "Go thither flying," for they say that Ayar Auca had developed some wings; "and seating thyself there, take possession of the land seen from that heap of rocks. We will presently come and settle and reside." When Ayar Auca heard the words of his brother, opening his wings, he flew to that place which Manco Capac had pointed out; and seating himself there, he was presently turned into stone, being made the stone of possession. In the ancient language of this valley the heap was called cozco, whence the site has had the name of Cuzco to this day.

The Llama's Warning

AN OLD PERUVIAN MYTH relates how the world was nearly left without an inhabitant. A man took his llama to a fine place for feeding, but the beast moaned and would not eat, and on its master questioning it, it said there was little wonder it was sad, because in five days the sea would rise and engulf the earth.

The man, alarmed, asked if there was no way of escape, and the llama advised him to go to the top of a high mountain, Villa-coto, taking food for five days. When they reached the summit of the hill all kinds of birds and animals were already there. When the sea rose the water came so near that it washed the tail of a fox, and that is why foxes' tails are black! After five days the water fell, leaving only this one man alive, and from him the Peruvians believed the present human race to be descended.

The Myth of Huathiacuri

AFTER THE DELUGE the Indians chose the bravest and richest man as leader. This period they called Purunpacha (the time without a king). On a high mountain-top appeared five large eggs, from one of which Paricaca, father of Huathiacuri, later emerged. Huathiacuri, who was so poor that he had not means to cook his food properly, learned much wisdom from his father, and the following story shows how this assisted him.

A certain man had built a most curious house, the roof being made of yellow and red birds' feathers. He was very rich, possessing many llamas, and was greatly esteemed on account of his wealth. So proud did he become that he aspired to be the creator himself; but when he became very ill and could not cure himself his divinity seemed doubtful. Just at this time Huathiacuri was travelling about, and one day he saw two foxes meet and listened to their conversation. From this he heard about the rich man and learned the cause of his illness, and forthwith he determined to go on to find him. On arriving at the curious house he met a lovely young girl, one of the rich man's daughters. She told him about her father's illness, and Huathiacuri, charmed with her, said he would cure her father if she would only give him her love. He looked so ragged and dirty that she refused, but she took him to her father and informed him that Huathiacuri said he could cure him. Her father consented to give him an opportunity to do so. Huathiacuri began his cure by telling the sick man that his wife had been unfaithful, and that there were two serpents hovering above his house to devour it, and a toad with two heads under his grinding-stone. His wife at first indignantly denied the accusation, but on Huathiacuri reminding her of some details, and the serpents and toad being discovered, she confessed her guilt. The reptiles were killed, the man recovered, and the daughter was married to Huathiacuri.

Huathiacuri's poverty and raggedness displeased the girl's brother-in-law, who suggested to the bridegroom a contest in dancing and drinking. Huathiacuri went to seek his father's advice, and the old man told him to accept the challenge and return to him. Paricaca then sent him to a mountain, where he was changed into a dead llama. Next morning a fox and its vixen carrying a jar of *chicha* came, the fox having a flute of many pipes. When they saw the dead llama they laid down their things and went toward it to have a feast, but Huathiacuri then resumed his human form and gave a loud cry that frightened away the foxes, whereupon he took possession of the jar and flute. By the aid of these, which were magically endowed, he beat his brother-in-law in dancing and drinking.

Then the brother-in-law proposed a contest to prove who was the handsomer when dressed in festal attire. By the aid of Paricaca Huathiacuri found a red lion-skin, which gave him the appearance of having a rainbow round his head, and he again won.

The next trial was to see who could build a house the quickest and best. The brother-in-law got all his men to help, and had his house nearly finished before the other had his foundation laid. But here again Paricaca's wisdom proved of service, for Huathiacuri got animals and birds of all kinds to help him during the night, and by morning the building was finished except the roof. His brother-in-law got many llamas to come with straw for his roof, but Huathiacuri ordered an animal to stand where its loud screams frightened the llamas away, and the straw was lost. Once more Huathiacuri won the day. At last Paricaca advised Huathiacuri to end this conflict, and he asked his brother-in-law to see who could dance best in a blue shirt with white cotton round the loins. The rich man as usual appeared first, but when Huathiacuri came in he made a very loud noise and frightened him, and he began to run away. As he ran Huathiacuri turned him into a deer. His wife, who had followed him, was turned into a stone, with her head on the ground and her feet in the air, because she had given her husband such bad advice.

The four remaining eggs on the mountain-top then opened, and four falcons issued, which turned into four great warriors. These warriors performed many miracles, one of which consisted in raising a storm which swept away the rich Indian's house in a flood to the sea.

Paricaca and the Invention of Irrigation

HAVING ASSISTED in the performance of several miracles, Paricaca set out determined to do great deeds. He went to find Caruyuchu Huayallo, to whom children were sacrificed. He came one day to a village where a festival was being celebrated, and as he was in very poor clothes no one took any notice of him or offered him anything, till a young girl, taking pity on him, brought him ***chicha*** to drink. In gratitude Paricaca told her to seek a place of safety for herself, as the village would be destroyed after five days, but she was to tell no one of this. Annoyed at the inhospitality of the people, Paricaca then went to a hill top and sent down a fearful storm and flood, and the whole village was destroyed.

Then he came to another village, now San Lorenzo. He saw a very beautiful girl, Choque Suso, crying bitterly. Asking her why she wept, she said the maize crop was dying for want of water. Paricaca at once fell in love with this girl, and after first damming up the little water there was, and thus leaving none for the crop, he told her he would give her plenty of water if she would only return his love. She said he must get water not only for her own crop but for all the other farms before she could consent. He noticed a small rill, from which, by opening a dam, he thought he might get a sufficient supply of water for the farms. He then got the assistance of the birds in the hills, and animals such as snakes, lizards, and so on, in removing any obstacles in the way, and they widened the channel so that the water irrigated all the land. The fox with his usual cunning managed to obtain the post of engineer, and carried the canal to near the site of the church of San Lorenzo.

Paricaca, having accomplished what he had promised, begged Choque Suso to keep her word, which she willingly did, but she proposed living at the summit of some rocks called Yanacaca. There the lovers stayed very happily, at the head of the channel called Cocochallo, the making of which had united them; and as Choque Suso wished to remain there always, Paricaca eventually turned her into a stone.

The Shepherd and the Daughter of the Sun

IN THE SNOW-CLAD CORDILLERA above the valley of Yucay, called Pitu-siray, a shepherd watched the flock of white llamas intended for the Inca to sacrifice to the Sun. He was a native of Laris, named Acoya-napa, a very well disposed and gentle youth. He strolled behind his flock, and presently began to play upon his flute very softly and sweetly, neither feeling anything of the amorous desires of youth, nor knowing anything of them.

He was carelessly playing his flute one day when two daughters of the Sun came to him. They could wander in all directions over the green meadows, and never failed to find one of their houses at night, where the guards and porters looked out that nothing came that could do them harm. Well! the two girls came to the place where the shepherd rested quite at his ease, and they asked him about his llamas.

The shepherd, who had not seen them until they spoke, was surprised, and fell on his knees, thinking that they were the embodiments of two out of the four crystalline fountains which were very famous in those parts. So he did not dare to answer them. They repeated their question about the flock, and told him not to be afraid, for they were children of the Sun, who was lord of all the land, and to give him confidence they took him by the arm. Then the shepherd stood up and kissed their hands. After talking together for some time the shepherd said that it was time for him to collect his flock, and asked their permission. The elder princess, named Chuqui-llantu, had been struck by the grace and good disposition of the shepherd. She asked him his name and of what place he was a native. He replied that his home was at Laris and that his name was Acoya-napa. While he was speaking Chuqui-llantu cast her eyes upon a plate of silver which the shepherd wore over his forehead, and which shone and glittered very prettily. Looking closer she saw on it two figures, very subtilely contrived, who were eating a heart. Chuqui-llantu asked the shepherd the name of that silver ornament, and he said it was called *utusi*. The princess returned it to the shepherd, and took leave of him, carrying well in her memory the name of the ornament and the figures, thinking with what delicacy they were drawn, almost seeming to her to be alive. She talked about it with her sister until they came to their palace. On entering, the doorkeepers looked to see if they brought with them anything that would do harm, because it was often found that women had brought with them, hidden in their clothes, such things as fillets and necklaces. After having looked well, the porters let them pass, and they found the women of the Sun cooking and preparing food. Chuqui-llantu said that she was very tired with her walk, and that she did not want any supper. All the rest supped with her sister, who thought that Acoya-napa was not one who could cause inquietude. But Chuqui-llantu was unable to rest owing to the great love she felt for the shepherd Acoya-napa, and she regretted that she had not shown him what was in her breast. But at last she went to sleep.

In the palace there were many richly furnished apartments in which the women of the Sun dwelt. These virgins were brought from all the four provinces which were subject to the Inca, namely Chincha-suyu, Cunti-suyu, Anti-suyu and Colla-suyu. Within, there were four fountains which flowed towards the four provinces, and in which the women bathed, each in the fountain of the province where she was born. They named the fountains in this way. That of Chincha-suyu was called Chuclla-puquio, that of Cunti-suyu was known as Ocoruro-puquio, Siclla-puquio was the fountain of Anti-suyu, and Llulucha-puquio of Colla-suyu. The most beautiful child of the Sun, Chuqui-llantu, was wrapped in profound sleep. She had a dream. She thought she saw a bird flying from one tree to another, and singing very softly and sweetly. After having sung for some time, the bird came down and regarded the princess, saying that she should feel no sorrow, for all would be well. The princess said that she mourned for something for which there could be no remedy. The singing bird replied that it would find a remedy, and asked the princess to tell her the cause of her sorrow. At last Chuqui-llantu told the bird of the great love she felt for the shepherd boy named Acoya-napa, who guarded the white flock. Her death seemed inevitable. She could have no cure but to go to him whom she so dearly loved, and if she did her father the Sun would order her to be killed. The answer of the singing bird, by name Checollo, was that she should arise and sit between the four fountains. There she was to sing what she had most in her memory. If the fountains repeated her words, she might then safely do what she wanted. Saying this the bird flew away, and the princess awoke. She was terrified. But she dressed very quickly and put herself between the four fountains. She began to repeat what she remembered to have seen of the two figures on the silver plate, singing:

Micuc isutu cuyuc utusi cucim.

Presently all the fountains began to sing the same verse.

Seeing that all the fountains were very favourable, the princess went to repose for a little while, for all night she had been conversing with the *checollo* in her dream.

When the shepherd boy went to his home he called to mind the great beauty of Chuqui-llantu. She had aroused his love, but he was saddened by the thought that it must be love without hope. He took up his flute and played such heart-breaking music that it made him shed many tears, and he lamented, saying: "Ay! ay! ay! for the unlucky and sorrowful shepherd, abandoned and without hope, now approaching the day of your death, for there can be no remedy and no hope." Saying this, he also went to sleep.

The shepherd's mother lived in Laris, and she knew, by her power of divination, the cause of the extreme grief into which her son was plunged, and that he must die unless she took order for providing a remedy. So she set out for the mountains, and arrived at the shepherd's hut at sunrise. She looked in and saw her son almost moribund, with his face covered with tears. She went in and awoke him. When he saw who it was he began to tell her the cause of his grief, and she did what she could to console him. She told him not to be downhearted, because she would find a remedy within a few days. Saying this she departed and, going among the rocks, she gathered certain herbs which are believed to be cures for grief. Having collected a great quantity she began to cook them, and the cooking was not finished before the two princesses appeared at the entrance of the hut. For Chuqui-llantu, when she was rested, had set out with her sister for a walk on the green slopes of the mountains, taking the direction of the hut. Her tender heart prevented her from going in any other direction. When they arrived they were tired, and sat down by the entrance. Seeing an old dame inside they saluted her, and asked her if she could give them anything to eat. The mother went down on her knees and said she had nothing but a dish of herbs. She brought it to them, and they began to eat with excellent appetites. Chuqui-llantu then walked round the hut without finding what she sought, for the shepherd's mother had made Acoya-napa lie down inside the hut, under a cloak. So the princess thought that he had gone after his flock. Then she saw the cloak and told the mother that it was a very pretty cloak, asking where it came from. The old woman told her that it was a cloak which, in ancient times, belonged to a woman beloved by Pachacamac, a deity very celebrated in the valleys on the coast. She said it had come to her by inheritance; but the princess, with many endearments, begged for it until at last the mother consented. When Chuqui-llantu took it into her hands she liked it better than before and, after staying a short time longer in the hut, she took leave of the old woman, and walked along the meadows looking about in hopes of seeing him whom she longed for.

We do not treat further of the sister, as she now drops out of the story, but only of Chuqui-llantu. She was very sad and pensive when she could see no signs of her beloved shepherd on her way back to the palace. She was in great sorrow at not having seen him, and when, as was usual, the guards looked at what she brought, they saw nothing but the cloak. A splendid supper was provided, and when every one went to bed the princess took the cloak and placed it at her bedside. As soon as she was alone she began to weep, thinking of the shepherd. She fell asleep at last, but it was not long before the cloak was changed into the being it had been before. It began to call Chuqui-llantu by her own name. She was terribly frightened, got out of bed, and beheld the shepherd on his knees before her, shedding many tears. She was satisfied on seeing him, and inquired how he had got inside the palace. He replied that the cloak which she carried had arranged about that. then Chuqui-llantu embraced him, and put her finely worked *lipi* mantles on him, and they slept together. When they wanted to get up in the morning, the shepherd again became the cloak. As soon as the sun rose, the princess left the palace of her father with the cloak, and when she reached a ravine in the mountains, she found herself again with her beloved shepherd, who had been changed into himself. But one of the guards had followed them, and when he saw what had happened he gave the alarm with loud shouts. The lovers fled into the mountains which are near the town of Calca. Being tired after a long journey, they climbed to the top of a rock and went to sleep. They heard a great noise in their sleep, so they arose. The princess took one shoe in her hand and kept the other on her foot. Then looking towards the town of Calca both were turned into stone. To this day the two statues may be seen between Calca and Huayllapampa.

The Princess and the Shepherd

FAR OVER THE ANDES, in the little valley of Laris, there once lived a shepherd-boy. His name was Acoya-napa. He was kind and gentle to his flocks of white llamas which he tended for the Inca to sacrifice to the Sun. In the mountain pastures, high above his home, Acoya-napa strolled, day after day, behind his flocks, playing softly upon his flute.

It happened, one day, while Acoya-napa was playing to his flocks, that two daughters of the Sun, beautiful princesses, were wandering through the fields. They drew near at the sound of the music. They saw the gentle shepherd resting at his ease, and they asked him about the llamas.

Acoya-napa had not seen them, until they addressed him, and he thought: "It may be that they are spirits from the mountains," and so he fell upon his knees before them. He dared not answer their questions about the llamas. But they reassured him.

"Do not fear us, for we are the children of the Sun, whose flocks thou carest for, and we wander over the green meadows or through the wide pastures on the mountains all the day long. When the grey twilight steals over the land, then we seek one of the mansions of our father, the Sun, for he has many palaces where we rest the night long. But, we may not enter until the guards have examined us to discover whether there he any necklaces or fillets about us. For should we carry such things with us into the palace of the Sun, great harm would come to us."

By this time, the shepherd's fear had died away, and he talked with the princesses and played sweetly for them until the rays of the sun drew nearer to the earth and cast beautifully coloured lights upon the snow-capped mountain-tops. Then Acoya-napa said:

"Twilight draws near, I must lead my flocks to their fold." And as he turned from them, the elder princess, Chuqui-llantu, detained him. She had been impressed by his grace and gentleness, and she felt a strange reluctance at having him leave her.

"What is thy name?" she asked, "and where dost thou live?"

And the shepherd pausing, answered her, "My name is Acoya-napa, and I live in the sheltered valley of Laris."

Then again Chuqui-llantu delayed his going, asking him about the plate of silver which he wore over his forehead. There were two figures very skilfully carved upon it, that were eating a heart between them. Chuqui-llantu held the plate toward the sunlight, examining it closely, and then returning it to the shepherd, took leave of him and set out for the palace of the Sun with her sister. But all the way home, she could talk of no one but the shepherd. And she described the silver plate which glittered upon his forehead.

When the princesses reached the palace, the guards examined them, and finding nothing harmful about them, allowed them to enter. They found the women of the Sun preparing the evening meal, but Chuqui-llantu would not join them, she was weary, she told them, and desired rest.

When Chuqui-llantu was alone in her room, she gave way to her thoughts of the shepherd lad. And, at last, these thoughts grew into longings. Then she fell asleep, and a strange thing happened. In her sleep, a bird appeared before her and said:

"Why dost thou mourn, fair princess?"

"Ah, little bird," the princess answered, "I mourn for that for which there is no remedy."

"Only tell me thy trouble," said the little bird, "and I will give to thee a remedy for it."

So Chuqui-llantu told the little bird about the shepherd lad who guarded the white flock. "And I must die," she said, "for there is no cure for me but to go to him whom I love; and if I do so, then my father, the Sun, will order me to be put to death."

"Now follow my directions," said the little bird, "and all will be well with thee. Go at once to the garden and sit between the four fountains and sing there those thoughts thou dost have uppermost in thy mind. If the four fountains repeat the words after thee, then mayest thou safely do that which thy soul desirest."

Then the princess awoke. She was all alone in her chamber. There was no little bird there. She was terrified. However, the word of the little bird kept ringing in her ears, and she quickly dressed and hastened to the garden of the four fountains.

"Now what shall I say," thought the princess. Then she remembered the gleaming silver plate that Acoya-napa wore upon his forehead, and she described that in a little song. She had no sooner finished her singing, than to her amazement, the four fountains repeated after her, her very words. *Then* Chuqui-llantu knew that all would be well, that in some way she would be permitted to marry the gentle shepherd lad. So with a light heart, the princess of the Sun returned to her chamber and was soon fast asleep.

Now, Acoya-napa, the shepherd of the white flock, could not free his mind of the thought of the great beauty of Chuqui-llantu. Love was stirring his heart and he was downcast, for there was no hope. He took his flute and played such sad music that he shed tears, murmuring, "*Ay! ay! ay!* for the unlucky shepherd. Now, truly, am I approaching the day of my death. For there is no remedy for me, and there is no hope."

The shepherd's mother in the valley of Laris, knew by her magical power that sorrow had seized her son, and she knew that he must die unless she could help him. So early in the morning she hastened up the mountain-side to the little hut beside the sheep-fold, and there she found Acoya-napa asleep, his face wet with tears. She awakened him, saying:

"Do not be so sad, my child, for I will surely find a remedy for thee." Then she went among the rocks of the mountain-side and gathered herbs which would be a cure for his grief. She collected a great quantity of them and was cooking them, when she saw coming toward the sheep-fold, the two princesses of the Sun. She hastily took off her magical cloak and covered Acoya-napa with it, making him invisible.

Just at that moment the princesses paused at the entrance of the little hut. When they saw the old woman within, Chuqui-llantu said:

"Couldst thou give us to eat, good dame? We have wandered far over the mountain-side and have hunger."

The old woman, kneeling before them, replied: "Truly nothing have I but a dish of herbs. But to that thou art welcome."

Then the princesses sat in the doorway and ate of the herbs, and Chuqui-llantu looked about the hut, hoping to see that one who held all her thoughts. "Ah, he must be with his white flocks," she concluded. Then she spied the cloak. It was woven in a strange, fanciful pattern, and it attracted her attention.

"What a beautiful cloak," she said, looking at it. "Where didst thou get it?"

"It came to me by inheritance," the shepherd's mother answered. "It once belonged to a woman beloved by Pachacamac, the deity of the valley."

Then Chuqui-llantu longed to have the cloak, and at length, begged it of the old woman. And when she finally possessed it her liking for it grew stronger. Soon she took leave of the old woman, and, holding the cloak carefully, wandered over the mountain pastures with her sister, filled with a longing to be with Acoya-napa.

All this while, the shepherd was invisible inside the magical cloak which hung over the princess's arm. And when the maidens returned to the palace of the Sun the guards examined the cloak but thought that no harm could come of it, so it befell that Chuqui-llantu laid it over a chair in her chamber. And there, that night, she wept, telling the cloak of her love for the gentle shepherd. Then quiet slumber comforted her. In the night she awoke, and she saw in place of the cloak, the shepherd-lad, gazing sadly upon her. The princess was filled with fear.

"How didst thou enter the palace?" she asked.

"By means of the magical cloak which thou didst carry so carefully," he answered. "Now, hereafter, I have the power to become the cloak at will."

Then the two made plans to escape, the next day, from the country of the Sun. Early in the morning just as the sun was brightening the mountain-tops the princess started out from the palace with her cloak over her arm. She wandered through the mountain slopes until she entered a ravine, and then, feeling secure from any watchful eye, she placed the cloak upon the ground beside her. At once the shepherd-lad stood before her.

But in the distance, there had followed the princess, a guard of the royal palace, and when he saw the shepherd, he gave the alarm with loud shouts, and hastily pursued them. The lovers fled high up the mountain until, at last, weary and fainting they climbed a giant rock, and in their weariness they fell asleep.

Now, it befell, that the Sun, travelling through the heavens, looked down upon the mountain side, and saw his beautiful daughter, Chuqui-llantu, asleep upon the high rock with the shepherd of the white flocks. And the Sun was filled with anger, and a sound like thunder filled the whole earth, awakening the sleepers.

The lovers arose from the rock and looked toward the town of Calca which lay at their feet. At that instant a strange horror seized them, and when the princess would fain have spoken to her lover, the power of speech had flown! She tried to turn to him, but she could not move. The shepherd, too, stood immovable.

And there upon the high rock overlooking Calca, may be seen to this day, the shepherd of the white flocks and the princess of the Sun.

The Love of Cusi-Coyllur – Joyful Star

THE INCA, PACHAEUTIC, had a beautiful daughter, Cusi-Coyllur – Joyful Star. The child had grown to womanhood and as yet had not been pledged in marriage.

Until the day when Joyful Star first saw Ollanta, her life had been one of peaceful content with her mother. This day she was wandering heart-free in her garden, when she came upon him. Cusi-Coyllur saw at once by his dress that he was one of the chieftains; and Ollanta, for the first time, saw the princess Joyful Star, whose beauty and grace were so celebrated in song. Behold, they loved.

Now both Ollanta and Cusi-Coyllur knew that their love was not lawful. For a chieftain with no royal blood in his veins had no right to aspire to the hand or the love of a daughter of the Inca. So they kept their love secret.

At length Joyful Star became the wife of Ollanta, and no one knew. They were happy now, but in the midst of their happiness Ollanta was sent upon an expedition by the Inca, who had no suspicion of their marriage.

With Ollanta absent, Joyful Star grew sad and silent, and at last, sorrowing over her loneliness, she confessed to her mother her love and her marriage.

One day Ollanta returned to her. "We must have our marriage declared publicly," he said.

"It may be that my father will have us put to death," Cusi-Coyllur objected. So it seemed better to gain the consent of the Inca before making their marriage known.

So Ollanta, seeking an audience with the Inca, bravely declared his love for Cusi-Coyllur, and asked the Inca's gracious consent to their marriage. But his pleading was met with scorn, and Ollanta, defying him, left his presence to raise the standard of rebellion.

Now Ollanta was a powerful chieftain and soon had caused a general uprising of malcontents, who looked to him to establish a new order of rule. After long warfare Ollanta was victorious, in the end defeating one of the royal generals.

This being accomplished, there was opportunity to flee to some place of safety with Cusi-Coyllur, and there to live their life of happiness free from all danger. *But Cusi-Coyllur had disappeared*! No one could tell Ollanta where she was, whether she were dead or alive. Search where he might, not the slightest trace of her could be found. So the years passed.

Now it happened that in the midst of the confusion of war and bloodshed, Cusi-Coyllur – Joyful Star – had given birth to a daughter. Ollanta, leading the rebel forces could not give her protection, and Joyful Star knew that her father would inflict punishment upon her, perhaps the severest torture, when he discovered the truth. But, at least, she possessed those first joys of motherhood – whatever might come to her, he could not take from her those hours when she held her baby to her bosom.

"How beautiful!" she whispered. "Why, that shall be her name!" And so the child was called Yma Sumac, How Beautiful.

Then her punishment swiftly descended upon Cusi-Coyllur. The child was taken from her – her baby, How Beautiful. Had she been put to death? No one vouchsafed a word to the frantic mother. She scarcely noticed that they had placed her in a dungeon in the dark convent. Where was her child, her daughter? Where was Ollanta, her husband? She crouched on the floor of the dungeon, groaning and sobbing. And so time dragged wearily along until years had passed.

Yma Sumac, How Beautiful, had been taken to the same convent to be reared. Mother and child were within the same walls, each ignorant of the presence of the other. This was a part of the punishment of Cusi-Coyllur that the Inca had pronounced upon her. As Yma Sumac grew old enough to play in the convent garden, she would very often hear moans and sobs from some place within the walls. The child would approach the wall and listen, her heart rilled with a strange unrest and pain. At last she went to her guardian, Pitu Salla.

"While I am at play in the garden there come to me strange sounds like some one groaning and sobbing. And I am rilled with longing to go to that one in sorrow. It is some woman. Who is that one so sorrowful? Something tells me that I know her."

But Pitu Salla evaded the questions. Much as she loved Yma Sumac, much as she desired to bring mother and child together again, there was always present before her the threats of terrible tortures and death made by the Inca when he gave these two into her keeping. No, Yma Sumac should never know; Cusi-Coyllur should never know; her days in the dreary dungeon must wearily pass, filled with pain and longing.

As Yma Sumac grew older it became more difficult to evade her questions and to resist her pleadings. At last, in despair, Pitu Salla told her the story of her mother, Cusi-Coyllur, Joyful Star.

Yma Sumac's pleadings to be allowed to go to her mother were now continuous and heartbreaking. But Pitu Salla feared the Inca too much to allow this.

Just at this time, however, came the word that the Inca was dead and that Yupanqui, his son, Cusi-Coyllur's brother, had succeeded him. *Then* Pitu Salla hastened to grant the prayer of the child.

No word of this was told to Cusi-Coyllur, who throughout the long days and weeks and years had mourned for her child and for Ollanta. Pitu Salla led the child to her mother's dungeon and opened the door. Yma Sumac stepped softly over the threshold. There before her was the sorrowful one, her mother.

"My mother," she said ever so gently. And then Cusi-Coyllur held her child in her arms once again.

"Yma Sumac, my child, my daughter!" she whispered again and again.

Throughout all these years Ollanta had been vainly searching for Cusi-Coyllur, Joyful Star. But no trace of her could he discover. And when the death of the Inca caused another uprising, Ollanta again led the revolutionists, determined to gain power, at least long enough to find Cusi-Coyllur. But this time defeat came to Ollanta, and he with many others was taken prisoner.

When Yupanqui, the new Inca, heard of Ollanta 's capture, he had the prisoner brought before him, for he had long known of the marriage of his sister and Ollanta, and had wished to bring them together again.

The Inca had just given Ollanta his freedom, when there came before him the little maiden, Yma Sumac, How Beautiful. In her earnestness she knelt before the Inca, not noticing the presence of Ollanta, and pleaded for her mother's freedom, and that they might be permitted to live together. She told Yupanqui of their long years of imprisonment and how, now that she had been restored to her mother since the death of the Inca, her mother had but one sorrow and that was for Ollanta, her husband.

Yupanqui placed the child in Ollanta's arms. "This is your father, my child," he said. "This is Ollanta. And now we will go to your mother Cusi-Coyllur."

There in the convent prison, Cusi-Coyllur and Ollanta found each other. Their child, Yma Sumac, How Beautiful, had brought them together, and the great darkness of Cusi-Coyllur's life gave place to gleaming sunshine.

The Paccari-tampu Myth

THERE IS A MYTH which was told to all the Spanish authors by their native informants, and is retailed by them with some variations, the most authentic version being that officially received from the Incas by Sarmiento. While the Titicaca myth was obviously invented to account for the ancient ruins and statues, and has no historical value, the Paccari-tampu myth is as certainly the outcome of a real tradition, and is the fabulous version of a distant historical event.

We are taken to the country of refuge at Tampu-tocco, where one side is protected from invasion by the deep gorge of the Apurimac. The fugitives of long ages back had multiplied. The descendants were more civilized, therefore more powerful than their neighbour's, and the time had come for the acquisition of better and more extensive territory. The idea of windows in the following myth was perhaps suggested by the word *Tocco*, the meaning of which is a window in Quichua. The district is called Paccari-tampu, or the 'Tavern of the Dawn,' in the legend, and Tampu-tocco is the hill with the three openings or windows, called Maras, Sutic, and Ccapac.

The legend relates how, out of the Maras window came a tribe with the same name, from the Sutic window came a tribe named Tampu. Out of the central Ccapac window came four august personages, all bearing the title of Ayar, a designation of several of the ancient kings. There were Manco, the princely; Ayar Auca, the fighting or joyful Ayar; Cachi, the salt Ayar; and Uchu, the pepper Ayar. With them were their four wives, Occlo, the august princess; Huaco, the warlike princess; Ipacura, the elder aunt; and Raua.

The four children of the sun, with their four wives, consulted together and came to a momentous decision: "We are born strong and wise, and with the people who will follow us we are powerful. We will go forth to seek more fertile lands, and when we find them we will subdue the people, making war upon all who do not receive us as their Lords." There was a considerable force at their command besides the two tribes who are said to have issued from the windows on the hill of Tampu-Tocco, named Maras and Tampu. Eight other *ayllus* or lineages were mustered under the banner of the Ayars, whose names were preserved. The Chavin tribe served under the salt Ayar. With it were the Arayraca tribe, the Cuycusa, the Masca, the Uru, and the Sañoc. The Tarpuntay was probably the priestly and sacrificial caste, while the Huacay Taqui *ayllu* was also a religious body conducting ceremonials and musical festivals. The gathering of these ten tribes together seems to have been a veritable exodus under the leadership of the Ayars. For they not only took with them their arms, but also their movable property, wives and children.

Their way was north-east for not more than twenty-five miles, for no doubt Cuzco was their goal from the beginning, well known to them as a desirable central position where megalithic buildings gave evidence of former occupation by the ancient civilizers. Starting from their homes at Tampu-tocco their movements were slow and deliberate, even stopping to sow and reap. The Ayar Manco was the leader. He took with him a golden staff. When the soil was so fertile that its whole length sank into the rich mould, there was to be the final resting-place. He also had with him a bird like a falcon, carried in a hamper, which all the people looked upon as sacred. It does not appear whether it was alive or artificial, but it was the Ayar's familiar spirit called Huauqui,or brother.

Their first march took this army of empire builders to a place called Huanacancha, where there was a long halt, and the next sojourn was at Tampu-quiru and Pallata, contiguous villages. Here they remained for several years sowing and reaping crops. But they were not satisfied with it, and moved on to another valley, called Hais Quisru.

The story proceeds to relate the way in which Manco got rid of his three brothers, so as to rule alone. The salt Ayar is described as so cruel and oppressive that the brothers feared that their followers would desert and leave them alone. He was so dexterous with the sling, and so strong that with each shot he pulled down a mountain and filled up a ravine. The existing ravines on the line of march were made by the salt Ayar in hurling rocks. The Inca Garcilasso tells us that the meaning of salt (Cachi), as applied to this Ayar, signifies instruction in rational life. His teaching must have been rather vigorous. We are told that his brothers feared him, and conspired to take his life.

They made a plot alike cunning and cruel. They called the salt Ayar to them and told him that some precious insignia had been forgotten, and left in the cave whence they came, called Ccapac-Tocco. These were the golden vases called Tupac Cusi, and the Napa, a sacred figure of a llama. They said that it would be for the good of all if he would go back and fetch them. At first he refused, but the strong-minded Mama Huaco rebuked him with stinging words "How is it that there should be such cowardice in so strong a youth as you are?" she exclaimed. "Get ready for the journey, and do not fail to return to Tampu-tocco, and do as you are desired." He was shamed by these words, and set out with a companion named Tampu-chacay, who was an accomplice of the fratricides. When they arrived the salt Ayar entered the cave to fetch the treasures, which were not really there. His treacherous companion, with great celerity, rolled a rock against the opening and sat upon it, so that the salt Ayar might remain inside and die there. The outraged prince exerted all his mighty strength to move the rock. His cries made the mountains tremble. But all was of no avail. With his last breath he denounced the traitor, declaring that he should be turned into a stone and never return to report the success of his crime. To this day the traitor stone may be seen by the side of the Ccapac-tocco. The salt Ayar was thus disposed of. Next came the turn of the pepper Ayar.

The army of the Ayars continued their very deliberate advance, and came to a place called Quirirmanta, only a few miles from the valley of Cuzco. Here there was a hill which, according to Sarmiento, was afterwards called Huanacauri. According to the legend, the brothers saw a sacred *Huaca* or idol on the hill, and proposed to take it away with them. The pepper Ayar was induced to approach it, and when he came in contact with the idol he was himself converted into stone.

He just had time to say: "Go, happy brothers. When you celebrate the *Huarachicu*, I shall be adored as the father of the young knights, for I must remain here for ever" Garcilasso explains that the name of pepper (*Uchu*) was applied to this Ayar as symbolically meaning the delight experienced from leading a rational life. Huanacauri or Huayna-captiy became one of the most sacred *Huacas* of the Peruvians. The word seems to have reference to the great festival when the youths received a sort of knighthood, the ceremony being performed near the *Huaca*. *Huayna* means a youth. *Cauri* is corrupt and has no meaning, but *Captiy* is the present subjunctive of the auxiliary verb. Here the unfortunate pepper Ayar was kept in memory, and received adoration at the great annual festival of arming the youths, for many generations.

Ayar Manco had now disposed of two of his brothers. The turn of the joyful or fighting Ayar was to come next. Meanwhile the march continued *festina lente*; and two years were passed in sowing and reaping at a place called Matahua, just within the Cuzco valley. Then it is related that Ayar Manco hurled his golden staff as far as Huanay-pata, where it sank into the earth. By this they knew that the land was fertile and suited for settlement. But first the joyful Ayar must be disposed of. A pile of stones was in sight, where the temple of the sun afterwards stood. Manco told his last remaining brother, who was winged, that he must fly thither and take possession of the territory. The joyful Ayar did so, and when he sat on the mount, lo and behold! he was turned into a stone. This cairn or mound was called Cuzco, whence the name of the future city. The word means literally a clod of earth, or hard, unirrigated land. Cuzquini is to level or break clods of earth.

Whether the three Ayars were disposed of in this miraculous way, or whether their lives were taken without a disturbance of the laws of nature, Manco now had no rival. He occupied a strong position with his army, near the joyous Ayar's fatal Cuzco, and forcibly subdued the Alcavisas and other former settlers in the valley.

This Paccari-tampu myth is, I believe, founded on an important historical event. It records the march of those descendants of the ancient civilizers who took refuge at Tampu-tocco. They were empire builders marching to Cuzco, with their religious beliefs and ceremonies, their insignia of royalty, their traditions of laws and customs, and their household gods.

The fertile vale of Cuzco, several miles in length, and surrounded by mountains, is in latitude 13° 30'S. and 11,380 ft. above the level of the sea. Over its site rises the imposing hill of Sacsahuaman, with the ancient cyclopean fortress on the eastern side. This famous mount is separated from the hills on either side by deep ravines, down which two torrents flow, called the Huatanay and Tulu-mayu. Reaching the level ground which forms the site of Cuzco, they often overflowed their banks, causing swamps and injuring the land. Eventually they form a junction, and the united stream flows down the valley to join the Vilcamayu. It was at the junction of the torrents, about a mile from the foot of the Sacsahuaman, that Manco established his settlement. Here he erected the House of the Sun, called Inti-cancha, but for a long time it was more a fortress than a temple. He and his successors subdued the former inhabitants of the valley, and the ten tribes from Tampu-tocco occupied their lands. These *ayllus*, or tribes, formed the fighting strength of the restored rule. Some of them, as the dominion extended, went further afield. The Maras tribe gave its name to the village of Maras, on the plateau overlooking the lovely vale of Vilcamayu. The Uru tribe was established at Urupampa, in the vale itself; and the Tampu tribe further down the same valley.

The date of the event recorded in the Paccari-tampu myth may be placed at about four centuries before the Spanish conquest, in 1100 CE or thereabouts. Sarmiento places it at 565 CE, by making each generation cover a century.

There is practical unanimity among all authorities with regard to the names of the four first successors of Manco. They were Sinchi Rocca, Lloque Yupanqui, Mayta Ccapac, and Ccapac Yupanqui. Most of these names are merely titles. The actual names are Rocca, Lloque, and Mayta. For the fourth only titles are given, and no personal name. The kings continued to live within the fortified Inti-cancha, dividing the land between the torrents into four quarters, to be occupied by their followers: namely Quinti-cancha, or the angular place, where the torrents join; Chumpi-cancha, or the place of stone heaps, perhaps buildings; Sayri-cancha, or the place where the Sayri plant was cultivated and

Yarampuy-cancha, another place for cultivation. These four kings undertook no great enterprise. Mayta Ccapac alone showed any energy, by finally subjugating the tribes in the Cuzco valley. The kings at the Inti-cancha were respected by the surrounding chiefs as children of the sun, and for their superior knowledge and civilization. Envoys were sent to them, some with submission, and they wisely cemented alliances by marriages with daughters of their more powerful neighbours. The marriages with sisters was a much later custom of their prouder and more imperially minded successors.

Apparently these early successors of Manco, owing to a certain superiority, occupied a position of priority, scarcely of suzerainty, over a very loose confederacy of surrounding tribes speaking the same language. But this was not what was contemplated by the Ayar Manco, who had filled the minds of his tribes with ambitious ideas. There was a feeling of unrest and discontent, the very opportunity to be seized by a highly gifted adventurer, if time should produce one.

Rise of the Incas

THERE WAS A FEELING OF UNREST among the descendants of the conquering tribes led by the Ayars to Cuzco. Vice was unchecked, the leaders of the people remained inert in the Inti-cancha, and no progress was made. Yet the people themselves were still vigorous, only needing a resolute chief, with a genius for command, to guide and direct their destinies.

Among the discontented there was an ambitious lady, said to have been of the blood-royal, who, in consultation with her sister, one of the most noted sorceresses of that day, resolved to effect a revolution. Her name was Siuyacu, or the 'gradually increasing ring.' She was shrewd, cautious, and determined.

Her son Rocca was to be the instrument to effect the revolution she contemplated for the good of her people. He was a youth in his twentieth year, well formed, handsome, valiant, and with a mind filled with lofty ideals. Already he was the leader of the young men who were discontented, and among his intimates he was called Inca or Lord.

The lady Siuyacu thus opened the subject to her son. "My son," she began, "you have a knowledge of the very happy estate enjoyed by our ancestors, when they occupied themselves in military exercises, and lived in conformity with the will of our great father the sun, and of the Supreme Creator Illa Tici Uira-cocha. By this path the city flourished, there was a succession of many kings, the realm was extended, the course of events was prosperous, and we always triumphed over our enemies, of which things our *quipus* are full. All this is now changed. The country is in the miserable state in which you see it. But I have determined that you shall be king. I trust in the aid of the Supreme Creator, that he will favour my plans, and I trust that you, by your valour and wisdom, will be the Restorer of the city and the kingdom to its ancient prosperity."

She ceased. Tears flowed from her eyes as she waited anxiously for her son's reply. There was a long pause. Rocca appeared to be deep in thought. After a time the valiant youth delivered his answer. "Mother and Lady!" he said, "what you have proposed must be for the common good of all the realm. As to what you have said of me, I dutifully accept your judgement. I declare to you that I am ready to give my life a thousand times that your noble aspirations may be fulfilled."

His mother was satisfied, for she knew the resolution of her son if he once undertook an enterprise, that with him there would be no turning back, and she was impressed with his wisdom in accepting counsel, and with his capacity in the execution of a carefully prepared scheme. She embraced him, declaring that she hoped no less of his valour and high spirit. She impressed him with the absolute necessity of silence, and charged him to follow exactly the instructions he would receive from herself and his aunt, the sorceress.

The lady Siuyacu next gave an account to her sister of this interview with her son, dwelling on the attention he had given to her words, and on his willingness to enter into her plans. His attitude promised success, and the sisters determined to take action without delay. The sorceress employed certain artisans, who were sworn to secrecy, to beat out a great number of square pieces of fine gold, with small holes perforated at each corner. They then sewed them on to a long garment, reaching from the neck to the heels, with numerous brilliant precious stones between the golden plates. The whole shone like the rays of the sun. The sisters then made several trials with the youth, to decide upon the way in which he should appear. At last they took him to a cave called Chingana, in the side of the Sacsahuaman hill, which overlooks the city. They dressed him in the gold-embroidered robe, and told him, at the end of four days, to appear at noon, on the height that dominates the whole city, so that the people might see him, and then to return to his hiding-place, where sufficient food had been provided.

The two sisters then declared to the people that, while their son and nephew, Inca Rocca, was sleeping in the house, the sun came down and carried him up to heaven enveloped in its rays, saying that he would soon return as king and favoured child of the great luminary. The solemn statement was confirmed by six members of the family who were witnesses. Partly on account of these assurances, partly because they had long looked upon Rocca as a child of destiny, most of the people believed the story. If there were any doubts they were soon dispelled.

Great numbers of people came from far and near to hear the news. On the fourth day sacrifices were offered to the sun from early morning, with earnest prayers that the youth might be restored.

Immense crowds were in the open space before the Inti-cancha. The hour of noon arrived. The busy hum of voices ceased. There was an awed silence, for there, on the summit of the Sacsahuaman hill, in the sight of all men, stood a golden figure glittering in the sun's rays. Then it suddenly disappeared, but thousands had seen it. The effect was indescribable. It must be Rocca, without doubt, and the sun had shown him, in answer to their prayers.

At nightfall the lady Siuyacu was at the Chingana, instructing her son to appear again, in the same way, at the end of two days, and then hide himself as before. During the interval the people were in suspense, and full of anxiety to see the end of such wonderful events. After two days the golden figure was again seen, for a few moments, on the summit of the Sacsahuaman hill. The feelings of the people were wrought up to the highest pitch of excitement. Siuyacu seized the fateful moment. She announced that the Supreme Creator, Illa Tici, had told her to go to the cave Chingana, where she would find her son. He was to be taken to the temple, where the people would hear the divine message from his lips, and must obey him in all things as one inspired by the Deity. The people prepared themselves by dressing as for a festival, amidst the most enthusiastic rejoicings. Then nearly the whole population, led by the lady Siuyacu, rushed up the hill, along the walls of the megalithic fortress, to the Chingana cave. Under a carved stone they found young Rocca reclining, apparently asleep. He awoke, and, rising to his feet, he told the people, with an air of great authority, that they must repair to the temple, where, by command of his father the sun, he would give them the message he had received.

The return of the people was more solemn. There was an awed silence. Rocca was seated on a golden throne within the temple. The vast crowd was eager to hear the message. A profound silence prevailed throughout the vast concourse of listeners as he rose to speak. These are said to have been his words: "No one can doubt, my friends, the special love which my father the sun feels for us. When he weakened the power of this realm so that it fell to pieces, he took care to provide a remedy. It was vice and sloth which consumed its grandeur, and reduced it almost to a vanishing point. Our policy was turned into a system of each man being his own master, leaving us to be satisfied with the thought that once we had a government. The tribute which every province used to pay, is replaced by disdain. You yourselves, instead of performing duties of men, follow the path of animals, you have become so effeminate that you have forgotten what a sling or an arrow may be.

"My father the sun has permitted this downfall, and yet has preserved you from falling into slavery. Now his providence will apply a remedy. His command is that you must obey me in all things, as his son. My first decree is that you must apply yourselves to warlike exercises. This you must do, for it was by discipline and exercises that our ancestors became Lords of the World, as our Quipucamayocs tell us. Thus occupied, idleness will be driven away, you will become accustomed to obedience, you will recover what has been lost, and you will finally regain the glory that has departed. In my father the sun you will have support. His rays will not dry up the land, nor will the moon deny its rains, evils from which our country has suffered at various times. My laws will be those of the ancient kings, and will not be new inventions. The happy feature of my promises is that they come from my father the sun, and cannot fail. The punishment of disobedience will be thunder that will terrify you, tempests to afflict you, rains to destroy your crops, and lightning to deprive you of life."

Rocca said all this with such solemnity that no one dared to dispute his words. The whole people proclaimed him their sovereign by acclamation, and the revolution was completed. He began to reign with the title of Inca Rocca. His first act was to remove from the Inti-cancha, which ceased to be the royal residence, and was given up entirely to the temple for the service of the sun. The Inca moved to the upper part of the town, and fixed his residence in an ancient building of the megalithic age. In its wall is the huge stone of twelve corners.

This interesting tradition is told by Montesinos, and is probably near the truth, for there are indications of a revolution of some kind, in Acosta, Morua, and other writers, at the time of Rocca's accession.

An important measure of the new sovereign was the division of people of every district into upper and lower, Hanan and Hurin. Great importance was attached to this arrangement, though it is not quite clear on what grounds it was instituted, and what purposes it was intended to serve. In Cuzco it was decreed that all the descendants of Inca Rocca should be Hanan Cuzcos, and settle in the upper part of the city. Half the *ayllus* which marched to Cuzco with Ayar Manco were also to be Hanan Cuzcos. These were:

Chavin
Arayraca
Sañoc
Tarpuntay (sacrificer)
Huacay Taqui (sacred music)

Perhaps these five tribes had shown more devotion to the cause of the new ruler than the others. The descendants of Rocca's predecessors were all to be Hurin Cuzcos, and to live in the lower part of the city. The other five original *ayllus* were also Hurin Cuzcos:

Tampu (settled at Ollantay-tampu)
Cuycusa
Masca (Mascani, I search)
Maras (settled at Maras)
Uru (settled at Urupampa)

Probably the division into upper and lower was connected, in some way, with the military exercises which were rigorously enforced by Inca Rocca. The descendants of the ten original *ayllus* mustered upwards of 20,000 fighting men. Several military expeditions were undertaken, and several neighbouring tribes were subdued – Muyna, Pinahua, Cayto-marca, and others – though their territories were not then permanently occupied. But the foundations were laid for a great army, destined to conquer and subjugate the whole Andean region. The ten original *ayllus* were the old guard, round which the rest of the army was formed. The exercises were continuous, and the Inca's son, Vicaquirau, and nephew, Apu Mayta, the two greatest generals the American race has produced, were trained under the eye of the Inca Rocca. It was their prowess and military skill that, during the three following reigns, created the empire of the Incas.

In all respects Inca Rocca appears to have been the pioneer of empire. The last recorded appearance of the lady Siuyacu was when she urged her son to lose no time in suppressing the vicious and slothful habits of the people. He made severe laws with this object, which were rigorously enforced. He also erected schools called *Yacha-huasi* to train youths as accountants, and recorders of events. The walls of the Inca's schools still resist the efforts of time. The grand city of later Incas was commenced under the auspices of Rocca. The torrents of Huatanay and Rodadero, rushing down the ravines on either side of the Sacsahuaman hill, had hitherto periodically overflowed their banks, and there were ponds and swamps, one of them on the site of the present cathedral of Cuzco. The Inca Rocca confined the torrents within solid walls, drained the site of the future city, and led off conduits to irrigate the valley. Thus the surrounding country, by a system of terrace cultivation and irrigation, was enabled to support a much larger population.

The custom of boring their ears and enlarging the lobes until they were a great length, which prevailed with the Incas, their relations, and the ten *ayllus*, obtained for them the name of *Hatun-rincriyoc*, or great-eared people, which the Spaniards turned into *Orejones*. The latter word is constantly occurring in the early chronicles and narratives, and is a convenient word to use in writing of the Inca nobles. The Incas and their *Orejones*, then, by their greater power and civilization, and their prestige as children of the sun, had attained to a certain predominance over most of the neighbouring tribes. Yet some stoutly maintained independence, even within a dozen miles of Cuzco, and some, like the Ayamarcas, were hostile and defiant.

The Stolen Child

A STRANGE AND UNLOOKED-FOR EVENT cast a shadow, though only for a brief period, over the Inca Rocca's life. He had married a very beautiful girl named Micay, the daughter of a neighbouring chief who ruled over a small tribe called Pata Huayllacan. She was the mother of four princes: Cusi Hualpa, the heir, Paucar, Huaman, and Vicaquirau, the future general.

We are told that Micay, the Inca's wife, had previously been promised by her father to Tocay Ccapac, the powerful chief of the Ayamarcas, a much more numerous tribe than the Huayllacans. Her marriage with the Inca caused a deadly feud between those two tribes. Hostilities were continued for a long time, and at last the Huayllacans prayed for peace. It was granted, but with a secret clause that the chief of the Huayllacans would entice away the Inca's eldest son and heir, and deliver him into the hands of his father's enemy, the chief of the Ayamarcas. If this condition was not complied with, Tocay Ccapac declared that he would continue the war until the Huayllacans were blotted out of existence.

These Ayamarcas were at one time a very powerful tribe, in a mountainous region about twenty miles S.S.W. of Cuzco ; while the Huayllacans were in a fertile valley between the Ayamarcas and that city.

In accordance with the agreement, a treacherous plot was laid. An earnest request was sent to the Inca that his heir, the young Cusi Hualpa, might be allowed to visit his mother's relations, so as to become acquainted with them. Quite unsuspicious, the Inca consented and sent the child, who was then about eight years of age, to Micucancha, or Paulu, the chief place of the Huayllacans, with about twenty attendants. The young prince was received with great festivities, which lasted for several days. It was summer time. The sun was scorching, and the child passed his time in a verandah or trelhs work, called *arapa*, covered with bright flowers.

One day it was announced that the whole tribe must march to some distance to harvest the crops. As it was still very hot, the Huayllacan chief insisted that the young prince should remain in the shade, and not accompany the harvesters, who had to go a considerable distance under the blazing sun. The prince's attendants consented, and all the tribe, old and young, boys and girls, marched up the hills to the harvesting, singing songs with choruses. All was bright sunshine, and their *haylli*, or harvest song, was in praise of the shade:

Seek the shadow, seek the shade,
Hide us in the blessed shade.

Yahahaha,
Yahaha.

Where is it ? where, where, O where?
Here it is, here, here, O here.

Yahahaha,
Yahaha.

Where the pretty cantut blooms,
Where the chihua's flower smiles,
Where the sweet amancay droops.
Yahahaha,
Yahaha.

There it is! there, there, O there!
Yes, we answer, there, O there.
Yahahaha,
Yahaha.

The child listened to the sounds of singing as the harvesters passed away out of sight, and then played among the flowers, surrounded by his personal attendants. The place was entirely deserted. When the sound of the singers had died away in the distance there was profound silence. Suddenly, without the slightest warning, the warcry "Atau! Atau!" was heard in all directions, and the little party was surrounded by armed men. The Orejones struggled valorously in defence of their precious charge until they were all killed, when the young prince was carried off.

Tocay Ccapac waited to hear the result of his treacherous raid in his chief abode, called Ahuayracancha, or 'the place of woof and warp.' When the raiders returned they entered their chief's presence, with the young prince, shouting "Behold the prisoner we have brought you." The chief said, "Is this the child of Mama Micay, who should have been my wife?" The Prince answered, "I am the son of the great Inca Rocca and of Mama Micay." Unsoftened by his tender years, or by his likeness to his beautiful mother, the savage chief ordered the child to be taken out and killed.

Then a strange thing happened. Surrounded by cruel enemies with no pitying eye to look on him, young Cusi Hualpa, a child of eight years, stood up to defy them. He must show himself a child of the sun, and maintain the honour of his race. With a look of indignation beyond his years he uttered a curse upon his captors. His shrill young voice was heard amidst the portentous silence of his enemies. "I tell you," he cried, "that as sure as you murder me there will fall such a curse upon you and your children that you will all come to an end, without any memory being left of your nation." He ceased, and, to the astonishment of his captors, tears of blood flowed from his eyes.

"*Yahuar huaccac*!" "*Yahuar huaccac*!" "He weeps blood," they shouted in horror. His curse and this unheard-of phenomenon filled the Ayamarcas with superstitious fear.

They recoiled from the murder. Tocay Ccapac and his people thought that the curse from so young a child and the tears of blood betokened some great mystery. They dared not kill him. He stood up in their midst unhurt.

Tocay Ccapac saw that his people would not kill the young prince then, or with their own hands at any time, yet he did not give up his intention of gratifying his thirst for vengeance. He resolved to take the child's life by a course of starvation and exposure. He gave him into the charge of shepherds who tended flocks of llamas on the lofty height overlooking the great plain of Suriti, where the climate is exceedingly rigorous. The shepherds had orders to reduce his food, day by day, until he died.

Young Cusi Hualpa had the gift of making friends. The shepherds did not starve him, though for a year he was exposed to great hardships. No doubt, however, the life he led on those frozen heights improved his health and invigorated his frame.

The Inca was told that his son had mysteriously disappeared, and that his attendants were also missing. The Huayllacan chief expressed sorrow, and pretended that diligent searches had been made. Inca Rocca suspected the Ayamarcas, but did not then attack them, lest, if the child was alive, they might kill him. As time went on the bereaved father began to despair of ever seeing his beloved son again.

Meanwhile the prince was well watched by the shepherds and by a strong guard, which had been sent to ensure his remaining in unknown captivity. But help was at hand. One of the concubines of Tocay Ccapac, named Chimpu Urma, or 'the fallen halo,' had probably been a witness of the impressive scene when the child wept blood. At all events, she was filled with pity and the desire to befriend the forlorn prince. She was a native of Anta, a small town at no great distance from Cuzco. As a friend of Tocay Ccapac she was free to go where she liked, within his dominions and those of the chief of Anta, who was her father.

Chimpu Urma persuaded her relations and friends at Anta to join with her in an attempt to rescue the young prince. It had been arranged by the shepherds and guards that, on a certain day, some boys, including Cusi Hualpa, should have a race up to the top of a hill in front of the shepherds' huts. Hearing this, Chimpu Urma stationed her friends from Anta, well armed, on the other side of the same hill. The race was started, and the prince reached the summit first, where he was taken up in the arms of his Anta friends, who made a rapid retreat. The other boys gave the alarm, and the jailers (shepherds and guards) followed in chase. On the banks of a small lake called Huaylla-punu, the men of Anta, finding that they were being overtaken, made a stand. There was a fierce battle, which resulted in the total defeat of the Ayamarcas. The men of Anta continued their journey, and brought the prince safely to their town, where he was received with great rejoicings.

Cusi Hualpa quite won the hearts of the people of Anta. They could not bear to part with him, and they kept him with great secrecy, delaying to send the joyful news to the Inca. Anta is a small town built up the side of a hill which bounds the vast plain of Suriti to the south. There is a glorious view from it, but the climate is severe. At last, after nearly a year, the Anta people sent messengers to inform the Inca. The child had been given up for lost. All hope had been abandoned. Rocca examined the messengers himself, but still he felt doubt. He feared the news was too good to be true. He secretly sent a man he could trust, as one seeking charity, to Anta, to find out the truth. The Inca's emissary returned with assurances that the young prince was certainly liberated, and was at Anta.

The Inca at last gave way to rejoicing, all doubt being removed. Principal lords were sent with rich presents of gold and silver to the chief of Anta, requesting him to send back the heir to the throne. The chief replied that all his people wished that Cusi Hualpa could remain, for they felt much love for the boy, yet they were bound to restore him to his father. He declined to receive the presents,but he made one condition. It was that he and his people should be accepted as relations of the Inca. So the young prince came back to his parents, and was joyfully received. Inca Rocca then visited Anta in person, and declared that the chief and his people were, from henceforward, raised to the rank of Orejones. The Huayllacans made abject submission, and, as Cusi Hualpa generously interceded for them, they were forgiven. Huaman Poma furnishes a curious corroboration of the story of the stolen child. Of all his portraits of the Incas, Rocca is the only one who is portrayed with a little boy. Huaman Poma did not know the story of the kidnapping and the recovered boy – at least, he never mentions it. All he knew was that only Inca Rocca was to be portrayed with a little boy.

Inca Rocca died after a long and glorious reign, during which he firmly laid the foundations of a great empire. His son Cusi Hualpa succeeded at the age of nineteen. He was commonly known by his surname of Yahuar Huaccac, or 'weeping blood.' His reign was memorable for the changes that took place in the system and objects of Inca warfare. The campaigns were no longer mere raids on hostile or rebellious tribes. The Inca's brother, Vicaquirau, and his cousin, Apu Mayta, were administrators quite as much as generals. Every attack on a hostile tribe ended in complete annexation. As the fame of the generals spread, the greater number of tribes submitted without resistance. Those who resisted were made terrible examples of, and if necessary a garrison was left in their principal place. The Ayamarcas were entirely crushed. Thus the Inca realm was every year extended, and at the same time consolidated.

Cusi Hualpa had five sons: Pahuac Hualpa Mayta, so named from his agility as a runner; Hatun Tupac, Vicchu Tupac, Marca Yutu, and Rocca. The Huayllacans, unimpressed by the pardon for their former treachery, conspired to make Marca Yutu the successor of his father, because he was more nearly related to their chief. With this object they enticed Pahuac Hualpa into their power and murdered him. For this there could be no forgiveness, and the tribe was entirely wiped out of existence by the Inca's generals. The second son, Hatun Tupac, then became the heir.

The new heir to the throne had, rather blasphemously, added to his real name of Hatun Tupac, the surname of Uira-cocha, which was that of the Deity. One reason that is given was that, being at Urcos, a town about twenty-five miles south of Cuzco, a vision of the Deity appeared to him in a dream. When he related his experience to his attendants next morning, his tutor, named Hualpa Rimachi, offered congratulations and hailed the young prince as Inca Uira-cocha. Others say that he took the name because he adopted the Deity as his godfather, when he was armed and went through other ceremonies at the festival of Huarachicu. Be this how it may, he always called himself Uira-cocha. His father, mindful of the debt of gratitude he owed to the people of Anta, married his heir to a daughter of their chief, and niece of his deliverer, Chimpu Urma. The lady's name was Runtu-caya.

In the fulness of time Cusi Hualpa (Yahuar Huaccac) was succeeded by his son Hatun Tupac, calling himself Uira-cocha. The policy of the two great generals was continued, and the whole region between the rivers Apurimac and Vilcamayu, the Inca region, was annexed and consolidated into one realm under the Inca. The names of Uira-cocha's sons by Runtu-caya were Rocca, Tupac, and Cusi. By a beautiful concubine named Ccuri-chulpa the Inca had two other sons named Urco and Sucso. For the sake of Ccuri-chulpa he favoured her children, and even declared the bastard Urco to be his heir. His eldest son was a valiant young warrior, trained in the school of Vicaquirau and Apu Mayta, and, when his age was sufficient, this prince Rocca became their colleague. Cusi was the most promising youth of the rising generation, endowed with rare gifts, beautiful in form and feature, of dauntless courage and universally beloved.

Three Inca Prayers

HYMNS AND PRAYERS were addressed by the Inca to their various gods. The sense of some of the most celebrated of these supplications is as follows:

To Viracocha

Viracocha, Lord of the Universe!
Whether male or female,
at any rate commander of heat and reproduction,
being one who,
even with His spittle, can work sorcery,
Where art Thou?
Would that Thou wert not hidden from this son of Thine!
He may be above;
He may be below;
or, perchance, abroad in space.
Where is his mighty judgment-seat?
Hear me!
He may be spread abroad among the upper waters;
or, among the lower waters and their sands
He may be dwelling.
Creator of the world,
Creator of man,
great among my ancestors,
before Thee my eyes fail me,
though I long to see Thee;
for, seeing Thee,
knowing Thee,
learning from Thee,
understanding Thee,
I shall be seen by Thee,
and Thou wilt know me.

The Sun – the Moon;
The Day – the Night;
Summer – Winter;
not in vain,
in orderly succession,
do they march to their destined place,
to their goal.
They arrive
wherever
Thy royal staff
Thou bearest.
Oh! Harken to me,
listen to me,
let it not befall
that I grow weary
and die.

To Viracocha

O conquering Viracocha!
Ever-present Viracocha!
Thou who art without equal upon the earth!
Thou who art from the beginnings of the world until its end!
Thou gavest life and valour to men, saying,
"Let this be a man."
And to woman, saying,
"Let this be a woman."
Thou madest them and gavest them being.
Watch over them, that they may live in health and in peace.
Thou who art in the highest heavens,
and among the clouds of the tempest,
grant them long life,
and accept this our sacrifice,
O Creator.

To Pachacamac

O Pachacamac!
Thou who hast existed from the beginning,
Thou who shalt exist until the end,
powerful but merciful,
Who didst create man by saying,
"Let man be,"
Who defendest us from evil,
and preservest our life and our health,
art Thou in the sky or upon the earth?
In the clouds or in the deeps?

Hear the voice of him who implores Thee,
and grant him his petitions.
Give us life everlasting,
preserve us, and accept this our sacrifice..

Myths of the Pueblo Indians

Introduction

THE PUEBLO PEOPLES are Native Americans, such as the Hopi and Zuni tribes, located in the southwest regions of what is now the United States. They speak Uto-Aztecan languages and are said to be descended from the ancient pre-Columbian Ancestral Puebloans. Like their Aztec, Mayan and Inca neighbours to the south, the Pueblo Indians, located today primarily across New Mexico and Arizona, are renowned for their rich culture, traditions and strong religious beliefs.

As with many other Native American peoples, the tales passed down from generation to generation by the Pueblo Indians feature a strong focus on animals and the supernatural. In the pages that follow are stories collected by Charles Lummis (1859–1928), mostly from the Isleta Pueblo people of New Mexico, in which you will encounter devils and witchcraft, humans transformed into animals and giants that meet their match against smaller, more cunning foes.

The Antelope Boy

ONCE UPON A TIME there were two towns of the Tée-wahn, called Nah-bah-tóo-too-ee (white village) and Nah-choo-rée-too-ee (yellow village). A man of Nah-bah-tóo-too-ee and his wife were attacked by Apaches while out on the plains one day, and took refuge in a cave, where they were besieged. And there a boy was born to them. The father was killed in an attempt to return to his village for help; and starvation finally forced the mother to crawl forth by night seeking roots to eat. Chased by the Apaches, she escaped to her own village, and it was several days before she could return to the cave-only to find it empty.

The baby had begun to cry soon after her departure. just then a Coyote was passing, and heard. Taking pity on the child, he picked it up and carried it across the plain until he came to a herd of antelopes. Among them was a Mother-Antelope that had lost her fawn; and going to her the Coyote said:

"Here is an *ah-bóo* (poor thing) that is left by its people. Will you take care of it?

The Mother-Antelope, remembering her own baby, with tears said "Yes," and at once adopted the tiny stranger, while the Coyote thanked her and went home.

So the boy became as one of the antelopes, and grew up among them until he was about twelve years old. Then it happened that a hunter came out from Nah-bah-tóo-too-ee for antelopes, and found this herd. Stalking them carefully, he shot one with an arrow. The rest started off, running like the wind; but ahead of them all, as long as they were in sight, he saw a boy! The hunter was much surprised, and, shouldering his game, walked back to the village, deep in thought. Here he told the Cacique what he had seen. Next day the crier was sent out to call upon all the people to prepare for a great hunt, in four days, to capture the Indian boy who lived with the antelopes.

While preparations were going on in the village, the antelopes in some way heard of the intended hunt and its purpose. The Mother-Antelope was very sad when she heard it, and at first would say nothing, But at last she called her adopted son to her an said: "Son, you have heard that the people of Nah-bah-tóo-too-ee are coming to hunt. But they will not kill us; all they wish is to take you. They will surround us, intending to let all the antelopes escape from the circle. You must follow me where I break through the line, and your real mother will be coming on the northeast side in a white *manta* (robe). I will pass close to her, and you must stagger and fall where she can catch you."

On the fourth day all the people went out upon the plains. They found and surrounded the herd of antelopes, which ran about in a circle when the hunters closed upon them. The circle grew smaller, and the antelopes began to break through; but the hunters paid no attention to them, keeping their eyes upon the boy. At last he and his antelope mother were the only ones left, and when she broke through the line on the northeast he followed her and fell at the feet of his own human mother, who sprang forward and clasped him in her arms.

Amid great rejoicing he was taken to Nah-bah-tóo-too-ee, and there he told the *principales* how he had been left in the cave, how the Coyote had pitied him, and how the Mother-Antelope had reared him as her own son.

It was not long before all the country round about heard of the Antelope Boy and of his marvellous fleetness of foot. You must know that the antelopes never comb their hair, and while among them the boy's head had grown very bushy. So the people called him *Pée-hleh-o-wah-wée-deh* (big-headed little boy).

Among the other villages that heard of his prowess was Nah-choo-rée-too-ee , all of whose people 'had the bad road.' They had a wonderful runner named *Pée-k'hoo* (Deer-foot), and very soon they sent a challenge to Nah-bah-tóo-too-ee for a championship race. Four days were to be given for preparation, to make bets, and the like.

The race was to be around the world. Each village was to stake all its property and the lives of all its people on the result of the race. So powerful were the witches of Nah-choo-rée-too-ee that they felt safe in proposing so serious a stake; and the people of Nah-bah-tóo-too-ee were ashamed to decline the challenge.

The day came, and the starting-point was surrounded by all the people of the two villages, dressed in their best. On each side were huge piles of ornaments and dresses, stores of grain, and all the other property of the people. The runner for the yellow village was a tall, sinewy athlete, strong in his early manhood; and when the Antelope Boy appeared for the other side, the witches set up a howl of derision, and began to strike their rivals and jeer at them, saying, "Poch! We might as well begin to kill you now! What can that *óo-deh* (little thing) do?"

At the word "*Hái-ko*!" ("Go!") the two runners started toward the east like the wind. The Antelope Boy soon forged ahead; but Deer-foot, by his witchcraft, changed himself into a hawk and flew lightly over the lad, saying, "We do this way to each other!" The Antelope Boy kept running, but his heart was very heavy, for he knew that no feet could equal the swift flight of the hawk.

But just as he came half-way to the east, a Mole came up from its burrow and said:

"My son, where are you going so fast with a sad face?"

The lad explained that the race was for the property and lives of all his people; and that the witch-runner had turned to a hawk and left him far behind.

"Then, my son," said the Mole, "I will be he that shall help you. Only sit down here a little while, and I will give you something to carry."

The boy sat down, and the Mole dived into the hole, but soon came back with four cigarettes.

Holding them out, the Mole said, "Now, my son, when you have reached the east and turned north, smoke one; when you have reached the north and turn west, smoke another; when you turn south, another, and when you turn east again, another. *Hái-ko*!"

The boy ran on, and soon reached the east. Turning his face to the north he smoked the first cigarette. No sooner was it finished than he became a young antelope; and at the same instant a furious rain began. Refreshed by the cool drops, he started like an arrow from the bow. Half-way to the north he came to a large tree; and there sat the hawk, drenched and chilled, unable to fly, and crying piteously.

"Now, friend, *we* too do this to each other," called the boy-antelope as he dashed past. But just as he reached the north, the hawk – which had become dry after the short rain – caught up and passed him, saying, "We too do this to each other!" The boy-antelope turned westward, and smoked the second cigarette; and at once another terrific rain began. Half-way to the west he again passed the hawk shivering and crying in a tree, and unable to fly; but as he was about to turn to the south, the hawk passed him with the customary taunt. The smoking of the third cigarette brought another storm, and again the antelope passed the wet hawk half-way, and again the hawk dried its feathers in time to catch up and pass him as he was turning to the east for the home-stretch. Here again the boy-antelope stopped and smoked a cigarette – the fourth and last. Again a short, hard rain came, and again he passed the water-bound hawk half-way.

Knowing the witchcraft of their neighbours, the people of Nah-bah-tóo-too-ee had made the condition that, in whatever shape the racers might run the rest of the course, they must resume human form upon arrival at a certain hill upon the fourth turn, which was in sight of the goal. The last wetting of the hawk's feathers delayed it so that the antelope reached the hill just ahead; and there, resuming their natural shapes, the two runners came sweeping down the home-stretch, straining every nerve. But the Antelope Boy gained at each stride. When they saw him, the witch-people felt confident that he was their champion, and again began to push, and taunt, and jeer at the others. But when the little Antelope Boy sprang lightly across the line, far ahead of Deer-foot, their joy turned to mourning.

The people of Nah-bah-tóo-too-ee burned all the witches upon the spot, in a great pile of corn; but somehow one escaped, and from him come all the witches that trouble us to this day.

The property of the witches was taken to Nah-bah-tóo-too-ee; and as it was more than that village could hold, the surplus was sent to Shee-eh-whíb-bak (Isleta), where we enjoy it to this day; and later the people themselves moved here. And even now, when we dig in that little hill on the other side of the *charco* (pool), we find charred corn-cobs, where our forefathers burned the witch-people of the yellow village.

The First of the Rattlesnakes

NOW THERE IS A TAIL TO YOU, *compadre* [friend]," said old Desiderio, nodding at Patricio after we had sat awhile in silence around the crackling fire.

Patricio had a broad strip of rawhide across his knee, and was scraping the hair from it with a dull knife. It was high time to be thinking of new soles, for already there was a wee hole in the bottom of each of his moccasins; and as for Benito, his shy little grandson, *his* toes were all abroad.

But shrilly as the cold night-wind outside hinted the wisdom of speedy cobbling, Patricio had no wish to acquire that burro's tail, so, laying the rawhide and knife upon the floor beside him, he deliberately rolled a modest pinch of the aromatic *koo-ah-rée* in a corn-husk, lighted it at the coals, and drew Benito's tousled head to his side.

"You have heard," he said, with a slow puff, "about Nah-chu-rú-chu, the mighty medicine-man who lived here in Isleta in the times of the ancients?"

"*Ah-h*!" (Yes) cried all the boys. "You have promised to tell us how he married the moon!"

"Another time I will do so. But now I shall tell you something that was before that – for Nah-chu-rú-chu had many strange adventures before he married Páh-hlee-oh, the

Moon-Mother. Do you know why the rattlesnake – which is the king of all snakes and alone has the power of death in his mouth-always shakes his *guaje* before he bites?"

"*Een-dah*!" chorused Ramon and Benito, and Fat Juan, and Tomas, very eagerly; for they were particularly fond of hearing about the exploits of the greatest of Tée-wahn medicine-men.

"Listen, then, and you shall hear."

In those days Nah-chu-rú-chu had a friend who lived in a pueblo nearer the foot of the Eagle-Feather Mountain than this, in the Place of the Red Earth, where still are its ruins; and the two young men went often to the mountain together to bring wood and to hunt. Now, Nah-chu-rú-chu had a white heart, and never thought ill; but the friend had the evil road and became jealous, for Nah-chu-rú-chu was a better hunter. But he said nothing, and made as if he still loved Nah-chu-rú-chu truly.

One day the friend came over from his village and said:

"Friend Nah-chu-rú-chu, let us go to-morrow for wood and to have a hunt.

"It is well," replied Nah-chu-rú-chu. Next morning he started very early and came to the village of his friend; and together they went to the mountain. When they had gathered much wood, and lashed it in bundles for carrying, they started off in opposite directions to hunt. In a short time each returned with a fine fat deer.

"But why should we hasten to go home, friend Nah-chu-rú-chu?" said the friend. "It is still early, and we have much time. Come, let us stop here and amuse ourselves with a game."

"It is well, friend," answered Nah-chu-rú-chu; "but what game shall we play? For we have neither *pa-toles*, nor hoops, nor any other game here."

"See! we will roll the *mah-khúr*, for while I was waiting for you I made one that we might play" – and the false friend drew from beneath his blanket a pretty painted hoop; but really he had made it at home, and had brought it hidden, on purpose to do harm to Nah-chu-rú-chu.

"Now go down there and catch it when I roll it," said he; and Nah-chu-rú-chu did so. But as he caught the hoop when it came rolling, he was no longer Nah-chu-rú-chu the brave hunter, but a poor Coyote with great tears rolling down his nose!

"Hu!" said the false friend, tauntingly, "we do this to each other! So now you have all the plains to wander over, to the north, and west, and south; but you can never go to the east. And if you are not lucky, the dogs will tear you; but if you are lucky, they may have pity on you. So now good-by, for this is the last I shall ever see of you."

Then the false friend went away, laughing, to his village; and the poor Coyote wandered aimlessly, weeping to think that he had been betrayed by the one he had loved and trusted as a brother. For four days he prowled about the outskirts of Isleta, looking wistfully at his home. The fierce dogs ran out to tear him; but when they came near they only sniffed at him, and went away without hurting him. He could find nothing to eat save dry bones, and old thongs or soles of moccasins.

On the fourth day he turned westward, and wandered until he came to Mesita. There was no town of the Lagunas there then, and only a shepherd's hut and corral, in which were an old Quères Indian and his grandson, tending their goats.

Next morning when the grandson went out very early to let the goats from the corral, he saw a Coyote run out from among the goats. It went off a little way, and then sat down and watched him. The boy counted the goats, and none were missing, and he thought it strange. But he said nothing to his grandfather.

For three more mornings the very same thing happened; and on the fourth morning the boy told his grandfather. The old man came out, and set the dogs after the Coyote, which was sitting a little way off; but when they came near they would not touch him.

"I suspect there is something wrong here," said the old shepherd; and he called: "Coyote, are you coyote-true, or are you people?"

But the Coyote could not answer; and the old man called again: "Coyote, are you people?"

At that the Coyote nodded his head, "Yes."

"If that is so, come here and be not afraid of us; for we will be the ones to help you out of this trouble."

So the Coyote came to them and licked their hands, and they gave it food – for it was dying of hunger. When it was fed, the old man said:

"Now, son, you are going out with the goats along the creek, and there you will see some willows. With your mind look at two willows, and mark them; and to-morrow morning you must go and bring one of them."

The boy went away tending the goats, and the Coyote stayed with the old man. Next morning, when they awoke very early, they saw all the earth wrapped in a white *manta*.

"Now, son," said the old man, "you must wear only your moccasins and breech-clout, and go like a man to the two willows you marked yesterday. To one of them you must pray; and then cut the other and bring it to me."

The boy did so and came back with the willow stick. The old man prayed, and made a *mah-khúr* hoop; and bidding the Coyote stand a little way off and stick his head through the hoop before it should stop rolling, rolled it toward him. The Coyote waited till the hoop came very close, and gave a great jump and put his head through it before it could stop. And lo! there stood Nah-chu-rú-chu, young and handsome as ever; but his beautiful suit of fringed buckskin was all in rags. For four days he stayed there and was cleansed with the cleansing of the medicine-man; and then the old shepherd said to him:

"Now, friend Nah-chu-rú-chu, there is a road. But take with you this *faja*, for though your power is great, you have submitted to this evil. When you get home, he who did this to you will be first to know, and he will come pretending to be your friend, as if he had done nothing; and he will ask you to go hunting again. So you must go; and when you come to the mountain, with this *faja* you shall repay him."

Nah-chu-rú-chu thanked the kind old shepherd, and started home. But when he came to the Bad Hill and looked down into the valley of the Rio Grande, his heart sank. All the grass and fields and trees were dry and dead – for Nah-chu-rú-chu was the medicine-man who controlled the clouds, so no rain could fall when he was gone; and the eight days he had been a Coyote were in truth eight years. The river was dry, and the springs; and many of the people were dead from thirst, and the rest were dying. But as Nah-chu-rú-chu came down the hill, it began to rain again, and all the people were glad.

When he came into the pueblo, all the famishing people came out to welcome him. And soon came the false friend, making as if he had never bewitched him nor had known whither he disappeared.

In a few days the false friend came again to propose a hunt; and next morning they went to the mountain together. Nah-chu-rú-chu had the pretty *faja* wound around his waist; and when the wind blew his blanket aside, the other saw it.

"Ay! What a pretty *faja*!" cried the false friend. "Give it to me, friend Nah-chu-rú-chu."

"*Een-dah*!" (No) said "Nah-chu-rú-chu. But the false friend begged so hard that at last he said:

"Then I will roll it to you; and if you can catch it before it unwinds, you may have it."

So he wound it up, and holding by one end gave it a push so that it ran away from him, unrolling as it went. The false friend jumped for it, but it was unrolled before he caught it-

"*Een-dah*!" said Nah-chu-rú-chu, pulling it back. "If you do not care enough for it to be spryer than that, you cannot have it."

The false friend begged for another trial; so Nah-chu-rú-chu rolled it again. This time the false friend caught it before it was unrolled; and lo! instead of a tall young man, there lay a great rattlesnake with tears rolling from his lidless eyes!

"We, too, do this to each other!" said Nah-chu-rú-chu. He took from his medicine-pouch a pinch of the sacred meal and laid it on the snake's flat head for its food; and then a pinch of the corn-pollen to tame it. And the snake ran out its red forked tongue, and licked them.

"Now," said Nah-chu-rú-chu, "this mountain and all rocky places shall be your home. But you can never again do to another harm, without warning, as you did to me. For see, there is a *guaje* in your tail, and whenever you would do any one an injury, you must warn them beforehand with your rattle."

"And is that the reason why Ch'ah-rah-ráh-deh always rattles to give warning before he bites?" asked Fat Juan, who is now quite as often called Juan Biscocho (John Biscuit), since I photographed him one day crawling out of the big adobe bake-oven where he had been hiding.

"That is the very reason. Then Nah-chu-rú-chu left his false friend, from whom all the rattlesnakes are descended, and came back to his village. From that time all went well with Isleta, for Nah-chu-rú-chu was at home again to attend to the clouds. There was plenty of rain, and the river began to run again, and the springs flowed.

The people plowed and planted again, as they had not been able to do for several years, and all their work prospered. As for the people who lived in the Place of the Red Earth, they all moved down here, because the Apaches were very bad; and here their descendants live to this day."

The Man Who Married the Moon

AMONG THE PRINCIPAL HEROES of the Tée-wahn folk-lore, I hear of none more frequently in the winter story-tellings to which my aboriginal neighbours admit me, than the mighty Nah-chu-rú-chu. To this day his name, which means 'The Bluish Light of Dawn,' is deeply revered by the quaint people who claim him as one of their forefathers. He had no parents, for he was created by the Trues themselves, and by them was given such extraordinary powers as were second only to their own. His wonderful feats and startling adventures – as still related by the believing Isleteños – would fill a volume. One of these fanciful myths has interested me particularly, not only for its important bearing on certain ethnological matters, but for its intrinsic qualities as well. It is a thoroughly characteristic leaf from the legendary lore of the Southwest.

Long before the first Spaniards came to New Mexico (and *that* was three hundred and fifty years ago) Isleta stood where it stands to-day – on a lava ridge that defies the gnawing current of the Rio Grande. In those far days, Nah-chu-rú-chu dwelt in Isleta, and was a leader of his people. A weaver by trade, his rude loom hung from the dark rafters of his room; and in it he wove the strong black *mantas* which are the dress of Pueblo women to this day.

Besides being very wise in medicine, Nah-chu-rú-chu was young, and tall, and strong, and handsome; and all the girls of the village thought it a shame that he did not care to take a wife. For him the shyest dimples played, for him the whitest teeth flashed out, as the owners passed him in the plaza; but he had no eyes for them. Then, in the naïve custom of the Tée-wahn, bashful fingers worked wondrous fringed shirts of buckskin, or gay awl-sheaths, which found their way to his house by unknown messengers – each as much as to say, "She who made this is yours, if you will have her." But Nah-chu-rú-chu paid no more attention to the gifts than to the smiles, and just kept weaving and weaving – such *mantas* as were never seen in the land of the Tée-wahn before or since.

The most persistent of his admirers were two sisters who were called *Ee-eh-chóo-ri-ch'áhm-nin* – the Yellow-Corn-Maidens. They were both young and pretty, but they 'had the evil road' – which is the Indian way of saying that they were possessed of a magic power which they always used for ill. When all the other girls gave up, discouraged at Nah-chu-rú-chu's indifference, the Yellow-Corn-Maidens kept coming day after day, trying to attract him. At last the matter became such a nuisance to Nah-chu-rú-chu that he hired the deep-voiced town-crier to go through all the streets and announce that in four days Nah-chu-rú-chu would choose a wife.

For dippers, to take water from the big earthen *tinajas*, the Tée-wahn used then, as they use today, queer little ladle-shaped *omates* made of a gourd; but Nah-chu-rú-chu, being a great medicine-man and very rich, had a dipper of pure pearl, shaped like the gourds, but wonderfully precious.

"On the fourth day," proclaimed the crier, "Nah-chu-rú-chu will hang his pearl *omate* at his door, where every girl who will may throw a handful of corn-meal at it. And she whose meal is so well ground that it sticks to the *omate*, she shall be the wife of Nah-chu-rú-chu!"

When this strange news came rolling down the still evening air, there was a great scampering of little moccasined feet. The girls ran out from hundreds of gray adobe houses to catch every word; and when the crier had passed on, they ran back into the store-rooms and began to ransack the corn-bins for the biggest, evenest, and most perfect ears. Shelling the choicest, each took her few handfuls of kernels to the sloping *metate*, and with the *mano*, or hand-stone, scrubbed the grist up and down, and up and down, till the hard corn was a soft, blue meal. All the next day, and the next, and the next, they ground it over and over again, until it grew finer than ever flour was before; and every girl felt sure that her meal would stick to the *omate* of the handsome young weaver. The Yellow-Corn-Maidens worked hardest of all; day and night for four days they ground and ground, with all the magic spells they knew.

Now, in those far-off days the Moon had not gone up into the sky to live, but was a maiden of Shee-eh-whíb-bak. And a very beautiful girl she was, though blind of one eye. She had long admired Nah-chu-rú-chu, but was always too maidenly to try to attract his attention as other girls had done; and at the time when the crier made his proclamation, she happened to be away at her father's ranch. It was only upon the fourth day that she returned to town, and in a few moments the girls were to go with their meal to test it upon the magic dipper. The two Yellow-Corn-Maidens were just coming from their house as she passed, and told her of what was to be done. They were very confident of success, and told the Moon-girl only to pain her; and laughed derisively as she went running to her home.

By this time a long file of girls was coming to Nah-chu-rú-chu's house, outside whose door hung the pearl *omate*. Each girl carried in her left hand a little jar of meal; and as they passed the door one by one, each took from the jar a handful and threw it against the magic dipper. But each time the meal dropped to the ground, and left the pure pearl undimmed and radiant as ever.

At last came the Yellow-Corn-Maidens, who had waited to watch the failure of the others. As they came where they could see Nah-chu-rú-chu sitting at his loom, they called: "Ah! Here we have the meal that will stick!" and each threw a handful at the *omate*. But it did not stick at all; and still from his seat Nah-chu-rú-chu could see, in that mirror-like surface, all that went on outside.

The Yellow-Corn-Maidens were very angry, and instead of passing on as the others had done, they stood there and kept throwing and throwing at the *omate*, which smiled back at them with undiminished luster.

Just then, last of all, came the Moon, with a single handful of meal which she had hastily ground. The two sisters were in a fine rage by this time, and mocked her, saying:

"Hoh! *P'áh-hlee-oh*, you poor thing, we are very sorry for you! Here we have been grinding our meal four days and still it will not stick, and you we did not tell till to-day. How, then, can you ever hope to win Nah-chu-rú-chu? Pooh, you silly little thing!"

But the Moon paid no attention whatever to their taunts. Drawing back her little dimpled hand, she threw the meal gently against the pearl *omate*, and so fine was it ground that every tiniest bit of it clung to the polished shell, and not a particle fell to the ground.

When Nah-chu-rú-chu saw that, he rose up quickly from his loom and came and took the Moon by the hand, saying, "You are she who shall be my wife. You shall never want for anything, since I have very much." And he gave her many beautiful *mantas*, and cotton wraps, and fat boots of buckskin that wrap round and round, that she might dress as the wife of a rich chief. But the Yellow-Corn-Maidens, who had seen it all, went away vowing vengeance on the Moon.

Nah-chu-rú-chu and his sweet Moon-wife were very happy together. There was no other such housekeeper in all the pueblo as she, and no other hunter brought home so much buffalo-meat from the vast plains to the east, nor so many antelopes, and black-tailed deer, and jack-rabbits from the Manzanos as did Nah-chu-rú-chu. But he constantly was saying to her:

"Moon-wife, beware of the Yellow-Corn-Maidens, for they have the evil road and will try to do you harm, but you must always refuse to do whatever they propose." And always the young wife promised.

One day the Yellow-Corn-Maidens came to the house and said:

"Friend Nah-chu-rú-chu, we are going to the *llano* to gather *amole*. Will you not let your wife go with us?"

"Oh, yes, she may go," said Nah-chu-rú-chu; but taking her aside, he said, "Now be sure that you refuse whatever they may propose."

The Moon promised, and started away with the Yellow-Corn-Maidens.

In those days there was only a thick forest of cottonwoods where are now the smiling vineyards, and gardens, and orchards of Isleta, and to reach the *llano* the three women had to go through this forest. In the very centre of it they came to a deep *pozo* – a square well, with steps at one side leading down to the water's edge.

"Ay!" said the Yellow-Corn-Maidens, "how hot and thirsty is our walk! Come, let us get a drink of water."

But the Moon, remembering her husband's words, said politely that she did not wish to drink. They urged in vain, but at last, looking down into the *pozo*, called:

"Oh, Moon-friend! Come and look in this still water, and see how pretty you are!"

The Moon, you must know, has always been just as fond of looking at herself in the water as she is to this very day, and forgetting Nah-chu-rú-chu's warning, she came to the brink, and looked down upon her fair reflection. But at that very moment, the two witch-sisters pushed her head foremost into the *pozo*, and drowned her; and then filled the well with earth, and went away as happy as wicked hearts can be.

Nah-chu-rú-chu began to look oftener from his loom to the door as the sun crept along the adobe floor, closer and closer to his seat; and when the shadows were very long, he sprang suddenly to his feet, and walked to the house of the Yellow-Corn-Maidens with long, strong strides.

"*Ee-eḥ-chóo-ri-ch'áhm-nin*," he said, very sternly, "where is my little wife?"

"Why, isn't she at home?" asked the wicked sisters as if in great surprise. "She got enough *amole* long before we did, and started home with it. We supposed she had come long ago."

"Ah," groaned Nah-chu-rú-chu within himself; "it is as I thought – they have done her ill." But without a word to them he turned on his heel and went away.

From that hour all went ill with Isleta, for Nah-chu-rú-chu held the well-being of all his people, even unto life and death. Paying no attention to what was going on about him, he sat motionless upon the very crosspiece of the *estufa* ladder – the highest point in all the town – with his head bowed upon his hands. There he sat for days, never speaking, never moving. The children that played along the streets looked up to the motionless figure, and ceased their boisterous play. The old men shook their heads gravely, and muttered: "We are in evil times, for Nah-chu-rú-chu is mourning, and will not be comforted. And there is no more rain, so that our crops are drying in the fields. What shall we do?"

At last all the councillors met together, and decided that there must be another effort made to find the lost wife. It was true that the great Nah-chu-rú-chu had searched for her in vain, and the people had helped him; but perhaps some one else might be more fortunate. So they took some of the sacred smoking-weed wrapped in a corn-husk and went to Shée-wid-deh, who has the sharpest eyes in all the world. Giving him the sacred gift they said:

"Eagle-friend, we see Nah-chu-rú-chu in great trouble, for he has lost his Moon-wife. Come, search for her, we pray you, if she be alive or dead."

So the Eagle took the offering, and smoked the smoke-prayer; and then he went winging upward into the very sky. Higher and higher he rose, in great upward circles, while his keen eyes noted every stick, and stone, and animal on the face of all the world. But with all his eyes, he could see nothing of the lost wife; and at last he came back sadly, and said:

"People-friends, I went up to where I could see the whole world, but I could not find her."

Then the people went with an offering to the Coyote, whose nose is sharpest in all the world; and besought him to try to find the Moon. The Coyote smoked the smoke-prayer, and started off with his nose to the ground, trying to find her tracks. He trotted all over the earth; but at last he too came back without finding what he sought.

Then the troubled people got the Badger to search, for he is best of all the beasts at digging – and he it was whom the Trues employed to dig the caves in which the people first dwelt when they came to this world. The Badger trotted and pawed, and dug everywhere, but he could not find the Moon; and he came home very sad.

Then they asked the Osprey, who can see farthest under water, and he sailed high above all the lakes and rivers in the world, till he could count the pebbles and the fish in them, but he too failed to discover the lost Moon.

By now the crops were dead and sere in the fields, and thirsty animals walked crying along the dry river. Scarcely could the people themselves dig deep enough to find so much water as would keep them alive. They were at a loss which way to turn; but at last they thought: We will go to P'ah-kú-ee-teh-áy-deh, who can find the dead – for surely she is dead, or the others would have found her.

So they went to him and besought him. The Turkey-buzzard wept when he saw Nah-chu-rú-chu still sitting there upon the ladder, and said: "Truly it is sad for our great friend; but for me, I am afraid to go, since they who are more mighty than I have already failed; but I will try." And spreading his broad wings he went climbing up the spiral ladder of the sky. Higher he wheeled, and higher, till at last not even the Eagle could see him. Up and up, till the hot sun began to singe his head, and not even the Eagle had ever been so high. He cried with pain, but still he kept mounting – until he was so close to the sun that all the feathers were burned from his head and neck. But he could see nothing; and at last, frantic with the burning, he came wheeling downward. When he got back to the *estufa* where all the people were waiting, they saw that his head and neck had been burnt bare of feathers – and from that day to this the feathers would never grow out again.

"And did you see nothing?" they all asked, when they had bathed his burns.

"Nothing," he answered, "except that when I was half-way down I saw in the middle of yon cottonwood forest a little mound covered with all the beautiful flowers in the world."

"Oh!" cried Nah-chu-rú-chu, speaking for the first time. "Go, friend, and bring me one flower from the very middle of that mound."

Off flew the Buzzard, and in a few minutes returned with a little white flower. Nah-chu-rú-chu took it, and descending from the ladder in silence, walked to his house, while all the wondering people followed.

When Nah-chu-rú-chu came inside his home once more, he took a new *manta* and spread it in the middle of the room; and laying the wee white flower tenderly in its centre, he put another new manta above it. Then, dressing himself in the splendid buckskin suit the lost wife had made him, and taking in his right hand the sacred *guaje* (rattle), he seated himself at the head of the *mantas* and sang:

Shú-nah, shú-nah!
Aí-ay-ay, aí-ay-ay, aí-ay-ay!
(Seeking her, seeking her!
There-away, there-away!)

When he had finished the song, all could see that the flower had begun to grow, so that it lifted the upper *manta* a little. Again he sang, shaking his gourd; and still the flower kept growing. Again and again he sang; and when he had finished for the fourth time, it was plain to all that a human form lay between the two *mantas*. And when he sang his song the fifth time, the form sat up and moved. Tenderly he lifted away the over-cloth, and there sat his sweet Moon-wife, fairer than ever, and alive as before!

For four days the people danced and sang in the public square. Nah-chu-rú-chu was happy again; and now the rain began to fall. The choked earth drank and was glad and green, and the dead crops came to life.

When his wife told him how the witch-sisters had done, he was very angry; and that very day he made a beautiful hoop to play the *mah-khúr*. He painted it, and put strings across it, decorated with beaded buckskin.

"Now," said he, "the wicked Yellow-Corn-Maidens will come to congratulate you, and will pretend not to know where you were. You must not speak of that, but invite them to go out and play a game with you."

In a day or two the witch-sisters did come, with deceitful words; and the Moon invited them to go out and play a game. They went up to the edge of the *llano*, and there she let them get a glimpse of the pretty hoop.

"Oh, give us that, Moon-friend," they teased. But she refused. At last, however, she said:

"Well, we will play the hoop-game. I will stand here, and you there; and if, when I roll it to you, you catch it before it falls upon its side, you may have it."

So the witch-sisters stood a little way down the hill, and she rolled the bright hoop. As it came trundling to them, both grasped it at the same instant; and lo! instead of the Yellow-Corn-Maidens, there were two great snakes, with tears rolling down ugly faces. The Moon came and put upon their heads a little of the pollen of the corn-blossom (still used by Pueblo snake-charmers) to tame them, and a pinch of the sacred meal for their food.

"Now," said she, "you have the reward of treacherous friends. Here shall be your home among these rocks and cliffs forever, but you must never be found upon the prairie; and you must never bite a person. Remember you are women, and must be gentle."

And then the Moon went home to her husband, and they were very happy together. As for the sister snakes, they still dwell where she bade them, and never venture away; though sometimes the people bring them to their houses to catch the mice, for these snakes never hurt a person.

The Moqui Boy and the Eagle

SOME OF THE FOLK-STORIES told in Isleta were evidently invented in other pueblos, whence the Tée-wahn have learned them in their trading-trips. There is even a story from the far-off towns of Moqui, three hundred miles west of here and ninety miles from the railroad. The Moquis live in northeast Arizona, in strange adobe towns, perched upon impregnable islands of rock, rising far above the bare, brown plain. They are seldom visited and little known by white men. All the other Pueblo towns and tribes have changed somewhat in the present era of American occupation; but the Moquis remain very much as they were when the first Spaniard found them – three hundred and fifty years ago. They retain many customs long extinct among their kindred, and have some of which no trace is to be found elsewhere. One of the minor differences, but one which would be almost the first to strike a stranger, is the absence of captive eagles in Moqui; and this is explained by the following folk-story:

The Eagle is Kah-báy-deh (commander) of all that flies, and his feathers are strongest in medicine.

So long ago that no man can tell how long, there lived in Moqui an old man and an old woman, who had two children – a boy and a girl. The boy, whose name was Tái-oh, had a pet Eagle, of which he was very fond; and the Eagle loved its young master. Despite his youth, Tái-oh was a capital hunter; and every day he brought home not only rabbits enough for the family, but also to keep the Eagle well fed.

One day when he was about to start on a hunt, he asked his sister to look out for the Eagle during his absence. No sooner was he out of sight than the girl began to upbraid the bird bitterly, saying: "How I hate you, for my brother loves you so much. If it were not for you, he would give me many more rabbits, but now you eat them up."

The Eagle, feeling the injustice of this, was angry; so when she brought him a rabbit for breakfast the Eagle turned his head and looked at it sidewise, and would not touch it. At noon, when she brought him his dinner, he did the same thing; and at night, when Tái-oh returned, the Eagle told him all that had happened.

"Now," said the Eagle, "I am very tired of staying always here in Moqui, and I want to go home to visit my people a little. Come and go along with me, that you may see where the Eagle-people live."

"It is well," replied Tái-oh. "To-morrow morning we will go together."

In the morning they all went out into the fields, far down in the valley, to hoe their corn, leaving Tái-oh at home.

"Now," said the Eagle, "untie this thong from my leg, friend, and get astride my neck, and we will go."

The string was soon untied, and Tái-oh got astride the neck of the great bird, which rose up into the air as though it carried no weight at all. It circled over the town a long time, and the people cried out with wonder and fear at seeing an Eagle with a boy on his back. Then they sailed out over the fields, where Tái-oh's parents and his sister were at work; and all the three began to cry, and went home in great sorrow.

The Eagle kept soaring up and up until they came to the very sky. There in the blue was a little door, through which the Eagle flew. Alighting on the floor of the sky, he let Tái-oh down from his back, and said:

"Now, you wait here, friend, while I go and see my people," and off he flew.

Tái-oh waited three days, and still the Eagle did not return; so he became uneasy and started out to see what he could find. After wandering a long way, he met an old Spider-woman.

"Where are you going, my son?" she asked.

"I am trying to find my friend, the Eagle."

"Very well, then, I will help you. Come into my house."

"But how can I come into so small a door?" objected Tái-oh.

"Just put your foot in, and it will open big enough for you to enter."

So Tái-oh put his foot in, and, sure enough, the door opened wide, and he went into the Spider's house and sat down.

"Now," said she, "you will have some trouble in getting to the house of your friend, the Eagle, for to get there you will have to climb a dreadful ladder. It is well that you came to me for help, for that ladder is set with sharp arrow-heads and knives of flint, so that if you tried to go up it, it would cut your legs off. But I will give you this sack of sacred herbs to help you. When you come to the ladder, you must chew some of the herbs and spit the juice on the ladder, which will at once become smooth for you."

Tái-oh thanked the Spider-woman and started off with the sack. After awhile he came to the foot of a great ladder, which went away up out of sight. Its sides and rungs were bristling with keen arrow-heads, so that no living thing could climb it; but when Tái-oh chewed some of the magic herb and spat upon the ladder, all the sharp points fell off, and it was so smooth that he climbed it without a single scratch.

After a long, long climb, he came to the top of the ladder, and stepped upon the roof of the Eagles' house. But when he came to the door he found it so bristling with arrow-points that whoever might try to enter would be cut to pieces. Again he chewed some of the herb, and spat upon the door; and at once all the points fell off, and he entered safely, and inside he found his Eagle-friend, and all the Eagle-people. His friend had fallen in love with an Eagle-girl and married her, and that was the reason he had not returned sooner.

Tái-oh stayed there some time, being very nicely entertained, and enjoyed himself greatly in the strange sky-country. At last one of the wise old Eagle-men came to him and said:

"Now, my son, it is well that you go home, for your parents are very sad, thinking you are dead. After this, whenever you seen an Eagle caught and kept captive, you must let it go; for now you have been in our country, and know that when we come home we take off our feather-coats and are people like your own."

So Tái-oh went to his Eagle-friend and said he thought he must go home.

"Very well," said the Eagle; "get on my neck and shut your eyes, and we will go."

So he got on, and they went down out of the sky, and down and down until at last they came to Moqui. There the Eagle let Tái-oh down among the wondering people, and, bidding him an affectionate good-by, flew off to his young wife in the sky.

Tái-oh went to his home loaded down with dried meat and tanned buckskin, which the Eagle had given him; and there was great rejoicing, for all had given him up as dead. And this is why, to this very day, the Moquis will not keep an Eagle captive, though nearly all the other Pueblo towns have all the Eagle-prisoners they can get.

The Drowning of Pecos

TWENTY-FIVE MILES SOUTHEAST OF SANTA FÉ, New Mexico, lie the deserted ruins of the ancient *Pueblo* town of Pecos. The village was finally abandoned by the Indians in 1840; and their neat houses of adobe bricks and stone, and their quaint adobe church, have sadly fallen to decay. The history of the abandonment of Pecos is by no means startling; but the Indian tradition – for they have already added this to their countless myths – is decidedly so. The story is related by two aged Pecos Indians who still live in the ***pueblo*** of Jemez.

"Now, this is a true story," said my informant, an Isleteño, who had often heard it from them.

Once Pecos was a large village, and had many people. But it came that nearly all of them had the evil road, and in the whole town were but five True Believers (in the Indian religion). These were an old woman, her two sons, and two other young men. Agostin, her elder son, was a famous hunter, and very often went to the mountains with a friend of his who had an evil spirit – though Agostin was not aware of that.

One day the friend invited Agostin to go hunting, and next day they went to the mountains. Just at the foot they found a herd of deer, one of which Agostin wounded. The deer fled up the mountain, and the two friends followed by the drops of blood. Half-way to the top they came to a second herd, which ran off to the right of the trail they were following, and the evil-spirited friend went in pursuit of them, while Agostin kept on after the one he had wounded.

He came at last to the very top of the mountain, and there of a sudden the trail ceased. Agostin hunted all about, but in vain, and at last started down the other side of the mountain.

As he came to a deep *cañon* he heard singing, and, peering cautiously through the bushes, he saw a lot of witch-men sitting around a fallen pine and singing, while their chief was trying to raise the tree.

Agostin recognized them all, for they were of Pecos, and he was much grieved when he saw his friend among them. Then he knew that the deer had all been witches, and that they had led him off on a false trail.

Greatly alarmed, he crept back to a safe distance, and then hurried home and told his aged mother all that had happened, asking her if he should report it to the Cacique.

"No," said she, with a sigh, "it is of no use; for he, too, has the evil road. There are but few True Believers left, and the bad ones are trying to use us up."

Among the five good people was one of the *Cum-pah-whit-lah-wen* (guards of the medicine-men); and to him Agostin told his story. But he also said: "It is of no use. We are too few to do anything."

At last the bad people falsely accused the old woman, saying that her power was more than that of all the medicine-men put together (which is a very serious charge, even to-day, among the Indians); and challenged her to come before all the people in the medicine-house and perform miracles with them, well knowing that she could not. The challenge was for life or death; whichever side won was to kill the others without being resisted.

The poor old woman told her sons, with tears, saying: "Already we are killed. We know nothing of these things, and we may make ready to die."

"Nay, Nana," said Agostin. "Despair not yet, but prepare lunch for Pedro and me, that we go to other villages for advice. Perhaps there the medicine-men will tell us something."

So the mother, still weeping, made some tortillas, and, strapping these to their belts, the young men set out.

Pedro, the younger, went east, and Agostin took the road to the north. Whatever person they met, or to whatever village they came, they were to seek advice.

When Agostin came to the foot of the mountains, he was very thirsty, but there was no water. As he entered a gorge he saw Hyo-kwáh-kwah-báy-deh, a little bird which builds its nest with pebbles and clay in the crannies of the cliffs, and is of exactly the same colour as the sandstones. He thought, "Ah, little bird, if you could speak I would ask you where there is water, for I am fainting with thirst, and dare not eat, for that would make it worse!"

But the little bird, knowing his thought, said:

"Friend Agostin, I see that you are one of the True Believers, and I will show you where there is water; or wait, I will go and bring you some, for it is very far." And off he flew.

Agostin waited, and presently the little bird came back, bringing an acorn-cup full of water. Then Agostin's heart sank, and he thought: "Alas! what good will that drop do me?"

But the little bird replied: "Do not think that way, friend. Here is enough, and even more; for when you drink all you wish, there will still be some left."

And so it was. Agostin drank and drank, then ate some tortillas and drank again; and when he was satisfied, the acorn-cup was still nearly full.

Then the little bird said: "Now come, and I will lead you. But when we come to the top of the mountain, and I say, 'We are at the top,' you must say, 'No, we are down in the mountain – at the bottom of it.' Do not forget."

Agostin promised, and the little bird flew in front of him. At last they were at the top, and the little bird said:

"Here we are, friend, at the top."

"No," answered Agostin, "we are down in the mountain – at the bottom of it."

Three times the little bird repeated his words, and three times Agostin made the same answer.

At the third reply they found themselves in a room in the mountain. There was a door in front of them, and beside it stood a *Cum-pah-whit-lah-wíd-deh* (guard), who said to Agostin – for the little bird had disappeared:

"Son, how came you here, where none ever think of coming? Do you think you are a man?"

Agostin told the whole story of the witches' challenge, and of how he had gone out to seek advice, and of how the little bird had brought him here, and the guard said:

"You are coming with the thought of a man; so now come in," and he opened the door.

But when Agostin entered the inner room, which was so large that no end could be seen, he found himself in the presence of the Trues in human shape.

There sat the divinities of the East, who are white; and of the North, who are blue; and beyond them were the sacred animals – the mountain lion, the eagle, bear, buffalo, badger, hawk, rabbit, rattlesnake, and all the others that are of the Trues. Agostin was very much afraid, but the guard said to him:

"Do not fear, son, but take the heart of a man, and pray to all sides." So he faced to the six sides, praying. When he had finished, one of the Trues spoke to him, and said:

"What can it be that brought you here? Take the heart of a man and tell us."

Then Agostin told his whole story; after which the Trues said to him:

"Do not be worried, son. We will help you out of that."

The principal True of the East said:

"Son, I will give you the clothes you must wear when you are in the medicine-house for the contest of power"; and he gave Agostin four dark-blue breech-clouts and some moccasins for himself and the three other good young men, and a black *manta*, (robe) and pair of moccasins for his mother.

"Now," said the True, "the evil-spirited ones will have this medicine-making contest in the *estufa*, and when you enter, you five, you must all be dressed in these clothes. The people will all be there, old and young, and there will hardly be room for you to stand; and they will all sneer at you and spit upon you. But do not be sorry. And take this cane to hold between you. Let your mother take it with one hand at the bottom, then the Whit-lah-wíd-deh's hand, then her other hand, and then his other hand; and last your brother's hand, your hand, then his other hand, and your other hand at the top of all. And when you say, 'We are at the top of the mountain,' he must answer, 'No, we are down in the mountain – at the bottom of it.' This you must keep saying. Now go, son, with the heart of a man."

Then the Whit-lah-wíd-deh led Agostin out, and the little bird showed him the way down the mountain.

When he reached home it was the afternoon of the appointed day, and in the evening the medicine-making contest for life or death was to come. In a little while the younger brother arrived, with his new clothes and moccasins torn to shreds; for he had travelled far in a rough country, without meeting a soul from whom to ask advice.

Agostin called together the four other True Believers, and told them all that had happened and what they must do, giving them the sacred clothing.

In the evening they went to the *estufa*, which was crowded with the witch-people, so that they had barely room to stand.

Then the evil-spirited ones began to make medicine, and turned themselves into bears, coyotes, crows, owls, and other animals. When they were done, they said to the old woman:

"Now it is your turn. We will see what you can do."

"I know nothing about these things," she said, "but I will do what I can, and the Trues will help me."

Then she and the four young men took hold of the sacred cane as the Trues had showed Agostin.

"We are on the top of the mountain," said he.

"No," answered his brother, "we are down in the mountain – at the bottom of it."

This they said three times. At the third saying the people heard on all sides the *guajes* of the Trues. At the same moment the ladder was jerked violently up out of the room, so that no one could get out.

Then the two brothers repeated their words again, and at the third saying the thunder began to roar outside, and all could hear plainly the singing and the *guajes* of the Trues. It began to rain violently, and the water poured down through the roof-door, and the lightning stuck its tongue in. The brothers kept repeating their words, and soon the water was knee-deep. But where the five True Believers stood, holding the cane, the floor was dusty. Soon the flood came to the waists of the witch-people, and then to their necks, and the children were drowning. Then they cried out to the old woman:

"Truly, mother, your power is greater than ours. We submit."

But she paid no attention to them, and her sons continued their words, and the water kept pouring in until it touched the very ceiling. But all around the five it stood back like a wall, and they were on dry ground.

At last all the evil-spirited ones were drowned. Then the rain ceased and the water departed as fast as it had come. The ladder came down through the roof-door again, and the five True Believers climbed out and went to their homes.

But it was very desolate, for they were the only survivors. Their nearest relatives and dearest friends had perished with the other witch-people. At last they could no longer bear to live in the lonely valley, and they decided to live elsewhere. On the way the old mother and one of the men died. Agostin went to the pueblo of Cochití, and Pedro and the Whit-lah-wíd-deh settled in the *pueblo* of Jemez, where they are still living (or were in the spring of 1891).

Such is the Indian version of the abandonment of the great pueblo which Coronado – that wonderful Spanish explorer – found in 1540. As a matter of fact, the Hyó-qua-hoon, or people of Pecos, had dwindled away by war, epidemics, and the like, until only five were left; and in 1840 these lonely survivors moved to other *pueblos*, and abandoned their ruined town forever. But the story is very valuable, not only for the glimpse it affords of some of their most secret beliefs, but also as showing how folk-stories of the most aboriginal stamp are still coined.

Witchcraft is still a serious trouble in all the *pueblos*, despite the efforts of the medicine-men, whose special duty it is to keep down the witches. One little *pueblo* called Sandia is dying out – as many others have done before it – because the medicine-men are quietly killing those whom they suspect of being witches. In 1888 a very estimable Indian woman of that town was slain by them in the customary way – shot through from side to side with an arrow – and this form of execution is still practised.

In Isleta they fear the Americans too much to indulge in witch-killing, for Albuquerque is only a few miles away. But it is only a little while ago that a young Isletan who was accused spent three months in the neck-stocks in our aboriginal prison, and much of the time had to, 'ride the horse,' sitting with his legs crossed upon the adobe floor and the heavy weight of the stocks pressing him down, a torture worthy of the Inquisition. The case was kept out of the American courts only by the payment of a large sum to his parents by his accusers.

One whose eyes or lids look red is always regarded with suspicion here, for witch-people are supposed not to sleep at night, but to change themselves into animals and roam over the world. Eccentric actions also lay one open to accusation; and when I first came here I was dangerously near being classed with the witches because, to amuse my dusky little neighbours, I imitated various animal cries to their great edification, but to the very serious doubt of their elders. The fact that they doubt whether Americans know enough to be first-class witches was largely instrumental in saving me from serious danger.

The Ants that Pushed on the Sky

A VERY ANCIENT AND CHARACTERISTIC STORY about the origin of Isleta is based on the historic fact that part of its founders came from east of the Manzano Mountains, from one of the prehistoric pueblos whose ruins are now barely visible in those broad plains.

Once upon a time there lived in one of those villages (so runs the story) a young Indian named Kahp-too-óo-yoo, the Corn-stalk Young Man. He was not only a famous hunter and a brave warrior against the raiding Comanches, but a great wizard; and to him the Trues had given the power of the clouds. When Kahp-too-óo-yoo willed it, the glad rains fell, and made the dry fields laugh in green; and without him no one could bring water from the sky. His father was Old-Black-Cane, his mother was Corn-Woman, and his two sisters were Yellow-Corn-Maiden, and Blue-Corn-Maiden.

Kahp-too-óo-yoo had a friend, a young man of about the same age. But, as is often true, the friend was of a false heart, and was really a witch, though Kahp-too-óo-yoo never dreamed of such a thing.

The two young men used to go together to the mountains to get wood, and always carried their bows and arrows, to kill deer and antelopes, or whatever game they might find.

One day the false friend came to Kahp-too-óo-yoo, and said:

"Friend, let us go to-morrow for wood, and to hunt."

They agreed that so they would do. Next day they started before sunrise, and came presently to the spot where they gathered wood. Just there they started a herd of deer. Kahp-too-óo-yoo followed part of the herd, which fled to the northwest, and the friend pursued those that went southwest. After a long, hard chase, Kahp-too-óo-yoo killed a deer with his swift arrows, and brought it on his strong back to the place where they had separated. Presently came the friend, very hot and tired, and with empty hands; and seeing the deer, he was pinched with jealousy.

"Come, friend," said Kahp-too-óo-yoo. "It is well for brothers to share with brothers. Take of this deer and cook and eat; and carry a part to your house, as if you had killed it yourself."

"Thank you," answered the other coldly, as one who will not; but he did not accept.

When they had gathered each a load of wood, and lashed it with rawhide thongs in bundles upon their shoulders, they trudged home – Kahp-too-óo-yoo carrying the deer on top of his wood. His sisters received him with joy, praising him as a hunter; and the friend went away to his house, with a heavy face.

Several different days when they went to the mountain together, the very same thing came to pass. Kahp-too-óo-yoo killed each time a deer; and each time the friend came home with nothing, refusing all offers to share as brothers. And he grew more jealous and more sullen every day.

At last he came again to invite Kahp-too-óo-yoo to go; but this time it was with an evil purpose that he asked. Then again the same things happened. Again the unsuccessful friend refused to take a share of Kahp-too-óo-yoo's deer; and when he had sat long without a word, he said:

"Friend Kahp-too-óo-yoo, now I will prove you if you are truly my friend, for I do not think it."

"Surely," said Kahp-too-óo-yoo, "if there is any way to prove myself, I will do it gladly, for truly I am your friend."

"Then come, and we will play a game together, and with that I will prove you."

"It is well! But what game shall we play, for here we have nothing?"

Near them stood a broken pine-tree, with one great arm from its twisted body. And looking at it, the false friend said:

"I see nothing but to play the *gallo* race; and because we have no horses we will ride this arm of the pine-tree – first I will ride, and then you."

So he climbed the pine-tree, and sat astride the limb as upon a horse, and rode, reaching over to the ground as if to pick up the chicken.

"Now you," he said, coming down; and Kahp-too-óo-yoo climbed the tree and rode on the swinging branch. But the false friend bewitched the pine, and suddenly it grew in a moment to the very sky, carrying Kahp-too-óo-yoo.

"We do this to one another," taunted the false friend, as the tree shot up; and taking the wood, and the deer which Kahp-too-óo-yoo had killed, he went to the village. There the sisters met him, and asked:

"Where is our brother?"

"Truly I know not, for he went northwest and I southwest; and though I waited long at the meeting-place, he did not come. Probably he will soon return. But take of this deer which I killed, for sisters should share the labours of brothers."

But the girls would take no meat, and went home sorrowful.

Time went on, and still there was no Kahp-too-óo-yoo. His sisters and his old parents wept always, and all the village was sad. And soon the crops grew yellow in the fields, and the springs failed, and the animals walked like weary shadows; for Kahp-too-óo-yoo, he who had the power of the clouds, was gone, and there was no rain. And then perished all that is green; the animals fell in the brown fields; and the gaunt people who sat to warm themselves in the sun began to die there where they sat. At last the poor old man said to his daughters:

"Little daughters, prepare food, for again we will go to look for your brother."

The girls made cakes of the blue corn-meal for the journey; and on the fourth day they started. Old-Black-Cane hobbled to the south, his wife to the east, the elder girl to the north, and the younger to the west.

For a great distance they travelled; and at last Blue-Corn-Maiden, who was in the north, heard a far, faint song. It was so little that she thought it must be imaginary; but she stopped to listen, and softly, softly it came again:

Tó-ai-fóo-ni-hlóo-hlim,
Eng-k'hai k'háhm;
Eé-eh-bóori-kóon-hlee-oh,
Ing-k'hai k'háhm.
Ah-ee-ái, ah-hee-ái,
Aim!

(Old-Black-Cane
My father is called;
Com-Woman
My mother is called.
Ah-ee-ái, ah-hee-ái,
Aim!)

When she heard this, Blue-Corn-Maiden ran until she came to her sister, and cried:

"Sister! Sister! I think I hear our brother somewhere in captivity. Listen!"

Trembling, they listened; and again the song came floating to them, so soft, so sad that they wept – as to this day their people weep when a white-haired old man, filled with the memories of Kahp-too-óo-yoo, sings that plaintive melody.

"Surely it is our brother!" they cried; and off they went running to find their parents. And when all listened together, again they heard the song.

"Oh, my son!" cried the poor old woman, "in what captivity do you find yourself? True it is that your father is Old-Black-Cane, and I, your mother, am called Corn-Woman. But why do you sing thus?"

Then all four of them began to follow the song, and at last they came to the foot of the sky-reaching pine; but they could see nothing of Kahp-too-óo-yoo, nor could their cries reach him. There, on the ground, were his bow and arrows, with strings and feathers eaten away by time; and there was his pack of wood, tied with the rawhide thong, ready to be taken home. But after they had searched everywhere, they could not find Kahp-too-óo-yoo; and finally they went home heavy at heart.

At last it happened that P'ah-whá-yoo-óo-deh, the Little Black Ant, took a journey and went up the bewitched pine, even to its top in the sky. When he found Kahp-too-óo-yoo there a prisoner, the Little Black Ant was astonished, and said:

"Great *Kah-báy-deh* (Man of Power), how comes it that you are up here in such a condition, while your people at home are suffering and dying for rain, and few are left to meet you if you return? Are you here of your free will?"

"No," groaned Kahp-too-óo-yoo; "I am here because of the jealousy of him who was as my brother, with whom I shared my food and labour, whose home was my home, and my home his. He is the cause, for he was jealous and bewitched me hither. And now I am dying of famine."

"If that is so," said the Little Black Ant, "I will be the one to help you"; and he ran down to the world as fast as he could. When he got there he sent out the crier to summon all his nation, and also that of the *In-toon*, the Big Red Ants. Soon all the armies of the Little Black Ants and the Big Red Ants met at the foot of the pine, and held a council. They smoked the *weer* and deliberated what should be done.

"You Big Red Ants are stronger than we who are small," said the War-Captain of the Little Black Ants, "and for that you ought to take the top of the tree to work."

"*Een-dah*!" (No) said the War-Captain of the Big Red Ants. "If you think we are the stronger, give us the bottom, where we can work more, and you go to the top."

So it was agreed, and the captains made their armies ready. But first the Little Black Ants got the cup of an acorn, and mixed in it corn-meal and water and honey, and carried it up the tree. They were so many that they covered its trunk all the way to the sky.

When Kahp-too-óo-yoo saw, his heart was heavy, and he thought: "But what good will that very little do me, for I am dying of hunger and thirst?" "Nay, friend," answered the Captain of the Little Black Ants, who knew his thought. "A person should not think so. This little is enough, and there will be some left."

And it was so; for when Kahp-too-óo-yoo had eaten all he could, the acorn-cup was still nearly full. Then the ants carried the cup to the ground and came back to him. "Now, friend," said the Captain, "we will do our best. But now you must shut your eyes till I say '*Ahw*!'"

Kahp-too-óo-yoo shut his eyes, and the Captain sent signals down to those at the foot of the tree. And the Little Black Ants above put their feet against the sky and pushed with all their might on the top of the pine; and the Big Red Ants below caught the trunk and pulled as hard as they could; and the very first tug drove the great pine a quarter of its length into the earth.

"*Ahw*!" shouted the Captain of the Little Black Ants, and Kahp-too-óo-yoo opened his eyes; but he could see nothing below.

"Shut your eyes again," said the Captain, giving the signal. Again the Little Black Ants pushed mightily against the sky, and the Big Red Ants pulled mightily from below; and the pine was driven another fourth of its length into the earth.

"*Ahw*!" cried the Captain; and when Kahp-too-óo-yoo opened his eyes he could just see the big, brown world.

Again he closed his eyes. There was another great push and pull, and only a quarter of the pine was left above the ground. Now Kahp-too-óo-yoo could see, far below, the parched fields strewn with dead animals, and his own village full of dying people.

Again the Little Black Ants pushed and the Big Red Ants pulled, and this time the tree was driven clear out of sight, and Kahp-too-óo-yoo was left sitting on the ground. He hastily made a bow and arrows and soon killed a fat deer, which he brought and divided among the Little Black Ants and the Big Red Ants, thanking them for their kindness.

Then he made all his clothing to be new, for he had been four years a prisoner in the bewitched tree, and was all in rags. Making for himself a flute from the bark of a young tree, he played upon it as he strode homeward and sang:

Kahp-too-óo-yoo tú-mah-quee,
Nah-chóor kwé-shay-tin,
Nah-shúr kwé-shay-tin;
Kahp-too-óo-yoo tú-mah-quee!

(Kahp-too-óo-yoo has come to life again,
Is back to his home coming,
Blowing the yellow and the blue;
Kahp-too-óo-yoo has come to life again!)

As he walked and sang, the forgotten clouds came over him, and the soft rain began to fall, and all was green and good. But only so far as his voice reached came the rain; and beyond all was still death and drought. When he came to the end of the wet, he played and sang again; and again the rain fell as far as his voice was heard. This time the Fool-Boy, who was wandering outside the dying village, saw the far storm and heard the singing. He ran to tell Kahp-too-óo-yoo's parents; but nobody would believe a Foolish, and they sent him away.

When the Fool-Boy went out again, the rain fell on him and gave him strength, and he came running a second time to tell. Then the sisters came out of the house and saw the rain and heard the song; and they cried for joy, and told their parents to rise and meet him. But the poor old people were dying of weakness, and could not rise; and the sisters went alone. When they met him they fell on their knees, weeping; but Kahp-too-óo-yoo lifted them up and blessed them, gave an ear of blue corn to Blue-Corn-Maiden, and to Yellow-Corn-Maiden an ear of yellow corn, and brought them home.

As he sang again, the rain fell in the village; and when it touched the pinched faces of the dead they sat up and opened their mouths to catch it. And the dying crawled out to drink, and were strong again; and the withered fields grew green and glad.

When they came to the house, Kahp-too-óo-yoo blessed his parents, and then said: "Little sisters, give us to eat."

But they answered, "How? For you have been gone these four years, and there was none to give us rain. We planted, but nothing came, and today we ate the last grain."

"Nay, little sisters" he said. "A person should not think so. Look now in the storerooms, if there be not something there."

"But we have looked and looked, and turned over everything to try to find one grain."

"Yet look once more," he said; and when they opened the door, lo! there was the storeroom piled to the roof with corn, and another room was full of wheat. Then they cried for joy, and began to roast the blue ears, for they were dying of hunger.

At the sweet smell of the roasting corn came the starving neighbours, crowding at the door, and crying:

"O Kahp-too-óo-yoo! Give us to taste one grain of corn, and then we will go home and die."

But Kahp-too-óo-yoo handed to each an ear, and said:

"Fathers, brothers, go now to your own houses, for there you will find corn as much as here." And when they went, it was so. All began to roast corn and to eat; and the dead in the houses awoke and were strong again, and all the village sang and danced.

From that time there was plenty of rain, for he who had the power of the clouds was at home again. In the spring the people planted, and in the fall the crops were so great that all the town could not hold them; so that which was left they brought to Shee-eh-whíb-bak (Isleta), where we enjoy it to this day.

As for the false friend, he died of shame in his house, not daring to come out; and no one wept for him.

The Sobbing Pine

ANOTHER FOLK-STORY told by the Quères colony in Isleta also relates to Acoma, perched upon the great round cliff in its far, fair valley.

Among the folk-lore heroes of whom every Quères lad has heard is Ees-tée-ah Muts, the Arrow Boy. He was a great hunter and did many remarkable things, but there was once a time when all his courage and strength were of no avail, when but for the help of a little squirrel he would have perished miserably.

On reaching manhood Ees-tée-ah Muts married the daughter of the *Kot-chin* (chief). She was a very beautiful girl and her hunter-husband was very fond of her. But, alas! she was secretly a witch and every night when Ees-tée-ah Muts was asleep she used to fly away to the mountains, where the witches held their uncanny meetings. You must know that these witches have dreadful appetites, and that there is nothing in the world of which they are so fond as boiled baby.

Ees-tée-ah Muts, who was a very good man, had no suspicion that his wife was guilty of such practices, and she was very careful to keep him in ignorance of it.

One day, when the witch-wife was planning to go to a meeting, she stole a fat young baby and put it to cook in a great *olla* (earthen jar) in the dark inner room. But before night she found she must go for water, and as the strange stone reservoir at Acoma is a laborious half-mile from the houses, she would be gone some time. So, as she departed with a bright-painted *tinaja* upon her head, she charged her husband on no account to enter the inner room.

When she was gone Ees-tée-ah Muts began to ponder what she had said, and he feared that all was not well. He went to the inner room and looked around, and when he found the baby cooking he was grieved, as any good husband would be, for then he knew that his wife was a witch. But when his wife returned with water, he said not a word, keeping only a sharp lookout to see what would come.

Very early that night Ees-tée-ah Muts pretended to go to sleep, but he was really very wide awake. His wife was quiet, but he could feel that she was watching him. Presently a cat came sneaking into the room and whispered to the witch-wife:

"Why do you not come to the meeting, for we await you?"

"Wait me yet a little," she whispered, "until the man is sound asleep."

The cat crept away, and Ees-tée-ah Muts kept very still. By and by an owl came in and bade the woman hurry. And at last, thinking her husband asleep, the witch-wife rose noiselessly and went out. As soon as she was gone, Ees-tée-ah Muts got up and followed her at a distance, for it was a night of the full moon.

The witch-wife walked a long way till she came to the foot of the Black Mesa, where was a great dark hole with a rainbow in its mouth. As she passed under the rainbow she turned herself into a cat and disappeared within the cave. Ees-tée-ah Muts crept softly up and peered in. He saw a great firelit room full of witches in the shapes of ravens and vultures, wolves and other animals of ill omen. They were gathered about their feast and were enjoying themselves greatly, eating and dancing and singing and planning evil to mankind.

For a long time Ees-tée-ah Muts watched them, but at last one caught sight of his face peering in at the hole.

"Bring him in!" shouted the chief witch, and many of them rushed out and surrounded him and dragged him into the cave.

"Now," said the chief witch, who was very angry, "we have caught you as a spy and we ought to kill you. But if you will save your life and be one of us, go home and bring me the hearts of your mother and sister, and I will teach you all our ways, so that you shall be a mighty wizard."

Ees-tée-ah Muts hurried home to Acoma and killed two sheep; for he knew, as every Indian knows, that it was useless to try to escape from the witches. Taking the hearts of the sheep, he quickly returned to the chief witch, to whom he gave them. But when the chief witch pricked the hearts with a sharp stick they swelled themselves out like a frog. Then he knew that he had been deceived, and was very angry, but pretending not to care he ordered Ees-tée-ah Muts to go home, which the frightened hunter was very glad to do.

But next morning when Ees-tée-ah Muts awoke he was not in his own home at all, but lying on a tiny shelf far up a dizzy cliff. To jump was certain death, for it was a thousand feet to the ground; and climb he could not, for the smooth rock rose a thousand feet above his head. Then he knew that he had been bewitched by the chief of those that have the evil road, and that he must die. He could hardly move without falling from the narrow shelf, and there he lay with bitter thoughts until the sun was high overhead.

At last a young Squirrel came running along the ledge, and, seeing him, ran back to its mother, crying:

"*Nana*! *Nana*! Here is a dead man lying on our ledge!"

"No, he is not dead," said the Squirrel-mother when she had looked, "but I think he is very hungry. Here, take this acorn-cup and carry him some corn-meal and water."

The young Squirrel brought the acorn-cup full of wet corn-meal, but Ees-tée-ah Muts would not take it, for he thought:

"Pah! What is so little when I am fainting for food?"

But the Squirrel-mother, knowing what was in his heart, said:

"Not so, *Sau-kée-ne* [friend]. It looks to be little, but there will be more than enough. Eat and be strong." Still doubting, Ees-tée-ah Muts took the cup and ate of the blue corn-meal until he could eat no longer, and yet the acorn-cup was not empty. Then the young Squirrel took the cup and brought it full of water, and though he was very thirsty he could not drain it.

"Now, friend," said the Squirrel-mother, when he was refreshed by his meal, "you cannot yet get down from here, where the witches put you; but wait, for I am the one that will help you."

She went to her store-room and brought out a pine-cone, which she dropped over the great cliff Ees-tée-ah Muts lay on the narrow ledge as patiently as he could, sleeping sometimes and sometimes thinking of his strange plight. Next morning he could see a stout young pine-tree growing at the bottom of the cliff, where he was very sure there had been no tree at all the day before. Before night it was a large tree, and the second morning it was twice as tall. The young Squirrel brought him a meal and water in the acorn-cup twice a day, and now he began to be confident that he would escape.

By the evening of the fourth day the magic pine towered far above his head, and it was so close to the cliff that he could touch it from his shelf.

"Now, Friend Man," said the Squirrel-mother, "follow me!" and she leaped lightly into the tree. Ees-tée-ah Muts seized a branch and swung over into the tree, and letting himself down from bough to bough, at last reached the ground in safety.

The Squirrel-mother came with him to the ground, and he thanked her for her kindness.

"But now I must go back to my home," she said. "Take these seeds of the pine-tree and these piñon-nuts which I have brought for you, and be very careful of them. When you get home, give your wife the pine-seeds, but you must eat the piñons. So now, good-by," and off she went up the tree.

When Ees-tée-ah Muts had come to Acoma and climbed the dizzy stone ladder and stood in the adobe town, he was very much surprised. For the four days of his absence had really been four years, and the people looked strange. All had given him up for dead, and his witch-wife had married another man, but still lived in the same house, which was hers. When Ees-tée-ah Muts entered she seemed very glad to see him, and pretended to know nothing of what had befallen him. He said nothing about it, but talked pleasantly while he munched the piñon-nuts, giving her the pine-seeds to eat. Her new husband made a bed for Ees-tée-ah Muts, and in the morning very early the two men went away together on a hunt.

That afternoon the mother of the witch-wife went to visit her daughter, but when she came near the house she stopped in terror, for far up through the roof grew a great pine-tree, whose furry arms came out at doors and windows. That was the end of the witch-wife, for the magic seed had sprouted in her stomach, and she was turned into a great, sad Pine that swayed above her home, and moaned and sobbed forever, as all her Pine-children do to this day.

The Magic Hide and Seek

I FANCY I MUST HAVE BEEN DOZING after that hard ride; for when a far-away, cracked voice that could be none other than Grandfather Ysidro's said, "***Kah-whee-cá-me, Lorenso-kaí-deh!***" I started up so hastily as to bump my head against the whitewashed wall. That may seem a queer sentence to rouse one so sharply; and especially when you know what it means. It meant that old Ysidro had just finished a story, which I had altogether missed, and was now calling upon the old man next him to tell one, by using the customary Pueblo saying:

"There is a tail to you, Father Lorenso!"

Kah-whee-cá-me is what a Tée-wahn Indian always says in such a case, instead of 'Now you tell a story, friend.' It is not intended as an impolite remark, but merely refers to the firm belief of these quaint people that if one were to act like a stubborn donkey, and refuse to tell a story when called on, a donkey's tail would grow upon him!

With such a fate in prospect, you may be sure that the roundabout invitation thus conveyed is never declined.

Grandfather Lorenso bows his head gravely, but seems in no haste. He is indeed impressively deliberate as he slowly makes a cigarette from a bit of corn-husk and a pinch of tobacco, lights it upon a coal raked out of the fireplace by his withered fingers, blows a slow puff eastward, then one to the north, another to the west, a fourth to the south, one straight above his head, and one down toward the floor. There is one part of the United States where the compass has six cardinal points (those I have just named), and that is among these Indians, and in fact all the others of the Southwest. The cigarette plays a really important part in many sacred ceremonies of the Pueblos; for, as I have explained, its collective smoke is thought to be what makes the rain-clouds and brings the rain; and it is also a charm against witches.

Having thus propitiated the divinities who dwell in the directions named, Lorenso looks about the circle to see if all are listening. The glance satisfies him – as well it may. There are no heedless eyes or ears in the audience, of which I am the only white member – and a very lucky one, in that I, an 'Americano,' am allowed to hear these jealously guarded stories, and to see the silent smoke-prayer which would never be made if a stranger were present. There are seven aged men here, and nine bright-eyed boys – all *Isleteños* (inhabitants of Isleta). We are huddled around the fireplace in the corner of the big, pleasant room, against whose dark rafters and farther white walls the shadows dance and waver.

And now, taking a deep puff, Lorenso exclaims:

"*Nah-t' hóo-ai*!" (In a house.) It has nothing to do with the story; but is the prologue to inform the hearers that the story is about to open.

"Ah-h-h!" we all responded, which is as much as to say, "We are listening – go on"; and Lorenso begins his story.

Once upon a time there was a Tée-wahn village on the other side of the mountain, and there lived a man and his wife who thought more of the future of their children than did the others. To care better for the children they moved to a little ranch some distance from the village, and there taught their two little sons all they could. Both boys loved the outdoors, and games, and hunting; and the parents were well pleased, saying to each other:

"Perhaps some day they will be great hunters!"

By the time the elder boy was twelve and the younger ten, they both were very expert with the little bows and arrows their father carefully made them; and already they began to bring home many rabbits when they were allowed to go a little way from home. There was only one command their parents gave about their hunts; and that was that they must never, never go south. They could hunt to the east, north, and west, but not south.

Day after day they went hunting, and more and more rabbits they killed, growing always more expert.

One day when they had hunted eastward, the elder boy said:

"Brother, can you say any reason why we must not go south?"

"I know nothing," replied the younger, "except what I overheard our parents saying one day. They spoke of an old woman who lives in the south who eats children; and for that they said they would never let us go south."

"Pooh!" said the elder, "I think nothing of *that*. The real reason must be that they wish to save the rabbits in the south, and are afraid we would kill them all. There must be many rabbits in that *bosque* (forest) away down there. Let's go and see – they won't know!"

The younger boy being persuaded, they started off together, and after a long walk came to the *bosque*. It was full of rabbits, and they were having great sport, when suddenly they heard a motherly voice calling through the woods. In a moment they saw an old woman coming from the south, who said to the boys:

"*Mah-kóo-oon* (grandchildren), what are you doing here, where no one ever thinks to come?"

"We are hunting, Grandmother," they replied. "Our parents would never let us come south; but to-day we came to see if the rabbits are more numerous here than above."

"Oh!" said the old woman, "this game you see here is *nothing*. Come, and I will show you where there is much, and you can carry very large rabbits home to your parents." But she was deceiving them.

She had a big basket upon her back, and stooping for the boys to get into it, she carried them farther and farther into the woods. At last they came to an old, battered house; and setting the basket down, she said:

"Now we have come all the way here, where no one ever came before, and there is no way out. You can find no trail, and you will have to stay here contented, or I will eat you up!"

The boys were much afraid, and said they would stay and be contented. But the old woman went into the house and told her husband – who was as wicked as she – to get wood and build a big fire in the *horno*. All day long the fire burned, and the oven became hotter than it had ever been. In the evening the old witch-woman raked out the coals, and calling the boys seized them and forced them into the fiery oven.

"*Tahh-kóon-nahm*?" (Is that so?) we all exclaimed – that being the proper response whenever the narrator pauses a moment.

"That is so," replied Lorenso, and went on.

Then the old woman put a flat rock over the little door of the oven, and another over the smoke-hole, and sealed them both tight with clay. All that night she and her husband were chuckling to think what a nice breakfast they would have – for both of them were witch-people, and ate all the children they could find.

But in the morning when she unsealed the oven, there were the two boys, laughing and playing together unhurt – for the *Wháy-nin* had come to their aid and protected them from the heat.

Leaving the boys to crawl out, the old woman ran to the house and scolded the old man terribly for not having made the oven hot enough. "Go this minute," she said, "and put in the oven all the wood that it will hold, and keep it burning all day!"

When night came, the old woman cleaned the oven, which was twice as hot as before; and again she put in the boys and sealed it up. But the next morning the boys were unhurt and went to playing.

The witch-woman was very angry then; and giving the boys their bows and arrows, told them to go and play. She stayed at home and abused the old witch-man all day for a poor fire-maker.

When the boys returned in the evening, she said:

"To-morrow, grandchildren, we will play *Nah-oo-p'ah-chée* (hide-and-seek), and the one who is found three times by the other shall pay his life."

The boys agreed, and secretly prayed to the Trues to help them –for by this time they knew that the old man and the old woman "had the bad road."

The next day came; and very soon the old woman called them to begin the game. The boys were to hide first; and when the old woman had turned her eyes and vowed not to look, they went to the door and hid, one against each of its jambs. There you could look and look, and see the wood through them – for the Trues, to help them, made them invisible. When they were safely hidden they whooped, "*Hee-táh*!" and the old woman began to hunt, singing the hide-and-seek song:

Hee-táh yahn
Hee choo-ah-kóo
Mee, mee, mee?
(Now, now,
Which way,
Went they, went they, went they?)

After hunting some time she called:

"You little fellows are on the door-posts. Come out!"

So the boys came out and 'made blind' (covered their eyes) while the old woman went to hide. There was a pond close by, with many ducks on it; and making herself very little, she went and hid under the left wing of the duck with a blue head.

When they heard her "*Hee-táh*!" the boys went searching and singing; and at last the elder cried out:

"Old woman, you are under the left wing of the whitest duck on the lake – the one with the blue head. Come out!"

This time the boys made themselves small and crawled into the quivers beside their bows and arrows. The old woman had to sing her song over a great many times, as she went hunting all around; but at last she called:

"Come out of the quivers where you are!"

Then the witch made herself very small indeed, and went behind the foot of a big crane that was standing on one leg near the lake. But at last the boys found her even there.

It was their last turn now, and the old woman felt very triumphant as she waited for them to hide. But this time they went up and hid themselves under the right arm of the Sun. The old witch hunted everywhere, and used all her bad power, but in vain; and when she was tired out she had to cry, "*Hee-táh-ow*!" And then the boys came down from under the Sun's arm rejoicing.

The old witch, taking her last turn, went to the lake and entered into a fish, thinking that there she would be perfectly safe from discovery. It did take the boys a great while to find her; but at last they shouted:

"Old woman, you are in the biggest fish in the lake. Come out!"

As she came walking toward them in her natural shape again, they called: "Remember the agreement!" and with their sharp arrows they killed the old witch-woman and then the old witch-man. Then they took away the two wicked old hearts, and put in place of each a kernel of spotless corn; so that if the witches should ever come to life again they would no longer be witches, but people with pure, good hearts. They never did come to life, however, which was just as well.

Taking their bows and arrows, the boys – now young men, for the four 'days' they had been with the witches were really four years – returned home. At the village they found their anxious parents, who had come to ask the Cacique to order all the people out to search.

When all saw the boys and heard their story, there was great rejoicing, for those two witch-people had been terrors to the village for years. On their account no one had dared go hunting to the south. And to this day the game is thicker there than anywhere else in the country, because it has not been hunted there for so long as in other places. The two young men were forgiven for disobedience (which is a very serious thing at any age, among the Pueblos), and were made heroes. The Cacique gave them his two daughters for wives, and all the people did them honour.

"Is that so?" we responded; and Lorenso replied, "That is so," gathering his blanket and rising to go without 'putting a tail' to any one, for it was already late.

I may add that the game of hide-and-seek is still played by my dusky little neighbours, the Pueblo children, and the searching-song is still sung by them, exactly as the boys and the old witch played and sang – but of course without their magical talent at hiding.

The Quères Diana

THERE IS A FRAGMENTARY QUÈRES FOLK-STORY which bears internal evidence that its heroine was the mother of the Hero Twins – that is, the Moon. The adventure described here is one of those which befell the Moon-Mother, as related in several myths; though it has been varied, evidently by some later story-teller, and the identity of the heroine does not appear at first sight. It is a story common to all the Quères, and is undoubtedly ancient; but as I heard it first in Isleta its scene is laid in Laguna, a pueblo only two hundred years old.

Once upon a time the Tah-póh-pee of Laguna had a daughter, who was the belle of the village. She was very fond of hunting, and killed as much game as any of the young men. Several miles south of Laguna is a very large sandstone dome rising in the plain, and in the heart of this rock the Governor's daughter had hollowed out a room in which she used to camp when on her hunting-expeditions.

One day there came a snow that covered the ground so that one could easily track rabbits, and taking her bow and arrows she started off to hunt.

She had unusual luck, and by the time she reached the hunting-lodge she was loaded down with rabbits. The evening was very cold, and she was hungry; so, going into the rock-house, she built a fire on the hearth and began to roast a rabbit. Just as it was cooking a strong west wind came up and carried the savory smell from her chimney far to the east, till it reached a dark cavern in the Sandia Mountains, fifty miles away. There lived an old giantess, the terror of all the world, and when she caught a whiff of that sweet meat she started up and rubbed her big red eye.

"Um!" she cried, "that is good! I am going to see where it is, for I have had nothing to eat to-day."

In two steps she was at the rock-house, and, stooping down, she called at the door: "*Quáh-tzee*? (How are you?) What are you cooking in there?"

"Rabbits," said the girl, dreadfully scared at that great voice.

"Then give me one," shouted the old giantess. The girl threw one out at the door, and the giantess swallowed it at a gulp and demanded more. The girl kept throwing them out until all were gone. Then the giantess called for her *manta* (dress), and her shawl and her buckskin leggings, and ate them all, and at last said:

"Little girl, now you come out, and let me eat you."

The girl began to cry bitterly when she saw that great savage eye at the door, which was so small that the giantess could not get her huge hand in. She repeated her commands thrice, and when the girl still refused to come out, picked up a great boulder and began to hammer the rock-house to pieces. But just as she had broken off the roof and stooped to pick out the girl, two hunters chanced to pass and hear the noise. They crept up and shot the giantess through the neck with their strong arrows and killed her, and, bringing new clothes for the girl, took her home safely to Kó-iks (the native name for Laguna), where she lived for many years.

The Hero Twins

THAT THE HEROES of 'The Magic Hide-and-Seek' were really the Pueblo Castor and Pollux, the twin offspring of the Sun-Father and the Moon-Mother, is more than probable. For some reason which I do not know, these demigods do not figure as clearly in the Tée-wahn myths as among the other Pueblos, the Navajos and the Apaches; but that they are believed in, even in Isleta, there can be no doubt. They were the ones who led mankind forth from its first home in the dark centre of the earth. The rainbow is their bow, the lightnings are their arrows. Among the other Pueblos there are countless folk-stories about these Hero Twins; and the following example myth will quickly remind you of the boys who played hide-and-seek. It is told in Isleta, though I have never heard it from the Tée-wahn people there. Ever since the great drouth of a generation ago, about one hundred and fifty Quères, starved out from the pueblos of Acoma and Laguna, have dwelt in Isleta, and they are now a permanent part of the village, recognized by representation in the civil and religious government, though speaking an altogether different language. Tée-wahn and Quères cannot understand each other in their own tongues, so they have to communicate in Spanish.

Máw-Sahv and Oó-yah-wee, as the Hero Twins are named in Quères, had the Sun for a father. Their mother died when they were born, and lay lifeless upon the hot plain. But the two wonderful boys, as soon as they were a minute old, were big and strong, and began playing.

There chanced to be in a cliff to the southward a nest of white crows; and presently the young crows said: "Nana, what is that over there? Isn't it two babies?"

"Yes," replied the Mother-Crow, when she had taken a look. "Wait and I will bring them." So she brought the boys safely, and then their dead mother; and, rubbing a magic herb on the body of the latter, soon brought her to life.

By this time Máw-Sahv and Oó-yah-wee were sizable boys, and the mother started homeward with them.

"Now," said she when they reached the edge of the valley and could look across to that wondrous rock whereon stands Acoma, "go to yonder town, my sons, for that is Ah-ko, where live your grandfather and grandmother, my parents; and I will wait here. Go ye in at the west end of the town and stand at the south end of the council-grounds until some one speaks to you; and ask them to take you to the Cacique, for he is your grandfather. You will know his house, for the ladder to it has three uprights instead of two. When you go in and tell your story, he will ask you a question to see if you are really his grandchildren, and will give you four chances to answer what he has in a bag in the corner. No one has ever been able to guess what is in it, but there are birds."

The Twins did as they were bidden, and presently came to Acoma and found the house of the old Cacique. When they entered and told their story, he said: "Now I will try you. What is in yonder bag?"

"A rattlesnake," said the boys.

"No," said the Cacique, "it is not a rattlesnake. Try again."

"Birds," said the boys.

"Yes, they are birds. Now I know that you are truly my grandchildren, for no one else could ever guess." And he welcomed them gladly, and sent them back with new dresses and jewelry to bring their mother.

When she was about to arrive, the Twins ran ahead to the house and told her father, mother, and sister to leave the house until she should enter; but not knowing what was to come, they would not go out. When she had climbed the big ladder to the roof and started down through the trap-door by the room-ladder, her sister cried out with joy at seeing her, and she was so startled that she fell from the ladder and broke her neck, and never could be brought to life again.

Máw-Sahv and Oó-yah-wee grew up to astounding adventures and achievements. While still very young in years, they did very remarkable things; for they had a miraculously rapid growth, and at an age when other boys were toddling about home, these Hero

Twins had already become very famous hunters and warriors. They were very fond of stories of adventure, like less precocious lads; and after the death of their mother they kept their grandmother busy telling them strange tales. She had a great many anecdotes of a certain ogre-giantess who lived in the dark gorges of the mountains to the South, and so much did Máw-Sahv and Oó-yah-wee hear of this wonderful personage – who was the terror of all that country – that their boyish ambition was fired.

One day when their grandmother was busy they stole away from home with their bows and arrows, and walked miles and miles, till they came to a great forest at the foot of the mountain. In the edge of it sat the old Giant-woman, dozing in the sun, with a huge basket beside her. She was so enormous and looked so fierce that the boys' hearts stood still, and they would have hidden, but just then she caught sight of them, and called: "Come, little boys, and get into this basket of mine, and I will take you to my house."

"Very well," said Máw-Sahv, bravely hiding his alarm. "If you will take us through this big forest, which we would like to see, we will go with you."

The Giant-woman promised, and the lads clambered into her basket, which she took upon her back and started off. As she passed through the woods, the boys grabbed lumps of pitch from the tall pines and smeared it all over her head and back so softly that she did not notice it. Once she sat down to rest, and the boys slyly put a lot of big stones in the basket, set fire to her pitched hair, and hurriedly climbed a tall pine.

Presently the Giant-woman got up and started on toward home; but in a minute or two her head and *manta* were all of a blaze. With a howl that shook the earth, she dropped the basket and rolled on the ground, grinding her great head into the sand until she at last got the fire extinguished. But she was badly scorched and very angry, and still angrier when she looked in the basket and found only a lot of stones. She retraced her steps until she found the boys hidden in the pine-tree, and said to them: "Come down, children, and get into my basket, that I may take you to my house, for now we are almost there."

The boys, knowing that she could easily break down the tree if they refused, came down. They got into the basket, and soon she brought them to her home in the mountain. She set them down upon the ground and said: "Now, boys, go and bring me a lot of wood, that I may make a fire in the oven and bake you some sweet cakes."

The boys gathered a big pile of wood, with which she built a roaring fire in the adobe oven outside the house. Then she took them and washed them very carefully, and taking them by the necks, thrust them into the glowing oven and sealed the door with a great, flat rock, and left them there to be roasted.

But the Trues were friends of the Hero Twins, and did not let the heat harm them at all. When the old Giant-woman had gone into the house, Máw-Sahv and Oó-yah-wee broke the smaller stone that closed the smoke-hole of the oven, and crawled out from their fiery prison unsinged. They ran around and caught snakes and toads and gathered up dirt and dropped them down into the oven through the smoke-hole; and then, watching when the Giant-woman's back was turned, they sneaked into the house and hid in a huge *olla* on the shelf.

Very early in the morning the Giant-woman's baby began to cry for some boy-meat. "Wait till it is well cooked," said the mother; and hushed the child till the sun was well up. Then she went out and unsealed the oven, and brought in the sad mess the boys had put there. "They have cooked away to almost nothing," she said; and she and the Giant-baby sat down to eat. "Isn't this nice?" said the baby; and Máw-Sahv could not help saying, "You nasty things, to like that!"

"Eh? Who is that?" cried the Giant-woman, looking around till she found the boys hidden in the *olla*. So she told them to come down, and gave them some sweet cakes, and then sent them out to bring her some more wood.

It was evening when they returned with a big load of wood, which Máw-Sahv had taken pains to get green. He had also picked up in the mountains a long, sharp splinter of quartz. The evening was cool, and they built a big fire in the fireplace. But immediately, as the boys had planned, the green wood began to smoke at a dreadful rate, and soon the room was so dense with it that they all began to cough and strangle. The Giant-woman got up and opened the window and put her head out for a breath of fresh air; and Máw-Sahv, pulling out the white-hot splinter of quartz from the fire, stabbed her in the back so that she died. Then they killed the Giant-baby, and at last felt that they were safe.

Now the Giant-woman's house was a very large one, and ran far back into the very heart of the mountain. Having got rid of their enemies, the Hero Twins decided to explore the house; and, taking their bows and arrows, started boldly down into the deep, dark rooms. After travelling a long way in the dark, they came to a huge room in which corn and melons and pumpkins were growing abundantly. On and on they went, till at last they heard the growl of distant thunder. Following the sound, they came presently to a room in the solid rock, wherein the lightning was stored. Going in, they took the lightning and played with it awhile, throwing it from one to the other, and at last started home, carrying their strange toy with them.

When they reached Acoma and told their grandmother of their wonderful adventures, she held up her withered old hands in amazement. And she was nearly scared to death when they began to play with the lightning, throwing it around the house as though it had been a harmless ball, while the thunder rumbled till it shook the great rock of Acoma. They had the blue lightning which belongs in the West; and the yellow lightning of the North; and the red lightning of the East; and the white lightning of the South; and with all these they played merrily.

But it was not very long till Shée-wo-nah, the Storm-King, had occasion to use the lightning; and when he looked in the room where he was wont to keep it, and found it gone, his wrath knew no bounds. He started out to find who had stolen it; and passing by Acoma he heard the thunder as the Hero Twins were playing ball with the lightning. He pounded on the door and ordered them to give him his lightning, but the boys refused. Then he summoned the storm, and it began to rain and blow fearfully outside; while within the boys rattled their thunder in loud defiance, regardless of their grandmother's entreaties to give the Storm-King his lightning.

It kept raining violently, however, and the water came pouring down the chimney until the room was nearly full, and they were in great danger of drowning. But luckily for them, the Trues were still mindful of them; and just in the nick of time sent their servant, Tee-oh-pee, the Badger, who is the best of diggers, to dig a hole up through the floor; all the water ran out, and they were saved. And so the Hero Twins outwitted the Storm-King.

South of Acoma, in the pine-clad gorges and mesas, the world was full of bears. There was one old She-bear in particular, so huge and fierce that all men feared her; and not even the boldest hunter dared go to the south – for there she had her home with her two sons.

Máw-sahv and Oó-yah-wee were famous hunters, and always wished to go south; but their grandmother always forbade them. One day, however, they stole away from the house, and got into the *cañon*. At last they came to the She-bear's house; and there was old Quée-ah asleep in front of the door. Máw-sahv crept up very carefully and threw in her face a lot of ground chile, and ran. At that the She-bear began to sneeze, *ah-hútch! ah-hútch!* She could not stop, and kept making *ah-hútch* until she sneezed herself to death.

Then the Twins took their thunder-knives and skinned her. They stuffed the great hide with grass, so that it looked like a bear again, and tied a buckskin rope around its neck.

"Now," said Máw-sahv, "We will give our grandma a trick!"

So, taking hold of the rope, they ran toward Acoma, and the bear came behind them as if leaping. Their grandmother was going for water; and from the top of the cliff she saw them running so in the valley, and the bear jumping behind them. She ran to her house and painted one side of her face black with charcoal, and the other side red with the blood of an animal; and, taking a bag of ashes, ran down the cliff and out at the bear, to make it leave the boys and come after her.

But when she saw the trick, she reproved the boys for their rashness – but in her heart she was very proud of them.

The Hungry Grandfathers

A DISOBEDIENT CHILD is something I have never seen among the Pueblos, in all the years I have lived with them. The parents are very kind, too. My little ***amigos*** in Isleta and the other Pueblo towns – for they are my friends in all – are never spoiled; but neither are they punished much. Personal acquaintance with a spanking is what very few of them have. The idea of obedience is inborn and inbred. A word is generally enough; and for extreme cases it only needs the threat: "Look out, or I will send for the Grandfathers!"

Now, perhaps you do not know who the Grandfathers are; but every Pueblo youngster does. It has nothing to do with the 'truly' grandpa, who is as lovely an institution among the Tée-wahn as anywhere else. No, the *Abuelos* were of an altogether different sort. That name is Spanish, and has three applications in Isleta: real grandparents; the remarkable masked officials of a certain dance; and the bad Old Ones. These last are called in the Tée-wahn tongue *T'ai-kár-nin* (Those-Who-Eat-People). They were, in fact, aboriginal Ogres, who once sadly ravaged Isleta.

The *T'ai-kár-nin* had no town, but dwelt in caves of the lava mountain a couple of miles west of this village – the *Kú-mai* hill. It is a bad place at best: bleak, black, rough, and forbidding – just the place that a properly constituted Ogre would choose for his habitation. In the first place, it is to the west of the town, which is 'bad medicine' in itself to any Indian, for that point of the compass belongs to the dead and to bad spirits. Then its colour is against it; and, still worse, it is to this day the common stamping-ground of all the witches in this part of the country, where they gather at night for their diabolical caucuses. Of its serious disrepute I can convey no better idea to the enlightened and superstition less American mind than by saying that it is a sort of aboriginal 'haunted house.'

So the hill of *Kú-mai* was a peculiarly fit place for the Ogres to dwell in. Deep in its gloomy bowels they huddled on the white sand which floors all the caves there; and crannies overhead carried away the smoke from their fires, which curled from crevices at the top of the peak far above them. Ignorant Americans would probably have taken it for a volcanic emission; but the good people of Shee-eh-whíb-bak knew better.

These Ogres were larger than ordinary men, but otherwise carried no outward sign of their odious calling. Their teeth were just like anybody's good teeth, and they had neither 'tushes' nor horns nor hoofs. Indeed, except for their unusual size, they would have been easily mistaken for Indians of some distant tribe. But, *ay de mi*! How strong they were! One could easily whip five common men in a bunch – "men even as strong as my son, Francisco," says Desiderio; and Francisco is as stout as a horse.

They were people of very fastidious palates, these Ogres. Nothing was good enough for them except human flesh – and young at that. Their fare was entirely baby – baby young, baby brown, and baby very fat. They never molested the adults; but as often as they found an appetite they descended upon the village, scooped up what children they could lay their hands upon, and carried them off to their caves. There they had enormous *ollas*, into which half a dozen children could be thrown at once.

There seemed to be some spell about these Ogres – besides their frequent hungry spells – for the Pueblos, who were so brave in the face of other foes, never dared fight these terrible cave-dwellers. They continued to devastate the village, until babies were at a premium, and few to be had at any price; and the only way the people dared to try to circumvent them was by strategy. In time it came about that every house where there were children, or a reasonable hope of them, had secret cubby-holes back of the thick adobe walls; with little doors which shut flush with the wall and were also plastered with adobe, so that when they were shut a stranger – even if he were a sharp-eyed Indian – would never dream of their existence.

And whenever arose the dreaded cry, "Here come the *T'ai-kár-nin*!" the children were hustled, shivering and noiseless, into the secret recesses, and the doors were shut. Then Mr. Ogre could come in and peer and sniff about as he liked, but no chance to fill his market-basket could he find. And when parents were forced to go away and leave the babies behind, the poor young ones were inclosed in their safe but gloomy prisons, and there in darkness and silence had to await the parental home-coming. These inconveniences were gladly borne, however, since they preserved the children – and we all know that preserved baby is better than baby-stew. It was, of course, rather rough on the Ogres, who began to find all their belts most distressfully loose; but no one seemed to consider their feelings. They were pretty well starved when the Spaniards came and delivered the suffering Isleteños by driving off these savage neighbours. This looks suspiciously as if the whole myth of the Ogres had sprung from the attacks of the cruel Apaches and Navajos in the old days.

There was one queer thing about these Ogres: on their forages they always wore buckskin masks, just like those of the *Abuelos* of the sacred dance. Their bare faces were seen sometimes by hunters who encountered them on the *llano*, but never here in town. It was in connection with these masks that Isleta had a great sensation recently. The Hungry Grandfathers had been almost forgotten, except as a word to change: the minds of children who had about quarter of a mind to be naughty; but interest was revived by a discovery of which my venerable friend Desiderio Peralta was the hero.

This dear old man – news of his death has come to me as I write this very chapter – was a remarkable character. He was one of 'the oldest inhabitants' of New Mexico – older than any other Indian among the twelve hundred of Isleta, except tottering Diego; and that is saying a great deal. His hair was very gray, and his kindly old face such an incredible mass of wrinkles that I used to fancy Father Time himself must have said: "No, no! You apprentices never do a thing right! Here, *this* is the way to put on wrinkles!" and that he then and there took old Desiderio, for a model, and showed the journeymen wrinkle-makers a trick they never dreamed of. Certainly the job was never so well done before. From chin to hair-roots, from ear to ear, was such a crowded, tangled, inextricable maze of furrows and cross-harrow lines as I firmly believe never dwelt together on any other one human face. Why, Desiderio, could have furnished an army of old men with wrinkles! I never saw him smile without fearing that some of those wrinkles were going to fall off the edge, so crowded were they at best!

But if his face was *arrugada*, his brain was not. He was bright and chipper as a young blackbird, and it was only of late that a touch of rheumatism took the youth out of his legs. Until recently he held the important position of Captain of War for the pueblo; and only two years ago I had the pleasure of going with two hundred *other* Indians on a huge rabbit-hunt which was under his personal supervision, and in which he was as active as any one, both on his feet and with the unerring boomerang. His eyes were good to find about as much through the sights of a rifle as anybody's; and on the whole he was worth a good deal more than I expect to be some seventy years from now. He was a good neighbour, too; and I had few pleasanter hours than those spent in talking with this genial old shrivel, who was *muy sabio* in all the folk-lore and wisdom of his unfathomable race; and very close-mouthed about it, too – as they all are. Still, there were some things which he seemed willing to confide to me; and he always had an attentive listener.

Desiderio was not yet too old to herd his own cattle during the season when they roam abroad; and, while thus engaged, he made a discovery which set the whole quiet village agog, though no other outsider ever heard of it.

One day in 1889 Desiderio started out from the village, driving his cattle. Having steered them across the *acequia* and up the sand-hills to the beginning of the plain, he climbed to the top of the *Kú-mai* to watch them through the day – as has been the custom of Isleta herders from time immemorial. In wandering over the rocky top of the peak, he came to a ledge of rocks on the southeast spur of the hill; and there found a fissure, at one end of which was a hole as large as a man's head. Desiderio put his face and his wrinkles down to the hole to see what he could see; and all was dark inside. But if his eyes strained in vain, his ears did not. From far down in the bowels of the mountain came a strange roaring, as of a heavy wind. Desiderio was somewhat dismayed at this; for he knew at once that he had found one of the chimneys of the Ogres; but he did not run away. Hunting around awhile, he found in the fissures of the rocks some ancient buckskin masks – the very ones worn by the Ogres, of course. He put them back, and coming to town straightway told the medicine-men of the Black Eyes – one of the two parties here. They held a *junta*; and after mature deliberation decided to go and get the masks. This was done, and the masks are now treasured in the Black Eye medicine-house.

I have several times carefully explored the *Kú-mai* – a difficult and tiresome task, thanks to the knife-like lava fragments which cover it everywhere, and which will cut a pair of new strong shoes to pieces in an afternoon. It is true that in this hill of bad repute there are several lava-caves, with floors of white sand blown in from the *llano*; and that in these caves there are a few human bones. No doubt some of the savage nomads camped or lived there. None of those famous *ollas* are visible; nor have I ever been able to find any other relics of the Hungry Grandfathers.

The Accursed Lake

A WAY TO THE SOUTHEAST OF THE MANZANO MOUNTAINS, two days' journey from my pueblo of Isleta, are the shallow salt lakes. For scores of miles their dazzling sheen is visible – a strange patch of silver on the vast brown plains. They are near the noblest ruins in our North America – the wondrous piles of massive masonry of Abó, Cuaray, and the so-called 'Gran Quivira' – the latter the home of the silliest delusion that ever lured treasure-hunters to their death. The whole region has a romantic history, and is important to the scientific student. From that locality came, centuries ago, part of the people who then founded Isleta, and whose descendants dwell here to this day. Perhaps you would like to know why those lakes are salt now – for my Indian neighbours say that once they were fresh and full of fish, and that the deer and buffalo came from all the country round to drink there. The story is very important ethnologically, for it tells much of the strange secret religion of the Pueblos, and more concerning the, method of initiating a young Indian into one of the orders of medicine-men – both matters which men of science have found extremely difficult to be learned. Here is the story as it is believed by the Tée-wahn, and as it was related to me by one of them.

Long ago there was still a village east of Shoo-paht-hóo-eh, the Eagle-Feather (Manzano) Mountains, and in it lived a famous hunter. One day, going out on the plains to the east, he stalked a herd of antelopes, and wounded one with his arrows. It fled eastward, while the herd went south; and the hunter began to trail it by the drops of blood. Presently he came to the largest lake, into which the trail led. As he stood on the bank, wondering what to do, a fish thrust its head from the water and said:

"Friend Hunter, you are on dangerous ground!" and off it went swimming. Before the Hunter could recover from his surprise, a Lake-Man came up out of the water and said:

"How is it that you are here, where no human ever came?"

The Hunter told his story, and the Lake-Man invited him to come in. When he had entered the lake, he came to a house with doors to the east, north, west, and south, and a trap-door in the roof, with a ladder; and by the latter door they entered. In their talk together the Lake-Man learned that the Hunter had a wife and little son at home.

"If that is so," said he, "why do you not come and live with me? I am here alone, and have plenty of other food, but I am no hunter. We could live very well here together." And opening doors on four sides of the room he showed the Hunter four other huge rooms, all piled from floor to ceiling with corn and wheat and dried squash and the like.

"That is a very good offer," said the astonished Hunter. "I will come again in four days; and if my Cacique will let me, I will bring my family and stay."

So the Hunter went home – killing an antelope on the way – and told his wife all. She thought very well of the offer; and he went to ask permission of the Cacique. The Cacique demurred, for this was the best hunter in all the pueblo, but at last consented and gave him his blessing.

So on the fourth day the Hunter and his wife and little boy came to the lake with all their property. The Lake-Man met them cordially, and gave the house and all its contents into the charge of the woman.

Some time passed very pleasantly, the Hunter going out daily and bringing back great quantities of game. At last the Lake-Man, who was of an evil heart, pretended to show the Hunter something in the east room; and pushing him in, locked the great door and left him there to starve – for the room was full of the bones of men whom he had already entrapped in the same way.

The boy was now big enough to use his bow and arrows so well that he brought home many rabbits; and the witch-hearted Lake-Man began to plot to get him, too, out of the way.

So one morning when the boy was about to start for a hunt, he heard his mother groaning as if about to die; and the Lake-Man said to him:

"My boy, your mother has a terrible pain, and the only thing that will cure her is some ice from T'hoor-p'ah-whée-ai (Lake of the Sun), the water from which the sun rises."

"Then," said the boy, straightway, if that is so, I will take the heart of a man (that is, be brave) and go and get the ice for my little mother." And away he started toward the unknown east.

Far out over the endless brown plains he trudged bravely; until at last he came to the house of Shee-chóo-hlee-oh, the Old-Woman-Mole, who was there all alone – for her husband had gone to hunt. They were dreadfully poor, and the house was almost falling down, and the poor, wrinkled Old-Woman-Mole sat huddled in the corner by the fireplace, trying to keep warm by a few dying coals. But when the boy knocked, she rose and welcomed him kindly and gave him all there was in the house to eat – a wee bowl of soup with a patched-up snowbird in it. The boy was very hungry, and picking up the snowbird bit a big piece out of it.

"Oh, my child!" cried the old woman, beginning to weep. "You have ruined me! For my husband trapped that bird these many years ago, but we could never get another; and that is all we have had to eat ever since. So we never bit it, but cooked it over and over and drank the broth. And now not even that is left." And she wept bitterly.

"Nay, Grandmother, do not worry," said the boy. "Have you any long hairs?" – for he saw many snowbirds lighting near by.

"No, my child," said the old woman sadly.

"There is no other living animal here, and you are the first human that ever came here."

But the boy pulled out some of his own long hair and made snares, and soon caught many birds. Then the Old-Woman-Mole was full of joy; and having learned his errand, she said:

"My son, fear not, for I will be the one that shall help you. When you come into the house of the Trues, they will tempt you with a seat; but you must sit down only on what you have. Then they will try you with smoking the weer, but I will help you."

Then she gave him her blessing, and the boy started away to the east. At last, after a weary, weary way, he came so near the Sun Lake, that the *Whit-lah-wíd-deh* of the Trues saw him coming, and went in to report.

"Let him be brought in," said the Trues; and the *Whit-lah-wíd-deh* took the boy in and in through eight rooms, until he stood in the presence of all the gods, in a vast room. There were all the gods of the East, whose colour is white, and the blue gods of the North, the yellow gods of the West, the red gods of the South, and the rainbow-coloured gods of the Up, the Down, and the Centre, all in human shape. Beyond their seats were all the sacred animals – the buffalo, the bear, the eagle, the badger, the mountain lion, the rattlesnake, and all the others that are powerful in medicine.

Then the Trues bade the boy sit down, and offered him a white *manta* (robe) for a seat; but he declined respectfully, saying that he had been taught, when in the presence of his elders, to sit on nothing save what he brought, and he sat upon his blanket and moccasins. When he had told his story, the Trues tried him, and gave him the sacred weer to smoke – a hollow reed rammed with *pee-en-hleh*. He smoked, and held the smoke bravely. But just then the Old-Woman-Mole, who had followed him underground all this way, dug a hole up to his very toes; and the smoke went down through his feet into the hole, and away back to the Old-Woman-Mole's house, where it poured out in a great cloud. And not the tiniest particle escaped into the room of the Trues. He finished the second *weer* without being sick at all; and the Trues said, "Yes, he is our son. But we will try him once more." So they put him into the room of the East with the bear and the lion; and the savage animals came forward and breathed on him, but would not hurt him. Then they put him into the room of the North, with the eagle and the hawk; then into the room of the West, with the snakes; and lastly, into the room of the South, where were the Apaches and all the other human enemies of his people. And from each room he came forth unscratched.

"Surely," said the Trues, "this is our son! But once more we will try him."

They had a great pile of logs built up ('cob-house' fashion), and the space between filled with pine-knots. Then the *Whit-lah-wíd-deh* set the boy on the top of the pile and lighted it.

But in the morning, when the guard went out, there was the boy unharmed and saying: "Tell the Trues I am cold, and would like more fire."

Then he was brought again before the Trues, who said: "Son, you have proved yourself a True Believer, and now you shall have what you seek."

So the sacred ice was given him, and he started homeward – stopping on the way only to thank the Old-Woman-Mole, to whose aid he owed his success.

When the wicked Lake-Man saw the boy coming, he was very angry, for he had never expected him to return from that dangerous mission. But he deceived the boy and the woman; and in a few days made a similar excuse to send the boy to the gods of the South after more ice for his mother.

The boy started off as bravely as before. When he had travelled a great way to the south, he came to a drying lake; and there, dying in the mud, was a little fish.

"*Ah-bóo* (poor thing), little fish," said the boy; and picking it up, he put it in his gourd canteen of water. After awhile he came to a good lake; and as he sat down to eat his lunch the fish in his gourd said:

"Friend Boy, let me swim while you eat, for I love the water."

So he put the fish in the lake; and when he was ready to go on, the fish came to him, and he put it back in his gourd. At three lakes he let the fish swim while he ate; and each time the fish came back to him. But beyond the third lake began a great forest which stretched clear across the world, and was so dense with thorns and brush that no man could pass it. But as the boy was wondering what he should do, the tiny fish changed itself into a great Fish-Animal with a very hard, strong skin, and bidding the boy mount upon its back, it went plowing through the forest, breaking down big trees like stubble, and bringing him through to the other side without a scratch.

"Now, Friend Boy," said the Fish-Animal, "you saved my life, and I will be the one that shall help you. When you come to the house of the Trues, they will try you as they did in the East. And when you have proved yourself, the Cacique will bring you his three daughters, from whom to choose you a wife. The two eldest are very beautiful, and the youngest is not; but you ought to choose her, for beauty does not always reach to the heart."

The boy thanked his fish-friend and went on, until at last he came to the house of the Trues of the South. There they tried him with the *weer* and the fire, just as the Trues of the East had done, but he proved himself a man, and they gave him the ice. Then the Cacique brought his three daughters, and said:

"Son, you are now old enough to have a wife, and I see that you are a true man who will dare all for his mother. Choose, therefore, one of my daughters."

The boy looked at the three girls; and truly the eldest were very lovely. But he remembered the words of his fish friend, and said:

"Let the youngest be my wife."

Then the Cacique was pleased, for he loved this daughter more than both the others. And the boy and the Cacique's daughter were married and started homeward, carrying the ice and many presents.

When they came to the great forest, there was the Fish-Animal waiting for them, and taking both on his back he carried them safely through. At the first lake he bade them good-by and blessed them, and they trudged on alone.

At last they came in sight of the big lake, and over it were great clouds, with the forked lightning leaping forth. While they were yet far off, they could see the wicked Lake-Man sitting at the top of his ladder, watching to see if the boy would return, and even while they looked they saw the lightning of the Trues strike him and tear him to shreds.

When they came to the lake the boy found his mother weeping for him as dead. And taking his wife and his mother – but none of the things of the Lake-Man, for those were bewitched – the boy came out upon the shore. There he stood and prayed to the Trues that the lake might be accurst forever; and they heard his prayer, for from that day its waters turned salt, and no living thing has drunk therefrom.

The North Wind and the South Wind

NEARLY EVERY NATION has its folk-lore concerning Jack Frost and his anti-type. The cold North Wind is always the enemy of man, and the warm South Wind always his friend. The Quères pueblos of Acoma and Laguna have an allegorical folk-story, in which the good spirit of heat defeats his icy-hearted rival.

Once, long ago, the *ta-pó-pe* (governor) of Acoma had a beautiful daughter, for whom many of the young men had asked in vain, for she would have none of them. One day there came climbing up the stone ladder to the cliff-built pueblo a tall and handsome stranger. His dress glistened with white crystals, and his face, though handsome, was very stern. The fair *kot-chin-á-ka* (chief's daughter), bending at a pool in the great rock to fill her water-jar, saw and admired him as he came striding proudly to the village; and he did not fail to notice the dusky beauty. Soon he asked for her in due form; and in a little while they were to be married.

But, with the coming of Shó-kee-ah – for that was the name of the handsome stranger – a sad change befell Acoma. The water froze in the springs and the corn withered in the fields. Every morning Shó-kee-ah left the town and went away to his home in the far North; and every evening he returned, and the air grew chill around. The people could raise no crops, for the bitter cold killed all that they planted, and nothing would grow but the thorny cactus. To keep from starving, they had to eat the cactus-leaves, roasting them first to remove the sharp thorns. One day, when the *kot-chin-á-ka* was roasting cactus-leaves, there came another handsome stranger with a sunny smile and stood beside her.

"What dost thou there?" he asked; and she told him.

"But do not so," said the young man, giving her an ear of green corn. "Eat this, and I will bring thee more."

So saying, he was gone; but very soon he returned with such a load of green corn as the strongest man could not lift, and carried it to her house.

"Roast this," he said, "and when the people come to thee, give them each two ears, for hereafter there shall always be much corn."

She roasted the corn and gave it to the people, who took it eagerly, for they were starving. But soon Shó-kee-ah returned, and the warm, bright day grew suddenly cold and cloudy. As he put his foot on the ladder to come down into the house (all Pueblo rooms used to be entered only from the roof, and thousands are so yet) great flakes of snow fell around him; but Mí-o-chin, the newcomer, made it very warm, and the snow melted.

"Now," said Shó-kee-ah, "we will see which is more powerful; and he that is shall have the *kot-chin-á-ka*." Mí-o-chin accepted the challenge, and it was agreed that the contest should begin on the morrow and last three days. Mí-o-chin went to consult an old Spider-woman as to the best way to conquer his powerful rival, and she gave him the necessary advice.

Next day the people all gathered to see the trial of strength between the two wizards. Shó-kee-ah 'made medicine', and caused a driving sleet and a bitter wind that froze all waters. But Mí-o-chin built a fire and heated small stones in it, and with them caused a warm South Wind, which melted the ice. On the second day, Shó-kee-ah used more powerful incantations, and made a deep snow to cover the world; but again Mí-o-chin brought his South Wind and chased away the snow. On the third day Shó-kee-ah used his strongest spell, and it rained great icicles, until everything was buried under them. But when Mí-o-chin built his fire and heated the stones, again the warm South Wind drove away the ice and dried the earth. So it remained to Mí-o-chin; and the defeated Shó-kee-ah went away to his frozen home in the North, leaving Mí-o-chin to live happy ever after with the kot-chin-á-ka, whom he married amid the rejoicing of all the people of Acoma.

Doctor Field-Mouse

It was the evening of the 14th of March. In the valley of the Rio Grande, that stands at the end of the winter. Now it is to open the big mother-canal that comes from the river to all the fields, giving them to drink after their long thirst; and now to plow the ***milpas***, and to uncover the buried grape-vines, and make ready for the farmer's work.

As the door opened to admit stalwart Francisco to the big flickering room where we were all sitting in silence, the long, shrill wail of a Coyote, away up on the Accursed Hill, blew in after him on the boisterous March wind. The boys pricked up their ears; and bright-faced Manuelito turned to his white-headed grandfather, and said:

"*Tata*, why is it that Too-wháy-deh always howls so? Perhaps he has a pain; for he has been crying ever since the beginning of the world – as they told us in the story of the Fawns and the She-Wolf."

"What, Unknowing!" answered the old man, kindly. "Hast thou never heard of the Coyote's toothache, and who was the first medicine-man in all the world? It is not well not to know that; for from that comes all that we know to cure the sick. And for that, I will tell-but it is the last story of the year. For to-morrow is *Tu-shée-wim*, the Spring Medicine-Dance; and the snakes are coming out from their winter houses. After that, we must not tell of the Things of Old. For it is very long ago; and if one made a mistake in telling, and said that which was not all true, *Ch'áh-rah-ráh-deh* would bite him, and he would die. But this one I will tell thee."

In the First Days, when the people had broken through the crust of the earth, and had come up out of their dark prison, underground, and crossed Shee-p'ah-póon, the great Black Lake of Tears, they came to the shore on this side. Then it came that all the animals were made; and very soon the Coyote was sent by the Trues to carry a buckskin bag far south, and not to open it until he should come to the Peak of the White Clouds. For many days he ran south, with the bag on his back. But there was nothing to eat, and he grew very hungry. At last he thought: "Perhaps in this bag there is to eat." So he took it from his back, and untied the thongs, and looked in. But there was nothing in it except the stars; and as soon as the bag was opened they all flew up into the sky, where they are to this day.

When the Trues saw that Too-wháy-deh had disobeyed, they were angry, and made it that his punishment should be to wander up and down forever, howling with the toothache and finding no rest.

So Too-wháy-deh went out with his toothache, running all over the world groaning and crying; and when the other four-feet slept he could only sit and howl. Because he came to talk with the other animals, if they could not cure him, they caught the toothache too; and that is the reason why they sometimes cry. But none have it like the Coyote, who can find no rest.

In those times there were no medicine-men in the world – not even of the people – and the animals found no cure.

Time passing so, it came one day that T'hoo-chée-deh, the smallest of Mice, who lives in the little mounds around the chapparo-bush, was making his road underground, when he came to a kind of root with a sweet smell. T'hoo-chée-deh was very wise; and he took the root, and put it with others in a buckskin pouch he carried under his left arm.

In a few days Kee-oo-ée-deh, the Prairie-Dog, came with his head all fat with toothache, and said:

"Friend Field-Mouse, can you not cure me of this pain? For all say you are very wise with herbs."

"I do not know," answered T'hoo-chée-deh. "But we will try. For I have found a new root, and perhaps it is good."

So he mixed it with other roots, all pounded, and put it on the cheek of Kee-oo-ée-deh; and in a little, the toothache was gone.

In that time it was that there was so much toothache among the animals that the Mountain Lion, Commander of Beasts, called a council to see what should be done. When every kind that walks on the ground had met, he asked each of them if they had found no cure; but none of them knew any. The Coyote was there, howling with pain; but all the other sick were at home.

At last it was to the Field-Mouse, who is the smallest of all animals, and who did not wish to seem wise until all the greater ones had spoken. When the Mountain Lion said, "And thou, T'hoo-chée-deh – hast thou a cure?" he rose in his place and came forward modestly, saying: "If the others will allow me, and with the help of the Trues, I will try what I found last."

Then he drew from his left-hand bag the roots one by one; and last of all, the root of the chee-ma-hár, explaining what it had done for Kee-oo-ée-deh. He pounded it to powder with a stone, and mixed it with fat; and spreading it on flat leaves, put it to the Coyote's jaw. And in a little the pain was gone.

At that the Mountain Lion, the Bear, the Buffalo, and all the other Captains of Four-feet, declared T'hoo-chée-deh the Father-of-All-Medicine. They made a strong law that from that time the body of the Field-Mouse should be held sacred, so that no animal dares to kill him or even to touch him dead. And so it remains to this day. But only the birds and the snakes, who were not at the Council of the Four- feet, they do not respect T'hoo-chée-deh.

So the Field-Mouse was the first medicine-man. He chose one of each kind of four-feet to be his assistants, and taught them the use of all herbs, and how to cure pain, so that each might practise among his own people – a Bear-doctor for the Bears, and a Wolf-doctor for the Wolves, and so to all the tribes of the animals.

Of those he taught, there was one who was not a True Believer – the Badger. But he listened also, and made as if he believed all. With time, the teaching was done; and T'hoo-chée-deh sent all his assistant doctors home to their own peoples to heal. But whenever one of them was asked with the sacred corn-meal to come and cure a sick one, he always came first to get the Father, the Field-Mouse, to accompany and help him.

But all this time Kahr-naí-deh, the Badger, was not believing; and at last he said to his wife:

"Now I will *see* if Old T'hoo-chée-deh is really a medicine-man. If he finds me, I will believe him."

So from that day for four days the Badger touched no food, until he was almost dead. And on the fifth day he said:

"*In-hlee-oo wáy-ee*, wife of me, go now and call T'hoo-chée-deh, to see if he will cure me."

So the Badger-wife went with meal to the house of the Field-Mouse, making to be very sad; and brought him back with her. When they came, the Badger was as if very sick and in great pain.

T'hoo-chée-deh asked nothing; but took off the little pouch of roots and laid it beside him. And then rubbing a little wood-ashes on his hands, he put them on the stomach and breast of the Badger, rubbing and feeling. When he had felt the Badger's stomach, he began to sing:

Káhr-nah-hlóo-hlee wee-end-t'hú
Beh-hú hoo-báhn,

Ah-náh káh-chah-him-aí
T'hóo-chee-hlóo-hlee t'oh-ah-yin-áhh
Wee-end-t'hú heh-hú hoo-báhn.

(Badger-Old-Man four days
Has the hunger-killing,
To know, to know surely
If Field- Mouse-Old-Man
Has the Medicine Power.
Four days, four days,
He has the hunger-killing.)

When he had finished rubbing and singing, he said to the Badger:

"There is no need of a remedy. In my teaching I found you attentive – now be true. You have wasted, in trying my power. Now get up and eat, to make up for the lost. And do not think that way again."

With that, he took his pouch of roots and went home. As soon as he was out of the house, the Badger said to his wife:

"My wife, now I believe that Mouse-Old-Man *has* the Power; and never again will I think *that* way.»

Then the Badger-wife brought food, and he ate – for he was dying of hunger. When he had eaten, the animals came in to see him, for they had heard that he was very sick. He told them all that had been, and how T'hoo-chée-deh had known his trick. At that, all the animals were afraid of the Field-Mouse, and respected him more than ever – for it was plain that he indeed had the Power.

Time passing so, it came that one day the Men of the Old made *nah-kú-ah-shu*, the great round-hunt. When they had made a great circle on the *llano*, and killed many rabbits, some of them found T'hoo-chée-deh, and made him prisoner. They brought him before the *principales*, who questioned him, saying:

"How do you gain your life?"

"I gain it," he answered, "by going about among the animals who are sick, and curing them.'"

Then the elders said: "If that is so, teach us your Power, and we will set you free; but if not, you shall die."

T'hoo-chée-deh agreed, and they brought him to town with honor. For twelve days and twelve nights he and the men stayed shut up in the *estufa*; for two days fasting, and one day making the medicine-dance, and then fasting and then dancing again, as our medicine-men do to this day.

On the last night, when he had taught the men all the herbs and how to use them, and they had become wise with practice, they sent T'hoo-chée-deh out with a strong guard, that nothing should harm him. They set him down at the door of his own house under the chapparo. A law was made, giving him full liberty of all that is grown in the fields. To this day, all True Believers honor him, so that he is not called small any more. When they sing of him in the sacred places, they make his house great, calling it *koor-óo-hlee naht-hóo*, the Mountain of the Chapparo. And him they call not T'hoo-chée-deh, the Field-Mouse, but *Pee-íd-deh p'ah-hláh-queer*, the Deer-by-the-River, that he may not seem of little honor. For he was the Father of Medicine, and taught us how to cure the sick.

"*Tahb-kóon-ahm*?" cried the boys. "Is *that* why the Coyote always cries? And is that why we must never hurt the Field-Mouse, but show him respect, as to elders?"

"That is the very why," said Manuelito's grandfather, gravely; and all the old men nodded.

"And why—?" began 'Tonio. But his father shook his head.

"*Tah*! It is enough. *Tóo-kwai*!"

So we stepped out into the night to our homes. And from the *Kú-mai*, black against the starry sky, the howl of Too-whá́y-deh, wandering with his toothache, swelled across the sleeping village of the Tée-wahn.

El Dorado

Introduction

THE FINAL STORIES of this collection derive from Frona Eunice Wait's fascinating exploration of the El Dorado myths, which had roots in Mexican and South American cultures and later evolved through European gold-fevered misconceptions – the former usually evoking a gentler, more spiritual incarnation of a mythical chief or legendary figure, the latter conjuring up a literal, materialistic idea of a city or even an empire.

Thus you will be taken to the island of Atlantis where you will encounter a mythical man named Golden Hearted, and travel with him on his journey to the mainland where he becomes a powerful figure in the cultures of many tribes. From there, we witness the arrival of the Spanish explorers and conquistadors, whose mere presence and relentless search for the riches of the South and Central Americas threatens the traditional way of life for the gentle people they encounter, and forever changes the landscape of this remarkable part of the world.

The Happy Island

A LONG TIME AGO there was a beautiful island close by the place in the east where the sun rises. The sea was all around it, and at noonday the sun in the sky seemed to slant just above it. Being near the equator and in a tropic clime the winds were soft and warm and full of the odour of sweet flowers. Sometimes the sea was smooth and clear as glass and then the goldfish and sea mosses floated near the surface and glittered in the sunlight.

At night the moon came out big and round like a silver ball and the stars shone very clear because there was no smoke nor fog in the air. In the moonlight the queer little flying fish would jump up out of the water and dart forth and back in the funniest way as if they were playing some kind of game. Their tiny wet wings glistened like silver gauze, and, when everything else was still, made a peculiar whirring sound by all flapping at once.

The beach was strewn with quantities of conch and abalone shells, also other species of all shapes and sizes and they were as dainty in color as it is possible to imagine. The children of the Happy Island often held the larger ones to their ears to listen to the murmurs and complaints of the insects and other forms of life living inside them. This was only a fancy, but many sea shells do have a soft musical cadence if we care to hear it. Some poets believe that they were the first musical instruments, and that the inhabitants of the sea send messages ashore in this manner.

The ferns grew almost as tall as the trees and there were hundreds of birds skimming through the air, or flitting through the branches singing and chattering and having a very happy time. They were not afraid because no one threw stones at them or tried to frighten them. Everybody was glad to see them put up their little bills and ruffle up their throats in singing, or else spread out their wings and splash water all over their backs while they stood on a pebble or twig taking a morning bath. The people said that when the birds were twittering and chirping they were talking to each other. When they were singing they were telling God how thankful they were for the warm sunshine and plenty to eat.

There was a wonderful city in the centre of the island named the City of the Golden Gates because it was surrounded by a high wall of very thick stones, with a great number of gates of gold through which the animals and people passed in and out. Here lived the Old Man of the Sea, as the king was called, and his son was a beautiful youth known as the Golden Hearted because he was so gentle and kind. He was a swift runner and could shoot well with a bow and arrow and was strong enough to wrestle with a big man, but he preferred to make gold ornaments and vessels for his father and was often permitted to go into the king's treasure house to watch the workmen polish the precious gems which they found in great abundance by digging into the mountains near the city.

The people knew all about white and black pearls and how to get them from the bed of the ocean. In full sight of the island was a large reef of pink and white coral and the young prince went there many times to see the curious little insects building their graceful, airy houses over some rock hidden by the water. He sometimes imagined that he heard the mermaids calling to him. What he really did hear was the wind dashing the waves in and out of the coral chambers as if it were determined to wash them away. The reef was an excellent place to fish, and the Golden Hearted and his companions had many a fine day's sport there while the divers were searching for the pearl oysters. He fished with a drag-net made by himself, and he could let it out and haul it in again like a regular sailor. He never killed any of the fish, and the divers would not give him the pearls they found because they were compelled to kill the oysters to get them, and this they said made the pearls unlucky and was the reason why they are round and shining like tear drops. The miners brought him all the emeralds they could find, because this was the happiness-bringing stone. Its colour is like the soft grass in the springtime, and they wanted him to be always young and have everything his heart desired.

The royal gardens were his special care and in them he was allowed to cultivate any kind of tree or plant or grain. Then from them he must learn the names and habits of the trees producing the best wood for building houses, what plants were good to heal the sick, and all about the grains useful for food either for man or animals. Every flower that had a perfume grew in a separate part of the garden, and those shedding their fragrance at night only were in a bed by themselves. He was required to know the difference between single and double species and why there is such a difference in the same family of plants.

Honey bees, big-winged butterflies, crickets and beetles hid in the flowers or flew above them, and these all taught a lesson to the young prince who had no other books. The honey bee was an industrious little fellow continually building a piece of comb or else filling it with honey. The butterfly, on the other hand, did not work at all but changed from an ugly grub into a caterpillar and finally into a gorgeous butterfly with spotted wings and bright eyes. The king told his son that the butterfly was like a soul – the immortal part of ourselves – and he wished him to be as busy as the bee, and to do no more harm to other creatures than does the pretty butterfly.

The cricket was a cheerful, merry chap, usually singing at the top of his voice, and the beetle tried to push all of the dirt out of the garden. If he found anything he did not like he would roll and tumble with it, even if it were much bigger than himself. This amused the Golden Hearted very much, and when he grew tired of his own occupations he would run out into the garden and watch the beetles.

One day he went into the splendid throne-room where his father was giving audience to some wise old men who were foretelling what was going to happen to the king and the people of the Happy Island. They urged the king to send some member of his household to the strange land over the sea, toward the setting sun, where the people were in barbarism.

The Golden Hearted was much interested and thought here was an opportunity to do some good for the weak and helpless. Springing forward he said:

"Dear father, let me go. I am able to sail the seas and am willing to devote my life to teaching these poor people how to live like brothers."

The king felt proud of the young prince, but he loved him so dearly that it was hard to let him go, and also hard to refuse such a noble, manly request.

"Do you know, my son, this will entail a great deal of hardship and self-denial?" he asked.

"Yes, father, but God intends us to earn all the good things in life; He will not give them to us for nothing. That is His good law, which makes us healthy, happy and wise – three of the most precious possessions in the world."

"Go, my Golden Heart, and may God bless and keep you always," said the king. "Take a green-throated humming-bird for your guide, and when you find the land, journey on until you come to a place where a cactus grows at the base of a rock and there is a golden eagle soaring in the air above it. Halt there and found a city, and name it in honour of the sun."

Then all the wise men begged to go with him, and for days after there were great preparations made for the departure of the king's son. At daybreak one morning he set sail in a snake-skin boat, and all the inhabitants came with the king to throw flowers and emeralds into the sea because they wished to show respect to the Golden Hearted. It was their method of blessing him and wishing him good luck. The whole shore line, as far as he could see, was lighted up by bonfires where the people burned resin and perfume to commemorate his going.

At the water's edge stood the old sea king with his long white hair and beard blowing in the wind. By his side was a cream-white horse with three plumes in the top of its bridle reins and a square, red blanket edged with deep fringe on its back. Crowns and moons and stars of gold and silver were scattered over the blanket to show that the horse belonged to the royal prince. Back of the king was a long line of young warrior priests mounted on white horses, with red blankets, and carrying reversed spears in their hands. They bowed their heads when the poor old father leaned over on the horse's neck and cried as if his heart would break as the boat with his only son in it pushed off from the shore. Snatching a torch from the hand of an attendant, the Golden Hearted waved it on high. Fire with them was a symbol of wisdom, and when the king saw it, he answered the signal by waving a torch, and the warrior priests flashed their spears in the bright sunlight, and the people sent up a deafening shout.

This meant that they were willing to sacrifice their future king for the good of a strange race of men who needed a teacher to show them how to cultivate the land and how to build cities and live civilized. The people of the Happy Island would not send a common man for a teacher. No, indeed; they gave the best they had – their dearly loved prince with the golden heart – to help their less fortunate neighbours. And he gave up all luxury and comfort because he would rather be useful, than live in ease as a king. The name of the island was Atlantis, and the new country was our own – America.

Zamna, the Eye of the Sun

"HO THERE! WHO COMES TO US IN A CANOE?" cried the people in the strange land when the Golden Hearted and the wise men arrived from the Happy Island. Many of the natives ran away and others hid in the bushes because they were afraid they were going to be killed. None of them were ever so badly frightened in their lives, and none had ever seen white men before.

"Do you come to fight us? Are you warriors?" they asked.

"I am your friend, not your foe," answered the young prince kindly, and holding a white flag high over his head. "To be a warrior is to have been in many battles, and I never marched a day under the banner of the king, my father. I come wholly in peace."

"He is only a lad. Surely we need not fear him," said the people coming back to crowd around him on shore and to examine his boat and clothes with much curiosity. "Why, then, are you here?" they finally asked.

"I am sent by my father to teach you the Good Law."

"We already know how to shoot an arrow through the heart of an eagle. We have taken many captives in battle, and are a scourge to our enemies," they answered proudly. They were still suspicious of their visitors.

"You crush a worm without mercy, never thinking it has the same right to live as you have, and that in itself it is more wonderful than all these things," said the Golden Hearted, reprovingly.

The natives were greatly astonished. Never had they heard any one speak like this, and they could not imagine what sort of young man he was. If he did not like the chase, and was not a warrior, and did not believe in killing things, they could not understand him at all.

"What do you mean by the Good Law? What is it anyhow?"

"It is to be gentle and kind to all creatures, and to treat your neighbour as if he were your brother. You must be just to the plant, to the bull, to the horse and to the dog. The earth too has a right to be cultivated. Neglect it, and it will curse you; fertilize it, and it will show gratitude in a thousand ways. May your fields bring forth all that is good to eat, and may your countless villages abound with prosperity."

The Golden Hearted was so modest and sincere in speech and so well mannered that they were pleased with him, and were beginning to feel quite friendly. The wise men also said many nice things to them and did all they could to make the situation pleasant.

To show appreciation and to welcome the young prince, the natives gave him a handful of fireflies, because light with them was a symbol of order, peace and virtue. This was a delicate, pretty compliment and so delighted the Golden Hearted that he scattered them all over his head. When they lit in his soft, wavy, yellow hair, their bulging eyes and gauzy wings sparkled like diamonds and they did not try to fly away because he sang to them:

"Firefly, firefly! bright little thing,
Light me to bed and my song I will sing.
Give me your light as you fly o'er my head
That I may merrily go to my bed.
Give me your light o'er the grass as you creep
That I may joyfully go to my sleep.
Come little firefly, come little beast,
Come and I'll make you tomorrow a feast;
Come, little candle, that flies as I sing,
Bright little fairy bug – Night's little king.
Come, and I'll dance as you guide me along,
Come, and I'll pay you, my bug, with a song."

Each fly has four spots, one back of each eye and under each wing which it can make as bright as candle light when it chooses. Its body is about an inch and a half long.

When the prince put the fireflies in his hair, the natives present touched the ground with their right hands and placed them over their hearts in token of respect. He, in turn, gave them the white flag he carried because it was an emblem of peace, friendship, happiness and prosperity, as well as purity and holiness, and he intended to bring them all of these things.

"What is your wish?" asked the natives of each of the wise men.

"We desire to bathe in the warm surf of these shores and then to make a thank offering for our safe arrival and your kindly greeting," they answered.

Criers with shrill trumpets and drums ran up and down the beach to call in the fishing boats.

"The men wearing skirts are coming into the sea," they shouted, and the Golden Hearted and his followers looked at each other with a smile when they heard what the criers said. The natives wore only breech clouts and feather and shell ornaments, much like the Indians of today. Never before had they seen men wearing long white robes, beards and high-crowned hats without rims, and having a square black cloth hanging over the shoulders in the back like a veil.

"Is there something else needed to make you more content and comfortable?" asked the criers when the fishermen had all come ashore.

"We need wood and stones to build an altar for our sacrifice," replied the Golden Hearted.

While the newcomers were splashing in the surf, the porters brought arms full of wood, and stones large and small and piled them near the boat and waited to see what the visitors would do with them.

"Why do you wear skirts like women?" they next inquired, as the bathers were putting on their robes after a long swim.

"Because we work for humanity," said the young prince. "No man is really great who has not developed a woman's tenderness in his heart, and that our fellows may know that we have this quality, we wear skirts and robes."

This is why in our day the king and priest and judge wear long gowns. The king rules men, women and children alike; the judge administers the law for all of them, and the minister prays for the good as well as the bad. For this reason we should respect their robes when we see them.

The natives did not know the name of the young prince but when they saw him take a piece of mica and hold it over a bit of cotton until the sun set it on fire, they exclaimed "Zamna!" meaning 'Eye of the Sun,' and this was what they called him while he lived in that country. The wise men had placed some copal on top of the altar they had made of wood and stone and it was not long before the cotton and copal began to burn. As it did so, the Golden Hearted pointed with his finger to a ray of the midday sun. First he and his followers held their arms high overhead, then they sat in a squatting position and recited all the incidents of their journey. Finally they all prostrated themselves on the ground and returned thanks for their safety and good health. Rising to their feet, the wise men began to chant with bared heads and faces turned toward the east.

The natives thought this a very strange performance and debated among themselves whether it could be part of the Good Law they were soon to learn.

"Do you come to destroy our old faiths, and to bring us a new god?" they asked as the wood on the altar burned low and the chanting ceased.

"To attack any form of worship is like fighting darkness with a stick. The only way to overcome the blackness of night dwelling in men's hearts is to kindle a light – and the light of the world is love," responded the Golden Hearted as he slipped his arm through that of the native who had asked him the question. "I did not come to quarrel with you. I want you to think of me as a brother ready and willing to serve you always. In my father's kingdom, the man who serves faithfully in any capacity is the one most honoured. Take this cross to the chief of your village and say to him that He who is the Dew of Heaven, Lord of the Dawn, and of the Four Winds, sends his only son with a message of peace and good will to all his people. Show him the red hand painted in the centre and tell him that it is not meant to convey strength, power and mastery, but that it is raised thus as an act of supplication."

As the swiftest courier in the group was girding a red sash tightly around his waist making ready for a quick run, the fishermen came up from their huts and invited the travellers to come and share their humble noonday meal. The Golden Hearted was glad to accept the extended hospitality, not because he had no provisions of his own, but because he valued their good opinion and was ready to do whatever he thought would please them.

They were a gentle, kindly folk, these simple fishermen. Not only were they industrious, but they were polite and reverential to their superiors and as happy as a lot of children when they found the strange prince under their roof. In all the after years they would have been willing to die for him.

The wise men of his company were so strict in their habits that they refused to eat the flesh of any animal, and their simple meal was soon finished. But while every one else was at the table they performed a sacred dance in a pompous and solemn style, circling around the Golden Hearted who sat by himself. They had green palms in their hands and every once in a while they would bow to the prince. In a peculiar sing-song way they chanted a long poem telling about the history of the Happy Island.

Imagine how funny they must have looked whirling round and round with their long robes, black veils and wide sleeves filled with the wind. They kept on their high hats and with their long beards and hair flying in every direction, it was no wonder that the fishermen and other people laughed and thought it was some kind of game. The dancers were not at all offended, and when the natives asked if they knew how to play ball, they answered good naturedly:

"No, but we would like very much to learn."

"Come out here into the alley and we will teach you. By and by you may give us lessons in many things, but we are going to give you the first one."

Then they all laughed, and so did the young prince and the wise old men.

The alley where they played ball was one hundred feet long and had smooth, white-washed walls about twelve feet high in the centre, but lower at each end where there was a rectangular nook for the players to rest. The walls were quite thick at the base but tapered toward the top which was finished with battlements and turrets.

Before the game began, the oldest player among them threw the small, solid, India-rubber ball four times around the alley muttering some words to himself all the time. The owner of the ground made the old man a trifling present, and then the game began in good earnest.

The rule was to hit the ball only with the knee, elbow or shoulder, not with the hands nor feet. The wise men with their long gowns and veils had a hard time keeping up with the native players, who wore very little clothing and were quick and sure footed. Two on each side played at a time, and the great point was to send the ball against the opposite wall or else over it as often as possible without allowing it to touch the ground. There were two referees; one being the Golden Hearted and the other, the oldest player.

Everybody shouted and laughed at the clumsy playing of the wise men who tried ever so hard to imitate the things they saw the others doing. It was a great effort for them and they panted and blowed as they ran. Very often they tumbled heels over head by stepping on their skirts in front. Then they would all go down together in a heap, one on top of the other, and the referees would have much to do before they could get them all straightened out again. It was jolly good fun, but required considerable time and patience even for an expert player to send the ball over the wall with either his elbow, knee or shoulder.

In the centre of the wall on each side was a huge stone carved with images, having a hole in the centre barely big enough for the ball to go through. Whoever was skilful enough to make a drive through one of them, not only won the game for his side, but was entitled to the cloaks of all those present. Of course, this was a very difficult feat to accomplish and made quite a hero of the man who succeeded, so every player tried for the honour.

This day the young native who first hailed the Golden Hearted when he landed, by a lucky toss of the elbow sent the ball flying through the hole on the wise men's side. In a moment the spectators scrambled down from their seats and ran away as fast as they could go. The wise men stood looking after them in wide-eyed astonishment, and before they had time to get out of the alley the victor stripped them of their veils and then their tall hats looked like a piece of stove pipe with a cover over one end of it.

The Golden Hearted insisted that each man should give back whatever he had won in a bet on the game, and for each loss of this kind he gave both winner and loser a present, and promised to teach their sons and daughters how to weave cloth having figures in it. In such a way he taught them how to count, and to this day they have no other method of reproducing a pattern perfectly. Each stitch must be counted and only a certain number of each colour put in, and all this must be carried in the head. The weavers are not allowed to write it down.

At nightfall the runners came in breathless with haste to say that the chief of the village was sending a councillor and official guide to welcome and escort the strange white men to his dwelling. But the Golden Hearted was not in a hurry to leave the fishermen and common people with whom he had spent the day, except for a short visit. When he returned he taught them how to make sun-dried bricks with which to build houses, also to shape the round water jars of brown pottery and how to ornament them and the gourds they drank from.

The wise men assisted him in all this, and in time, the natives not only built comfortable houses for themselves but learned how to fashion many pretty designs of cornices and wall decorations out of stucco which they tinted many colours.

The first thing he did when he went to the village was to make the chief king, and then he ordered some of the wise men who were architects and engineers to lay out a splendid city and help the natives to build it. Before he came there were nothing but trails from one part of the country to the other and the simple tradesmen did not know how to exchange their wares. The Golden Hearted became the patron of the builders and traders and lived many years with the people of Aztlan.

While in that country, he occupied himself with the building of a sacred temple dedicated to those who served the Good Law. It had four beautiful halls facing the four cardinal points of the compass. That on the east was the Hall of Gold and its walls were almost covered with plates of the precious metal having delicately-chased pictures over its shining surface. To the west was the Hall of Emeralds and Turquoises where many gems were studded into the plaster. The south hall was finished in silver while the northern hall was made of jasper stuck with colored shells in curious patterns. In each room there was a tapestry of yellow, blue, white and red feather mosaic that was as fine as a painting and in some cases perfectly represented men and animals. In front of the main entrance for many years stood a winged lion cut out of granite holding an image of the Golden Hearted in his mouth.

The name of the city was Mayapan and the king who had been merely a village chief was the celebrated Cocomes of the olden times.

Cholula, the Sacred City

IT WAS IN THE TONITUAH, or great sun age, that the wise men and the Golden Hearted built the Memento for Generations, on the plains of Puebla. It is not so high, but is twice as long as any other pyramid in the world, and is truncated, that is to say, it has four terraces which are reached by long circular staircases. On top there is an acre of ground on which once stood a wonderful teocalli or temple, built by the wise men, and dedicated to the Golden Hearted. Each generation added something to the beauties of the Sacred City, Cholula, which sprang up near the pyramid, and for all time it will be one of the most wonderful things ever done by primitive men, who did not have our kind of implements to work with.

The Golden Hearted lived in Cholula twenty years, and during that time he taught so many men how to make fine filigree work in gold and silver that there were whole streets filled with them, and the ornaments they made were famous for delicacy of design and finish.

There was also a mountain of outcry, where the laws enacted by him were proclaimed by runners, but it is difficult to say whether this was Orizaba, with her conical snow-capped head far to the east, or whether it was huge Popocatepetl, or his twin sister who stood like colossal sentinels to guard the enchanted regions.

"It is necessary to construct a calendar stone, so that the people will know when to hold festivals, and what ceremonies to perform," said the son of Guatamo to the Golden Hearted, one day while the long line of men were passing bricks by hand from the lower to the upper terrace of the pyramid which they were trying to finish.

"I have been thinking about it," he replied, "and have decided to ask a certain old woman, and her husband, to help select the signs."

"Be sure to make them plain to the people and appropriate to the subject," said the son of Guatamo, who had now become the chief adviser of the Golden Hearted. All of the wise men were still called *Nahuas*, or wizards, and the Golden Hearted was their plumed serpent, or wise king.

In the evening of that day, the Golden Hearted approached the hut of a famous soothsayer and story-teller – the old woman he wished to consult about the calendar. Standing in front of the door of the hut he said:

"A humble applicant claims thy assistance in a matter of great import to thy fellows now and for all time. Wilt thou kindly hear me?"

"Since it is always for thy brothers and never for thyself thou art constrained to invoke aid, I am honoured by thy confidence," she said. "I have long been expecting thee."

"Then thou knowest that I wish to invent a calendar which can be cut in enduring stone?" he asked, considerably surprised that she should already know his thoughts.

"Yes," she said, "and so well do I understand thy wishes and needs that I have the first sign ready for thee." Motioning him to follow her into an inner room, she showed him a water-snake she had painted on a piece of parchment, and continued:

"Make it the sign of the serpent, the symbol of wisdom, since thou art come to teach brotherhood to all our tribes."

A queer hunchbacked old man sat huddled up in a corner looking over a set of parchment leaves lying on a table before him, and muttering to himself in a low tone.

"My husband must make the next selection," said the old crone, going up to him and taking a paper out of his hands. "He makes it two cones," she continued, examining the design closely.

"Now it is my turn to choose," said the Golden Hearted, "and I will select the three houses from this pile, and make that the third sign."

They took turns about until twelve signs were chosen, then the Golden Hearted said:

"I will make the last design myself, but not until my time of departure is at hand."

"Before going, do not forget to inscribe the face of the pyramid, and also to explain its import fully," said the story-teller as the Golden Hearted was leaving her hut.

"Thou art better able than I am to tell the hidden significance of that wonderful pile," he answered.

"But it is thy duty; shirk it not," she said with decision.

Not long afterward he called all the workmen and their families together and said:

"There has now come a time in my life when I must live in seclusion away from the thoughts and occupations of my associates. But before going up on top of the pyramid to live alone until the altars in its temples are ready to receive the sacred fire, I will tell you why we have tarried so long and made such a wonderful structure. It is really a pillar of the Cosmos, or world, and is a centre of fire which is the essence of all life."

The name pyramid means a place of fire or a volcano, and the Goddess Pele, of the native Hawaiians, is the spirit of the volcano.

"A pyramid," continued the Golden Hearted, "is the ideal form of the principle of stability because it cannot be destroyed. An earthquake will not shake it down, nor can it be set on fire. Being so big at the bottom and so heavy it is secure from floods of water, nor can the wind possibly blow it over. Neither time nor the elements will have any influence on this cunningly constructed pile, and for this reason it is like a noble character, which no adverse circumstance ever changes."

Approaching the front of the pyramid, he pulled down a cloth hanging over the inscription cut in symbols on the face of a huge piece of granite.

BEFORE THE LIGHT WAS OBSCURED THIS MEMENTO FOR GENERATIONS WAS BUILT BY SERPENT KINGS. THEY WERE SCATTERED OVER THE EARTH TO CARRY TRUTH AND WISDOM. THEY WILL COME AGAIN TO RECEIVE THE TREASURES HIDDEN IN MY BOWELS. THEN ALL MEN WILL SPEAK AND HEAR THE GREAT IMPERISHABLE TRUTH.

The next morning the Golden Hearted called his little band of wise men around him and said:

"In the Bundle of Wonderful Things given me by Guatamo, I find my father's final command. It imposes seclusion upon me in this spot. The temple requires a central spire and I shall build and cover it with pure gold. Go thou to the valley and make thy life apart from me. I love thee well, and shall miss thee sadly, but I have need to be alone."

"What wilt thou have us do?" asked the son of Guatamo.

"Go thou amongst thy fellows and teach them the arts of peace. Show them how to coax fertility anew out of the soil, and strengthen civil power until I call thee."

It was several months before the spire was finished, and then it required several days to make a llama of beaten silver as an emblem of suffering innocence to put on the altar. The llama seated upon the back of an eagle was rescuing a rabbit from the fangs of a rattlesnake.

"This quaint symbol shall represent the unequal conflict between the good and bad things in life, but the llama compelling the serpent to give up its prey means that good shall finally triumph," said the Golden Hearted, to himself, as he put the offering in place on the altar.

"I have only a few days more in this beautiful spot, then must I return to good King Cocomos, my life-long friend and follower. Well indeed has he kept his promise to me, and not only are his subjects blessed with all the arts of civilization, but they are a shining example to other less favoured races. I must offer a fitting sacrifice," he continued, "on this newly erected altar before I go."

There were eight altars in the temple on top of the pyramid, and at sunset on the last day of his stay, the Golden Hearted placed the llama on the one facing the east. At the same time the son of Guatamo headed a procession of wise men at the base of the pyramid, who slowly climbed to the top. They performed sacrifice on each terrace as they ascended, and did not reach the temple until midnight.

The Golden Hearted was alone in the great dark structure intently watching the constellation of the Pleiades directly overhead. As Alcyone, the dim star in the centre of the group, approached the zenith, he sprang forward with a glad cry and vigorously swinging a copper hammer made the sparks fly from a piece of flint. The son of venerable Guatamo held the bit of cotton over it and carefully nursed the fire into a blaze. As the light streamed up toward the heavens shouts of joy and triumph burst forth:

"Once more the children of men receive a direct ray from the spiritual sun! Awake! awake! and hear the glad tidings!"

Runners with torches lighted at the blazing beacon sped in every direction carrying the cheering element to all parts of the country. Long before sunrise it was brightening the altars and hearthstones in every house. The Golden Hearted prayed before the eastern altar, and then took an affectionate farewell of the young priest of the Order of Quetzalcoatl left in charge, but before descending, he gazed long at the matchless scenery below. Soft spring verdure lay on all sides, and he drew courage and inspiration from that fact. At the foot of the pyramid he said:

"Be of good cheer. A long era of peace and prosperity is for thee and thine. Let this knowledge be thy secret refuge lest thou be tempted to depart from the way. Grieve not for me, in the fullness of time I will come again."

Then he set out for the Kingdom of Tlapalla, accompanied by four youths of noble birth. At the water's edge he took leave of them saying:

"Guard well the temple and the sacred fires, for when I come again, I will bring disciples with me who shall possess and rule the land."

When the four youths returned to Cholula and told all their master had said to them, the people divided their province into four principalities and gave the government to the four young nobles. Ever after, four of the descendants of these youths continued to rule as priests of the Order of Quetzalcoatl in the sacred city until the Spaniards came, which we will know all about when we read the story of 'El Dorado, the Golden.'

One of the first things done by the noble youths when they became rulers was to make a statue of the Golden Hearted in a reclining position, because they said that he had gone to sleep in the bosom of the sun. When the wind blew they said he was sweeping the roads, and that he was the god of fertility. Not any place else in the new world was there so much reverence and respect paid to a statue as to this one of the Golden Hearted which was for ages kept in the temple he built on the top of the pyramid. For hundreds of miles around people came to do reverence to it, and even if it did have a black face, the ancient Aztecs always called him their 'Fair God.' And to this day the calendar stone and many other wonderful things in Mexico are said to have been made by him.

Tulla, the Hiding Nook of the Snake

NO DOUBT YOU REMEMBER that the wise men built a Dark House in Nachan to hold the National Book, and such other treasures as the Golden Hearted did not wish to carry with him. And you also remember that he left a number of wise men in charge, and that he promised to return. The great pyramid at Cholula was not all finished, but it was far enough along so he could leave the son of Guatamo to go on with the work while he paid a visit to his old friends in Nachan.

When he arrived there, he found a splendid city having whole houses of silver, others of turquoise, some of white and red shells and some of rich feathers. Cotton grew there in all colours, so it was not necessary to dye it, and the people were rich and prosperous. A great and mighty king ruled them, but he finally grew jealous because the people seemed to think that all their good fortune came from obeying the commands given them by the Golden Hearted when he visited them as a mere youth.

They did everything in their power to honour the good prince. When he promulgated a new law, they ran to the mountain tops and proclaimed it in a loud voice, and then the swift-footed couriers dashed through the country with lighted torches and repeated it to every one they met. One day a young man came to him and said:

"Good prince, be on your guard. The king no longer loves you."

"Why do you say this to me?" asked the Golden Hearted.

"Because I know he plots to injure you. He is angry because you are helping the wise men build Tulla. He calls it the Hiding Nook of the Snake to show contempt for you."

"Again I ask why do you say such things to me?" There was so much reproach in the tones of the voice of the Golden Hearted that the young man hung his head and stammered:

"Forgive me, but I wanted you to know there is danger for you here, and I am ready to serve you faithfully."

The Golden Hearted made no reply, but taking a thoroughly-dried cactus needle from a shelf, stuck it through his ears and was beginning to pierce his tongue when the young man sprang forward and caught his hand.

"Why, good prince," he cried in a startled voice, "do you maltreat your poor ears and tongue? It is I who have spoken evil, not you."

"But I listened, and that is an offense against the Good Law. Do you think I will not punish myself for disobedience?"

"Oh," said the young man, with tears streaming down his face, "the sight of blood makes my heart ache, and I, too, will be punished." And with that he stuck cactus needles through his ears and tongue.

"My friend," said the Golden Hearted, "I thank you for your kind thought of me, but I must beautify Tulla even if it does displease the king, and he is right in calling it the Hiding Nook of the Snake, because it will be a treasure-house of the wisdom inherited from the philosophers and wise men of your race. You should always bear in mind that a serpent is a symbol of wisdom, and not a thing to despise. The king compliments me, even though he knows it not."

The young man went out of the room with the thorns still sticking in his ears, and when he spat blood, his companions said:

"Why does your mouth bleed?" and he answered:

"Because I have been speaking evil of some one."

"Open your mouth and let us see," they said.

"It is only needful to examine the tongue. I have pierced it with the sharp needle of the cactus."

"Who gave you leave to do such a thing?"

"No one," he answered, "but when the Good Prince inflicted that penalty on himself for merely hearing what I said, I could do no less than follow his example."

"And we will do likewise," they said, and in after years, every devotee of the teachings of the Golden Hearted punished himself in this manner for evil speaking or listening to others saying unkind things of a fellow creature.

Of course we know that the king really was jealous of the Golden Hearted, and was determined that he should not stay long in Tulla, which bade fair to rival his own city with which it was connected by the secret passageway containing the Dark House. During the years of his absence, the wise men left in Nachan had been at work on this wonderful city, and it was very beautiful indeed, even before the Golden Hearted saw it at all. When he came the inhabitants received him with great rejoicing, and then the king of Nachan began to be afraid that he would have too great a following.

The king had no excuse to fight the Golden Hearted, because he always put his fingers in his ears when they talked of war in his presence, and under no circumstances would he have been made king himself. He only wanted to teach and help the people in a peaceable and kind way.

The king knew all this, but he was uneasy and wanted the Golden Hearted to go away. So he hired a native wizard to play a cunning trick upon the Golden Hearted. Disguising himself as one of the wise men, the wizard went to his house and said to his servant:

"I wish to see and speak to your master."

"Go away, old man, you cannot see the prince for he is sick. You will annoy him and cause him heaviness."

"But I must see him," persisted the pretended old man.

"Wait a moment and I will ask him," said the servant, and he went and told the Golden Hearted that a strange old man was determined to see him.

"Let him come in," said the sick man.

Tottering up to the bedside as if he were very feeble, the intruder said with well-feigned sympathy:

"How are you, my lord? Here is a medicine I have brought for you."

"You are welcome; I have been expecting you for many days," and the Golden Hearted held out his hand in a friendly manner.

"How is your body, and how is your health?" again asked the visitor, seating himself by the bedside.

"I am exceedingly sick. All my body is in pain, and I cannot move my hands nor my feet."

"The medicine I have is good and wholesome. If you will drink it you will be healed and eased at heart." As he said this, the wizard held up a small silver cup and put a white powder in it. "Drink this and you will then have in mind the toils and fatigues of death, and of your departure."

"Where have I to go?" cried his listener in surprise.

"To Tlapalla (which was their name for the Happy Island), where The Old Man of the Sea is waiting for you. He has much to tell you, and when you return you will be young and handsome. Indeed you will be a mere boy again." Seeing that the Golden Hearted merely stared at him, he said: "Sir, drink this medicine."

But the sick man did not wish to do so.

"Drink, my lord, or you will be sorry for it hereafter," urged the wizard.

"No, no; I will not drink it."

"At least rub some on your brow and taste a sip." So the Golden Hearted drank a little to try it, saying:

"What is this? It seems to be a thing very good and savoury. Already I feel myself healed. I am well."

"Drink some more, my lord, since it is good. The more you drink, the better you will feel."

The sick man swallowed considerable more and then he was drunk. It was not medicine at all that the wizard gave him, but a white wine made from the maguey plant and the powder he put in it was to make the Golden Hearted believe that he must go away.

For days after he was very sad and wept continuously, but he began to get ready to leave Tulla. No matter what was said to dissuade him, he could never get rid of the idea that he must take all of his followers and go as quickly as possible.

The wise men, seeing that he was determined, gathered up all the picture writings they had made as a record of their journeys, and putting them into an ark, carried it swung on a pole with them. Before leaving, they called the people together and said:

"Know that the Golden Hearted commands you to remain here in these lands of which he makes you master and gives you possession. He goes to the place whence he and we came, but he will return to visit you when it shall be time for the world to come to an end. You must await him in these lands, possessing them and all contained in them since for this purpose came we hither. Remain, therefore, for we go with the Golden Hearted."

The Departure of the Golden Hearted

THE POISONED WINE worked in the brain of the Golden Hearted and caused him to do many singular things. For instance he burned all the beautiful houses built for him by the wise men and ordered much of his treasure to be buried in the mountains and ravines. When he left Tulla, he took all the bright-plumaged singing birds with him, and would only allow nineteen of the wise men to go with him.

Two of these knew all about fishing, and two knew about farming, and one was a weather prophet who studied the clouds and winds, and could foretell storms, while all the rest were priests who kindled the sacred fires and taught the people the Good Law.

As soon as the King of Tulla found he was leaving, he took an army and followed after him, laying the country waste and taking captive as many of the people as he could find.

"Good prince, why do you not let us make war upon your and our enemy?" the warriors often asked him, but he always put his fingers in his ears and replied sadly:

"You do not understand the Good Law, my friend. The only way to overcome hate is with love. It is fully time for me to return to Tlapalla."

He travelled on until he came to a place where there was a great tree, high and very thick. Here he sat down to rest.

"Bring me a mirror," he said to his servant, and when he saw his face reflected in it, he cried out:

"Take it away. I am already old." Then the wise men knew that the drug in the wine was making him mad again and they did not try to hinder him when he began throwing stones at the tree.

"I will make these stones stick into your bark until you look like a porcupine and the wind cannot blow them out," he said, and for a long, long time, the tree was pointed out to travellers as being enchanted, because the god of wind had hurled his wrathful breath upon it. From all accounts the tree was full of sharp rocks from top to bottom and must have looked very queer indeed.

The flute players tried to divert his attention as they marched along the wood, but he was very weary and finally sat down to rest on a stone by the roadside.

"O, Thou of infinite mercy and compassion, dry the hot tears that flood and burn my face," he said brokenly as he looked toward Tulla. People now say that his tears marked and ate into the stone, and that the print of his hands is still to be found on it.

After he had reached a very wide river and had commanded his followers to help build a bridge across it, he was met by some men who tried to stop him.

"Where are you going?" they asked, "and why do you leave your city? To whose care will you commend it, and who will do penance in it?" The Golden Hearted answered them firmly:

"You can in no wise hinder me, for I must go."

"But where are you going?" they insisted.

"To Tlapalla," he answered.

"For what purpose are you going?"

"The sun calls me," he said.

"Go then," they replied, "but leave behind all the mechanical arts, the melting of silver, the working of precious stones and of masonry, picture writing, feather work and other crafts." And then they would have robbed him, but he threw all his rich jewels into a fountain. Among his tormentors was the pretended old wizard who tried to induce him to drink more wine.

"No, I can not drink it. I can not even taste it again," he said, and that night in his sleep he turned his head from side to side and tore his hair with his hands.

The next morning in passing between a volcano and the snowy mountain tops, all his servants being hunchbacked, died of cold, and he had no way to get down the steep mountain side except to slide in a squatting position with his feet close together.

In one place he stopped and built a square stone court for ball play, and taught the people how to play the game. Now it is said that he drew a line through the centre of the court, and that made the deep gash in the mountains still to be seen.

In another place he threw a dart at a tree and pierced it in such a manner that it looked like a cross, and after that a cross was called 'The Tree of Our Life,' in memory of this event. Some say that he built houses with certain underground passageways where he hid picture writing and records of his teachings, and just before arriving at the water's edge, he set up and balanced a great stone so that it could be moved with one's little finger, but a whole multitude could not displace it.

No doubt you remember the village chief where the Golden Hearted went when he first arrived from the Happy Island, and also that he sent this chief a cross with a hand in the centre. Now that he was going home again, the Golden Hearted thought he would visit the chief and see how he and his people were progressing.

Imagine his surprise in finding that they had dedicated a temple to him, and that in the middle of the square tower was a terracotta statue of himself dressed as a warrior holding an arrow in his hand, and because the statue was hollow they thought it was an oracle. His name in their language was Cukulcan, but the common people called him 'The Working Hand,' and had great respect for a huge stone cross erected in the turreted courtyard in front of the temple, which had a big red hand in the centre.

When the Golden Hearted went among the people, he found that they remembered everything he had told them, and that on the anniversary of his coming great crowds of people came on a pilgrimage to the oracle statue in the temple. It did no good for him to tell them that he was simply an elder brother and teacher come to give them aid in a simple, kindly way. They believed he was sent by God, and for ages after the people made pilgrimages to this shrine, and held it in very great esteem.

Realizing that it was time for him to go down to the sea coast among the fishermen he had first seen, he went to the temple service one morning, and after praying before the altar, picked up a sacred Tunkel and sang them a prophetic song of farewell:

Ye men of Itza hearken to the tidings
Listen to the forecast of this cycle's end,
Four have been the ages of the world's progressing
Now the fourth is ending and its end is near,
A mighty lord is coming, see you give him honour,
A potent lord approaches to whom all must bow
I, the prophet, warn you, keep in mind my boding,
Men of Itza mark it, and await your lord.

"Waste not your time in idle repining," he said in farewell, "I go for purification, but will surely come again."

He only spent time enough on the seashore to build and provision a *balsa*, or boat with sails, and then he said "good bye" to the fisherfolk, and sailed away toward the east with a few of the wise men for companions. Just before he stepped into the boat he turned to the wise men, who were to remain and said:

"It wrings my heart to part from you, but there is need for you to stay here in order to complete the tasks already begun." As he embraced and kissed each one on the cheek he named their special duty, and had no fear that his orders would not be fully carried out.

"You must go to the son of Guatamo, and tell him my work is finished."

To another he said:

"You must go about and teach in my stead. I will come again, but at another time."

It was difficult for him to persuade the fisherman not to accompany him.

"Have no fear. Mine is a staunch bark capable of riding the storm and stress of the angry sea. Farewell, beloved, I will return to you, when the time and seasons are propitious."

The people on shore turned again and again to throw kisses to him, while the fishermen in their little boats put out to sea with him, and strained their vision to catch a last glimpse of his flower-laden *balsa*.

The wise men and priests in the temples whereever he had been, began at once to guard the sacred fires and to watch and pray for his safe return. Lest they should forget his sayings they engraved them on stone, and taught them to the people so that his name was a household word for generations. His was the only civilization known in the Americas before the advent of the white men.

El Dorado, the Golden

WE HAVE READ SOMEWHERE that 'in 1492 Columbus sailed the waters blue,' and we know that the big Exposition held in Chicago in 1893 was to commemorate the four hundredth anniversary of the discovery of America, but no one can possibly tell how long it was after the Golden Hearted sailed away, until Columbus came.

And nobody knows where the Golden Hearted went.

He said he was going to Tlapalla, which we know meant the Happy Island, but no one can find it any more, and there are traditions which say that the island, with all its inhabitants, sank in the ocean. This may be why the Golden Hearted never came back again. Of course the wise men and the primitive people in the Americas believed that he would return because he said he would, and they watched and waited all the long years from one generation to another. Many times bright and promising young men, just out of the universities, or fresh from victories on the battle fields, would take the vows of a priest, and give up all their hopes and ambitions to serve in the temples erected in honour of the Golden Hearted. They did not know anything more about him than we do, but they had faith in him.

They said:

"All the good we know comes from him, and when he returns all wrongs will be righted and every heart made to rejoice. He will give us everything we wish for."

Several times during the year whole nations would fast and do severe penance to induce him to come quickly. Not one of them could be made to believe that he was dead.

"No, no," they said, "he is asleep in the bosom of the sun. He will surely come again; he promised us he would."

Then they would get the idea that he was offended, and the kings would order great sacrifice to be made to appease him. In some places I am sorry to say they offered the quivering, bleeding hearts of human beings by the hundreds, but still he did not come. In other places they remembered his gentleness and only laid fruit, flowers and perfumes on the sacred fire altars which they still kept burning. There were many places where they carefully preserved his sayings by cutting them in sign language on the stones of the temples, and every child was taught to imitate his virtues and follow his example.

For several years before Columbus arrived the priests and wise men had been prophesying that the Golden Hearted was soon to return, that the sun was bringing him back, accompanied by companions like himself, who would rule over them. Not even the great-great-grandfathers of the men then living had seen the Golden Hearted, so they did not know how he looked, but their traditions said that he was a bearded white man, and we shall see by and by what a curious mistake this led them to make about the first white men who came to them after the discovery of America.

Before we can understand how such things could happen, we must remember that the people in Europe did not know there was an America, and that many of them had very queer ideas about the shape of the earth. Some said it was four-cornered and square like a dry goods box, and others thought it was round and flat like a plate, surrounded by water which finally changed into vapour and mist, and that whoever ventured far out into the misty clouds fell through and went – heaven knows where!

In the quaint old Italian city of Genoa was born a little boy named Christopher Columbus, who was to change all this, and be the innocent cause of much suffering to the descendants of the races who had been visited by the Golden Hearted. When a mere lad at school, he was greatly interested in boats, and he not only studied geography and history, but read all the books of travel he could find, and dreamed night and day of a great long voyage he was going to make on the ocean some time. He did not waste his time fishing and playing on the beach like other boys, but picked up the chips that washed ashore and examined them very carefully, because he believed that if there was an unknown land some where in the west, that the waves would bring something ashore from there. He was really quite an old man before he found anything, but one day he picked up some strange chips at Cadiz that had been cut by hand, and then he knew he was right.

Sailors always do have wonderful tales to tell about the sea, and in those days they were so superstitious that they were sure that there were huge monsters living in the distant waters just waiting to eat up any sailor foolish enough to venture near them. There was not one of them willing to listen to Columbus, when he tried to explain that the earth is round like an orange, and that we live on the outside of it. He said to them repeatedly:

"If we sail west steadily, we shall in time arrive back at the place from which we started." Finally, not only the sailors, but the people in the streets pointed their fingers at him and said:

"There goes the crazy old man, who thinks the world is as round as an apple."

The more he talked and reasoned and argued and even drew maps to prove that he was right, the more everybody shook their heads and called him crazy.

Columbus was about to give up in despair because he was very poor, and there seemed to be no way by which he could demonstrate that his theory of the shape of the earth was correct.

And now comes a curious coincidence.

He was a very devout Christian, and felt certain that the inhabitants of this strange country in the west had never heard of our God nor of his beloved son Jesus, and his heart was fired with zeal to reach these poor heathens and tell them the story of the Christ.

About this time some influential friend secured an audience for him with the King of Portugal, but it did no good to tell his story to the rich monarch, who was neither of a scientific nor a religious turn of mind, and he might as well have talked to the wind. Utterly discouraged Columbus decided to go to Spain, which is a near neighbour of Portugal, and see if he could not induce the famous King Ferdinand and Isabella, the queen, to give him boats to make his longed-for voyage. The queen especially was very pious and was much interested in Columbus' story about the heathens, but the ministers of her court laughed at Columbus and said:

"It is a foolish dream which can never be carried out."

Almost heart-broken Columbus silently turned his back on the Spanish capital and walked a long way to a seaport called Palos, where there was a queer old convent in which strangers were made welcome by the kind monks living in it. Knocking upon the gate, he said to the porter:

"Will you please give me a bit of bread and a drink of water."

Fortunately, the prior, a learned man and an intimate friend of Queen Isabella came along, and was quick to see that Columbus was no common beggar. He invited him in, and after listening quietly and thoughtfully to his visitor's plan of crossing the ocean to convert the heathen to Christianity, he borrowed a mule and rode miles across the country to the castle where the Queen was staying and persuaded her to help Columbus.

"It is your duty," he said. "God has given you riches and many blessings that you may assist your fellow men, and these strange people know nothing of our God, and they need teachers to help them find the right way of living."

Queen Isabella was so impressed with what he said that she immediately petitioned the Royal Treasurer to give Columbus money to make his voyage of discovery.

"Your majesty, there is no money to spare," was the polite answer of the Treasurer, who, like all the rest of the court, thought Columbus was a visionary dreamer if not crazy.

"Very well," she said. "I will pawn my crown jewels," and she did. This was a most noble and courageous act on her part, for a queen in those days was scarcely considered dignified or respectable without splendid crown jewels to wear on public occasions, but she was bent upon sending the gospel of Christ to the heathen in America. Does it not seem strange that the Golden Hearted and the Queen of Spain should be credited with the same desire to help the people of the Americas, and that they lived hundreds of years apart and could never have known of each other, and that one incident is a fact of history and the other only a legend?

But as soon as Columbus secured the money another difficulty arose. No sailor could be found who would risk his life on an unknown sea with such a crazy old man. Finally Queen Isabella had to promise liberty and full pardon to the convicts in the prisons before Columbus could get any one to go with him. It was a terrible thing for him but he had a brave heart, and the monks from the convent at Palos sent some of their number with him to teach the natives.

On and on, the three caravels, the *Santa Maria*, the *Pinta* and *Nina*, sailed without finding land, until their provisions were getting low and the crews of convicts were about to mutiny and kill Columbus. In order to keep them quiet he told them wonderful stories of the riches of this land they were trying to find.

"You can have all the gold, and silver, and precious gems you can carry," he promised them. In an instant you could see the cunning and greed in their wicked faces. They did not care whether the earth was round or flat, nor what became of the natives, if they only had gold, and then they would gather around Columbus and question him closely about the size of the nuggets and precious stones. Of course he could only guess at it, but he knew that to save his life he must say something, so he replied:

"I firmly believe that there are immense pieces of solid gold to be found there, and that it is abundant."

Some thought they would find it in lumps as big as a house, and they all expected to pick up hands full of gems just anywhere. Columbus had strained his eyes looking for the land until he was nearly blind, but one night he imagined he saw a glimmer of light ahead. Where there was light there must be land, he thought. So he called one of the sailors to him and asked him what he saw.

"A light! a light!" cried the sailor joyfully. But it was not until nearly two o'clock in the morning that the commander of one of the other boats started the cry:

"Land! Land ahead!"

You can imagine what excitement there was on all the caravels, and how thankful Columbus was. The padres gathered around him, and as he sprang ashore, he dropped on his knees and stooped and kissed the ground. Even the sailors forgot about the gold while he and the padres prayed and thanked God for giving mankind a new world.

Immediately the flag of Spain was planted and the land claimed for King Ferdinand and Isabella, but wonderful indeed were the things surrounding them. Men and women of a bronze colour crowded around them and offered them strange, but delicious fruits and flowers and brought them food and water. In his first letter to Queen Isabella, Columbus said of them:

"There is not in all the world a better people nor a better land. Their converse is ever sweet and gentle, and is accompanied by a smile. They truly love their neighbour as themselves."

Finding them docile and kind the padres set about teaching them, and the simple natives were very willing listeners. It was quite a long time before they could understand each other well, but the padres told the story of the Christ the first time they held a service, which was on a Sunday. Remembering the precepts of the Golden Hearted, the faces of the natives lighted up understandingly when they heard the words of Jesus which bade them be loving and kind to each other, and they nodded their heads and exclaimed:

"El Dorado! El Dorado!"

At least that is what the ignorant convict sailors thought they said. The words 'El Dorado' in Spanish, which was their mother tongue, meant 'The Golden,' or 'The Gilded One.' We know they were eager and greedy to find gold and that they had been told to help themselves freely to all they could get, so they immediately began to question the simple natives.

"Yes, yes; we have plenty of gold," the natives said, in surprise, because they did not value it at all, except for ornaments, and they ran to fetch some for their visitors. When they saw how glad it made the sailors, they were happy and content as a lot of children, and they not only brought all they had, but told where there was plenty more to be found.

The Child of the Sun

NONE OF US HAVE FORGOTTEN about the Children of the Sun, and the city of Cuzco founded by the Golden Hearted, or of his ruling over them as Manco-Capac, the powerful one. He went into their country which we call Peru before he had ever seen Mexico, but the Spaniards came to the ancient city of Tenochtitlan before they knew anything about Cuzco. It was not long after the death of Montezuma until the Spaniards heard about the riches of the Children of the Sun, and they were determined to find that country.

The Aztecs did not help them any because they no longer looked upon them as sent from Heaven but as ruthless destroyers borne along on the backs of fierce animals swift as the wind, and carrying weapons in their hands that scattered death and destruction everywhere. The Aztecs learned to hate the Spaniards bitterly, and when we came to study their history we shall know why. Even their own historians do not pretend to deny that they fell upon the poor Aztecs sword in hand and robbed them of all the treasures they had, besides taking their lands away from them.

Some say that Francisco Pizarro was a cousin of Hernando Cortez who conquered the Aztecs, but all agree that he was an ignorant swineherd, who could neither read nor write, and whose parents were not respectable. While he was not actually a convict he belonged to the low class, and the men going with him to search for the new El Dorado among the Children of the Sun, were really no better. Cortez had some hidalgoes, cavalliers and knights with him because men of good family often came to the Americas on the first voyages after Columbus, but Pizarro collected a band of cut-throat adventurers who were just as greedy and ignorant as he was. All the exploring they did was simply to search for gold, and they did not care what methods they used to get it. The simple natives with their naked defenseless bodies, and bows and arrows were no match for men covered with steel armour, mounted on horseback and armed with guns and cannon. Balboa had already found the Pacific Ocean, and Pizarro knew that the Children of the Sun lived in that direction, so he rigged out a vessel and sailed along the coast trying to find them. At the first place he landed the natives said to him:

"Why do you not stay at home and till your own land instead of roaming about to rob others who have never harmed you?"

But the savages wore some heavy gold ornaments, and Pizarro asked eagerly:

"Have you more of this?"

"Yes, we have a little more," they said, and as they were weighing some of the metal their chief struck the scales with his fist, scattering the nuggets all over the floor.

"If this is what you prize so much that you are willing to risk your lives to attain it, I can tell you of a land where they eat and drink out of vessels of gold, and where there are great quantities to be had for the asking."

"Where is this rich country?"

"It is ten days journey toward the south and is ruled by the Child of the Sun."

The Spaniards were nearly mad with joy because now they said:

"All our fond dreams are about to be realized." They were in such a good humour that they gave the natives some glass beads and some live chickens. When they turned the rooster loose, he crowed, and then the simple natives clapped their hands in glee, and asked:

"What is it saying?"

It sounded as if the rooster said:

"How do you do, sir!" which the natives thought was very funny indeed. Then they wanted to know what the cannon said. One of the men set up a target and fired at it shivering the board into fine splinters. The loud noise, the flash of smoke and powder, frightened the poor natives nearly to death. Some of them fell flat on their faces, and others ran into the woods as fast as they could go, screaming:

"Our good Manco-Capac is coming back to us angry."

That night the old men huddled the terrified people together and said to them:

"Do you remember when the comet flamed through the sky; when the earthquake shook the land, and there was a rainbow around the moon?"

"I well remember," said one of the old men, "that a thunderbolt fell on one of the Incas' royal palaces setting it on fire, and I saw an eagle chased by several hawks hovering in the air over Cuzco. Our king saw it too, and while he looked at it the eagle fell dead at his feet."

"It is no use to resist these strangers," said an envoy from the Inca, who had arrived in time to hear the last statement. "Seven years ago when the father of our king died, he called his son to his bedside and told him that white and bearded strangers were coming to overturn the Empire. And as you know, our great oracle has foretold the return of Manco-Capac at the close of the twelfth dynasty of the Incas. That day is at hand, so do not quarrel with the strangers."

No one showed a disposition to disobey him, and in a short time he stood before Pizarro saying:

"I bring you greetings from the Inca, Child of the Sun, who rules this land. He wishes me to ask why you come, and from what country."

"Our home is far across the sea," responded Pizarro, "and we serve a rich and powerful prince who has heard of the Child of the Sun, and sends us to pay our respects to him."

This was not the truth for the King of Spain knew nothing whatever of Pizarro's wicked intentions, nor did he know about Cortez either until long after poor Montezuma was dead and his country laid waste. But when men turn out to be wholesale robbers they do not care whether they tell the truth or not.

"Our Inca is at his favourite baths and wishes to know when you will arrive, so that he may provide suitable refreshments for you."

"We will come at once," said Pizarro.

"It would be better to wait a few days," said the king's messenger. "Our Inca is keeping a sacred fast, and we cannot disturb him until it is finished." The Spaniards had no respect for the king's wishes or his privacy, so they made ready to follow the messenger. While they were dividing the presents of llamas, sheep and gold goblets among themselves some of the soldiers said:

"This dog of a king may have thousands of followers. What can a handful of men like we are, do against so many? Suppose they should try to fight us?"

Pizarro happened to overhear them and replied:

"Let every one of you take heart, and go forward like a good soldier. God ever protects his own, and will humble the pride of the heathen and bring him to a knowledge of the true faith – the great end and object of this conquest."

It was the first time he had spoken of conquest, but the soldiers remembered the complete success of Cortez in Mexico and only needed to be told that the natives were to be Christianized to make them certain that the home authorities would not interfere with them, so they shouted:

"Lead on! wherever you think best we will follow with good will."

The few padres in the company were sincere in their wish to teach the natives and so was the King of Spain, but neither of them could control the actions of such men as Pizarro and his adventurers, now ready to pounce down on the mild and inoffensive people like a band of hungry wolves. When they got up on the top of the mountain and looked down, the landscape had the appearance of a huge checker-board cut into squares by canals and evergreen hedges. A wide river rolled through the meadows, like a narrow silver ribbon, while across the valley were the famous hot baths with steam and vapour rising from them in the clear air. Along the slope of the hills a white cloud of tents covered the ground for several miles, where the Child of the Sun, and his court were encamped.

Pizarro with banners streaming and the sparkle of armour glittering in the sun, galloped into the city with blare of trumpets and lances fixed. The Inca was in a camp near by, but the rude Spaniards broke in upon his fast, and a brother of Pizarro almost rode him down with his horse. Giving the bridle a sudden jerk he brought the horse to his haunches, so close to the Inca, that the horse snorted with fear, but the brave king did not move a muscle, although he had never seen a white man in armour nor a horse before in his life. Seeing that he could not frighten him Pizarro's brother said haughtily:

"What is your royal will? My brother desires that you visit him."

Without raising his eyes from the ground where he had kept them as a mark of respect to his visitor, the Inca smiled and said:

"Tell your captain, that I am keeping a fast, which will end tomorrow morning. I will then visit him with my chieftains. In the meantime let him occupy the public buildings on the square till I come, when I will order what is to be done."

Turning to his attendants he continued:

"Give our brothers food and drink, and have their quarters made ready for them."

That night Pizarro put all his cannon in place and boldly planned to take the Inca prisoner in his own pleasure garden. He ordered his soldiers to hide in the plaza, and wait until the Inca arrived. As soon as he was in the great square they were suddenly to spring out and put the natives to the sword, and capture their king.

It was late in the day before the Inca got all his court in splendid array, and then he sent word to Pizarro that he was coming in state.

"I am much pleased to hear it," said Pizarro. "Let your king come anyway he will; he shall be received as a friend and brother. Let him sup with us and sleep in our quarters tonight."

When once in motion the Inca's retinue had on so many gold ornaments that they blazed like the sun. Some wore showy stuffs in white and red with gold and silver embroidery, while others were dressed in white and carried silver maces in their hands. The Inca wore the royal *borla*, or crown on his head, with the Quetzal feathers in the back and the long red fringes across the forehead. Over him was a canopy representing a rainbow, to show that he was a Child of the Sun, and a follower of Manco-Capac, who we know was the Golden Hearted. He was seated on a gold throne which was placed in a litter and carried by four noble youths, in gorgeous liveries. Around his neck was a splendid gold necklace set with large emeralds. Looking around and not seeing anyone the Inca asked in surprise:

"Where are the strangers?"

At this moment a padre came forward and demanded that he give up his power and become a subject of Spain. He also told the king that he must become a convert to Christianity. The eyes of the Inca flashed fire as he replied:

"I will be no man's tributary. Your prince may be great; I do not doubt it when I see that he has sent his subjects so far across the waters. I am willing to hold him as a brother. As for my faith, I will not change it. My God still lives in the heavens and looks down on his children. By what authority do you make such demands upon me?"

The padre handed the Inca a bible but as the thought of the insult offered came over him, the Inca threw it to the ground and said angrily:

"Tell your comrades that they shall give me an account of their doings in my country. I will not go from here until they have made me full satisfaction for the wrongs they have committed."

A soldier turned to Pizarro and said:

"Do you not see that while we stand here wasting our breath in talking to this dog full of obstinate pride that the fields are filling with Indians. Let us set on at once."

Pizarro saw that the hour had come, and waving a white scarf which was the appointed signal he and his soldiers sprang into the square, shouting the old war cry of Cortez:

"Santiago! and at them!"

The poor natives in their holiday dress and fine jewelry were wholly unarmed, because they were coming to make a visit, and had no way to defend themselves. When they tried to escape they found they were hemmed in on all sides by the stone buildings facing the plaza, and nobody knows how many thousands of them were killed. They were stunned by the roar of the cannon, choked by the smoke, trampled under the horses' feet, and their naked bodies hacked to pieces with swords.

The Spaniards seemed bent upon killing the Inca, but his loyal subjects caught hold of the horses' bridles and saddle blankets, and even the legs of their riders to prevent them from hitting the Inca. Some offered their own bodies to the lances – anything to save the king who was stunned and bewildered. As the men who were carrying him were killed, the litter lurched to one side and he fell to the ground. Instantly the imperial *borla*, or crown, was snatched from his head; his hands were securely tied, and he was hustled, a prisoner, into a building nearby. Then the soldiery robbed and pillaged as much as they pleased, even carrying off the plate from the Inca's table.

Realizing that it was gold that the Spaniards wanted, the Inca began at once to try to buy his freedom.

"I will cover the floor of this room with gold if you will release me," he said, to Pizarro. Seeing that the soldiers smiled at this, he added:

"I will fill the room full, as high as I can reach," standing on tip-toe and stretching his arm against the wall. Pizarro agreed to accept that amount of gold, but demanded double that amount of silver, and would only allow the Inca two months' time to collect it in. The Spaniards kept close watch over him, and as soon as the amount was all paid in, Pizarro accused the unhappy captive of trying to stir up an insurrection. The Inca was surprised and indignant; saying:

"You have me in your power. Is not my life at your disposal? What better security have you for my fidelity? It is very far to my capital at Cuzco, but that you may be satisfied that I am proceeding in good faith, send some of your own people there."

The Spaniards sacked and pillaged Cuzco when they got there, taking seven hundred plates of gold from the walls of the temple dedicated to the Golden Hearted. Besides this, there were heavy cornices of gold, fountains, birds, fruit, vegetables, tables, statues, slabs, basins and panels of pure gold; which, when melted down made millions of dollars.

Never before did anybody in the wide world pay such a ransom. But Pizarro had no intention of setting the Inca free. Pretending to be very suspicious, he suddenly appeared before the Inca, and said:

"What new treason is this you are meditating against me? Me, who has been so brotherly and kind to you?"

"Why do you mock me," replied the Inca. "Am I not a captive in your hands? How could I conceive such a design as you speak of when I would be the first victim? You little know my people, if you think they would attempt such a thing against my will."

Pizarro was determined to get rid of him, so he trumped up twelve charges against him, and, after a mock trial, sentenced the helpless Inca to be burned at the stake.

When told of his fate, the poor king said to Pizarro, with tears streaming down his face:

"What have I, or my children done, that I should die like this? And from your hands – you who have received only benefit and kindness from me and my people."

The doom of the Inca was sounded by trumpet in the same square he had innocently entered to visit his strange white brother, and two hours after sunset he was led out by torch-light and burned to death.

To make sure that there was no danger of an uprising in the distant parts of the country, Pizarro sent an officer to finish collecting the ransom and find out the actual condition. While he was gone Pizarro had the Inca executed. When the officer returned, he said:

"I have met with nothing but kindness on the way. There has never been any attempt at an uprising."

And this was the truth.

The Gilded Man

THERE WERE NONE WILLING TO SAY "God forgive him," is what history tells us of the end of Pizarro, whose throat was cut by some of the men he quarreled with over the treasures they had taken from the Children of the Sun, and I do not believe that any one was ever sorry that he perished like a wretched outcast. Of course, one of his brothers had heard of El Dorado, and he began to inquire closely of the Indians whether there really was such a person.

"Yes, there is," he was told, "and this chief smears himself all over with a sweet-smelling gum and sprinkles his body with fine gold-dust until he looks like a shining statue."

"Where does this chief live?"

"Not far from here, and his people are very rich in gold and emeralds."

This was what the Spaniards wanted to hear, and the Children of the Sun hoped by this means to get rid of their hated conquerors. We remember the visit of the Golden Hearted to the Zipa of the Muscas, and we see, by the unfriendly feeling of their neighbours, that they were still quarrelsome.

"We will go and find the Valley of the Gilded Man," said the brother of Pizarro, to his soldiers, who were getting tired of being idle. "I am told that there are wealthy regions to the north, east, and south of us, where the people go about covered with gold-dust, and where there are no mountains or woods."

This pleased the greedy adventurers very much, and it was not long before there was quite an army of them ready to start. But they did not know that they were going into a country where there were cannibals – savages ready to kill and eat every one of them, and that they fought with poisoned arrows. The Muscas were obliged to fight these people, but they traded with them, because there was no gold in their own land, and they prized it highly as an offering in honour of the Golden Hearted. They had quantities of salt which they pressed into little round cakes, like sugar loaves, and carried over beaten paths to market. Besides this, they wove beautiful cotton cloth, and managed to get large quantities of gold and silver and emeralds by trading with the cannibals.

They had not forgotten what the Golden Hearted taught them about hammering the gold, or casting it into tasteful shapes, and they not only wore it for ornaments, but used it to decorate the outside and inside of their temples. It was near the anniversary of his departure, and there were many pilgrims from neighbouring tribes who had come to cast emeralds into the lake at Gautavita in his honour. On the mountain tops surrounding the lake beacon lights were burning, and the sacred fires on the altars in the temples had never been allowed to go out. As each band of pilgrims came into the city, the Zipa welcomed them, saying:

"Tomorrow, comrades, we will go in solemn procession to the lake, and commemorate the departure of Bochica, and his purification afterward. We have made his heart very sad by our misdeeds, but from his home in the sun he can look down upon us, and see that we still adore and worship him."

The next day, at noon a solemn procession approached the lake. In the lead walked bronze-coloured men, without any clothing, but whose bodies were covered with red paint, as a sign of deep mourning, and they wailed in a most sorrowful manner. Behind them were warriors decorated with gold and emeralds, wearing bright feathers in their gold head-dresses, and carrying mantles of jaguar skins over their arms. Some of them were singing, while others shouted joyfully or blew on horns and pipes, and conch shells. Close to them were priests in black robes, with white crosses on them, and tall black hats, like those worn by the wise men. In the rear was the Zipa riding in a kind of gilded wheelbarrow hung with disks of gold. His naked body had been anointed with a resinous gum, and covered all over with fine gold-dust.

Arrived at the shore, the Gilded Man and his companions stepped upon a *balsa* gay with streamers and loaded with flowers, and rowed out into the middle of the lake. There the Zipa, who was the Gilded Man, plunged into the water and washed off all the gold-dust. While he was doing this his companions, with music and singing, threw in the gold and emeralds they had brought out on the lake for that purpose. Coming back to the shore the Zipa said:

"Do no more work for this day, but make merry with singing, dancing and feasting, as if the gentle, kind Bochica were with you again."

All this time Pizarro's brother, and his greedy soldiers, were wandering around in the mountains trying to find the Gilded Man. If they could have seen him covered with gold at the festival, they would probably have tried to skin him alive to get the gold dust on his body. One of the padres, who came to convert and teach the natives, writing to the king of Spain, said:

"I do not believe that the men taking part in the expeditions in search of the Gilded Man, would have tried so hard to get into Paradise."

Further on in his letter the padre describes the terrible hardships and suffering the men had to undergo. After telling about their failure to find El Dorado, he says:

"The men and officers returned to us nearly naked. In the warm rain their clothes had rotted on their backs, and were torn into shreds by the thickets they had crawled through on their hands and knees. Their feet were bare and wounded by the thorns and roots in the pathways, and their swords were not only without sheaths, but were eaten up with rust. Hunger compelled them to kill and eat their horses and dogs."

While this had been going on in Peru, the King of Spain was busy sending out men for the same purpose. The story of the Gilded Man was known over all Europe, and other nations, besides Spain, were trying to find him. Some German bankers had loaned the king large sums of money for the privilege of searching for El Dorado, and the first white men to visit Gautavita was a band of Germans sent out by the banking house. They wanted slaves as well as gold, and were just as merciless and cruel as the Spaniards. In fact, any man having money enough to buy boats, or to provision men, stole off into the woods and went in search of the Gilded Man. The country was overrun with armed bands of adventurers who were ready to commit any kind of crime for the sake of gain. Whoever offered resistance was killed, and they were suspicious and jealous of each other, as well as of the Indians.

After Pizarro's brother made such a miserable failure, and had to endure such bitter hardships one would expect his friends and associates to be careful about making another venture, but they knew of the German invaders, and then it was a race to see who would get hold of the Gilded Man first. Either side would have killed him and burned and pillaged the city, so the Indians had learned to distrust and hate all white men, and they made war on both the Spaniards and Germans whenever they had an opportunity.

A young Spanish lieutenant, named Quesada, was the real conqueror of the Muscas, and, as might have been expected, he murdered the Zipa and robbed Gautavita, and every other village in the kingdom. He was as hard-hearted with his men, as he was with the Indians, and after five hundred of them had died from exposure on the way, they found themselves surrounded on all sides by overflowing rivers. Weeping and dejected they sought Quesada, saying:

"We beseech you to send us back to Peru. Instead of gold, only hunger, misery and death await us here. The Gilded Man only exists in the distorted fancy of those who believe the lying tales of the Indians."

At this juncture they stumbled on to a path with huts, at intervals, by the wayside, filled with the white cakes of salt said to come from the home of the Gilded Man, and they also found some cotton cloth.

"We are on the right road at last," said Quesada, to his dispirited soldiery. "Prove faithful now, and we shall soon stand face to face with El Dorado." With a significant nod of the head, he added: "You know what that means to fearless men, like yourselves, and you can trust to the generosity of your captain for a rich reward."

The prospect of getting plenty of gold soon caused the men to forget all about their troubles, but the Zipa not only fought them stubbornly, but when he was finally compelled to abandon Gautavita, there was no treasure to be found. The Muscas had either buried all their gold and emeralds, or thrown them into the lake. Great, indeed, was the disappointment of the Spaniards, and for his own safety Quesada soon planned another expedition against a neighbouring tribe of Indians. The strange chief was surprised and captured in the Council House, and with him perished all of the notable men of the tribe. The soldiers found some gold and some very fine emeralds, but when they went to sack the Temple of the Sun, which had a thatched roof, they carelessly set the dry leaves on fire, and burned all the plate and other treasures it contained. Bands of armed men rode hither and yon looking for the Zipa, whom they now believed to be the Gilded Man. He kept in very close hiding, and no amount of torture, or promises of reward could make his followers tell where he was, or where the gold ornaments and vessels were hidden.

"He is in the mountain fastnesses, where he has a house made of gold," declared some irresponsible Indians, glad to get rid of the cruel Spaniards.

"Where is the house located?" Quesada asked, eagerly.

"Some of the Indians say it is in the north, some say the south, some say near by, and others far away," answered his servant.

"Very well, we will search in all directions until we find the miserable dog, and when we do it shall go hard with him."

It took them several months to hunt him down, and when they did find him he could not be induced to tell anything about the treasures.

"I have a house of gold in the sun where my master and lord, Bochica lives. I go to him, whom I have faithfully served all my life."

After his death a new governor was sent from Peru, and he undertook to drain the lake to get the treasures of gold and emeralds which had been thrown into it in honour of the Golden Hearted. The Muscas were told that the new Governor would be kind to them if they would tell where they had hidden their wealth, but one of their priests said:

"Do you think a river will run up hill?"

The new Governor, hearing the remark, turned to him, and said:

"No, it is not possible for water to run up hill. Why do you ask such a foolish question?"

"How then, do you expect me to believe in the existence of a white man who will be just to us? One thing is quite as possible as the other."

And to this day no one knows what became of the riches of the brave Muscas, but it is said that they still remember the Golden Hearted, and in secret, offer gold and emeralds in his honour.

The Amazon Queens

WE SHOULD ALL GET VERY TIRED I am sure if we tried to follow the Spaniards into every nook and corner of the New World where they went in search of El Dorado, but we are interested in knowing that the name Costa Rica means the rich coast, because it was one of the El Dorado regions, and in Panama, the little narrow strip of land which unites North and South America, they expected to find a Castle of Gold, while the Island of Porto Rico is also one of the homes of El Dorado. It made no difference to the Spaniards whether the natives in these places had heard of the Golden Hearted or not. They only wanted to find the riches of the country, and would not have listened to any teaching other than that brought by the padres. So for years and years they kept on making mistakes and undergoing the most terrible hardships trying to acquire sudden wealth.

One of the stories that is very queer was that about the Amazon Queens. Columbus wrote of them, and this is what he said:

"On the first island discovered on the voyage from Spain to the Indies, no men are allowed to live. The female warriors do not follow any womanly occupations, but use bows and arrows of cane, and cover as well as arm themselves with brazen plates, of which they have many."

He says nothing of their having great wealth, but Cortez also heard of them, and wrote to the King of Spain that the island was ten days distance from a province in Mexico, and that many persons had gone there and seen the women warriors. He concludes his letter by saying:

"I am told that these fighting women are rich in pearls and gold."

This news was quite enough to start the Spaniards on a search for the island, and, as usual, the Indians gave them much contradictory information about its location. Some said it was north and some said it was south, so exploring parties were sent in both directions. A man by the name of Guzman came up into Mexico as far north as Sinaloa, looking for this wonderful island, and his march was one of devastation and murder. He not only compelled the Indians to accompany him as slaves to do all the drudgery, but tortured such chiefs as he thought had gold, and in many cases killed them because they either did not give it to him quickly enough, or in as large quantities as he wanted. The farther north he went the poorer the natives were.

"Instead of a rich island inhabited by soldierly women," he exclaimed, in disgust, "I find a few insignificant villages occupied by women and children, because the men have all fled to the mountains. In the whole country there is not a trace of gold, pearls or treasures of any kind."

Along the way he found very scant supplies of gold, and this made him furious, for he returned to the city of Mexico poorer than when he left it.

Pizarro and his followers in Peru heard of the Amazon Queens, and so did Sir Walter Raleigh and the German adventurers, but their country was said to be along the banks of a very wide river in South America. The Indians called them the Great Ladies, and the river has since been named the Amazon in their honour.

"If the Great Ladies do not invite you to visit them, it is a very dangerous thing to attempt," said the Indian guides to Orellana, the man who discovered the Amazon river, and was the first to sail its entire length.

"Why do you say that?" asked Orellana.

"Because they are tall, strong-limbed and fair, and are great fighters. They wind their long hair across their foreheads in thick bands, and defend themselves well."

"What kind of weapons do they use?" queried the Spanish soldiers, when they could stop laughing at the Indians for being afraid of a lot of women.

"They shoot with blow-pipes, bows and arrows, and have a war-club that they wield with great vigour," answered the Indians, with serious faces.

"Are they always so hostile to men?"

"Only the grandfathers of this generation have seen them, and none save the Kings of the Borderers ever venture near their habitation."

"How are the Kings of the Borderers received by these strange women?"

"They meet them at the frontier of their possessions with bows and arrows in their hands, but after an exchange of pledges the Great Ladies invite the men to come and feast and dance with them. Sometimes they stay a month, and then the Queens escort them to the edge of their land, and send them home loaded with presents."

"What kind of presents do they give?" asked the Spaniards, suddenly taking a great interest in what was being said.

"There are gold ornaments in plenty, and emeralds and pearls, besides the grains of gold carried in eagle quills."

"We will capture these Great Ladies," interrupted the Spaniards, excitedly. "We will teach them their proper places when we get hold of them. Why do you Indians allow them to live in such a manner?"

"Our forefathers have taught us to hold them in great veneration, because they live in a Mansion of the Sun. Long years ago they were Virgins of the Sun, but in the wars between the different tribes they were allowed to separate from the rest and live in a community by themselves."

"Do they build houses?"

"They have temples, and keep the sacred fires burning on the altars, as was done in olden times."

"Who rules them, and what do they do with their boy babies?"

"They select their own queen, and the boy babies are given to the Kings of the Borderers; they only keep girl babies in their tribe, and when they grow up they become either warriors or priestesses."

"How do they support themselves?"

"By hunting, fishing, weaving cloth and trading with their neighbours."

"Where do they get their riches?"

"From the mountains of Parima, where they have secret storehouses filled with treasures they have been hoarding for ages."

This pleased the Spaniards very much, and quite decided them to make a raid upon that country. Even after they had talked the matter over fully among themselves they recalled the Indians and questioned them still further.

"Would you be afraid to undertake to fight these strange women?" they asked, when they saw that the guides were unwilling to accompany them.

"No, we are not afraid, but we are enjoined to let them alone. None of us would ever think of disturbing them. They are very fierce, and will kill any man that they do not like."

"But you could easily conquer women warriors," urged the Spaniards, now eager to commence the journey.

"It would not be so easily done as you imagine," said the guides, shaking their heads doubtfully. "The Great Ladies wear thick shields and cover their clothes with metal discs which turn away an arrow point."

"We can easily overcome that protection with our guns, and we are not commanded to respect them," replied the Spaniards.

"You will find that they have deep underground retreats to which they fly in times of danger, and they are known to be excellent shots."

Just then a party of prospectors returned from the mountains where they had been looking for gold. Among the things they brought was a number of thin, flat green stones with holes pierced in each end, showing that they had been used for ornaments. The Indian guides said at once they were the same kind of emerald as that worn by the Amazon Queens for an amulet against disease.

"How did you succeed in getting them?" they asked.

"From some Indian pedlars we met with packs on their backs. They said the stones would cure the spleen, and we have been wearing them ever since."

"Did you have any difficulty in persuading the pedlars to part with them?"

"No; they said they got them from a tribe of women warriors many leagues to the south, but we did not believe them."

"It is all true," said the guides, "and these Great Ladies have been in that land a very long time."

"If we can find enough of these spleen stones to make our trip profitable we do not care whether we meet the Great Ladies or not," said the prospectors, when told of the proposed trip in search of the Amazon Queens.

As the party pushed forward into the tangled thickets, they found cocoanuts, and plantains, ripe and ready to eat, and they also found some very juicy little canteloupes growing on a vine, but none of the Indians living on, or near the Amazon river, could tell them where to find the Queens. They searched up and down the banks for a hidden passageway which was said to guard the entrance to their mountain home, but to all questions the river made no answer. To the disappointed Spaniards it looked angry, sullen and relentless in the untamed might of its turbid waters.

"It seems to be always summer here," said the weary soldiers, "but one would die of malarial poisoning if compelled to stay long."

Some of the guides felt sorry for the sick men, and went into the woods and brought them sarsaparilla bark, and made them a tea of it.

"Drink this," they said, "because it will cure your sickness which comes from the head. If your heart was strong with love for your brothers you would find blessings in this land. As it is you seek to plunder and rob the Great Ladies, but the Sun is their father, and he will make the mountains, trees and rocks hide them and their treasures."

"It is no use to look for these women any longer. We shall all die before we can reach them," said the leader, wearily.

And no one to this day knows just where the Amazon Queens lived.

The Seven Cities of Cibola

THE NAHUAS IN MEXICO were really a sect of wise men descended from those that came with the Golden Hearted. They believed that they originated in Seven Caves, which were not locations at all, but was only a way of saying that human beings have seven wonderful qualities. They might have thought so because we can see, feel, taste, hear and smell, and have instinct and are able to reason, or it may have been something else. At any rate, it did not mean actual caves, but was a symbol. In later times when people were not so wise, they said it was seven tribes instead of caves, and when the Spaniards heard about it they managed to twist it into seven cities, and immediately conceived the idea that great riches and gold could be found in them. When questioned on the subject the Indians said:

"To the far north there are seven wonderful cities where the people make arrowheads of emeralds and take the sweat off their bodies with scrapers of pure gold, and have jewelled gates, and turquoise ornaments over their doors."

"Do these men know how to work precious stones and metals?" asked the Spaniards eagerly.

"There are long streets filled with jewellers who make rings for the ears, nose and arms," they said. "Forty days must you journey to reach this land, and you must travel through a desert where there is neither water nor food to be had."

The first Spaniard to attempt the search for the Seven Cities was the cruel Guzman, who looked north for the Amazons. He had with him quite an army, and his men were so excited over the stories they heard that they scarcely took time to eat or sleep on the way. They hoped every day to find the cities, but instead of this the country grew more desolate, the road more difficult, and the cities still farther to the north. Then the Spaniards began to complain, and said:

"We have been deceived, and shall all die in this bleak land. Let us return to Mexico." And they did. For six years no one had the courage to seek the Seven Cities.

Then something very strange happened.

Into a little seaport where Cortez had ordered some ships built to explore the western coast, came wandering four strange men. They were barefooted, and had no clothing except some old, dirty skins with the hair worn off in spots. Their heads were a perfect mass of tangles, and their beards reached almost to the knees. Falling flat on their faces before the first white man they saw, they cried out in a loud voice:

"Thank God! We are safe at last!" When the astonished Spaniard turned to look at them, they seized his hands and kissed them, and springing to their feet danced and shouted for joy.

"These are escaped maniacs," said the people, gathering around to look at them. "Whatever shall we do with mad men?"

"No, no! You do not understand. We are poor wanderers who have been lost for years among the Indians."

"Let us take them to our Captain. There is something very strange about this," said the Spaniards, and they started at once.

"Who are you?" asked the Captain, rudely, looking with disgust at their dirt and rags.

"I am a noble of Castile who came to help conquer Florida, and my name is De Vaca," said the oldest man. "The fleet was wrecked and all were lost except my companions here, and me. All the years since we have been with the Indians."

"I do not believe a word of it," said the Captain. "Put these fellows in prison until we find out about them. They may be criminals."

For three months they lay in prison, and then the Alcalde came and released them.

"Tell me your story," he said.

"When the ships were lost," responded De Vaca, "we swam to the mainland, and were captured by the Indians. They were a poor, starved tribe who lived on roots and berries, and often went days without a mouthful. We had with us a rattle, and this, with our beards, made them think we came from Heaven, and were great medicine men. They fell on their faces before us and gave us all they had. We asked them to take us where the sun sets, but they refused, and we pretended to be very angry, until they finally let us go. After months of wandering we came to a land of plenty, where the people were wealthy, and wore beautiful plumes in their head-dresses. They brought us five emeralds cut into arrow-heads, and many fine turquoises, and beads made of coral. When I asked where they got these stones, they pointed to some lofty mountains toward the north and told us the gems came from there, and that near them were large cities, with houses three or four stories high. I did not go there because I heard that toward the sunset were other men of my kind, and I longed once more to look upon the face of a Spaniard."

"Of course," said the people, as they talked the matter over, "these are the same cities Guzman tried to find. He did not go in the right direction, but we know where they are," and many were eager to set out at once. But the Viceroy was a quiet and careful man.

"There have been many lives lost already," he said, "and it will be best not to hurry. I shall not send an army there until I am sure."

Then he thought of a padre, named Fray Marcos, who had lived much among the Indians of the north, and he sent for him, and said:

"Perhaps there lies to the north as rich a nation as Mexico or Peru. If so it must be conquered for the Church and the King of Spain. You know how to speak to the Indians, and it might be that they would let you come among them and learn the truth. Will you undertake to do so?"

"God giving me strength I will," said Fray Marcos, with enthusiasm.

"Very well. The negro Stephen, who was with De Vaca is here, and is willing to be your guide. If you come to any great city do not send back word, but return yourself and tell me about it. Make all your plans and set out as soon as possible."

Fray Marcos did as he was told, but it was several months before anything was heard of him. One day a traveller, in a monk's gown, came walking into the same seaport that De Vaca had visited.

"It is Fray Marcos, who went in search of the Seven Cities! Did you find them! Are they full of wealth? Where is the negro Stephen?"

Fray Marcos would not answer their questions.

"I have much to tell, but my news is for the Viceroy himself," said the padre, and he started for the city of Mexico. When there he said to the Viceroy:

"The Indians came out to meet and welcome me everywhere. They had food ready for me, and where there were no houses, they built bowers of trees and flowers that I might rest safe from the sun. I spent four days journeying through a desert, and then I found some Indians who marvelled much to see me. They thought, because I was white and wore a gown, that I must have come from Heaven. I asked them if they knew of any great kingdom where there were seven large cities, and they told me that farther on were high mountains with wide plains at the foot where the people lived in cities and clothed themselves in cotton. I sent Stephen ahead three-score leagues, and charged him to send back Indians to bring me news of his success. If the country was poor and mean, he was to send me a cross no longer than my hand; if it were a goodly place the cross was to be two lengths of a hand, and if he found what he sought he was to send me a large cross. In four days a messenger came from Stephen bearing a cross as high as a man. He brought news of a mighty province called Cibola, thirty days journey northward from the town where Stephen was. In this province there are seven great cities governed by one Prince."

"You should have followed at once to make sure that all these things were true," said the Viceroy, now very much interested.

"I did," responded Fray Marcos. "Each day messengers came to me carrying large crosses and giving more particulars concerning Cibola. Finally I entered a valley where there were many people, and all of them had turquoises hanging from their noses, and ears, and collars of the same three or four times double around their necks. Then I had to go through another desert, and was beginning to get very tired when one day there came running to me, an Indian in great fright – his body covered with sweat and dust, and his face showing extreme sadness. He said that the day before Stephen had reached Cibola, and had sent guides into the city with presents for the chief, and to let them know he came in peace. But the great Lord of the City flew into a rage and dashed the presents to the ground. He drove the messengers out in fury, and said he would kill them if they came back again. He said, too, that he would kill Stephen. But the negro was not afraid, and went directly into the city. Instantly they were seized and cast into a prison, where they were kept all night without anything to eat or drink. The next morning Stephen and his guides tried to escape, but the people killed all of them except one other and the messenger who came to me. These two were struck down and left for dead, but were only stunned, and when the angry people went away they crept out in the night, and made their escape."

"What did you do then, Fray Marcos?" asked the Viceroy.

"So great was my grief that it seemed for a moment as if I should die, but when my guides began to weep and lament I gave them the presents I intended for the Lord of Cibola, and resolved to go and see the city, even if I could not enter it. I travelled one day and came to a round hill, which I climbed. Looking down I saw the beautiful city of Cibola."

"And the houses, were they as the Indians told you?"

"Yes, my lord; they were built of stone four stories high, and glistened in the bright sunshine. The people were fair and dressed in white. Greatly was I tempted to risk my life and go down to them, but I contented myself with planting a cross and hurrying here to tell you what I had done."

"That was right, Fray Marcos," said the Viceroy, "and now it is time to send an army."

The first person the Viceroy thought of to lead the soldiers was a brave nobleman, named Coronado, who sat by his side. He had been listening eagerly to all that Fray Marcos had to tell. Turning to him the Viceroy said:

"It is my wish that you should command my forces and conquer this Kingdom of Cibola. I desire you to make ready at once."

"Fray Marcos simply confirms what Guzman and De Vaca have already told us," replied Coronado, "and I accept your commission with one proviso."

"And what may that be?" asked the Viceroy, with a smile.

"That you allow me to bear the expenses of the entire expedition."

"Very well, and when you find Cibola I will make you its governor and give you all the treasures you find except what justly belongs to the King of Spain, and his representatives and soldiers taking part in the enterprise."

So great was the excitement over Fray Marcos' story of the new El Dorado, that Coronado scarcely knew what to do with the volunteers of all classes who came flocking into camp determined to go with him. He not only spent all his own money, but borrowed all he could get and provided for every one in splendid style. They marched out in glittering armour, on prancing horses with lances gleaming in the sunshine and banners flying gayly. They were all in high spirits because they expected to return in a short time loaded with gold and jewels.

But it was very different when they reached the desert and mountains, for they did not know how to bear the fatigue of such a journey, nor how to care for their horses, cattle and sheep. The animals died rapidly, and the soldiers got into many fights with the Indians who resented being robbed and badly treated. On they went through what we now call Arizona, over almost the same road that Fray Marcos had travelled, and found, instead of the fine, glittering city they expected, only a few houses of one of the Zuni Indian villages.

The hearts of the Spaniards sunk as they gazed upon it. Calling some of the men, Coronado said:

"Go in to the people of the city, and say that we come to defend and join with them in friendship."

They went and delivered Coronado's greeting, but were received with scorn.

"We did not ask you to come, and your chief had no right to send you. This is our land, and we can defend it. If you attempt to stay here we will kill every one of you." Even as the soldiers, carrying the message, turned to go away the people of Cibola began firing arrows at them. Coronado quickly gave the command to attack, which the Indians answered by a shower of arrows and stones which they sent down from their high-walled houses. They seemed bent upon killing Coronado; twice they felled him to the ground, but he recovered and led the charge with an arrow sticking through his foot.

"Santiago! and at them!" he shouted, as he rode forward in the last assault.

"Santiago," echoed his soldiers, close at his heels. When the Indians saw the horses coming at full speed into their village, they threw down their bows and arrows, and fled in every direction.

Then the Spaniards almost cried with anger and disappointment. The houses were really made of stone, but there were no jewels, no gold, no treasures of any kind – nothing, in fact, but a poor, miserable Indian pueblo, or village, built upon a high ledge of rocks, miles away from the fields of corn, beans and squashes, upon which they lived. All the Indians in that part of the United States built their houses in pueblos, or villages, but not one of them had any treasures. They irrigated the dry, sandy soil and tilled their fields, and were a simple, kindly people, until the greedy Spanish soldiers drove them into rebellion which has left their country bare and desolate, even to this day..

Biographies & Text Sources

The stories in this book are drawn from a number of original sources, many of which are from the nineteenth and early twentieth centuries. They are often based on the author's first-hand accounts of tales narrated to them by indigenous people, while others are the author's own observations and interpretations of the cultures, manuscripts and archaeological evidence. As previously noted, they may be problematic due to the colonial or Christian perspectives and biases of their era, but we ask the reader to bear this in mind while acknowledging their intrinsic value as records of tales and information that might otherwise have been lost.

Hartley Burr Alexander
Myths of the Chibcha
(Originally Published in *The Mythology of All Races,* 1920)
Hartley Burr Alexander (1973–1939) was a philosopher, author, scholar, educator, iconographer and poet. Born in Nebraska to a Methodist family, Alexander came to distrust Christianity and developed an interest in First Peoples of the Americas, their religions and spirituality. Alexander wrote prolifically on the subjects of Native American philosophy, lore, mythology and art. One of his best-known works is the poem 'To a Child's Moccasin (Found at Wounded Knee)', which stood in stark contrast to the prevailing negative views and treatment of Native Americans by the US government and American society of the time.

Hervey Allen
The Bride of Huitzel: An Aztec Legend
(Originally Published in 1922)
Hervey Allen (1889–1949) was an American author, poet and educator. Born in Pittsburgh, Pennsylvania, he served in the US Navy from 1909 to 1911. He later joined the Pancho Villa Expedition along the US's border with Mexico, from which he drew inspiration for his first book, *Ballads of the Border* (1916). His best-known work is his historical fiction novel *Anthony Adverse* (1933), which is regarded among literary critics as a model for the modern American historical novel.

Anthony F. Aveni
Foreword
Anthony F. Aveni is the Russell Colgate Distinguished University Professor of Astronomy, Anthropology, and Native American Studies, Emeritus, at Colgate University, in Hamilton, New York. Aveni helped develop and now is considered one of the founders of cultural astronomy, in particular for his research into the astronomical history of the Aztec and Maya Indians of ancient Mexico. He has done similar research in North America, Peru, Israel, Italy and Greece. Aveni has involved his students in research through regular field trips to Central America and Peru to study history, hieroglyphic writing, calendars and architecture. In 2004, Aveni was the recipient of the H.B. Nicholson Award for Excellence in Mesoamerican Studies. He has more than 300 research publications to his credit, including articles in *Science* magazine, *American Scientist*, *The Sciences*, *American*

Antiquity, *Latin American Antiquity* and *The Journal of Archaeological Research*. Aveni has written or edited more than 40 books, including *Conversing With the Planets*, a work that weaves together cosmology, mythology and the anthropology of ancient cultures, and *Nasca: Eighth Wonder of the World*.

Padraic Colum
The Twin Heroes and the Lords of Xibalba; Quetzacoatl; Quetzacoatl's Enemy; The Gods of the Azteca; The Azteca; Viracocha; The Llama-Herder and the Virgin of the Sun
(Originally Published in *Orpheus: Myths of the World,* 1930; © Padraic Colum, reprinted by permission of the Estate)
Padraic Colum (1881–1972) was born in County Longford, Ireland. He wrote prolifically as a poet, biographer, novelist, playwright, dramatist, children's book author and folklore collector. A prominent figure in the late nineteenth-century Irish Literary Revival, Colum developed connections with numerous well-known Irish writers including James Joyce and W.B. Yeats. His first book, a poetry collection entitled *Wild Earth,* was published in 1907. Later living in the US, Colum ventured into prose fiction and children's books, and taught at Columbia University and CCNY.

Inca Garcilaso de la Vega, El Inca
[More on] The Festival of the Sun; The Legacy of Inca Yupanqui Pachacuti
(Originally Published in *The First Part of the Royal Commentaries of the Incas,* 1871)
Inca Garcilaso de la Vega, also known as El Inca, (1539–1616) was born in Cusco, Peru, before moving to Spain aged 21. He was the son of a Spanish conquistador and an Inca noblewoman, and grew up during the beginning of Spain's conquest. Vega is best known for his work on the history, society and culture of the Incan civilization. He also penned a chronicle on the Florida expedition of Hernando de Soto.

Ruth Warner Giddings
The Walking Stone; Five Friends of Takochai; The Snake People; Kaiman; The Big Bird; The Death of Kutam Tawi
(Originally Published in *Yaqui Myths and Legends,* 1959)
Author Ruth Warner Giddings published her collection *Yaqui Myths and Legends* in 1959, marking the first such collection to be published on the folk tales and traditions of the Yaqui people. The Yaquis are a southwestern Native American tribe in the Sonoran Desert. With populations in Arizona and Mexico, the Yaquis hold a strong folkloric tradition that has been influenced by the Spanish conquest which began in the seventeenth century.

Diego de Landa and William Gates
Construction of the Houses of Yucatan. Obedience and Respect of the Indians for Their Chiefs. Headgear and Wearing of Garments; Food and Drink of the Indians of Yucatan; Painting and Tattooing of the Indians. Their Orgies, Wines and Banquets. Their Comedies, Music and Dances
(Originally Published in *Yucatán Before and After the Conquest, 1937)*
Diego de Landa (1524–79) was a Spanish Franciscan Bishop. Based at the Roman Catholic Archdiocese of Yucatán, de Landa led a campaign to eradicate practices of idolatry among the indigenous peoples. This culminated infamously in de Landa's burning of nearly all existing Mayan codices, which had preserved the Mayan writing system, culture, religion

and history. His own documentation of the Maya now comprises the majority of current knowledge on the civilization. The 1937 edition of his book *Yucatán Before and After the Conquest* was translated by William Gates, an Americanist and scholar.

Charles Fletcher Lummis
The Antelope Boy; The First of the Rattlesnakes; The Man Who Married the Moon; The Moqui Boy and the Eagle; The Drowning of Pecos; The Ants that Pushed on the Sky; The Sobbing Pine; The Magic Hide and Seek; The Queres Diana; The Hero Twins; The Hungry Grandfathers; The Accursed Lake; The North Wind and the South Wind
(Originally Published in *Pueblo Indian Folk-Stories,* 1910)
Charles Fletcher Lummis (1859–1928) was born in Lynn, Massachusetts. Moving to the Southwest, he developed a passion for the region and its indigenous peoples, and he wrote extensively on these cultures. As a writer, journalist and activist, he advocated for the rights of Native Americans and the preservation of their cultures. Lummis created the Sequoya League, a Native American rights group, and he battled the US Bureau of Indian Affairs. In 1907 he founded the Southwest Museum of the American Indian in Los Angeles.

Anne Cary Maudslay and Alfred Percival Maudslay
Chichén Itzá; Tikál and Menché
(Originally Published in *A Glimpse at Guatemala,* 1899)
Anne Cary Maudslay (d. 1926) was an author and the granddaughter of American statesman Gouverneur Morris. Husband and fellow author Alfred Percival Maudslay (1850–1931) was a British diplomat, archaeologist and explorer. He is most notable for his surveying and documentation of Mayan ruins. Marrying in 1892, the couple travelled to Guatemala for their honeymoon, where they conducted field work for Harvard University's Peabody Museum. Their work was published as *A Glimpse at Guatemala* in 1899.

Sir Clements Markham
Ttahua-Ntin-Suyu
(Originally Published in *The Incas of Peru,* 1912)
Sir Clements Markham K.C.B. (1830–1916) was an English geographer, writer and explorer. Serving as secretary of the Royal Geography Society from 1863 to 1888, and later the society's president for a further twelve years, Markham organized the British National Antarctic Expedition of 1901–04. He is known for spurring the nineteenth-century revival of Britain's interest in exploring the Antarctic, as well as his prolific writings on geography, travel and history. He also produced English translations of numerous Spanish works including Pedro Sarmient de Gamboa's *History of the Incas.*

Philip Ainsworth Means
Three Inca Prayers
(Originally Published in *Ancient Civilizations of the Andes,* 1931)
Philip Ainsworth Means (1892–1944) was an anthropologist and historian, born in Boston, Massachusetts. He is notable for his anthropological and archaeological work in Peru, which focused on the Incan civilization. As Director of the National Museum of Archaeology in Lima, Means oversaw excavations and published numerous works on Incan culture and Spanish conquest. Among his best-known publications is *Ancient Civilizations of the Andes* (1931), one of the first books detailing the culture and history of the Incas.

Emelyn Newcomb Partridge
Miss Pound-the-stones; The Princess and the Shepherd; The Love of Cusi-Coyllur
(Originally Published in *Joyful Star: Indian Stories for Camp Fire Girls,* 1915)
Emelyn Newcomb Partridge (1869–1963) was a Canadian author, psychologist and lecturer. Born in Nova Scotia, Partridge attended school in Worcester, Massachusetts, and later worked as a clinical psychologist in Boston. In 1954 she founded a school for mentally disabled children in Virginia. Partridge primarily wrote children's fiction which focused on Native American themes, including *Glooscap The Great Chief, And Other Stories: Legends of the Micmacs* (1913) and *Joyful Star: Indian Stories for Camp Fire Girls* (1915).

Guy Cadogan Rothery
Amazons of America
(Originally Published in *The Amazons,* 1910)
The Amazons, by Guy Cadogan Rothery (1863–1940), is one of the few books whose central focus is the Ancient Greek myth of the Amazons. Exploring various indigenous cultures through the lens of this myth, Rothery examines in the chapter 'Amazons of America' the Spanish conquistadors' perception of the native South American peoples they encountered as proof of this myth.

Pedro Sarmiento de Gamboa
Viracocha and the Coming of the Incas; Death of Pachacuti Inca Yupanoui
(Originally Published in *History of the Incas,* 1907)
Pedro Sarmiento de Gamboa (1532–92) was a Spanish explorer, historian, author, astronomer, and mathematician. He sailed to 'New Spain' (present-day Mexico) in 1555, marking the beginning of his career in exploration. He later joined an expedition which resulted in the discovery of the Solomon Islands. In 1572, the fifth Viceroy of Peru, Francisco de Toledo, commissioned Sarmiento de Gamboa to write a history of the Incan civilization. The resulting work, *History of the Incas,* preserved meticulous details of the Incas' culture and history.

Dr Nicholas J. Saunders
Some introductory material
Nicholas J. Saunders studied archaeology at the universities of Sheffield and Southampton, and anthropology at Queens' College Cambridge. He has held teaching and research posts in the USA, Trinidad, Jamaica, Argentina and Mexico, specializing in pre-Columbian archaeology and anthropology. He is currently Emeritus Professor in the Department of Anthropology and Archaeology at University of Bristol.

Charles M. Skinner
Sacrifice of the Toltecs
(Originally Published in *Myths and Legends of Our Own Land,* 1896)
Charles Montgomery Skinner (1852–1907) was an American writer, playwright and journalist, who wrote on a wide range of topics, such as natural history and socialism, but also published collections of myths, legends and folklore, including *Myths and Legends of Our Own Land* (1896).

Lewis Spence
The Popol Vuh
(Originally Published in *The Popol Vuh: The Mythic and Heroic Sagas of the Kichés of Central America*, 1908)
The Religion of the Ancient Peruvians; Peruvian Ritual and Worship
(Originally Published in *The Mythologies of Ancient Mexico and Peru,* 1907)
James Lewis Thomas Chalmers Spence (1874–1955) was a scholar of Scottish, Mexican and Central American folklore, as well as that of Brittany, Spain and the Rhine. He was also a poet, journalist, author, editor and nationalist who founded the party that would become the Scottish National Party. He was a Fellow of the Royal Anthropological Institute of Great Britain and Ireland, and Vice-President of the Scottish Anthropological and Folklore Society. He published many books, of which *The Myths of Mexico & Peru* (1913) is one of relevance to this volume.

Frona Eunice Wait
The Happy Island; Zamna, the Eye of the Sun; Cholula, the Sacred City; Tulla, the Hiding Nook of the Snake; The Departure of the Golden Hearted; El Dorado, the Golden; The Child of the Sun; The Gilded Man; The Amazon Queens; The Seven Cities of Cibola
(Originally Published in *The Stories of El Dorado,* 1904)
Frona Eunice Wait (1859–1946) was an American author and journalist who published numerous books as well as articles for various newspapers and magazines. Following the death of her second child in 1880, Wait began her career in journalism. Working at the *Santa Rosa Republican* and later the *San Francisco Examiner,* she was one of just two women journalists on staff. She later became an associate editor for the *Overland Monthly*..